Bravo Fortissimo

GLENN GOULD

THE MIND OF A CANADIAN VIRTUOSO

HELEN MESAROS M.D.

Heritage Special Edition
American Literary Press
Baltimore, Maryland

Bravo Fortissimo Glenn Gould

Library of Congress
Cataloging-in-Publication Data
ISBN-13: 978-1-56167-985-0

Library of Congress Card Catalog Number:
2007943597

Published by

Heritage Special Edition
American Literary Press

8019 Belair Road, Suite 10
Baltimore, Maryland 21236

Manufactured in China

To Don

May you find this book stimulating and fun to read.

With every good wish

In Toronto
April 23, 2008

To my parents
Milinka and Dragi

To my grandchildren
Hanna, Maya and Emma

author

Bravo Fortissimo Glenn Gould

Library of Congress
Cataloging-in-Publication Data
ISBN-13: 978-1-56167-985-0

Library of Congress Card Catalog Number:
2007943597

Published by

Heritage Special Edition
American Literary Press

8019 Belair Road, Suite 10
Baltimore, Maryland 21236

Manufactured in the United States

ACKNOWLEDGMENTS

First and foremost, I owe my gratitude to Dr. Dorothea Dobbs Gaither, psychologist of Toronto, a loyal friend and dedicated editor of this book. Dorothea not only edited the manuscript once, but went over the everchanging text several times in order to be on top of all possible errors. She also played the role of "sidekick," a compatible, professional partner in discussions about Gould.

My sincere thanks to the Glenn Gould Estate, particularly to Mr. Stephen Posen, the executor of the estate, for allowing me to pursue unlimited research in the music archives of Glenn Gould at the Library and Archives Canada.

I am deeply thankful to all Gould relatives who participated in my research by not only being interviewed over the telephone, but who entertained me at their homes and provided invaluable information about the life and work of Glenn Gould. Moreover, they befriended me and let me into the most intimate corners of Gould's background. These kind individuals are: Mr. Russell (Bert) Gould, Glenn's father, and his second wife, Mrs. Vera Dobson Gould, now both deceased, who gave me hours of their valuable time in their warm home environment; Ms. Jessie Greig, Gould's first cousin who loved and admired him throughout his life. Ms. Greig died from cancer, which she attributed to the stress induced by the loss of her favorite cousin. I am equally thankful to Mrs. Betty Greig Madill, Mr. John Greig and Dr. Tom Johnson, Gould's first cousins, who spent their earlier years with him, and to Glenn's uncle, Dr. Grant Gould, who hosted my daughter Dr. Marianne Mesaros McKinley and myself at his home in California, sharing precious information about his nephew, Glenn Gould.

My thanks go to Mrs. Elsie Lally Feeney and Mrs. Edna Meyer, who in the role of nannies showed much care and empathy toward Glenn as a child.

I am especially grateful to Mr. Ray Roberts and his wife, for their supportive presence in Gould's life and his post-Gouldian contribution in maintaining a positive image of his friend and patron, Glenn Gould.

Many thanks to Mr. Robert Fulford for being one of the first volunteers for a formal interview about his friend from childhood, Glenn Gould.

My cordial thanks go to Mr. Andrew Kazdin, who on a busy day traveled to Manhattan and paid expensive parking just to engage in a lengthy interview with me. Mr. Kazdin was one of the first individuals with whom I shared my original findings about Gould's Jewish ancestry. Mr. Kazdin exploded in positive emotions, saying: "If you asked me to come here just for this single piece of information, it would have been worth my effort." He was also amused by Gould's ability to hide it from him. "I wondered about Glenn having some Jewish blood in him, but he covered it so well that he even fooled me."

My very special thanks to Mr. Bob Silverman, Gould's loyal friend over the last ten years of his life. Mr. Silverman hosted me at his home in Vermont for several days in order to reflect on his experiences with Gould through hours of marathon conversations.

I would like to thank Mr. Verne Edquist and his wife for hosting me in their home for new insights about Glenn Gould.

I am grateful to all staff of the Glenn Gould Archives at the Library and Archives Canada in Ottawa, who assisted me in the long weeks of research on their premises. Among them, Ms. Jeannine Barriault, Ms. Cheryl Gillard and Dr. Timothy Maloney were particularly helpful. Equally, my thanks go to the archives of Sony Classical and Ms. Faye Perkins; the Canadian Broadcasting Corporation in Toronto, and to Steinway Hall in New York, all of whom made it possible for me to do uninterrupted research. Mr. Peter Goodrich of Steinway Hall provided useful literature and participated in a candid interview.

My special thanks to the Toronto-based concert pianist, Mr. Anton Kuerti, for his frankness in a lengthy interview at my home.

Gould's female friend, Ms. Margaret Pacsu, joined me at my home for a very open and genuine interview, for which I will always be indebted. Likewise, another of Gould's loyal friends, the opera singer, Miss Roxolana Roslak, shared valuable humorous and somber stories about the virtuoso.

I am thankful to Mr. Malcolm Lester, the literary advisor to the Glenn Gould Estate, who was available to discuss with me the intricate world of publishing. My heartfelt thanks to Dr. Michael Rosenbluth, a psychiatrist in Toronto, a colleague and a sincere supporter of my work on Gould's biography, by supplying rare news articles of which I was not aware.

My thanks to a large number of friends, relatives and colleagues who provided ongoing interest and moral boost in the long years of book preparation. To name but a few: Mr. Voja Devic, Mr. Jim Curtis, Dr. Amira Bishai, Ms. Amy Sum, Ms. Ada Hefter, Dr. John Gaither, Dr. Les Kiraly, Dr. Marianne McKinley, Ms. Elvira Arevalo, Mr. John Massin, Ms. Leslie Fairfield, Ms. Pauline Hui, Ms. Morgan Flury, Dr. Elen Mak, Dr. Ruth Baruch, Dr. Allan Rosenbluth, Dr. Philip Morton, Dr. Larry Chad, Dr. Joel Jeffries, and Dr. Vladimir Diligenski.

This work would not be possible without the invaluable ongoing assistance of my son, Dr. Luke Mesaros, a chiropractor in Toronto, who over the years looked after all technical aspects of my work.

Finally, this book is a "thank you" note for Gould's inspirational presence in the music world of the twentieth century.

Helen Mesaros

In Toronto, December 2007

CONTENTS

Chapter I	PRELUDE	1
	Glenn's Radio Debut	1
Chapter II	THE FORERUNNERS OF FAME	7
	The Family Tree of the Gould Family	7
	Florence Greig and Her Family of Origin	8
	Russell Herbert Gold and His Ancestors	15
Chapter III	THE CHILDHOOD OF A CONCERT PIANIST	25
	Glenn's Infancy	25
	Notes About Gifted Children	29
	The Boyhood of a Prodigy	34
	The Beginning of the End	47
	The Principal Music Teacher—Alberto Guerrero	53
Chapter IV	THE GROWING PAINS OF ADOLESCENCE	57
	Pianist in Short Pants	57
	Glenn and Guerrero	64
	The Dynamics of Adolescence	74
	"The Nice Genius"	79
Chapter V	INROADS TO FAME	85
	The Genius Tested	85
	The Psychology of Gould's Piano Technique	90
	The Keyboard Master Arrives	96
Chapter VI	GLENN GOULD MAKES MUSIC	103
	Gould's American Debut	103
	The Concert Pianist Par Excellence	111
	The Gould-Steinway Affair	125
	More Piano Conquests	133
Chapter VII	THE INNER WORLD	145
	The Gould Triangle	145
	The Emergence of Symptoms	154
	The Grieg Myth	159
	Performance Anxiety	164
Chapter VIII	GOULD AS A YOUNG MAN	171
	Farewell to Youth	171
	String Quartet Op. 1	177
	Communication at a Distance	184
	The King is to Blame	190

Chapter IX	THE GOLDBERG VARIATIONS	201
	The Essence of Creation	201
	The Greatest Live Performance	210
	Gould on the "Goldbergs"	213
Chapter X	THE CEREMONY OF PERFORMANCE	217
	That Special Piano Chair	217
	Gould at the Grand Piano	231
Chapter XI	THE MUSIC CIRCLE	241
	Glenn Gould and Leonard Bernstein	241
	Other Music Associates	256
Chapter XII	TURNING THIRTY	269
	Gould in the Driver's Seat	277
	The Playful Puritan	281
Chapter XIII	THE TALES OF STRATFORD	291
Chapter XIV	BOWING OUT	307
	The End of Gould's Public Performance Career	307
	Goodbye Stage Fright	312
Chapter XV	LOVE AND SEXUALITY	321
	Touch Me, Touch Me Not	321
	In Search of Love	325
	The Mystery of Fetishism	334
	Real Love Stories	338
Chapter XVI	REAL AND IMAGINED ILLNESS	345
	To Be Ill or To Be Healthy	345
	Detriments of Narcissism	357
	In Search of Truth	362
Chapter XVII	THE VOLLEY OF CREATIVITY	367
	Gould as a Distinguished Canadian Broadcaster	367
	Recording Philosophy and Fame	378
Chapter XVIII	THE LAST TEN YEARS	383
	Andante Sostenuto	383
	Lento: Lament for the Lost Mother	390
	Bravo Fortissimo	407
Chapter XIX	FINALE	413
	Requiem for a Canadian	413
Chapter XX	PHOENIX RISING	423
	Gould as the Most Famous Canadian Artist	423
Endnotes		439
Index		467

Chapter I

PRELUDE

GLENN'S RADIO DEBUT

December 5, 1938

Dear Glenn,
Congratulations on a fine performance on the occasion of your radio debut. Your fans look forward to having you oftener from now on—so keep up the good work.

The boys from South House[1]

This is one of countless letters received by a six-year-old child star, Glenn Herbert Gold, the future international concert pianist, Glenn Gould. This exceptional boy stirred up excitement, not only in his peers from South House but in the entire Toronto east end community where he was born and raised. The radio, as a new electronic gadget, just came into being in the early 1920s, and the Canadian Broadcasting Corporation (CBC) had been recently established in 1936, all of which made the presence of the little radio guest even more sensational. There was this grade-one student, already known as a child prodigy, who was playing classical music live on the piano, and the owners of radio sets in Toronto and its vicinity could hear him instantaneously.

Sitting at home on a Sunday afternoon and listening to the radio was a favorite pastime in pre-World War II Canada, particularly in the wintertime. This was a way to relax after a hard working week or to have fun after dutiful Sunday morning church services. Radio program had universal appeal, and people of all ages flocked around to listen to this novel and wonderful apparatus. Being such a powerful medium of telecommunications, even a single appearance of an artist on the radio could make him or her famous within hours of broadcasting.

For Glenn, fame began earlier. At the age of five, he was already known to local circles through his live church appearances. There were at least two dozen musical performances before he was six years old, which usually involved his parents singing hymns, solo or in duet, with Glenn at the piano as the accompanist. The most distinguished was Glenn's live debut on June 5, 1938, in Uxbridge, Ontario, the hometown of the Gold family, when he appeared in the United Church before a congregation of 1,600 people. This was a Golden Jubilee in celebration of the thirtieth anniversary of the Business

Men's Bible Class in Uxbridge, founded by Glenn's grandfather, Thomas G. Gold. Glenn's name was publicized in the program notes with the flattering headline "Five year old Master Glenn Gold at the Piano," and on June 9, the local paper, *The Uxbridge Times Journal*, reported the following news:

> ... Former Uxbridge artists, in the persons of Mrs. Erma Brownscombe Croskery and Mr. and Mrs. R. H. Gold greatly delighted the audience with their splendidly rendered numbers each one being well received. Then, too, were the several numbers rendered by the little five-year-old son of Mr. and Mrs. Gold, Glenn, by name, who quickly impressed the audience that there was something of a musical genius in the making. All his numbers were splendid, but the two original compositions of the little chap were quite remarkable in one so young, and foreshadowed one of the country's talented composers in the not too distant future.[2]

This stunning live debut in Uxbridge in the month of June, and then his radio debut in Toronto in December of the same year, consolidated Glenn's new role as music wonderchild. Here is another more personable response to Glenn's radio success from his paternal aunt, Winifred Johnson:

> Sunday P.M.
>
> Dear Glenn,
>
> We heard your broadcast at Blackwater tonight and we were so proud of you. Barry sat as close to the radio as he could get and listened spellbound with such a pleased grin on his face. After he heard you he turned around and said "Grandma I can play the drum."
>
> It was Grand Glenn. I'll bet Santa Claus will be pretty good to you after that.
>
> Heaps of Love and a great big kiss
>
> Auntie Freda[3]

There was also a sweet letter from his two-year-younger cousin Barry:

> Dear Glenn,
>
> I heard you over the radio and I liked you.
>
> I am at grandma's. I've got one of my aeroplanes down at Blackwater's. The propeller will go round in the wind but the aeroplane won't fly. It was one Daddy made.
>
> Barry[4]

While Barry enjoyed hearing his cousin playing the piano, he also had other things in mind, like his intriguing toy airplane. Glenn, on the contrary, had to abide by a busy daily schedule of practicing the piano and preparing for live and radio performances and to worry about his public image. He had to make a choice between playing the little preludes that tickled his music curiosity or playing with those fantastic toys that awakened his boyish needs. Though Glenn clearly would have rather pursued them both with a near equal passion, this was technically impossible. Music won the contest. For Glenn, playing the piano was his ultimate fun. From relative anonymity, the novice pianist stepped into an absolute whirlwind of media exposure. His name then became newsworthy, and the press referred to him in glowing terms as the wonder child of the beaches. On account of Glenn, his parents were flooded with requests and offers from local churches and social gatherings to appear in their music programs. Many such propositions had to be turned down, as the Gold trio simply could not keep up with all of them. Being a child star is a rare gem anywhere and at anytime. In the late 1930s, the ten-year-old Shirley Temple was the most famous child movie star. At the same time, the six-year-old Glenn, in a more modest way, was undoubtedly the Canadian child star in the genre of classical music.

There is only a handful of children who could accomplish that kind of momentum of drawing the instant attention to themselves. At the age of five to six, most children are eased off from the carefree comfort of kindergarten into the more serious world of grade school. This process is natural and, in most cases, it tends to be smooth and exciting. Gifted children are exceptions to the rule, inasmuch as once their endowment is shared with the public, from then on they will be expected to give more of themselves over and over again. Being a child celebrity, though a very rewarding experience to the parents, relatives and people at large, may complicate, even interfere with the normal progress of the young artist by virtue of high and unnatural expectations.

Complicated or not, Glenn at the tender age of five, forged ahead into public life. So, on that pleasant and festive day of June 5, 1938, the preschool boy had his name first published for posterity. The six words of the concert program "Master Glenn Gold at the Piano," was an understated hint of Glenn Gould's future life achievement.

Glenn was born in the Ontario capital city of Toronto on September 25, 1932, as the only child of Russell Herbert Gold[5] and Florence Greig. Ever since a baby, he showed a profound interest in the music that surrounded him. Music from the radio that was often turned on to entertain him, sounds from the piano played by his mother and the voices of both his parents practicing hymns and ballads were his constant environment. His mother, Florrie, was musically gifted, and so was his paternal grandmother, Alma Gold, which genetically predisposed Glenn to be musical himself. Glenn's father, Bert, reminisced in this way:

> From a very early period of his life, Glenn showed quite clearly that he had innate musical talents that no responsible parent could overlook. As a baby a few days old, he would flex his fingers almost as if playing a scale. As soon as he was old enough to hold on his grandmother's knee at the piano, he would never pound the keyboard as most children will with the whole hand striking a number of keys at the same time, instead he would always insist on pressing down a single key and holding it down until the resulting sound had completely died away. The fading vibration entirely fascinated him.[6]

Music was pushing from within and stimulating his mind from without. It was Florrie who detected the early buds of Glenn's extraordinary music abilities and nurtured them to bloom. She introduced him to the piano by playing guessing games. At first she played with Glenn at the piano by letting him strike a note with his tiny finger and then telling him the name of each note. Then she would ask him to repeat it: "Glenn, honey, give me an A. Good boy. How about middle C? Now something harder, give me all the G's. That's it, you are doing very well." Both the mother and her toddler son were mutually amused; she by his consistent perfect pitch and rapid acquisition of basic music skills and he by her attentiveness and the endless tonal possibilities. Florence unconsciously became a pediatric music pedagogue whose playful methods may be viewed as a precursor to the present well-established and sensible Suzuki method of early music training. She was also indirectly modelling for her son by actively practicing the piano in front of him, by singing, and by teaching the piano to young students.

Her husband, Bert, also participated in that indirect modelling, though to a lesser extent, by singing solo or in duet. Glenn's life from day to day was suffused with music. By the age of five, he not only read staff notation, but performed before church audiences, which required the complex blend of music and social skills. Even more, he wrote little compositions and then played them as an addendum to the scheduled program. Witnesses say that Glenn was disarmingly charming during his early performances. Mothers often used him as an example and coaxed their children to be like Glenn. "Isn't he a darling?" they uttered with a sigh. "See how nicely he is playing, wouldn't you like to play like that some day?" In his early performing life, there was a good equilibrium between Glenn, the performing artist, and the audience. He loved to play for them and they gave him their full-hearted support and adoration through applause and cheers. This all contributed to the fact that the first six years of Glenn's life, building up to his radio debut, unfolded with ease toward making him a star. As always, the steps to stardom have an engendered risk of overdevelopment in one direction at the expense of other personal needs. Glenn was being conditioned into a highly responsible role of distinction in music, which went hand in hand with an aura of specialness and pride. This is partly illustrated in a letter written to his mother after Glenn's radio appearance, by her niece, Bettsy Greig:

> December 5, 1938
>
> Dear Aunty:
>
> Just a line to let you know that we heard the program yesterday afternoon and that the Greigs as a family are pretty proud of Glenn.
>
> We thought that he did splendidly.
>
> We are very proud of him and think he has a wonderful future in store for him.
>
> ... you can certainly be proud of Glenn. Of course, there might be a little family pride in our opinion of Glenn, but there is a great deal of admiration.
>
> Lots of love
> Bettsy Greig[7]

All of a sudden, Glenn was showered with praise and a multitude of letters from everywhere. In another letter by a relative of Florrie's from Mount Forest, in reference to Glenn's radio debut, Glenn was complimented not only for his playing but also for announcing his music:

Mount Forest, Monday

Dear Flossie and All:

Just a hurried note to tell you that we heard Glenn very clearly yesterday. Auntie Jean[8] came down and laid on the chesterfield all afternoon, so she would be able to hear Glenn. We did enjoy it so much and we hope we will be able to listen to him soon again. He spoke out very distinctly and he certainly played beautifully.

Sincerely
Margaret[9]

An aura of happiness in his relatives was all around this auspicious child. Glenn became spokesman for both the Gould and Greig clan, a little persona grata of the east end of Toronto and an honorary citizen of Uxbridge. In the span of the next twenty years, Glenn outgrew the boundaries of his hometown and raised himself to the status of a world-class music figure. This biography is dedicated to finding out all that we can. By using documented facts and psychological insights, it is hoped that the person behind the legendary name of Glenn Gould will be better known and understood.

Chapter II

THE FORERUNNERS OF FAME

THE FAMILY TREE OF GLENN GOULD

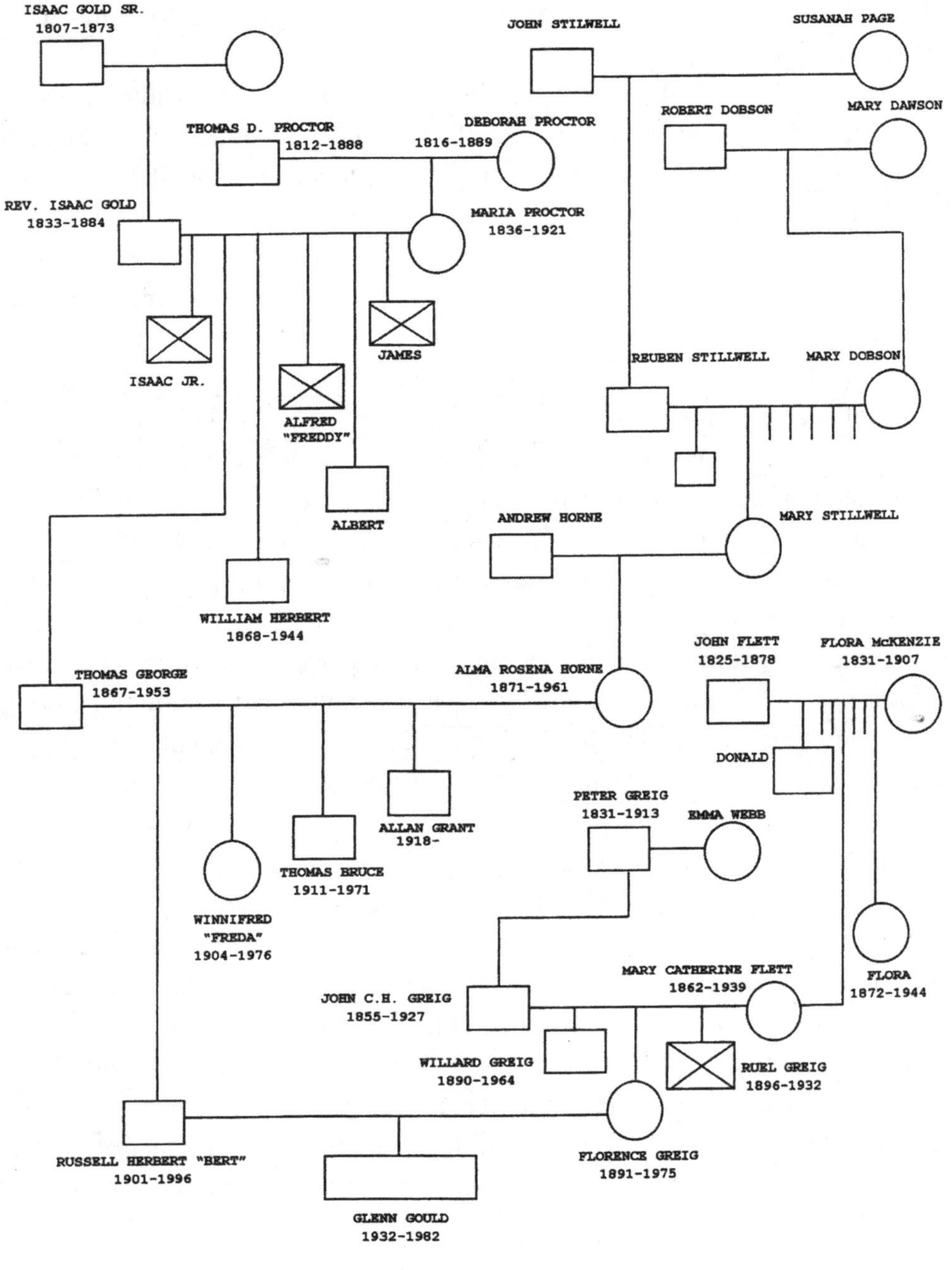

FLORENCE GREIG AND HER FAMILY OF ORIGIN

> The family only represents one aspect, however important an aspect, of a human being's functions and activities. ... A life is beautiful and ideal or the reverse, only when we have taken into our consideration the social as well as the family relationship.
>
> Havelock Ellis[1]

This is a sketch of the colorful lives of Glenn's predecessors within the half century before his birth. The goal is not just to rescue them from anonymity but to gain a much deeper understanding of Glenn through the recognition of their strengths and shortcomings. The way we are is determined by many influences, from heredity, from the psychosocial environment and the constant interplay between the two. Our endowments, as well as our disorders and maladaptive traits, are often passed down from one generation to another.

The most influential person in Glenn's life, both genetically and psychologically, was certainly his mother, Florence E. Greig. Florrie, as she was affectionately called, was born on October 31, 1891, in Mount Forest, Ontario.[2] She was a second generation Canadian. Her grandfather, Peter Greig, came from Aberdeenshire, Scotland, as a young man and settled in the small community of Arthur, in what later became the Province of Ontario. This is where he worked as a shoemaker and established his family. One of his ten children, John C. H. Greig, was the father of Florrie and grandfather of Glenn Gould.

John Greig was born in Hamilton, Ontario. He married Mary Flett, who also was of Scottish descent. As a schoolteacher by profession, John made meager wages, and his family had to move from town to town in Ontario in search of jobs and accommodation. He was described by his granddaughter, Jessie Greig, as a stern and scrupulous man, often prone to arguments and anger when challenged.[3] John and Mary had three children: Willard, Florence and Ruel. John was a typical father of his time. He showed little demonstrative warmth and demanded prim and proper behavior from his children. John and Mary were quite old-fashioned. Born in the heart of the Victorian age, they fully embraced the rigid social and ethical values of their time, including their prohibitive mind set and strong religious beliefs. Consistent with this, John and Mary brought up their children in the moralistic spirit of obedience with an emphasis on social manners. Some of John's positive qualities were his sound intelligence and a keen sense of music, which earned him the position of precentor, which was the name of the choir leader in his church.

Florrie's mother, Mary Flett, was born in 1862 in the tiny community of Mount Forest, Ontario, as the second oldest of seven children. She also was educated and worked as a schoolteacher before she was married. Mary's father, Florrie's grandfather, John Flett, was a carpenter by trade. He emigrated from Scotland and settled in Mount Forest, Upper Canada. Mary had a hard life, marked by losses and sadness. When she was seventeen years old, her beloved father, John, died from injuries in a building construction accident while working on the roof of the local Bank of Montreal. This tragic event left his wife, Flora MacKenzie, widowed and in a state of permanent, deep mourning from which she never recovered. As the eldest daughter, Mary Flett, the future grandmother of Glenn, had to take over in looking after the household and younger siblings to replace her bereaved mother. Mary herself was grief-stricken and unable to let go of her prolonged sorrow. In 1899, when Mary was thirty-seven years old, she lost her younger sister, Helen. The tragedy of this premature loss was compounded with the previous loss of her father. Those two untimely losses in the Flett family fell upon them as a dark veil of melancholia and was deeply set in their minds, never to be resolved. Mary's inherent grief was brought, as a part of her unfinished family mourning, into her future marriage and family life. Mary ended up being an austere person, always somewhat unhappy looking and self-absorbed.[4] Like her husband, John Greig, she was deeply religious, and she, too, placed great importance on social propriety and rigorous self-control. Her stern and somber demeanor made her emotionally distant and unavailable to her three children, Willard, Florrie and Ruel, which set the stage for their future emotional vulnerabilities. Mary Flett Greig, who had unfinished emotional business from her family of origin, including her unending grief and depressing outlook, was also a person who helped raise her grandson, Glenn Gould. Being one of the instrumental figures in his early childhood development, some of her personal qualities and traits became reflected and perpetuated in him.

While Florrie's life was gradually unfolding in this quiet rural area of Ontario, the society around her was experiencing exciting events and propulsive changes. As the nineteenth century was coming to its conclusion, North America was vigorously expanding in view of its population as well as in industry, science and culture. Only a few years before Florrie's birth, in 1882, the "Age of Electricity" brought about by Thomas Edison began in North America, representing a quantum leap for humankind. A little earlier, in 1876, the momentous invention of Alexander Graham Bell, the telephone, revolutionized people's lives. This new apparatus exponentially improved the mode of communication over distance. In the next year, 1877, the Bell Telephone Company was founded and, in less than one hundred years, life would be totally unimaginable without the telephone. Once it was established, many individuals worldwide, including Glenn Gould, would depend on the use of the telephone as a predominant means of interpersonal communication.

Such major discoveries like the telephone and electricity immeasurably improved the lives of people. A myriad of other clever inventions flowered in the emancipated countries of the Western Hemisphere. Soon after the revolutionary spread of electrical light bulbs, Edison's ceaseless mind endowed the world with the first motion picture camera, setting forth a new and powerful communication medium. This invention made it possible to film significant events around the globe and to produce artistic motion pictures, hence bringing news and entertainment much closer to the general public. With the advent of Emil Berliner's gramophone in 1887, music was no longer a one-time experience. Rather, it became memorized and solidly engraved, not only on records but also in the minds of people who could then listen to it at their discretion many times over. Florrie Greig, who showed an early talent for vocal and instrumental music, was one of the growing number of phonograph listeners. She was truly swept up by the contagious enthusiasm of the budding twentieth century, offering her a wider horizon of opportunities for personal pleasure and self-development than was available to the generation that preceded her.

Historically, this was the sunset of the long-lasting Victorian Age, whose characteristics had a rippling effect throughout the British Empire and its colonies, including the Dominion of Canada. In the first decade of Florrie's life, the international arena was dominated by the mightiest in foreign powers at the time, the British Empire, which, with its numerous scattered colonies, took up one fifth of the globe. In 1897, as the nineteenth century marched to its finale, "Good Queen" Victoria, celebrated her "Diamond Jubilee," which was the peak of her full and productive reign of some sixty-four years. Such a long and enduring physical presence of a reigning monarch, and more importantly, the strong symbolic meaning of the same, gave British subjects a sense of stability. Queen Victoria's personal and historical aura and the strong governing system that evolved around her left a deep imprint on the politics, culture and the lifestyle of her subjects. Nearly everything from the arts and architecture to fashion, social structure and behavior was fashioned by the orderly Victorian style.

Politically, the queen was a symbol of regal supremacy and unity of the Empire. In a more focused psychological sense, she held the scepter of the social standards and morality of her people. Queen Victoria, who in reality gave birth to nine children, was perceived by millions of her adopted compatriot-children as a strict and conditionally benevolent mother. The queen was seen as all-approving to those loyal and obedient subjects and conversely, all-disapproving, even punitive, to the nonconforming ones. Over the long decades, the queen was turned into a symbol of prudence and purity and became an object of mass idealization, as if she were a saint. In this sense, the symbol of the "Good Queen" became deeply incorporated into the individual and collective societal conscience of her subjects. It was left up to the generations of the twentieth century in Britain and North America to gradually modify and dilute those idealized but harsh moral norms into more realistic social attitudes and relaxed ways of living.

There was another concern over this ubiquitous role model. Following the sudden loss of her beloved husband, Prince Albert, who died of typhoid fever in 1861, Queen Victoria lapsed into prolonged, unresolvable mourning for twenty-five years. In the first decade of this bereavement, the queen resorted to seclusion in Windsor Castle, refused to make public appearances and wore black, which she continued to do until the end of her reign. Prolonged grief does not allow for the acceptance of the loss, its resolution and the successful continuation of life. It presents itself as an emotional hindrance to the mourner and to those around. In that sense, the queen's pathological grief, as it is termed today, was self-defeating and made her emotionally unavailable to her subjects.

In scientific literature concerned with the mourned and unmourned death of loved ones, it is found that adequate mourning is required in order for healthy acceptance of the loss and proper adjustment to life thereafter. George Pollock, who dedicated several decades of his life to studying this subject, calls this the mourning-liberation process. He says:

> ... the mourning-liberation process [is] a normal, necessary, universal, transformational process that permits us to adapt to change (which is loss), loss of meaningful figures, loss of home, loss of resources, loss of physical and emotional-mental health.[5]

When healthy mourning is achieved, the mourner can preserve personal integrity and make further progress in life. Conversely, when mourning is prolonged and unresolvable, it poses an obstacle in emotional functioning and individual growth. Such mourners are not fully able to liberate themselves from the unhealthy ties with the deceased and not able to adapt to the loss. It appears that Queen Victoria, as well as many of her contemporaries, like Mary Flett and her mother, by lapsing into protracted mourning, were not able to successfully end it and get on with their lives, which affected the future generations.

The society in which Florence Greig was born and raised was permeated by rigid morality, typified by authoritarian father figures and benevolent yet stern and self-sacrificing mothers. It was a society of patrons and patronizing relationships; fierce religiosity; parishes and parochialism. This society was in many ways strong and progressive but also vulnerable and begging for changes. The New World was determined to make such changes and to be emancipated from those powerful Victorian ties.

While Florrie was watching the world change at an incredible pace, her parents were troubled by personal problems and abject poverty. Florence Greig was the middle of three siblings, positioned between her brothers. Willard was one year older than Florrie, and Ruel was six years her junior. It is said that Willard Greig, the future uncle of Glenn Gould, was "bright and sharp as a whip" and "one could tell as early as in his childhood that he was going to be a scholarly and distinguished individual."[6] Indeed, he was an exemplary student in school and quite ambitious with respect to his future career. Due to the economic poverty of his family, Willard worked all through his youth on various jobs such as trapping furs in the wilderness and as a laborer for the railway. By so-doing, he saved enough money to put himself through law school in Toronto. Willard got married to Blanche Simpson, from Thessalon, Ontario, and fathered four children: Elisabeth (Betty), Willard Jr. (Simpson), Jessie and John Greig. All of Willard's children, and, in particular, Betty and Jessie, played an important role in the lives of their aunt, Florrie, and their first cousin, Glenn. Willard was very gifted rhetorically and had an excellent sense of humor.

"What was your father like as a person?" I asked Jessie Greig.

"He was a typical Scotsman. My father had a photographic memory and he was able to recite the whole book of Psalms from the Bible. He was really sharp. He had a high IQ bordering on genius. Glenn was a lot like him," Jessie said with a sense of pride.

"How do you know that your father had a high IQ?" I asked Jessie.

"I know because he had his IQ professionally tested and it turned out to be in the high superior range,"[7] Jessie said confidently. Jessie's older sister, Betty, also confirmed that Glenn was often compared to her father. On the whole, there seems to be a family consensus that Glenn inherited his superior intelligence and fabulous gift of speech from his maternal uncle, Willard Greig.

During those politically stable and expansive times toward the end of the nineteenth century, wealth was rapidly accumulating in the hands of individuals in the New World, such as successful industrialists, professionals, bankers and businessmen. South of the Canadian border, the United States of America was a rapidly expanding, capitalistic world power that would soon surpass the power and hegemony of Britannia. At the turn of the century, technology was in its full force of expansion. Spearheaded by Henry Ford, the car industry was booming. Arts and entertainment were also flourishing parallel to the growth of capitalism in the United States and Canada. Local theaters and concert halls multiplied. In 1891, the year of Florrie's birth, Carnegie Hall opened in New York City, which was soon to become a mecca for classical music lovers in North America. Only two years later in 1893, Massey Music Hall opened in Toronto as a counterpart to Carnegie Hall. Times were changing rapidly, and when the queen died in January 1901, it marked the beginning of the slow but sure transformation of Victorian-style society into a more modern, liberated and democratic society.

Florrie Greig grew up in such a dynamic and shifting social milieu. The new hybrid society of Canada evolved from the influences of British and American society and from a myriad of cultures from all over the world. Being a contemporary of such great men as Bell, Edison, Ford and Carnegie, Florrie was a prime witness to the technological and cultural upheaval in North America. She was dazzled by these inventions but, more specifically, she was able to listen to music from the gramophone and study comfortably under electric lights. Not everybody could go to Carnegie Hall and Covent Gardens to see and hear great performances, but more people than ever before had access to music recordings and could watch world news on the screen, and thereby more intensely participate in the fabric of life. Florrie was among the first consumers of these new media. She became a walking encyclopedia about the music stars of the day. She adored the exquisite operatic voice of the Italian tenor, Enrico Caruso, and the Russian bass opera superstar, Feodor Chaliapin. She became an avid gramophone fan and a record collector.

Thanks to the philanthropic mogul of the day, Andrew Carnegie, who infused social culture with generous donations, a number of concert halls mushroomed across the States, fully equipped with costly music instruments for their orchestras. Carnegie, as a generous benefactor, furnished over seven thousand churches with expensive organs for the convenience and pleasure of millions of churchgoers. In this way, he single-handedly and most decisively nurtured the spread of both secular and spiritual music in North America. Obviously, with the advent of the radio, the gramophone, the motion picture camera, and the generosity of Carnegie and many other philanthropists, music was no longer a local group experience. It became accessible to people of all ages and of different socioeconomic backgrounds.

The Greig family moved around northern Ontario and resided in the vicinity of Manitoulin Island. They lived in a tiny community, Nestorville, near Thessalon on the northern shore of Georgian Bay. The two older Greig children, Willard and Florrie, were both musical just like their father. In grade school, they had a hard task of having to walk from Nestorville to their school located in Thessalon, often in very cold weather conditions. At an early age, Willard became skillful at fishing and in his early teens he became very good at trapping for fur. By selling pelts, he was able to supplement the modest and unstable income of his father. Willard and his sister, Florrie, were both very curious children who yearned for self-improvement. Florrie was naturally musically gifted to the great delight of her father, John. He gave her her first singing lessons. She was fascinated by his beautiful voice, the great number of hymns he knew and his choir-leading ability. Young Florrie identified deeply with her father's music aspirations and became his fervent student and follower. The scope of Florrie's music talent went beyond her father's. With his encouragement, she was sent to Sault Ste. Marie for a few private piano and voice lessons. Often, her lessons were financed from Willard's petty cash budget earned from trapping wild animals. This is how the themes of classical music studies and animal fur as a resource for pursuing them became interwoven early in Florrie's life and then later on in the life of her son, Glenn Gould.

Through her music education, Florrie became acquainted with the history of music, technical piano, and voice studies. Her interest extended in the field of diction, proper speech, and enunciation, many of the fine qualities that she later passed on to her son, Glenn. Florrie studied piano music with profound interest, even taking stoic pleasure in drilling scales. Clementi's sonatinas, Czerny's technical and pedagogic music pieces and Bach's *Little Clavier* were all perfected under her youthful fingers. There was more and more music to learn. When her family was poor and struggling to make ends meet, Florrie kept practicing on the old upright church piano until payments for more music lessons could be afforded. As a child, she listened to the family legend being retold about a probable shared ancestry between her father's Greig family and that of the famous Norwegian composer, Edvard Grieg. Incidentally, when Grieg died in 1907, the teenage Florrie, inspired by the family myths of relation to the great composer, gathered a greater momentum to dedicate herself to a more advanced study of music. In the same year, 1907, Florrie lost her beloved grandmother, Flora Mackenzie Flett. With the deaths of Edvard Grieg, her musical ego ideal, and the passing of her Grandma Flora, Florrie Greig seems to have entered a new stage of her life. Until then she was playful, like a little girl who had fun with music. After this turning point, she somehow became more grown up and determined to pursue music as a career. Moreover, Florrie behaved as if she had a mission to accomplish; the mission being to become a distinguished musician herself, akin to Edvard Greig, whom she regarded as her great musical relative. With such emotionally charged determination, at the age of sixteen, Florrie broke away from her rural family and arrived in Toronto with a great fantasy-mission in her mind. She moved in with her maternal aunt, Flora Flett. In the course of the next eighteen years of living together, the two relatives became very close. This was a step up on the emotional ladder from the tense, worrisome and reserved environment of her parental home.

Flora Flett was named after her mother, Flora Mackenzie Flett, who was related to William Lyon Mackenzie, the famous Canadian politician, rebel and the first mayor of Toronto in 1834. His grandson, William Lyon Mackenzie King, was three times Prime Minister of Canada, from 1921 to 1930 and from 1935 to 1948. Flora Flett was very proud of her heritage and her family ties to the prime minister. She was politically minded and greatly identified with Agnes MacPhail, who was the first woman member of the House of Commons in Canada. Flora Flett lived at 38 Kenneth Avenue and worked as a professional seamstress in her salon located nearby on Bloor Street. As a couturier, she produced garments for well-to-do customers of the affluent west end of Toronto. This is where her sixteen-year-old niece, Florrie Greig, joined her in the largest and most dynamic city of Ontario. For Florrie, this was a turning point where she separated from her conservative parents and the economic and cultural poverty of their environment to begin a life nourished by arts and entertainment evolving in a modern city. Florrie was driven by her inner quest for emotional independence, by her talent for music and a firm belief in her mission. By far, Florrie preferred life in Toronto with her more compassionate and open-minded aunt to her overly regimented life with her parents. Here she was able to attend classical music concerts at Massey Hall and go to movie theaters. She diligently studied music and gave solfeggio, vocal, and piano lessons to young pupils. At the same time, she took classes in music to upgrade her piano technique. Her brother, Willard, always came to her rescue whenever she was short of cash by paying for her advanced music education. In her twenties, Florrie was sought after as a music teacher. She prepared children for their exams at the conservatory, which they often passed with honors. To enhance her income, she traveled by train to the small communities of Bradford and Uxbridge to teach instrumental and vocal music and to prepare local choirs for special public performances. It was she who endlessly taught Clementi and Czerny finger technique and eagerly played the works of Diabelli for four hands with her students. Being a fervent listener of her father's singing in church, she gradually fell in love with the music of worship. She sang hymns with pious passion and dedication. Florrie's own voice developed into a beautiful, rich, and clear mezzo soprano. It was suitable for operatic and belcanto performance but was not sufficiently trained to go beyond the level of a church and choir vocalist. As a teacher, Florence Greig was also strict and methodical, just like her father. As an adult choral director, she was also strict and formal, emphasizing the importance of discipline. Despite her short-lived, teenage rebellion against her parents, Florence very much identified with their moralistic spirits and, in a broader sense, with the ethical values of the Victorian Age. Though she was interested in classic music, Florence Greig never formalized her music education, nor did she ever become a professional pianist.

On the political arena following the death of Queen Victoria, her oldest son became King Edward VII. Upon King Edward's death, his second son ascended the throne as King George V. During his time, Great Britain was among the first nations to enter World War I in August 1914 with Germany. Canada, as a part of the British Dominion, entered the war simultaneously. The Canadian government fought against conscription and delayed it, but enlistment was fiercely pursued and thousands of Canadian soldiers were sent abroad to European battlefields. The forerunner of modern radio was used by the military as a new means of electronic telecommunication. The chilling news of the war was relayed intercontinentally from the European front to Canada. The infamous battles of Ipres and Passchendalle caused mass bloodshed, destroying the lives of several hundred thousand soldiers in their prime. French, British, and Canadian Allied troops were slaughtered in the trenches by poisonous gas, artillery and infectious diseases. Many Canadian mothers and fathers were draped in black for the loss of their beloved sons in the horror of this war. This was the world climate of Florrie Greig's young adulthood as she tried to establish herself in the field of music, at a time when music was not foremost on the minds of Canadians.

In 1916 Florrie's brother, Willard Greig, as a young lawyer moved to Uxbridge, Ontario. He joined the law practice of Col. Samuel C. Sharpe, who soon went to serve overseas.[8] Willard had a congenital heart murmur and could not enlist. Upon return from the war, Col. Sharpe tragically ended his own life by suicide, which left Willard in charge of the entire law practice. He eventually purchased it, and for the next forty-five years Willard Greig led a productive life as a town solicitor. In 1919, Willard's father, John Greig, retired and moved to Uxbridge with his wife and their youngest son, Ruel, and permanently settled there. Florrie, who resided in Toronto, often took a train to Uxbridge to visit her parents and to rehearse with the local church choir. She had become a pristine young woman, a devout churchgoer and, above all, a keen vocal director.

While much is remembered about Florrie's older brother, Willard, very little is known about her younger brother, Ruel Peter Greig. Not only does Ruel remain a mystery to current researchers, but he was totally unknown to Glenn. Apparently, at some point, Ruel moved to Vancouver, where he lived with his wife and two daughters, Geraldine and Alberta. He died prematurely in June 1932 at the age of thirty-six when his older sister, Florrie, was pregnant with Glenn. This meant that at the time of Glenn's birth, in September 1932, both his mother and grandmother, Mary, were bereaved around the loss of Ruel. Curiously, Glenn never learned anything from his mother or other sources about his Uncle Ruel. This information became a family secret that was carefully kept from him. Long after his mother passed away, Glenn accidentally found out from his cousin, Jessie Greig,[9] that he once had an uncle who died before his birth. Glenn felt greatly hurt and betrayed by his mother.

Glenn's oldest cousin, Betty Greig Madill, remembered her uncle:

"I was told that Ruel was a 'good-time-Charlie' always ready to join a party, but he really did not have any direction in life," Betty recalled.

"It seems that he ran away from the family, as if there is a sense of shame about him. Do you know why Glenn's mother never talked about him to Glenn?" I asked cautiously about this private family matter.

"Unfortunately, I don't know, because the subject never came up while Aunt Florrie was alive and because this all happened when I was a teenager and before Glenn was born. He simply disappeared and he was never spoken about again,"[10] Betty finished this sad story.

Was Ruel ostracized or disowned by his family, or did he reject them? Though Glenn would never know, Ruel seemed like the "black sheep" of the Greig family, always surrounded by the veil of secrecy. Glenn was an unwilling recipient of his mother's grief and guilty conscience for Ruel's unhappy ending. These unspoken and unresolved feelings in his family of origin were registered in Glenn's subconscious mind and followed him like a shadow throughout his entire life.

RUSSELL HERBERT GOLD AND HIS ANCESTORS

> Yes, I am a Jew, and when the ancestors of the right honorable gentleman were brutal savages in an unknown island, mine were priests in the temple of Solomon.
>
> Benjamin Disraeli[11]

Uxbridge was the hometown of the well-respected Gold family. The house at 36 Franklin Avenue, where Willard Greig, the town solicitor, used to live and where his sister, Florrie, used to visit on weekends, was only steps away from the Gold residence at 69 Second Avenue, where Tom and Alma Gold resided with their four children. Their oldest son, Russell Herbert Gold, later became the father of Glenn Gould. Tom, who was an admirer of great British statesmen, picked the name Russell for his firstborn son, after Lord John Russell, while his middle name came from Tom's younger brother, William Herbert. Bert, as Russell Herbert was universally called, was born on November 22, 1901. Bert was a sturdy and energetic boy who attended both primary school and high school in his native Uxbridge.

"What was your life like as a child?" I asked Bert.

"I would say very quiet. We had two horses and two cows. I had to look after the cattle. Sometimes, I had to get up early in the morning to milk the cows. In those days, we didn't have a car, but we used a horse, and we owned a buggy," Bert remembered.

"What about your social life as a boy?"

"I played with kids whenever I could. We'd chase butterflies, and we played hide-and-seek and leapfrog; often we'd play a ball game."

"What was your manner of playing as a teenager?" I asked.

"I had a Shetland pony which I enjoyed very much. When we were older, we'd go to Lake Scugog fishing. It was a lot of fun. I had a nice childhood, I can't complain at all,"[12] Bert stated with a sense of contentment.

Bert's father, Thomas G. Gold, was born in 1867, the year of the Confederation of Canada, in Paisley, Ontario, as the second son to his parents, Reverend Isaac Gold and Maria Proctor. In 1882, when Tom was fifteen years of age, his older brother, Isaac, Jr., ran away from home to Australia, where he soon died. Tom's youth was one of hardship and losses. In 1886, his father, Rev. Isaac, crushed by the death of Isaac Jr., died suddenly from a heart attack at the age of 51. Not yet recovered from the grief, in the following year, Tom lost his younger brother, Alfred "Freddy" Gold, who drowned in the local pond. This "saddest accident occurred in the evening when Fred and his friend William went skating on the local pond. The thin ice instantly broke down and the two youths disappeared under the water."[13] After this tragedy, the twenty-year-old Tom was gravely distressed. In his deep sorrow, from which he never fully recovered, he hung a hook on the wall above the fireplace, where it stayed for many years to come. This was the hook used to pull Freddie's body from the water. Bert and his siblings grew up aware of the hook and the tragic end of their Uncle Freddy. In the future, Glenn Gould also would become aware of the hook and the story behind it. Because of Freddie's accident, Glenn's parents never encouraged him to skate.

In 1891, following the tragic loss of her son, Freddy, to drowning, Maria Proctor Gold, the widow of Reverend Isaac Gold, purchased the house at 69 (presently 73) Second Avenue in Uxbridge and moved in with her three remaining sons, Tom, William Herbert and Albert. The loss of his father, Isaac, and two brothers, Isaac Jr. and Freddy, put enormous responsibility on Tom, who according to the tenets of his time and being the eldest surviving son had to become the chief caretaker of his family at the tender age of nineteen. Bert said with compassion in his voice while referring to his father, Tom: "My dad, at an early age, had to get out and hustle in order to support his mother and two surviving brothers, Will and Albert."[14]

As a young man, Tom Gold married Lily Gould, the granddaughter of Joseph Gould, the founder of Uxbridge. Lily, like many other young women, died at childbirth in 1898, along with her newborn, leaving Tom a childless widower. Those untimely losses of cherished family members left on Tom a deep penchant of sadness and seriousness for the rest of his life.

In search of inner peace and financial security, Tom turned to religion and business. In 1900, he remarried to Alma Horne. Two years later, Tom entered the fur business and worked in a prestigious Toronto fur house, first as a manager and later as a partner of Mansfield and Gold. In 1912, Maria Proctor Gold signed over the house at 69 Second Avenue in Uxbridge, Ontario, to her older son, Tom. Maria and her two younger sons then moved into the house next door, which Maria owned. She died of old age in 1921 and was buried in Bond Head, near Newton Robinson, Ontario, which was the hometown of her family of origin, the Proctors.

Tom and Alma Gold turned the house into their permanent home. Gradually, the house was adapted and refurbished to suit their personal needs and social status. Details like stained-glass windows, tapestry and oil paintings added to the warmth of the house and its people. The living room was dominated by a grand piano, which was among the first such instruments built in the local Uxbridge Piano Factory.

In 1913, Tom established his own fur salon on Melinda Street in downtown Toronto. The witnesses remember that a number of hunters and trappers from all over the county used to come to Tom's house in Uxbridge and unload in front of his door stacks of raw pelts skinned off wild animals. Apparently, the sight of blood and the stench that emanated were quite gruesome. Tom then purchased the goods in bulk and selected the pelts for the local tannery. After the tanning, the leather and fur were shipped to his Toronto fur salon.[15] As time went on, the wholesale of goods became more sophisticated and was done through the distributors of fur directly sold to Tom Gold's fur salon in Toronto. Curiously enough, one of Tom's early business associates was Willard Greig, not necessarily in the matter of law but in the matter of the fur business. Willard, as an excellent trapper and hunter, used to sell his goods to Tom Gold. Willard's youngest son, John Greig, related a rare anecdote that typifies the frontier mentality of the early twentieth century in Canada:

"Mr. Greig, what do you remember about your father's business with Tom Gold?" I asked John Greig during my Christmas visit to Uxbridge.

"My father had a couple of polar dogs named Grit and Tory. He took those dogs everywhere in Ontario, trapping and hunting in all kinds of weather. They were husky dogs, very rough and capable. They could pull sleds and had no fear of anything," John said with certainty.

"When did your father stop trapping and hunting?" I asked.

"He never did. Even with his successful law practice, my father never stopped hunting and trapping. At first, it started as a business. He used to sell the animal skins to Tom Gold. Later on, it was more like a sport or a hobby," said John.

"What else do you remember?" I was fascinated by the story.

"Well, do you know how Florrie and Bert met?" John asked me.

"I think I do. They had met in Uxbridge in the church choir," I said.

"In fact, they had met much earlier and under different circumstances. You see, there was this occasion when my father [Willard] and his sister, Florrie, arrived by train at Union Station in Toronto, along with Grit and Tory," said John.

"Really, what for?"

"They carried the goods for Tom's Fur Salon on Melinda Street." John was enthralled in his own story.

"Please go on," I urged him.

"The story goes that Tom had a black cat who sat around idling in his salon. When Grit and Tory arrived, they developed an instant dislike for the black cat. They chased the cat around; it got to be very rough and they tore the poor cat into pieces in front of everybody. My father tried to stop them but it was too late. Bert was there, too." John had a clear memory of this unfortunate story.

"You mean, Grit and Tory killed the Gold cat in the middle of the fur salon in front of the four people?" I was stunned by the image, which seemed more like a scene from a Farley Mowat story about the Canadian wilderness.

"Yes, the dogs simply collided with the cat. And this is how Bert and Florrie met for the first time,"[16] John said.

"Unbelievable. Do you know whether Glenn knew this story?" I asked.

"I am sure he did. Everyone else in the family knew it because the story was retold at different family events," John replied adamantly.

If Glenn knew this shocking story about uncle Willard's dogs, what was his reaction? Was he compelled to replay the fatal chase in his daydreams? Was he appalled? Did he assume guilt feelings from his elders for the death of his grandfather's cat? We will always wonder.

At the same time, while pursuing this unsavory part of his fur business, Tom also led a very fulfilling and rich spiritual life. He worked avidly for the Methodist Church in Uxbridge as a Sunday school teacher and the local preacher. Tom Gold became a distinguished and upstanding citizen of Uxbridge. He lived a long and rewarding life and had the pleasure of watching his firstborn grandson, Glenn, grow and develop into a famous music personality. On his side, Glenn had a distinct opportunity to know his Papa Gold and learn from him about Canadian history.

Tom's wife, Alma, was the only child of Andrew Horne and Mary Stillwell from the tiny community of Saintfield, near Uxbridge.[17] Her father taught primary school and music and was her first music teacher. She took music classes in piano and organ and played both instruments very well. When "Allie," as her parents affectionately called her, was a teenager, she rode a bicycle. Unlike her female friends, she belonged to a local bicycle club. Alma brought to the Gold family her hope chest with the dowry furnished by her fairly well-to-do father. But more importantly, she possessed fine personal assets such as an energetic and vivacious spirit and her natural music talent. Before her marriage to Tom, following in the footsteps of her father, Andrew, she taught primary school and music in Greenbank and Uxbridge. During her marriage, Alma continued to give private piano classes and to coach the junior choir. She played the organ faithfully every Sunday at the nearby Methodist Church, which later became the Trinity United Church. Alma pursued many social and music activities and served as an accompanist at the piano for the Business Men's Bible Society, founded and presided over by her husband, Tom. At that time, the Bible was read daily and prayers were said regularly at meals and at bedtime. Sundays were dedicated to church going and worship services, which often were attended twice daily, once in the morning and at seven in the evening. At home, Alma ran a busy and dynamic household by raising four bright and musical children, entertaining relatives and hosting countless parties.

"I understand that your mother was very outgoing and that your house was referred to as a 'hive of music?'" I asked Mr. Gould.

"Yes, we always had guests and we always had music in the family. On Sunday evenings, usually after the church service, we had our neighbors over, and my mother played the piano and everyone was singing,"[18] Bert was happy to recall.

Bert, the firstborn of his mother, became the apple of her eye. In turn, Bert grew up to adore and respect her as the most valued person of his life. He emulated many positive qualities of his mother, particularly her vitality, sense of humor and musicianship. As an adult, Bert's choice of a musically and religiously minded older wife was largely determined by his subconscious need to surround himself with those valued qualities of his mother.

From his infancy on, Bert was exposed to his mother's music endeavors, which inspired and encouraged him toward both instrumental and vocal music. "My mother always tried to give me piano lessons but that was just not my instrument,"[19] Bert confessed. He was then started on violin lessons, and by his teens he was able to play in the local orchestra; the same one in which his mother was a soloist at the piano. His violin practices did not "soften" his masculine strengths, and Bert did not hesitate to engage in physical fights with other boys when his honor was at stake. Nor did his friends easily dare to tangle with him. Bert's violin career did not last long. After a finger injury in his mid-teens, he stopped playing altogether and never resumed his violin studies again.

Bert was mechanically minded. He was very good at building and repairing things. As a young lad he was handsome and socially outgoing. Bert was dating girls, staying out late at night and coming home inconspicuously through the back door of the house. He also pursued many hobbies. Fishing became one of Bert's favorite pastimes, which he practiced for many years until his son, Glenn, pressured him to stop. Unlike his younger brother, Bruce, Bert rarely engaged in hunting trips, and when he did, it was mostly hunting ducks, grouse and rabbits. He had no desire for trapping, which contrasted with his future lifelong occupation as a furrier.

Bert's likeness to his father, both in looks and behavior, was striking. He spent a great deal of time with him in various manly activities. On top of his robust physical disposition, Bert was a curious and daring teenager, who at the age of fourteen drove his "father's Chevrolet, the first car of the kind that appeared in an Oshawa car dealership, which was the closest city to Uxbridge."[20] Bert chauffeured his father to and from Toronto, where Tom Gold's fur salon was located.

"I find your story most interesting. Please tell me more about your teenage driving adventures," I pleaded with Mr. Gould.

"Well, I would put on my long trousers to look older than fourteen, in case we were stopped by police." Bert sounded somewhat mischievous.

"Were you ever caught?" I asked with a smile.

"No, not really. In those days the number of cars on the roads was scarce and the traffic regulations were quite lenient, so I was never caught for driving underage."[21] Bert spoke as if he had won a round. The father-son tandem worked quite well, and when Bert was in his early twenties, he started working for his father as manager of the fur business. For some thirty years, they enjoyed a mutually supportive relationship and saw each other on a daily basis at work.

Bert Gold was born in the family house at 69 Second Avenue, in Uxbridge, Ontario. This interesting and unique-looking two-story house with wood clapboard siding and two bay windows, one on each floor, has stood out for its beauty for over a hundred years. Particularly attractive is the facade, with its Grecian columns on the front verandah and the upper-story balcony. It was Tom Gold who ornamented this previously simpler-looking house by building the columns and balconies to match his successful business status as a furrier. While most of the other houses on Second Avenue were replaced by more contemporary bungalows, the former Gold family house, along with the Palmer house across the road, withstood the test of time, and both still compete with new dwellings in their architectural and esthetic merits. The presence of the elegant Gold family house contributed greatly to the attractiveness of Second Avenue. Only steps away is the end of the street, the end of the town and the beginning of corn fields and green meadows with wild flowers like goldenrod, daisies, poppies and trumpet creepers that quiver in the wind like waves on the ocean. That kind of panoramic landscape helps generate a feeling of equanimity and personal security in its inhabitants. Such was the original environment where Bert Gold was born and raised, and where his son, Glenn, was a frequent visitor in his childhood and youth.

Bert's three younger siblings were also musical. His sister, Freda, was started on the piano by their mother, Alma. The same was true for their baby brother, Grant, who was born much later, when Alma was forty-seven years of age. Alma was only able to provide basic piano education to her children, and when they achieved a certain level of training, she hired professional piano teachers for them. In 1924, when Grant was six years old, his mother, Alma, invited Florrie Greig, who was a visiting music teacher in Uxbridge, to pay them a visit at home in order to assess Grant's musicality. When Florrie came, she met Bert Gold at their home. Hence their paths crossed again. Alma had no idea that Bert and Florrie would soon strike a relationship and be married. At some point in 1930, when Grant was about twelve years old, he was enrolled in formal piano classes with Florrie Greig, who was by that time already married to his older brother, Bert, and had become a member of the Gold family.

Yet, the most musically gifted Gold child was the third-born, Bruce, who was self-taught and capable of playing several brass instruments, at first trumpet and saxophone. He went on developing skills in playing bugle and tuba, which he continued throughout his adult life. Bruce became a member of the local orchestra and the marching band. "He was a town celebrity; he could play any instrument he set his hands on,"[22] said John Greig, who knew Bruce very well.

Like his staunch, churchgoing parents, Bert also became involved in church activities, including regular Sunday worship services. He was musically gifted and had a warm baritone voice, which helped him become a member of the male quartet. By listening to the hymns his mother played, Bert himself developed an aptitude for both music and religion. It was during those church-oriented activities and song rehearsals when the paths of Bert Gold and Florrie Greig first crossed. He was the singer and she was everything else, the organizer, choir conductor, promoter and often the piano accompanist.

"What do you remember about the time when you met Glenn's mother?" I asked Mr. Gould.

"She was our choir leader and she used to prepare our vocal quartet. We did a lot of anniversary work in churches; our group became quite well known and invitations came from all over Northern Ontario," Bert said.

"Please, tell me a little more about your shows?" I pleaded.

"Well, Glenn's mother and I used to sing a great deal in duet, and we sang ballads at private lawn parties within a fifty-mile radius. We used to hire an elocutionist, Ella Montgomery, to come with us and do the skits."[23] Bert was somewhat reserved while still enjoying our conversation.

Bert's mother, Alma, led a dynamic life filled with her family, music and church. As a skillful pianist and organist, she lived long enough to see her first-born grandson, Glenn Gould, achieve unprecedented fame as a world-class pianist. It was a rare phenomenon and privilege that a pianistic grandmother was able to relate to and enjoy the incredible musical talent of her famous grandchild. She enjoyed talking about Glenn's music accomplishments with him personally and with others, offering comments and unconditional positive regard. Alma also read Glenn's critical reviews and often saved newspaper clippings that she thought would interest him. It appears that Alma's genuine love of music and her musicality were both passed on to her first-born grandson. This shows that Glenn's genetic roots to music could be traced to the Horne family and not only to the Greigs.

Going back to one generation earlier, Reverend Isaac Gold, the father of Tom and great-grandfather of Glenn, was an interesting but elusive character. Born in the state of Maine, where his parents temporarily settled, he came to the Dominion of Canada in his early twenties with his father, Isaac Gold Sr.[24] So far, nothing is known about Reverend Isaac's mother, not even her name or the time of her death. Reverend Isaac frequently moved from one place to another and traveled a great deal, defying the problems that a traveler of the Victorian Age had to endure. He not only traveled extensively in North America, but he went back and forth to England, the original homeland of the Gold family. His father, Isaac Gold, Sr., came from Fording Bridge, near Salisbury in England. Like his great contemporary, British Prime Minister Benjamin Disraeli, and many other Jewish families who renounced their faith, Reverend Isaac Gold, too, converted to Christianity at the age of twenty-three. Soon after the adoption of his new faith, Isaac was ordained in Quebec and acquired his first circuit of several congregations. He immigrated with his father to Ontario, where they permanently settled. He became a Methodist minister, and in this capacity he was reassigned to a different community every four years, exposing him to a variety of parishes such as Arthur, Paisley and Caledon. He married Maria Lucy Proctor, the daughter of Thomas and Deborah Proctor of Newton Robinson.[25] The Gold couple gave birth to six sons, of which the first five survived, whereas the sixth son, James, died at the age of one month in September 1873. Soon after, in November of the same year, Isaac Gold Sr. died. Shortly after his death, Reverend Isaac embarked on a four-month journey to England via France. It is curious that Reverend Gold would depart overseas during the winter, leaving his bereaved wife, who just lost her baby, at home with five young children. It is possible that an inheritance was the motivating reason for him to visit his father's birthplace.

Following the loss of his oldest son, Isaac Gold, Jr., who died in Australia due to unknown causes, Reverend Isaac took sick and had to retire from his ministerial job at the Oakwood Methodist Church, near Lindsay, Ontario. He then moved to Uxbridge in 1886, where he soon died and where his family permanently settled.

The town of Uxbridge grew from the initial settlement of Dr. Christopher Beswick in the year 1806. In the course of the next eighty years, Quaker families from Pennsylvania and other brave pioneers from the British Isles and the United States populated the area. This fast-growing community achieved the status of town in 1885 by an order in council. The leading force in the growth of the town is considered to be Joseph Gould, who also became the first reeve. His parents, who were of Irish extraction, immigrated to Canada by way of Philadelphia. Joseph's family name was Gold. According to his own story, Joseph found in a Webster spelling-book that the word "G-o-l-d " stood for a metal, whereas the word "G-o-u-l-d" was a man's name. On a "whim," Joseph decided to change his last name. He said: "And so I commenced writing the name GOULD, and in a few years the whole family did the same."[26] While this naive reason may have been true, it is likely that there may have been much deeper reasons for the name change. Be reminded that the society of the Victorian Age was branded by widespread prejudice and parochialism. When Ontario was pioneered, people clung to their respective religious and national communities and to their socioeconomic classes. Mixed marriages were looked upon as risky and outlandish, whereas class aloofness and segregation were practiced as safe and habitual. There were very few Jewish settlers in Ontario at that time. While they were able to accomplish a solid economic and cultural status, it was much harder for them to blend and to achieve social distinction. On the contrary, when it came to politics, leadership and social prestige, it was unpopular to be of Jewish descent. Understandably, some of the ethnic minority immigrants who were not able to withstand the ethnic and anti-Semitic tension resorted to measures such as changing the family name, renouncing their faith and converting to another more acceptable religion in order to conform to the majority. It is likely that Joseph Gold, as did many other families motivated by demographic reasons, changed his Jewish-sounding name to a more anglicized name, Gould. The ambitious Joseph Gold, by transforming his name to Gould, gained a degree of security and freedom from possible anti-Semitic attitudes, which all helped him embark on a successful political career. In the identity of a gentile, Joseph "advanced, as he grew to manhood through all the gradations of path master, municipal councilor, school trustee, and warden, to the honor of a seat in Parliament as representative of his native county."[27] Joseph's five sons, Isaac, Harvey, Charles, Jonathan and Joseph, all became distinguished and influential citizens in Uxbridge.

A century later, Tom and Bert Gold followed the same pathway of the name change. No family kinship has been proven between the families of Joseph (Gold) Gould and Reverend Isaac Gold. It is possible that Reverend Isaac Gold, in choosing Uxbridge as the place of his permanent residence, was partly motivated by the prosperity of the county and, in part, encouraged by the presence of the influential Gould family, whose former surname, Gold, he shared. The attraction between the Gold and Gould families materialized when Tom Gold married Lily, the daughter of Joseph E. Gould. With Lily's death, this liaison formally was broken.

Situated about forty-one miles northeast of Toronto, on the way to Lake Simcoe, Uxbridge had a fortunate geographical location since it was so close to both rural and urban areas. The town was encircled by a belt of rich farmland, excellent for a variety of grain crops. The abundance of cattle and plentiful virgin woods are only some of the many assets of this rich county. In the course of the nineteenth century, the town was expanding rapidly. Churches and industries mushroomed in and around the town. The saw and grist mill, the woolen mill, the piano factory, and the mechanic institute were distinguished structures that enriched this community. In 1873, this was a little bustling "boomtown" with a solid population of 1,617. Construction of the Toronto and Nippissing Railway was a great contribution to the mobility and strategic development of Uxbridge. In 1901, there was yet another important edifice added to Uxbridge— the music hall, which was opened for the community's cultural needs.[28] The Uxbridge Music Hall housed many concerts, and various members of the Gold family performed there, such as Glenn's grandmother, Alma, his father, Bert, and uncle, Grant. Glenn himself frequented the music hall as a visitor. In brief, this was the social environment where Reverend Isaac Gold, the great-grandfather of Glenn Gould, settled in the late 1800s.

A word is to be said about the fur industry in the nineteenth century, which was one of the major resources for the livelihood of the growing population of settlers. The Canadian frontier and, in a more narrow sense, the Ontarian wilderness, or bush, offered an abundance of animals as a source of food, leather and fur. The ecology between North Americans and their natural environment was, for the most part, well balanced in the nineteenth century. Hunting and fishing were characteristic for the frontier and necessary for survival. The Ontario soil was excellent for agriculture and livestock. A number of tanneries were opened to process the hides of domestic animals into commercially usable, high-quality cow and calf leather, sheep and lamb skin. Earlier, in 1670, the Hudson's Bay Company was founded in order to coordinate and distribute fur both locally and to export it to England. In 1869, the Dominion of Canada took over control of the entire bay area and the Hudson's Bay Company. The main occupations of the settlers in the bay area were connected to trapping, fishing, lumbering and related industries. Typical frontier fur posts were opened to facilitate the fur trade. In Canada, the most commonly used pelts were those of raccoon, rabbit, fox, opossum, beaver, mink, and seal. Gradually, the fur that served to meet basic needs for clothes and shelter became a commodity for the accumulation of capital in the hands of individuals and to meet the demands for luxury and prestige items. It was in this social and economic milieu when Tom Gold, Glenn's paternal grandfather, decided to become a furrier.

The end of World War I in 1918 signaled the time for Canadians to heal the wounds of multiple losses. The postwar peace provided an incentive for vigorous industrial and cultural development all across North America. This was also a time to celebrate the blood-earned peace, to educate, entertain and build families. In November 1920, the first radio public broadcasting company opened in Pittsburgh, Pennsylvania, and in the next two years another 500 radio stations proliferated in America. In 1922, Bert Gold made the pages of local history by bringing the first radio receiver to the town of Uxbridge. Despite a bout of economic depression after the War, the North American economy and industry continued to grow and expand. Media expansion, transmission and telecommunication of information, music and news, all through telegraphy, the gramophone, motion pictures, the radio and the performing arts, were rapidly evolving and becoming a new necessity for a quality life. Owning a radio set meant having a broadened vista of the world. It provided a wonderful opportunity for learning and entertainment. These were the times when the Toronto-based music teacher, Florrie Greig, was teaching music and organizing choirs in the small communities of Uxbridge and Bradford in Ontario. The Gold and Greig families were distinguished and socially affluent in Uxbridge. They also lived in close physical proximity. In April 1923, owing to ill health, Florrie resigned from the choir leader position at the Uxbridge Methodist Church,[29] but she continued to visit her mother in Uxbridge. Around that time, Bert's love relationship with his girlfriend was broken on her initiative. Feeling dejected and on the "rebound," he started seeing Florrie, of whom he had fond memories from their choir days. Encouraged by her warmth, Bert asked Florrie for her hand in marriage, and they became betrothed. On October 31, 1925, Bert Gold and Florence Greig were married in Toronto on her birthday. He was almost twenty-four years of age, and she was ten years his senior. Bert was a young, attractive-looking businessman, working for his father in a promising downtown Toronto fur business. He was considered to be from a good home with favorable prospects for the future. Florence was a sister of the town solicitor, Willard Greig, and was also considered to have come from a morally upstanding home. She was plain in her looks but ambitious and musical.

Bert's parents did not approve of this marriage and did not come to the wedding. To them, Florrie seemed too old and unattractive. Regardless of this original disapproval, Florrie and Bert worked their way back into the hearts of the Gold family. Bert continued to work as the manager in his father's fur store, but he could no longer drive his father to and from work. This meant that Tom Gold, though reluctantly, had to commute between Uxbridge and Toronto by train. Tom eventually made fewer trips to Toronto, giving more control of the business to his son. Bert and Florrie resumed visiting their elders in Uxbridge on the weekends and taking part, this time as guests, in Sunday church services. Only a year after her wedding, Florrie's father, John Greig, had a stroke and died in February 1927. His death caused profound bereavement in his family, which typically could not be resolved. In the beginning of June 1932, when Florence was almost six months pregnant with Glenn, there was a celebration of the twenty-fifth anniversary of the Uxbridge Bible Class founded by Tom Gold. On this occasion, Florrie sang a recital of old hymns that portrayed the mood of the day and reflected her extreme personal austerity and commitment to the Christian faith. This is how on June 5th, 1932, *The Lindsay Daily Post*, described the event:

Anniversary of Uxbridge Bible Class (25)

> ... Organized 25 years ago by that greatly beloved layman, Thomas G. Gold, of Uxbridge, this class has grown in influence and numbers until its annual anniversary is an occasion greatly looked forward to by all men who have the privilege and pleasure of attending ... The soloists for the day were Mr. and Mrs. R.H. Gold of Toronto, with Miss Isabel Alexander as accompanist. Their solos and their duets were greatly enjoyed during all three services. At the close of the afternoon service, Mrs. Gold sang a medley of old hymns which just captivated the large congregation: "What Can Wash Away My Sins, Nothing But The Blood Of Jesus," "Draw Me Nearer, Nearer, Nearer, Blessed Lord," "If You Want Peace, Joy and Power, You Will Find It At The Cross Of Jesus," "In The Cross, In The Cross, Be My Glory Ever," ending in that grand old hymn, "Shall

> We Meet Beyond The River," which struck so tenderly the chords of the human heart that you could almost feel that there came an answer a great refrain from all present, " Yes, We'll Gather At The River" ... The twenty-fifth anniversary was a signal triumph for this great organization and a lasting tribute to Mr. Thomas G. Gold, the teacher ...[30]

Clearly, both Florrie, referred to as Mrs. R. H. Gold, and her father-in-law, Thomas G. Gold, were the stars of this religious festivity. Florrie was six months pregnant at the time of this austere recital. Only three weeks later, Florrie was thrown into deep mourning again following the sudden death of her younger brother, Ruel. Her moods ranged from the bliss of pregnancy to her deeply personal and suppressed sorrow. No one would ever know the extent of her remorse and repentance over her family's attitude toward her estranged brother. Again, her unborn child was exposed to her deep sorrow. The worst part was that Florrie kept her feelings about Ruel to herself and never mentioned him in front of Glenn. By being arcane about this major family event, she unconsciously passed onto Glenn the burden of unfinished emotional business from her own family. These were some of the most important psychological and social dynamics predating Glenn's birth and influencing him in the future.

Chapter III

THE CHILDHOOD OF A CONCERT PIANIST

GLENN'S INFANCY

The Child is [the] father of the Man
William Wordsworth[1]

Glenn was born in his parents' home at 32 South Drive in the east end of Toronto. His birth was a long and anxiously awaited event as his mother, Florence, was nearly forty-two years of age. The birth took place on the second floor in the Gould's master bedroom and was assisted by the family physician, Dr. Sisely, a midwife, and Elsie Lally, the newly hired live-in help. Not too long before this successful pregnancy, Mrs. Gould had a miscarriage that caused her enormous grief and apprehension about possible childlessness. The Gould couple was doing well financially and socially, but they both felt incomplete without a child. Since this was well before any advances in reproductive technology, the Goulds were left to their own devices in the matter of conception. Because this pregnancy may have been their last chance, every precaution was taken to bring it to full term. For the first time in their lives, a maid was hired to relieve Mrs. Gould from undue exertion in the last months of pregnancy. The happiest of all events occurred on September 25, 1932, when Mrs. Florence Gould smoothly delivered a healthy baby boy, to the great joy of her husband and herself.

"How did you choose Glenn's first name?" I asked Mr. Gould during one of our many conversations.

"I never saw it in print but my wife named him after a dear friend of hers, Mrs. Robert Glenny," Mr. Gould recalled.

"Why was your wife taken with Mrs. Glenny? Was there anything special about her?" I inquired.

"I don't think so. I know she wasn't musical. It's just that they were very close,"[2] Mr. Gould answered.

Mr. Gould's story about the origin of Glenn's name is compounded with another version of her friend, Pearl, according to which Florence fantasized about having a son named Glenn long before she was married and much before she knew Mrs. Glenny. The middle name, Herbert, was of a more concrete origin and was given with respect to family tradition after his father's middle name, Russell Herbert, and his granduncle's name, William Herbert. So the child was named by combining a name that was his mother's chosen favorite and a middle name that connected this baby boy to the paternal side of his family.

At Glenn's birth, Dr. Sisely noticed with astonishment that the newborn's tiny fingers kept spreading and flexing as if he were playing the piano. According to the family legend, Dr. Sisely exclaimed prophetically: "This little boy will be a pianist some day or a doctor, one or the other!" It appears that Dr. Sisely's comment was more flattering and casual than scientifically based. In pediatric neurology, it is normal for babies to have purposeless movements of fingers and arms as a sign of incomplete development of their central nervous system. Despite such reasoning, no other compliment could be more fitting to Glenn's mother, who was fatigued from childbirth but gratified by having a baby boy who might be musical.

It was Florence Greig who longed to become a distinguished keyboard performer herself. Unluckily, her dreams remained unfulfilled. Her niece, Betty Greig Madill, remembered:

"Aunt Florrie wanted to be a pianist herself. Ever since she has been a child, that's all she wanted to be," Betty emphasized.

"As far as I know, she never finished formal piano studies, did she?" I asked.

"No, you are right, she never did. She tried to pass her ATCM [examination] but failed. She was heartbroken. They [her parents] had very little money and could not afford regular piano lessons. Poor Aunt Florrie, she only got a few lessons but this was not enough. Mostly, she had to study on her own,"[3] said Betty.

Since Florrie's efforts to obtain a degree of Associate of the Toronto Conservatory of Music, so-called ATCM, did not come to fruition, she remained personally unfulfilled in the realm of piano music. At some point, Florrie started fantasizing about having a son who would be a great pianist some day. A letter from Pearl (last name unknown), her friend from youth, testifies that Florrie's wishful speculation predated by far the birth of her child. Pearl's letter, congratulatory in nature, was written on the occasion of Glenn's New York City debut in 1955 when he reached international fame. It alludes to those early hopes of his mother in this way:

> Dear Florrie, Chatham, February 2,1955
> ... Florrie do you recall one day when you were my guest in Moncton ... You told me some day you were going to marry and have a little boy and his name would be Glenn. I said I suppose he will be musical. You quickly said I'll see to that with a twinkle in your eye. I shall never forget that day. You were never satisfied with just anything, you wanted only the best, the old saying 'hitch your wagon to a star.' I am indeed happy for you that your dreams have come true. Seldom is a dream remembered so clearly in so long a time, but I remember as if it were yesterday.[4]

Pearl's letter proves that Florrie was emotionally very much invested with the idea of having a famous musical son. Her chief mission was to pass the music torch of the Greig family on to her child. Mindful of this, Florence pursued a variety of musical activities during her pregnancy. She played the piano daily with fervor; listened to records from her sizable collection and sang a variety of popular ballads. Florrie most often played Bach's music, particularly preludes and toccatas, but not infrequently she would lapse into the music of Mendelssohn and Mozart. She was convinced that the more music she heard and played, the better it would be for her future child, so that he might be musically inclined. In this regard, Florrie Greig Gould may be considered as a forerunner of modern theorists who have explored fetal responses to music. Her hypothesis was never published, but practically, by exposing her yet unborn child to music, she formulated her belief in early auditory stimulation of the fetus. A myriad of sophisticated studies confirm what Florence believed. The general consensus of this current research suggests that the "human infant may perceive music or aspects of it from the third trimester of intrauterine life."[5] Further, there are findings that support the idea that a fetus not only can experience music but is able to familiarize itself with specific music melodies.[6] Hence, it is not accidental that Glenn, when he grew up, became such a supreme interpreter of Bach's music, as his mother played and sang it for him like a lullaby before and after he was born.

Back to the Gould family, the entire running of their household was geared toward the needs of the little newcomer. Mr. Gould personally attended his wife after their son's birth. He prepared hearty breakfasts for her that he himself took to her room, even though the eager and helpful Elsie was standing by. This special mother of this very special and only son was to be attended with the best of care. Mary Flett Greig, the maternal grandmother, arrived from Uxbridge to help look after the baby. The three women in attendance devoted themselves to catering and fussing over the baby's every need. It was a busy, action-filled environment. Elsie, who was nineteen years old at the time, had the task of going for daily walks with Glenn, wheeling him in a pram down the hilly neighborhood streets. Her job was to entertain him and make sure that the little boy was out in the fresh air, which was considered good for his developing lungs.

Glenn was a very attractive baby. His beautiful rosy face, like that of a little cherub, was encircled by ringlets of golden blond hair. On the street, when passersby spotted Glenn in his baby carriage, they often made passionate utterances like: "Oh, what a gorgeous-looking baby!" When at home, Elsie habitually sang little nursery rhymes holding him in a white wicker rocking chair in the sun room.[7] She also looked after the stacks of his baby clothes and diapers, which had to be meticulously cleaned and ironed. Grandma Mary took pleasure in holding Glenn and keeping him company, often in his sleep, to protect him from the shock of waking up alone. And, of course, there was the chief caregiver of this precious infant, his ever busy and concerned mother, Florrie. Baby Glenn was showered with physical attention, ceaselessly cuddled, and pampered by those three devoted women. The familiar smile on his father's face was seen only in the evening when he came home from a lengthy day of work. Glenn was also a first-born grandchild to his paternal grandparents, Tom and Alma, who adored and lavished much attention upon him too.

Along with his physical growth, Glenn was developing musically. Florrie practiced the piano and sang hymns during her pregnancy as well as after Glenn's birth, and Glenn was very familiar with the fine lilt of her voice. From the beginning the baby was saturated with organized sounds in the form of vocal and instrumental music, be it from the radio or performed live in front of him. Since he was regularly taken to church, Glenn frequently listened to rich pipe organ sounds and choir voices. The habitual family visits to his grandparents in Uxbridge were also music-oriented. Music was used to entertain Glenn, to teach him, to help him sleep, to keep him quiet, and to cheer him up. Every day was filled with music. The tiny boy was held at the piano before he was six months old. Several of Glenn's relatives believed that he was endowed with a gift for music. Consequently, they felt obliged and somewhat driven to do everything in their power to help shape and enhance his raw music talent. As a result, Glenn was always coaxed, praised and influenced in the direction of music. On his side, he responded to his cheerleaders jovially and curiously. Even though Glenn did not need to be cajoled toward music, he enjoyed all the attention and interest bestowed upon him. This pattern of interaction—attention sought, attention given—between Glenn and others was a pattern that survived into his adulthood.

Developmental milestones in Glenn's infancy were quite advanced. Both his early language skills and ability to sit and walk came easily and earlier than in average infants. At six months, he cheerfully played peek-a-boo and soon after pat-a-cake. His sense of humor and playfulness gave a picture of an unusually bright little boy. Glenn was bubbly and knew several words by the age of one, which hinted at his great future verbal acuity. As an infant, he nicknamed his nanny, Elsie Lally, as Lollipop and proceeded to call her that throughout his entire life. Elsie's face lit up when she reminisced about Glenn's infancy:

"What was Glenn like as a baby? There are several types of babies described at birth. Was he happy and sociable, or was he more on the quiet side? Can you tell me whether he was easy to handle or was he a handful?" I asked Elsie.

"Well, when he was tiny, he didn't give us any trouble. I used to play with him right from the beginning and he liked that. He smiled at me, and wanted me to pick him up. I still remember his toothless face. I used to squeeze him and kiss him all over and he laughed," Elsie recalled with a smile.

"It seems Glenn was very playful as a baby, wasn't he?" I asked.

"Oh yes. He was very outgoing, you could tell, because he always wanted someone around to play with." Elsie enjoyed memories about baby Glenn.

"What was he like as an older baby, a year old or so?" I pursued this pleasant conversation.

"Oh, the older he got the more active he was. As a baby, he could've been ten or eleven months old, Glenn used to tease me, pull my nose and make it disappear and then he pretended to give it back to me," Elsie said affectionately.

"What else do you remember?" I asked.

"Well, Glenn wanted to play hide-and-seek and used to chase me around. When he finally got a hold of me, he giggled and asked me to pick him up as a reward for being a winner in the game. I loved to play with Glenn because he made me laugh and he was so cute,"[8] Elsie happily recalled.

Baby Glenn seemed to enjoy being in the limelight among adults, whom he amused by showing off his charm, sense of self-importance and strong-willed mind. He was a playful and interactional child who sought the presence of others. In this sense, it was said that "he took after his paternal grandmother, Allie," who had a vivacious and sociable personality. Glenn was often photographed by his granduncle, professional photographer, William Herbert Gold. "Uncle Will," as he was fondly called, left behind a wealth of endearing portraits of Glenn as a document of his boyhood.

Besides music, Glenn's childhood was filled with a procession of toys to amuse and entertain him. Among them, he consistently favored a variety of stuffed dogs. It is curious that at a time when most infants and their parents preferred teddy bears, Glenn never owned one. Perhaps his fascination with toy dogs and, later on, with real dogs came from the dedication of his extended family to dogs. Glenn's father was brought up with a dog guarding his cradle. Glenn was photographed from his infancy on with a dog posing at his side and then, for the next couple of decades, was inseparable from his own two loyal dogs. Still, having toy dogs and real dogs does not preclude owning a teddy bear. Though we will never know for sure, it appears that Glenn's mother, out of her preference, decided to exclude teddy bears from her son's assortment of toys.

His mother's upright piano, like the plush stuffed animals and real dogs, soon became a focus of Glenn's constant curiosity and play. Baby Glenn was allowed to press the keys and amuse himself with the fading sounds. Once Glenn was able to master all the "baby stuff," including toilet training, by the age of two, his mother introduced him to more mature musical exercises. Florence, who already trained many young children in music, had a very methodical way of teaching. Her gift was particularly utilized when Glenn "came of age" to be taught music. She could hardly wait to introduce him to the piano, not just as a toy but in a more meaningful and organized way. The earliest training she pursued with Glenn consisted of note recognition, imitating little tunes, and the use of guessing games. This proved to be an excellent pedagogical tool that helped take Glenn further into the world of music sounds. Bert Gould remembered those lovely mother-child games:

> He would go to a room at the far end of the house and his mother would strike a difficult cord on the piano in the living room. Invariably, Glenn would call the correct answer.[9]

By the time Glenn was three years of age, his mother was convinced that he had perfect pitch and a preternatural talent for music. To corroborate her wishful beliefs, Florrie sought a professional consultation from a distinguished music pedagogue of that time whose name is now forgotten. Such a consultation was expensive. Glenn's father deemed it extravagant and refused to pay for it. Florrie became petulant and sat on the stairs pouting in protest against her husband's decision until he gave in. Finally, the consultation took place, and it was confirmed that Glenn was indeed gifted.[10] Encouraged by this professional opinion and by the anecdotes of other famous pianists, like Joseph Hofmann and Artur Rubinstein, who were started on early music training, but mostly guided by her own motives, Florrie Greig Gould began formal music lessons with the three-year-old Glenn. Thus, the shaping of a young artist began.

NOTES ABOUT GIFTED CHILDREN

> Art is a jealous mistress.
>
> Ralph Waldo Emerson[11]

This essay is specifically concerned with the psychology of children who are being prepared for a career as a performing pianist. One of the prerequisites to becoming a professional concert pianist is to start and pursue early music training, preferably before the age of five. This is because the piano technique should be grasped while the little hands are in their formative years. Once the child's musicality is recognized, the next step is to engage the child in very intense, even rigorous music training, in order to shape, reshape and perfect the raw music talent at the instrument. Selection of a suitable teacher is another important ingredient in the music training of a future performing artist. There are reputable piano teachers who specialize in guiding gifted students into their distinguished performing careers.

Children who are started on the career of an instrumental soloist may end up maturing rapidly in the area of music, whereas their social development may lag behind. Unlike their non-career-oriented peers, these youngsters have to make an unnaturally fierce commitment to music, often at the expense of other developmental needs. Playing an instrument is a form of play that could be a source of fun and imagination to the total satisfaction of a young music artist. Rehearsing and perfecting a music piece at the instrument is not necessarily fun but more a goal-oriented task. Such playing is more a matter of structure and discipline in the service of achievement and conquest. Sometimes, playing and studying music for performance could be a matter of obsessive drive at the expense of pleasure and other more genuine rewards. The young pianists who are subjected to vigorous music training with emphasis on structure and discipline are at risk of being deprived of the spontaneous playing of music or playing with their peers or toys. Moreover, they are specifically restricted from playing with dirt, sand and mud, and from engaging in rowdy physical sports and games in order to protect their hands from possible injuries. These children, by being very busy, do not have enough spare time to play freely. One of the advocates of child psychology, D.W. Winnicott, said in his work *Playing and Reality*:

> ... it is play that is the universal, and that belongs to health; playing facilitates growth and therefore health; playing leads into group relationships.[12]

Another major developmental scholar, Erik Erikson, stresses the same point:

> For to "play it out" is the most natural self-healing measure childhood affords.[13]

The link between play and health has been established beyond any doubt. Conversely, those children who have been deprived of fun and play are liable to suffer emotional consequences from this loss. Gifted children are not different from average children in their need to play. This is why heavy structured channeling in the direction of their gift is in various degrees at the expense of spontaneous play. During their music conditioning, those children often harbor unfulfilled longings for ordinary games and the company of their peers at the playground. Those unmet longings to play freely become masked by the seriousness of the discipline in practicing and studying music. Their play is being disrupted, but the adults around them justify it by regarding them as special and different from other children. Once again, the wisdom of Erik Erikson speaks on behalf of children's needs:

> The antithesis of play disruption is play satiation, play from which a child emerges refreshed as a sleeper from dreams which "worked."[14]

One wonders if young pianists are ever allowed to be satiated in their child's play? Not only may young pianists be disrupted in their specific need to play, but often there is a more profound and general disruption of their development. In the families where there is an overemphasis on music, where one or both parents are heavily music-oriented, where there is an embedded expectation for the child to be a musician, the child's natural development is disrupted by channeling most energies toward one activity at the expense of all others. The same child, left to his or her own preferences, might generate a different spectrum of interests and practices. The over-directed child likely has over-invested parents who pursue their own agenda as opposed to supporting their child's natural and unforced progress.

The age of three is commonly associated with what is called in the field of developmental psychology "first individuation." In normal development, the process of gradual emotional separation and individuation of the child from birth on is supposed to be achieved by the age of thirty-six months, or in many children even earlier.[15] This means that the child is able to gain a sense of his or her own individuality by the age of three. Such a child could be left to play by himself or could stay at kindergarten or a day-care center without being in distress in the temporary absence of his mother. This inner peace and sense of security is made possible through the acquired ability of the child to retain and keep the image of his mother (or primary caretaker) in his mind as a steady and constant person/constant object. A sense of object constancy and one's own individuality account for the psychological milestone of human growth known as "first separation and individuation."[16] Those children who, for various reasons, cannot successfully individuate because they are too emotionally attached to the parent(s) or parent substitutes, and cannot hold a constant inner image of the parent (object), continue to experience every minor separation from the primary caretaker with a sense of dread and inner distress. This very uncomfortable state of mind is referred to as separation anxiety.

In the case of early music training starting around the age of three or four, which is the age of striving toward one's own individuality, over-ambitious and rigid parents, by putting a priority on discipline and compliance above the child's spontaneous needs, unconsciously may interfere with the natural process of mental growth. By being controlling, invasive, and even punitive, these parents clash with their child's natural need to explore the world. This all inhibits the child's opportunity to explore music on his or her own and even to fantasize freely, which are necessary ingredients of successful emotional growth and individuation. Rigidity and lack of parental sensitivity to the child's needs may become a source of inner frustration to the child. The conflict between parental expectations and the child's ability to meet them may resolve itself in the course of personal and music growth of the young individual. Unfortunately, in some cases, it may lead to an unhappy ending and be responsible for the dissolution of a promising music career. This may be one of the explanations why some gifted children are unable to keep up and live up to their innate music talents in their adult years.

Contrary to possible childhood losses incurred by rigorous music training, there are many advantages to being a young and precocious musician. Those little music artists are esteemed and valued by their parents, relatives and their immediate community because of their extraordinary music talent, their achievement and their potential for future greatness. Inevitably, there is an aura of being special around them that serves as a broad source of self-esteem. Gifted children are showered with praise, applause and publicity, which all act to further their productivity and their sense of self-confidence.

There is a common tendency in achieving parents to wish for their children to follow in parental footsteps. Such a wish may be sensibly expressed and transferred to the child through positive modeling and encouragement. This is accompanied by the underlying unconscious mechanism of identification with a significant love object. The power of identification with parent or parent substitute is uncanny. As they say, like father like son. Glenn Gould in many of his manners, personality traits, self-image, choice of occupation, recreation, and socializing style did not take after his father. Instead, a lack of identification with the same sex parent occurred. As a result, Glenn, at first in his childhood and then in the course of his entire life, was unable to come to terms with his father. This had a negative impact on Glenn as a person and on his future career as a concert pianist. In the realm of having a passion for music, Glenn's mother served him as the model for primary identification. Also, he unconsciously identified with her strict moral values, puritanism, tendency toward rational thinking, and emotional inhibition. Glenn's mother, by being dedicated to discipline and the drive for achievement, for the most part was unable to treat music as play and recreation but took it extremely seriously, as a goal and duty.

Genetically, it was said that in terms of his exceptional photographic memory and particularly his verbal intelligence, Glenn took after his maternal uncle, Willard Greig, and that his musicality was related to the notable musical talent in both maternal and paternal families. But there was something original in Glenn, quite unlike any of his relatives, something beyond the mechanism of identification and heredity. He was endowed with a natural musical talent. Thus, a multifaceted background is operating and is responsible in the formation of this great artist. In Glenn's case, there was the psychological mechanism of identification with the music aspect of his parent (mother) and a biological mechanism of genetic transmission of musical talent from his mother, paternal grandmother and paternal uncle, Bruce. But, above all, there was in him a unique creative gift that was the product of many contributing factors, and this gift was unshared with others.

Pursuance of the intense music training and the appropriate selection of music teachers are two of the most important external factors in the making of a distinguished music artist. The role of parents and, particularly, the nature of the relationship between gifted children and their parents are the most important internal factors. Who wants to be a concert pianist, the child or the parent? Who is introducing the child to music classes and under what circumstances? Is there a coercion factor or not? Is there an ulterior motive on the part of the parent(s) or not? Upon reviewing biographies of thirty great performing music artists, I found that most of them were introduced to music by their parents between the ages of three and six. Two other possibilities appear to be less common: when the future great artist is introduced to music after the age of six or even at a later, adolescent age; or the least frequent situation of when the young child leads the parents in the direction of music achievement. Typical examples of the first situation would be those of the famous classic pianists Clara Schumann and Joseph Hofmann. It is well documented that both of them were deliberately and methodically trained for the career of concert pianist by their respective fathers, Friedrich Wieck and Casimir Hofmann. The parents of Artur Rubinstein boarded him out at the age of three into the care of a music teacher. The ambitious mother of Van Cliburn eagerly started her son's piano training at the age of three. The mother of Leon Fleisher, who herself was not musical, had decided that her son was going to be a great pianist. Fleisher started his piano training at the age of four-and-a-half and gave his first piano recital at the age of eight. He wrote:

> ... there was nothing "normal" about my childhood. I never went to school; I did all my academic work under the guidance of tutors, and I believe there was a big advantage to that. Yet I must admit that what one learns as a person, about life, about interaction with others, one gets by going to school with other people, and that was missing in my education ...[17]

It seems that some parents are driven to phase their children into music training immediately after their toilet training. One wonders whether such early organized training is more to do with the wishes and needs of the parents or the child. Is the child of three or five years of age able to make a decision about becoming a great pianist and then follow through? Mostly not, but the parent is. In reality, most often the parent(s) have decided for the child on the choice of a music career. While early music training may be positively correlated with music achievements, it is likely associated with the built-in risk factor of an adult ulterior motive. Overzealous parents inadvertently may overlook the child's natural pace and force their own tempo upon the child.

In the second most common situation, an older child or an adolescent, guided by their elders or through their own initiative, decide on studying music. Such teenagers largely rely on their natural talents and personal ambition. While parental and social supports are needed as facilitators, in this case they are not at the core of one's own success. Ivo Pogorelich, encouraged by his father, began piano classes at the age of seven in his native Yugoslavia but was sent to Moscow at the age of eleven for more advanced piano studies. Music artists such as Ignacy Paderewski, Igor Stravinsky, and Leonard Bernstein, driven by their own ambition and love of music, relied on their own talents and pursued their music training in their teens, often despite their parent's wishes and expectations.

Less commonly, gifted children could be so precocious and strongly self-motivated that they become propelled to fame spontaneously through their own resources and at a very early age. For example, British pianist Dame Myra Hess, who has no musical background and was not pressured to study piano, was driven by her own music gift to fame. Similarly, American pianist Rosalyn Tureck showed passion for music in her early childhood. She insisted to her parents that she be given piano lessons. An even more remarkable example would be that of Spanish pianist Alicia de Larrocha, who at the age of two urged her aunt to teach her how to play the piano. In these cases, the elements of parental ulterior motive, purposeful modeling, and high expectations placed on these children were all absent. The goal here is not to deem one of these situations as better than another but mainly to observe the differences and to caution all those concerned about the possible psychological pitfalls associated with music training of gifted children.

In the most common example, when the parents take initiative to train the child in the direction of music, the outcome is quite complex. Is the parent predominantly emotionally invested in the child for his or her own unfulfilled needs or more for the child's needs and wishes? Grandiose parents are likely to reinforce the success of their children in order to obtain personal gratification. Those parents who live vicariously through their offspring may confuse them by idealizing and overvaluing special qualities in them, particularly their talent for music. At the same time, they may overlook and even devalue their other abilities and needs. The prospect of fame may be so blinding that parents may not see the child for the fame. In an over-ambitious quest for prestige and success, parents and teachers may subject youngsters to coercive training, which may lead to various problems related to their self-esteem and issues of over- or under-compliance. Most musicians and psychologists would agree that rigid and punitive training may help create a good instrumentalist but an unhappy person. One of the adverse outcomes possible would be a lasting and plaguing presence of insecurity and anxiety around performing for others. Strict music training may frustrate the child's natural disposition and love of music, leading to a variety of complications ranging from personal discontent to more specific artist-related problems. Such a child may completely miss his natural path.

The results could be much better if the child is empathetically and gently guided ahead in music training. For best results, early training ought to be made as easy and comfortable as possible and be balanced with the rest of the child's needs such as the basic need to play with peers. "Good enough" and sensitive parents and/or teachers likely are able to create such an atmosphere for "comfortable enough" conditioning of the child into a performing artist/concert pianist, so that the child does not have to end up trading fame for a stolen childhood.

THE BOYHOOD OF A PRODIGY

Lord, give us the peace that the Earth cannot give.

There is no doubt that the close-knit relationship between Glenn and his mother served as the basic soil where the seed of his musicianship was planted. Glenn, too, like Clara Schumann and Joseph Hofmann, was rushed into early music training, driven by the interwoven forces of his own personal gift of music and parental ambition. Unfortunately, the risk factor of an ulterior motive was present, stemming from his mother's unfulfilled wishes to become a concert pianist herself. Armed with an irrepressible drive, Florence Gould started her son's music training at the age of three. It is said that Glenn was able to read music symbols around the age of four, which was earlier than he knew the letters of the alphabet. The discovery of music came quite naturally to Glenn and was accompanied by his insatiable curiosity to find out more about it. It is an understatement to say that Glenn was a fast learner. The first music book from which he studied was *Keyboard Town* by Louise Robyn. Florrie's introductory teaching method consisted of guessing games and playfulness at the keyboard and was consistent with her interest and skills in the vocal arts of speech and singing. Spoken and singing tones and words were interchangeably mingled with her keyboard lessons and demonstrations. Glenn sang too, matching his tiny voice with the robust piano tones. Guessing games were extensively applied in his early training, in which Glenn was supposed to guess and label various piano tunes or the notes sung by his mother. The little, brilliant boy picked up all music symbols with an amazing speed. Soon he could guess any do, re, mi, fa in solmization or any C, D or E of the diatonic scale. At this young age, between the ages of three and five, Glenn received from his mother a fair amount of praise, with only a few restrictions. Glenn was allowed to amuse himself at the piano and to compose his own little tunes. Nobody knew at the time that Florrie devised a long-term study plan for her son. According to this plan, Glenn was given some leeway as a warm-up period to entering more seriously structured music studies that began shortly after his fifth birthday. Up to this point things developed smoothly and as predicted. Indeed, at the age of five, Glenn performed at a long list of music debuts, both as a soloist and accompanist at the piano. By this age he knew not only several piano exercises, but he was able to play many popular ballads and hymns in synchrony with his parents' singing. The musical Gould trio performed informally at their garden parties at the cottage[18] and formally in churches in Toronto and Uxbridge. Edna Meyers, Glenn's baby sitter for the summer 1938, recalled:

"At the cottage, they [the Goulds] used to put on concerts on their lawn for the public. There were benches for neighbors to sit on and all three of them would perform. Glenn used to play beautifully. He was five years old at the time."

"How did Glenn come across to you?" I was interested whether Glenn looked strained or put upon.

"Oh, no. Glenn looked very happy. He wasn't shy at all. He loved to play for others."[19] Edna was obviously impressed by Glenn.

This was the first glimpse the world had of this gifted boy at the piano. The protective privacy and anonymity of his parental home gave way, and he became known at the cottage and in the local congregations in Toronto as a child prodigy. Following the *Keyboard Town* mastery, Glenn went through a succession of basic music pieces and books for young beginners. He was introduced to baroque music earlier than the average student, having listened since infancy to his mother's piano and vocal practices of Bach's music. At the age of six, Glenn played Bach's little menuets from *Anna Magdalena Notebook*. He discovered the beauty of Bach's ornaments and particularly fell in love with the trills, which he interpreted so skillfully that one could tell he had a very special talent for this type of music.

Glenn's concerted, voluntary efforts at the piano and his mother's dedication as a coach came to full fruition. In February 1940 the young pianist took his first examination at the Toronto Conservatory of Music, achieving first class honors in grade three piano. Glenn was only seven years old. In the same year, Glenn was enrolled in additional studies of music theory with Leo Smith, who taught Glenn until 1947. The scope of Glenn's collective music knowledge was expanding rapidly. The works of Mozart such as Sonatina in C Major, Diabelli Sonatina in F Major, and Clementi Sonatina in G Major were all practiced with ease and learned properly. Within the same year, still at the age of seven, Glenn passed grade four in piano with the following, rather typical evaluation of his existing skills:

Grade IV Piano

	Maximum	Marks Obtained
Accuracy (including Notation, Time Values, Fingering, Touch)	24	21 ½
Musicianship, General Effect	32	27
Memory	8	8
Technical Requirements (scales etc.)	20	17
Ear Test	8	7 ½
Sight Reading	8	8
	100	89

[Signed] Reginald G. Green
A promising young boy[20]

From that time on, Glenn's wagon was really hitched to a star. The music examiner, Mr. Green, accurately predicted that he was a "promising young boy." The review of this evaluation points to Glenn's consistency in high marks, particularly in memory, ear test, and sight reading. These high marks were suggestive of his high natural cognitive ability, which was an enduring component of Glenn's talent and one of the predictors of his future greatness. By the age of seven, he already stood out among his peers as an advanced musician.

The Gould family led an orderly and rather structured life. The work and churchgoing ethos were their predominant values. Both parents kept quite busy with their occupations, religious practices, and social activities. There was a degree of relaxation in their lives, but that too was somewhat structured and repetitive. Shortly after Glenn's birth, his father personally built a cottage on the east side of Lake Simcoe on the then uninhabited, tranquil shore called Uptergrove. This small enclave was in the vicinity of Orillia, Ontario, the historic town where Samuel de Champlain first landed in the early 1600s. Bert Gould made a fortunate choice by buying a piece of waterfront bush land, rich in graceful birch trees, conifers, and a variety of dense shrubs. Bert personally cleared this prime but rugged property and built for his family a simple stucco frame cottage, which was to become the focal point of many happy days over the next four decades. A humble road sign was erected with an arrow pointing to the "R.H. Gould's Cove."

The practice of going to the cottage on the weekends or at any other spare time became a built-in component in the life of the Gould family. Most of their recreational life had to do with not just visiting but living in that cottage whenever possible. Cottage-going is so widely practiced in Ontario that one could make a case for the study of behavioral cottage-psychology. Having a cottage is not only a symbol of economic status but plays a major part in the Canadian sense of identity. Cottage life provides closer contact with nature and, in that, closer contact with one's own inner, instinctual self. Despite the availability of technological amenities, in a cottage one is more likely to improvise and create, to reflect and relax, to play and fantasize. Though partly urbanized, cottage country is still a wonderful opportunity for a less formal life with fewer urban restraints.

Traveling back and forth to the Uptergrove cottage was combined with a stopover en route to Glenn's paternal grandparents, Alma and Tom Gold, in Uxbridge. This was usually a rather intense family experience during which Glenn encountered various paternal relatives and friends. Glenn's Uncle Bruce was there as well as Aunt Freda and her son Barry, who became Glenn's playmate. Glenn's father reminisced on these unforgettable Uxbridge times with a smile on his face. "Glenn was a tenderhearted boy. He played tirelessly with my nephew, Barry. Glenn was five and Barry was three. They played with little automobiles and toy planes. Glenn often gave his toys to Barry. They were buddies and both cried when we had to leave and go home."[21]

Glenn's Uncle Bruce was the talented musician who was equally good at playing several brass and wind instruments. Glenn loved to hear him play and he used to sing along and conduct while Uncle Bruce was playing for him. This was one of the high points of his visits to his grandparents. Glenn's grandmother, Alma, was another interesting person to meet. She was a town socialite known for her hospitality, culinary specialties, and music entertainment. She organized many holiday dinner parties for her extended family, and often a few other guests were invited. The Gold residence, among other amenities, had a manicured bowling green and a gorgeous professionally maintained rose garden. While the others enjoyed Sunday afternoons at the Gold Shangri-La, Glenn seemed to be somewhat overstimulated by it. There were picture-taking sessions, the music hour at grandma's piano, adult bowling sessions, laughter, discussions and lots of jokes and humor. From Glenn's point of view, Grandma's rhubarb-apple pie and strawberry frappe were delicious and her piano entertainment along with Uncle Bruce's wizardry on brass instruments were very enjoyable. Best of all, the presence of his first cousin, Barry, his dearest buddy, meant that the two of them could play happily together until the supper interrupted their games. This was all different from the "cool" environment at his home, fostered by his mother to help him focus on his piano studies. The same was at his cottage, where the natural tranquillity and modest social interaction with his peers and the neighbors altogether accounted for a slow-paced lifestyle. The home of his grandparents in Uxbridge was anything but slow-paced. Glenn was not used to the joie de vivre of the flowery garden and crowds of visitors even when they were not total strangers. While he was happy to play and listen to music, he was overwhelmed by the social euphoria and the party-like atmosphere. Though he was not a complete non-joiner, he preferred to socialize in moderation rather than to be in such a "hot" and exuberant place. He longed to return home and to the quietness at the cottage, which were more suited to his tender psyche.

In his first six years of life, other than to Uxbridge and Uptergrove, Glenn occasionally was taken to another small Ontario town, Mount Forest. This town could be considered the headquarters of the Flett family, and it is where Florrie's uncle resided. Donald Flett owned greenhouses and had a dog Glenn adored and played with from the time he was a baby. Glenn had much fun petting the dogs and chasing after them, one was the dog of Uncle Donald and the other was Glenn's personal dog who was always taken along on family trips. Florrie felt very close to her Uncle Donald, and Glenn himself looked up to him as a grandfatherly figure.

Once Glenn was at the cottage, there was a lot to do there, from riding his tricycle, which later was replaced by a bicycle, to playing with the six neighboring McDonald boys, out of whom Duncan became his closest companion. Reluctantly, the fun of playing and mingling with his friends had to give way to the demands of his piano training. His parents equipped the cottage with a piano so that Glenn would not be away from his practice time. At that stage of his life, from age six to ten, there was a growing number of restrictions. Glenn was conditioned to watch his hands, to use them sparingly for chores and errands other than playing the piano. Naturally, he had to refrain from touching and grabbing sharp, heavy, or dirty objects. Glenn eventually gave up riding his bicycle in order to avoid the risk of falling down or running into things and damaging his face and hands. Even swimming was gradually deemed to be dangerous, as Florrie believed that cold water could potentially ruin the hands of a future pianist. The pastime of playing outdoors became more and more limited as the demanding schedule of Glenn's music studies inevitably interfered with his natural child's need "to play it out" as a self-healing function.

Wherever Glenn went, the music was always present, and it became ingrained in the back of his mind as an object of love, an expectation to meet, and a personal goal to reach. The pursuit of music became as constant a thing as one's own daily physiological functions and need for food and water. It appears that in the first six years of Glenn's life, the visits to the cottage were a matter of fun with a fair bit of music structure. As time went on, this proportion gradually reversed to the pervasive study of music interspersed with brief periods of play and relaxation.

At home in Toronto, there was even more regimentation. Glenn was regularly taken to Sunday church services and weekly activities. In public, he was known as a well-behaved and immaculately dressed child. His wardrobe was carefully designed and sewn by his mother, whose sense of fashion and style was greatly influenced by her aunt, Flora Flett, a professional couturier in Toronto. Glenn's clothes were in the high and formal style of the day. Elegant suits made of white satin or black velvet, crisp white shirts, polka dot ties, white knee-highs, black patent shoes; these were but some details of the outfits he wore for his church visits and little performances at the piano. His mother tutored him in the social etiquette of the day to refine his demeanor. The whole presentation of Glenn at the age of six, with both his natural and acquired charms, was that of Little Lord Gould.

Another major structure added at that time to Glenn's life was the milestone of starting school. The year 1938 was a double turning point consisting of music debuts on the radio and before live church audiences, and it also marked Glenn's personal debut as a first grade pupil. Unlike his budding music career that was a source of happiness for him, his introduction to elementary school was not such a blissful experience. Glenn went to the Williamson Road Public School located within a five-minute walking distance from his home. This is how Glenn later described his fiasco at the start of public school:

> I went wrong early ... When I was six, I managed to persuade my parents that mine was an uncommonly sensitive soul, which ought not to be exposed to the boorish vandalism I perceived among my contemporaries. Consequently, my 1939-1940 season was made more agreeable by the improvisation of a private tutor.[22]

Glenn's initiation to school was so traumatic that his memory of it became skewed and blocked. Apparently, according to his school records, Glenn started grade one on time in 1938. In the following academic season, 1939 to 1940, he officially went to grade two but missed forty-two days of school. When Glenn said, "I went wrong early," he referred to his erratic attendance due to his spurious ailments. The real cause of Glenn's school avoidance was his high separation anxiety, which was manifested in the form of "school phobia." Glenn seems to have been in a constant state of dread about parting from his familiar environment at home and having to function in what he perceived as a hostile school situation. In grade two, Glenn's overall marks were in the eighty-percent range, but his "social studies were a disappointment," as his teacher put it. Though he was allowed to skip a full grade and was promoted to grade four, Glenn simply could not relax and enjoy school; he spent mornings literally counting the seconds. Glenn truly suffered anytime he was in school. On their side, his parents, too, were ambivalent about their son's going to school. Florence placed much emphasis on music, which could be taught at home. Most of all, she was worried about Glenn's health and was unable to let go of him. Bert also had mixed feelings on the subject. This stemmed from the fact that his own mother, Alma, did not allow her youngest son, Bert's baby brother, Grant, to attend grade school, but personally taught him at home. Eventually, Glenn's paternal uncle, Grant, began to attend school regularly in his teens when he came of age for high school. When Glenn started school, a special arrangement was made for him by his father, who negotiated the following deal with the school principal:

> Throughout his entire school years at Williamson Road Public School and Malvern Collegiate, he continued this half-day routine with the afternoon devoted entirely to music. We, as parents, were very fortunate to be able to hire teachers to come to our own home in the evening and give Glenn instruction in the subjects he had missed in the afternoon classes. By this method, Glenn was able to keep abreast of all his school work.[23]

Obviously, the Goulds were overprotective of their only child. It appears that in their search for an optimal school arrangement for their son, they made a costly error. By introducing Glenn to a "half-day routine," they subconsciously and inadvertently transferred onto him their own personal anxieties and dependency needs from their own childhoods. This is how Glenn entered his serious music training with an added emotional burden that was soon going to spread and surface in the form of his many emotional problems.

While Glenn enjoyed listening to music and playing the piano each afternoon, he was clearly unable to enjoy his mornings at school. He was apprehensive, and the whole social experience with his peers was most uncomfortable for him. While other boys engaged in intense play like tobogganing, hockey, or simply playing with marbles on the ground, Glenn stood aside with his hands tucked in his pockets, watching his playmates in action. For, by this time, his mother's anxious daily warnings of "watch your hands," "watch your eyes," "don't touch dirt," were deeply etched in his mind and incorporated into his own code of self-protective behavior. To illustrate the above point, Glenn's cousin, Betty, who was his senior by fifteen years, told a story which typifies his childhood:

> Once I took Glenn for a sleigh ride. Glenn was very excited when I pushed him down a small hill. When we came home, Aunt Florrie was very upset with me and chastised me for taking Glenn on the snow. She said that it was very thoughtless to take Glenn for a sleigh ride as his face and hands could have been ruined in the cold. I was stunned and I apologized to her. It seemed to me that a sleigh ride was such a normal thing to do.[24]

This upsetting event ended with a tacit understanding that there would be no more sleigh rides for Glenn. Imagine the child Glenn gazing through the frosty living room window. The sight he saw was probably similar to those classic winter post cards portraying the bliss of children's play in the snow. Meanwhile, he was allowed to spend only short periods of time playing in the backyard and on the driveway of his house, where his play was rationed and supervised by his mother. He was not encouraged to join the play of other children because of ever-anticipated dangers. Instead, he watched them with a nostalgia and envy of a lost childhood. Glenn seemed preordained to stay at home and prepare for his "higher calling" to fame. By the age of six, the young pianist was already an unwilling subject in a Faustian bargain. He had to face a tough and rather unnatural choice—to be an ordinary boy or to be an extraordinary musician. In an optimal situation, Glenn could have the best of these two worlds integrated into one, to play with toys and children but also to play the piano. As it was, his situation was not optimal but had an inherent risk of a serious bias toward music at the expense of his many childhood needs. This bias did not originate in Glenn but was passed on to him from the significant adults in his early life.

In addition to being short of play, going to school was the worst stress in Glenn's life. Grasping the basics of arithmetic was easy enough, and he was on an equal footing with his classmates in this subject. His reading skills were excellent, and his vocabulary was far advanced. But having to sit in a classroom full of children and interact and participate was an anxiety-laden experience for him. Glenn perceived the normal playful behavior of his classmates as "boorish vandalism." He thought of their kind of play as aggression and, indeed, harbored enormous fear of aggressive impulses sensed in himself and/or in others. This will be explored in more detail in the upcoming story about fishing. Actually, while in school, Glenn could relate to some classmates while he avoided others. During his grade school years, he was most industrious and special as a pianist, unlike any other peer in his native land, but socially he was not popular or sought out by others. Glenn's academic performance also was blemished by emotional blocks and impasses in his early development. For instance, he excelled in mathematics and reading skills, since in those he was free of people-related conflicts. In other subjects, where Glenn was expected to conform, such as writing skills, notably the principles of grammar and neatness, he was rather sloppy, which resulted in lower marks. This set the stage for ongoing struggles with teachers and recurring feelings of anger and guilt about mediocre school performance. Glenn ended up being highly anxious, particularly on Sundays in the face of starting another five-day cycle of school. Glenn, who attended Sunday evening church services, remembered very well the minister's words at the conclusion of the benediction: "Lord, give us the peace that the Earth cannot give." This subtle petition became Glenn's metaphor for social fear and avoidance. It helped him to justify the search for peace in himself, within the deep confines of his home and music. For Glenn the earth, or in his case, the school was a most disquieting place. Going to school, an act that could fill Glenn with a sense of challenge and contentment, became an arduous, even a tortuous task. There were numerous reasons leading up to Glenn's unhappiness in school. The main reason was that he was brought up in an overprotective manner, which did not leave room for him to properly separate and individuate as a person. There were also external stressors that contributed to his social and school avoidance. The most important among them were: the change of his family name, the loss of close relatives, and the external socioeconomic hardships associated with the start of World War II.

First is the name change. In the late 1930s, Glenn's parents worked fervently on changing their family name from Gold to Gould. Through the centuries, changing the surname commonly was practiced across the world. The reasons varied from the most benign ones, such as for esthetic improvement of the name, to the most serious ones, such as to disguise one's own ethnic background or to protect one's status or life. The immigrants to North America often had their awkward and long surnames replaced or abbreviated by the officers at the port of entry. The purpose was to adapt them to the existing Anglo-Saxon population and facilitate more suitable everyday communication and pronunciation. Like others, Jewish settlers also were known to have changed their family name to protect themselves from anti-Semitic attitudes. A name change alone would often open the door to a more peaceful and prosperous life. Sometimes, the family name would be preserved but the religious affiliation would change by way of conversion to Christianity.

As World War II approached, Glenn's family became sensitive to the advantages of a name change. The initiative was taken by Glenn's mother but accepted by the rest of the family. Like many other families in Europe and North America fearing persecution, Florrie felt that it was unpopular and unsafe to carry on with a Jewish-sounding name like Gold. Elsie Lally Feeney illustrated this point:

> In summer 1932, I was looking for a job. Somebody gave me the address of Mrs. R. H. Gold, who was expecting a child. I went there for an interview. I knocked on the door and the pregnant woman appeared. I said: "Hello. Are you Mrs. Gold?" She said: "Yes, but we are not Jews."[25]

Florrie, who apparently was very insecure about the name, had rationalized that Glenn, should he become a famous public figure, would be better off with a more Anglo-Saxon sounding name. She was encouraged by many similar situations in the history of great men related to change of religion or family name. Florrie knew the story of Joseph Gould of Uxbridge, whose birth name was also Gold. She was aware that the fathers of the British prime minister, Benjamin Disraeli, and the composer, Felix Mendelssohn, renounced Judaism, converting to Christianity, in order to assure safer and more successful futures for their sons. In Glenn's case, his great-grandfather, Isaac Gold, converted to Christianity, but he did not change his family name. Once, in one of our lengthy conversations with Mr. Bert Gould, I brought up the topic of the name change:

"When did the name change take place?" I asked.

"Oh, I am not sure. I have the original document in my safety box and if you are interested I'll get it for you," Mr. Gould replied.

"Great! I'd really like to have a look at it. What prompted you to change the name?" I pursued the same topic.

"Oh, we were long overdue. Most of other families with the name Gold had already changed their name. So, we did the same," Mr. Gould answered boldly.

"But why? Is it because it sounded Jewish?" I asked cautiously.

"No, 'Gold' is not a Jewish name. It is an old English name,"[26] Mr. Gould stated. If I were more bold, I could have questioned Mr. Gould further by saying:

"I believe that your grandfather, Reverend Isaac Gold, was of Jewish descent." Instead, I sensed that Mr.Gould, at the age of ninety, was still protective of this family secret and reluctant to discuss such a private matter. The truth was that Glenn's mother, Florrie, led by the reality of the existing societal prejudices and by her own anxieties, put the name change mechanism into motion. She engaged her brother, Willard Greig, the solicitor of Uxbridge, to draw up the legal papers to that effect. The final document, which became accessible only after Mr. Gould's passing, reads:

IN THE SUPREME COURT OF ONTARIO DEED POLL

> Witnesseth by this Deed which is intended to be filled and enrolled in the Central Office of this Court at Osgoode Hall, Toronto, I, the undersigned Thomas George Gould, of the City of Toronto, in the County of York, Merchant, and formerly called Thomas George Gold, a natural born British Subject, do hereby absolutely renounce and abandon the use of my said surname of Gold and in lieu thereof, assume as and from the date hereof the surname of Gould.
>
> 16th day of December A.D., 1938[27]

This event of the name change had a profound emotional impact on Glenn. Being a perceptive child and a thinker by nature, Glenn picked up on various subtleties related to the name change. He sensed his mother's anxiety and her crusading influence in this matter, and he was aware of the tension in the family building up in the style of pros and cons related to the name change. Glenn was afraid of any potential conflicts and outbursts of anger in his family. Worst of all, he did not know how to explain to his friends why his name was changed. If his name was not of Jewish origin as he was told, then why change it; if it was, then why deny it? This was all too much and too unclear for a six-year-old boy. He had one more reason to hide and avoid group situations where the questions could be asked for which he had no straight answers. His granduncle, William Herbert Gold, a photographer who by that time retired in Uxbridge, refused to alter his name. His presence was a constant reminder of some secretive and unfinished family business.

The second major emotional stress in Glenn's life had to do with losses through death. In March 1939 Glenn's maternal grandmother, Mary, passed away after a short illness. Soon after, in the month of May, her younger brother and Glenn's granduncle, Donald Flett, the owner of the interesting dogs and greenhouses, and former mayor of the town of Mount Forest, also died. Florrie was emotionally very attached to her Uncle Donald, who was a partial father figure to her. Glenn, too, was fond of him. The loss of these two close senior relatives at once was very stressful and called for appropriate mourning. Glenn's mother, by way of her cold and reserved character, was unable to grieve properly, nor was she able to help her six-year-old son in his bereavement. As a result, Glenn ended up feeling abandoned and very frightened. He developed a fear of being left all alone and became even more clingy with his mother. A child of six years of age still does not have a clear concept of death and needs a supportive environment to get over the bewildering and undefined fear. Now that Mary and Donald went to heaven, as Glenn was told, would his mother go with them? Glenn feared the potential loss of his mother. His preexisting separation anxiety became almost paralyzing and made him reluctant to leave his mother at home and go to school like other anxiety-free children. By staying home in his mother's proximity, Glenn felt reassured that she was still there for him. This, in part, was responsible for Glenn's solitary living at home and his social avoidance.

The third emotional deterrent to going to school was related to the growing national apprehension in the face of World War II. Simultaneously with the Gold family's efforts at a name change, Canadian soldiers were being recruited for the upcoming war. The hovering threat of war became layered upon Glenn's preexisting emotional vulnerabilities and aggravated his separation anxiety, which was played out in school and elsewhere by social avoidance.

For Glenn, staying at home was the only comfortable and appeasing situation he knew. At home, Glenn preferred to wear very casual, loose clothes, and insisted on being shoeless and not wearing a belt. This was the place where his separation anxiety was warded off by the reassuring familiarity of his surroundings. On a healthier note, Glenn had an innate predisposition toward music, and his home happened to be the optimal place for exploring the limitless treasures of piano music. Such ultimate comfort at home and at the cottage played a major role in the formation of his future artistic success. Also, there were quality times when Glenn genuinely felt good in the company of his mother and enjoyed a healthier aspect of his relationship with her. On her side, she at times also was able to relax and focus on Glenn in a more empathic way.

Other than his mother and music, there was another world at home that served as a major object of love and attachment to Glenn, a small community of his beloved pets. Glenn had a lovely parakeet that he named "Mozart" but called him affectionately "Motzy." Then there were three goldfish graced with names of composers, Haydn, Bach and Chopin, idling around in the decorative aquarium placed near the piano. The real star among those favored animals was Glenn's English setter, Nick, who enjoyed special privileges that no other person or dog in the family ever had. He was allowed to sit at Glenn's feet during his lengthy and grueling piano practices. This everyday domestic scene of Glenn working at the piano, while Motzy the parakeet pattered around and majestic Nick sat at his feet, became an integral part of Glenn's life. It became incorporated into his unconscious mind as a symbol of comfort, the pacifier that always worked for him. Glenn clung to this image and whenever anxious, even in his adult life, was compelled to reenact it in one way or another, over and over again.

At home, Glenn encountered a familiar gestalt, pleasant and reassuring to his frail sense of self. It included Glenn at the piano, his mother coaching him in the comfortable living room in the presence of pets. That all accounted for a unique and soothing "stimmung."[28] The music was a go-between, a vehicle of intimate communication. The mother and son were alone for hours on end, collaborating or arguing in the medium of the transmuting sounds of music. The familiar stimmung at home was far preferable to any other situation. In the words of Donald Winnicott, it played the role of Glenn's "transitional world,"[29] which remained active between Glenn and his mother like a buffer zone. The living room was akin to the safe and insulated atmosphere in the womb. The music, like amniotic fluid, was a medium, a space filler that served to alleviate friction, to communicate, to maintain life. This explains why Glenn, as a future great concert pianist, was in a constant search to recreate a "womb-like security" while performing and recording.

When Glenn was nine years old, the dynamic Fulford family moved into the house next door. One of their four children, Robert, became Glenn's classmate at the Williamson Road Public School. The two boys quickly developed a degree of closeness and played together, usually when Glenn had a break from his lengthy piano practices. Sometimes, Bob was taken to the Goulds' cottage to keep Glenn company, which gave him an opportunity for an intimate look into his friend's life.

H. M. "Do you remember ever meeting Glenn's grandparents?"

R. F. "Yes, I do. Once my brother Wayne and I went to Uxbridge for Thanksgiving. Florence was there; she sang some songs, and Glenn's grandmother was there, I think. Bert was recording their voices. Glenn's grandfather was there. He was a little, old man; everybody called him 'Papa Gold.'"

H. M. "Are you sure they called him 'Papa Gold' and not 'Papa Gould?'"

R. F. "Of course. Glenn always used to call him 'Papa Gold.' Later on I asked Glenn why did they change the name into Gould and he said because 'we didn't want people to think that we were Jewish.'"[30]

In this capacity as a close observer, Bob, who later became a distinguished Canadian columnist, evoked memories of his famous friend in his book, *Best Seat in the House*:

> ... Glenn avoided the games all the rest of us played. So far as I know he never touched a football or a baseball, and if you threw one to him—out of ignorance, or to tease him—he would silently step back and let it fall to the ground. He knew what his long, graceful hands were for, and it wasn't baseball. He understood that this in itself made him a strange kid, and sometimes in conversation he playfully magnified his aversion to balls of all kinds, even to the word itself.[31]

H. M. "Was Glenn not allowed to play, or could it be that he did not wish to play?"

R. F. "He was different than the rest of us. For example, we had two languages in 1942. One was the language of adults and another was the language of boys, which was full of obscenities. When my mother was around or my sisters, we were perfect

> little lads. But my mother could control me only when she was around. As soon as she was a hundred yards away, I'd use my boy language. At the age of 10, I was bilingual. In Glenn's case, he totally internalized his mother's prudishness. She could control him even when she was not around. That is why he avoided to play with us and never used obscene language."[32]

If Glenn was not at par with his schoolmates at play or in the content of speech, he was far ahead of them in music. While going to grade school was a laborious task, he had pursued his music studies with passion and vigor. In the span of a little over three years between ages eight and eleven, Glenn finished six grades in piano, from grade five to ten. In this period, Glenn covered the sizable piano literature. *Czerny's School of Velocity* guided his excellent sense of rhythm into technical mastery. Bach's *Little Clavier* took a special status in Glenn's mind, reaffirming his deep ties with Bach's music. At the age of eight, Glenn played very technically complex pieces for a youngster, such as Kuhlau's Sonatinas in A Minor and G and the beautiful but tricky Consolation by Felix Mendelssohn. Many other demanding works of music followed: Bach's partitas, more Clementi, more Diabelli, Scarlatti, Kuhlau. Mozart's sonatinas gradually led to more mature sonatas. The masterworks of Beethoven were added to Glenn's list of mental acquisitions. Moving along, Glenn went through the compositions of Grieg, Chopin, and Couperin. This overall achievement is quite remarkable within such a short period of time, and piano students know the seriousness and task mastery required to learn such music works heading toward the advanced levels of grades nine and ten. To remind the reader, in 1944, when Glenn was preparing for his grade 10 piano examination, he was in grade seven public school and only eleven years of age. A major task for him was to bridge the sizable gap between being a boy in his preteens and being a master of music in his class. In the conservatory's grade ten, Glenn had to conquer a large selection of mature and demanding music works. He learned the famous "Spinning Song," op. 67, no. 34, by Felix Mendelssohn, which is one of forty-eight music pieces titled "Songs Without Words." The "Spinning Song" is described as "a really difficult piece, requiring accurate rotational control."[33] A succession of other music compositions recommended for grade-ten piano students followed: Mozart Sonata in F Major, KV280; Rachmaninoff's Elegie op. 3, no. 1, a beautiful lyric piece and the more demanding Beethoven Sonata in C Minor, op. 10, no. 1. It is said of this latter music piece that "the finale is more taxing, needing good fingers, accurate staccato and firm rhythmic control."[34] All of these music works had to be perfected until approved by his teacher. This was a most unusual feat for a child.

Earlier on, at the age of eight, Glenn embarked on yet another project. He undertook the study of the pipe organ in addition to his piano training. The studies commenced in 1940 with Frederick C. Silvester and lasted until 1945. Keeping up with two instruments, one of them at the top level, another one close behind, was highly demanding for the sensitive eight-year-old youngster. The idea for organ studies was born in the mind of Glenn's mother, Florrie, and grandmother, Allie. Since Florence and her mother-in-law, Alma, were dedicated organists who favored Bach's music, they liked the idea of having an organist in the family. It was a nice but emotionally taxing idea. Glenn's day-to-day schedule was already crowded with the formidable task of studying the piano. Why then add to his stress level and take away from his spare time? Like his mother, Glenn also had his personal motive to learn to play the pipe organ. He was a regular churchgoer and listener of organ music on the radio, notably Sunday-morning concerts by the greatest American organist, E. Power Biggs. Glenn, who resented anything boisterous, found in organ music remedial solace always needed for his ever-present anxieties. Once he started playing, he became very successful at it, breezing through a succession of grades and exams. Here is a sample of Glenn's exemplary marks:

Grade VI Organ

	Maximum	Marks Obtained
Accuracy	25	23
Rhythm, Phrasing and Musicianship	25	23
Control of Instrument	12	10
Pedal Scales (studies)	10	9
Sight Reading	10	9
Ear Test	10	10
Questions	8	5
	100	89

Healey Willan[35]

As a grade school student, Glenn was turning into the "busiest kid on the block." Along with his piano and organ studies, he took exams in music theory, solo singing and sight singing, where he obtained first class honors. To top it all, Glenn took part as a competitor at annual Kiwanis Music Festivals, winning scholarships and trophies. There was even more activity each October when he was awarded top medals at the TCM Graduation Exercises held at Convocation Hall, often for two or three grades he pursued simultaneously. Congratulatory handshakes and diplomas were given ceremoniously by such music dignitaries and scholars as professors Leo Smith and Healey Willan and the celebrated conductor Sir Ernest MacMillan. Being acknowledged publicly was a great reward for Glenn and his parents, who were sitting in the audience. Every achievement and new medal also meant more anxiety and greater expectation of the performing artist.

To boost his music life and whet his appetite, Glenn's mother took him to musical movies and a variety of concerts and told him anecdotes about great composers and performers. She often referred to Mozart as a child prodigy and compared her son to him. At home, Glenn had a growing collection of gramophone records and often listened to the New York Philharmonic performing on the radio. As early as age six, he was taken to Massey Hall in Toronto to see the legendary Joseph Hofmann in a piano recital. Glenn reflected upon this event by saying:

> The only thing I can really remember is that, when I was being brought home in the car, I was in that wonderful state of half-awakeness in which you hear all sorts of incredible sounds going through your mind. They were all orchestral sounds but I was playing them all, and suddenly I was Hofmann. I was enchanted.[36]

The daily regime of keeping up with two instruments, school and evening tutorials left little free time for leisure activities. There were only a few sports that Glenn pursued in moderation in his childhood; swimming, bicycling and boating. While the first two were given up gradually earlier in his life, boating continued into his twenties. When interviewed at the age of twenty-three, shortly after his American debut, Glenn admitted candidly:

> Ever since a child I've been fascinated by boats. One of my earliest dreams is operating a fleet of boats on Lake Simcoe. I saw myself sometimes as the captain of a water-taxi service between the islands and the mainland, other times as the owner of a houseboat.[37]

What a modest fantasy. Glenn wished to be nothing more than the captain of a water-taxi service. This was miles apart from being a famous piano virtuoso. Glenn was not supposed to use boats with oars, as those would be hard on his hands, so he only used motorboats. There, sitting at the helm, he felt fulfilled and self-assured. Simply, he felt in charge. Navigating a boat is reminiscent of a naval occupation. In reality, Glenn's Uncle Grant was a navy officer during the war. Glenn secretly admired his honorable occupation and fantasized about being a commander himself. Yet, this fantasy was not strong enough to become a reality and to outweigh his firmly grounded identity as a musician.

The growing child Glenn had a lot with which to contend. Shortly before his seventh birthday, on September 3, 1939, Great Britain and France entered World War II as allies. Canada followed their example on September 10. Glenn became very curious about the war. As a true radio fan, he followed the news from the battlefield with the fervor of an adult. To supplement his information bank, Glenn used to cut out newspaper clippings with pictures and text about the war, particularly navy operations. Often, Glenn pretended to be a radio reporter, and in this role he would make up imaginative, somewhat humorous stories about ocean combat, involving sly amphibious assaults, colossal aircraft carriers and deadly torpedoes. Glenn conjured up dramatic images of the war, and, in his child's play, fantasized war scenes using his own toys to recreate battles between a Messerschmitt and a Spitfire—German and British fighter planes, combating submarines and warships. Here is Glenn's vivid autobiographical story, which evokes his war-related fantasies:

> ... when I was eight my idea of a movie was something with a plot—preferably a plot with a war theme. My favorites featured shots of German battle cruisers, emerging grim and gray from fog banks in Norwegian fjords, and with cuts to the blacked-out bridge of some hapless British destroyer where Clive Brook or John Clements or Jack Hawkins might say something like: "Men, we are about to engage the Scharnhorst and Gneisenau. I need to tell you that their range exceeds ours. But the First Lord has ordered us to hold the beasts at bay, and that we shall do at any cost."[38]

Not bad for an anxious and sheltered boy! By playing war games, Glenn dealt with his own pent-up aggression toward those whom he perceived as an enemy. His father felt the pinch of the war. Bert worked as a manager of Gold Standard Furs but his business slowed down. Fur coats, just like china and crystal, were luxuries that did not sell well in wartime. Meanwhile, the expense for his son's education rose steeply from year to year. There was a general belt-tightening, and meat and other basic necessities were rationed and obtained through food stamps. Florrie resented the wave of frugality with which she was only too familiar from her own childhood. She insisted on Glenn having all the comforts of quality clothes, tutorials, and piano lessons, often supplied at her own expense. Glenn, on his side, was thriving on music. At the age of nine, he received this letter:

> Mr.Glenn Gould: July 17th, 1942
>
> We have pleasure in informing you that the mark you received in your recent examination for grade VIII Piano was the highest in the Province of Ontario. This entitles you to the Canadian Silver Medal.
>
> With congratulation on your splendid work, and best wishes for your future success, I am,
>
> Yours sincerely,
> Examination Registrar[39]

THE BEGINNING OF THE END

> Great geniuses have the shortest biographies.
>
> Ralph Waldo Emerson[40]

Along with his growing musical expertise, Glenn unconsciously was developing a variety of peculiar personal characteristics. A skillful eye could observe a number of psychological symptoms and somewhat odd behavior, most of them fully formed and observable by the age of six. There was school avoidance, social shyness, fear of the dark and fear of being abandoned. The major problem behind these symptoms was high separation anxiety, which was an offshoot of his excessive emotional attachment to his mother. The normal process of individuation was delayed, and from the age of six to ten Glenn was still unable to emancipate himself from his strong ties to his mother. The inner conflict between his dependency needs and his need for autonomy resulted in an outbreak of symptoms in the form of anxiety and social phobia. These symptoms of anxiety, avoidance and shyness were the forerunners of his future fully-formed Social Anxiety Disorder. By not going to school full time, Glenn was practicing solitude rather than social life. The natural act of going to school is associated with the opportunity to learn and organize, to share and communicate, to play and create; in other words, to expand intellectually and emotionally. On the surface, going to school part time was in the service of music studies but, on a more profound level, it had to do with being emotionally intertwined with his mother, while his father was for the most part both physically and emotionally absent. Nobody recognized at the time that Glenn had a dysfunctional family. From year to year, the school principals were reluctant to grant Glenn such outstanding privileges of partial school attendance not because they understood Glenn's family problems but because it was against their policy. This is why some external pressure was applied to convince them that Glenn's partial absence from school was justified. Here is a letter written to the school authorities when Glenn was ten years old, as a part of the campaign to allow his part-time attendance:

> To Whom It May Concern: January 30th, 1943
>
> Master Glenn Gould is studying Organ, Harmony and History at the Conservatory, and is also preparing examinations in Piano and Sight-Singing. He is

> an unusually talented student, having won the Provincial medals for the highest marks in all the piano examinations he has taken in the past 3 years. He has recently commenced the study of the Organ, and though he promises equally well in that field, an adequate amount of time for practice is only available on the Conservatory organs during the daytime, when he is at school.
>
> We understand that he is well ahead with his school work, and if on that account he could be allowed time off from school, it would greatly facilitate his musical education. His parents are also quite willing to obtain private tutors in his school subjects to make up for any work which he might lose on this account.
>
> Fred Silvester
> Examination Registrar[41]

Musical education was given a higher priority than Glenn's general education and personal growth. Having tutors in the evening was taxing for Glenn. He was frail and easily fatigued by his grueling daily schedule. Staying at home was necessary to practice the piano but also to alleviate his high social anxiety. Glenn started feeling physically indisposed even though he did not seem to have any real physical illness. Florrie always focused heavily on her son's physical condition. Glenn, too, increasingly became preoccupied with his health. He did not care about the fitness of his body but rather lived in fear of becoming ill. Gradually, he developed a pattern of expressing his emotions through feeling indisposed or being in pain of some kind. A complex, clandestine psychosomatic disorder set in, which in adulthood dominated his life and interfered with his progress. This psychosomatic bent was deeply rooted as far back as Glenn's infancy.

Being raised by several doting adults, Glenn became an early target of their overindulgence. Florrie suffered from a solicitous fear of her only son catching a cold or some other nasty infection, or, worst of all, becoming ill with consumption. She would often remind Glenn to "put on a sweater" or "put on a hat, or else you might catch a cold." Glenn developed a real phobia of catching a cold and a phobia of germs. This led to his overcompensatory behavior of germ avoidance, and he took hypochondriac measures of self-protection. Elsie Lally related her vivid memories about the roots of Glenn's problems:

"Was there anything disturbing to you about Glenn as a baby? Does anything stand out in your mind?" I asked Elsie during my visit to her home on Doncaster Avenue.

"Did Mr. Gould tell you about the cod-liver oil?" she asked.

"No, he didn't. What happened?" I wondered.

"Well, when Glenn was young, his mother used to give him cod-liver oil every day. She pushed the spoon into his little mouth, you know. And I had to stand there and watch him gag and spit the darn thing out, and he cried and carried on because he didn't want to swallow it," Elsie lamented.

"It sounds to me that he had no choice but to swallow," I remarked.

"Of course, he had to! I was so sorry for him. So, I always had a spoon of yellow sugar ready and I gave it to him and he felt a little better."[42] Elsie sounded more consoled.

Though Elsie understood that the cod-liver oil was given as a prevention against rickets, she could not help feeling for Glenn's plight. She was annoyed with Mrs. Gould for forcing this most "horrid" liquid upon her son. The dynamics of this conflict between the two important caregivers are quite interesting. On the one hand, there was this rigid and over-responsible mother forcing vitamins on her precious child, as she believed this was good for him. On the other hand, in juxtaposition, there was this nineteen-year-old nanny who deeply identified with Glenn's misery and literally felt his nausea as her own. Almost sixty years later, while Elsie recounted the story to me, she relived the original feelings of panic and disgust around the event, as well as anger with Glenn's mother for what she had done to her son. It follows that Glenn, in this case, was exposed to a "bad mother" who made him gag, and a "good mother" who deeply felt for him and gave him sugar. Events like this reinforced Glenn's very distinct feelings of love and hate, which were already noticeable in his preschool years. Glenn internalized the images and meanings of "good" and "bad" in a split fashion, which he was never quite able to put together and integrate into one. As a result, Glenn perceived things and people in a black-and-white fashion with no possibilities in between.

Another interesting detail in analysis of this episode is that Florrie was a proponent of natural healing. She herself avoided taking pills and throughout her life, even in her old age, was quite reluctant to see a doctor. Elsie Lally was a person with a phobic fear of swallowing tablets to the point of refusing them even when she had a serious medical condition requiring oral medication. It means that the two women responsible for Glenn's upbringing passed onto him their own exaggerated fears and concerns. Glenn internalized aspects of their rigidity, and he, too, became overconcerned and self-preoccupied with his body. His own rigidity went in the other direction of constantly looking for remedies for both his real and imagined illnesses.

Florrie had ongoing worries, not only about Glenn's respiratory organs but about his appetite, digestive system, posture, and any body discomfort in general. She believed that respiratory infections were preventable by putting on layers of warm clothes and by eating fruit and vegetables containing vitamins. If children in general resent the phrase "eat your vegetables," then Glenn had good reason to despise it even more, as this dictum was so commonly uttered at his home. While some of Florrie's ideas relating to the intake of fresh food were positive and are widely propagated today, her patronizing manner, excessive worries, and disciplinary "must" approach were all intrusive. Glenn resorted to protest and defiance, particularly in the matters of food, in order to preserve some autonomy. He became a very finicky eater with a generally poor appetite. He also developed food fads and eating rituals. These defenses all became much worse in adulthood.

Similar problems with opposition behavior developed in relation to Glenn's body posture. Glenn was prone to slouching, and he seemed forever to be looking for a support for his body in order to hold it up. Elsie Lally remembered that when Glenn was sitting on the couch he would lapse into a semi-horizontal position, leaning on his elbow and propping his head with his hand. "His mother hated it." Elsie recalled. "She was after him all the time. She'd say, 'Glenn, can't you sit up for once? Sit up straight, please. You don't have a jelly-spine!'"[43] Robert Fulford confirmed that Florrie constantly tried to correct his posture. "Glenn, sit up straight" or "stand up straight." These remarks were not very helpful. Glenn did not only slouch at the table or on the couch, but proceeded to do it at the piano. He simply was never able to overcome his habitual slouching.

As Glenn was growing up, he was acquiring distorted perceptions of his human environment and developing an increasing protest against it. He was exposed to doting and domineering adults, who often frustrated him by hindering his own desires and need for expressing his feelings. Even in the realm of music, which was his optimal way of self-expression, Glenn was confined and restricted by his seniors. Increasingly, after the age of six, he had to play only what was prescribed for him. His mother did not allow him to hit a wrong note, to frolic or to improvise at the piano. When he "misbehaved," his mother would slam down the piano lid, saying, "That's it for today." For Glenn, this was much worse than any other form of punishment. With no other recourse to expressing emotions freely, Glenn unconsciously resorted to holding them back. It was particularly difficult for him to contend with his feelings of anger. Gradually, defense mechanisms developed to protect him from disagreeable emotions. Indeed, on the surface, Glenn looked calm and non-angry. His brilliant intellect was always there to rescue him from untoward emotions. In protest against adults, Glenn engaged in rational and self-righteous debates.

When having no acceptable outlets for his thoughts and emotions, Glenn often ended up being physically ill. As early as at the age of eight, he started having occasional headaches. Glenn reported that at the age of nine, after watching the movie *Fantasia*, he developed a massive headache. Upon arrival home, he took himself to bed without having supper. Presumably, Glenn was stressed out by this overwhelming and over-stimulating film. This could have been a tension headache or an attack of migraine. In both instances, the emotional stress or a number of physical causes such as atmospheric pressure, food he ate, motion pictures and colors of the movie may have been implicated. In psychotherapeutic practice, it is noticed that those individuals with stress-related headaches may improve in the course of treatment by developing the ability to express strong feelings of anger, shame, guilt, humiliation and grief and by learning the principles of assertiveness and relaxation. Glenn was simply unable to release his stifled feelings. In rare instances, when Glenn brought himself to express his mental anguish, he did it in an impulsive way through temper tantrums or through ongoing protest against those whom he perceived as oppressive.

Human aggressive impulses are an integral part of life. Glenn perceived aggression as entirely negative and spent his life in disavowal and denial of aggressive impulses in himself. What he saw as aggression was often a quite normal component of human survival. For example, he saw fishing as a form of aggression toward the helpless fish. In Glenn's eyes, all fishermen were despicable and wicked. Meanwhile, fishing is the closest and perhaps the oldest preserved contact with land and water, and fish are a direct and free source of fresh food, unaltered by technology or selling practices. Fishing is a basic and ancient activity that is as old as humanity.

From the time Glenn was six years old, he vehemently opposed fishing. A photograph of Glenn at the age of five shows him happy with a victorious smile on his face while holding a medium-sized pike on a hook. Glenn's baby-sitter, Edna Pollard, nee Meyers, of Uxbridge was hired for the summer to look after him at the cottage. She recalled that Mrs. Gould was sick at the time and "spent most of her time in the attic, occasionally coming down and then going up the ladder again."

"Glenn and I, we used to go fishing. We fished from a motorboat and he was able to ride it. He was only five years old," Mrs. Meyers recalled.

"Did he show any fear of fishing?" I valued her recollections.

"Not at that time. We were fishing quite a lot. I have a picture of myself from that time holding a muskellunge. I caught it there when I was at the cottage," she proudly replied.

"Have you noticed anything else unusual or abnormal about him?" I asked.

"No, not at all. He was a normal little boy. In fact, he was above average. Can you imagine riding a boat at the age of five? He knew exactly what to do."[44] Edna had no doubts in Glenn's abilities.

Within the next year, Glenn's sense of self-confidence was shaken by the stress of going to school and the loss of relatives. Along with that, he was becoming more attached to his pets and more sensitive to animals' rights. He assumed a role of protecting animals whenever he thought that they were subjected to some type of injustice. Here is how Glenn as an adult reminisced about the time when he was six years old and the neighbor took him fishing with his children:

> We went out in the boat and I was the first to catch a fish. And the little perch came up and started wiggling about, I suddenly saw this thing entirely from the fish's point of view—it was such a powerful experience. I picked up my fish and said I was going to throw it back. At that moment, this has remained with me as a sort of block against people who exert influence over children. The father suddenly pushed me back into my seat, probably for the sensible reason that I was rocking the boat.
>
> Then, he took the fish out of my reach, at which I went into a tantrum and started jumping up and down, stomping my feet and pulling my hair and stuff like that. And I kept it up until we got in to shore. I refused to speak with those children for the rest of the summer, of course, and I immediately went to work on my father to convince him he should abandon fishing. It took me ten years, but this is probably the greatest thing I have ever done.[45]

Glenn identified with the helpless fish who, according to him, suffered in the face of the human need to catch and kill. The temper tantrum served as a child's dramatic protest against adults who were seen as predatory aggressors. This revolutionary behavior could be related back to Glenn's male family members who were hunters, fishermen and furriers, and he perceived those occupations as insensitive and cruel. He could not reconcile the images of his beloved "Papa Gold" and his own father, Bert, with the images of purchasing animal skins from trappers and hunters and turning them into fur coats. Glenn hated the fact that his father and grandfather were furriers and that his uncles, Willard Greig and Bruce Gould were both avid hunters. Willard's youngest son, John Greig testified:

"We were all hunting in those days. I remember when Uncle Bert [Gould] once went hunting and he got a deer," said John.

"If everyone was hunting in the country and that was considered to be normal, then why do you think Glenn hated hunting so much?" I asked.

"It was just a quirk that he picked up in his life,"[46] John responded without any trace of ambivalence.

For better or worse, Glenn became a defender of animals and an opponent to his elders. In his mind, Glenn saw fishing and hunting as an adversarial and immoral act of killing. One wonders whether Glenn considered that people of the First Nations and the settlers depended on the animal world for their survival? Blinded and tormented by his deep-seated conflict between loving and hating his elders, Glenn projected his resentments onto all hunters, furriers and fishermen of the world. He was never quite able to resolve his indignation.

Related to this exaggerated perception of human brutality, Glenn also showed an unusual sensitivity toward colors, particularly the color red. The color red happens to be not only the most stimulating color of the chromatographic spectrum but also is emotionally significant because of its broad symbolic meaning. It symbolizes patriotic and revolutionary spirit, often portrayed in stately symbols like flags, pins and badges. It stands for the heart, as the central motor of the circulatory system, for blood, as a vital body liquid, and through that it represents the fervor and vitality of life in general. The color red is often used to designate love as portrayed through Valentine's cards, roses, and carnations given to loved ones. In nature, there is an abundance of the color red seen in songbirds such as cardinals with their beautiful red plumage, and in flowers, tropical fish and a variety of fruits and vegetables. Also, the color red may be used as a symbol of destructive aggression seen in bloody battles, rage, or a sanguine temperament. The red cape in Spanish bullfights is used to irritate the bull, provoking a savage battle, causing the bloody sight of a wounded animal and, eventually, its death. When Glenn thought of the color red or was exposed to the sight of it, he did not think of it as a symbol of love or patriotism. His first mental association was with blood and bleeding. He felt violated by the color red, which reminded him of wounded fish caught on a hook and wounded animals trapped and killed by hunters. It got to the point that Glenn, as a grown-up, favored only a few selected colors such as charcoal gray, "battleship gray" and dark blue. Glenn's peculiar attitude toward colors served a defensive purpose. His protest and rage against perceived human aggression were unconsciously displaced and projected outward as a protest against fishing and hunting of helpless animals, chased after and hunted down by his relatives and countrymen.

Between the ages ten and twelve, Glenn showed himself to be extremely bright and industrious. He was still under his parents' wings. His nanny, Elsie, was no longer living with them. She got married and had children of her own, but continued to work for the Goulds on a part-time basis. Bert Gould remembered: "She was like a daughter to us. She was trustworthy and my wife was very good to her, gave her food and clothes to take home. Once, I even gave her a fur coat as a gift. When Glenn went to live on St. Clair Avenue, she went to clean his apartment for him."[47]

At ten, Glenn was a pale and slender grade school student still dressed in knee highs and short pants. Betty Greig Madill explained: "Glenn wore short pants longer than his peers. My Aunt Florrie wanted him to wear short pants to look younger, to look like a child. But the funny thing is that he looked younger than his classmates, anyway."[48] Why did Florrie insist on Glenn wearing the short pants? Was it out of fear that Glenn may grow up fast and leave the parental nest? In that case, she needed to console herself that he was still a child as symbolized by his boyish looks. Or, was it out of her vanity and a need to show off Glenn as a young prodigy? The younger he was, the more sensational he was as a pianist. The truth was that Glenn, in his music progress, was far ahead of his personal growth. In the realm of music, he was brilliant, while on the personal plane, he needed more personal strength and more social life.

At the age of ten, Glenn was in love with music, deciding that he was going to pursue it as a career to the great delight of his mother. At the same time, Glenn's father was not so sure about this career choice for his son. Although he supported his wife and supplied financial sponsorship for his son's studies, he was not convinced totally that this approach was best for Glenn. Betty Greig-Madill recalled: "Bert was very concerned that music was going to turn Glenn into a sissy. This is not strange in the least. I was concerned about my older son, David, who too was very musical and used to take piano lessons from Florrie. She had great hopes for him to become an accomplished pianist, but I didn't want this as his career. So, David went on studying medicine and became a doctor."[49] Bert was an ordinary man with broad interests and a straightforward love of life, and he could think of many other career options for his son. He knew he was going to inherit the fur business from his father but was fully aware that Glenn was never going to be his business partner. Florrie and Glenn had chosen music as the one and only appropriate career choice. Bert acquiesced to their decision for Glenn to become a concert pianist. It was too late for changes and there was no turning back.

THE PRINCIPAL MUSIC TEACHER—ALBERTO GUERRERO

A dream of every teacher is to be able to hatch the next Glenn Gould.

R. Murray Schafer[50]

Florrie had increasing difficulty teaching Glenn in higher grades as he exceeded her music knowledge. Toward the end of his grade nine piano, she sought consultation with a few music elders with respect to her son's future music training. One of them was Sir Ernest MacMillan, a prominent music personality and conductor of the Toronto Symphony Orchestra since 1931, who "was knighted by King George V in 1935, the only Canadian musician ever to be so honored."[51] For a long time, Florrie idolized MacMillan for his prodigious music achievements as an organist, composer and music director. She valued him as the best advisor. Two other respectable counselors to Florrie were Healey Willan and Frederick Silvester, both professors of pipe organ studies. The consensus of the little informal council was that it would be best for Glenn to take advanced music classes with Alberto Guerrero, uniformly considered one of the foremost piano teachers in town. Alea iacta est![52]

In 1943, Glenn was introduced to Guerrero and started the challenge of the senior music program at the Toronto Conservatory of Music (TCM), which later became known as the Royal Conservatory of Toronto (RCT). The school was located on the southwest corner of College Street on the elegant and spacious University Avenue, just opposite the Queen's Park Parliament Building. Up to this time, Glenn had been educated by his mother, who in 1943 was aged fifty-two. She was then being replaced by a principal teacher, Guerrero, aged fifty-six. There was a transition taking place from the world dominated by females in his earlier childhood to a male-dominated world. In addition to Leo Smith and Frederick C. Silvester, who taught Glenn music theory and organ, there was Guerrero, seen at least twice weekly at the conservatory. The previously small and familiar stimmung of Glenn's living room marked by the presence of his mother was ambitiously expanded and filled with the more formal presence of a male teacher. Glenn was also physically dislodged from his home and had to spend time away at the downtown Conservatory building.

There is a dearth of biographical data about Alberto Garcia Guerrero, and a good deal of what we know comes from writings of John Beckwith,[53] Canada's renowned composer and Guerrero's former student, as well as from the testimonies of a number of Guerrero's other piano students. Before meeting the ten-year-old music prodigy, Guerrero had a substantial music career behind him. He was born in Chile in 1886 and immigrated to Canada in 1919 at the age of thirty-three. A gifted musician himself, he used to give piano concerts in his native country but was also multitalented and active as a conductor, music critic and teacher in the capital of Santiago, Chile. Upon coming to Toronto, he became a successful music teacher at the Toronto Conservatory of Music with a particular interest in gifted and advanced children. While he was still in Chile, Guerrero at first studied to be a priest and lived in a seminary for a while. He also embarked on medical studies with a special interest in human anatomy and physiology. Though he ended up becoming a pianist, his valuable knowledge of physiology helped him to understand the work of hands and fingers at the piano. Guerrero was a member of the Five Piano Ensemble that flourished in Toronto in the mid 1920s along with Vigo Kihl, Ernest Seitz, Norah de Kresz and Reginald Stewart. Guerrero had a rich performing career. He gave concerts at the Toronto Massey Hall and frequent recitals at the University of Toronto's Hart House. Guerrero is to be credited for introducing to the Canadian audience the works of the moderns—composers like Ravel, Debussy, Hindemith, Schoenberg, and Stravinsky. Among his former pupils were Canadian composers R. Murray Schafer, Oskar Morawetz and John Beckwith; pianists Ray Dudley, Pierrette LePage, William Aide and Arthur Ozolins.

Glenn Gould became the most famous of all of Guerrero's pupils. From the age of ten onward, Glenn spent his afternoons at the conservatory with his teacher. Florrie used to accompany him to and from the conservatory, while Bert gave them a ride and dropped them off. She then spent time waiting for Glenn as long as it took. At some point, to keep busy during the waiting time, Florence took a course herself in vocal studies with David Dick Slater at the same conservatory. Later, when Glenn was older, from his teens on, he traveled unaccompanied by streetcar.

Glenn was relieved from having his mother as a teacher. As he was becoming more advanced in his studies, he could less and less tolerate her limitations, both personal and in the field of music. Moreover, he was no longer complying with her conventional rules as he required more freedom of music expression. At first Glenn looked up to his teacher with admiration and respect, hoping to have found an ally in him in his music views. Guerrero, in turn, at first admired his gifted student, looking forward to pass on to him all his craft. Here was a rare chance for Glenn amid the war and economic hardships to quench his natural thirst for music by being guided by a concert pianist himself. In the first half of the Glenn-Guerrero liaison their relationship was amiable and well-balanced. Glenn was impressed by Guerrero's virtuosity at the keyboard, by his versatility, the wealth of his experience, and by his intimate knowledge of keyboard literature. It was not just a matter of a student-teacher relationship but there was a flavor of camaraderie and pleasure in each other's company. The Guerreros also had a cottage on Lake Simcoe, and when Glenn was older, he often dashed in his motorboat across the lake to bring his teacher over to his home for socializing. The two of them engaged in long and lively discussions, invariably about music, and played games like monopoly and cards. They developed a competitive interest in playing croquet. This is a lawn game played with mallets, balls, stakes and wire arches called wickets. It has elements of polo, golf and billiards. The aim is to drive the ball, by striking it with a mallet, through each wicket in turn until the ball makes a complete circuit in the field and strikes the home stake.

"Glenn and Mr. Guerrero played it [croquet] tirelessly often into the night," Mr. Gould remembered, laughing.

"Were they quiet through the game?" I asked.

"Quiet, are you kidding? They talked nonstop for hours. Sometimes, I stopped by to watch them play but I was really busy doing my gardening. Once, I made a point of eavesdropping just to get an idea of what they were talking about," Mr. Gould said.

"I guess they talked about music. That must've been the foremost thing on their minds." I imagined Glenn and his teacher in their music-related conversation.

"Of course, it goes without saying, they talked about music. But would you believe that they also talked politics, the [Second World] War, they talked about Germany being a perpetrator and they both admired [Sir Winston] Churchill." Mr. Gould was quite amused.

"This seems a very serious dialogue. Was it always like that, intellectual and serious?" For a moment I questioned whether Glenn had enough fun.

"Absolutely not. It was mixed. They could cover a variety of themes. All of a sudden, they would switch to telling jokes. I remember Mr. Guerrero using some Spanish words while telling Glenn some funny anecdotes from his native country."

"What was their reaction to the jokes?" I asked.

"They laughed so much, that they made me laugh, and I didn't even know what the joke was about. They had a lot of fun together."[54] Mr. Gould had fun himself retelling the story.

The child of eleven and the teacher of fifty-seven shared ample time together. Before, Glenn lived in unison with his mother; then Guerrero became a stand-in figure. Under Guerrero's auspices, Glenn practiced ferociously for his final grade ten piano. The harvest of their mutual, enthusiastic efforts came to fruition when on June 17, 1944, Glenn passed his grade ten piano examination with eighty-four percent. Here is what the adjudicators had to say about Glenn's playing:

Grade X Piano

Bach Allemande	Fluent playing with care. Violent in the nuances in places. It should go along quite peacefully.
Haydn	First class in many respects with a fine authority. The tendency to run ahead too fast in places detracted from an otherwise outstanding performance. The detail work really quite remarkable.
Adagio	Tonally rather brittle and not always spaced well. Keep the short values softer as they overload the phrase.
Liszt	Overbrilliant at times and virtuosity displaced charm and delicacy, but from many standpoints it was a quite remarkable performance.
Schubert	Watch the long values. Tonally very musical. Candidate is unusually musically gifted![55]

The eleven-year-old preadolescent Glenn was much younger looking than his chronological age. He was still typically dressed in short pants and knee-high socks. By contrast, he was incomparably more mature in his music outreach than his peers. His tally of achievements by now was a dozen medals and three scholarships. Immediately after passing grade ten piano, Glenn was awarded the Heintzman Piano Scholarship to the value of one hundred dollars for the academic season of 1944 to 1945. On October 28, 1944, the *Toronto Evening Telegram* reported:

> Glenn Gould, son of Mr. and Mrs. R. H. Gould, was presented with three medals at the annual TCM graduation exercises at Convocation Hall. At the age of

> 11, Glenn won the medals for the highest standing in the Province of Ontario, in grade X piano and grades VIII and VI organ.[56]

On this very promising note, Glenn, guided by Guerrero, was prepared to climb to even greater heights in music through his teen years.

Chapter IV

THE GROWING PAINS OF ADOLESCENCE

PIANIST IN SHORT PANTS

> I think I should have no other mortal wants, if I could always have plenty of music. It seems to infuse strength into my limbs and ideas into my brain. Life seems to go on without effort, when I am filled with music.
>
> George Eliot[1]

Glenn's initiation to the most turbulent time of human life—adolescence—was marked by a string of powerful music-related events. While his childhood was fairly secluded and more evenly paced, his teens unfolded propulsively, exposing him to many challenges. In this remarkable decade spanning from the age of twelve to twenty-one, the natural developmental milestones were encountered simultaneously with the unnaturally vigorous progression of his music studies. Such intense artistic growth is what made Glenn's teens so intricate and different from that of most of his peers.

The year 1945 represented a major turning point for Glenn. On the personal level, it was highlighted by the onset of puberty, and as an artist it meant the beginning of organized and broad music exposure to the public. On March 10, 1945, the Kiwanis festival winners program was aired by the CFRB radio station, and thousands of listeners were able to hear the young prodigy playing the piano. Being a local East York wunderkind, Glenn stepped into a much wider and more responsible circle of fame. By then, Glenn's frequent appearances in churches, on the radio, and at festivals made him stand out in the public eye, not as a passing fancy but as a serious performing artist who was there to stay. As an emerging concert pianist, he was showered with letters from fans and offers for new engagements. All of a sudden, Glenn realized that piano playing, with its many abstract and noble advantages, was also lucrative. After his radio broadcast, a CFRB official wrote:

> March 19, 1945
> Rogers Radio Broadcasting Company Ltd.
>
> Dear Glenn,
>
> On behalf of this station, and in appreciation of your excellent performance this afternoon, would you please accept the enclosed gift with a hope that it may

assist you in the furtherance of your chosen career.

May we wish you continued success,
W. Campbell
Director of Music[2]

The victory at the Kiwanis Music Festival enabled Glenn to win the Gordon V. Thompson scholarship one more time. As well, the entire spring of that year was dedicated to intense piano studies pending his final music exam. The gigantic stepping stone was mastered in June, when Glenn, at the age of twelve, passed with flying colors the piano examination for the Toronto Conservatory of Music Associateship and won the A.T.C.M. diploma with the highest marks in the Dominion of Canada. His mother's unfulfilled dream to obtain the same degree in music herself became a reality expressed in the remarkable achievement of her son. Again Glenn scored another record in Canada by becoming the youngest student ever to pass this most advanced piano examination. One normally does not expect to find a piano virtuoso in short pants and among elementary school students. Glenn was a rarity even in the small and privileged group of young concert pianists. In the same year Glenn finished grade eight. His classmate, Doris Townsend, described her vivid memories of their friendship:

> I well remember Glenn and was very fond of him. We became good friends at Williamson Rd. Public School, where we both had the same teacher, in grade eight, Mr. Laughlin. He played the piano in class, and I would sing the odd time. He told me before my music teacher did about my music exams (results) at the Toronto Conservatory of Music. We used to have some nice talks at recess, as we were both sort of loners. I remember asking him why he didn't join in the games, and he told me he couldn't because his hands were insured. I could never get over how he did so well in school, when he was absent so often. He was a genius of course, but I didn't realize it then.[3]

At the same time, while Glenn was climbing the heights of musical success, World War II was coming to an end. In August, atomic bombs were dropped on the Japanese cities of Hiroshima and Nagasaki. On September 2, 1945, shortly before Glenn's thirteenth birthday, the formal surrender of the enemy forces was signed and the ghastly war officially ended. One wonders how Glenn felt during the spring-summer period of that year. He was competing and winning at the festival and passing his final piano examination while fierce life-and-death battles were being fought. The same radio station that broadcast Glenn's piano performance also aired the news from the war, which he followed whenever possible. Naturally, Glenn felt jubilant about the Allies' military advances and victories. But how did he feel about his own musical victories when young men not so much older than he were perishing in the war? When at the age of twenty-nine Glenn was interviewed by Bernard Asbell,[4] he stated that in his teens he wanted "to be a composer" and that "everything else was a little bit frivolous." Implicitly, playing the piano for Glenn may have felt as frivolous. Further on in the same interview Glenn stated: "From the age of thirteen on, I absolutely refused to take any examination to enter any kind of competitive undertaking."[5] Though Glenn did not live a life of a Jewish boy and did not celebrate a bar mitzvah, being thirteen gave him renewed strength to make an irrevocable and independent decision:

no more piano competitions. Glenn saw competition as a form of aggression, and he judged playing the piano for the sake of competing and not producing anything new and noble as a rather trivial activity. The war, as the epitome of aggression, left Glenn with a lasting disgust toward human aggressive tendencies. He thought the war was abominable. He was fully aware that the war produced poor economic conditions and that his piano studies were extravagantly expensive. Moreover, his Uncle Grant valiantly participated in the war and had suffered a crushing wound to his chest. Glenn was very proud of his uncle and collected newspaper clippings related to him. The following excerpt from *The Globe and Mail* of September 13, 1944, is from Glenn's collection:

> Surgeon Lt. Grant Gould of Uxbridge, Ontario
> Ship's Doctor Aids Heroes of Regina
>
> ... Canadian corvette Regina hit a mine and sank in 28 seconds. Two men were killed and 27 were missing after the sinking of Regina. Lt. Grant Gould performed a surgery aboard of the rescue ship on a man from the Regina. He used a butcher knife and an ordinary table. The amputation was successful and the sailor's life was saved.[6]

When many years after the heroic event, Dr. Gould was interviewed, this is what came out:

"Dr. Gould, did you know that Glenn admired your heroism during the war and that he kept a file on you with the clippings?" I asked.

"A file? This is new to me. I never thought that Glenn was very interested in me. When he came to Vancouver for a concert, I was waiting for him at the airport and brought him to my home. I offered him my piano for rehearsal. Glenn said that my piano was nice but it was too cold in my living room." Dr. Gould sounded hurt.

"What happened, then?" I asked.

"Glenn didn't stay with us but insisted on going back to his hotel, so I gave him a ride there." Glenn's uncle obviously never reconciled his differences with his nephew.

"Yet in his teens, Glenn looked up to you very much, didn't he?" I reminded Dr. Gould that his ties to Glenn were very close and deep-rooted.

"Well, I can't say that he did but this is probably because he could not be open about it. You see, his mother wanted him to keep his focus on music and not on anything else. She was very strict as a piano teacher and Glenn was afraid of her reaction. If he really liked me, as you say, he was not able to show it."[7] Glenn's uncle concluded his rather unhappy testimony.

While the war was not responsible for Glenn's emotional problems, it certainly contributed to them by making him feel more anxious and guilty. By his teens, Glenn was showing signs of inhibition of feelings and moral suffering. He was harsh with himself, imposing rigorous self-discipline in the matter of pursuing music, and he was quite critical, even sarcastic, toward others. In the long run, all this had a negative impact on his future as a performing artist.

There was another, more personal source of emotional turmoil for Glenn. During this period of winning competitions, he was also exposed to his mother's grief around the loss of her beloved aunt, Flora Flett. When Flora died in July 1945 after a long and debilitating illness, Florrie entered a state of deep and inconsolable sorrow. The story goes that during the war years, Flora Flett became totally blind and physically enfeebled, which called for extensive bedside nursing. Florrie very much wanted to take care of her aunt, but her husband vehemently opposed this, which created a fair degree of tension in the Goulds' house. As a result, Aunt Flora was sent to her native Mount Forest, where she was looked after by her nephew, Boyd Flett.[8] In this duel between his two embittered parents, Glenn sided with his mother and resented his father's totalitarian attitude. With Flora's death, her role as a mother substitute to Florrie and as the last living link with the senior Fletts were forever lost. For Glenn, whose inner feelings resonated with those of his mother, the passing of his great aunt stirred up old emotional ties with his maternal family of origin. Florrie, who on her side never fully resolved her personal dependency needs for her relatives, was gravely bereaved by the loss.

Glenn, on the surface, typically did not show signs of acute distress, but he was quite shaken underneath, as he was able to feel his mother's pain. The young pianist camouflaged his whole internal world of fear and grief so well that his pain was not recognized by others. Yet it was that same complex and troubled inner life that governed him in creation, determined his mood, led him down the paths of victories, or pushed him into great personal losses. Inability to mourn his numerous losses left Glenn with a collection of emotional scars. He became more unsure of himself, more timid and evasive of close relationships and more odd in his dress.

Amid the emotional turmoil related to losses, there was a bright event on the horizon. If Glenn and his mother lost their beloved Flora Flett, they gained the presence of Florrie's niece, Jessie Greig. In the fall of 1945, Jessie ran away from home. She came to Toronto and moved in with the Gould family upon the invitation from her Aunt Florrie. History repeated itself. Akin to Florrie, who many years ago ran away from her family and came to Toronto to live with her aunt, Flora Flett, the nineteen-year-old Jessie dealt in a similar way with her need for autonomy.

"What were the circumstances of your arrival to Toronto and moving in with the Gould family?" I asked Jessie during my visit to her home in Oshawa.

"All my junior life was spent in Uxbridge. After I graduated from high school, my father wanted me to study law. I wanted to be a teacher. So I ran away from home, which was the most rebellious thing I've ever done in my life, and I enrolled in the Teachers' College," Jessie replied.

"What happened next?" I asked.

"Well, Aunt Florrie invited me to move in with them, which was very, very nice of her. I accepted her offer and I stayed with them for a year. It worked out really well for all of us. Glenn would be twelve, going on thirteen, at that time," Jessie summed it up.

"How did you get along with Glenn?" I asked directly.

"He and I became closest friends. I was like a sister to him. Aunt Florrie used to tell me that she wished I was her daughter," stated Jessie with pride.

"Yet, Glenn was immersed in his music and I presume he had very little social time. How did that affect you?" I was interested in the impact of Glenn's busy schedule on others.

"I'd hear him practice till late at night. He played beautifully and I always stopped to listen to his music," Jessie reminisced with pathos.

"Yes, of course, but was it ever too much for those living around?" I asked.

"Oh no, it wasn't too much." Jessie sounded a bit hurt.

"I remember that when I practiced the piano for hours in our one-bedroom flat, this was rather rough on my parents. My father could not listen to the radio and my mother was overwhelmed by me practicing music pieces and scales over and over again. I wonder whether this was your experience with Glenn?" I shared with Jessie my personal trials and tribulations around piano practicing while trying to get her to open up on the subject.

"No, no, I am telling you, it wasn't. Glenn did not practice scales. I never resented his practice," Jessie said. "What a lovely way to fall asleep with him playing the piano."[9] Jessie added a new perspective on piano studies.

At the same time Glenn entertained his first cousin, he had to face another turning point in his life. In September 1945 he started high school. The change from the previously sheltered and familiar public school environment to the more socially and academically challenging high school dynamics produced in him a fairly serious adjustment reaction. While most students were excited by the novelty of change and took it in stride, Glenn entered his new school, Malvern Collegiate Institute, with doubts and apprehension. He was intellectually able to relate well on a one-to-one basis, but group experience on any level, within the extended family, at church, or at school, was intimidating to him. In Glenn's life, there was an almost total absence of chumming around, gathering with others on the sports field, or any previous group camping experience. In the same year, 1945, there was the following modest announcement in the local paper about the opening of the so-called "Our Boys' Camp:" "It is with fresh hope that the Kiwanis Club of Guelph now looks forward to the opening of the greatly improved boys camp site." The camp was located on Bellwood Lake, fifteen miles north of the town of Guelph. The ad offered a selection of "land and aquatic sports, cross-country hikes, nature study, woodcrafts, campfires and pow-wows [that] will be under supervision ..." As a recent Kiwanis winner, if Glenn had gone to the camp, he would have been a music star there. He would have had a chance to relax from daily routines, to improvise for his fellow-campers and to share with them his original guessing games in which he excelled. Most of all, he would have had a prime opportunity for social experience. Adolescents, just like children, need conditions appropriate to their age to play and keep busy in the very way suggested in the camp advertisement. Participating in summer camps with peers plays a major role in social development of young people. Campers can afford to be carefree and enjoy the bliss of life, and still assume specific personal and social responsibilities as a bridge to the future. The sense of camaraderie is advanced. Young people have fun by engaging in prankish humor and sexual themes. Camping is a medium of discovery and a practicing field where youth can display limitless wit, vitality, and a sense of adventure. Belonging to a group of friends, a school club, or going to camp is a precursor of adult socializing and membership as an "in grouper."[10] Participation in group activities helps to create a social identity and is an irreplaceable source of pleasure. Glenn was always removed from such group activities by practicing solitude or dyadic relationships at best. If it had been up to him, Glenn would have skipped high school altogether, but as a future concert pianist he needed, or so he was told, a well-rounded education. This is why Glenn submitted to attending high school. He was reluctant but acquiesced to what his parents and society expected him to do.

If Glenn was stunted socially, his music career was booming. On April 10, 1947, the fourteen-year-old virtuoso gave a piano recital at the Conservatory Concert Hall. He played beautifully before all his music teachers, including Alberto Guerrero, and before his parents a treat that would not often be available to them in the future. Glenn performed the following piano compositions:

Sonata in E flat	Haydn
Allegro	
Adagio	
Finale—Presto	
Two Preludes and Fugues	Bach
B flat minor	
C sharp major	
Sonata in D major, op. 10, no. 3	Beethoven
Presto	
Largo e mesto	
Menuetto—Allegro	
Rondo—Allegro	
Impromptu in F sharp major	Chopin
Andante and Rondo Capriciosso	Mendelssohn[11]

On December 3, 1947, Glenn appeared as a guest artist in Hamilton, Ontario, where he played with the Toronto Symphony Orchestra directed by Sir Ernest MacMillan, interpreting Beethoven's Concerto no.1 in C Major, op. 15. These, and several other piano and organ public concerts, were all given by Glenn during his high school education.

Malvern Collegiate Institute is located on the east side of Malvern Street, half a mile north of Lake Ontario. It is surrounded by a quiet residential neighborhood spread over an attractively groomed, hilly landscape. In the 1940s, Malvern was known as a reputable high school in the east-end community. Demographically, the students gravitating to this school were predominantly white, of Anglo-Saxon extraction and mostly affiliated to with various Protestant churches. Those who belonged to an ethnic minority, like Theresa Stratas, the future renowned opera singer, were rare. For Glenn, the school was conveniently close, being only a ten-minute walk from home. The interior dynamics at Malvern[12] were remnants of the former Victorian society that propagated strict moral standards and overemphasis on academic achievement, hierarchy and discipline, rather than on social and humanitarian progress. The school authorities, embodied in the personage of the principal, fostered at Malvern a traditional atmosphere of formality with the accent on order and adherence to often-outdated school rules. All three Malvern principals in the late 1940s appeared to be rather authoritarian leaders who fostered the atmosphere of obedience and regimentation. There were sporadic attempts by the teachers to relax existing stringent disciplinary practices. For example, the teacher of Latin language, Stewart Niece, introduced half-day outings in order to appease the discontent and defiance of students. For this he was reprimanded by the principal, who put an end to the interesting social excursions.[13]

Some gifted and sensitive students at Malvern felt particularly deprived of recognition and empathy from their school mentors. There was a sense of rising dissatisfaction in some students, which contributed to a high dropout rate. Robert Fulford, Glenn's friend and schoolmate, admitted to his own disappointment in the school system. Fulford, a gifted writer who raised himself to a status of distinction in Canadian journalism and cultural life in general, experienced the Malvern school environment as unsupportive and oppressive. Ironically, the peak of human intelligence is at the age of sixteen, but the youth in the '40s and '50s had little of the sociopolitical power required to reform the existing school system. Fulford, an intelligent young man and a liberal spirit, and other similar students were not able to change nor come to terms with the school politics but often resorted to giving up school studies before matriculation.

Glenn Gould, who entered Malvern Collegiate as a full-scale concert pianist, experienced similar discontent. Within the next few years he won distinction as a classical pianist and became a celebrity among his countrymen, while receiving little special attention from his school community. He, too, felt a need for more understanding and personalized support. Instead, at Malvern, there was an air of skepticism around him. Glenn had a formal privilege endorsed by the principal for part-time morning school attendance, but the official school support seemed to have ended at that. Although these two remarkable men, Fulford and Gould, were not able to complete their training at Malvern, proportionally many more students were. Those other students were seemingly more adaptable and able to make use of opportunities that the school offered. The academic curriculum was indeed rigid and demanding but obviously conquerable by the majority of students. There were sports practiced like rowing, football and baseball; the school choir and many other extra-curricular activities were offered, which helped to balance the poor interaction and authoritarian pedagogical style. As noted before, Glenn developed emotional impasses in the course of his childhood, which in his teens were played out in the form of social shyness and his high vulnerability to any external stress. The relatively unsupportive school community was perceived by Glenn as rejecting and injurious. Subsequently, he felt so unhappy while in high school that every day of attendance felt like a major chore. As a famous public figure, Glenn referred in his interviews to the times when he had recurring school-related nightmares. Glenn stretched his school tolerance maximally and kept going to school for the sole motive of pleasing his parents. Nevertheless, no amount of stretching was enough to sustain him until graduation, and he stopped going to school short of his requirements for matriculation. Neither was Glenn able to overcome his inner obstacles and endear himself to the social school environment, nor were the school authorities capable of empathizing and reaching out to their unique student. There was a mutual failure in their interpersonal relation. Glenn the teenager, who was already hailed at Massey Hall, who was so often a subject to the media and who was praised and publicized in the wider society, appeared infrequently in concerts at his own school. This deprived him of a chance for more interaction with and more appreciation by his schoolmates and teachers. His first concert given at Malvern was on November 11, 1948, when Glenn played the organ on Remembrance Day. He was sixteen years old at the time. This was for him more a spiritual than a virtuoso-type of experience. Here are the excerpts from that concert program:

> November 11, 1948
>
> Malvern Collegiate Institute, Toronto
> Dedication and Memorial Service
>
> Dedication [to] students of Malvern Collegiate who served and those who gave their lives during W.W.II.

Prayer: Almighty and Eternal God before whom all nations rise and fall, and who doth behold the passing of all generations may be true to the highest when we find it and particularly to the sacrificial love of our fellow men. We thank Thee for those men who nobly fought and dearly won the battle for freedom and righteousness. Especially do we thank Thee for those who showed a love as great as any human possesses, in giving up their lives for their friends. In great humility we would dedicate this organ to their memory, through Jesus Christ our Lord. Amen.

Organ recital Dupuis
Mr. Glenn Gould[14]

This event most likely stirred mixed feelings in Glenn. The organist in him was satisfied in integrating his music achievement with the useful cause of commemoration. The person in him, endowed with a harsh conscience, may have felt remorseful for "those men who nobly fought and dearly won the battle for freedom ..." Like his guilt-laden Christian forebears, notably his mother and grandmother, who kept making sacrifices in life to expiate their guilt feelings, Glenn, too, inescapably felt a burden of his personal moral suffering reinforced by the minister's prayers and benediction.

GLENN AND GUERRERO

> Glenn, I can't teach you anything because you've already learned everything by yourself.
>
> Alberto Guerrero[15]

Unlike most of his peers that attended one school, Glenn had another equally demanding school with which to contend. He used to spend entire afternoons at the Royal Conservatory of Music. To Glenn, the morning session spent at Malvern was a nadir, whereas the afternoons spent at the conservatory were a vaulting point of his day. Every day he impatiently waited for his rendezvous with music. Such a dichotomy of nonmusical ebbs and musical flows, or hated school vs. beloved school, was never integrated in Glenn's mind into a whole and acceptable reality.

In the course of nine years, Glenn spent his afternoons on the third floor of the conservatory with Alberto Guerrero. Lilly Mech remembered:

> Glenn Gould and I studied piano together ... His teacher's studio was one door away from my teacher's and we would sit on hard wooden chairs just feet apart from each other. He was a tall good-looking kid, lanky, almost gaunt, shy to the extreme, preoccupied, with his genius already a burden.
>
> ... At 14, after Glenn Gould had won the Kiwanis music competition in piano with an extremely high mark and a prize of $100, as well as an acknowledgment by the music critics that he showed promise, he was on his way to

> importance. His coach, Alberto, recognized this and accorded him the privilege of entering the studio upon arrival.
>
> ... Glenn seemed to caress each note—each sounded heavy and very melodious. Added to this was either his humming or loud singing, most often not in tune with his piano. He would often play at an exaggeratedly slow tempo. At this time he was working on Bach, often with Alberto's loud voice running a commentary.[16]

Even when Guerrero was not there in body, he was certainly present in Glenn's thoughts, feelings and piano technique. Guerrero is here regarded to have been the single most influential non-family person, both in Glenn's music development and personal life as an adolescent. The appearance of Guerrero on the scene was most inspiring, and Glenn looked up to him as the key-holder to the magic world of music. Guerrero was a window to new music explorations, and Glenn sat at that window absorbing the vistas his magician teacher opened up to him.

R. Murray Schafer, distinguished Canadian composer and music educator, was also Guerrero's student. We met in Rochester, New York, where he participated in the conference on "Music, Growth and Aging." He reminisced:

"I am actually a failed pianist. I studied with Guerrero only about two years. He was sympathetic enough toward me. He was quite gentle and genial."

"Did he exert any pressure on you with respect to your piano practice?" I asked Schafer while he was comfortably smoking his pipe.

"Not at all. He did not force me to practice the piano; no technical exercises and no emphasis on scales. And he did not try to correct my posture. I suppose Guerrero treated me differently as I studied composition and not the art of performing,"[17] explained Schafer.

Perhaps Guerrero was more lax with his student-composers than with future concert pianists. His other famous student, William Aide, does not think of Guerrero as being gentle. "He [Guerrero] was not a modest man. I don't think that he was altogether benevolent. He was extremely tough on me ... He told me that I was too moral to be a pianist, that I was scrupulous, that I didn't have enough intensity or purpose and that I never perfected a thing."[18]

In the beginning, Gould had an insatiable need to spend time with Guerrero and to absorb the knowledge of his worldly mentor, both his approach to music and his general wisdom. Guerrero was a sounding board and an excellent partner in conversation who was able to meet Glenn's high rhetoric needs. As Glenn in his earlier childhood needed to spend hours on end with his mother, this necessity was then in part transferred to his teacher. When Glenn outgrew his mother's scope of music, he required a more advanced music partner and more independence to discover music for himself. At that time, Glenn seemed to have had a closer bond with Guerrero than other students. Such closeness between Glenn and Guerrero lasted until Glenn's mid-adolescence. Glenn enjoyed the status of a special student to a special teacher. The feelings were mutual. Guerrero had a daughter, Melisande, but did not have a son of his own. He embraced Glenn and subconsciously designated him as an heir to his wealth of music achievement. Like the old J. S. Bach, who passed his music knowledge onto his sons, Guerrero had a fatherly instinct to do the same. Passing one's own trade or wealth onto the next generation makes mortals feel less mortal. With Glenn around, Guerrero felt reassured that his intimate love and knowledge of music would be relayed to an appropriate recipient. Glenn, on his side, having a distant relationship with his own father, was in a constant search for a benevolent father figure, which at the beginning he found in Guerrero. So, Glenn and Senor Guerrero worked seriously at the piano but also felt a sense of kinship. They spent time together well beyond the scheduled music classes, even during weekends and holidays at their nearby cottages. A boy of fourteen and man of sixty were involved in a close father-son type of a bond. Guerrero supplied what Glenn's father could not. While Bert Gould possessed many fine personal qualities, he was unable to relate deeply to his son's genius. At first Glenn, just as his friend Murray Schafer, perceived Guerrero as a well-meaning person, except that Glenn, unlike Murray, went much further in his emotional interaction with his teacher. He had experienced him as a father figure and constantly sought him out in order to recapture the emotional losses that occurred in the relationship with his own father. Evidently, Guerrero became a significant love object in Glenn's life. The process of unconscious identification with Guerrero was underway. Glenn emulated his teacher's music philosophy, his music technique and creative approach to the keyboard.

Having a "fatherly" weakness for his favorite pupil, Guerrero went through the overprotective stage with Glenn. It happened that, around the same time Glenn's music career was ascending and the demands of his performing career were growing rapidly day by day, Glenn was becoming more sickly. Periodically he complained of body aches, be it headaches, neck aches, or achy sensations in his hands. This is when Glenn discovered that putting on an extra piece of clothing, like a sweater, or wearing woollen gloves would make him feel better and would appease his body pains. Glenn remembered that his beloved grandmother, Alma Gold ("Grandma Allie"), often used to warm her hands on the kettle steam before sitting down at the piano. Glenn's father, Bert, confirmed: "My mother believed that this was helpful for her arthritis. By keeping her fingers warm and limber, she was always ready to play for you." Indeed, between the ages of thirteen and fourteen, Glenn was toying with the idea of wearing gloves before playing the piano. This was not a firm habit at that time but more a matter of experimentation. Guerrero was there too, witnessing Glenn's evolving concerns and corresponding protective devices Glenn used to cope with his discomfort. Not only did Guerrero not put Glenn at ease on the subject, but he actively encouraged him to wear gloves and to even soak his hands in warm water, particularly in cold weather and before performing. Guerrero and Glenn were in collusion against the rest of the world. Glenn's mother thought that her son was overreacting and tried to dissuade him from wearing extra clothes and gloves. She did not want Glenn to be outlandish and vastly different in that sense than other pianists she knew and valued. In spite of her concerns, Glenn never abandoned this behavior, and in his twenties he developed a strange and full-blown habit of wearing warm clothes and woollen gloves even in mild weather.

If one thinks of Glenn's mother as being ambitious by introducing her three-year-old son to regular piano classes, then one has to think of Guerrero as even more ambitious for creating a concert pianist at the age of twelve.[19] Guerrero was always aware of Glenn's prodigious music gift and threw himself full force into the working relationship with his student. The first thing Guerrero noticed was that Glenn exhibited an unusual habitual behavior at the piano, such as fidgeting and slouching, which had to be given up and replaced with more disciplined and conventional posture. To have to correct posture at the piano is a fairly common task piano teachers encounter at the junction when they receive a student from less sophisticated training to a more advanced program. Guerrero soon found how difficult it was to challenge Glenn's behavioral acquisitions. He applied several approaches in order to have Glenn stop his "platform antics," as Guerrero sarcastically called them, but these were all in vain. Glenn continued to slouch, hum and sing at the piano. Guerrero was a good pedagogue who capitalized on patience and perseverance, hoping that sooner or later Glenn was going to polish his physical manners. After all, Glenn was rapidly grasping the special finger technique of his teacher and was doing marvelously as a young virtuoso. The posture issue could be taken care of later. He could not have been more wrong. It was Guerrero's idea for Glenn to study Beethoven's G Major Piano Concerto. Indeed, at the age of twelve Glenn started learning the concerto by memorizing the scores and by comparative listening to the records of Artur Schnabel. In the course of the next two years, Glenn mastered the concerto through diligent, hard work into a finished product—the public performance. Here, at this early stage in the student-teacher relationship, is where the first rift of three occurred between them. Guerrero, for didactic and personal reasons, wanted Glenn to model after Rudolf Serkin's interpretation of Beethoven's music. Serkin, who taught piano at the Curtis Music Institute in Philadelphia, appealed to Guerrero both as a person and musician. Had Glenn been an "ordinary" budding concert pianist, he would have accepted his teacher's suggestions, like it or not, until he had become an independent concert pianist. Obviously, Glenn was anything but "ordinary." In addition to his abundant music talent, he was opinionated and headstrong. The competition with his valued mentor had begun. These were the first arguments between the two. Glenn was quite rigid when it came to arguing. His point was crystal clear to him. Schnabel was his model and his way of playing Beethoven's Fourth Concerto appealed to Glenn. End of discussion.

Guerrero was stunned with such an open and stubborn protest from his student. The teacher proceeded to exert subtle pressure on Glenn to do what was expected of him. It was in vain. Glenn's mind was firmly made up. He used Schnabel's approach to Beethoven's monumental music piece but, indeed, formed his own concept of interpretation. This way he felt free of restraints and had a degree of creative and personal autonomy from Guerrero. Why should he rely on Guerrero's concept when he had his own? Clearly, in this case, Glenn felt emotionally and musically more predisposed to Schnabel's music.

Artur Schnabel, "one of the greatest teachers in history,"[20] was an authority on interpreting Beethoven's music. He was a student of the most famous European piano teacher, Theodor Leschetizky. Schnabel, like Gould, was a performing virtuoso at the age of twelve; but unlike Gould, he did not attend high school in order to dedicate himself entirely to music. Gould empathized with this aspect of Schnabel, and through this he paid respect to Leschetizky as a supportive teacher. Gould emulated Schnabel's way of playing Beethoven's music, since through Schnabel he had a direct sense of kinship to Beethoven himself in the following way:

Beethoven —taught→ Czerny —taught→ Leschetizky —taught→ Schnabel
Gould identified with Schnabel's style

The message directed to Guerrero was filled with meaning. By identifying with Schnabel and not with his teacher on the concerto issue, Glenn paradoxically showed how much he was in need of his autonomy and how much he relied on the support and understanding of his teacher. But, in this particular case, his teacher offered him neither. Glenn was very sensitive to the issue of emotional support; once he felt it was not there, he felt hurt and abandoned. Guerrero, on his part, had no clue what Glenn's needs were. He simply disapproved and dissociated himself from his student once the student was disobedient. This resembled Glenn's original emotional interaction with his mother, who approved of him when he behaved but rejected him when he did not. Guerrero, by dissociating from Glenn's choice of playing the concerto, reacted exactly like Glenn's mother would have reacted. Following the two years of meticulous studying and practicing of the Beethoven Concerto no. 4, Gould was ready to perform it before the local public. On November 29, 1945, he played the first movement in a two-piano arrangement, Guerrero playing at the second piano. This was a sort of dress rehearsal, designed primarily for Guerrero to scrutinize his student's performance capacity. Gould passed the test and appeared as soloist playing the opening of the same concerto at Massey Hall on May 8, 1946, with Ettore Mazzoleni conducting the Conservatory Symphony Orchestra.

To sum up the Schnabel affair, here are Gould's reflections described in his lively autobiographic piece written when he was thirty-eight years old:

> ... for two years I have been in possession of an RCA album—acquired with funds painstakingly set aside from my allowance—featuring Artur Schnabel, Frederick Stock, the Chicago Symphony ...
>
> ... Almost every day during the two years ... I faithfully traced every nuance of the Schnabelian rhetoric ...
>
> ... as the concert date approached, my own Schnabel impersonation had acquired such awesome authenticity that my teacher, a scholar scarcely noted for his indulgence of student power, compelled me to hand over my album with the sort of pedagogical high-handedness ...[21]

Gould then explained how he tricked Guerrero in order to appease him by playing for him "Serkinesque dispatch," or Rudolf Serkin's rendition of Beethoven's Fourth Concerto, which he had heard on the radio; this met with Guerrero's approval. Gould reminisced further:

> ... and my good professor pronounced himself entirely satisfied with my progress, my tractability, and his own expertise in the field of tutorial psychology.[22]

Alas, at the concert, Gould gave his rendition modeled after Schnabel. The student won the first round:

> ... I felt in high spirit, my teacher was shattered, and the press on the whole was quite kind.[23]

This was a ferocious psychological warfare between the two fine musicians. The statements referring to Guerrero, like "a scholar scarcely noted for his indulgence of student power," or "my teacher was shattered," are loaded with meaning. Glenn resented Guerrero for betrayal and retaliated by making a fool out of him. He simply fought for autonomy as a person and authenticity as a virtuoso.

Meanwhile, Guerrero endeavored to mold Glenn his way. It was a dramatic power struggle resulting in the first emotional rift in their relationship.

What did the critics have to say? Throughout his entire music career, Gould received a lot of positive, dazzling feedback from the critics. Here at the start of the thirteen-year-old pianist's career, there is a prototype of the positive feedback embodied in the critical writing of Edward W. Wodson:

> The boy's playing showed how beautiful piano music can be, how glorious Beethoven writing for the piano is, and how awesome are the ways of genius in a child. For Glenn Gould is a genius ... his butterfly hands made the piano sing as only De Pachman [sic] used to do. He showed the music lover that scale passages and arpeggios on the humble piano may have spiritual as well as technical beauty and character. His phrasing was eloquent as poetry chanted by the poet himself.[24]

Another critic, Augustus Bridle of *The Toronto Daily Star,* gave us an idea of the public response: "...thrice curtain-called, for a stiff single nod to the crowd."[25]

There was also some less generous feedback from other critics. Allen Sangster commented with caution:

> Glenn Gould's offering was the opening movement of the Beethoven G Major Piano Concerto. Not too much dynamic range here, phrasing a little choppy and sometimes puzzling to one familiar with Schnabel, but with obvious possibilities.[26]

Gould was vulnerable to that kind of depreciative criticism, particularly to the ambiguous allusion to Schnabel. Some twenty-four years later, he attributed to Sangster these bitterly distorted words (which Sangster never said):

> Beethoven's elusive Fourth Concerto was left in the hands of small child last night. Who does the kid think he is, Schnabel?[27]

Years after the fact, Gould still suffered emotional consequences of his Schnabel affair. In it he was injured by Guerrero and, to a lesser degree, by Sangster. He was never able to resolve his conflicts around this episode, in which he felt let down by Guerrero. This kind of polarized critique of Gould's artistry by his teachers and professional critics, at times positive to the extreme, negative even hostile at other times, set the stage for his lifelong love-hate relationship with his teacher and with professional critics.

Despite the rising tension with Guerrero, Glenn's phenomenal growth as a musician went on unblemished. Letters of support, greetings and music offers kept coming. His music school rewarded him one more time for his exceptional efforts:

Toronto Conservatory of Music, July 27, 1946

Dear Glenn,

I have pleasure in informing you that the Ada Wagstaff Harris Scholarship to the value of $250.00 has been awarded to you for the academic season 1946-47. It is understood that you will continue to study with Mr. Guerrero.

Faithfully yours,
Ettore Mazzoleni
Principal[28]

There is very little of Guerrero's archives saved pertaining to Gould. The following letter is one of the few that survived. Though not properly dated, it appears to have been written in August 1946, shortly after the turmoil of Glenn's performance at Massey Hall. It reads:

Dear Glenn, August 26 [1946]

Mr. Ealton, the Manager of the Toronto Symphony, called me by telephone today and said that you have been chosen to play in the opening concert of Secondary School series, the nineteenth and twentieth of November. You would play the G Major Beethoven [concerto] complete. Sir Ernest will conduct. There is a nominal fee of $75. Mr. Ealton would like you to see him next week some time, to confirm all this.

I have missed very much a game of croquet and, almost, one of monopoly. Though I suspect what I really miss is the lovely place and kind hospitality.

Please give my best regards to mother and father.

Sincerely
Alberto Guerrero[29]

Was Guerrero always so businesslike, much as in this letter, or was he being put off by Glenn's disobedience at Massey Hall? If Guerrero had at least some warm and exciting feelings for Glenn, he could have said something more personal like, "I have missed a game of croquet with you, Glenn," instead of putting it so impersonally, or he could have simply said, "I missed you Glenn, and I am looking forward to seeing you in September." This was not the case. As to the concert that Guerrero referred to, it took place not in October but in April next year and not with MacMillan but with Bernard Heinze as conductor. Another interesting thing about this letter is that it was written in black ink. Glenn, in the course of his entire life, wrote exclusively with the black-ink felt pen, which seems to have been a habit that he took on from Guerrero.

On October 28, 1946, shortly before his mother's fifty-fifth birthday, Gould received the TCM Associate Diploma at the Toronto Conservatory of Music graduation exercises at Convocation Hall, University of Toronto. His beaming parents were in the audience, as was Alberto Guerrero. Hence, Glenn became a fully certified concert pianist at the age of fourteen, which is a dream of many a parent and teacher which only rarely comes true. Was Glenn's freshly acquired ATCM diploma a gift for his mother's birthday, or was it a symbolic note of gratitude to his teacher? Perhaps it was the harvest of this extraordinary tripartite team, a crowning result of enduring dedication, and a labor of love. Florence Greig Gould, Glenn Gould and Alberto Guerrero rode the avenues of history together until this autumn day in 1946. This convocation was a turning point. Glenn was supposed to leave his elders behind and leap into the world of artistic individuation.

Conflicts or not, as a teenager Glenn was amazingly successful as a musician. His music achievements were steadfastly growing, and he was spearheading into the echelons of musical fame. The news of Glenn's unique acquisition of the title as the youngest certified concert pianist in Canada transcended its boundaries. He received this flattering letter:

> Buckingham Palace, October 2, 1946
>
> The Lady-in-Waiting is commanded by the Queen to thank Mrs. Samuel Jeffrey for her letter and to say that her Majesty was interested to read of the little Canadian boy who is such a clever musician.[30]

At that stage of early adolescence, Glenn was still pursuing comprehensive studies of two music instruments—the pipe organ and the piano. This colossal task was both mentally and physically taxing for his delicate constitution. At first, Glenn managed to keep on top of these demands by way of insatiable curiosity and music talent. His enormous enthusiasm held his attention for the organ for six years, after which point Glenn had to stop playing the organ to concentrate solely on his piano studies. By the age of thirteen, Glenn was an accomplished organist. His debut as a performing soloist was indeed as an organist, at Eaton Auditorium on December 12, 1945, and not as a pianist. He presented the following program:

Mendelssohn's last organ sonata	Bach fugue G-minor
Dupuis concerto	Bach prelude

What was the driving force behind Glenn's comparative studies in organ and piano? Often gifted children are involved in parallel studies of two instruments. One of his early music models, American pianist Rosalyn Tureck, enrolled in studies of harpsichord and clavichord on top of her central piano studies, which she pursued successfully with relative ease. In the course of her music career, Tureck gradually evolved from performing artistry to a career of musicology and music philosophy. It appears that, regardless of the artist's enormous enthusiasm and love of music, one cannot humanly perform at the top level on more than one instrument. Orchestral musicians are able to switch from one instrument to another and still offer a high quality of performance, but concert soloists are hardly able to keep up with the demands of their careers playing more than one instrument on the solo performing level.

While Glenn became acquainted with the work and biography of Rosalyn Tureck in mid-adolescence, he started playing the organ at the age of nine. As mentioned earlier, Glenn's mother, grandmother, and Sir Ernest MacMillan appear to have been crucial motivators backing Glenn's organ study. Glenn himself was a voracious music student with a strong natural impulse toward generating and reproducing music. He embraced rather than resisted the proposal of his mother to study the organ. The piano is known as a more worldly instrument, whereas the organ is more associated with spiritual music and is not normally used for interpretation of popular music. Florence was drawn to the organ as a "pure" instrument, residing in churches to enhance religious events. Eventually, Glenn abandoned his studies of the pipe organ. The piano, his first love, remained the chief instrument of his creative expressiveness for the rest of his life.

It is unknown what Guerrero had to say about Glenn's organ studies. When they first met, Glenn was already in the process of studying organ. Guerrero had a strong Catholic religious background, yet in his adulthood he turned to a more secular life. He preferred piano unambiguously to any instrument. We will never know whether Guerrero ever passed comments explicitly to Glenn. What is more likely was that Guerrero showed implicitly that Glenn's piano studies ought to have the highest priority. Everything else, including the organ and high school studies, were to take a back seat. Consistent with the influence of his teacher, as well as with the reality of this highly demanding task, Glenn eventually stopped his organ studies in 1947 at the age of fifteen while pursuing his advanced grade nine. His mother's second dream for him to become a certified organist was shattered.

The relationship between Gould and Guerrero was predominantly positive at the beginning, reaching its peak in the middle of Glenn's teens, ages sixteen to seventeen, when it started gradually declining to its vanishing point. One of several contributing factors was the introduction of music manager Walter Homburger to Gould's life.

Walter Homburger immigrated to Canada from Karlsruhe in Germany. He studied accountancy but enjoyed listening to music as a hobby. In his middle age, he became Canada's leading impresario and retired at the age of sixty-three as a manager of the Toronto Symphony Orchestra. This is how Homburger described meeting Glenn Gould, at the age of twenty-one, and becoming his music manager:

> I had plenty of free time before I was married. So, I used to go to the Kiwanis Festival at Eaton Auditorium morning, noon and evening. That's where I heard Glenn Gould for the first time, in 1946,[31] playing Beethoven's Fourth Piano Concerto with his teacher, Alberto Guerrero, at the second piano. He was only fourteen years old, but I thought he was phenomenal and went right away to talk to his parents. I had never done anything like that before, but he was starting to do the odd concert and I began to arrange them for him.[32]

Other than his father, school teachers and tutors, Walter Homburger was the fourth important adult male figure in Glenn's fifteenth year of life; after his organ teacher, Frederick Silvester, his music theory teacher, Leo Smith, and Guerrero. Before Walter came along, Glenn's father acted on his son's behalf as manager and as public relations person. When young but suave Homburger introduced himself, Mr. and Mrs. Gould were cautious yet flattered by his offer. While Guerrero still looked upon Glenn as a student who had a long way to go to mature and perfect his musicianship, Homburger looked upon Glenn as an artistic commodity and a delightful business venture. Homburger had a thick German accent, a solid work discipline, and an air of formality. Being such a conventional type of a person, Homburger went through a great deal of hardship in relationship to his teenage client. Glenn was his most promising music artist but was the most complex and most difficult one to understand. Homburger claimed seniority in business experience, Gould claimed uniqueness, often refusing to conform to general managerial rules. To Guerrero, the presence of Homburger was distracting Glenn from his main focus as a music student. To Glenn, the relationship with Homburger provided a window to fame and independence as a concert pianist. This drama in the triangle between the gifted student, music teacher and the manager is well described in the novel *Madame Sousatzka* by Bernice Rubens. The protagonist, Madame Sousatzka, is a loving but also possessive music teacher and unfulfilled pianist who holds onto her gifted student, Marcus. At the moment when the music manager appears on the scene, arranging a public concert for Marcus, the relationship between the teacher and the student was compromised. For Glenn, like Marcus, it was reassuring and flattering to have a manager and be a young and paid concert pianist with multiple offers and engagements. For Guerrero, one can only speculate that he had concerns about losing control and influence over his special student.

With the arrival of Homburger, Glenn had four significant adults to juggle interpersonally—his parents, Guerrero, and Homburger. All four were conventional, proper individuals who had limited ability to understand and handle Glenn as a person. The personality clashes within that pentagonal system occurred on an ongoing basis. With Guerrero, Glenn had the best, the longest, the most fervent discussions about cultures of the world. Glenn learned from Guerrero like from no other person, but also competed with him like with no one else. While Guerrero expanded Glenn's music grasp, Homburger added a more worldly dimension to Glenn's socially narrow exposure. As with Guerrero and earlier with his parents, the clashes with Homburger were inevitable. When at the age of twenty-three, as an acclaimed pianist, Gould was asked about Homburger, this is how he qualified their relationship:

> My agent Walter Homburger, of International Artists. Walter heard me play in the Kiwanis Festival in 1947—nine years ago—and asked my parents if he could represent me. My parents insisted there should not be exploitation of me simply as a youthful prodigy, that I shouldn't be pushed until I was ready. Walter agreed, his theory being the artist should be learning as much as possible in his teens. After success arrives there is no more time.
>
> Walter and I never disagree about anything except money, pianos, programming, concert dates, my relations with the press, and the way I dress. He insists I sometimes appear to be playing the piano with my nose, and is delighted when I am criticized in the press for my appearance.[33]

Although Gould humorously referred to his squabbles with Homburger, one can deduce the seriousness of the problem underneath. Homburger preferred Gould to follow the standard concert repertoire for pianos; to be more diplomatic, cooperative and amiable with the press; and to be more normal in his appearance. Homburger was a conformist who attempted to fit into the social and business standards of his time. He had ordinary expectations of his client to conform himself. Naturally, Gould and Homburger often disagreed due to their personal differences. It is more worrisome that Gould saw Homburger as "mean" by saying, [Homburger] "is delighted when I am criticized in the press for my appearance." If Homburger was really irritated by Gould's appearance and made sarcastic comments on this account, then the pianist perceived his manager as unsupportive and punitive in the same way he perceived the critics. This is why Gould built some animosity toward his manager, which became more manifest in his post-concert years.

Gould was a music genius but socially inexperienced and somewhat raw in his artistry. Guerrero was a seasoned performer and influential music pedagogue. Homburger was an astute music business promoter. A team of those three capable men could have been maximally productive personally and musically. Instead, their interpersonal conflicts became a major obstacle. Young Gould claimed centrality as a music star, and he was not about to give it up or to give in to his teacher or manager. After all, he managed to control his father in the matter of fishing; similarly he had to find how to control these two influential men. Predictably, Glenn applied his odd and omnipotent behavior as a defense in relationships with his two music partners. Despite such turbulent interpersonal dynamics, Gould, coached by Guerrero in music and Homburger in business, continued to forge ahead toward greater musical conquests.

THE DYNAMICS OF ADOLESCENCE

> We are now eager to trace the steps of individuation during adolescence.
>
> Peter Blos[34]

While Glenn was a flourishing teenage artist his inner mind was in the state of flux. Currently, adolescence is considered as a distinct stage in human development. Peter Blos, one of the pioneer scholars of adolescence, summed up the importance of this phase:

> The core of individual personality begins to coalesce in childhood and then crystallizes in adolescence, which provides a second chance to complete the work of the earlier stages of psycho social development.[35]

In an earlier paper, Blos put forward a concept of a so-called "second individuation" that takes place in adolescence. He said:

> I propose to view adolescence in its totality as the second individuation process, the first one having been completed toward the end of the third year of life with the attainment of object constancy.[36]

The term "individuation" refers to the "shedding of family dependencies." In a practical sense, through their emotional growth, adolescents are depending less and less on their primary caretakers and making a shift toward "external and extrafamilial love and hate objects." Earlier, in reviewing Glenn's childhood, some impasses were noted around his first individuation. Here was a chance for Glenn to do some reworking on his previously acquired emotional problems. Since he was a teenage celebrity, Glenn had inordinate opportunities to meet interesting people, develop meaningful friendships and practice new challenges that could have allowed him to overcome his childhood anxieties. The psychological growth accomplished through a successful second individuation serves as a fulcrum in the architectural edifice of one's personality.

Another major dynamic phenomenon in adolescence that is inseparable from second individuation is the formation of the ego identity. Erik Erikson, a distinguished expert on adolescence, proposed the concepts of identity crisis and ego identity. He said that adolescents have to reach for and rely on their peers for support and understanding, as they themselves are going through the identical process of development. The group of peers or the group of friends becomes an ego ideal that serves as a temporary synthesizer of the disorganized aspects of the inner self. Being an "in-grouper," Erikson proposed, provides temporary ego strength. Conversely, being on the outskirts of the group weakens ego identity, setting the stage for "role confusion." Those fortunate teenagers who successfully negotiate their adolescence will emerge with a stable sense of social identity—on the personal, family, societal and vocational levels. They will then enter their young adulthood more or less knowing who they are, where they came from, and where they are going next. The aim is to develop a firm social ego identity and not an ego diffusion or ego confusion.

Anna Freud pointed to two major characteristics of adolescents: their global inner turmoil and their reemergence of instinctual drives. Here is what she had to say about the unending flux and contradictions in the life of adolescents:

> ... it is normal for an adolescent to behave for a considerable length of time in an inconsistent and unpredictable manner; to fight his impulses and to accept them; to ward them off successfully and to be overrun by them; to love his parents and to hate them; to revolt against them and to be dependent on them; to be deeply ashamed to acknowledge his mother before others and, unexpectedly to desire heart-to-heart talks with her; to thrive on imitation of an identification with others while searching unceasingly for his own identity; to be more idealistic, artistic, generous, and unselfish than he will ever be again, but also the opposite: self-centered, egotistic, calculating.[37]

Although adolescence can be an exciting time, it can also be a very painful state of inner unrest, even under the best of circumstances. To complicate things, there is the stormy appearance of instinctual impulses. "Normal" adolescent girls and boys experience rapid shifts in their mood and behavior from one extreme to the other. They live under the duress of individuation while working on consolidation of their ego identity and enduring the onslaught of their sexual drives. Yet they are still able to manage their own mercurial interior dynamics and enter young adulthood with relief and stability. In a practical sense, when adolescence as a distinct stage is mastered, it results in one's comfortable individuation from parental bonds; the ability to enjoy a social life; to hold a job; to belong to a group of individuals with similar interests and affiliations; and to be comfortable with intimacy and one's own sexual identity. Successful resolution of adolescence leads to an appropriate career choice with a stable sense of satisfaction with one's chosen vocation.

Occupationally, Gould had a prevalent identity as a musician. The art of music is a vast province in which one has to find one's own comfortable niche. When it came to Glenn's identity in that province, he struggled with it throughout the entire two decades of his public concerts, from the age of twelve, when he appeared on the stage, to the age of thirty-two, when he stepped down. During this exceptional time, Glenn collected praise and recognition but also angst and heartache. Honestly, Glenn had mixed feelings with respect to his occupational identity as a concert pianist. In his interview with Bernard Asbell, which took place in New York City in 1962, Glenn summed up his painful conflict over his choice of a music profession that weaved through his formative years:

Gould: Throughout my teens I rather resisted the idea of a career as a concert pianist.
Interviewer: Resisted?

Gould: Yes, it seemed like a kind of superficial thing, some sort of pleasant adjunct to a scholastic interest, you know. I imagine that only a career that was musicologically motivated was worthy and that everything else was a little bit frivolous. I saw myself as a sort of Renaissance Man, capable of doing many things. I obviously wanted to be a composer. I still do. Performing in the arena had no attraction for me. This was, at least in part, defensive. Even from what little I then knew of the politics of the business, it was apparent that a career as a solo pianist involved a competition which I felt much too grand ever to consider facing.[38]

Analysis of this rich paragraph uncovers the inner confusion related to his career choice. Gould was at the pinnacle of his pianistic achievement when he was interviewed at age twenty-nine, yet he was ambivalent and insecure about being a concert pianist. Be reminded that it was his mother who transferred her personal wishes and goals onto her son. He identified with some of her strengths but could not escape internalizing some of her limits in the form of restraints. Gould told us through the interview with Asbell that he had bigger and broader career aspirations. It follows that if he had been freer from restrictions with respect to his future vocational identity, his innate genius could have guided him to a more open-ended multi-musicological career. He could have been anything, from being a concert pianist, composer or conductor, to a true musical Renaissance man on a grand scale. In this powerful identity crisis, the young and brilliant artist inadvertently shared with the world his feelings of loss of who he wanted to be and what he was capable of doing. He sensed the inherent danger of his unconscious conflicts around being a performing artist. Implicitly, Gould told us that he was forced into a very narrow role; that he was cheated, deprived and robbed of his true God-given abilities; and that he was disillusioned and angry about these restrictions. He could not tell us how this all happened, with whom he was angry, and how he would have changed things. He only shared with us a slice of his suffering, his role confusion, from which he could not find a way out.

In the course of his developmental years, the emotional tension between Glenn and the outer world was gradually getting worse. When he was young, his parents feared that he, as a child prodigy, may be exploited, just as the great composer Mozart and the pianist Joseph Hofmann were. Glenn internalized the fear of exploitation and became overly controlling of his environment, particularly around the concert performance and in response to his critics, friends and associates. This all was suggestive of his insecurity and distrust of others. On the one hand, Glenn was raised to be a public figure of great stature; on another, he had many mixed feelings and trepidation around this very identity. It was as if he were raised in a "glass house," watching and remote-controlling the world from inside out but not connecting with it intimately and freely. Glenn lacked the basic life, social and business skills required for everyday living. He could not endure any degree of interpersonal roughness or confrontation and shunned those who gave him a hard time or when he thought they did. Fortunately, Glenn was endowed with superior intelligence and a vast music gift, which to a point compensated for his identity problems.

Related to social maladjustment, young Glenn exhibited an array of peculiar habits that were widely publicized and lumped together under the umbrella term of eccentricities. His behavior ranged from the "soft" childhood tendencies of slouching, fidgeting and headstrong opinions to the more hard-core posturing and mannerisms at the piano; all noticeable in his teens and more pronounced in adulthood. In his late adolescence, the first signs of oddities appeared in the form of self-grooming and in the way he dressed. For example, Glenn started wearing gloves and a winter wardrobe even in hot weather. In all this he differed in a major way from his peers. The term "eccentricity," so overused by the press in reference to Gould, is a misnomer, a nonspecific term with a number of possible meanings, yet none of them is clearly discernible. Gould's so-called eccentricity is a complex syndrome that deserves careful, in-depth analysis that will be pursued in ensuing chapters. It is fair to say that Glenn's underlying emotional conflicts, stemming from his early childhood, and then perpetuated through further stages of growth into adolescence, were responsible for his peculiar habits. In short, these oddities served as a defense against, as well as a way of coping with, those inner conflicts. The conflicts were in four major areas; conflicts over dependency needs, over aggressive drives, over sexual urges, and over identity issues. Unresolved conflicts gave rise to stage performance anxiety and existential depression, which became clinically manifested in his teens. Just like other frustrated teenagers who rely on their behavioral expression of nervousness by being restless, chewing their nails, daydreaming, or having a short attention span, Glenn also developed a number of expressive ways to cope with his frustrations constantly rising from within.

First, to address Glenn's depression. Sigmund Freud considered depression to be anger and aggression turned inward and directed against the self. Modern psychiatry considers several types of depression, focusing on biological, or more specifically on the biochemical origin of depression. Adolescence is a stage of powerful transition from a sheltered life to an independent existence. As such, it is normal to have a degree of apprehension and sadness around the loss of childhood joys and around acquisition of growing responsibilities. In Glenn's teen years, he did not experience just the normative depression but rather a clinically observable one. For instance, Glenn's dread of going to school, his social withdrawal and overt sensitivity to rejection, his distrust, his surmounting guilt feelings and strong sense of humiliation whenever he "failed" were but some of many signals of his evolving clinical depression. This condition had its precursors in his childhood as it was played out in his sorrow about fish dying from fishing, his temper tantrums and his avoidance of "cruel" children and adults. All this was predictive of his future depressive state of mind. Unfortunately, his feelings of dejection were misinterpreted and described with dismissive adjectives such as odd, idiosyncratic and, finally, eccentric. The public was oblivious of Glenn's inner maelstrom. Worse, the professional critics, press and academic observers were often annoyed and judgmental of Glenn's behavioral facade. They became blinded by and fixated on his superficial "eccentricities," which made it impossible for them to have an in-depth understanding of his versatile and many-layered personality.

One of the earliest published records of Glenn's idiosyncrasies on the stage was by Pearl McCarthy of *The Globe and Mail*. Following Glenn's appearance at Massey Hall on January 14 and 15, 1947, when he interpreted Beethoven's G Major Concerto with the guest conductor from Australia, Bernard Heinze, and the Toronto Symphony, McCarthy made this observation:

> The boy played it exquisitely. He is not a heavy tone, but delicacy of phrasing and timing give it a clear carrying power.[39]

Immediately after this brief positive feedback, McCarthy, in the same breath, focused on Glenn's behavior at the piano in a stern and pretentious fashion:

> ... Unfortunately the boy showed some incipient mannerism and limited his self-control to the period when he himself was playing. As he approaches adult status he will undoubtedly learn to suppress this disturbing fidgeting while his collaborators are at work.[40]

This early report by Pearl McCarthy may be regarded as a prototype of most later reviews by the press of Gould's music performance. The ambivalence of such reports could be summed up in the following sentence: "Glenn's playing is exquisite but his manners are poor." Hence, the Gouldian "platform antics," a term coined by Guerrero, or his mannerism or his eccentricities, were all totally misunderstood by his contemporaries. One can see that the stage was set for the interpersonal failure between Gould and his observers. The perennial trap that most music professionals and critics fell into was to assess his genius in the same pen stroke with his extra-musical behavior. Since Glenn's "eccentricities" were symptoms of his emotional disorder, they were comparable to any other physical disorder or disability. For example, if he had been one-eyed or one-legged, would the same critic say, "his playing is exquisite but his one-legged appearance is annoying to watch?" In other words, Glenn could not help being the way he was. He was simply at a loss to know how and why he turned out to be so vastly different from others. His behavior was more or less beyond his control.

Interestingly enough, it was Glenn's parents who set the original pattern of approval-disapproval in relationship to him. They valued his musicality but disapproved of his manners. In the same way, McCarthy's otherwise accurate assessment of Glenn's performance was also insensitive and unthoughtful. She offered the "but" feedback, which engendered her ambivalence toward him and was very reminiscent of his disturbing relations with his caregivers. Glenn was aware that he was not wholeheartedly accepted by others, which frustrated him and deepened his resistance to change and to improve. He intuitively felt that the message of his critics was: "Change your manners or else we won't love you and approve of you, regardless of the fact that you are the best." This reflects a punitive attitude of his elders to which he was sensitized. Every act of rejection with its implicit disapproval and punitiveness represented a psychological trauma for Glenn. The instigators of his emotional wounds were unaware of the damage they caused him and his future relationships.

From Glenn's point of view, his fidgeting at a concert on January 14, 1947, was justified. This is how he recounted the critical event:

> As a soloist ... as I was getting in my best dark suit prior to the concert, my father cautioned me not to play with Nick but that was of course easier said than done.[41]

Apparently Glenn, prior to the concert, and despite his father's warnings, played with his beloved English setter, Nick, whose long hair clung to Glenn's evening attire. When Glenn sat down to perform Beethoven's G Major Concerto, he found himself staring at his suit and plucking off Nick's hair whenever his hands were free. This came across to the audience as fidgeting and poor manners at the piano, which later was reflected in the critique of Pearl McCarthy. It is possible to imagine what was going through Glenn's mind while crossing the stage and sitting at the keyboard. Making a debut at the age of fourteen and playing with the more mature and experienced Toronto

Symphony musicians, and above all, interpreting such a serious and challenging music piece would be expected to be an anxiety-provoking event. Glenn played with Nick in order to appease his high performance anxiety, which had nothing to do with naughtiness and not obeying his father's wishes. When he crossed the stage and sat at the piano, his father was likely on his mind or at least in the back of it. By plucking off Nick's hair during the concerto, Glenn was obediently undoing the mess he created despite the admonishment he received. The misbehaving son, who caused his father unnecessary grief and shame, was fighting two parallel battles. First, he was trying to overcome the technical and artistic demands of this beautiful Beethoven concerto. He won this battle and was dubbed "exquisite." The second battle, which had to do with his son-father relationship and his relationship to the critical audience, was lost. Glenn's fidgeting and unruly picking of the hair was unfathomable and unacceptable to the critics. There was a high price to pay and Glenn walked off the stage split between being a promising pianist and the naughty boy who raised the eyebrows of adults. In hindsight, one can see through psychological analysis that Glenn's music future as a performer was signed and sealed at that point. It was quite predictable that the concert pianist, with such maladaptive stage manners, would not be able to last long on the stage. This very insight made Gould accurately predict that he would not last more than a decade as a performing artist but would have to retire by the age of thirty.

"THE NICE GENIUS"

Nulla dics sine linea.[42]

Along with the changes in psychological and social dynamics in adolescence, such as the formation of the ego identity, there are also massive psycho-sexual upheavals. These are marked by hormonal growth, bodily sexual maturation, and an awakening of instinctual sexual impulses. Suddenly, children step from their sexually quiescent stage into the powerful awareness of their rising libido. Normally, in the span of six to nine years after the onset of puberty, youths are able to gain mastery of their instinctual impulses and develop stable sexual identities.

Anna Freud explained that some adolescents, in their struggle to cope with their instinctual drives, go through a so-called "ascetic phase," during which they show inordinate fear of "the quantity rather than the quality of their instincts." She summed it up in the following observation:

> ... We have all met young people who severely renounced any impulses which savored of sexuality and who avoided the society of those of their own age, declined to join in any entertainment, and, in true puritanical fashion, refused to have anything to do with the theater, music or dancing. We can understand that there is a connection between the forgoing of pretty and attractive clothes and the prohibition of sexuality.[43]

Further on Freud, who also studied the function of the ego in relationship to the instinctual drives, concluded:

> Every time the instinct says, "I will," the ego retorts, "Thou shalt not," much as after the manner of strict parents in the early training of little children.[44]

How true these findings were for Gould! He certainly lived through an ascetic phase both socially and sexually. He refrained from social gatherings and from celebrating important events. Glenn always maintained his privacy and a safe social distance. Nothing much had changed since his childhood when he stood timorously aside watching his peers at play. As time went on, he showed more need for solitude. His next best option was to spend time with music-related friends and adult associates, whereas mingling with his peers was a distant third choice.

Robert Fulford was one of the few teenagers who maintained any social continuity with Glenn. Fulford is seen as the most reliable extra-family witness because of his fairly close relationship with Glenn in his formative years. Fulford not only made valuable and insightful observations of Glenn, but he documented his remembrances. He confirmed that Glenn was set apart from his peers in his musical accomplishments but also in his outward appearance and social behavior. Even Glenn's speech was unusually serious, intellectual, and devoid of slang and other language impurities. He deliberately avoided the use of "dirty words" or any terminology that would even remotely resemble obscenities. In terms of language and thought content, Glenn resorted to purism. Fulford remembered that even the word "balls" was banned from Glenn's vocabulary.[45] Fulford, with his budding journalistic identity and admiration for his interesting friend, gave a warm account of Glenn's music achievement. He wrote for the school gazette *9 Bugle*, dated April 3, 1946, that Glenn "won seven medals and three scholarships" [to date] and that his latest triumph was at the Kiwanis Festival, where he was called by one of the adjudicators a "wonder child." Fulford concluded his portrait of Glenn: "He is a confirmed bachelor at 13 ..."[46] This precise pronouncement of the young journalist, Bob Fulford, turned out to be a remarkably accurate forecast of Gould's future status as single. Even to this day, Fulford is in awe of his own prediction. He made it intuitively on the basis of his excellent perception and good common sense. In his comparative analysis of Glenn and others, Fulford noticed that Glenn refrained from dance, popular music, and dating girls. These activities, which are typical for adolescence, are worth exploring in more detail.

The youth of the 1940s, just like the youth of any other decade, had some distinct behavioral practices. This was a part of their own liberation movement geared to free them from the constraints of existing norms of social behavior. Teenage girls began to bare their legs and wore "bobby socks." The boys greased their hair. Dance became freer and wilder, such as the boogie-woogie, which was conducted at a breathless speed. Glenn, whose music ear recorded those familiar dance melodies from the radio, totally refrained from going to school dances or any other dance party. Even at home, where he was free to do what he pleased, he shied away from making rhythmic dance steps and moving his body to music.

"Have you ever seen Glenn dance at home?" I asked Jessie Greig.

"You have to understand that Glenn was always busy practicing the piano or he was simply away from home. And in that little time we spent together, we joked sometimes; this is what he liked. But to dance, no, I never saw him do steps to the radio music or any other music. You see, he never played popular music either," recounted Jessie.

"What did the two of you do when you were alone?" I asked.

"Glenn used to entertain me. He loved to be dog. So, he'd get down on his hands and knees pretending to be dog. He made me laugh. We had a lot of fun together. When Glenn was happy, he could be quite outgoing, you know,"[47] Jessie reminisced fondly.

Socially, at the age of fourteen, Glenn behaved as if he were still eight years old. Glenn did not participate in any of the societal fads of the '40s. He was for the most part too timid, too self-involved and too inhibited to join in. The whole movement typical for adolescence, fashion, hair style, dance, sports and others, passed him by while he stood aside watching. Something similar happened with Glenn vis-à-vis jazz music. In 1946, Fulford wrote that "he [Glenn] thinks jazz music is terrible." Despite heavy emphasis at home on classical music, Glenn was fully aware of the existence of popular music. From the time he was a young child, his mother discouraged him from any association with music other than classical music. She feared that Glenn's interest and taste for classical music may get contaminated by the exposure to jazz. Most of all, she feared that such music may draw Glenn away and redirect his interest elsewhere. This was confirmed by several of Glenn's relatives. Dr. Grant Gould, Glenn's youngest uncle, testified about Glenn's mother:

"Well, whenever she gave me piano lessons, she kept a ruler on the piano to give me a whack if I, by any chance, slipped into a few chords of popular music melodies."

"How did you feel about taking piano lessons in the first place?" I asked.

"Oh, I enjoyed playing the piano. And I loved classical music too, but I adored jazz music very much. I just couldn't understand why she was so dead-set against it,"[48] Dr. Gould pondered.

Jessie Greig and her older sister Betty both confirmed that music other than classical was undesirable in Gould's household. In Glenn's case, the ruler was not necessary because he got the message that jazz was bad for him. Glenn unconsciously internalized puritan values of his mother without challenging them. Though Glenn could prohibit his mind from loving popular music, he could not shut his ears from hearing it. He picked up on the Swing Era of the popular Benny Goodman band, which swept New York City in the early 1940s. Having a perfect sense of rhythm, Glenn knew exactly what the difference was in beat between the boogie-woogie and jitterbug. He was aware of bop and its protagonists, Dizzy Gillespie and Charlie "Bird" Parker, whom he mentioned in his adult writings. The presence of Bob Fulford, who loved jazz, became a collector of jazz records and devoted a part of his journalistic career to being a jazz critic, inadvertently contributed to Glenn's awareness of jazz music at first in his teens and then in his adult age. Did Glenn secretly admire the great jazz men without being able to consciously admit to it? It is likely that Glenn assumed his mother's attitude toward jazz while disregarding his own true feelings and liking for it. His true feelings were repressed. Such repression of his true self during his teens explains Glenn's sudden, explosive interest, when he was a grown man, in the popular singers Petula Clark and Barbra Streisand. Of course, Glenn could never catch up with the losses of his formative years. The loss of the opportunity to dance, play and sing popular music, to engage in youthful fashion and other teenage behavior, left him with unfinished business from this stage of development.

Courtship is also a normal part of adolescence. Some teenagers dread the upsurge of their instinctual impulses and try to overcontrol them. They avoid dating but immerse themselves in ascetic and intellectual endeavors. This means that by overuse of their thinking ability they try to cover their erotic and romantic interests. Most adolescents are eventually able to overcome their dread of their own sexual impulses. They go through the stages from being too inhibited to being less and less inhibited, until they gain a normal range of strength and mastery over their fears of sexuality and dating.

Glenn was particularly threatened by the emergence of his instinctual drives. By avoidance of dance, fashion, jazz music, sexual themes and dating, he practiced flight and repudiation of his instinctual impulses. He resorted to an ascetic lifestyle with a heavy emphasis on his intellectual and creative pursuits. A conflict developed within himself between hiding and expressing his intimate thoughts and feelings. The moral standards embedded in him were prohibitive. Glenn's tendency to use "pure speech" was an end result of his strict upbringing. Glenn was raised to be a nice boy, well-behaved, well-spoken and always clean, tidy and inoffensive. This was the ego-ideal of his mother, and to a lesser degree of other important family figures. Fulford accurately perceived that Glenn's mother wanted him to be a "nice genius" and was unable to accept and settle for anything else. In accordance with his ascetic approach to life, Glenn did not show signs of curiosity in matters of love and sexual issues. The phase of courtship, typical for adolescence, was missing in Glenn's life. While his classmates went through the fun and tribulations of dating, Glenn lacked the experiences of love, sex and intimacy. He turned to music as a major source of personal gratification. Strong instinctual energy was sublimated into his great intellectual and artistic pursuits. Hence, music and not another person(s) became his preferred personified love object. Music was allegorically looked upon as a human figure. Indeed, when Glenn played the piano in his adult life, he came across so passionately as if he were interacting with and courting the instrument. The music, not a man or woman, became the permanent, close companion in Gould's life. In reality, music is not a human being and can never replace one. Gould created an illusion for himself of having a love affair with music, idealizing it as a superhuman, super-spiritual structure, while at the same time denying the reality of his own biology and basic human needs.

Glenn's teenage problems, coupled with his clinical depression, had an adverse effect on his academic performance. His naturally high intellectual acumen and excellent memory capacity warranted nothing but a grade "A" academic performance. In reality, Glenn did not excel in school overall, but had inconsistent marks ranging from excellent to poor. This was more in keeping with his inner dynamics than with any type of intellectual impediment. In other words, when Glenn felt well and free of conflicts within a certain medium, he performed up to his high potential, and the converse is also true. Some of Glenn's teachers resented his privileged part-time school status and displayed a cold, if not cynical attitude toward him. Glenn was the type that, whenever he encountered lack of support or worse, overt criticism, he felt personally attacked and injured. To cope and defend himself, he would re-attack his "enemy" in his subtle but still antagonistic and defiant manner. Though he was well-read and had excellent rhetoric skills, Glenn scored poorly in English grammar, composition, and content of his written language. On top of that, his handwriting was untidy and illegible, which did not help his overall mark in English. Operating here was Glenn's defiance of disciplinary rules. Grammar and tidy handwriting are both governed by rules which Glenn attempted to modify and downgrade. This was very much akin to what Glenn later did in his music approach—changing, relaxing, and depreciating the rules of interpreting the music scores.

The following excerpt from an English essay written in grade thirteen illustrates Glenn's inner turmoil, as well as the critical response of his teacher:[49]

D- Description G. Gould 13 A

The abandoned room generated depression? Its spacious airiness, symbol of a former elegance, now reduced to vacant emptiness, entreated the heavy black curtain which dropped from the dusty window-frame to allow the sunlight to revitalize the interior, deep in pensive contemplation. A broken stool leaned against a protruding plaster chip on the wall. A chandelier chord hung loosely from the ceiling ~~as~~ like a pendulum without a clock robbed of its, purpose of existence, and for which time is not immaterial. Yet in spite of the heavy presence of omnipotent inevitability, the room was not calm. [An active motivation grasped its spirit as though in seeming submission it felt its past, not mediated on it.] And, as the November breeze flapped the black curtain, and a shade of sunlight appeared, the pendulum began to sway again.[50] Conclusion?

just stuff and nonsense

In the paragraph you are using words for their own sakes. The result is that your style is obscure and seems forced. What is the point of using vacant to modify emptiness. To me it seems redundant redundance.

This sample of Glenn's writing sums up his teen problems. It shows his isolation from the world and his deep inner disillusionment. It is as if the writer is old and desolate and there is no hint that he is youthful and enjoys life. The essay portrays Glenn's despondent and lonely feelings. The teacher's notes reveal total lack of attunement with Glenn. What Glenn attempted to say in 135 words could have been condensed in only three: "I am depressed." The teacher concentrated on assessing Glenn's English skills without noticing the person behind. Yet Glenn's gloom and doom were obvious and most unusual for a lad of his age. The teacher's comment may have been academically accurate, but was emotionally insensitive. Instead of showing concern about her student, the teacher responded sarcastically. The real question, "What is wrong with this young man to be writing such a dark essay?" remained unanswered. Here, like elsewhere in Glenn's relationships, the boat of mutual understanding was missed. The troubled adolescent did not reach out for help, neither did his beholders reach out to him. This unrewarding pattern of communication continued to prevail in Glenn's future relationships.

There was a pleasant epilogue to this wistful story. Several years after Gould's plight in school, when he became internationally famous, his English teacher, Harriet Ingham, wrote these words of recognition and covert apology:

> March 12, 1956
>
> ... One of these days I must hear you "in person" (as the expression goes) once having taught you English (or did I ?). Teachers are much like parents in this respect: that they will continue to see even geniuses as the young people they once knew. As a matter of fact, in your photograph in the "Telegram" you do not look any older than when you sat in a 13a classroom at Malvern.[50]

Chapter V

INROADS TO FAME

THE GENIUS TESTED

> The heights by great men reached and kept
> Were not obtained by sudden flight,
> But they, while their companions slept,
> Were toiling upward in the night.
>
> Henry Wadsworth Longfellow[1]

After Gould's performance of Beethoven's G Major Concerto, with conductor Bernard Heinze and the Toronto Symphony, Edward W. Wodson of *The Toronto Telegram* wrote on January 15, 1947:

> The grace and understanding of the boy were never at fault. Phrase after phrase of the loveliest pianism would answer orchestral finesse with a solo artistry no less masterly. He sat at the piano a child among professors, and he talked with them as one with authority. It was a joy to hear his beautiful playing and to see him so modest and so utterly self-forgetful.[2]

Wodson's vision was clear and undistracted by Gould's extraneous behavior. His farsighted evaluation of Glenn's performance was most encouraging. Glenn was only a teenager. He needed to hear the words of praise that helped him stay on the slippery road of concert pianism.

After this major achievement at Massey Hall, Glenn was ready to embark upon his next interesting project, recording his music. In the same year, he and his piano teacher amused themselves by making a private recording of Mozart's *Music for Piano, Four Hands*, as follows:

Allegro from Sonata in C Major, K. 521
Andante with 5 variations in G Major, K. 501
Allegro di molto from Sonata in F Major, K. 497
Fantasy in F Minor, K. 594

In total, it was over twenty-one minutes of recorded music. Inscribed on the record jacket were the names of the performing tandem: "Glenn Gould, Pianist – Alberto Guerrero, Pianist." Here was a remarkable occasion, when a fourteen-year-old lad and his sixty-year-old mentor performed as equals. There is no way to know how Glenn felt about this event. Was he on top of the world and truly enjoying the partnership with his teacher? Or did he feel patronized and anxious to obtain his autonomy as an independent music artist? What is known with certainty is that Guerrero and his student shared the love of classical music, and they were both excited about the novelty of recording. On the other hand, having gone through emotional friction over the Beethoven Fourth Concerto when Glenn played a "Schnabelian" rendition a year earlier, the two musicians had developed a degree of reservation toward each other. Thus, when the two sat side by side, they experienced a sense of complementary pleasure but also a degree of individualistic competition and reserve. Despite their ambivalent feelings during that historical event, the artistic pair subconsciously set a precedent for the future making of recorded music. Guerrero, as the patron of the arts and, in this case, a patron of Gould's artistry, introduced his protégé to the world of timeless, recorded music. From then on, the teacher stayed in the background, like a humble shadow; whereas his student leaped forward into the new dimension of recording artistry. In only a few years, Gould became a master of this newly discovered world of making recorded music.

On October 20, 1947, at the age of fifteen, Glenn gave his first public solo recital at the Eaton Auditorium in Toronto. This was his first commercial recital, and it was arranged by his manager, Walter Homburger. Symbolically, it was a present for his mother's upcoming 55th birthday. One can notice from the concert program the heavy presence of his teacher. Glenn played Couperin's Passacaille in Guerrero's transcription and works of Chopin, Liszt, and Mendelssohn that were all Guerrero's choices. A few years later, when Glenn became a renowned concert pianist, he no longer kept the three last composers in his repertoire. This meant that he emancipated and distanced himself from Guerrero's influence.

On December 3, Glenn made his first out-of-town appearance as a guest soloist in Hamilton, Ontario. At the McMaster Alumni Club, he played Beethoven's Concerto no. 1 in C major, Opus 15, with the Toronto Symphony conducted by Sir Ernest MacMillan. These two performances with the Toronto Symphony at Massey Hall and in Hamilton, and his noted recital at the Eaton Auditorium, unofficially earned Gould the title of a homegrown Canadian, Toronto-based pianist.

Gould's foremost and oldest love of composing, first expressed and tested when Glenn was five years old, reappeared in fuller force in his late teens. In the 1948 to 1949 period, Gould cut down the rate of his public appearances in order to focus on two major tasks. First, he got acquainted with the new music of the composers of the twentieth century. Second, he started composing his own music, as well as innovating different approaches to the music of others. By working studiously and simultaneously on those two tasks, Gould steadily developed his own style of music interpretation, which was to become specifically Gouldian in the future.

Driven by his innate music talent and inspired by the presence of his friend and composer, Oskar Morawetz, Gould produced, in 1948, his first distinguished music composition—a piano sonata. The piece remained nameless and unpublished during his lifetime. Gould was always insecure and often very self-critical when it came to composing. At times he felt quite disheartened while at other times he thought that he was pretty good and original at composing. This fluctuating self-image, good enough and not good enough, weakened his motivation and inhibited his otherwise strong natural impulse to compose music. In the next period, from 1949 to 1950, Gould produced another composition with the modest title *Five Short Piano Pieces*:

1. Allegretto   2. Andante   3. Allegretto   4. Presto   5. Andante

Again, this no-name product was typically downplayed by its composer. Shortly after, in 1950, Glenn gained enough self-esteem to create and then publicly perform his Sonata for Bassoon and Piano.

"Why bassoon?" asked Robert Fulford.

"When you have a friend who plays the bassoon, you compose for the bassoon," Glenn retorted.[3]

The comment referred to the bassoonist, Nicholas Killburn, with whom Gould premiered the composition at his *Recital of Contemporary Music* in Toronto.

This event represented a triple gesture of dedication. First, Glenn created a composition to acknowledge his friend at the time, which was a rare expression of his warm feelings. Second, inspired by the music of Paul Hindemith, Oskar Morawetz and Ernst Krenek, Gould composed his own music piece, thus showing his personal appreciation of these novel twentieth-century musicians. The third, and the most hidden gesture of dedication, was to his teacher, Guerrero, who himself had a taste for contemporary music that he passed on to Glenn. Guerrero introduced the works of German composer Paul Hindemith to Toronto audiences in the 1930s. He taught Glenn the music of both Hindemith and Arnold Schoenberg, which Glenn then perfected, adopted as his own, and championed throughout his music career. There is a definite continuum here noticed between the teacher and his student, akin to a father-son relationship. Gould unconsciously identified with some aspects of Guerrero and paid a subtle tribute to him in this recital, while he rejected other aspects.

There were also fierce arguments, competition and clashes between Glenn and Guerrero. It was in the last three years of Glenn's adolescence that a third emotional rift occurred between them. The previous two rifts occurred over Glenn's interpretation of Beethoven's Fourth Concerto, the so-called "Schnabelian" rendition; and over the hiring of Walter Homburger as his manager. The third major conflict occurred when Glenn, in search of his own music expression, took off in the world of artistic experimentation as a pianist. Glenn challenged Guerrero in the same way he had challenged his mother a decade earlier. It got to the point where Glenn interpreted everyone, from Bach to Mozart, Beethoven to Schoenberg, differently in concept from the way his teacher had taught him. From the psychodynamical point of view, Glenn's antagonizing behavior was a part of his personal growth, which reflected his attempts to differentiate and individuate from his teacher. There was a heavy price to be paid. The more Glenn developed his own style in his music, the more Guerrero disapproved. Bewildered, Guerrero consulted with his friend from Chile, international concert pianist Claudio Arrau, who suggested he leave Glenn alone. When many years later, Glenn's friend, Robert Silverman, interviewed Arrau on the subject, this is what he recalled:

R. Silverman: Almost unique among pianists was Glenn Gould because he seemed to have no problems of intensity in the studio setting. Did you ever meet him?

C. Arrau: Yes, he came to me when he was seventeen or eighteen. His teacher was a great friend of mine. He played for me at Guerrero's house. Guerrero did not know what to do with this genius. I remember most distinctly what a terrific impression he made upon me. His facility and musical expression were remarkable even at that age. Guerrero asked me what course he should follow and I told him to let him alone.[4]

Guerrero did not listen to Arrau and did not "let" Glenn alone. By that time, Guerrero was so hurt by his student's defiance that he could not forgive him. Paradoxically, Glenn's fame was soaring, while

Guerrero's positive attitude toward him was diminishing. Complicating this interpersonal conflict was Guerrero's exasperation with his student's posture at the piano. Guerrero abhorred Glenn's tendency to sit low, to slouch and fidget while performing. Like Glenn's mother, Florrie, Guerrero expected Glenn to be a "nice genius;" always humble and obedient. Neither Glenn's mother nor Guerrero were able to appreciate Glenn's inner need for emotional autonomy. Glenn subconsciously reacted toward his teacher as if he were his mother; the teacher reacted to his student ambivalently, admiring some qualities and vehemently disapproving of and rejecting his shortcomings. Guerrero was unable to be objective and maintain a position of professional neutrality and became too deeply emotionally entangled with Glenn. Their relationship gradually deteriorated until it stopped in the following year. It seems that Guerrero became so emotionally intertwined with his gifted student that he practically "invaded" him to the point of smothering. The student felt compelled to "throw" his invader out of his life. This was well illustrated by another great music teacher, Nadia Boulanger, in her comment about the American composer, Aaron Copland:

> A very long time ago, Copland was my student. To let him develop was my great concern. One could tell his talent immediately. The great gift is a demonstration of God. More the student is gifted, more you must be careful not to invade his self. But I hope that I did never disturb him, because then is no more to be a teacher, is to be a tyrant.[5]

The aim here is not to dub Guerrero as a tyrant but rather to find out the keys to a successful and even optimal teacher-student relationship.

At eighteen, Glenn was a widely sought after and busy teenager. A future great concert pianist cannot afford to be lackadaisical, so Glenn practiced piano pieces throughout the afternoons, evenings and into the early morning hours. Piano studies at Glenn's level were incredibly taxing and required an average of five to six hours daily, and more. It was at that time when Glenn started going to bed late. Where does one find so many hours to practice in a day filled with a demanding high school curriculum, homework, and a simple need to have fun? Glenn always managed to find time for music, even if it had to be at the expense of his sleep. At this young age, Glenn's output was enormous. He was able to play from memory over fifty distinguished music works from the piano literature of Couperin, Scarlatti, Haydn, Bach, Mozart, Beethoven, Cherny, Mendelssohn, Chopin, Brahms, Liszt, Schoenberg, Hindemith, Prokofiev and others, all on the public concert level. His astute manager, Walter Homburger, did not sit idly but organized a variety of music activities for Glenn. In addition to almost weekly performances in churches, galleries and music halls, there were those major events such as public recitals, along with radio and TV appearances.

On the morning of Christmas Eve 1950, Gould made his radio debut as a seasoned teenage pianist. He played Mozart's Sonata in B-flat Major, K. 281, and Hindemith's Sonata no. 3. For an adolescent, Glenn did very well by showing self-assurance in presenting an unusual music repertoire. By combining a great eighteenth-century composer with a relatively unknown twentieth-century composer, the young pianist daringly opened a new forum for conveying fresh ideas to the audience. Glenn enjoyed this radio appearance immensely. While he had been on the outside as a radio listener throughout his youth, this was his chance to be on the inside, intimately involved in the inner workings of this electronic medium of communication. Glenn was in a state of ecstasy. He was excited by everything in the studio: the equipment, the physics and mechanics of transmission, the task of the radio technicians and, in particular, the use of the microphone. His long-lasting love affair with the microphone had begun. During this debut, Glenn met thirteen-year-old Lorne Tulk, who was to become his friend and a lifelong associate in his radio and recording work. Most of all, Glenn enjoyed the anxiety-free state associated with working on the radio, which spared him from direct exposure to the audience. He knew that through the radio he would be evaluated on his musical merits and not on his stage-related behavior. From then on, the CBC studios on Jarvis Street would become one of Glenn's favorite places for his creative endeavors.

Homburger continued to look for new audiences for Glenn and arranged more out-of-town appearances. On November 26, 1950, the eighteen-year-old pianist gave a recital at the University of Western Ontario in London. This marked the beginning of Glenn's nomadic life as a concert pianist, with its inevitable drawbacks such as staying in hotel rooms, changing beds, and suffering endless travel fatigue. Glenn, who was used to the familiar and private comfort of his home, suddenly had to adapt to a completely different lifestyle, including changes in sleeping and eating habits. Moreover, he had to get used to a variety of bohemian practices that are part and parcel of fame, particularly the intense socializing after a concert at late-evening receptions.

In 1952, several developmental milestones occurred. First, piano studies with Guerrero ended. There is no available evidence about this event. The two men parted seemingly politely. It appears that both of them felt hurt and dissatisfied, as if something was missing and incomplete. What was missing in their relationship all along was that they could not express personal feelings of anger and disappointment with each other. Instead, they held back those strong feelings and remained emotionally cold toward each other, even throughout the act of parting. Their future telephone contacts lessened in frequency to a vanishing point by the mid 1950s.

The second major event in that year was Gould's successful television debut appearance on the Canadian Broadcasting Corporation as the first pianist in Canada to be televised during a live performance. Gould continued his love affair with radio and television for the rest of his productive life.

At the age of eighteen, Gould stopped going to church. In 1952, he attended grade thirteen courses but did not write the last exams. Gould also started gradually distancing himself from his high school friends and relatives. This marked the onset of his quest for creative solitude at the beginning of young adulthood. Glenn intuitively sensed that only by capitalizing on his tremendous personal, intellectual and artistic talents as major sources of his ego strength could he perhaps compensate for his interpersonal liabilities. Gould concluded his adolescence triumphantly as a great music artist in the making. On the personal level, he accomplished a degree of personal growth but not enough to complete the psychological task of the second individuation. In spite of this, he was able to use the challenges of his adolescence as building blocks toward his goal of becoming a Canadian virtuoso.

THE PSYCHOLOGY OF GOULD'S PIANO TECHNIQUE

The sound is all that matters ...

Mitsuko Uchida[6]

In his pre-fame period, between the ages of nineteen and twenty-two, Gould was spending more time at the cottage on Lake Simcoe, which he turned into his music studio. By staying there for weeks on end, he had the ideal tranquillity needed for playing and studying music in meticulous depth. From his early teens on, Gould developed a method of studying music by listening to the recording of a certain music piece; then learning the score away from the piano; practicing long hours at the keyboard; trying various approaches; and, finally, coming up with his own concept of interpretation. He then taped his different renditions of a learned music work on a tape recorder. By comparative listening of music recorded by other great pianists and his own taped versions, Gould was able to produce a range of interpretations, varying from the one exactly to the letter of the composer's wishes to others that he modified with respect to rhythm, dynamics and form. Most other distinguished concert pianists tend to adhere to the written text and to deliver one final version of a music piece without venturing into experiments. Gould was not a literalist. He clearly differed from the mainstream of his colleagues by studying music scores first away from the piano and by changing the concept in his mind. All of these differences accounted for his innovative approach. Only after this "mental" experience of music was Gould able to phase into the "physical" expression of a composition through his finger work.

Gould brought to the cottage the wealth of his cumulative music knowledge, which he had learned from Guerrero, as well as his own novel music ideas. In fact, he adopted many of his teacher's approaches to music and incorporated them into his own music technique and philosophy. Gould did not merely imitate Guerrero's approach to piano music but identified with it. In his adult life, Gould purported that he was self-taught. This was partially true, as he did offer original music interpretations. The fact that he learned from Guerrero, which he denied, was also true. Guerrero literally modeled for Glenn by playing parts of music in front of him and discussing the pros and cons of certain techniques. Also, Glenn heard Guerrero play in concerts in person at the conservatory and at the University of Toronto's Hart House. Like it or not, Guerrero's distinct music sound was etched in Glenn's mind and became amalgamated with his own. Even when Gould's music differed from Guerrero's, it was still related to it. Over the years, Guerrero earned credit by providing his student with universal and unbiased cross-sectional training through the five centuries of piano music literature.

In the world of athletics, competitors have to leave their coaches behind and attain their goals alone. Likewise, sooner or later, a trained pianist will have to walk onto the stage and sit at that grand instrument without the supportive presence of his mentor. A pianist, indeed, is a special breed who more often than any other instrumentalist is supposed to sit at the center of a spacious stage and perform alone. Even more, piano recitalists have to "sell" their music assets and entertain their spectators for hours on end. It is all like a long solo drama where expectations are high, nerves are tense and mistakes are not tolerated.

When in 1952, Glenn ended his formal music lessons with Guerrero, his mother vigorously disagreed with his decision, which Glenn took as a lack of her support. Guerrero opposed it too. Glenn's father remembered that the process was gradual, that Glenn went to his teacher's studio less and less often until he stopped.

"What was your wish for Glenn with respect to his studies with Guerrero?" I asked Mr. Gould during one of several visits to his home.

"I remember that his mother wanted him to continue. But I think that Glenn outgrew Guerrero's teaching. Even when Glenn was young, Mr. Guerrero used to say, 'Glenn, I can't teach you anything because you learned everything by yourself.'"

"What happened after they had parted?" I asked.

"Mr. Guerrero kept coming to visit us at the cottage, but Glenn was too busy at the time, so I guess they didn't see very much of each other"[7] said Mr. Gould.

By not formally releasing his student from didactic classes, the teacher implicitly gave his opinion that Gould was not ready. In reality, Guerrero was not ready to let go of Gould, thinking that his job was not quite finished, the job being to rid Glenn of his platform antics at the piano. Guerrero, who successfully taught Glenn music, was powerless to change his piano mannerisms. The ambitious teacher fell short of completing the task of making Gould into a "normal" virtuoso. Distinguished music pedagogue, William Newman, wrote:

> ... Working himself out of a job ... the teacher should help the student meet his pianistic challenges until eventually the student makes himself independent of formal teaching.[8]

In Gould's case, neither his mother, as his first piano teacher, nor Guerrero felt ready to let go of him. In fact, they *did not* help Glenn be independent but unconsciously fostered his dependence and "misbehavior." Glenn was left totally alone in his decision to break away from Guerrero. From the scholastic point of view, one can argue whether Glenn's decision to stop music lessons with Guerrero was timely or not. From the psychological standpoint, Glenn's attempt to separate from his dominant teacher and become his own person appeared to be necessary. As Gould put it himself:

> Our outlooks on music were diametrically opposed. He was a 'heart' man and I wanted to be a 'head' kid. Besides, nine years is long enough for anyone to be a student of the same teacher. I decided it was time for me to set out on my own snowshoes, and I developed an insufferable amount of self-confidence, which has never left me.[9]

One wonders why Gould, after breaking up with Guerrero, did not go elsewhere for some additional "post-doctoral" piano studies with another reputable music teacher. There is a three-pronged answer to this question. First, Gould was a master of the piano as it was. Second, he could not and would not change his approach to the piano as an instrument. For example, when the famous Polish pianist, Ignacy Paderewski, went as an older student to study piano with Theodor Leschetizky, who was at the time the most renowned teacher in Europe, the latter asked him to "forget" his old piano technique and learn a new one. Gould was neither able nor willing to challenge or "forget" his original piano technique. The third reason was non-musical, Gould simply could not see himself being away from home in an unfamiliar environment of another city for a long period of time.

Most great concert pianists have in common their rich educational background and the best piano teachers of their time. To name but a few distinguished Toronto pianists: William Aide studied with Guerrero but also with Beveridge Webster. Anton Kuerti studied with two great teachers, Edvin Bodky and Beryl Rubinstein, formerly students of Ferruccio Busoni. In addition, he studied with Mieczyslaw Horszowski, who was the longest living student of Theodor Leschetizky. Another Toronto pianist, Gould's contemporary, Patricia Parr, studied with Isabela Vengerova, who also was a student of Leschetizky. Even though Gould did not follow the examples of his colleagues who studied with several teachers, he still became the most famous Canadian pianist.

For Gould, leaving Guerrero also meant pursuing on a large scale and all on his own the performing music career for which he was trained. His independent life as a concert pianist began. Every time Gould ventured to do a concert, he took the risk of walking into a hornet's nest. Standing ovations, fame, publicity, requests for autographs and interviews, new offers and correspondence were all stimulating for his self-image but too challenging for his need for solitude. Another aspect of the hornet's nest was the "buzzing" feedback of the music critics, who hailed the quality of Gould's artistry but disapproved of his piano manners. Gould played into their annoyance by his tenacious habit of sitting low at the piano, by humming and singing audibly and by conducting with whichever hand was free. While Gould's platform mannerisms, in the narrow sense, were not a part of his piano technique, they helped him allay his stage fright and perform before an audience.

Piano theorist William Newman proposes that there are "four main playing mechanisms," which are: "playing by the finger working from the knuckle at its base, or the hand from the wrist, or the forearm from the elbow, or the upper arm from the shoulder."[10] Much is written on the subject of the proper use of the piano chair. Newman wrote: "It is best to sit only on the front half of the bench; covering the whole bench induces slumping." His final comment of interest on the subject of the piano chair is: "Sitting too low, which is perhaps the worst of two evils, constrains the finger action by raising the wrists and knuckles; sitting too high constrains the hand action by lowering the wrists and elbows."[11]

Other musicologists have less-conventional views of what the piano technique of performing pianists should be. Recently, Charles Rosen put forward an integrated approach to playing the piano, allowing for idiosyncratic methods suited to the individual needs of the performing pianists:

> ... almost all books on how to play the piano are absurd, and ... any dogmatic system of teaching technique is pernicious ... Not only the individual shape of the hands counts but even the shape of the entire body. That is why there is no optimum position for sitting at the piano, in spite of what many pedagogues think. Glenn Gould sat close to the floor, while Artur Rubinstein was almost standing up.[12]

Rosen gave many examples in support of the individual physical differences of the pianists:

> Josef Hofmann ... had a hand so small that he could reach no more than the eight notes of an octave, and Steinway built him a special piano in which the ivories were slightly narrower so that he could reach a ninth. His friend Sergei Rach-

> maninoff had a very large hand, as did Rudolf Serkin ... Horowitz played with his fingers stretched flat, and Jose Iturbi used to hold his wrist below the level of the keyboard.[13]

There were numerous attempts by music scholars and veteran critics to analyze Gould's way of playing the piano, particularly his hand position and his method of sitting. It is evident that Gould totally defied several conventional rules and tenets of piano playing, as suggested by William Newman and other scholars alike. Over a decade of his most intense formative years in music training, he developed a physically impossible piano technique. Not only did he sit lower at the piano, which is said to be the worst of two evils; not only did he slump, which is deemed unacceptable; but he used a chair with a back support instead of the conventional adjustable piano bench. Contrary to the expected failure of this type of sitting position, Gould developed and perfected a pure finger technique. Glenn's friend from the conservatory, John Beckwith, who became a distinguished music figure in Canada, pointed to the similarities between Glenn and Guerrero as pianists:

> Gould's physical appearance at the keyboard was in my view more like Guerrero's than was any other pupil's—the finger-angle very similar, the lowseated position similar too, though lower still in his mature years. His pure "finger technique" was also highly reminiscent of Guerrero's; his famous quick non-legato touch could be called an extension of it.[14]

In Gould's own words, he prefers the clarity of the sound:

> The fascination I have with staccato lines as opposed to legato lines is, in part ... an attempt to make an isolated legato moment a very intense occasion. I happen to adore the cleanliness, the clarity of texture that one gets when the prevailing touch is of a *détaché* nature.[15]

The other principal features of Gould's art of pianism are high velocity, clear finger separation and minimal use of pedals.

John Beckwith and the Toronto pianist and music scholar William Aide, both former students of Guerrero, made a comparative description of their teacher's method of playing on one side and Gould's piano technique on another. Beckwith agrees that Gould was a genius in possession of a "natural technique." Gould himself believed that a good deal of his piano technique was second nature. Regardless, having been in music training with Guerrero for nine years, Gould adopted two main features of his teacher's keyboard method: 1) a pure finger technique as opposed to a "weight technique," and 2) finger-tapping. The "pure finger technique" means that the main action of playing is executed by the fingers, with less employment of the hands, elbows and trunk. This technique was also characterized by finger separation, quick non-legato touch, or so-called playing in a détaché style. When practicing, Gould applied finger-tapping, where the fingers of one hand are tapped by the non-playing hand. William Aide provides this vivid description:

> The left hand taps the fingers successively to the bottom of the keys. The right-hand fingers are boneless; they reflex from the key bed and return to their original position on the surface of the keys. The left hand should tap near the tips of the right-hand fingers, either on the fingernails or at the first joint. The motion of the tapping should be as fast as possible. The second stage of this regimen is to play the notes with a quick staccato motion, one finger at a time, from the surface of the key, quick to the surface of the key bed and back to the surface of the key. This is slow practice, each note being separated by about two seconds of silence.[16]

Gould doggedly persevered at the piano until he polished this painstaking method of finger tapping. It helped that he enjoyed hearing the finished product, which made the tedious process of practicing worthwhile.

Though Gould applied both hands at the keyboard expertly, the power and agility of his left hand was special, and this hand was used most adroitly. Unlike the majority of great pianists in the past two centuries, Gould was left-handed, but at the piano he was ambidextrous. From the technical point of view, this is the most desirable gift a pianist could possess, the superior ability and equal control of both hands. In exceptionally difficult passages for the right hand, Gould used his adept left hand to execute them, turning them into cross passages. Gould's left-handedness was not hereditary. It is known that in the right-handed population the neurocentres of creative ability are, for the most part, stored in the right brain hemisphere, whereas the dominant motor, language and thinking functions are represented in the left side of the brain. By this token, Gould's brain functions would have been in reverse. It appears that Gould had the best of two worlds, which in part accounts for his giftedness. As a left-handed, or even better, an ambidextrous pianist, Glenn Gould could be compared to Franz Liszt and Joseph Hofmann, whose superior use of both hands accounted for the full expression of their virtuosity and genius at the piano. It is interesting that each of these two men stood out in the nineteenth and twentieth centuries, respectively, as the foremost pianists of the world. Gould's left-handedness is to be credited for his mastery of counterpoint, which puts much emphasis on the left hand. Even his professed dislike of some of Mozart's music had to do with this subject. Once Gould stated with a tinge of annoyance, "I mentioned to my teacher that I could not understand why Mozart would ignore so many obvious canonic opportunities for the left hand."[17] He obviously felt that in interpreting Mozart's music his left hand felt neglected and not as busy as he would have liked it to be.

While Gould's left-handedness was neuro-biologically determined, his performance mannerisms were more a function of his psychological development. Often music scholars and critics tended to ridicule Gould's piano mannerisms and consider them as attention-seeking devices. Toronto pianist Anton Kuerti[18] thinks of it as "affectation," believing that Gould could have given them up if he had so wanted. Gould's mannerisms at the piano can be seen as rituals, which are an obsessive and compulsive need to repeat certain habits and practices in order to alleviate and control his unbearable stage fright. Every effort to reduce those habits would increase nervous tension and interfere with producing good and coherent music. Gould himself was perturbed by his piano mannerisms, which is reflected in this pleading confession: "It's a terrible distraction. I would stop it if I could, but I can't. I would be like that centipede, I'd forget how to play the piano."[29] He genuinely feared giving up his piano-related rituals at the risk of forgetting or spoiling the music. In other words, Gould depended on his rituals, which served as a trade-off for his music performance. Mitsuko Uchida, one of the topmost pianist-interpreters of Mozart's music in the late twentieth century, commenting on piano technique argued:

> Purely technically speaking, everybody has a different metabolism, a different bone structure, different nervous system ... Some people think you have to curl fingers, some people think you have to stretch. Rubbish! ... The sound is all that matters, and so to make some sort of preconceived, moral premise about piano playing I am strongly against.[20]

If the sound is all that matters, then any piano technique ending in excellent quality music sound should be acceptable. By this model, Gould's critically acclaimed piano technique, which resulted in his critically acclaimed piano sound, is the only issue that matters. His extra-musical behavior did not really avert the piano sound but rather served as little pacifiers to his uneasy and conflicted inner world. Realistically, Gould's piano-related manners were of no serious consequence to the music or to its listeners. They became an integral part of his musicianship.

At times, Gould was frisky and full of self-confidence at the piano, and at other times he approached it gingerly and with various degrees of anxiety. There were some instances at the piano when Gould seemed to be sedate, apathetic, almost paralyzed-looking. His attitude or mood did not just depend on the demands of the interpreted music but was more correlated with his inner psychology. When Gould was freer of anxiety, freer of fear of being criticized and disapproved of, and when he felt more self-assured, he produced a finer quality of music performance. An example of that would be his memorable and completely successful concert tour in Russia. In this case, Gould was able to maintain a positive attitude through the entire eight concerts while the audience responded to him and to his performance with positive unconditional regard. As an end result, Gould's music was entirely enchanting and of the highest quality.

Gould had another innate talent that he developed to the fullest. He not only had excellent long-term memory for his previous mental acquisitions but also had a supreme haptic memory of his fingers. The haptic memory is facilitated by intensive and repetitive piano practice, during which both the mind and fingers remember the scores, fingering, sequences and other variables of a given music piece. In the end, the music that is memorized by the mind and by the fingers is played flawlessly by heart. Unlike some pianists who play from scores, or at least keep them on the piano in case of a momentary memory lapse, by rule Gould played from memory. He not only kept the music notes stored in his mind but often rehearsed measure by measure inside his mind without touching the piano. Only at the very end of learning a music piece would Gould sit at the piano, usually two to four weeks before a public performance, and practice by using his hands. This was a specific faculty unique to him and regarded to be an innate endowment. Gould's memory capacity was legendary. Both his mental and finger memory made it possible for him to reproduce and play music literature many years after his last practice and performance of the same. A famous illustration of this statement would be an event that occurred in Gould's post-concert career, when the renowned Italian pianist, Arturo Benedetti Michelangeli, was unable to go through with his performance for television of Beethoven's Concerto no.5, Emperor, in Toronto. Gould was given a telephone call on Thursday evening. The problem was explained, and he was asked to substitute for Michelangeli the next morning, on Friday, when the Toronto Symphony and the conductor, Karel Ancerl, were scheduled to work with Michelangeli. Gould's answer was affirmative and good-spirited. In the space of a few hours, Gould rehearsed the concerto he had not touched in four years. The program was aired on September 12, 1970. To everyone's amazement, Gould played Beethoven's concerto in front of the camera flawlessly and by heart.

Before concerts and recording sessions, Gould was in the habit of soaking his hands and wrists in hot water. Like a surgeon washing and scrubbing his hands before surgery, the concert pianist carried out his task of hand-soaking with a compelling commitment. It is said that Guerrero condoned this routine of his special student, but it was really Gould who exalted it and then pursued it relentlessly to the end of his music career. Warm-up exercises before a music performance are highly individualistic. Some great pianists practice the piano before their concerts in order to improve finger motility, whereas others take a break and rest their hands on the day of performance. Overt application of heat on one's hands is uncommon among top-ranking pianists, and there are only scattered examples of such a practice in the history of pianism. Sergei Rachmaninoff wore gloves and put his hands in an electrical muff to keep them warm and flexible before a performance. Those few who have chosen to apply heat usually behave as though it were their prerogative and private business, rather than to go about it as a public affair. Gould complained of suffering stiffness in his fingers due to an ailment called "fibrositis," which he believed was relieved after hand-soaking in hot water, allowing him to "play with newborn fingers." Instead of keeping it a personal affair, both Gould and many of his watchful critics by rule overfocused on his soaking practices, thereby creating an aura of confusion as to its meaning. At the end of this "hoopla," Gould looked like a very eccentric pianist. In reality, his hand-soaking habit was a necessary ritual that helped him relax and quell his inordinately high anxiety in the face of public performance. It did not add anything to his piano technique nor to his fame, but it certainly added to Gould's sense of self-confidence in surmounting the task of playing in public.

THE KEYBOARD MASTER ARRIVES

> Fulfilled our highest hopes. Guerrero's Bravo Fortissimo.
>
> Bert Gould[21]

On October 28 and 29, 1951, the nineteen-year-old Glenn Gould gave two concerts at the Orpheum Theatre in Vancouver, British Columbia. On both occasions he performed what was to him so familiar, the Beethoven Concerto in G Major, with William Steinberg conducting the Vancouver Symphony. The young virtuoso brought down the house and his ecstatic audience gave him a prolonged applause for producing such extraordinary music. There were cheers and curtain calls, to which he responded with modest bows and faint smiles. Glenn's mother, Florence, who accompanied him on that tour, appeared to be gratified to the fullest. Her son's unprecedented success in Vancouver was the best present she could have been given for her fifty-ninth birthday. At the reception after the concert, Mrs. Gould's face shone with pride. Her elegant attire, a long evening gown topped with a mink stole—reflected the greatness of this event. She was the center of attention while receiving compliments and questions from curious fans. When interviewed by the press, Florence Gould admitted with tremendous satisfaction that she was Glenn's only piano teacher until he reached grade nine. There also were congratulatory telegrams from well-wishers. Jessie Greig expressed her joy:

> Greetings. Hope you had good trip. Enjoy all sights and take an extra peep for your poor relative; best wishes for all concerned; I'll be listening and receiving audiences here; love to you both. Jessie Greig[22]

The most valued of all the praise was a telegram Glenn received from his father with this wording: "Fulfilled our highest hopes. Guerrero's Bravo Fortissimo. Excellent reception!" As always, Bert's regards for Glenn were rather formal, but surprisingly this time Guerrero presented his student with his laconic yet generous recognition. Glenn, as one can imagine, reveled in this particular "Bravo Fortissimo." After all these years of waiting for Guerrero's spontaneous and unqualified approval without "buts" and "shoulds" ("Yes, you played well, but your face was too close to the keys") he finally received an unconditionally positive message. True, Guerrero's praise could have been expressed personally and directly to Glenn over the telephone or by a letter rather than being squeezed into Mr. Gould's cablegram. For Glenn, even though he would not publicly admit to it, Guerrero's music opinion of him was of prime importance; it made him feel good when it was supportive and caused him to wither emotionally when it was negative or denied. Bert Gould shared his memories of this special event:

"What do you remember about Glenn's first concerts in Vancouver?" I asked Mr. Gould.

"The only thing I remember is that my wife went with Glenn to keep him company. They took the express train. My wife was very afraid of flying. She preferred to travel by land, you know," Mr. Gould admitted.

"At that time, your brother, Dr. Grant Gould, resided in Vancouver with his family. Do you know whether Glenn stayed at his uncle's place?" I asked.

"Oh no, not at all," Mr. Gould chuckled. "Glenn would never sleep at people's places. Never. It was bad enough having to stay in hotels, but at least he had his privacy there. He was rather nervous before each concert and he didn't want to talk to people and get sidetracted,"[23] Mr. Gould explained.

A few days before Glenn's conquest in Vancouver, the world-class pianist Artur Schnabel passed away in Switzerland on October 16. Gould always held Schnabel in high esteem and regarded him as a model for the interpretation of the Beethoven Concerti, particularly the Fourth Concerto, which he played in Vancouver. Although the two pianist-stars never met in person, Gould spent ample time listening and analyzing his predecessor's music records, until he himself accomplished "Schnabelian authenticity."[24] Before Schnabel's death, there was another loss with which Glenn had to reckon. In July 1951 the American composer of Austrian birth, Arnold Schoenberg, died in California. Gould had adopted Schoenberg's piano music into his own performing repertoire. In Gould's subconscious mind, with the passing of Schnabel and Schoenberg, he had a mission of being a successor and champion of both.

Along with his rapidly rising concert career, Gould's social responsibilities grew. His life seemed destined to be more outgoing and worldly. The young, formerly sheltered lad was thrust into the front echelons of fame. Inherent in the role of celebrity is not just the act of music performance but a required ability to demonstrate personal and social skills. Celebrities are expected to keep up with a variety of public demands, contracts, deadlines and unending public exposure. Reluctantly, Gould became not only a member of the music guild, but he took a special place in a broad socio-cultural medium as its most promising commodity. The inauguration into public music circles served as an opportunity to meet with a number of music associates and make a network of friends that was both stimulating and challenging. Often, Gould felt too exposed and impinged upon by those very expectations and demands upon him which, in the long run, partly accounted for his short career as a traveling concert pianist.

In the first part of his concert career, Gould collaborated with the Toronto Symphony directed by Sir Ernest MacMillan. Gould's association with MacMillan had started a few years earlier when Gould, as a child prodigy, was introduced to this great Canadian musician. MacMillan, who was the music director of the Toronto Symphony for twenty-five years, was a very influential international music figure. This relationship between Gould and MacMillan had a more emotional meaning than from a music-making point of view. It was Glenn's mother who looked up to MacMillan, whereas Glenn had a degree of reservation toward him. Yet, at this early stage, unlike in his adult years, Gould was able to keep in check his strong personal bias and create good quality performances together with MacMillan:

Gould's Concerts with Sir Ernest MacMillan and the Toronto Symphony

December 3, 1947	Hamilton	Beethoven Concerto #1
January 23, 1951	Toronto	Beethoven Concerto #1
March 6, 1951	Toronto	Weber Konzertstuck (125th anniversary of von Weber's death)
December 12, 1951	Toronto	Beethoven Concerto #2 (tribute to Schnabel)
March 29, 1955	Toronto	Bach D Minor; Strauss Burleske
March 21, 1956	Hamilton	Bach D Minor

This list of concerts reveals that MacMillan, like many other conductors in the future, acquiesced to Gould's preference and choice of performing music, consisting mostly of the works of Beethoven, Bach and modern composers of the twentieth century; in this case, Richard Strauss. In due course, such a combination of music would become a staple in Gould's performing repertoire.

The frequency of public appearances increased through Gould's teens. This was to be attributed to the initiative of his manager, Walter Homburger, who through a succession of contracts formalized a firm business relationship with his promising protégé. On April 1, 1951, the following major agreement was signed between the two men and cosigned by Gould's father:

1. Glenn Gould hereby appoints Walter Homburger as his sole and exclusive manager for the whole world. He authorizes him to act on his behalf at all times in connection with his professional engagements. He further authorizes him to make Engagements and Agreements and sign Contracts for him and on his behalf. Gould agrees to honor these Contracts and Agreements to the best of his ability.

2. It is understood that Gould cannot accept any engagement or enter into a contract unless they have been approved and confirmed by Homburger.
3. Homburger agrees to promote the professional career of Gould to the best of his ability in the best interest of his career.
4. It is understood and agreed that Gould will pay for all advertising material which is needed for the promotion of his career.
5. Gould agrees to pay Homburger the following commission on contracts or engagements:

    Concert appearances 20%
    Radio 15%
    Television 15%
    Motion Pictures 10%[25]

The agreement was valid for a period of two years, and it really was a two-edged sword. On the one hand, it opened up for Gould the heavy door of the complicated and privileged concert world but, on the other hand, it was confining and expensive. Gould was not only obliged to pay a hefty twenty-percent commission to Homburger, but he had to furnish other costs such as travel and promotional expenses; shipping and freight bills for the piano; concert hall rentals and taxes, all of which more than doubled his expenditures. Given the fact that the usual range of commission allotted to music managers varies from ten to twenty percent, it is obvious that the commission paid to Homburger was on the high side. There were several successive contracts signed between Gould and his impresario. The last one was in 1963, which ran for a period of five years.

"Walter Homburger was the first person who approached you, and he was someone with no previous managerial experience. What made you hire him?" I asked Bert Gould.

"He seemed to be a decent man. He was very interested in working with Glenn. My wife made sure with him that Glenn was not to be rushed to perform in public. We didn't want Glenn to be exploited in any way. Homburger seemed to understand our concerns,"[26] Bert Gould answered pragmatically.

The question still remains, why were there no negotiations by Glenn's parents or by Glenn himself that would have been more conducive to his rising fame? What made Gould keep Homburger as an exclusive manager for twenty years and maintain such an expensive contract throughout? It appears that the Goulds were flattered by Homburger's initial offer to manage their son's music career and instantly hired him. Blinded by their son's fabulous prospects as a virtuoso, they had overlooked other options and, even though they had claimed that they never rushed Glenn to perform publicly, it seems that they were eager to have him do just that. Motivated by their personal grandiose fantasies and needs, the Goulds, lacking awareness of Glenn's interpersonal over-sensitivity, hired for him a businessman of rigid character who had little capacity for understanding his client as a person. It seems that all that mattered was the business of public performance and the spread of fame. In the history of music, there are many unfortunate stories of parents who were greedy for the fame, money and status of their children. Even the greats like Mozart and Beethoven were unnecessarily forced and coerced by their fathers to perform in public. There are also numerous stories about ruthless and greedy music managers. In the case of the famous concert pianist, Joseph Hofmann, both his father, Kazimir, and his manager, Henry Abbey, forced him over-ambitiously to perform in frequent public concerts when he was only ten years old. They clearly exploited his talent and youth and treated him as if he were a gold mine for their own monetary gains. One cannot help but notice a flavor of personal fulfillment and parental ambition in the Goulds, who had their young son show off his piano artistry publicly when he was only five years old. Ten years later, by engaging Homburger as his manager, they proved how anxious they were to exhibit Glenn's virtuosity in public, this time in a more organized and proficient manner.

Gould, who was not able to assert himself with his parents, took the issue of having Homburger as his manager as a fait accompli. Though Gould was far too aware of the tension and personality clashes with Homburger, he was unable to challenge the contracts or replace him for two decades. The most Gould could do was to rebel against Homburger indirectly through concert cancellations and other "mischiefs." Also, he generally did not cope well with major changes and was in desperate need to keep his environment always the same. This all led Gould to maintain such a long and unhappy reliance on his manager.

In fairness to Homburger, he took on a substantial risk by entering a business contract with a young and unknown pianist, a risk he reduced somewhat by charging a high commission. During his business partnership with Gould, Homburger gradually developed his entrepreneurial skills and elevated himself to the status of an internationally known music manager. In his post-Gould career, Homburger managed such renowned piano artists as Alfred Brendel and Louis Lortie, and became an impresario of Toronto's Roy Thomson Hall. It is noted that personal managers of artistic stars are often under the stress of having to put up with countless unpredictable situations and attitudes of their associates and those they manage. Concert cancellations are a manager's nightmare, not only in terms of monetary loss but more as a source of psychological stress, including the uncertainty of their business from day to day and anxiety around rebooking engagements. Successful managers ought to have excellent public relations skills in order to endure in their "high-wire" balancing acts between their soloists and the patrons of music. Toronto-based concert pianist Anton Kuerti provided useful insights:

"What is the situation like today with respect to music managers?" I asked Mr. Kuerti.

"We don't see that many old-fashioned personal managers anymore. This occupation is on the brink of extinction, and a good number of performing artists opt for having booking agents."

"What is the nature of the liaison between an artist and his/her booking agent?"

"It is more businesslike, more professional, and there is not much possibility of exploitation of the artist," Mr. Kuerti clarified.

"Do you know Walter Homburger?" I asked.

"Yes, I do. I know him quite well," he answered.

"What do you think about the relationship between Gould and Homburger? Was it enhancing or restrictive?" I asked.

"Oh, that's hard to say. Walter is a good man but somewhat rigid. He really did a lot for Glenn. But Glenn was probably restricted by such long contracts," Mr. Kuerti candidly answered.[27]

On the whole and despite the interpersonal hardship, the association between Gould and Homburger was productive at the business level. Through Homburger's efforts, Gould got numerous concert engagements, which heightened his public exposure and fame. Financially, Gould did not earn much from concertizing. His major sources of remuneration were from his far-more-lucrative broadcasting and recording work.

Following the agreement with Homburger, Gould gradually wound down his music lessons with Guerrero until he stopped. In February 1952, shortly before breaking away from his teacher, Gould gave a recital in the Great Hall at Hart House in Toronto, which was where he saw Guerrero perform solo and with a chamber orchestra many times before. Gould's program included Sweelinck's Fantasia, Bach's Partita no. 1, Brahms' Intermezzi and Berg's Sonata op. 1. The sophisticated pianist delivered an unusual cross-section of baroque and romantic music represented by Bach and Brahms, respectively, and the contemporary music of Alban Berg. With the exception of Brahms' Intermezzi, Gould played the same program at his American debut three years later. By giving a recital at Hart House, sitting at the same concert grand piano as his teacher did years earlier and playing the music learned from Guerrero, Gould traveled the exact path of his mentor. On November 6, 1952, Gould made his debut-recital in Montreal, playing Bach's Partita no. 5, Beethoven's Sonata op. 101, Brahms' Intermezzi and Berg's Sonata op. 1. Eric McLean of *The Montreal Star* was positively excited and wrote this most complimentary headline:

GLENN GOULD AMAZES MONTREAL

A Debut on a Par of Importance with that of Isaac Stern or Kathleen Ferrier

McLean gently described Gould's idiosyncrasies at the piano:

> His technique is one which could not be recommended for all since it involves such a personal working out of problems. He sits so low at the keyboard that the line from the elbow to the fingers is almost hook-shaped. While playing he has some of Solomon's habit of leaning forward with the head turned to one side as though cocking an ear for the sound.[28]

At that time, there were frequent appearances in Gould's birthplace, Toronto, which was not the case in his later, more mature performing career. In the early 1950s, when Gould still maintained an amiable relationship with his school-mate, Robert Fulford, the two friends established a little music business together. They called it the New Music Associates. The purpose of it was to promote the twentieth-century music of Schoenberg, Berg, Hindemith, Morawetz and others. Bob Fulford was responsible for advertising, promotion and finances, while Glenn was the performing artist. This mini-music company managed to produce three concerts in Toronto. In the first concert, on January 4, 1951, Gould played works of modern composers: Hindemith Sonata no. 3, Morawetz Fantasy in D minor, Krenek Sonata no. 3 and two music pieces composed by Gould—*Five Short Piano Pieces* and *Sonata for Bassoon and Piano*, which Gould premiered along with his friend, Nicholas Kilburn, bassoonist to whom it was dedicated. The second concert of the New Music Associates was the Schoenberg Memorial concert on October 4, 1952, which was shortly after the breakup between Gould and his music mentor, Guerrero, who introduced him to Schoenberg's music four years earlier. In addition to playing Schoenberg's Piano Pieces op. 11 and Piano Suite op. 25, Ode to Napoleon Bonaparte, along with Victor Feldbrill conducting the chamber group, Gould also included reading of his essay "Arnold Schoenberg: A Commentary." This was his rhetoric debut in which he combined a music performance with an educational speech. Unlike the majority of other distinguished pianists who could not or would not relate to Schoenberg's music, Gould was mesmerized by it and gradually built it into his performing and recording repertoire.

In the third, the *All Bach Concert*, Gould performed with Maureen Forrester, famed Canadian contralto. Forrester remembered that the concert took place on October 16, 1954, a day after devastating Hurricane Hazel, which caused power failures, flooding and thirty-two deaths in Toronto. This weather calamity was also responsible for the fiasco of the *All Bach Concert*, where only fifteen spectators showed up. Gould and his partner, Fulford, were discouraged, which ultimately led to the dissolution of the New Music Associates.

In this pre-fame and post-Guerrero phase between 1953 and 1955, Gould composed his largest music piece, *The String Quartet*. While more space will be devoted to Gould's composing activity later, here in chronological order it is important to note that Gould composed music upon his withdrawal to the cottage and after his breakup with Guerrero. At the same time, his concert career was booming. It appears that the simultaneous separation from Guerrero and from his parents served as powerful stimuli to his creative accomplishments.

In 1953, the American composer of Austrian origin, Ernst Krenek, paid a visit to the Toronto Conservatory of Music, where he gave conducting master classes. The music students were flabbergasted by Krenek's "eccentric" behavior of walking on the street in sandals without socks, a practice unseen in the then-conservative Toronto. Gould was inspired greatly by the live encounter with Krenek, taking to his music and adopting it into his own music repertoire. His initial exposure to Krenek's music occurred earlier when Gould, under Guerrero's coaching, learned Krenek's Sonata #3. The young pianist was so amused and playful about the whole thing that he wrote a little poem that he sent to his friend at the time, John Beckwith. The poem was written in 1950 at "Marine Headquarters, Uptergrove, Ontario," as Gould referred in jesting spirit to his cottage, and it reads:

I've been studying Ernst Krenek's Sonata #3,
I'm sure that the score you'll be dying to see.
It's done in four movements, and it sure is not meek,
The first one embodies the 12-tone technique.[29]

In his mature career as a music writer, Gould corresponded with Krenek and published a paper with the humorous title "A Festschrift for 'Ernst Who???,'" in which he alluded to the obscurity of Krenek's music and to himself as being a rare person attracted to it. By championing Krenek's music, as well as the music of other contemporary composers like Hindemith and Schoenberg, Gould clearly was walking in the footsteps of his master-teacher, Alberto Guerrero.

Chapter VI

GLENN GOULD MAKES MUSIC

GOULD'S AMERICAN DEBUT

We know of no pianist like him at any age.
Paul Hume, *The Washington Post*[1]

Maturity of his interpretation is second to none.
Musical Courier[2]

As the contacts with Guerrero died out, the business relationship with Homburger intensified. The gradual climb-to-fame process was built up slowly but paid off in the best possible way—with a sudden breakthrough when Gould was catapulted to music stardom. It seemed to have happened quite randomly when Homburger booked for Gould a couple of American recitals in Washington, D.C., and in New York City. The Toronto-based pianist left Canada as modestly known but returned as an internationally acclaimed virtuoso. It was on January 2, 1955, at the age of twenty-two, that Gould made his American debut as a pianist at the Phillips Gallery in Washington, D.C. This elegant, red-brick, corner house encompasses the priceless art works known as "The Phillips Collection." In the early 1920s, the former owner of this mansion, Duncan Phillips, and his wife, Marjorie, graciously opened a section of their private home to the public. This was the beginning of the Phillips Gallery, which became a home for modern art, a cultural center and a tourist attraction in the American capital. Paintings like *The Repentant Peter* by El Greco and art pieces by such masters of the pallette as Paul Cezanne and Renoir and by American modernists such as Georgia O'Keefe, John Martin and Arthur Dove are but a few of some 2,500 art pieces that grace this peaceful gallery. The Phillips family, known for its philanthropy, thoughtfully included music as an essential component of their mostly visual art gallery by allocating a spacious room on the first floor as a music room. Through the decades, this room allowed a procession of fine musicians to display and share their artistry with audiences of over a hundred devotees. This dignified-looking room has dark oak paneling and ornamental trim. Because of its size and decor, it creates an intimate and elegant atmosphere for music performance. There is no podium and the piano is placed on the parquet floor, just steps ahead of the audience. This is where our young protagonist, Glenn Gould, made his American debut and embarked on his world career in music. The barriers to fame were broken within hours following Glenn's brilliant recital.

The news of Gould's success was spread through the pen of the well-respected music critic, Paul Hume, of *The Washington Post*, who wrote:

> Gould is a pianist with rare gifts for the world. It must not long delay hearing and according him the honor and audience he deserves. We know of no pianist like him at any age.[3]

The choice of Gould's piano program was most unusual. It was not chosen to please the audience with familiar music pieces but to educate, to call attention to his fresh concepts and to demonstrate his original piano technique. By presenting in the same recital the music of the Renaissance and Baroque periods combined with twentieth-century music, Gould announced his creative and innovative approach to classical music. He painted the old music with a new brush on a modern canvas. No longer having ties with Guerrero and having had no guidance or advice from other veteran-pianists, Gould was left to his own devices in the preparation and selection of the music for his debut. His chosen keyboard works of obscure composers, such as Gibbons, Sweelinck, Webern and Berg, were practically unknown to concertgoers in North America. The daring young pianist took a risk in performing them at such a vulnerable time in his career. He took a chance and succeeded. Everything worked: his strange program, his fabulous piano technique and the powerful, charismatic image he projected.

Gould felt accomplished and content after this performance but, like any other soloist, he was not immune to the anxiety pending another, perhaps even more critical, recital. On January 11, Gould made his debut in New York City, the mecca to which all artists aspire. He played at Town Hall, and his music program was a repeat of the one he had successfully executed in Washington. The historic Town Hall is located in the heart of Manhattan, on West 43rd Street, sandwiched between 6th Avenue and Broadway. It opened in 1921 to mark the victorious end of the suffragists' struggle for voting privileges for women. A wide spectrum of lectures and debates of leading philosophers and humanists took place at Town Hall. Such great individuals as Thomas Mann, Winston Churchill and Bertrand Russell spoke from its stage to enlighten the world. Gradually, Town Hall activities expanded to include nearly all forms of the performing arts; ranging from classical music recitals to vocal, jazz and pop concerts and ethnic celebrations. Famous music artists like Rachmaninoff, Paderewski, Landowska, Heifetz and Menuhin fascinated the world from the Town Hall stage. So did Glenn Gould. This remarkable place became Gould's destination on that freezing day. The audience was unusually small, with about seventy-five people. Since the artist was unknown, the concert was only modestly promoted, and the program was uninviting. Gould received a number of cheering telegrams from his Toronto fans who were not lucky enough to attend. His friends wrote:

> January 11, 1955
> Tonight New York will realize "All that Glitters is Gould." Best Wishes,
> Irene and Baily Bird[4]

Gould stayed at the Park Chambers Hotel at 63 West 58th Street in New York. A telegram came to this address from the "Staff of Thomas G. Gould," which was his father's fur business shop. Though

Glenn's beloved grandfather, Tom (Thomas G.), was long deceased, the fur business still carried his name and tender memories about him. Glenn was swamped with many other telegrams:

> January 11, 1955
> Wishing you deepest satisfaction of truly inspired performance tonight.
> Prayers. Bernice and Val Hoffinger[5]
>
> All our very warmest wishes for tremendous success tonight.
> Lois Marshall and Weldon Kilburn[6]

In spite of the unfavorable weather conditions, several members of the music elite, already charged by the news of Gould's memorable performance in Washington, came to see him in action. Such music personalities as the future renowned pianists Gary Graffman, Paul Badura-Skoda and Eugene Istomin were in the audience; so was David Dubal, musician and critic and David Oppenheim, the director of Columbia Records' Masterworks division. They all listened breathlessly to the most unusual of all pianists they ever had known. Gould was indeed different in nearly every aspect of his piano playing. The way he sat at the instrument in his low chair, his manual technique, his philosophy, the depth of music he delivered and the choice of the same, all were a new discovery for his audience. The excellent acoustics of Town Hall helped in the transmission of Gould's finest ornaments of baroque music and of his extra-soft and slow passages. While most pianists finish their recitals with a build up toward an impressive and vigorous finale, Gould ended his debut performance on a soft, anticlimactic note. Martin Canin, whom Gould had met a few months earlier at the Juilliard School of Music in New York, was in the audience. He recalled the following technical details:

> It was fabulous playing, if somewhat reduced in its effect on the meager audience ... because Glenn, in his desire to emulate the sound of the old instruments, played the Gibbons and Bach with the piano lid on the half-stick. And, as the first half, which finished with the Beethoven [Opus] 109, ended very softly, so did the entire program, which ended with the Berg Sonata, a work whose last measures contain a triple piano followed by a diminuendo. I sincerely doubt that before or since, has a pianist ended a New York debut recital on such a muted note.[7]

The chemistry between the performer and his astonished audience was maximized. Gould was not only noticed for his unique music repertoire and piano technique, but he was critically acclaimed as a new music persona with an unlimited future in the field of piano music. On the whole, press reviews were satisfactory but somewhat cautious. John Briggs of *The New York Times* reported:

> The challenging program Mr. Gould prepared was a test the young man met successfully, and in so doing left no doubt of his powers as a technician. The most rewarding aspect of Mr. Gould's playing, however, is that technique as such is in the background. The impression that is uppermost is not one of virtuosity but of expressiveness. One is able to hear the music.[8]

On this epic trip to Washington and New York, Gould had a small entourage with him, which was a rare treat that would not often be repeated on his ensuing concert tours. Even though the roads were icy and treacherous, Gould's parents drove on their own to join their son in his baptism of fire. Walter Homburger came along, too. Another important companion was inanimate in nature—Gould's private piano chair with the low seat and back support was brought from home. The use of such an uncommon chair, together with Gould's dark business suit, which he wore during his recital instead of formal attire, partly accounted for the relatively cool and guarded reception of the music critics. Gould introduced himself modestly and unpretentiously. While his two American recitals were not alluring, they were well recognized by music zealots. It was as if, unknowingly, he was auditioning for the title role in the "Who-is-the-Best-Pianist" drama.

In a very real sense, it was not so much Gould's two debut recitals but what followed immediately afterward. David Oppenheim of Columbia Masterworks, astonished by Gould's unique presentation of music, intuitively approached Homburger with an offer for a recording contract. As a result, Gould was invited to meet with the executive staff of Columbia Masterworks on West 30th Street. The meeting took place on January 12, 1955. Gould was presented with a generous contract to record classical music of his choice. Representatives of the leading American record company had a farsighted vision of Gould by perceiving him as a budding pianistic superstar. The contract between Gould and Columbia Masterworks ran with renewals for not less than the next quarter of the century. It launched him into the sphere of recording music and became the backbone of his entire music career. This was a totally unexpected but remarkable turn of events for the young concert pianist, who had just received the offer of a lifetime.

Gould's debut in the United States and, more importantly, his engagement by Columbia were responsible for his overnight success which afforded him a passport to future prosperity. There is an often-told story about Gould being encouraged by the enthusiastic Columbia management to record something of his choosing. Gould proposed Bach's *Goldberg Variations*. The story goes further to suggest that his new employers were not impressed. They proposed other pieces like Bach's Sinfonias or Inventions and pleaded with Gould, but his mind was firmly set. In June 1955, Gould returned to New York, where his first recording of Bach's *Goldberg Variations* took place in the CBS studios located in an abandoned Presbyterian church at 207 East 30th Street. His chosen producer was Howard Scott, who at that time was a director of A&R (artists and repertoire) for Columbia Masterworks.

Gould recorded the *Goldberg Variations*, which then became the bestseller in the classic music genre. At these recording sessions over a week's time, Gould displayed an array of rituals and extramusical behavior that baffled not only the recording crew but became a focus of the press and the music critics. He brought from Toronto his "equipment," as he called it, which consisted of an unusual supply of towels to wipe his hands after soaking them in hot water before sitting down at the keyboard. Furthermore, there was a stack of shirts and sweaters, which he frequently changed because of his profuse sweating while working at the piano; several bottles of pills, mainly sedatives and painkillers; and two bottles of Poland Water, as Glenn claimed high sensitivity to the New York tap water. The central part of his "equipment" was his folding, adjustable piano chair. A press release from Columbia Records summed up the rest of his unusual behavior:

> Gould at the keyboard was another phenomenon—sometimes singing along with his piano, sometimes hovering low over the keys, sometimes playing with

> eyes closed and head flung back ... After a week of recording, Glenn said he was satisfied with his recording stint, packed up his towels, pills, and bridge chair. He went 'round to shake hands with everyone—the recording director, the engineers, the studio man, the air conditioning engineer. Everybody agreed they would miss the cheerful "soaking" sessions, the Gould humor and excitement, the pills, the spring water.[9]

Idiosyncrasies at the piano did not stop Gould from a most successful completion of his first recording. When the record was released in January 1956, it was followed by raving reviews. Glenn's friend from childhood, Robert Fulford, sent him a curt note with an enclosed newspaper clipping:

> Glenn,
> Thought you might miss this in March *Atlantic*.
>
> R. Fulford

The clipping reads:

> Bach: Goldberg Variations
> (Glenn Gould, piano, Columbia Ml—5060: 12"). Glenn Gould, the twenty-two-year-old Canadian WUNDERKIND who dunks his forearms before performing, jigs around the studio during playback and writes his own very literate jacket-notes, also plays Bach very well indeed. In fact, here is probably the best set of Goldberg Variations this side of Wanda Landowska's. The piano sounds are as bright as Mr. Gould's future looks.[10]

The critics were stunned by the virtuosity of a young pianist who came out of the woodwork. Harold Schonberg of *The New York Times* wrote:

> Gould has skill and imagination, and the music appears to mean something to him. He also has a sharp, clear technique that enables him to toss off the contrapuntal intricacies of the writing with no apparent effort. Best of all, his work has intensity ... Obviously, a young man with a future.[11]

Many other sensational reviews by the national magazines showered universal praise upon the newly emerged pianistic star. *Time* magazine, which declared that Gould's recording of Bach's *Goldberg Variations* are Bach as the old master himself must have played them. *Life* magazine poetically dubbed Gould "The Music World's Young Wonder."

Gould's formula on the choice of music he performed was remarkably steady during the span of his concert career. It consisted of the works of J. S. Bach, L. van Beethoven and the "moderns"—Schoenberg, Hindemith, Krenek and Berg. Occasionally, Gould digressed from this formula to play the music of other composers, but the cornerstone of his performing repertoire was a selection of baroque and classical music, complemented by contemporary music pieces. There is an obvious avoidance of nineteenth-century romantic music. Gould thought of it as opulent, melodramatic, too touchy and too coiffured to the point of kitsch. It was baroque music that he felt was of consummate beauty, solemn and ethereal.

Out of all the world's composers, it was predominantly Bach's music that Gould preferred to play. J. S. Bach is the best-known and most prolific composer of the baroque era. Bach was a master of counterpoint[12] or contrapuntal music. Contrapuntal or polyphonic music features two or more voices or parts, each with an independent melody but all harmonizing. Bach also invented for it new elements in rhythm, harmony and style. The question is, what determined Gould's choice of baroque music? How did he become the most interesting interpreter of Bach's keyboard music in our time? Even more, how did he become such an innovative Bach scholar and revivalist of his music?

It seems that Gould's interest in Bach's compositions stemmed, first, from his own innate talent for contrapuntal music; second, from his early exposure to his mother's vocal and instrumental performances and, to a lesser degree, from his grandmother's playing of Bach's music in church; and third, from his personal moral convictions and need to recreate a sanctimonious atmosphere around himself.

While for most young students counterpoint in music is not such an appealing and smooth subject to practice and memorize, Glenn had a knack for it. He took formal studies in counterpoint at the conservatory, for which he earned his usual high marks, but it was his natural disposition that made him into its master. Gould's whole mind, particularly his auditory and visual perception, was well suited for this polyphonic or "many-voiced" music. Even his thought process was contrapuntal, as he was often doing several things simultaneously. For Glenn, to practice the piano, listen to the radio and do mental arithmetic at the same time was effortless and normal.

Gould's basic knowledge of Bach's keyboard music taught to him by his mother was reinforced and expanded by his music mentor, Guerrero, who introduced his student to Six French Suites, Six English Suites, Seven Partitas and Inventions and Sinfonias, all of which Gould perfected and played from memory. Partita no. 5 in G Major and Partita no. 6 in E Major became two of his favorite and most performed music pieces. The latter is known as the most technically demanding of the partitas because of the fingering problems and a need for a firm rhythmic grasp. Nothing stood in the way of Gould's insatiable exploration of Bach's keyboard music. He played Bach's Toccatas and Fantasias with supreme technical command and beauty. In his mid-teens Gould started preparing Bach's clavier concerti, out of which the Concerto in D Minor became his specialty, and he performed it frequently in his later international concerts. Last but not least, Gould topped his wide knowledge of Bach's keyboard literature with the complete mastery of the most attractive and complex of all Bach's works—Aria with Thirty Variations, known popularly as the *Goldberg Variations*.

Gould incorporated his mastery and love of Bach's music into his performances. Following his New York debut, the concert pianist spent the rest of his 1955-1956 performing season on his Canadian-American tour. On March 14, 1955, he played Bach's *Goldberg Variations* in Ottawa for the first time in a major recital. Gould delivered a stunning rendition of this masterpiece. In 1956, when Gould gave only twenty-three concerts, he added to his performing Bach repertoire *The Art of the Fugue*, which he successfully delivered in recitals in New York on May 7 and Delaware, Ohio, on November 2. In Hamilton, Ontario, Montreal, Quebec, and Winnipeg, Manitoba, along with other works, Gould played Bach's Italian Concerto and Bach's D Minor Concerto. In the same year, Gould appeared twice in Massey Hall in his native Toronto. The first time, he performed a recital, including the Sweelinck Fantasia and Bach's *Art of the Fugue*. Gould's avid fan, performing harpsichordist Jim Curtis, who was in the audience, wrote in his journal:

> The highlight of the evening for me was the Hindemith Sonata no. 3, a virile driving, closely knit composition of great beauty. The Bach suffered from excessive speed, though it possessed uncanny unity. As encores he [Gould] did some of the Goldbergs. We [Curtis and two friends] met him [Gould] afterwards and got three autographs! ...[13]

The second appearance at Massey Hall was on October 24, when Gould was a piano soloist in the performance of Beethoven's Second Concerto along with the Toronto Symphony directed by Walter Suskind. Again, his learned fan, Jim Curtis, made this lively entry in his music diary:

> ... Finally the moment arrived. Out came Glenn with his characteristic limp (in tails this time). He sat waiting for his entry in various positions, all of them the picture of complete nonchalance and relaxation. He kept shaking his hands vigorously, as if the circulation were not all he could wish for. As the music (Beethoven 2) neared the piano's entrance he gradually became involved, to the point of conducting the work for his own benefit (Walter Suskind was officially in charge). At last we heard the immaculate tone and sweeping line, that absolute sureness of touch that are his trademarks. I was completely entranced for the entire work. The lyricism of the Adagio was astounding. In the faster movements his humming was particularly audible ...[14]

After the concert, Curtis went backstage toward Gould's dressing-room to meet the virtuoso in person. Curtis immortalized this precious moment in his diary:

> To my great joy I found him, standing in the doorway chatting with some girls, all bundled up to his ears in a huge overcoat and scarf, with his hands well encased in heavy woollen gloves! I waited my turn and then spoke to him. I happened to mention my harpsichord and he was delighted. He turned his back on the rest of the line and proceeded to chat at some length with me about the instrument (he wants to get one!), about Greta (Kraus) etc. I was quite nervous, but managed to hold my own. He was the essence of kindness and graciousness, and his high cultivation of mind could almost be felt. What a great moment! I came home on air ...[15]

Gould continued to display his brilliance at the piano by interpreting works of Beethoven and Bach. Since 1953, Gould had in his performing repertoire Bach's fifteen sinfonias. According to Philipp Spitta,[16] Bach's scholarly biographer, Bach referred to his *Inventionen und Sinfonien* as "an honest guide" for "the lovers of the clavier." Spitta summarized that Bach "wished in the first place, to produce an exercise book for the clavier-player; but, with mechanical practice; to cultivate the pupil's artistic powers generally, both on the side of impromptu invention ... and on that of serious composition."[17] Quoted in Spitta's book were Bach's own words indicating that he wanted his students "not only to acquire good ideas, but also to work them out themselves and to gain strong predilection for and foretaste of composition."[18] Gould, who owned Spitta's book, was well versed in his representation of Bach's music ideas and absolutely reveled in having so much latitude to interpret the Sinfonias and Inventions in his own way. This type of music stimulated his personal talent for impromptu music expression. Fortified with Bach's two-century-old permission for freedom and reinvention, Gould played his music with unparalleled ability and beauty.

After Gould's recital at the Metropolitan Museum in New York on November 16, 1956, the press reviews duly credited his exquisite artistic prowess as an interpreter of Bach's music. *The Herald Tribune* proudly reported:

> The recital given by pianist Glenn Gould last night at the Grace Rainey Rogers Auditorium would have been remarkable if it had come from a veteran artist in his mature, middle years. Coming from a twenty-three-year-old, it was astounding. One does not expect such extraordinary control of resources from a comparative youngster, nor such precision and refinement of thinking.
>
> The program, which comprised works by Bach, Krenek and Hindemith, displayed these attributes functioning at the high level. In the Four Fugues from the "Art of the Fugue" and in the Fifteen Sinfonias by Bach, one reveled in the pleasure of actually experiencing, for a change, each line laid out in a different shade of tone, each echo and each expansion of an idea carried to its contrapuntal and emotional finishing point. There was no bombast; no sentimentality. Slow, singing passages moved one with their sincerity; the fast Sinfonias were downright dazzling in their steady, leggiero speediness.[19]

The writer for *Musical Courier* expressed his high regard for Gould's music in just one sentence: "The technical mastery of this artist is stunning; his colorfulness of touch can easily compete with that of the late Walter Gieseking, and the maturity of his interpretations is second to none."[20] In this decisive commentary, Gould was compared to the great German pianist of the first half of the twentieth century, Walter Gieseking, who died a few weeks before Gould's recital in New York. Gieseking was a remarkable pianist, who by the age of sixteen played all the major works of Bach and Beethoven. Gould, like Gieseking, was fast at sight reading and memorizing music. With the pianistic stars, Gieseking and Schnabel, gone; with Horowitz retired in 1953 and with ailing Joseph Hofmann to be dead in two years, the world's stage was becoming clear for Glenn Gould as the new pianistic mega-star.

After J. S. Bach, whose compositions Gould most frequently performed, his second favorite composer was Ludwig van Beethoven. Throughout his pianistic career, Gould persevered in performing and recording Beethoven's music, both as a soloist with an orchestra and in recitals. On March 15, 1956, he gave a memorable performance of the Beethoven Concerto in G Major at the Masonic Temple Auditorium in Detroit, Michigan, with Paul Paray conducting the Detroit Symphony. *The Detroit News* reported:

> So many things go into the building or breaking of historic careers that it is risky to report that a genius of the piano was here last night. But about 4,000 concert-goers loudly expressed that opinion after Glenn Gould played Beethoven's fourth piano concerto ... the ovation that followed the end of the concerto was the kind that occurs at historic events. He was called back six times.[21]

THE CONCERT PIANIST PAR EXCELLENCE

> Glenn Gould, in spite of his youth, is ... one of the best performers of Bach in the world.
>
> Isai Braudo
> *The Toronto Telegram*[22]

The period between 1957 and 1962 was the most productive in Gould's life as a performing artist. During this half dozen years, Gould toured a wide number of cities from coast to coast in North America and made three overseas journeys, totaling 206 major public concerts.[23] In this period, the busy pianist gave concerts in San Francisco in three consecutive years. On February 28 and March 1 and 2, 1957, he played for his San Francisco debut Bach's Concerto in F minor and *Burleske* by Strauss, along with the San Francisco Symphony conducted by Enrique Jorda. After a number of curtain calls and modest bows, Gould received greetings backstage. Among those who were anxious to meet him was a San Francisco resident, Dr. Peter Ostwald, who was a psychiatrist and violinist. Ostwald introduced himself to Gould as a friend of Martin Canin, pianist, whom Glenn had met earlier in New York. Ostwald was fascinated by Gould's personality, fondly recalling the event:

"Why did you wish to meet Gould so much?" I asked Ostwald during my first visit to San Francisco.

"Martin [Canin] told me all about his New York debut. He said to me, 'You absolutely must go to his concert, he [Gould] is exceptional at the piano but also quite a character.' So, he didn't have to tell me this twice. I was single at the time and I had just moved from New York to the West Coast. I also had a special interest in the music and psychology of performing artists, and I was very interested in Gould," Dr. Ostwald explained.

"As a psychiatrist, you are trained to look at people analytically. What was your first impression about Gould as a person?" I invited Dr. Ostwald to elaborate.

"I was stunned by his music. What a master with his fingers. In some ways he was like a kid, very personable and open. Yet he had this aura about him. He touched me so much that I often talked about him when I was in psychoanalysis,"[24] Dr. Ostwald said candidly.

The Gould-Ostwald acquaintance that started backstage developed into a friendly relationship that continued for the next twenty years. They made occasional telephone calls to each other, exchanged correspondence and met a few times in person.

Upon his return home to Toronto, Gould was busy getting ready for his first concert tour abroad. He was going on a major concert tour of Russia, Germany and Austria. Traveling overseas and performing in Europe was novel and exciting yet unnerving and anxiety-provoking. Gould feared that something might go wrong while he was away. He was afraid of being sick or of not being well received by the concert audiences and the critics. Despite his high anticipatory anxiety surrounding this journey, the 1957 concert tour in Russia became one of the highlights of Gould's career as a traveling virtuoso.

Gould arrived in Moscow accompanied by his manager, Walter Homburger. In the span of less then two weeks, from May 7 to May 19, he gave eight performances, four in Moscow and four in Leningrad. Going on prolonged trips was always much too hard for Gould, and Russia seemed so far away from home. For North Americans, the Soviet Union was a remote and mysterious country behind the "Iron Curtain." It was ruled by the oppressive Communist government, which placed restrictions not only on the freedom of speech but also on the liberality of artistic expression. The postwar political dictator, Joseph Stalin, died in 1953, to be succeeded by Nikita Khrushchev as the premier of the state. In 1956, just prior to Gould's pioneering Russian tour, Khrushchev started the process of gradual destalinization. This, among many other innovations, included the opening of the Russian borders for cultural exchanges with the West. Glenn Gould became the first pianist to be invited behind the Iron Curtain. The existing political climate in the Soviet Union, marked by cultural starvation and isolation from the rest of the world, made Russian audiences exceptionally receptive and grateful for having the rare chance to hear the North American virtuoso in person. Gould already had earned worldwide fame two years earlier, and the news of his uniqueness as a pianist had reached Russian music lovers. Such a pre-climate contributed to Gould's unprecedented music success, and his appearance was of the utmost mutual satisfaction for both the artist and his audiences. In Moscow, he played his favorite Bach pieces, Partita no. 6 and the *Goldberg Variations*. The eminent Soviet music critic, Elena Grosheva, reported:

> Above all, Mr. Gould is a musician of a profound intellect. You take this for granted, once you hear him play Bach. It can be safely said that Mr. Gould is the unmatched interpreter of the compositions of the great polyphonist. In any event, I find it hard to recall ever having heard such a living, inspired and, this needs to be emphasized, such a modern Bach. In Mr. Gould's interpretation it is Bach's profound humanism that comes first.[25]

In Leningrad, the director of the Conservatory, Yuri Bryushkov, gave this concise and appreciative commentary in response to Gould's recital:

> The Goldberg Variations by Johann Sebastian Bach, two intermezzos by Johannes Brahms and the third sonata by Paul Hindemith, which are rarely performed, are not intended to win easy success with the public. But Glenn Gould's penetrating rendition captivates his audience.[26]

Practically all reports from Russia were on the same theme of enormous adoration of Gould as a person and a very special music artist. Massive standing ovations called for a "marathon of encores." Gould was compared to Casals and was showered with bouquets of flowers tossed on stage along with voiced appreciations: "B-r-a-v-ooo, B-r-a-v-ooo," and many utterances shouted in Russian—" H-a-r-a-s-h-o-o-o, H-a-r-a-s-h-o-o-o, E-s-h-c-h-ooo, E-s-h-c-h-ooo."[27] Pianist professor Pavel Serebryakov, who earlier visited Canada, wrote:

> When Glenn Gould plays, one gets the impression of a whole orchestra playing and not a single piano. The 25-year-old musician charms his audiences both by his profound penetration into the piece performed and his superb technique. I was particularly stirred up by Bach's famous Goldberg Variations. These intricate pieces acquired a particular brilliance under the hands of Glenn Gould.[28]

Walter Homburger reported for the Canadian press:

> The last two concerts in Leningrad were, like the others, memorable occasions. Last Saturday Gould played the Bach D Minor Concerto and the Second Beethoven Concerto with the Leningrad Philharmonic. The concert was held in the Bolshoi Hall, Leningrad's largest, which has a seating capacity of 1,300. However, the management had sold an additional 1,100 tickets which meant that those 1,100 people stood through the concert, packed like sardines into every available space.[29]

None of the major reviews of Gould's concerts in Russia put emphasis on his piano mannerisms. It was as if they did not exist. Meanwhile, Gould, as always, sat in his low chair with its back support; his white shirt was not properly tucked in his pants, and his shirt tails stuck out during his numerous bows. Typically, he hummed while performing and flung his hands in conducting gestures, yet the press remained discreet, demonstrating overall unconditional positive regard for Gould. The message was loud and clear—the Russians were interested in Gould's artistic mastery and in him as a phenomenon. His posture at the piano was not to be judged, as it did not take away from his virtuosity. Results were maximal for both the audiences, who felt privileged to hear him play, and for Gould, who felt comforted by their acceptance and appreciation.

The visit to Russia brought out in Gould his best public relations skills. He was relatively relaxed, less self-conscious than usual and well motivated to follow through with his musical engagements. He acted not only as a great artist but also as a good-hearted diplomat for the West, who spontaneously charmed Eastern music connoisseurs. He gave two informal concerts for the Moscow and Leningrad Conservatory students, demonstrating for them the little-known music of Schoenberg, Webern and Krenek.

In the interest of objectivity, it is necessary to raise some questions with respect to Gould's music repertoire. Gould visited the Soviet Union at the time when the Communist Party looked upon Westerners as decadent and when contemporary German composers were not held in high esteem. On the contrary, they were associated with bourgeois Germany, the country that initiated two world wars. Yet Gould's music program in Russia consisted only of works by Germanic composers. While Bach, Beethoven and Brahms were accepted as "old" classics, the rest of them—Hindemith and composers of the Viennese school, Schoenberg, Krenek, Webern and Berg—were considered to be "decadent" and "unpopular." In his lengthy letter to Yousuf Karsh, this is how Gould described what happened at the Moscow State Conservatory, where he played for students:

> When I first announced what I was going to do, i.e., that I was going to play the sort of music that has not been officially recognized in the U.S.S.R. since the artistic crises in the mid-thirties, there was a rather alarming and temporary uncontrollable murmuring from the audience. I am quite sure that many of the students were uncertain whether it was better for them to remain or walk out. As it turned out I managed to keep things under control by frowning ferociously now and then and the only people who did walk out were a couple of elderly professors who probably felt that I was attempting to pervert the taste of the young. However, as I continued playing music of Schoenberg from his earliest years, almost until his death and following that, music of Webern and Krenek, there were repeated suggestions from the student body, mostly in the form of discreet whispers from the committee on the stage but occasionally the odd fortissimo suggestion from the audience that they would prefer to spend their time with Bach and Beethoven.[30]

What made Gould force unwanted music on the Russian students? By "frowning ferociously," he imposed pressure on them rather than entertaining and pleasing them. Earlier on in his pianistic career Gould played music of the Russian composers Prokofiev and Taneyev, and toward the end he recorded works of Scriabin and Glinka. One wonders why he could not prepare for this special event in Russia a music piece of a native composer as a gesture of recognition and respect. What made it so hard for Gould to play anything else but the atonal music of Schoenberg and Webern? One answer to this question would be that Gould's choice of music was not determined by spite or his political prejudice but rather it was his trademark. Gould never claimed a reputation as a crowd pleaser, and his main objective was to deliver good quality renditions of the "new" music, good according to his highly developed taste and standard. Another explanation would be related to Gould's self-centeredness in playing his favorite music while disregarding the needs and wishes of others. In this case, Gould exercised the narcissistic pursuit of perfection in music using the principle "art for art's sake" rather than art in the service of the people.

In both Soviet cities Gould made several acquaintances. One of them was Kitty Gvozdeva, Gould's hostess and translator in Leningrad, who practically "adopted" him as her symbolic music son. Gould and Gvozdeva exchanged records and sincere letters for many years to come.

In Moscow, Gould personally met the most famous Russian pianist of that time, Sviatoslav Richter, who came to see him backstage. Gould made a point of attending Richter's recital, to which he referred with the highest praise:

> The first time I heard him [Richter] play was at the Moscow Conservatory in May 1957, and he opened his program with the last of Schubert's sonatas—the Sonata in B flat major ... for the next hour I was in a state that I can only compare to a hypnotic trance. All of my prejudices about Schubert's repetitive struc-

> tures were forgotten ... I realized at that moment, as I have on many subsequent occasions while listening to Richter's recordings, that I was in the presence of one of the most powerful communicators the world of music has produced in our time.[31]

What an impact! Just as Richter admired Gould at his concert, Gould was hypnotized by Richter's interpretation of Schubert's music, which Gould had never favored before. Richter seemed to be the only person alive who could challenge Gould's negative views of romantic music. From then on, the two gigantic piano figures became instant mutual fans, a feeling they maintained for the rest of their lives.

Consistent with the all-encompassing fascination with Gould in Russia was a great plea for him to come back again: "Spasibo, Spasibo, Gospodin Gould," "Ne zabudnite nas, " "Dosvidanya."[32] Gould conquered many music minds and even more hearts among his new Eastern European audiences. The aftereffects of Gould's visit to the Soviet Union were powerful and long-lasting. Russian music lovers showed their approval and admiration by purchasing Gould's records, which were made available to Russian music stores in major cities. Music students were inspired by his ways of playing Bach, and the seasoned critics and scholars honored Gould with the highest appraisal of his musicianship.

Following this entirely musically successful tour in the Soviet Union, *The Toronto Telegram* printed on May 23, 1957, a special wrap-up report received from the Russian expert on Bach, professor Isai Braudo:

> Glenn Gould, in spite of his youth, is in my opinion, one of the best performers of Bach in the world. It is hardly possible to imagine a greater harmony in his rendition of Bach's most difficult works. He is a virtuoso even when he handles pieces written for the clavecin, which are very difficult to render on the piano. In truth, Glenn Gould is an outstanding pianist of our times.[33]

On the way back from Leningrad, Gould and Walter Homburger stopped in Berlin as a part of their concert itinerary. Gould, who from his childhood fervently followed radio news about World War II, was now able to see one of its historical headquarters. Berlin was the largest and one of the most beautiful European cities before the war, but it was shelled and crushed in battles with allied forces and rebuilt afterward. The infamous Berlin Wall was not built yet, so the magnificent Brandenburg Gate stood alone as a dividing marker between East and West Berlin. Dissimilarly to Russia, where Gould felt relatively comfortable performing, here in Berlin, the twin cradle of music achievement with Vienna, he experienced high stage fright in the face of playing with the fabled conductor Herbert von Karajan and the prestigious Berlin Philharmonic. In Gould's personal chronology, this encounter was the most significant one so far. It was exciting to meet with the charismatic figure of von Karajan, but it was also stressful to appear before the refined ears and scrutinizing eyes of seasoned Berlin concertgoers. In a succession of three concerts from May 24 to 26, Gould performed the Beethoven Concerto in C Minor, op. 37. A Berlin music critic wrote:

> This 25-year-old master pianist has the marvelous gift of presenting the music with such freshness as if it were being heard for the first time. We must

> count Gould among the very great pianists of our day ... The man has music in his blood and Beethoven in his fingertips. This performance of the C Minor Concerto, Beethoven himself, would most certainly have approved ... Gould is the reincarnation of an extremely romantic type of musician with a sensational virtuosity.[34]

Interestingly, Gould was referred to as a "romantic type of musician" when in reality he professed his dislike for romantic music of the nineteenth century. Intellectually, Gould rejected romantic music, but deep down he enjoyed it. These positive feelings were largely censored and repressed. Only in some rare instances, such as when listening to Sviatoslav Richter's rendition of Schubert's music, did Gould allow himself to feel spontaneous elation.

One of the most respected veteran-critics in Europe, H. H. Stuckenschmidt, was impressed by Gould's music appearance and provided this laudatory review:

> Actually Gould plays as if possessed physically by a thousand passions, a young man in the strange way of a trance, an artist on the edge of dream and reality. His technical abilities are fabulous; the fluency in both hands, the manifold dynamics, and the many colors of his touch represent a degree of mastery which I have not come across since the time of Busoni.[35]

Again, the critic saw Gould as "possessed ... by a thousand passions," which may be a synonym for his intense emotional experience of music. Stuckenschmidt compared Gould to Ferruccio Busoni, who was one of the greatest pianists at the turn of the century. He lived and gave recitals in Berlin and died there in 1924. Busoni is considered to be the first of the pleiad of brilliant modern pianists in the twentieth century, with Rachmaninoff and Hofmann to follow. As Gould's music career unfolded, he became one of the pleiades to emerge after Schnabel and Horowitz. The former chief critic for *The New York Times*, Harold Schonberg, wrote:

> Busoni's style at the keyboard must have been monumental and, for its day, eccentric. Critics, and also many of his fellow pianists, could not follow his ideas. He took nothing for granted and he restudied everything he played."[36]

Gould, like Busoni, was an avant garde pianist, a philosopher at the keyboard much ahead of his time, a master technician, innovator and eccentric.

For a young North American pianist, being compared in top music circles to the established performing master, Busoni, was a matter of graduation and valedictorian honor. If in Russia Gould was met with the dramatic "red carpet" reception, here in Berlin the response to him was more of level-headed admiration.

Other than being a concert pianist, Glenn also indulged in some quiet social time in Berlin. He practiced at Steinway House as usual and talked to the Steinway staff about the merits of various concert pianos. There he also met with pianist Gary Graffman, who practiced at Steinway, and the two spent some social time together. Gould made a personal visit to Captain Richard O'Hagan, who was stationed with the Allied Forces in Berlin. O'Hagan became Gould's fervent music fan and supporter. Gould found his presence helpful and referred to him as his aide-de-camp because Dick, as he called him, came to be quite handy in a variety of small errands, particularly as a Berlin guide to music stores. Their friendship continued through Gould's next two music tours to Berlin.

Despite all those rich personal experiences and public accolades in Berlin, Gould felt exhausted, even physically sick. This was partly due to the aftereffects of the emotional tension and stage fright he endured through the three concerts given, but mostly it had to do with a larger picture of his greatly augmented separation anxiety. Never before had Gould left his home for such an extended period of time and geographical distance, nor had he ever performed eleven times in nineteen days with extensive traveling in between.

By the time he left Berlin and arrived in Frankfurt for the weekend, Gould came down with his typical, nonspecific general malaise, consisting of body aches, fever, sinus congestion and fatigue. He was totally unaware of how homesick he was, but blamed his illness on trivial reasons such as poorly heated hotel rooms and fatiguing travel by airplane. Not admitting to himself that he was terrified of flying, he rationalized that because of his nasty "hay fever," it would have been better for him to take a train to Vienna, which was his next touring destination. So he took the train and traveled by himself from Frankfurt through the pastoral lands of Upper Bavaria, gazing through the windows at the "rolling hills, rivers, beautiful forests and any number of quaint little towns dominated by baroque churches."[37] Gould arrived safely in Vienna, where Homburger flew to meet with him. On June 3, 1957, immediately upon settling in at the Hotel Ambassador, he wrote his most affectionate and personable letter ever to be written to his parents. The letter began with an unusual "Dear Mouse-Possum-Bank" and contained a naive little drawing of a hound, a mouse and a possum climbing a dead tree trunk. The mouse, in his mind, was an endearing representation of his mother; the possum stood for his father, while the bank was his dog Banquo, named so after Banquo from Shakespeare's Macbeth. The content of this extremely playful letter, rich with psychological meanings, could be a subject of lengthy analysis, but the gist was that Gould missed his family and felt emotionally exhausted. Gould then made a sudden detour in his letter by writing about having a wonderful time in Europe and about "seriously thinking of taking up residence" there for six months in the next season. This little air of bravado ended in a rare outpouring of emotions:

> Now, may I close with a suggestion for you two. Why not plan and save now for a trip in Europe? Forget about going west—this is much more exciting. You (I address this to Daddy) are always talking about being a good traveller and not being tired by long trips, so you could certainly enjoy driving around as I hope to do. Besides, if my plans of the moment go through I shall be establishing my European residence (sounds imposing, what?) probably in Germany in the early fall of '58 (concert permitting) and you could come over and visit me.[38]

Glenn's writing style as seen in this paragraph is many-layered, contrapuntal. He is as witty as ever and he is uncustomarily emotional, a state rarely experienced and shared with others.

"Mr. Gould, what do you think about your son's fantasy to live in Europe and to have you and his mother visit him?" I asked Bert Gould.

"Glenn was a dreamer. I think he was very excited about his trip but he always wanted to come home. Besides, my wife would never go overseas, not by plane, anyway,"[39] Mr. Gould responded succinctly.

Obviously, Gould had concurrent positive and negative feelings about his European encounter. The child in Glenn wrote a playful letter garnished with the cute characters of a mouse and possum; the adventurer was fantasizing about a little castle amid the picturesque Bavarian landscape; and the mature musician in Gould had a natural instinct to be in the proximity of the music mecca of the world. After formally ending his letter, Gould kept adding postscripts and post-postscripts as if he were unable to let go of his parents. On the fantasy level, Gould had future plans that would be more adequately suited to his status as an international virtuoso, but on the inner level of emotional insecurity, there was a clear limit to his ability to follow through with his plans. Indeed, in reality, Gould never followed up on his fantasy of residing in Europe.

Vienna, the busy and elegant capital of Austria, situated on the river Danube, has a long reputation of fame in the field of music, general arts, psychology, fashion and commerce. Most of all, it confers a specific status and affinity for musicians. Everyone who is prominent in music has at least some relationship with Vienna. Music giants like Mozart, Haydn, Beethoven, Brahms, Schubert, Johann Strauss and Mahler all lived and worked in Vienna. Gould's preferred composer, Arnold Schoenberg, was born in Vienna, and Schoenberg's student, Anton von Webern, was also Vienna-based. Yet Gould somehow could not warm up to this city. He was more intimidated by its rich history, or at best, he was overwhelmed by the fervor of Vienna. He simply put it in the letter to his parents: "I find Vienna much less attractive than I imagined it. Too much rococo architecture for my rather severe tastes."[40] As always, when Glenn was emotionally stirred up, he projected his unhappiness outside on people or on his surroundings. Once again, the likely reason for his unhappiness was his rising stage fright which prevented him from maximally enjoying the occasion. Though musically Gould was so well prepared for his upcoming recital in Vienna, he still suffered from high anxiety. In other words, he had anticipated a possible performance-related disaster. On Friday, June 7, 1957, Gould performed at Mozart Hall at the Vienna Konzerthaus as a part of the annual Vienna Music Festival. His program consisted of Bach's fifteen Sinfonias, Beethoven's Sonata in E Major op. 109 and von Webern's Variations op. 27. As everywhere on this European tour, Gould's appearance stimulated enormous interest in music circles. Concertgoers, music scholars and instrumentalists from all over Austria and guests from abroad who gathered for the festival came to see Gould in action. Famous Vienna-based pianists Georg Demus, Paul Badura-Skoda and Alfred Brendel were in the audience. There was a cheering section of Canadians and such dignitaries as the Canadian ambassador in Vienna, J. S. MacDonald, along with members of the diplomatic corps in attendance. Not only did Gould's feared disaster never happen but he was endowed with the highest possible praise. A critic wrote:

> We do not know of anyone who can equal him in his interpretation of the great master [Bach] ... Up to the present time, Glenn Gould was practically unknown in Vienna. But we will never forget him after this concert yesterday. Although young in years, he has a technical perfection which borders on the miraculous.[41]

Gould's first European tour was entirely successful, and he returned home charged with positive regard and the most generous reviews and compliments. According to his own wish, Gould sneaked back to Toronto anonymously. His homecoming and marvelous achievements were only mildly acknowledged by the press and state officials. At the press conference, speaking of the Russian audiences, Gould stated that they were "terribly enthusiastic and extremely attentive," while the Berlin audiences, were "terribly dull, staid and respectable—just like Torontonians."

> Mr. Gould said his eccentric piano manners, which caused such a flurry of comments from North American critics went unnoticed in Europe. "I received none of the blasts about my eccentricities I get over here. Perhaps European critics are just more polite."[42]

The relative coolness of the official reception in Toronto was compensated for by a very dynamic public response. Gould was showered with letters of praise from all over Canada and from the countries he had just visited in Europe. They conveyed positive sentiments and often requests for more concerts and pleas for inscribed personal photographs and records. Busy as he was, for years Gould tried to keep up with the correspondence with his fans by personally answering each letter. As a reaction to Gould's first overseas tour, Walter Homburger received a number of propositions for future concert engagements, resulting in a second European tour in 1958 and two years' worth of advanced bookings.

Meanwhile, Gould devoted the rest of the 1957 performing season to touring American cities introducing Bach's *Goldberg Variations* as the central piece of his music repertoire. In recitals in Toronto on November 11, Pittsburgh and Cincinnati on November 16 and 20 and New York City on December 7, he championed his penetrating rendition on the "Goldbergs," cleverly combining them with the Haydn Sonata in E-flat Major, no. 49, and the Schoenberg Suite for Piano, op. 25. Bach's Aria with Thirty Variations calls for the interpretive power of a great pianist. Haydn's Sonata no. 49 was composed at the time of Mozart's death and is reflective in nature, revealing great depth of personal feeling. Schoenberg's difficult Suite for Piano, written in the twelve-tone method, calls for the highest degree of pianistic artistry. This piece reminded Gould of his organ-playing days and of his love of counterpoint and "cerebral" music, as opposed to "heartfelt" music. Here is an overall impression of Gould's playing summed up by the critic of *The Pittsburgh Post-Gazette*:

> The word "genius" is used sparingly in these columns as any faithful reader over the past twenty years can attest. But I find no substitute for it in describing Glenn Gould, the young Canadian pianist who gave the Music Guild audience at Carnegie Music Hall Saturday as sensational a display of solo pianism as has not been heard here since the young Horowitz made his debut.[43]

If Bach's music was Gould's foremost love, then his passion and deep attachment to Beethoven's music was his next love. Such a strong predilection for Beethoven's music was noticeable in Gould's teens, when at the age of twelve he began to study Beethoven's Concerto no. 4 and eventually performed it two years later at his concert debut in Toronto. Glenn invested hours of his youth, on a daily basis, in the company of Beethoven and his interpreter, Schnabel, acquiescing to their music and learning how to represent them both. By the time he was twenty years of age, he performed all five Beethoven concerti before the public. From then on, almost everywhere Gould performed in concert he either played a Bach concerto or one of the Beethoven concerti. In recitals, he usually kept one of Beethoven's pianoforte works in his repertoire. Most often it was the Sonata in E Major, op. 109, or less frequently, the Sonata in A-Flat Major, op. 110. The last five Beethoven sonatas are known to be some of the most profound music works ever to be composed for pianoforte, calling for a great deal of studious effort, depth of emotion and musical insight.

Shortly after Gould's return from Vienna, he appeared in a recital on August 17, 1957, at the Hollywood Bowl in Los Angeles. The critic, Raymond Kendall, of *The Los Angeles Mirror* left us this appraisal:

> If any further evidence were needed, Tuesday night's recital provided it: Pianist Glenn Gould is one of the most phenomenal musicians before the concertgoing public today ... Nowhere in last night's concert was Gould's recreative force more apparent than in the Beethoven Sonata. I haven't heard such Beethoven since Schnabel's best days; it soared and chanted, rushed on, thundered. It was as though Gould was possessed by a splendid demon ... No one who heard him Tuesday night would deny that Glenn Gould is a truly great pianist.[44]

Driven by a "splendid demon" is suggestive that Gould had a very deep and personal motive to play so magnificently. It could have been his often-denied love of Beethoven's music, love as great and personified as if it were felt toward another human being. It was passionate and highly expressive; it was perhaps fuelled by his feelings toward the most important person, his mother, who indeed introduced him to Beethoven's music, and to a lesser degree to Guerrero, who taught him the perfection of playing Beethoven. A Toronto pianist, Amy Sum, commented: "Gould played as if he had a phantom within himself, a compelling need to use music to exorcise the ghost from inside."[45] In this case, the phantom or the ghost is seen as the vast inner primal artistic force.

Gould had a particular affinity for Concerto no. 2 in B-flat, op. 19, which Beethoven composed when he was only twenty-five years old. In the first movement, Allegro con Brio, in Gould's famous fugal cadenza, a music admirer could recognize the theme from the finale of Beethoven's Symphony no. 3, *Eroica*, which is captivating in its beauty. For Gould to enjoy this concerto so much, there must be an element of personal identification with this music piece or with Beethoven himself at his young age. Keep in mind that Gould was in his early twenties himself when he composed his String Quartet no. 1, wishing to produce five more quartets just as Beethoven had accomplished a century and a half earlier. This means that Gould used Beethoven as a role model and identified with him as a great music father. Also, Gould was in his mid-twenties at the time of propagating Beethoven's Second Concerto and eventually selected it for his New York debut at Carnegie Hall in January 1957. This was his first collaborative appearance with the famous conductor, Leonard Bernstein, and the New York Philharmonic. The review from *The Herald Tribune* was high-spirited:

> Glenn Gould, the word has gone out, is an individualist. The report is not exaggerated. Saturday night he proved himself a unique figure both in his platform

> behavior and the manner of performance ... He made the work a hurtling virtuosi vehicle ... his rendition was so powerful, so full of assurance and authority that any objections one might have raised that Beethoven is being misrepresented, were quickly dispelled ... he is equipped with a dazzlingly accurate technique and a tone that retains its beauty as it progresses ... he is an enormously gifted musician and a pianist of spectacular attainments.[46]

By that time, some East Coast critics had established a rather biased attitude toward Gould, focusing on his piano-related manners, which made it impossible for them to fully enjoy his musicianship. *The New York Times* critic, Harold Schonberg, also quite preoccupied with Gould's extramusical behavior, was stern and tentative in acknowledging his music qualities:

> Glenn Gould, the spectacular young pianist from Canada, chose an unspectacular work for his debut with the Philharmonic Symphony ... Mr. Gould strolled on stage, sat at the piano, crossed his legs during the opening tutti, gazed calmly upon audience and orchestra, and then untangled his legs and got to work. He presented a sharp, clear-cut reading that had decided personality ... his interpretation was musical and logical ... to receive an ovation after a performance of the Beethoven B flat is not something that comes to every pianist.[47]

Shortly after their Carnegie Hall concert, the tripartite team of Gould, Bernstein and the New York Philharmonic recorded the same Beethoven Concerto no. 2 in conjunction with Bach's D Minor concerto. Schonberg, though still reserved, was far more positive in his critique of the recording. This time he only had to listen to it and not see Gould's unorthodox manners at the piano. He wrote:

> The results are beautiful. Both works emerge in a clear, unhurried, rhythmically precise manner, overall impression is one of well-balanced plasticity of piano merging with orchestra and veering out again, of fine ensemble and musical finesse.[48]

In most of the other places where Gould played Beethoven's Concerto no. 2, the reviews were unconditionally positive. After three consecutive concerts in Washington, D.C., at Constitution Hall (October 29 and 30, 1957) and at Lisner Auditorium (October 31), with Howard Mitchell and the National Symphony, critic Irving Lowens of *The Washington Evening Star* likened him to Chopin and expressed his highest regards for Gould:

> Mr. Gould is assuredly an artist in the romantic tradition, but he is not the romantic thunder of a Liszt. Rather, his is a romantic elegance of a Chopin—aristocratic, small-boned, expressive—and while listening to Mr. Gould's early Beethoven yesterday, with its pearly runs and exquisite phrasing, I could not help feeling that this must have been the way the great Pole must have once

> played ... For make no mistake about it, this pianist is music incarnate, and one of the most eloquent artists at work today.[49]

The year 1957 was successfully concluded by Gould's recital at Carnegie Hall. Again, Gould's friend, Jim Curtis, made this invaluable observation:

> ... Finally the recital (Carnegie Hall, New York). And what a recital! Undoubtedly the most enjoyable of Glenn's to date. The playing was superlative, evidence of great application these past two weeks, with a change of programme (the Schoenberg op. 25 Suite in place of the Haydn, and opening with the Sweelinck) and part of the 5th Partita as an encore. His movements were never before so utterly integrated with the sense and line of the music. Everyone (full house) was entranced, and cheered him wildly through seven curtain calls. He beamed radiantly, obviously enjoying the adulation. He wore tails, though a typically ill-fitting set. We talked to him afterwards ... and he told me he had had an accident with his car too, on the way to this very event; going too fast to catch the plane, he turned over in a snowdrift, unhurt, just shaken! We were within arm's reach of [Leonard] Bernstein, who was the first to greet him, embracing him warmly, saying "marvelous, boy," and inviting him to his place for lunch ...[50]

From the point of music accomplishments, the year 1958 was for Gould even more intense than the previous one. Public performances were scheduled in cities from coast to coast in Canada and the United States, where he continued to present his favorite and very familiar music program. In July, Gould appeared at the first annual Vancouver International Festival, where he had three extremely busy days. On July 23, he gave a recital playing Haydn Sonata in E-flat Major, Beethoven Sonata in A-flat Major and Bach's *Goldberg Variations*. Reporter, George Kidd, wrote an extensive article for *The Toronto Telegram*:

> Awkwardly he [Gould] stepped on stage, ill at ease in his white tie and tails. Quietly, shyly, he acknowledged the applause of the already keyed-up audience. Then he sat down to play. At his request a German Steinway had been shipped down from Vernon, B.C ...
>
> ... But he had his own folding stool that has gone with him wherever he has played, including Russia. He also had a carpet for his feet. He slumped before the instrument as quiet settled over the large theatre. And then he began to play, and the obvious idiosyncrasies were forgotten in the music that poured from him, head to toe.
>
> ... The Haydn was delightfully refreshing in its charming pattern and the Beethoven, sharp in contrast, was excitingly unfolded.
>
> Following intermission, to the now quite familiar Goldberg Variations ... In his complete understanding of the 30 variations there was a mature freshness that never wavered and an overall intelligence that was beautifully controlled.

> ... And then the storm broke. The audience recalled him over and over again.
>
> ... Then he sat down and played his encore—Alban Berg sonata in one movement, a most formidable task after the carrying of the printed program.
>
> ... And when he concluded it there was another five-minute round of applause before he was allowed to depart.[51]

On July 27, Gould was a soloist in a concert with the Vancouver Festival Orchestra and Irwin Hofman conducting. They played Beethoven Concerto no. 2. Finally, on July 30th, in a double bill concert with the CBC Chamber Orchestra and John Avison as conductor, Gould played Bach D Minor Concerto and Brandenburg Concerto no. 5.

In August 1958, Gould embarked on his second pilgrimage to Europe, this time for an ambitiously planned and extensive concert tour in six countries. The tour was supposed to last until mid-December and commenced in Salzburg with a concert appearance at the traditional annual festival established in honor of Mozart, who was born there. Gould played Bach's D Minor Concerto at Mozarteum's Konzertsaal, along with the Concertgebouw Orchestra conducted by Dimitri Mitropoulos. While he felt confident enough at interpreting Bach's piece, he was mortified at having to play Mozart's music before his native worshippers. As usual, Gould's emotional distress triggered physical illness like a safety valve, and he came down with a chest cold. This meant that his next recital, featuring Bach's *Goldberg Variations*, Mozart's Sonata in C Major, K. 330, and Schoenberg's Suite for Piano, op. 25, had to be canceled. Troubled by his inner conflicts, Gould was unable to relax in this ancient Austrian town and enjoy its Renaissance and Baroque architecture and endless number of cultural attractions. Instead, he withdrew to his hotel room, fantasizing about the serenity of the surrounding Alps.

Just imagine a hot August day in Salzburg, where flocks of tourists stroll in the narrow, cobblestone streets in its quaint downtown section. They are either likely to browse around and look for collectors' items, music souvenirs and purchase Mozart chocolates; or to cool off with a draft of beer at a sidewalk bistro. Preoccupied with his chest congestion, Gould was shopping around too, but unlike others, he was looking for an electrical heater! At first sight, this seems like a ludicrous thing to do. On closer examination, Gould's behavior was a sign of how diffident and out of place he must have felt. Whenever he was in such a state of mind, he was absorbed by his spurious ailments so he did not have to deal with his true feelings. In his unconscious, the heater became a self-soothing object, a magic solution for his plight of performing. It was simply supposed to ward off his overwhelming performance anxiety. Still focusing on his personal health issues, Gould wrote to his friend in Berlin, Captain Richard O'Hagan: "I caught a ferocious influenza in Salzburg through just such incommodious living as is prevalent throughout European hostelries and at the risk of making a nuisance of myself in all hotels this fall, I intend to keep warm and, if possible fit."[52] Eventually, Gould ended up buying two portable heaters in Salzburg and mailing them to O'Hagan in Berlin, with the intention to use them there in his hotel room. Somewhat improved from his illness and embarrassment from canceling the recital in Salzburg, Gould once again crisscrossed Europe, this time heading north to his next destination, Brussels, to be followed by more touring in West Germany and Sweden.

In 1958, Brussels hosted the International Exhibition from April to October. The exhibition complex was dominated by the 334-foot-high Atomium, a gigantic aluminum construction that represented the atomic structure of an enormously magnified metal molecule. This was Gould's first Expo. The theme of this World Fair was world peace and the peaceful use of atomic energy. The recently established Canada Council chose pianist Glenn Gould of Toronto and soprano Marguerite Lavergne of Montreal as cultural ambassadors at the Expo. On August 25, Gould appeared as a soloist at the piano. Once again, as in Salzburg, he performed Bach's Concerto in D Minor; this time with the Hart House string orchestra conducted by Boyd Neel. Gould was in a fairly good and relaxed mood while in Brussels, which meant that both the people and physical conditions were optimal, and he produced an excellent rendition of Bach's lovely D Minor concerto. *The Toronto Daily Star* reported:

> Gould gave a masterly interpretation of Bach's Concerto no. 1 in D Minor. He was particularly effective in bringing out all the joyous vigor of the first and last movement ... His unorthodox mannerisms—playing much of the time with his legs crossed and in pauses dropping his hands limply to his sides—startled his Belgian audience, but their unreserved applause showed admiration for his keyboard artistry.[53]

The same report concluded that guests at the performance were Senator Drouin, speaker of the Canadian Senate; Charles Hebert, Canadian ambassador to Belgium; and representatives of the Brussels diplomatic corps. By that time, Gould had been called a "genius" so often that the critical press became interested in how he felt about such high recognition. Dennis Braithwaite of *The Toronto Daily Star* asked Gould a pointed question:

D.B. You've been called a genius, Glenn. Do you feel like a genius? If you do, when did you first get that feeling?

G.G. That's a dirty question. I regard this word with great suspicion. I have never really got into the habit of using it myself, certainly not about myself and rather infrequently about other people. When I do use it about other people they're usually safely dead and they're usually composers. I don't recall using it about a pianist at all so I don't think I deserve it and honestly I don't really know what it means. I think that one should stick to relative terms of some kind.[54]

This is how modest and unaware of his greatness Gould was. There are also hidden guilt feelings in these words for not being a composer but "only" a pianist, and according to Gould, the pianist does not "deserve" the honor of being called a genius. At the same time, *Maclean's* magazine wrote:

> **WHO SAYS GENIUS DOESN'T PAY?**
>
> Pianist Glenn Gould is expected to reach the $100,000-a-year level in the next year—his busiest yet. A 25-concert pre-Christmas tour is taking him through Europe to Israel. A 22-concert spring tour will carry him across the U.S., with four junkets into Canada at Calgary, Edmonton, Montreal and hometown Toronto. Gould's fees have been upped from $ 1,250 to $ 2,000 a concert this season.[55]

THE GOULD-STEINWAY AFFAIR

"... your most celebrated artist [and] favorite son, Vladimir Guldowsky"
Glenn Gould[56]

Gould arrived in Berlin on September 17, 1958, and stayed there at his "stronghold," the Steinplatz Hotel. According to the original plan, this was supposed to be a sizable West Germany tour with about a dozen public appearances in major cities. The curiosity and excitement in music circles for this special occasion were on the rise. Captain O'Hagan hosted a party inviting music scholars and fans to listen to Gould's records and study his musicianship before seeing him in concert. Among them was the famous Berlin harpsichordist Silvia Kind. She attended both the dress rehearsal and one of the concerts held on September 21 and 22 at the Hochschule fur Musik in West Berlin. Gould played Bach's D Minor Concerto with Herbert von Karajan conducting the Berlin Philharmonic. Kind was truly fascinated by Gould's music:

> I recall going to the orchestral rehearsal preceding the concert. After the first few bars of the solo Karajan handed the baton to his concertmaster, sat down in the hall and listened deeply absorbed. The concert itself was fantastic—the audience seemed in part moved and in part astonished, for Glenn was a completely new and exciting phenomenon in the concert hall.[57]

After the rehearsal, Kind was introduced to Gould, which marked the beginning of their long friendship. Many years later, she reminisced with adulation:

"You obviously liked the way he played Bach's music. How did you feel about him as a person?" I asked Kind at the Glenn Gould Festival in Holland.

"I very much enjoyed his music, and I instantly liked him as a person. He was a kind young man with boyish looks," Kind answered without any doubt.

"What was it about you that appealed to Gould?" I reversed the question.

"He was so happy to hear that [Paul] Hindemith was my teacher. I think that he felt that we had something important in common. I told him how much I liked his recording of [Bach's] *Goldberg Variations*. Glenn suggested we should write to each other and exchange records and we did,"[58] said Kind. Eventually, Gould and Kind became friends through correspondence, and she was his lasting fan and scholarly partner for discussing baroque music.

Back to Gould and his Berlin triumph. This is what he wrote to Homburger:

> You have probably heard from Kollitsch that the concerts were a great success. The reviews were even better than last year or at least the ones I have so far seen were. (I am now the greatest pianist since Eduard Erdmann.) Unfortunately I made the mistake of saying I didn't know who Erdmann was which convinced everyone that Canada is indeed an isolated spot ...[59]

Dorothea von Ertmann [not Erdmann] was Beethoven's pupil, his assistant pianist and a fervent interpreter of Beethoven's piano works. Italian composer Muzio Clementi held her in high regard as a pianist. Gould was obviously not well informed and at the time of writing this letter he did not know who Ertmann was. Gould continued his letter to Homburger:

> Karajan was extremely cooperative and terribly enthusiastic. Von Westerman insisted that I come back next year which I told him would not be possible but I promised him definitely for 60-61 ...
>
> Phillips had come alive—greeted me at the airport with a bouquet of flowers and on stage ditto after each performance. They have arranged a press party in Hamburg. Isn't that fantastic.[60]

Having made an acquaintance with Silvia Kind, who gave him positive regard, and graced by the hospitality of Dick O'Hagan, Gould modestly celebrated his twenty-sixth birthday and maintained his spirits in a delicate balance. On the day of his birthday, Glenn wrote a postcard to his grandmother, Alma, in Uxbridge, Ontario.

> Dear Grandma, September 25, 1958
>
> The past year has been a great improvement in Berlin with many new buildings. It begins to recapture a little of the glory it must have had in pre-Hitler days. And the Philharmonic remains my dream orchestra. A great joy to play with them again.
>
> Many thanks for birthday remembrance.
>
> Love Glenn[61]

After the concert in Berlin, Gould dashed off on a brief but productive excursion to Sweden. In Stockholm, he was engaged to play in two concerts and two recitals, which he successfully performed. Stockholm, this thirteenth-century city, is dubbed "Venice of the North" to illustrate its landmarks, consisting of countless wharves and man-made canals. Gould was quite comfortable at Stockholm's Grand Hotel. He particularly enjoyed the waterfront dotted with all sizes of boats, a scene most reminiscent of his lake view cottage in Uptergrove. His schedule was unusually busy, and within a week he met the task of four performances and recording all the music pieces on his rich Stockholm program. On September 30 and October 5, Gould was a soloist at the Music Academy with George Ludwig Jochum conducting the Swedish Radio Symphony Orchestra. They played and recorded Mozart's Piano Concerto in C Minor and Beethoven's Concerto no. 2. On October 1 and 6, he gave recitals at the Music Academy, playing the piano music of Haydn, Beethoven and Berg. True, Gould sat at the piano on his low, beat-up chair with his legs crossed, true that his piano was raised on wooden blocks, but it was equally true that Swedish audiences loved his persona and greatly enjoyed his music. Had Alfred Nobel, who was born in Stockholm, remembered in his will the best musician of the year, Gould would certainly have been a strong nominee for his original ways of championing piano music. Dagens Nyheter of Sweden reported: "He is a pianistic genius. The refined culture which characterizes Gould's playing motivates his top ranking among the great younger pianists."[62]

On October 9, Gould appeared in Wiesbaden, a popular German spa since the time when Roman legionnaires proclaimed the curative power of its water. As a piano soloist, Gould played the Beethoven Concerto in C Minor, no. 3, with Wolfgang Sawallisch conducting an unidentified orchestra. The concert was a great success, and Gould, as the central figure, received standing ovations. In a colorful letter to his grandmother, he described the next portion of his itinerary:

> I drove from Wiesbaden to Cologne in a rented car and took the slow route up the Rhine castle country. It was quite worth the trip and in Cologne my window was opposite the famous Cathedral which is the most impressive 16th [century] architectural triumph I have seen in Germany."[63]

The concert in Wiesbaden and the ride through the countryside were the last leisurely activities before Gould was to experience his next emotional storm. In Cologne, despite the magnificent eye-pleasing view of the cathedral, he was again on the cusp of emotional collapse. Gould's sense of inner panic and his depressed mood got the best of him, surfacing in the form of an obscure but familiar pre-concert ailment, manifesting as a chest cold, with a high fever and fatigue. From Cologne, where his public appearance was canceled, Gould went to Hamburg, where he became quite clinically ill and confined himself to his room at the Hotel Vier Jahreszeiten to reconvalesce. The results of this dramatic health crisis were devastating. Gould did not set his hands on a piano for three weeks, and nine concerts had to be canceled in Cologne, Hamburg, Berlin and Vienna.

In any theater there is a number of curtains at the back of the stage. Similarly, in the human psyche there are layers of dynamics which, unlike the curtains in a theater, are all interacting together. These "curtains" made out of emotional dynamics are in the background of any behavior outwardly manifested on the "stage" of human relations. This metaphor may be of help in understanding Gould's episodic illness. One of those emotional layers was his ever-present separation anxiety, which occasionally sprang out in a vicious form. Another feature of Gould's inner psychology was his ongoing depression, which wreaked havoc in his life and caused him to be susceptible to frequent physical illness. These dynamics were deeply embedded in Gould's personality, featuring his power struggle and conflict with authority figures. Before describing the next mishap during Gould's German tour, or so-called "Hamburg crisis," it would be worthwhile to shed some light on Gould's underlying conflict with authority as a major facet of his personality. This conflict will be simply called "the Gould-Steinway affair."

With the exception of practicing on his Chickering piano and, for a short while, playing a Heintzman piano in his early teens, in his performing career Gould was exclusively a Steinway artist. From the inception of his international fame in 1955, or more precisely around the time of recording Bach's *Goldberg Variations* in May/June in the same year, Gould established a direct, personal and amiable relationship with the executive staff of the New York firm of Steinway & Sons. He purchased from them a nine-foot concert grand piano, Steinway CD 90. Before shipping this piano to Toronto, he requested that the Steinways make a number of alterations to it, stating that the piano was "too loose in action." The chief Steinway technician, William Hupfer, met those specific demands to a certain point in accordance with the Steinway company policy and his personal standards of tuning the piano. Unsatisfied, Gould asked for more changes, which Hupfer refused. Gould took it as a personal affront and felt gravely humiliated by Hupfer. This opened the door for a two-decade-long feud between Gould and the Steinway management. Gould's feelings were well summarized in his letter to Winston Fitzgerald, Steinway director of liaison to artists. He complained of "negligence" saying that "no artist of the undersigned stature has ever received such lack of consideration ..." In this lengthy letter, Gould requested further alterations to his CD 90, and even uttered a threat. Failing that, he reckoned:

> I shall be left no alternative but to avail of your oft-repeated offer to assist me in selling this nine foot delight and to return once more to my standing as a Heintzman artist.[64]

It is obvious that Gould had a very strong sense of what he wanted and even stronger feelings of what he did not want, yet was forced to do, to which he responded with an angry ultimatum. It would have been a relief if this unpleasant interpersonal exchange between Gould and Steinway had ended at this point. Instead, once the conflict was ignited, it only sparked a chain reaction that ran through all the years of their very productive business relationship. In the next year, 1957, the conflict soared to an even higher tension level. It all started in the month of February in Montreal, where Gould was visiting for a concert and where he discovered an ordinary Steinway piano at the local Eaton's store. He instantly believed it to be perfectly suited for his artistic needs. In reality, this piano was not authorized by its mother firm as CD (for concert department), which meant that it was not specifically built for concert performances. In his humorous letter to Winston Fitzgerald, Gould attempted to enlist his support:

> The piano, as I mentioned, is joshingly referred to as #266, since the poor piano has never been given the honor of bearing the illustrious trademark of Steinway and Sons—a CD insignia. Indeed is regrettable that one of the finest flagships in your fleet should be so deprived. It would be a gesture entirely worthy of the noble dedication of your company if, during the October visit of your most celebrated artist and your most glorious instrument if a dinner were held at which a bronze plaque might be unveiled on the lyre of #266 ... bearing the inscription: "this instrument maintained for the exclusive use of our favorite son, Vladimir Guldowsky." If you will inform me as to the hour and place of this dinner (the Oak Room at the Plaza would be appropriate) I will start to work on my address which I shall endeavor to keep within modest limits—certainly not exceeding 2½ hours.[65]

This letter portrays Gould's determination to get his way; it reflects his witty sense of humor and his love-and-hate relationship with Steinway. Just as he played a role of a symbolic artistic son to the Columbia Masterworks, Gould fantasized about being "favorite son" to Steinway. In his fantasy, he wished to be embraced and loved unconditionally by Steinway in the same way Vladimir Horowitz had been embraced. At the same time, Vladimir Guldowsky, the pen name in this instance for Gould, felt only like a "stepson" at best to Steinway, which met his basic needs but withheld the unconditional love and approval. By fighting for piano #266, Gould unconsciously fought emotional battles for underdogs, in this case, for the "poor" non-concert piano, forcing his symbolic and powerful "father," the Steinway firm, to approve of it and him. And, for those who wonder how this interesting exchange ended, this story will be carried a little further. This time, Gould won the round and got his way. He had the piano #266 shipped to New York for adjustment to suit his artistic needs, and he indeed used it for recordings and in several concerts. Eventually, this non-concert piano had the honor of being set on the stage at Carnegie Hall, and Gould played on it as a soloist on March 13, 14, and 16, 1958. He performed Bach's D Minor Concerto and Schoenberg's Concerto, with Dimitri Mitropoulos conducting the New York Philharmonic. To conclude this Gould-Steinway saga of piano #266, here are excerpts from Gould's letter to James Graham, the salesman in Montreal from whom Gould rented the piano. He began by thanking Graham for #266, which was a "godsend" to him:

> ... Messrs. Steinway have developed something of a block about fixing up the treble of that piano. They say that it cannot be adequately repaired without a complete rebuilding, which would almost certainly destroy the felicities of the action which I so much enjoy at the present.[66]

Gould continued his emotional outpouring by saying that Leon Fleisher also tried the same piano and agreed with him "that it possesses a really beautiful quality except for the upper register ..." but both of them agreed that said piano with "a little work and little money, [could] be put in really top-notch condition." Gould concluded his letter to Graham, dated July 8, 1958, which happened to be shortly before his tour to Germany, with a doleful awareness that he might have to give up this piano:

> But if it is Steinway's prerogative to refuse to do the job, except on their own terms, I just don't know what to do about it, and, as you can appreciate, I cannot undertake to buy the piano even at the very reasonable price at which you offered it to me, unless I feel assured that the rebuilding would be successful and that my investment would in that way be wise. It has been a very annoying experience because it is one of the few pianos in North America that I can honestly say that I adore.[67]

As always, once Glenn became emotionally attached to an object, he could not let go of it. The outcome was that either he clung to it permanently, like he did with respect to his piano chair, which he took with him on his tours, or if he had to let go of his object of love, it was at great personal emotional expense. This is exactly what happened with piano #266, which he desperately sought after in the 1957-1958 season, only to be forced to separate from it. This drama preceded his European tour, which meant that Gould was already greatly sensitized to any Steinway-piano-related stress. His conflicts continued to torment him. In Berlin, he came to the conclusion that he no longer enjoyed concert grand pianos in general and insisted on playing on a Steinway baby-grand piano that was used for rehearsals. In accordance with Gould's wishes, this piano was wheeled onto the stage for performance with Karajan. In Stockholm, Gould's conflict with Steinways erupted into a small scandal when he played and recorded on a Bechstein piano. In a letter from Stockholm to Homburger, Gould wrote about "the local Steinway dealer who is for some inexplicable reason rather annoyed that I am playing a Bechstein."[68] In another letter from Cologne, Gould penned these words: "I am now up to my neck in hot water with Kuhne (who wrote to remind me that I am sailing under the Steinway flag) and so this might be the most welcome fee I ever earned."[69] Kuhne was a top executive of the large Steinway firm in Hamburg.

Gould's initial idea, when he began his tour in Germany, was to rent a Steinway concert piano, either in Berlin or in Hamburg, and transport it to Vienna for his next concert and recording there. In the process of his growing frustrations, illness and stage fright, which all complicated his piano selection ordeal, he was at a loss to make up his mind and choose a piano. "I no longer like any of the large [Steinway] pianos here [in Berlin]. I find the action of all the full-size pianos unsympathetic ..."[70] The pianist's conflict around the issue of authority escalated as expressed further in his letter: "I am so furious with the Hamburg Steinway people that I am just ready to take any drastic action."[71] Needless to say, he did not take any drastic action, but got sick instead, which temporarily took care of everything. It spared him a confrontation with Kuhne; it precluded the piano selection; but most of all, it gave him a reason for a series of cancellations which saved him from his menacing stage fright. By this time, since his malady in Salzburg at the end of August, Gould claimed that he had lost about thirty pounds in two months, getting down to his teenage weight of 150 pounds. On account of his acute illness, which he claimed to be a right-sided bronchitis and viral nephritis, Gould retreated to Hamburg's Hotel Vier Jahreszeiten to recuperate. He was under doctor's care and was prescribed bed rest, whereas no medications were prescribed. During this time, he remained recumbent or he puttered around in his room producing reams of letters, most of them to his manager. He summed up his current status in the following paragraphs written to his grandmother on October 27, 1958:

> I have now been here for two weeks tomorrow and I will probably have to stay one week more. I am sure you know, I had some rather bad after effects of the flu—principally something called nephritis which is an infection of the kidney. Actually, I am now feeling very much better and probably because of the strict diet I am on (no protein for 10 days) and because of all the staying in bed, I feel more rested than for many weeks. So perhaps it was all for the best although it certainly made a great mess of this tour—altogether 9 concerts cancelled although two or three of them I will be able to do later in the year.
>
> Although I would like to get out of this damp climate (it rains almost every day here as in London), I am extremely comfortable at this hotel. I have two nice rooms looking out over the inner harbor—actually a small lake which they call the Alster, and the ferry boats dock just opposite my window. So it makes a fine view.[72]

And what was the reaction of others to Gould's behavior? As the press reports indicated, Gould's admirers felt vastly disappointed for having to forego the pleasure of seeing him making music. How did the Viennese feel at the prospect of Gould shipping to them a Steinway piano from Hamburg, as if they did not have appropriate concert pianos of their own? How did the Steinways feel about Gould playing a Bechstein in Stockholm and an old Steinway baby grand in Berlin, disregarding a wide choice of expensive concert grands? Moreover, how did the impresario, Herr Kollitsch, feel about Gould canceling three quarters of all his engagements in West Germany? There is plenty of evidence about the reaction of Kollitsch, who was incensed and "thunderstruck" by Gould's purported illness and seclusion in his hotel room. Kollitsch quickly traveled from Berlin to Hamburg. All his power of negotiation and persuasion were in vain, and he heavy-heartedly agreed to cancel a number of concerts in accordance with Gould's requests. It turned out that this was too costly a feat for Gould. From the income he had earned so far, which was 4,000 German marks for two concerts in Berlin, and 2,500 marks for the one in Wiesbaden, Gould had to pay Kollitsch around 300 marks as a penalty for cancellation. On top of that, he had to finance the services of two men playing the role of aides. This, together with his hotel expenses, left Gould without sufficient funds for living, and he urged Homburger to wire him $1,000. Most importantly, how did Gould feel about himself as a person and as an acclaimed musician for the "mess" he created and the anger he brought upon himself?

"How did the Steinway management feel about Glenn Gould's selectiveness of the pianos for his public concerts," I asked a high Steinway official in New York, Mr. Peter Goodrich.[73]

"I wouldn't be able to tell you that because his concert career was finished long before I came on board," Mr. Goodrich answered politely.

"The incident involving your chief piano tuner, Mr. Hupfer, which was widely publicized, is suggestive that there were some problems between Steinway and Mr. Glenn Gould," I persisted in the same line of questioning.

"Mr. Hupfer was a very nice man. Did you by any chance read this biographical article about Mr. Hupfer?" Mr. Goodrich changed the topic.

"No, I am sorry, I didn't. Do you happen to have a copy?" I asked.

"I don't have one right now but I would be happy to mail it to you." Mr. Goodrich was eager to help.

"Thank you, I appreciate it. One more thing about Gould. I enjoyed very much your Hall of Fame with portraits of great pianists, but I noticed that you don't have Gould's portrait." I did not hide my disappointment.

"Oh, we have one but I wouldn't know where we put it. We change them from time to time."[74] Mr. Goodrich was somewhat apologetic.

The ominous absence of Gould's portrait at the magnificent Hall of Fame at Steinway & Sons in New York spoke for itself. Gould did not play by the rules, which cost him a lot; in this case, it led to a strained relationship with the Steinway executives. He did not make efforts to be more flexible and diplomatic but was rather compelled to repeat his problems and suffer afterwards, which all contributed toward his early withdrawal from his public concert career.

Though Gould's lavishly planned tour in Germany was supposed to be the summit of his success, it had to be severely reduced to his appearances in Berlin and Wiesbaden only. Having recovered from the Hamburg crisis, Gould returned to Brussels as a stopover to Italy. There he met with Homburger, who flew from Toronto in order to accompany Glenn on the rest of the trip. Earlier on, while still in Hamburg, Gould tried to persuade his manager to cancel all concerts in Vienna and Israel, which Homburger vigorously refused to do. In anticipation of Homburger's wrath, Gould wrote to him: "I think I can already see you picking up an impassioned pen and writing me not to be a fool, or similar sentiments couched in softer, more soothing Homburgerian tones."[75] Somehow, the two men reached a compromise, through which the appearances in Vienna were irreversibly canceled but the Israel tour fortunately was saved, whereas out of several performances scheduled in Italy, those in Turin and Rome were cancelled, and Gould agreed to follow through with only one recital in Florence. This decrease in concerts was not so much due to Gould's capricious tendencies and his need to be in control but was more caused by his unstable depressive disorder.[76] His despondent mood was portrayed in his letter written at the beginning of this European tour to his friend Edward Viets, who invited him for Christmas:

> Dear Ted, September 9, 1958
> ... I am sure that you will not find it too unsociable if I discourage all ideas of entertainment at that time [Christmas]. I shall be just back from Europe, undoubtedly exhausted (I am exhausted before I leave) and I have a feeling that I would not be in any frame of mind for socializing at that time. So please, no dinners, no parties, no interviews, no photographers, no autograph hunters and no stage door Janes.[77]

"I am exhausted before I leave" is a telling statement pointing to the extent of Gould's fatigue, which along with his lack of energy to do things, insomnia and proneness to physical illness is suggestive that he was depressed. This melancholic testimony of Gould's letter referred to his last concerts scheduled for that year in Detroit, December 26 and 27, when he was invited to spend Christmas with Viets. Though it may have looked like Gould could stop giving concerts at any time due to his frequent bouts of malaise, he had enough resilience in him to carry on for another six years of his performing career.

After the "Hamburg crisis," the next destination of this busy tour was Florence. In this city, famous for its cultural heritage and inestimable art treasures, Gould not only was not in crisis but even modestly enjoyed himself. Though hardly practicing the piano in the previous five weeks, he gave a successful recital playing his beloved and familiar program—Bach's *Goldberg Variations*; Mozart's Sonata in C Major, K. 330 and Schoenberg's Suite for Piano, for which he was acknowledged with six curtain calls. He even did some basic sightseeing and socializing in Florence. His letter to Benjamin Sonnenberg II of New York, dated January 30, 1959, shows that Gould attended a reception hosted by Mrs. Goth. He described Mrs. Goth in this most complimentary way:

> All of her Grande Dame of Florence instincts came out by the end of the evening, she was suitably mollified and I quite liked her ... I gather from what other people have told me about her that she has done a great deal for composers and ex-patriots living there but I wonder if her philanthropies are entirely altruistic. In any case, she is a fascinating woman and I think basically a very kind one, so I am grateful to you for having arranged an introduction.[78]

It is curious why Gould wanted so much to play in Florence, while readily resisting appearing elsewhere in Italy. What motivated him to spend a social evening with Mrs. Goth? Through careful analysis of Gould's massive correspondence, which sprang from this tour in 1958, it is painfully evident that there was no exchange of letters between him and his mother. Meanwhile, his mother was the closest person in his life. Be reminded that her name was Florence and that her sixty-sixth birthday was on October 28, while Gould was still on his sick leave in Hamburg. It may very well be that the city's name, Florence, evoked deep feelings in the son for his mother. Having made her worried by being ill, he was now ready to cheer her up with a belated birthday gift, a successful recital in Florence. His visit to Mrs. Goth was a way to reconnect with his repressed feelings for his mother. One likely explanation for not writing to his parents was a deep sense of shame for being a "bad boy" by causing trouble with Steinway in Europe and by not honoring his duties with respect to the concert tour. Once Gould was able to materialize the performance in Florence and overcome his remorse, it gave him an incentive, a second wind, to go through the eleven concerts in Israel in the next eighteen days.

MORE PIANO CONQUESTS

For the truth is that Glenn Gould is a real musical genius ...
Haaretz, Israel[79]

As a creation of multiple historical and political forces and the activism of the Zionist movement, in 1948 Israel emerged as a newly-born state. Ben-Gurion was its founder and the first prime minister. Ten years later, when Gould and Homburger arrived in Tel Aviv, they were instantly able to spot the major difference between the placid situation they left behind in Canada and the tumultuous, military-focused atmosphere in Israel. Not fully reconciled to be living together within the confines of the same state, the indigenous Arabs and Israelis carried on a tense and hostile relationship that often ended in violent skirmishes. Israel was a land of warriors in which a majority of its male population and many young women wore soldiers' uniforms, carried firearms and had that typical fierce and ready-for-action look on their faces. The organized cultural pursuits and entertainment industry barely had started to develop in this new country. Tel Aviv, the nation's largest city and a port on the Mediterranean Sea, with less than half a million inhabitants in the late 1950s, happened to be within a short geographical distance from the West Bank, which was then still in the domain of the kingdom of Jordan. Hence, the arrival of the internationally famous pianist, Glenn Gould, was well publicized as a rare cultural treat for this new country in the Middle East. Gould stayed at the American resort called Herzliya-by-the-Sea, which was situated about fifteen miles north of Tel Aviv. He rented a car from the Hertz Company and proceeded to drive fearlessly, all by himself reaching the unsafe zone within steps from the Jordanian border.

Despite the relative danger, Gould pursued his driving adventures with flamboyance and ease. If anything, he was more ill at ease in anticipation of his upcoming public performances in Israel. Dumbfounded by, as Gould put it, the "rotten" piano at the concert hall in Tel Aviv, and disheartened to begin with, Gould could hardly go through the rehearsal of the Beethoven Second Concerto, which he was supposed to play with Jean Martinon conducting the Israel Philharmonic. Years later, in an interview with Jonathan Cott, Gould reflected on this rehearsal with self-derogation, saying that he "played like a pig." His well-known fastidious taste and need for an exclusive piano was brutally challenged, as here in this new and desert country there were only "desert" pianos with which one had to make do. Not throwing in the towel, Gould drove along the seashore viewing the crop of orange trees that extended all the way to the sand dunes in an attempt to relax and bring his consternation under control:

> So I sat in my car in the sand dune and decided to imagine myself back in my living room ... and first of all to imagine the living room, which took some doing because I'd been away from it for three months at this point. And I tried to imagine where everything was in the room, then visualize the piano, and ... this sounds ridiculously yogistic, I'd never done it before in precisely these terms ... but so help me it worked.[80]

Through this step-by-step psychological imagery,[81] he recalled what it was like to play on his Chickering piano in his preferred environment. By bolstering himself with self-hypnosis, Gould was able to regain a measure of inner peace and strength, enough to help him carry on with the performance. The virtuoso also had this extraordinary ability to go over his piano part and even to "re-create the admirable tactile circumstances" all inside his mind. Reassured and re-energized, and with little actual practicing, Gould interpreted Beethoven's Concerto no. 2 before the public with astonishing music artistry. Much like the Russians, the Israeli audience offered him euphoric and untarnished admiration. The critic of *Haaretz* was as ecstatic as the audiences were. He mused:

> The soloist, Glenn Gould, offers an opportunity to quote the famous music critic R. Schuman when he said: "Gentlemen, lift your hats; there is a genius," and in fact, such playing moves the listener to the depth of his soul by its almost religious expression. We have never heard anything like it in one of our concerts ... One must hear Glenn Gould. He is a musical sensation.[82]

Artur Minden, a lawyer in Toronto and the chairman of the United Jewish Appeal Study Mission, recorded:

> Tel Aviv—Glenn Gould, internationally celebrated Canadian pianist, played for one of the world's most critical audiences—and more than two thousand rose in a body to applaud him.
>
> Cheering, hundreds from the orchestra seats surged to the stage, and the soloist had to return from the wings seven times to acknowledge the continuing acclaim.
>
> In the audience were eighteen Canadians, all from Toronto, who had just completed a twelve-day United Jewish Appeal study mission, spending their last night in Israel.[83]

In Tel Aviv, Gould spent three pleasant evenings dining and debating music at the home of Abe Cohen, the manager of the Israel Philharmonic. A confirmed teetotaler, Gould declined to indulge in sipping on the authentic orange liqueur, Sabra, but was satisfied by quantities of chilled, nonalcoholic orange beverages made from this abundant, sun-raised fruit. Walter Homburger, who accompanied Gould, reported a few interesting anecdotes:

> Jerusalem, Dec. 6. ... Although Gould's schedule is a heavy one he has had

> many opportunities to experience the warm hospitality and friendly disposition of the Israelis. Earlier this week he made front page news in the local papers when it was discovered that, unannounced and unescorted, he had visited a communal settlement within one mile of the Jordanian border.
>
> Glenn was exploring the countryside in his rented car. He picked up a hitch-hiker, who turned out to be an immigrant from India, returning to his communal settlement. He directed Glenn to his homestead which consisted of dwellings for 100 families.
>
> Gould was invited in and offered tea. When he requested some milk his host, without batting an eye, rolled up his sleeves, set off for the barn and called over his shoulder; "just a moment, I'll get it." Gould still does not know whether he was served cow's or goat's milk.[84]

As Gould continued his musical tour in Israel, in the space of the next two weeks he dashed off to Jerusalem for a repeat of the Beethoven Concerto no. 2 at Edison Hall, and then to Haifa for a recital, to be back in Tel Aviv for several recitals. Again the enthusiastic critic of *Haaretz* wrote:

> For everybody who had the good fortune to attend the recital of Glenn Gould yesterday night at the Frederick Mann Auditorium, it was the greatest musical experience of his life. Gould is only 25 years old, but his playing is of a depth as if imbued with the accumulated knowledge of generations and generations of musicians ... For the truth is that Glenn Gould is a real musical genius, which is an infrequent occurrence in our era of many 'geniuses.'[85]

Once he returned to Toronto, Gould wrote a letter to Dick O'Hagan in Berlin, affectionately alluding to his visit to Israel:

> Even I ... with all the bourgeois thinking of my Western background, was in a very happy mental condition while I was there and felt myself very much attuned to stone huts, donkey carts, shepherds and flocks of goats. I think I might even go back as a tourist.[86]

Gould's music conquest in Israel was undisputed, and both his audiences and the music scholars honored him. After his return home, Gould was notified by the Department of External Affairs in Ottawa that he had been awarded the Harriet Cohen Bach Medal for excellence in music performance. Gould's rather controversial music year of 1958, full of high anxiety, yielded a great cultural achievement and finished on a positive note.

For Gould, 1959 could be dubbed as the year of the Beethoven concerti. It was also the year that brought him fresh laurels and represented the highest point of his concertizing productivity, with more than fifty major public performances. It is noted that great concert pianists average about a hundred concerts per year in order to make a living and to keep up the momentum of fame. There are also those hyperproductive ones, like the Russian pianist Sviatoslav Richter, who was capable of yielding up to two hundred major concerts in a year. Gould's output as a performing artist was, therefore, on the low side, which was consistent with his health issues. The older he grew, the less he was able to overcome the rigors of his demanding career.

Hardly rested from the lengthy European-Israeli tour and from a pair of Christmas concerts in Detroit, at the start of the new year, Gould was thrown into the whirlwind of his American tour. As always, the American audiences felt a sense of awe and privilege in anticipation of Gould's concerts. Meanwhile, the publicists rubbed their hands at the prospect of sensational reports on how to raise Gould to Olympic heights or how to besmirch him as they had never done to anyone before. Gould opened on January 2, 1959, in Minneapolis by playing the poetic Beethoven Concerto in G Major, no. 4, with Antal Dorati and the Minneapolis Symphony, and immediately after on January 5 and 6 in Houston, where he demonstrated his unmatched virtuosity in interpretation of the Beethoven Concerto in E-flat Major, no. 5, with Andre Kostelanetz and the Houston Symphony. From there he performed a successful recital in Pasadena, California on January 9, where he virtually mesmerized the audience with his stunning rendition of Bach's Goldbergs. As often before, a massive applause rose from the audience with shouts of "m-o-o-o-r-e" and "b-r-a-a-v-o-o-o," expressing their spontaneous unqualified regard for the man and his music. Gould continued to publicly display his remarkable piano artistry and his deep emotional attachment to Beethoven as a composer by continually playing and recording his compositions.

Having conquered the Berlin audiences with a successful piano performance of the Beethoven Concerto no. 3 with Karajan in the previous year, Gould played the same piece in San Francisco at the War Opera Memorial Hall on January 14, 15 and 16, 1959, with Enrique Jorda and the San Francisco Symphony. The renowned music critic, Alfred Frankenstein, of the *San Francisco Chronicle* wrote:

> Gould played Beethoven's third concerto. Before he did so, I was wishing that he selected something else, but afterward I was very happy with his choice, for he seems to be the only pianist in the world who knows what this concerto is all about.[87]

Frankenstein and San Franciscan spectators adored Gould. Something is to be said about the love affair between Gould and his San Francisco audiences. This was the third out of five concert-giving visits to San Francisco, whose music admirers could not get enough of Gould. The feeling was reciprocal, and if it had not been for the pianist's developing phobia of flying, he most likely would have returned to San Francisco after his concert career had ended. In this gorgeous city, Gould was even relaxed enough to pursue some sightseeing. He took a ride on the famous San Francisco open cable car and visited Fisherman's Warf. He could not get enough of the splendid view there, which was so reminiscent of the view from his own private dock at Lake Simcoe. "Please come back again!" was a familiar plea of San Franciscans for more eye-and-ear contacts with Gould. He did return, and on November 1 of the same year he gave a recital consisting of his music "delicatessen"—the works of Sweelinck, Schoenberg Suite for Piano, Mozart's Sonata in C Major, K. 330, and Bach's *Goldberg Variations*. The last appearance in San Francisco was in February 1963, when Gould, in a series of three concerts, delivered the Bach D Minor and the Schoenberg Concerto, together with Jorda conducting the San Francisco Symphony. Overall, it is estimated that more than 30,000 San Franciscans, many of them more than once, had the rare opportunity to hear Gould in person.

In the spring of 1959, Gould embarked on his third and last European tour, which was done in two separate trips. At first, in May, he performed in Berlin and London, while in August he performed in Salzburg and Lucerne. In West Berlin, Gould was on familiar ground at the Konzertsaal of the Hochschule Fur Musik, where he gave a flawless recital as a part of the Robert Kollitsch Series. Gould's loyal friend and devotee, Silvia Kind, recalled the event with compassion:

> The only public solo recital by Glenn that I attended was again one given in Berlin. I remember preludes and fugues from the Well Tempered Clavier, a wonderful swinging crystal clear Mozart, a splendid piece by Sweelinck, Beethoven's op. 110 (with the middle part standing out in the fugue!) and a marvelous Schoenberg. His appearance—strikingly young, lonely, shy, and sitting on his little low chair—almost moved me to tears.[88]

Though the Berlin experience was reassuring, it could not serve as an antidote to Gould's rising anticipation anxiety in the face of his London debut. As a part of the Beethoven Festival, the London project was indeed a monumental task of performing all five Beethoven concerti in a ten-day span. Gould appeared at the Royal Festival Hall with the London Symphony Orchestra conducted by Josef Krips. Together, they played the first four Beethoven concerti, whereas the performance of Concerto no. 5, *Emperor*, which is regarded to be the most brilliant and the most beautiful of all the Beethoven Concerti, had to be cancelled because of Gould's typical pre-concert ailment. Like the enchanted audiences of other countries, England too was watching Gould at the keyboard with the utmost interest and appreciation. The critic of *The London Telegraph* complimented: "I came away with the impression of a unique combination of exceptional musical gifts with a spiritual innocence and single-mindedness not common among professional pianists of any age."[89] *The London Times* reported:

> In fact he immersed himself wholeheartedly in the music as soon as he began to play, with no self-conscious thoughts of Mr. Gould at all, and had his audience spellbound with the immense musical concentration, the vividly refreshing imagination, and the sheer tonal beauty of the sounds he drew from his instrument ... Mr. Gould allowed us to hear this familiar music as if with new ears and a keen sense of wonder.[90]

Despite those isolated reports that honored Gould's music adequately, the general stiff-upper-lip tone of British critics was rather cynical. Once again, they betrayed the Canadian virtuoso by focusing heavily on his extra-musical behavior. In his home town, *The Toronto Star* reproduced the acerbic review of Gould's playing originally published by *The Manchester Guardian*, rather than choosing one of the more empathic reviews. In his letter dated June 30 to his journalist friend, Gladys Riskind, Gould revealed how hurt he was by the disloyalty of the *Star's* editors:

> ... they devoted an editorial to me, a very flattering and gracious editorial, but written in the manner of an apology. It took the tone that the London Press had overstated my mannerisms and that all good Canadians would rise with irate dis-

> pleasure at the slightest inference that I was anything other than the archetype of the well-scrubbed, gentlemanly boy next door. It seemed odd that it was also the *Star* that reproduced the *Manchester Guardian* to the exclusion of all others.[91]

Being a well-scrubbed, gentlemanly boy was the epitome of the well-behaved darling that Glenn was raised to be. This bothered him so much that he spent his entire lifetime undoing and rebelling against this model of himself in an attempt to build a new and unique identity.

The emotional injury to his self-esteem following the critical blast in London was amplified by the tragic loss of his cousin, Barry, on June 6, drowned shortly upon Glenn's return from England. Glenn, who was totally loyal to his clan, kept his grief deeply private, never referring to it in his letters. The emotional loss due to Barry's untimely death was devastatingly taxing on his already frail mental health. His friends and business associates expected him to carry on with a show of strength. As a virtuoso, Gould had to pretend that he was completely prepared for the second part of his European tour. Leaving on tour meant experiencing his phobia of flying once again, more separation anxiety, more solitude and unshared grief, not to mention his intolerance of the austerity of hotel rooms. All of this grief and anxiety had to be camouflaged. He fulfilled these expectations when one more time, on a hot summer day on August 25, Gould appeared in Salzburg at the Mozarteum in a solo performance of Schoenberg's Suite for Piano, Mozart's Sonata in C Major, K. 330, and Bach's *Goldberg Variations*. Given the extenuating circumstances, particularly his bereavement and high external stress, there was really no escape from becoming ill. By the time Gould arrived in Lucerne, Switzerland, he was exhausted enough to entertain a concert cancellation. This, of course, was quite risky and would likely have jeopardized his international reputation. The pianist had to force himself to go ahead with the concert despite his oppressive chest congestion and fever.

Lucerne, the ancient Swiss town on Lake Lucerne, is exceptionally picturesque in the summertime. Hemmed in by the towering Mount Pilatus and by its feudal walls and watchtowers, the city of Lucerne demonstrates more than ten centuries worth of historical monuments. Gould always had a passion for lakes and waterfronts, which reminded him of his home on Lake Simcoe. Just a year before, he enjoyed the lake view from his hotel room in Hamburg, and here in Lucerne he had a similar chance to view the lake and its busy sightseeing steamers. Gould's concert in Lucerne was a great success. Once again his music friend, harpsichordist Silvia Kind, made a point of attending this Gould-Karajan historical performance, and as an authentic eyewitness, she reported:

> The third time I heard Glenn was at the Lucerne Festival in August 1959, again with Karajan, and again in the Bach D-Minor Concerto. He arrived with a bad cold and fever and wanted to cancel the concert, but it was too late. When he appeared on the stage, he was very pale but his performance was absolutely wonderful. I remember that as I went backstage a great crowd tried to rush after him, but was held back. In any case, Gould always kept his precious and fragile hands to himself.[92]

The concert in Lucerne and Gould's overall music popularity stayed permanently engraved in the memory of the people. Decades after the fact, the Swiss press from time to time reports on

Gould's life, anything from little stories from his childhood to reviews of his post-mortem recording releases.

The last third of the 1959 concert season was marked by a busy concert schedule. Gould toured the United States from San Francisco to Denver, Atlanta and Syracuse to the Canadian cities of Winnipeg, Manitoba, and London, Ontario. His recital in Berkeley, California, where he championed his typical Gouldian program of the works of Berg, Schoenberg, Hindemith, Krenek and Morawetz, won over the minds and hearts of both audiences and critics. The press raved:

> A phenomenon is undoubtedly the best word one can use to describe the brilliant young Canadian pianist Glenn Gould. His performance last Sunday evening at the Harmon Gymnasium was nothing short of miraculous.[93]

In Cleveland, where he was already a legendary music hero to his fans, Gould once again thrilled his audiences. On November 26 and 28, he played the Schoenberg concerto and Bach's Brandenburg Concerto no. 5 with the Cleveland Orchestra conducted by Louis Lane. On November 27, Gould appeared in Severance Chamber Hall, as the composer at the performance of his own *String Quartet no. 1* played by the Symphonia String Quartet. The critic Klaus George Roy of *The Christian Science Monitor* wrote:

> In a dazzling sequence of protean transformation, 27 year old Glenn Gould astonished and delighted musical Cleveland over the Thanksgiving weekend. Within three days Mr. Gould appeared at Severance Hall as pianist, author, lecturer, historian, teacher, and composer, excelling in all.[94]

Be aware that at the same time Gould's triumph in Ohio occurred, his inner life was crowded with major emotional upheavals and losses. He just lost his cousin, Barry, and was quite worried about having to move soon out of his parental home. Underneath his public image, the piano wizard kept his tormenting emotions far from his spectators. Soon after this Cleveland music conquest, his teacher Guerrero died in November, which was followed by Gould's moving out of his parents' home and entering a new phase as a solitary artistic figure.

Beyond his public concerts and draining inner conflicts, Gould's life was rich and full with his radio and TV appearances; recording sessions for Columbia in New York; writing for music magazines and liner notes; correspondence with fans and colleagues, and his legendary, prolonged telephone calls. His contract with Columbia Masterworks stipulated the making of three recordings every two years. Since 1955, when Gould recorded the Goldbergs, he had several more records released. By 1960, Gould chose a few of Bach's works, such as Partita no. 5 and 6, Beethoven's Concerto no. 2, Bach's D Minor Concerto and others, which were recorded and released with Leonard Bernstein conducting the Columbia Symphony Orchestra. Simultaneously, Gould was also active in broadcasting and recording for the Canadian Broadcasting Corporation. By 1960, he released a few records, among them his own composition String Quartet, op. 1, and Brahms' Quintet in F Minor, op. 34, both with the Montreal String Quartet. These numerous activities, beyond his live concerts, took on a life of their own. Gould, the public entertainer at the keyboard, became a star in two autobiographical films made by the National Film Board of Canada. He was featured in a relaxed and casual way during a recording session in the New York Columbia Studio and at his summer cottage. These films, titled *Glenn Gould on the Record* and *Glenn Gould off the Record*, were shown repeatedly worldwide during his lifetime and after.

The last five years of Gould's performing career, from 1960 to 1964, were akin to a marathon runner's exhaustion in the last stretch, when extreme fatigue, leg cramps, and breathlessness result in a terrific inner temptation to quit and lie down. Glenn savored the idea of quitting and even made official predictions of retirement from the concert stage.

Having been overworked as a performing pianist in the previous year and having moved out of his parents' home, Gould entered the year 1960 in low spirits. In spite of that, he gave his first concert on March 2 at the Lyric Theater in Baltimore, playing with the Baltimore Symphony conducted by Peter Herman Adler. On that occasion, critic George Kent Bellows of *The Baltimore Evening Sun* offered this commendable review:

> Mr. Gould, playing Beethoven's Fourth Concerto, gave a magnificent performance, one that plumbed the emotional depths of the score, but one that in no way exaggerated ... And what a joy it is to have a young artist come along who neither bangs nor breaks the speed limit. Mr. Gould's deliberation was calculated, but all within the realm of good taste and awareness of architectural line. It was great playing and the audience was quite aware of it.[95]

In Baltimore, backstage at the theater, Gould met Dr. Joseph Stevens, psychiatrist and harpsichordist, who introduced himself as a friend of Dr. Peter Ostwald. From then on, Gould and Stevens became partners in many long telephone conversations. As a keyboard specialist, Stevens was of much interest to Gould because they shared the love of the piano and harpsichord literature. As a psychiatrist, Stevens had even more appeal to Gould, who was just going through a period of depression following the Steinway incident and the shoulder injury from which he was recovering. Gould's frequent telephone calls to Stevens reflected his need for reassurance and emotional support. While Gould befriended Stevens as a music friend, the two men never entered a professional therapeutic relationship, and Stevens never really became Gould's "doctor."

Hibernating through the winter, Gould partially recovered from his bout of depression and shoulder pain so that by the summertime he emerged with renewed self-confidence and a fresh music repertoire. His concerts in Stratford, Ontario, and Vancouver, British Columbia, highlighted the performing season. In Stratford, on July 24, Gould was brilliant in the performance of the Bach D Minor and the fifth Brandenburg Concerto in D Major no. 5 for clavier, flute and violin with Oskar Shumsky as a solo violinist and the National Festival Orchestra. Immediately after this concert, Gould flew to Vancouver, where he graced his loyal audiences with three appearances. On July 27, in a double-bill concert, he played Beethoven's Fourth Concerto and Mozart's C Minor with Louis Lane conducting the Vancouver Festival Chamber Orchestra at the Queen Elizabeth Theatre. For Gould, playing with Lane was most reassuring. Two days later, on July 29, there was another special and rare treat for the admirers of Gould's artistry. This was a recital featuring works of Beethoven, the Tempest Sonata, the Eroica Variations, and Berg's Sonata. The Tempest Sonata in D Minor op. 31, no. 2 is known to be one of Beethoven's greatest works. The Eroica Variations in E flat Major op. 35, are based on the original theme from Beethoven's *Prometheus*, and the same melody reappears in the finale of his Eroica Symphony. The Eroica Variations are famous for their impressive architecture, lack of embellishment, seriousness and thoughtfulness. The focus is on its heroic melody and the various ways of restating it.

Variations in music are a form of improvisation by the composer. Beethoven was known as an excellent improviser. He did not only compose music in the confines of his room, but played new music ad-lib in front of his audiences. Inspired by a certain theme, he had an irresistible pressure from within to play it in different forms or variations. When Beethoven was ad-libbing in his recitals, it was amusing for him and entertaining for his audience. Improvisation in classical music, or even more in jazz, represents a relative freedom of rules and restraints, permitting the expression of the immediate mood. In that, improvisation differs from interpretation proper, where an instrumentalist follows the prescribed text. Gould was exceptionally good at interpreting Bach's *Goldberg Variations* and, in this case, Beethoven's Variations, because in them he felt a sense of freedom and latitude. Though he did not improvise on them, he was able to recreate them, adding his own personal touch without major alterations to the script.

Following this successful recital in Vancouver, where he masterfully delivered both the Tempest and the Eroica Variations, Gould gave his third concert on August 2, and demonstrated his expertise in Schoenberg's music. He played selected Schoenberg songs, the Book of Hanging Gardens, Schoenberg's Suite for Piano and Ode to Napoleon Bonaparte with the Vancouver String Quartet. In his Suite for Piano, composed in 1924, Schoenberg made use of his newly invented twelve-tone technique and atonal music; whereas in Ode to Napoleon in 1943 he refined this technique and blended it with traditional tonal music. Arnold Schoenberg, along with other contemporary composers of the twentieth century, such as Stravinsky, Bartok, Prokofiev and Webern, represents a new, nontraditional style in music. These composers produced piano works that strongly de-emphasized the popular romantic style of the previous century and incorporated more intellectual, often unorthodox, elements into their music. The renowned American critic, Harold Schonberg, in his book *The Great Pianists*, put forward this concise commentary with respect to modern classical music:

> In the realm of the piano and pianists, it all meant that the concept of the Virtuoso-as-Hero was being retired to an honored place in history. As a replacement came the scholar-pianist, the musician-pianist, the re-creator of the composer's thought, the abdication of technique qua technique. Virtuosity indeed became something of a dirty word.[96]

Gould, himself a denier of the concept of virtuosity and romanticism in music, was particularly attracted to the cerebral aspects of Schoenberg's music. He greatly identified with Schoenberg's expressionist style at the piano and became an absolute performing master of the same. When Gould played Schoenberg's music, the critics were at a loss to compare his playing to any other simply because there was no reference point. While Schoenberg's music was unpopular and rarely played at public concerts, Gould researched it in depth, perfected it and kept delivering it to the broad public audiences; thereby, he evolved into a prophet and world authority on Schoenberg's piano music. Among his many projects are his extensive radio programs dedicated to Schoenberg and his music in ten parts in 1974, and *Schoenberg: the First Hundred Years—A Documentary Fantasy for Radio*.

In the same year, 1960, of significance were Gould's concerts in Detroit, where on October 12 and 13 he played Strauss's Burlesque, Beethoven's Concerto no. 2 and Bach's Fifth Brandenburg Concerto with the Detroit Symphony directed by Paul Paray. The reviews of Gould's piano artistry hailed him in a familiar manner. Josef Mossman of *The Detroit News* reported:

> Gould played the piano in Bach's Fifth Brandenburg Concerto and Beethoven's Second Concerto. In both, he displayed the profoundly searching musicianship that ranks him not only as a great young pianist, but as great among all pianists.[97]

On November 15, Gould gave a piano recital in Toronto at the Music Hall of his former music school, The Toronto Conservatory of Music, as a part of the "Artist Series." He performed two Beethoven works: Sonata, Opus 31, no. 2, and Eroica Variations, Opus 35. After the intermission he presented Brahms's Intermezzi and Berg's Sonata Opus 1. For this last piece, Gould wrote the following program notes:

> In 1908, a young man named Alban Berg produced a piano movement which must surely be considered among the most auspicious "Opus 1's" ever written. At the time Berg was 23 and completing his studies with the most demonic disciplinarian of the day, Arnold Schoenberg. In consigning his apprenticeship to Schoenberg, Berg made a wise choice. The intense, fervently romantic young Berg learned that whenever one honestly defies a tradition, one becomes, in reality, the more responsible to it ...[98]

This paragraph shows Gould's admiration for this music piece and identification with Berg as a composer who dared to defy tradition by departing from tonality to chromaticism. Gould became very personal when he stated that "whenever one honestly defies a tradition, one becomes ... more responsible to it," as if he was very familiar with the act of "defying a tradition" through his highly unorthodox interpretations of music. In the next paragraph, Gould says that sonata portrays:

> ... the language of collapse and disbelief, of musical "weltschmerz," the last stand of tonality betrayed and inundated by the chromaticism which gave it birth ...[99]

Again, Gould refers to the collapse of romantic trends in music, thereby supporting his own theory of inferiority of the nineteenth century's romantic music.

The concert season of 1960 appropriately finished with Gould's second appearance in Toronto, where on December 6 and 7 Gould performed at Massey Hall the Schoenberg concerto and Mozart's C Minor with Walter Susskind conducting the Toronto Symphony. John Beckwith of *The Toronto Daily Star* was greatly inspired by Gould's playing and wrote in superlatives:

Glenn Gould, the eighth wonder of the music world, returned to his native haunts last night to join Walter Susskind and the Toronto Symphony Orchestra at Massey Hall in superb, deeply thoughtful performances of piano concerti by Schoenberg and Mozart, such as should provide concertgoers with enough spiritual nourishment to last out the rest of the winter.[100]

Chapter VII

THE INNER WORLD

THE GOULD TRIANGLE

> If you have never been hated by your child, you have never been a parent.
>
> Bette Davis[1]

Those of Gould's fans who, despite what they know about him, are still puzzled and in search of answers, may want to engage in an in-depth study of his inner world, which holds the secrets and keys to a more satisfactory understanding. Why did he withdraw from the concert stage so early? What made him so eccentric and what was his real story behind and beyond the observable? This understanding is possible only by pursuing a detailed scientific analysis, which is often confusing and painstaking. In the end, this type of inquiry will reward the seeker with more truthful answers but, more importantly, will demystify Gould and bring him closer to his admirers.

The quality of parenting, particularly the nature of maternal care, is essential in the future emotional development of the child. Knowing more about Glenn also means having to know more about his mother-child relationship from his birth on. This is rather hard to accomplish because the Goulds were always so secretive about their personal lives. Neither Florrie nor Glenn left many obvious documents behind, like letters and diaries, to help understand the essence of their relationship. Fortunately, certain papers survived, and among those rare ones is Glenn's poem that he wrote to his mother for Valentine's Day, when he was seven and a half years of age. It reads:

Dear Mistress

1. Sometimes I'm as bad as can be,
   I run away quite often;
   But when I give you my sad look
   I know your heart will soften.
2. and when I'm home I try to show
   I'm really not so dumb,
   and when I get a pat from you
   I know you love me, Mum.

3. E'en when I'm given a gentle shove,
and Master Glenn says 'bother,
Get out of here you big old hound'
I know I got you, Mother.
4. 'Cause every day throughout the year
you're good to me dear Mummy
you fix my ears, and let me out
and make my dinners yummy.

Your setter
Nicky[2]

Glenn was quite a poet! If he had never made any other declaration of love to his mother, this poem would have been enough to show his love and attachment to her. In the scarcity of knowledge about Florence Greig Gould, Glenn's Valentine's card is considered to be a rare illustration of the mother-son relationship. In his other preserved Valentine's cards, written in his boyhood between the ages of six to ten, Glenn signed them with a pseudonym "your puppy." This kind of signature would stand for affectionate feelings toward his mother, akin to those extra-warm feelings felt for his dog, Nicky. Glenn wrote this poem as if it had been written by his dog. It follows that he found it much easier to express his deep loving feelings for his mother in this way than to express them more directly.

The title of Glenn's poem, "Dear Mistress," laid out between a printed red heart and a printed picture of a puppy dog is striking. This card is riddled with psychological meaning and points to his rich and dynamic inner world. Glenn referred to his mother as the mistress of the house or, from the dog's point of view, she would be the dog's mistress and, by inference, Glenn's mistress (or boss).

At the time when the poem was written, Glenn was spending his mornings at public school and his afternoons at home with his mother. Going to school was associated with high separation anxiety, whereas the afternoon part of his day was more anxiety-free. Glenn vehemently resented school as the epitome of forced socializing, and he skipped classes whenever possible. He by far preferred staying at home in the company of his mother. Being involved in such a close mother-son relationship brought about a number of psychological complications, such as mutual dependency, a power struggle between the mother and the son, and Glenn's tendency to be self-centered. Here is a sketchy account of how Glenn's egocentric behavior could have developed.

In the first three years of Glenn's life, there were three women looking after and doting on him. The chief caretaker was his mother; while the two other mother-substitutes were his live-in grandmother, Mary Flett, and his nanny, Elsie Lally. Glenn was treated as a privileged child, coddled and indulged by the three women. There was an ulterior motive for this triple emotional devotion, stemming from his mother's cogent belief that her son was special and destined for fame. Florrie admired her son's qualities, particularly his brightness and musical ear. She gradually idealized and overvalued Glenn's talents, which was echoed in the other two women, Mary Flett and Elsie Lally, who also treated Glenn as an exceptional child. Children who are indulged and idealized in this way may easily develop an overvalued image of themselves, which may result in the formation of a so-called "grandiose self." This term, according to the American psychoanalyst Heinz Kohut, refers to the "child's solipsistic world view and his undisguised pleasure in being admired ..."[3] The thesis here is that Glenn's personality was featured by self-centeredness and grandiosity.

Another distinguished American psychoanalyst, Otto Kernberg, suggested that one's grandiose self develops through the mental process of the fusion of: 1) the admired aspect of the child; 2) the fantasized version of oneself; and 3) the fantasized image of the loving mother.[4] According to this, Glenn's grandiose self formed through being overly admired by the significant people of his boyhood; to which he responded with his child fantasy of being great and being the central figure of his family and, in a broader sense, in the rest of the world. Furthermore, Glenn also developed an idealized image of his mother by fantasizing about her as being ever great, ever loving and ever available to him. The end product of such mental constructs was an illusion of being ever great himself, which is a central characteristic of the grandiose or the narcissistically invested self. Grandiosity is a defensive mental process that serves to defend against anger and envy toward ambivalent caretakers, who admire some aspects of the child but neglect others.

In this type of family constellation, where the caretaker idealizes and overvalues certain aspects of the child, the self-esteem of this child becomes contingent on admiration by others and on the self-love related to one's greatness. The operating formula is: "I am loved by others when I am great. I am rejected when I am not. I love myself when I am great; and I hate myself when I am not." The grandiose self becomes a valued and cathected aspect of the self, whereas the rest of oneself, which is not valued, is split off as an unfavored part of the dyad between the self and the love object. For example, in Glenn's real life his musicality was favored, while his ability for poetry, sports, comedy, and other ordinary abilities were hardly noticed. There was an internal split in Glenn where the grandiose self was constantly reinforced, while the rest of his non-grandiose self was not favored or was even rejected as bad. This internal split was responsible for his feelings of boredom and emptiness because a part of himself was devalued and lost. As an adult, Gould frequently felt unfulfilled and driven to look for new ways of gratification, only to be unfulfilled again. The grandiose self is unproductive and "does not charge the battery ..."[5]

Contrary to the dominant presence of his mother in Glenn's early years, his father's presence in real life was less intense. In Glenn's inner world, his nonmusical father was internalized as a rival rather than a soul mate. While the maternal presence was more responsible for the formation of the grandiose self, the paternal presence was more associated with the sense of personal inadequacy. It follows that right from the start, in the first three to five years of life, Glenn was emotionally handicapped in both dyadic relations, between the self and his mother and the self and his father. The image of the mother was internalized in an ideal way, and the image of the father was internalized in a hostile way, which was also not realistic. In both relations, Glenn was unable to develop a true self, nor to perceive the true qualities of others. Instead, he developed a false self, which was played out in future relationships with his friends, relatives, teachers and music associates and which was patterned on the basic idealistic prototypes of relations between himself and his parents. In simple words, neither the over-involvement with Glenn on the part of his mother, nor the under-involvement on the part of his father, enhanced Glenn's future emotional well-being.

Now that some aspects of Glenn's early subconscious dynamics have been furnished, it will be easier to understand Glenn's Valentine's poem, "Dear Mistress." What motivated his choice of word "mistress"? Why not simply "Dear Mum"? Did he express his tender feelings from the dog's point of view or his own submissive position vis-à-vis his mother as a person of power and authority? The themes of dominance and submission alternated in the mother-son relationship all along. Narcissistic investment in one's own child engenders the trend of dominance over the child but also a trend of submission to the child's specialness. In the first verse of Glenn's poem: "Sometimes I am bad as bad can be," he belittled and scorned himself as if he were not a good boy, which was his mother's attitude that he assumed. This could have been Glenn's unconscious portrayal of his "all-bad" aspect, the one that was split off and was unadmired and unapproved by his significant elders. The next reproachful line, "I run away quite often," reflected Glenn's fantasy to break away from the smothering ties with his mother. "Running away" was also necessary in order to pursue music and become his own person. Even though a part of the music world was shared with his mother, most of it was unique to him. Glenn's world of music was a limitless and private estate where he, as the sole owner, could run free and where trespassers were prohibited.

Glenn's next declaration in the poem, "when I am home I try to show, I am really not so dumb," is quite interesting. Where did he even get the idea to refer to himself as dumb, when in reality he had a razor-sharp mind? Did anybody refer to Glenn as dumb? This plea is suggestive of Glenn's doubting his own goodness, which was reflected in his constant need to be reassured and told that he was good. This is an example that Glenn at times experienced himself as being "all-good," which accounted for the grandiose part of him, and "all-bad," which represented the inferior part of him. He was torn by these polarizing inner states of mind and was unable to balance them out. Both of these experiences coexisted together.

In the latter part of the poem, Glenn became more direct in expressing his feelings: "I know you love me, Mum," and "you're good to me dear Mummy." By using endearing terms, Mum and Mummy, Glenn could no longer disguise his affection and express it from the dog's perspective, but he was doing it from his own child's view.

The end of Glenn's poem is quite realistic and not allegoric at all:

5. I really do appreciate,
and here have tried to say
How much I really love you
For your care from day to day.

The last verses are self-explanatory in the portrayal of Glenn's positive feelings for his mother. He signed the card as "Your setter Nicky," pursuing the idea of his dog writing the card. A puppy is the ultimate symbol of love and affection, and the image of the puppy is associated with softness and cuddling. Glenn, as the cute, little darling to his mother, was surely expressing tender feelings of his "puppy love" for her. "Puppy love" is an ambiguous term as it may designate the first romantic love in one's life, which usually occurs in adolescence. In that sense, Glenn may have subconsciously revealed his, possibly incestuous, love feelings toward his mother.

Other than his mother, the presence of Glenn's grandmother, Mary Flett, and her younger sister, Flora Flett, were also influential in Glenn's formative years. Mary Flett, by her way of doting on Glenn, also contributed to Glenn being so self-centered. Glenn's mother, Florrie, was quite dependent on her mother, Mary. In the same way, Florrie was emotionally intertwined with her youngest maternal aunt, Flora Flett, who was a mother substitute to her. This was Florrie's unfinished family business, which was then transferred onto Glenn. "The Flett triangle" appeared to be a closed interdependent social system that did not allow strangers to join in intimately, as seen in the following scheme:

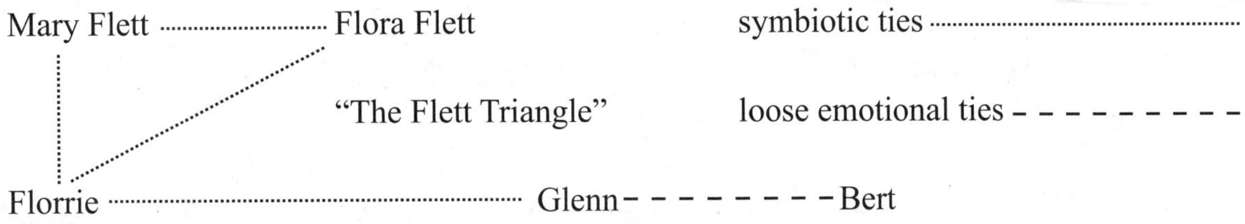

Bert Gould was an outsider of that close-knit female triangle. He never deeply bonded with his wife, who was enmeshed with her family of origin. By playing such a peripheral role in his family, Bert was in a clear minority among the Flett women in decisions related to his son's upbringing. Glenn was treated as an extension of his emotionally dependent mother, who belonged to a powerful union with her Flett relatives. So, through his mother, Glenn inadvertently became affected by his grandmother and his great aunt. By this token, Glenn was raised from the beginning to be more like his Greig-Flett relatives, while his emotional bonds to his Gould relatives were weaker. This had a confusing effect on Glenn, particularly on his self-image and his relationships with others.

While there were problems of overprotection coming from his mother's side, there was a different set of inherent and unreconcilable problems for Glenn from his father's side. Because of the overpowering presence of his mother and her relatives, Glenn was turned against the Gold clan. Glenn could not relate well to his father nor to his grandfather. He often wondered why his Papa Gold was involved in the "cruel" fur business. He could never understand why his father was involved in fishing and duck hunting instead of playing music or playing with him. Glenn could not answer those questions without stirring up strong emotions and even stronger judgments, and his parents were not able to appease his quizzical mind. He felt so set apart from his big, strong-looking father—the fisherman, the builder and the furrier. For Glenn, hunting and fishing were the two most abhorrent activities. Glenn was longing for more unconditional love, more closeness with his father and, above all, more quality time spent together.

So far two major aspects of Glenn's infancy have been described: the mutual dependence of Glenn and his mother and his egocentric behavior. Both were merely the forerunners of the growing set of problems encountered in the next phase of development between three and five years of age, which according to Sigmund Freud is called the "Oedipus complex."[6] This term is a derivative of the Greek legend of King Oedipus, told by Sophocles, one of the great tragic poets of ancient Greece, in his famous classic drama, *Oedipus Rex*. The central core of the story is that Oedipus, who was raised away from his parents, killed his father Laius, King of Thebes, and married his widow, Jocasta, not conscious of the fact that she was his mother. When Oedipus became aware of the incest with his mother, he resorted to self-punishment by blinding himself and forsaking his home. Shakespeare, who was familiar with Sophocles' work, incorporated the story into his famous drama *Hamlet*. Sigmund Freud, who was a fervent reader and student of both Sophocles and Shakespeare, incorporated the legend into his psychoanalytic theory. The Oedipus complex involves the psychology of the father-mother-son triangle. According to this theory, male children between age three and five emerge with strong affectionate feelings toward their mothers; they often become possessive of them and at the same time more antagonistic toward their fathers. Freud suggested:

> What, then, can be gathered about the Oedipus complex from the direct observation of children at the time of their making their choice of an object [of love] before the latency period? Well, it is easy to see that the little man wants to have his mother all to himself, that he feels the presence of his father as a nuisance, that he is resentful if his father indulges in any signs of affection towards his mother ...[7]

Successful resolution of this developmental stage results in identification with the same-sex parent. In healthy development, the boys of five to six years of age are likely to overcome their previous strong (infantile) sexual desires for their mother. They no longer need to be with their mother all the time, to monopolize her nor to hate and compete with their father for her love. At the end of successful growth, boys are able to accept their fathers and their own male identity. If there are problems in this developmental period, they may interfere with normal emotional growth of male children. Indulgent and overprotective mothers may hang onto their sons for too long, not allowing their independence. Freud thought that such unresolved problems remaining from the Oedipal situation are the source of anxiety and obsessive neurosis.

Young Glenn entered this stage by the age of three and encountered the problems on the part of his parents. His mother was forty-five years old and just had entered menopause, which added to her anxiety over aging and over running out of time. This meant that Glenn's initiation into the Oedipal stage was marked by his mother's aging and her compensatory grand plans for her only son's future. At the same time, his father was only thirty-five years of age, very attractive, athletic looking and successful socially and in business. Bert Gould was not in love with his wife, but he was rather in awe of her music talent. In the same way, Bert was in awe of his little boy who was so musically precocious. Under the pressure of his wife, Bert deferred to her decision to start Glenn's very early music training. Deep down, he would not have minded at all had his son shown interest in fishing, playing with toy soldiers, or even if he was going to become a minister, doctor or merchant like other members of his family. In short, Bert was only peripherally involved with his son, which made him a poor role model with which to identify.

Bert also had a personal motive in abdicating his rights in decision-making with respect to Glenn's music education. He himself was a son of a musical mother who taught the piano and introduced her children to music. Personally, Bert, like his father, showed no interest in the piano. His middle brother, Bruce, played several brass instruments and had a sustained love of music. The same was true for his youngest brother, Grant, who enjoyed piano music throughout his life. By relinquishing all decision making to his wife, Bert subconsciously paid respect to his own musical mother and acknowledged his guilty feelings over failing her as a musician. When his very persuasive wife announced that their son had a perfect musical ear and that she would train him to be a concert pianist, Bert acquiesced, disregarding his own personal wishes and aspirations.

In the literature on narcissistic personality disorder there are described three frequent characteristics of the parents of a future narcissistic child: "These children 1.were born into families in which father was viewed as a failure by mother; 2. these mothers treated their boys predominantly as narcissistic objects by overvaluing them as long as they promised to undo the humiliation of father's failure; 3. these boys experienced actual seduction by their mothers."[8] This more or less applies in Gould's case, where Florence was married to an ordinary business man and not to a distinguished musician. She also hated his family name and probable Jewish ancestry, which she endeavoured to disguise or change. Florence grafted onto her self the influences of great musicians she viewed as personal models, which she wished to pass onto her son. Norwegian composer Edvard Grieg was her ego-ideal to which she aspired. Florence even professed that she was related to Grieg through her ancestry, which was a family legend and more a product of her grandiose fantasy than a proven fact. The other admired music figures she idealized were the world-famous patriarchs of music, like the great conductor, Arturo Toscanini; opera singer, Enrico Caruso; and concert pianist, Joseph Hofmann. Florrie transferred her idealization of the music "fathers" onto Glenn, hoping that he might join the ranks of these elite. If he did, that would compensate for the deficit of not becoming a pianist herself and for having an ordinary husband.

From infancy, Glenn was exposed to his mother's lullabies, which she sang for him in her beautiful and soothing voice. Whether she told him the *Tales of Mother Goose* or sang him *Sonnets for the Cradle*, the boy was invariably mesmerized and couldn't have enough of them. In Greek mythology the nymphs were in possession of such beautiful singing voices that they were able to use them in seducing sailors travelling the seas. In poetry, the voices of singing birds, like the nightingale and canary, are referred to as symbols of beauty and auditory pleasure. Florrie, who introduced her child to fairy tales and lullabies, became a nymph and a nightingale in his mind, a godess-like figure with this superior harp-like vocal instrument in her voice box. For Glenn, she was the muse of song, the best vocalist and pianist he ever knew and, in that sense, his permanent ego-ideal. In his adult life, Gould's fascination with Wagner's Siegfried Idyll and Richard Strauss's operas and songs such as "Ophelia Lieder," as well as his adoration of singers Barbra Streisand and Petula Clark, were all related to his early fixation on his mother's glorious soprano voice.

Glenn was not only seduced by his mother's voice but also by her constant physical proximity. His insecurity and fear of the dark led him to crawl into his mother's bed at night in quest for reassurance that she was still there for him. By the age of five, he already had separation anxiety, and her physical presence was the most effective temporary remedy for it. On her side, Florrie was subconsciously unable to let go of her son. Seduction by voice was compounded by a degree of covert sexual seduction. The key document supporting this assertion was provided by Glenn's childhood friend, Robert Fulford:

"Once when I was at the Gould's cottage, Glenn told me that he slept with his mother on alternate nights, while his father slept with her otherwise, an arrangement that was made some years earlier," Fulford mentioned quite sincerely.

"How old were you at the time?" I asked.

"We were twelve years old but I remember it very well."[9]

Fulford memorized Glenn's confession as an anecdote. To the researchers, this event is of analytic importance as it sheds light on one of many family secrets that Glenn and his relatives protected. At the cottage, where there were fewer rules and restrictions, Glenn had the privilege of sleeping with his mother on alternate nights. Hence, Glenn and his father became rivals and competitors. Of course, Glenn's father was a potent and grown male, capable of having a sexual relationship with his wife, whereas Glenn was merely a child with repressed infantile sexual fantasies.

After the age of three, Glenn had to contend not only with his separation fear but also with his growing castration anxiety, which was a spin-off of the Oedipal situation. Castration anxiety is to be taken metaphorically rather than literally. It stands for fear of his father's masculine power and ability to punish him. Glenn could not properly internalize his father's masculinity, his sexual prowess and unquestionable genital primacy over his wife but remained in conflict with them.

This kind of triangular family structure, featuring emotional entanglement with the mother and insufficient positive identification with the father, prevented successful resolution of Glenn's Oedipal stage. During the first few years of Glenn's life, a number of unconscious pathological defense mechanisms evolved to help cope with the confusing situation with his parents and to defend against frustrations and emotional stress. One of the prominent early defense mechanisms of fending off a number of personal anxieties was the mechanism of omnipotent control, which is an unconscious tendency to control others through various means. As a child Glenn often behaved in a "smart Alec" fashion and always needed to get his way. Through this behavior, he was able to challenge his mother's power over him, as well as to compete more with his father. His mother's endless rules made him want to oppose them, which was done through occasional temper tantrums, self-righteous arguments and by peculiar behavior. Slouching at the piano was one of many symptoms of defending against his mother's disciplinary codes. Unfortunately, defiance in a dependent child is often followed by remorse and one or another form of suffering around disappointing and hurting the person to whom he was attached. This particular pattern of defiance followed by self-reproach continued to reoccur throughout Glenn's entire life. Obviously, Glenn required more involvement and more limit-setting by his father. Meanwhile, Bert abdicated his rights to disciplinary guidance of Glenn in favor of his wife, which placed enormous responsibility on her and which, in the long run, she was not able to handle. Instead of Glenn being able to fish along with his father on a boat, he threw temper tantrums and persisted in a lengthy campaign against his father's fishing. The end result was that his father finally gave in to Glenn, which meant that he submitted to his son's need for omnipotent control. Those complex inner and outer psychodynamics in the mother-son-father triangle helped reinforce and perpetuate self-aggrandizement, which carried into Glenn's adult life.

Contrary to the lay opinion, grandiosity as a personality trait, and narcissism as a broader psychological phenomenon, though they may account for some success in life, do not account for health and mental well-being. A grandiose self is deceiving to and restraining of one's own mental growth. It does not open vistas to the real world or to sincere interpersonal relationships but closes them; it does not provide freedom of thought, feeling and behavior but imposes limits. Grandiose leaders ranging from grandiose parents and bosses to grandiose politicians are more invested in their personal aggrandizement than in the genuine issues and needs of their followers. In this specific case, a parent pursuing her own grand aspirations had overlooked the child's personal needs for more spontaneous and uninterfered emotional progress. By rebelling, Glenn won an island of independence where his gift of music took over as his main driving force. The rest of his emotional territory remained occupied by emotional oppression, by alternating feelings of love and hate, by sickness and loneliness, all of which depleted his personal reserves. There was a ransom to be paid since the Oedipal triangle remained unresolved in the boy and later in the man. In the background of Glenn's personal drama, one can always notice his mother's overbearing presence and his father's ominous absence.

In his comprehensive book, *The Narcissistic Pursuit of Perfection*, Arnold Rothstein[10] elaborated on the complex dynamics of the narcissistically invested child, which were the same dynamics operating in Gould's life. He says: "Healthy individuals integrate their pursuits of perfection in adaptive manners." In describing the mother of future narcissistic individuals, Rothstein used the term "suppliant," meaning that parents may supply their child with narcissistic investment and invest in the child for their own sake and not for the child's best interest. They supply narcissistic fueling, which even though it is fueling, is still unhealthy. Individuals with narcissistic personality features are known to have poor anxiety tolerance, poor frustration tolerance, high sensitivity to disappointments and to any imperfection of the loved ones.[11] Rothstein's observation of his patients almost entirely applies to Gould. He was unusually sensitive to disappointments and was very intolerant of imperfection in himself and in others. His relationships were characterized by idealizing others at first and then denigrating and deserting them later, if and when they did not meet his inordinately high expectations. Gould lost many friends through this type of subconscious mental mechanism.

Closely related to narcissistic personality features are masochistic attitudes and behavior. Masochism is a human mental phenomenon that involves conscious and particularly unconscious forms of self-damage. There are two basic types of masochistic activities, known as sexual and moral masochism. In this section, the focus is on moral masochism as it relates to Gould. In the lay population, there is a prevalent opinion that children often become victims of their insensitive caretakers who cause them emotional harm in a variety of ways. The less known is another concept that puts emphasis on the "inner self-damaging tendencies,"[12] which is a mechanism that repeats itself over and over again in the course of one's own life and long after the original childhood trauma happened. This inner mechanism is responsible for ongoing self-abuse in some individuals, which is beyond their conscious control. Thesc individuals do not necessarily wish to suffer, but they still end up suffering in one or another way. The chief characteristic of moral masochism is the presence of a very harsh and tyrannical conscience (superego), which becomes critical and punitive of oneself (of the rest of the personality, called ego). In the process of conflict between the ego and superego, the former produces a countermeasure aiming to turn all the displeasure generated in the inner psyche into pleasure. This mechanism of turning inner misery, such as inner frustrations, guilt and sorrow, into more bearable, pleasurable experiences is psychic masochism—which means unconscious pleasure derived from displeasure. The only way to derive pleasure from displeasure is to make displeasure a pleasure. In Glenn's early childhood there were numerous self-defeating practices manifested in the form of social avoidance and lack of fun with peers, which were predecessors of his future self-damaging behavior. As an adult, Gould succumbed to a number of self-harming practices, ranging from wearing excessive clothes in warm weather to poor eating, poor sleeping and very poor self-upkeep habits. His persistent use of his peculiar piano chair, which attracted excessive criticism and ridicule, is also seen as a self-defeating or masochistic behavior. Gould was daunted by his hang-ups but was unable to change their merry-go-round pattern. Unfortunately, the way it often works in human psychology is that any maladaptive behavior or trait, if not modified and improved through some form of professional treatment, tends to get worse with the aging process. There is no evidence of Gould engaging in psychotherapy to help alleviate his inner tendency toward self-defeat. This left him stuck and doomed to repeat his odd behavior over and over again.

THE EMERGENCE OF SYMPTOMS

> Holistic medicine has arisen as a viable medical practice in recognition of the unity of mind and body, of muscular tensions which arise from stress ...
>
> Hans Selye[13]

It was always hard for Glenn to express his feelings freely, those of anger and grief in particular. He was raised in the spirit of the Victorian society with an emphasis on politeness and good manners. His mother, Florrie, was even visibly put off by Glenn's smallest flashes of anger. She also disapproved of his sulking and stubbornness, which were more quiet forms of protest, not to mention his temper tantrums, which she abhorred. A variety of disciplinary methods such as corrections, reprimands and even coercion were applied to stop Glenn from showing his wrath in front of her, or what was even more unacceptable, in public. Glenn's cousin, Jessie Greig, said that such a style of child rearing was very common in those days and that she too was brought up in the spirit of obedience and "not talking back." This is what Jessie revealed:

"Do you remember in what way Glenn's mother punished him when he misbehaved? Did she hit him or send him to his room?" I asked Jessie.

"I don't recall that I ever saw Aunt Florrie smack Glenn over the head or pull his ear, which in those days was not uncommon. She kept a ruler, though, on the top of her piano, which I suspect she used on her music students," Jessie said somewhat apologetically.

"How do you think she disciplined Glenn?" I inquired.

"Well, it was all in her voice. She used to give Glenn a look of disapproval, and she would not talk to him afterwards for a while. She could be so cold and stern when she disapproved of something, just like my Grandma Greig. I feel badly telling you this because they were good people,"[14] Jessie responded sadly.

Glenn's nanny, Elsie Lally Feeney, confirmed that Mrs. Gould expected others to behave at all times. She remembered some delicate details from Glenn's early childhood:

"I was scared myself when Mrs. Gould was mad. She chilled me to the bone a few times. When she asked me to do something, I had to say, 'Yes, Mrs. Gould,' 'As you wish, Mrs. Gould,' and I had to do things her way," Elsie confessed.

"Can you be more specific? What did she do? Did she raise her voice?" I asked.

"Well, that's the thing. She didn't yell at you at all; she just gave you a look and then she'd walk away from you. I think, this hurt more than if she'd slap you."[15] Elsie got this long repressed anger against Mrs. Gould off her chest.

Unhappily, Glenn was exposed to frequent episodes of silent treatment by his mother. In this atmosphere, Glenn gradually learned to keep his emotions in check. He himself became terrified of his mother's cold, disagreeable feelings and afraid of his own reactive anger and fury. He was even more afraid of being unable to hold these "ugly" feelings back and possibly explode in wrath in front of others. This is how he developed a defense against his own anger, by making conscious attempts to suppress it. Glenn hardly revealed anything personal with his relatives and friends. Even so, on one rare occasion Glenn shared an anecdote with Andrew Kazdin, his record producer for fifteen years. Kazdin preserved Gould's story for posterity:

> Just once he [Gould] talked about a traumatic incident that happened in his childhood. Apparently he had committed some infraction of the family rules and was engaged in an argument with his mother. He revealed to me that at the height of his rage, he felt that he was capable of inflicting serious bodily harm on this woman, perhaps even committing murder. It was only a fleeting spark of emotion, but the realization that he had, even for a split second, entertained the notion frightened him profoundly. He had suddenly come face to face with something within him that he did not know was there.[16]

Glenn "snapped" in response to his mother's demands to behave. In the second round, he became alarmed by his own hostile feelings toward her. Had his mother been able to tolerate his anger and help him get over it without feeling guilty, that would have been the better of the two possible scenarios. She could have said, "Glenn, I am sorry, I didn't mean to upset you, and I can see that you have reason to be angry," which would have settled the matter. In this case, there was a different scenario in which Glenn felt terrible for having acted out his negative feelings toward his mother. Florrie did not accept Glenn's anger and usually responded to him with a silent treatment. This accounted for Glenn's bad feelings about himself, which became unresolvable, and he carried these negative feelings into his adulthood. It is known that children who are emotionally intertwined with their parents often have grave difficulties coming to terms with anger within and/or outside of themselves. This is because their aggressive impulses are systematically thwarted and discouraged from expression by primary caretakers, which inevitably leads to inhibition of affect and to a variety of adversarial ways of coping with aggression. This is how Kazdin ended Gould's story:

> The experience caused him [Gould] to retreat into serious introspection, and when he emerged, he swore to himself that he would never let the inner rage reveal itself again. He was determined that he would live his life practicing self-control. Glenn concluded by saying that he had been successful in this endeavor and that he had never lost his temper since that first day so many years ago.[17]

For Glenn, holding and controlling anger like that was very hard and caused him to suffer. Modern child psychology recognizes the value of verbal expression of any emotion, be it love, shame or anger, and advocates that parents need to listen and hear what their children are trying to express. Open and sincere rapport in parent-child relationship contributes to the mental well-being of the children.

In the absence of appropriate skills for channeling and expressing feelings directly, Glenn was left with a narrow choice of handling his emotions in a more passive, indirect and controlling way. In this, he heavily leaned on his intellectual abilities in order to think through his personal problems and as a mode of communication with others. Early in his childhood, Glenn discovered that if he were not allowed to express his feelings, he could at least put forward his opinions and then argue his point rationally. His elders did not favor this behavior either but justified it and compromised because he was so clever and special. By so doing, they played into his need to be more rational and reserved rather than to express feelings. As time went on, Glenn was increasingly compelled to be right in his opinions; to win and dominate debates with his partners at work and play. Some of his friends described him as arrogant, even provocative in his self-righteousness, and often exhausting to his conversational partners. Indeed, Glenn was able to speak for hours; preferably over the telephone, where he could convey his thoughts and sparkling intellect. Glenn's need to control his partners was merely his way of channeling aggression in the absence of other more adaptive ways of coping.

At the same time, Glenn's verbal intelligence and his brilliant ideas were unique and fascinating. There were a number of contradictions about him that were often projected onto others. Some became bewildered by his arrogance and others were charmed by him. This refers back to Glenn's inner split into "all-bad" or "all-good" parts, which was never properly integrated. As a consequence, these aspects of himself were projected onto others, who then experienced him in positive or negative ways. In the period between six and eleven years of age, which happened to overlap with the war, Glenn became greatly interested in the radio news, in imagining combat situations and watching real-life movies rather than fairy tales and cartoons. This is how Gould reminisced in his paper Stokowski in Six Scenes on the time when he was eight years old:

> ... my parents informed me that I was going to see "Fantasia," that it was in color and all about music, and that I would get to hear one of the world's greatest conductors. At the time, I had only seen one movie in color—"Snow White" and I hadn't been too thrilled with that; besides, everybody knew that the really good movies—the ones with plots, and enemy agents, and German battle cruisers—were in black and white. The "all about music" part did not please me either. I went though because I figured that maybe this great conductor would be taking his orchestra to entertain troops at Dunkirk and that they would all be blown to smithereens by some nice, black Stukas that would come out of the clouds all of a sudden and drop their 500-pounders while the Messerschmidt 109's strafed the beach.[18]

By publishing this remarkable article in which he described his association with Maestro Stokowski, Gould also let his public into his very personal experience. He let us know about his preferences; that he did not have a need to see a movie "all about music," but that was rather his mother's need; that he preferred real-life stories to fairy tales. Just like present-day children who like to watch movies and TV shows with violent content where the "good guys" are fighting "bad guys" using a variety of sophisticated tools and weapons, eight-year-old Glenn handled his aggressive impulses through the images and fantasies of power, revenge and victory. This is to be regarded as part of his masculine identification with his father and other males in his family, and stands for normal psychosocial development. This attempt at healthy adjustment was dodged by Glenn's parents, particularly his mother, who was compelled to direct and redirect him to music. After seeing *Fantasia* Glenn became physically ill:

> ... I went home depressed, feeling faintly nauseous, and with a first headache I can remember I told my parents I couldn't eat my dinner, and went to bed hoping that I could rid my mind of that awful riot of color. I tried to imagine that I'd just closed down the conning-tower hatch on some cool, gray submarine

and that I would soon submerge beneath the midnight blue waters of the North Atlantic.[19]

In this passage, Glenn has bared his soul by admitting to his depression, feeling sick to his stomach, and to having a migraine-like headache. In other words, he developed "symptoms" or became symptomatic and physically ill. As a consequence, he went to bed without supper and without practicing his beloved piano. Glenn was so emotionally exhausted by the conflict with his parents and the action of the movie that he had to resort to strong self-soothing images of an ocean submarine surrounded by perfect silence. Later in his life, Gould always preferred darkened rooms and recording studios in order to reenact this womb-like security.

The movie, *Fantasia*, as a Disney classic can be used as a framework to demonstrate the outbreak of Glenn's psychosomatic symptoms. When *Fantasia* as a full-length film in Technicolor was first released in 1940, it was the state of the art in animation, technology and music, which were all perfectly synchronized together. Though it was a cartoon and presumably geared for light entertainment, it was so rich and novel that it must have been quite overwhelming for the young and inexperienced viewers of the early 1940s, for they did not have the television and movie sophistication as do their counterparts of the 2000s. In this film, the famous American conductor, Leopold Stokowski, appears as the conductor of the Philadelphia Orchestra playing the music of Bach, Beethoven, Stravinsky and other composers for the sound track, but both the conductor and musicians are shown only in the form of black silhouettes. It follows that Glenn felt tricked by his parents when told that he was going to *see* Leopold Stokowski. *Fantasia* is not focused on the people at all but on the magic display of dazzling colors and animated images of geometric shapes, flowers and animals, which are constantly moving about and dancing. There is also a graphic portrayal of primitive prehistoric scenes of planetary disasters, floods, ocean furies; of great turtles and archaic birds and primitive reptile-like dinosaurs roaming the earth. There is a great deal of aggression between the animals, where a gigantic tyrannosaurus standing tall on his hind legs is in savage combat with an equally huge stegosaurus. Eventually, all these animals perish from heat and dehydration, leaving only footprints and skeletons behind. This particular segment is accompanied by Stravinsky's music "Rite of Spring," which is at times as violent, dramatic and imposing as the visual story itself. In another part of the movie, a piece by Modest Mussorgsky, "A Night on Bald Mountain," is played along with terrifying scenes of devils and other Mephistophelian figures of darkness. There are also gentle and playful parts, where cute mushrooms and water lilies perform pirouettes to Tchaikovsky's Nutcracker Suite. All is presented in truly amazing, vivid colors like crimson red, glaring orange and all imaginable shades of pink. These astonishing scenes may be an absolute delight for both youngsters and adult viewers but not necessarily for the eight-year-old Glenn, who felt totally overstimulated by the perceptual onslaught of visual, auditory and kinetic stimuli. He responded to it by developing motion sickness, a state of horror and a massive headache. Glenn was particularly sensitive to the violent scenes of life-and-death fights accompanied by brutal music and to the evil creatures causing harm to the innocent. The emotional trauma was so severe that Glenn, for the rest of his life, hated the music of both Stravinsky and Mussorgsky, which in his unconscious mind represented brutalizing terror.

By this time, Glenn was in a complex psychological predicament. He already had a background of power struggles with his parents, who repeatedly told him what to do. He had suffered from a long-lasting fear of the dark, fear of crowds, and he had a visual oversensitiveness to bright colors. Though Bert and Florrie may have been well-meaning and uninformed about the movie content, it still stands that they were not able to relate to Glenn's fears or his preferences. While the act of watching *Fantasia* cannot be held responsible for causing Glenn's sickness, it certainly served as a catalyst that triggered the outbreak of physical symptoms. This episode set the stage for future reoccurrences of physical ailments whenever he was in similar stressful situations. Glenn's future intolerance of colors, his many psychosomatic reactions to stressful situations and other consequences could be traced back to this multi-traumatic experience associated with seeing *Fantasia.*

There was another independent event that occurred around the same time that also facilitated the outbreak of psychosomatic symptoms. This was reported by the renown Canadian writer and media personality, Pierre Burton, who interviewed Gould at the cottage in the winter 1961:

> When he was a boy of eight, a schoolmate standing near him was physically ill. All eyes turned on the wretched child and from that instant on Gould was haunted by the specter of himself being ill in public. That afternoon he returned to school with two soda mints in his pocket, a small tousled boy on guard against the moment when he might lose face.[20]

This description corroborates much of the other evidence that Glenn, at the age of eight, had several fully-blown symptoms brought on by emotional stress. In this case, Glenn helped himself with soda mints to supposedly calm his queasy stomach and to be able to cope with his obsessive fear of vomiting in front of others, which would humiliate him. From that point on, Glenn discovered that whenever he was in similar distress, he could always intervene by swallowing pills and potions to appease his inner tension. This set the stage for his progressive oral dependence on pills to soothe himself and ward off anxiety, which manifested in the form of prescription drug dependence in his adult years.

It was evident that Glenn in his early childhood was recruited into the army of those people who react to emotional stress by being physically ill. Joyce McDougall, in her book, *Theaters of the Body*, described how the "theater scripts" are written in the unconscious of some young children at a preverbal age. Those scripts have a permanent effect on them in the form of psychosomatic reactions, symptoms and one or another major physical illnesses. She offers this observation:

> All of us use action instead of reflection when our usual defenses against mental pain are overthrown. Instead of becoming aware that we are guilty, anxious or angry, we might overeat, over drink, have a car accident or a quarrel with our neighbor or our life-partner or, weather permitting fall victim to a flu! These are simple examples of "expression in action," through which one disperses emotion rather than thinking about the precipitating event and the feelings connected to it.[21]

Glenn was more often than not unconnected to his inner emotion. His intellectual thinking prevailed over his need to reflect and get in touch with his feelings, which set the stage for strong physical symptoms during times of stress throughout his life.

THE GRIEG MYTH

> I don't know who my grandfather was; I am much more concerned to know what his grandson will be.
>
> Abraham Lincoln[22]

In the literature on Gould, there are common references pointing to the kinship between Gould's mother, Florence Greig, and the famous Norwegian composer, Edvard Grieg. Presumably, the paternal great-grandfather of Florence Greig was a cousin of Edvard Grieg. The rumors of such family relatedness were spread by Florrie herself, who as the most accomplished musician of her Ontario-based Greig family and as the mother of the future world-famous Glenn Gould was most invested in the Grieg legacy. Without much solid proof and encouraged by the vague family legend, but mostly by her own wishful belief, Florence went on reiterating and exaggerating the family myth. When Grieg died in 1907, the fifteen-year-old Florrie, who was well on her path of studying music, began compiling newspaper clippings, letters and other memorabilia creating a file on him. By her deep conviction that she was a blood relative of the famous composer, she perpetuated her own ambitious fantasy of being born into an exceptionally musically gifted family. This vast emotional cathexis served as an incentive for her to relentlessly pursue music and to carry and pass the music torch on to her son. Glenn was raised and nurtured by his mother's prophecy and the Grieg story, which he took for granted. He even referred to Grieg as "Cousin Edvard." Though Glenn was mostly doing it in jest, he was still serious enough in giving credence to this elusive subject and even endeavoring, particularly in his writings, to convince others of its merits:

> A Confidential Caution to critics: Gentlemen, Edvard Grieg (1843-1907) was a cousin of my maternal great-grandfather. My mother, nee Florence Greig, maintained, as did all the Scottish branch of the clan, the 'ei' configuration while Grieg's great-grandfather, one John Greig, crossed the North Sea in the 1740's, settled in Bergen, and inverted the vowels so as to afford a more appropriately Nordic ring to the family name.[23]

Gould was in error as it was not John but rather Alexander Greig who crossed the North Sea and settled in Norway. Gould, who was an avid researcher otherwise, did not do his homework well enough when it came to the Grieg subject, as if it suited him not to find an error and demythologize his past.

Edvard Grieg is by far the greatest composer and music figure of Norway. He was born in Bergen to his father, Alexander Grieg, who was a seafood merchant, and to his very musical mother, Gesine Judith Hagerup. His ancestry is well documented and could be safely tracked back to his Scottish roots. As a child, Edvard showed an inclination to music, and his mother, Gesine, taught him the basics of the piano. Her younger sister was married into the musically distinguished Bull family, which provided encouragement and direction for Edvard's future music career. It was Ole Bull, the renown Norwegian violinist, who arranged for Edvard to enter the Leipzig Conservatory when he was fifteen years old. At the age of twenty-three, Grieg became conductor of the Philharmonic Society of Christiania (now Oslo, the capital of Norway) and soon after, at the age of twenty-four, he became a founder of the Norwegian Academy of Music. In the same year he married his first cousin, Nina Hagerup, who as an opera singer inspired Grieg and publicly performed his songs. At the age of twenty-six, Grieg composed his most important large-scale work, the Piano Concerto in A Minor, which was an instant success. His rapid outstanding achievements in the field of music were well appreciated by the Norwegian Government, which awarded Grieg with a lifelong grant to help devote himself entirely to music composition. Grieg composed an array of over one hundred songs to German, Norwegian and Danish words. These songs are known for their lyricism and their authentic Norwegian melodies, and many of them were set to poems and dramas by his friends Henrik Ibsen and Hans Christian Andersen. His major orchestral works are the *Peer Gynt Suites*, *Norwegian Dances*, *Holberg Suite*, and *Lyric Suite*, originally written for piano but orchestrated later.

By drawing a parallel between Grieg and Gould, there are many similarities but also major differences. Gould, like Grieg, was raised to be the greatest music son of his native country. Gould was a child prodigy who earned a license as a concert pianist at thirteen, and became internationally acclaimed at twenty-two. As a child he started composing little music pieces, and at the age of twenty-three he published his most important composition—*The String Quartet*. Unlike in Grieg's case, Gould's music career did not unfold smoothly and straightforwardly; he never fully developed as a composer, nor did he receive in his formative years any substantial financial support from the Canadian Government.

Florence and Glenn were well acquainted with Grieg's biography. Though Glenn was flattered by the professed connection with his "Cousin Edvard,"[24] he was resentful of his mother's overemphasis of the subject. Florrie was in the habit of comparing Glenn to her ideal music figures, like Mozart, Hofmann and Grieg. Glenn felt that he did not need to be compared to others because he himself was an original. The flip side of the coin of those self-confident feelings was a sense of shame and humiliation for not being able to become a composer of Grieg's stature. Inevitably, Glenn ended up having mixed feelings about Grieg or, more precisely, he projected his ambivalent feelings felt toward his mother onto Grieg, who was long dead and had no bearings on this interpersonal conflict. The end result was that Gould never embraced Grieg as a composer, and though he was familiar with Grieg's works, he avoided playing them in public. Gould made a point of not playing or recording Grieg's songs; while at the same time he took pleasure in interpretation of songs composed by Arnold Schoenberg and Richard Strauss. By blatantly ignoring Grieg's songs, Gould indirectly expressed a silent protest toward his over-ambitious mother and retaliated by hurting her feelings. The subconscious psychological process of a power struggle between mother and son that was set off in childhood carried on into his adult life. Gould had to face his old and deep-seated conflict—whether to submit and obey his mother or break away from her expectations in favor of his autonomy. This conflict caused him much distress and was never resolved. Driven by his inner resistance and a need to rebel, Gould kept disregarding Grieg's music and kept delaying performing it for others. In the interview with Bernard Asbell, Gould was able to put his most inner feelings into words:

Interviewer: I have heard that you may record the Grieg concerto.

Gould: We've talked about it. If I do it, it will be out of family pride. He's a relative, a first cousin of my mother's grandfather.

Interviewer: Do you like the piece?

Gould: It's certainly a piece that—given all my convictions—ought not to appeal to me. I have tried to convince myself that I have a duty to perform in doing it.[25]

It was Karl Ancerl, a conductor of the Toronto Symphony, who helped Gould in his inner dilemma by directly encouraging him to record Grieg's *Piano Concerto in A Minor*. In his letter to Carl Little, it looked as if Gould reached a firm decision and had a full intention to record it: "As you know I'm recording Uncle Edvard's concerto with the Cleveland Orchestra in September ..."[26]

The pinnacle of Gould's inner quandary around the Grieg issue presented itself in his paralyzing inability to follow through with the recording of Grieg's best composition, the Piano Concerto in A Minor. In 1971, long after his performing career had ended, the management of Columbia Masterworks offered Gould the chance to re-record the Beethoven Concerto no. 5 in E-flat Major, known as the *Emperor*, this time in stereo. Gould was seemingly quite agreeable also to prepare for the same recording session Grieg's Piano Concerto in A Minor. The choice of the place of recording was the Severance Hall in Cleveland, Ohio, partly because Gould was so fond of it from the time when he had appeared there in concerts in 1957 and 1959. Along with Gould as the piano soloist, this project included the Cleveland Orchestra and Karl Ancerl as conductor. Given that Gould was familiar with the territory, with the music and the people involved, and that he was quite comfortable working with Ancerl, the odds were favorable that this double concerto project was going to be a smashing success. As Gould himself put it, this was going to be "a cameraman's delight." To completely satisfy the piano soloist, Columbia also arranged for the "Gould Piano," Steinway CD 318, to be shipped from the recording studio in New York to Cleveland's Severance Hall. When everything was set and ready for recording, Gould called in sick! Torn by his deep love-and-hate feelings, he was unable to go through with the recording. Inevitably, this was disabling and frustrating for him and for his associates. Gould's music producer, Andrew Kazdin, remembered this anticlimactic event:

> Alas, at practically the last moment, Gould called me with the sad story that he had contracted the flu or some other illness that would necessitate canceling the recording. Naturally we wondered whether we were hearing the truth or not. But then, what difference would it make? If Glenn did not want to go to Cleveland, certainly we would not force him. We simply had to accept the excuse and set about picking up the pieces.[27]

Kazdin was obviously annoyed with what he suspected was Gould's wayward behavior. Meanwhile, it was not that Gould did not want to go to Cleveland but rather that he was not able to overcome his inner conflict, to record or not Grieg's masterpiece, to please or not please his mother. Gould was not fully conscious of this battle within himself. He only felt unmotivated and hindered by something obscure and overpowering. This unconscious pit of conflict was responsible for the devastating end result. Gould felt perplexed and physically indisposed. He lacked stamina to follow through and finally had to cancel what could have been a promising recording. The stress from decision-making made him physically ill. Gould deprived himself of what could have been a remarkable achievement, both musically and personally, by winning a victory over his masochistic needs.

The cancellation of the Cleveland recording session had unfortunate repercussions. It left Gould's music associates in a state of dismay. There was also a threat of penalty for not fulfilling the contract. On the positive side, there was general willingness to rebook the recording at a later date. In due course, the attempts at rescheduling were interfered with by various external reasons. During that period, Karl Ancerl suddenly died, which added further to the inevitable collapse of the entire project. The final outcome was negative, Gould never recorded the Grieg concerto. He dealt with his inner anguish by reaching an emotional compromise. Gould settled the matter by recording one of Grieg's compositions, which helped to appease his mother's disappointment but also to assuage his own mixed feelings. He selected the Sonata for Piano op. 7 in E Minor, which is one of Grieg's lesser-known works. This is what Gould said in his liner notes furnished for this recording:

> The Sonata, of course, though hardly a repertoire staple, is played and recorded from time to time, and some of you may well feel that my response to it is at almost perverse pains to underline those dour, curiously dispassionate qualities of Ibsenesque gloom that I feel to be on predominant display in even the earliest work of Cousin Edvard.[28]

Even this brief commentary is steeped in ambivalence. At first, Gould put down the sonata, then he told us that he went out of his way to convey the bulk of its meaning, "dispassionate Ibsenesque gloom," and finished the paragraph by reminding the reader of his connection to "Cousin Edvard." The underlying love and hate feelings first experienced with his parents continued to spread and exist in his adult direct and indirect relationships.

The question remains. Why did Gould have to suffer such turbulent dynamics vis-à-vis Edvard Grieg when there is not even firm evidence of a family connection? The extensive research of Gould's cousin, Betty Greig Madill, and my personal research show that the genealogical connection between Florence Greig and Edvard Grieg cannot be proven. The following analysis will demonstrate the salient weakness of the Grieg myth. The research available to date points to two main characteristics: 1. The genetic relationship between Florence Greig and Edvard Grieg cannot be proven because of the absence of information on the generations between John Greig in position 1a and John Greig in position 4a, which are missing links; 2. Even if future researchers would favorably decode the "missing links," the relationship between Florence and Edvard would be remote and statistically insignificant. The following chart shows the presence of the "missing links" in the family tree of Florence Greig:

The Lines of Descent of Florence Greig and Edvard Greig

1a John Greig 1b
1703—1774, Cairnbulg, Scotland

(unproven) 2a. gr.gr.gr.gr. grandfather (of G. Gould) ?	Alexander Greig 2b. 1739—1803
"missing links"	
(unproven) 3a. gr.gr.gr. grandfather (of G. Gould) ?	("The immigrant" to Norway) John Grieg 3b. 1772—1844
4a. John Greig, gr. gr. grandfather date of birth unknown (Scotland, had 10 children) (proven)	Alexander Grieg 4b. 1806—1875
5a. Peter Greig, gr. grandfather 1831—1913, Aberdineshire, Scotland (the immigrant to Canada)	Edvard Grieg 5b. 1843—1907
6a. Charles Holman Greig, grandfather 1855—1927	
7a. Florence Greig 1892—1975	
8a. Glenn Gould 1932—1982	

The "missing links" in positions 2a and 3a, make it impossible to prove that Glenn Gould is a direct descendant of John Greig (1703-1774). This means that his professed genetic connection to Edvard Grieg also cannot be proven.

The Grieg myth infringed on Glenn's normal development in his childhood, and it continued to burden him in his adulthood. This was not a benevolent story told to him in passing by his mother, Florence, but an aspect of her obstinate fantasy of grandeur. Glenn's mother had overlooked many weaknesses and errors of the Grieg myth. She failed to conduct her own research in order to find out the truth but passed on to Glenn slipshod information. Florence missed the fact that in Edvard Grieg's family the music talent was on the side of his mother, Gesine Hagerup, to whom she was not related. She also denied the importance of the genetic distance and that in the best scenario, her grandfather could have only been the second cousin to Grieg, in which case, Florence Greig and Edvard Grieg would be relatives four times removed, whereas Glenn Gould and Edvard Grieg would be five times removed. This would really be a very distant relation. Placing emphasis on the Grieg connection was a template of deceit, which was emotionally damaging to

Glenn. This inflated story triggered in Glenn haughty fantasies and mixed love-and-hate feelings. The Grieg myth, though intriguing, was only a fallacy that distracted Gould from the healthier focus in his life.

PERFORMANCE ANXIETY

> An opera begins long before the curtain goes up and ends long after it has come down. It starts in my imagination, it becomes my life, and it stays part of my life long after I've left the opera house.
>
> Maria Callas[29]

Glenn began his performing career at the age of five before a large church congregation. He accompanied his parents at the piano while they sang the songs of worship in duet. Though this was a church service and not an entertainment show, their success was splendid and the tiny pianist was well-noted and admired. Glenn was a little wunderkind, but he also was a model-child displayed on the church podium in his fancy Lord Fauntleroy-like suit. Glenn was launched as a showpiece, but at that stage of his young life he thoroughly enjoyed being shown off. While the choir and the solo singers, like his parents, served as the backbone of the liturgy music, Glenn, the child-star, appeared in church as a delightful little dessert to the main course. He was welcomed by the appreciative church audience, who loved him unconditionally for whatever he delivered. There was practically no risk of failure but only astonishment and well-wishing for this gifted child. Even if Glenn were to hit a wrong note, the audience would likely have loved him just the same. The sweetness and innocence of a preschool boy, his bravery, but, most of all, the wonderment of such a little musician captivated the affection of the Toronto East End audiences.

In the course of human development children go through the rapprochement stage at the age of approximately one year. This is when they behave as if they are central and super-special to their parents and the rest of their social circle. This interaction between an infant and others is described in the literature as a "love affair with the world." In the further process of normal human development, the child learns how to relinquish the aura of being super special by realizing that other children and adults are also important; that no one person is the center but rather only a part of this big and integrated world. Glenn was a gifted child, at first valued by his family and then sought and validated by his early audiences. It is as if, because of all this attention and praise, little Glenn's rapprochement stage was extended, so that by the age of five or six he was still able to have the thrill of a love affair with the audience. Glenn felt anxiety-free while he securely mirrored himself in the smiling faces of the church-goers. At the same time, at home, where demands on Glenn were multiplying by the day, where the supervision was strict and often disapproving, his anxiety was rising proportionally. Indeed, Glenn's many anxieties and fears did not start on the church platform but originated in the family triangle.

Performance anxiety or, in common parlance, stage fright is a ubiquitous human experience that exists in many individuals who have to appear and perform before an audience. Anxiety is an uncomfortable inner experience marked by a variety of undesirable symptoms. Anxious individuals often have shortness of breath or smothering sensations, heart palpitations, muscle tension, body aches and restlessness. Anxiety, when persistent, is also a very tiring condition that may cause a sense of mind-and-body fatigue. Commonly, during the anxiety phase, one's concentration may be severely impaired and the person often feels keyed-up, irritable and easily startled. Because of a dry mouth, anxious individuals are often thirsty and need to sip on liquids like water or coffee. They may have profuse sweating of the palms or may have the sensation of cold and clammy hands. Those with performance anxiety may have any of the above symptoms or several of them combined.

In stage fright, as a specific form of heightened anxiety, there is the added burden of obsessive thoughts and obsessive fear of failure, fear of being disliked, defamed and rejected. Glenn Gould experienced many of those anxiety symptoms without being aware what they were. Before performing on the stage, he suffered severe back and neck tension, muscle pains, and felt nervous and agitated. His hands were cold, which made him develop a habit of wearing gloves at any time and soaking his hands in hot water before a performance. He suffered a dry mouth, which caused him to keep a glass of water on the top of the piano, enraging many critics and musicians. His stomach felt bloated and gassy, which was responsible for his habit of wearing oversized clothes and beltless trousers. Gould did not know that he was afflicted with such a common condition of the civilized world, nor did his beholders have any concept of what he was experiencing. Gould referred to his anxiety in descriptive terms. Before his concerts he was often invited by his music associates and fans to participate in social activities. They invited him to attend dinner parties, to visit their homes, to sleep over, to play their pianos or to be interviewed. In his letter to Marjorie Agnew of November 6, 1956, Gould responded to her lunch invitation in this way:

> As it happens, the week of my Vancouver concert, I am also playing in Spokane and Winnipeg—a different program each time. Since you must surely remember how fidgety I get when preparing programs at such close proximity, I know that you will agree that it would be risky for me to commit myself to any other engagements at the moment.[30]

And soon after, on November 22, he declined an invitation of his uncle, Dr. Grant Gould, who resided in Vancouver and invited him to his home:

> Dear Uncle Grant,
> ... As you know, I have a tendency to become rather crotchety under pressure and I think it is best to keep all extra curricular interviews to a minimum.[31]

By using terms like "fidgety" and "crotchety," Gould described his inner anxiety, which was most uncomfortable for him. He coped with this problem through different strategies, one of them being social avoidance. By isolating himself and concentrating heavily on music, Gould was able to keep a good deal of his anxiety under control and to carry on with public performance.

Joseph Roddy left us a perceptive description of what Gould was going through hours before his debut at Carnegie Hall in February 1962, where he played Beethoven's Second Concerto with Leonard Bernstein as conductor with the New York Philharmonic. Gould told Roddy that he planned to arrive after the intermission, close to 9:30 that evening, just minutes before his solo piano role in order to avoid listening to the music of the first part. He explained:

> Before Bach I can listen to Strauss, Frank, Sibelius, jukeboxes – anything. But nothing before Beethoven. I have to wind myself into a kind of cocoon before playing him. I go in like a horse with blinders.[32]

Roddy proceeded to give us a humorous but benevolent account of how Gould spent his last three hours before this historic performance in New York. Without being aware, Roddy furnished this detailed but painstaking account of Gould's coping rituals in the face of a highly anxiety-provoking event:

> At seven-thirty in his [hotel] room, Gould got out of bed, slipped off the two pairs of mittens he had been wearing, and proceeded to perform the concerto twice. There was a piano in the room, but he didn't touch it. Instead, he paced about, playing the solo part with his fingers, conducting the orchestra part with his chin, and singing both at the top of his voice. The hand-soaking rite, a quieter activity, started at about eight-thirty and lasted almost an hour. A bare minute or two before Gould was due to perform, he arrived at Carnegie Hall ...[33]

Gould was having an intense bout of stage fright. The performing artist at such a high level was going through a virtual torture by shivering in bed, feeling restless and unwell. Stage fright is often seen even in the performing veterans on the stage. The Chilean-born concert pianist Claudio Arrau had an unabating performance anxiety throughout his impressive and long concert career. He relied on ongoing professional treatment to help him cope with anxiety. The famous American pianist Rudolf Serkin suffered high performance anxiety in the form of being sick to his stomach before concerts. His son and equally famous concert-pianist, Peter Serkin, also is subject to stage fright. It was noted that on one occasion he suffered such a paralyzing bout of panic, that he had to be physically pushed out on the stage.[34] Even the great Maestro, Vladimir Horowitz, had recurring inner fears including a dread of having an accident of some sort while on the stage. He too needed professional help, which made it possible for him to carry on his rich concert career. One of the foremost concert-master violinists in the world, Jasha Heifetz, once discussed with his students the intricacies of stage fright. He said: "It's easy for you. All that you have to do is to go out there and play your best. When I go out there, I have to play like Heifetz all the time." Performing artists have to live according to a certain image of themselves, created by them and their audiences. Performing at a lesser image is not acceptable and would be instantly rejected in one way or another.

In scientific literature, stage fright is seen as a complex syndrome with multiple dynamics and roots. One of the important dynamics underlying stage fright is incomplete emotional separation and emancipation from the close attachment with parents or their surrogates. Those performing artists who have never accomplished fuller emotional autonomy will likely be reliving their separation issues in their adult career each time they go on tour, as they change cities, hotels, etc. "A significant portion of the stage fright experience is a recapitulation of the child's fear of asserting himself as a separate individual against the regressive pulls of symbiosis."[35] The performing artist-soloist has the task of assertion as an individual and the task of pursuing his or her artistry alone. A few could do it with no anxiety, and most could do it in spite of the anxiety.

Stage anxiety before a performance may be so severe as to induce a tremor of the hands, knee trembling, stiffness of the body and more, which all may jeopardize and impair the quality of the music. Solo pianists have an extraordinary challenge to face by having to perform alone under the glare of reflectors. Their sense of aloneness is equaled only by a few similar, anxiety-provoking situations in life, such as being on the operating table or having to parachute in unknown enemy territory, both of which are associated with a sense of dread and anticipation of the worst kind. Those concert pianists who suffer severe stage fright often have a fantasy of running away, being somewhere else and avoiding the performance. Despite their subjective feeling of having "jelly-legs" and other anxiety symptoms, they are expected to march firmly toward the piano positioned in the middle of a spacious stage and exude an aura of self-confidence. The recitalist quickly may be perceived as being hesitant and unsure, which then might be reflected in the morning's press and lead to a chain of untoward effects. This means that a pianist has to conceal the entire discomfort of the stage fright and project a self-assured image with the following message: "I am O.K. and ready to give the best of myself for your convenience and entertainment."

Glenn Gould was greatly predisposed to stage fright. One of the major reasons was his high separation anxiety dating from the time of his boyhood. His sufferings as a performing artist were quite predictable though never recognized. There was a big contrast between Glenn's childhood experience as a pianist on the risk-free church platform and corresponding feelings of his teens when he began to play on a formal concert stage. In church, Glenn felt safe while being together with his parents before the humble and uncritical congregation. On the real concert podium, Glenn the teenager was all alone at the piano, while his mother and the official critics sat in the audience. This was for him an anxiety-inducing environment, much different from his preferred hideaway at home.

Other inner dynamics accountable for stage fright are those of discomfort around the artist's exhibitionism and the public's voyeurism. Often, performers resent the audience for watching their every move and the prying critics who peep into the privacy of their lives and personal aspects of the artistic performance. Developmentally, voyeurism in children is related to the primal scene of their parents, which means, seeing them in an act of intimacy, particularly love making. Children soon learn that they must not take a peek at their parents' privacy, which implies that their voyeurism is prohibited. If they keep intruding, or even if they keep wishing to peep, and keep fantasizing about what their parents do when alone, they may have to pay for it by feeling guilty. An adult performer with unresolved voyeuristic issues usually ends up with severe misgivings about being watched by thousands of inquisitive eyes. Yet the performer, once again, must disregard his own strong feelings of resentment and go on with the show, which partly accounts for his performance anxiety. The task of performing involves the act of exhibiting one's own person, talent and skill. If the performer is inhibited and bashful, then there will be an inherent conflict within the self. The pressure to be great is high, but in the performer's mind there is a cluster of nagging doubts: "What if I make a mistake, or a faux pas of some sort; what if I come across as foolish or a buffoon; what if they don't like me?"[36] This fear of being imperfect is related back to the original childhood fear of being chastised and rejected by the significant adults. This is why many performers usually have increased stage fright when their parents, teachers or other senior figures known to them are in the audience. This was certainly very true of Glenn, who, as early as in his teens, dreaded the presence of his parents in the audience. This fear gradually became more severe and obsessive in its quality. Gould, as a seasoned concert pianist, went out of his way to prevent his family members and friends from attending his concerts. Worse, he himself avoided going as a viewer to concerts to watch other pianists perform because he identified with their fear so strongly, to the point of reliving his own.

Stage fright is seen also as an offshoot of castration anxiety. The performers by virtue of being on stage are often vulnerable, as if they were naked and stripped of all strengths. At the bottom of such vulnerability and insecurity is the fear of being humiliated and condemned by the critical audience, who may be viewed as punitive and "castrating." In fact, the performer only projects his own unresolved castration anxiety onto onlookers.

Exhibiting oneself may be easily associated with the sense of shame and guilt. Performers often have a strong sense of self-consciousness, which makes them acutely aware of their bodies. They frequently feel exposed, naked, even indecent, and they feel that others may see right through them, which all aggravates their preexisting feeling of shame. Among performers, there is also a fear of loss of self-control, making a blunder, or worse, losing one's own sphincter control and being gravely humiliated.

The sense of guilt in the performer is related to attempts to be the best, to be superior to others, also to being immodest and boastful and for conquering all rivals. The performer may feel guilty over the inner aggression that is at the bottom of competitiveness and attempts at conquest. Both dynamics of shame and guilt were strongly represented in Gould's unconscious psyche. He felt terribly exposed to others and avoided piano competitions whenever he could. In the end, he hid not only by withdrawing from the stage but by hiding from people socially in his day-to-day life.

This was a sketchy account of some inner psychodynamics implicated in stage fright. There are other approaches to the enigma of anxiety. According to a biological view, the anxiety is an end result of disturbed neuroreceptors in the brain. The fact that anxiety responds well to medication from the chemical group called benzodiazepines, means that there are specific neuroreceptors in the brain for these particular drugs. Some of these drugs are very popular presently, such as: Diazepam (Valium), which is good as a muscle relaxant, and Lorazepam (Ativan), commonly used for anxiety. In Gould's times, Valium was the "bestseller," and he was prescribed Valium for his chronic muscular tension caused by anxiety. It was observed that on some occasions during his performing career Gould was not himself. He looked as if he was on some drugs, "flat" and a bit "dazed." At his recital in Windsor, Ontario, in March 1956, Gould was perceived as being "quiet and sedate" and even not well prepared for his performance. It appeared that Gould medicated himself, perhaps with Valium or some other sedative, which made him look nonchalant and incapacitated him to play optimally. It is not to say that Gould was irresponsible by appearing in front of his fans under the influence of drugs, but that he was so petrified and panic-stricken before the performance that he had to resort to some measures of relief. In the absence of other techniques, such as relaxation, light calisthenics, meditation and self-hypnosis, he practiced what was known to him, swallowing remedies and potions.

The performer must be upbeat enough to perform in public. A normal high amount of adrenaline in the blood stream is necessary for a successful performance. Performers cannot be phlegmatic and placid, nor can they be high-strung and jumpy. Therefore, a good deal of innate self-regulation and self-control is needed to accomplish a desired end result, a successful performance. Those who lack self-confidence need to acquire learned techniques in order to appear on stage in the optimal state of mind. Gould was born perhaps three decades too early, at the time when physical exercises and relaxation were not widespread. He had access to a few popular treatment modalities, to psychotherapy, to hypnosis and to psychotropic medication. Revolutionary changes in the 1970s and onward turned North Americans into a more sophisticated society with respect to the mind-body connection. People at large became more physically active through sports, jogging, exercises and gymnastics, with more emphasis on self-awareness and self-actualization by practicing yoga, meditation, proper diet, by engaging in personal and group psychotherapy and behavior modification.

By building up the performance toward its finale, the performer is unconsciously driving to the symbiotic-like moment of oneness with the audience. When the virtuoso finishes the last and often his best music piece of the recital, when the audience greets the performer with standing ovations and shouts of admiration, both the performer and the audience reach the peak of their relatedness, which is akin to the symbiotic oneness between the mother and child.

In this very activity of performance, the libidinal energy is transformed or sublimated in the music achievement. A recital is akin to the sexual act. It starts with foreplay and is gradually worked up to the climax of the finale. Indeed, the ovations at the end of a successful concert are equivalent to the sexual orgasm, except, here in the concert hall, sex is not felt and experienced but is sublimated into the feelings of ecstasy, pleasure, buoyancy and emotional merging with the performer. When the audience responds in synchrony with the performer, they will, in the end, experience the mental arousal and thrill of the performance. Gould was so scared of this type of end result that he often endeavored to produce anticlimactic finales to his music. Remember that he ended on a low note at his debut recital in Washington, D.C., and in New York City in 1955. In the same vein, in February 1962 Gould published an article in *Musical America* titled "Let's Ban Applause,"[37] in which he gave us many clues as to how he felt about public performance, both on the part of performing musicians and on the part of responsive audiences. He first compared the music theater to a "comfortably upholstered Roman Coliseum" and then wrote: "I have come to the conclusion, most seriously, that the most efficacious step which could be taken in our culture today would be the gradual but total elimination of audience response."[38] He proposed the program "GRAADAK," an abbreviation of the Gould Plan for the Abolition of Applause and Demonstrations of all Kinds.[39] The program would start by scheduling "applausless concerts each Friday, Saturday and Sunday. These three days with their inherent liturgical connotations, are best able to evoke a suitable reverent state of mind." In further elaboration of this poignant statement, Gould suggested for the solo pianist to be equipped with "a sort of a lazy-Susan device which would transport him and his instrument to the wings without his having to rise." At the end of this proposal, Gould admitted with regrets that he could not really put this program forward in Toronto because he "would be confronted with the age-civic antagonism for the local boy with a vision."[40]

By using the metaphor of the Roman Coliseum, Gould revealed that in his inner experience, the music theater was equal to an arena where there are battles and games for the pleasure-seeking audiences and their aggressive needs. Gould's sensitivity to any image of aggression culminated in his proposal of GRAADAK, where he proposed a quiet and solemn church-like atmosphere at concerts, where the audience would refrain from applause because Gould thought of it as immoral. The lazy-Susan device would help the anxiety-stricken solo pianist to cope with his "sea-legs" and lightheadedness and save him from having to bow in front of others. It is painfully obvious that Gould's elaborate construction of his GRAADAK was but a defensive camouflage of his inner anxieties and their underlying conflicts related to stage performance.

After publishing this article, Gould went another step further in fighting against the concept of public performance and the public's applause—he actually implemented an applausless concert at the Stratford Music Festival. Eric McLean of *The Montreal Star* reported in July 1962 these interesting observations:

> Glenn Gould told the audience in the Stratford Festival Theatre that he had a favor to ask of them. He admitted that his request was an unusual one, and that it was the sort of thing associated with memorial services for royalty, not with an ordinary concert. At the end of the seven fugues he would play the chorale which Bach composed on his death bed, after which the audience was asked not to applaud.

McLean continued his empathic and insightful story of Gould's experiment in the following way:

> The effect was electric ... It was an attention-getting trick, but one which cannot be altogether condemned since it attracted as much attention to Bach as it did to Mr. Gould. The audience listened with their nerve-ends, and what they heard was a performance of which no other living keyboard artist, to my knowledge, is capable.[42]

When Gould gradually realized that he was in the minority in his strange music-related views and behavior, and when he could no longer control his surmounting stage anxiety, in April 1964 he abruptly stopped his public performing career. Most of his contemporaries had no idea about his inner struggles and weariness but simply thought he went on a sabbatical and was going to return soon. Unfortunately, Gould's stage fright rendered him permanently disabled for public performance.

In conclusion, this was Gould's real story behind and beyond the observable. Gould's crusade for applausless concerts is suggestive of his avoidance of any emotional thrill and his attempts to tone down his act of showing off in order to lessen the underlying feelings of shame and guilt. His stage fright was equal to a chronic disease that never goes away, from which there is no reprieve, no pardon and no permanent remedy. For Gould, the concert stage was perceived as a circus arena in ancient Rome where the performing gladiators were the victims of the voracious masses. Gould, who felt guilty about any sign of his own aggression, was highly sensitized to the perceived aggression in others.

Nevertheless, the universal reality is that the stage, with all its foibles and contradictions, is not a savage product but a call of civilization; a tool of mass media and a call for a healthy mastery. It is a benevolent battlefield where the human instinctual drives are transformed or sublimated into beautiful and worthwhile cultural achievements. The concert pianist is faced with the enormous task to accomplish a motor mastery of the instrument, to conquer all the aspects of a music work, to overcome vicious stage fright and its preexisting roots, and to entice the critics and the audience at large. In spite of that, the stage is an irreplaceable and undying medium of social communication that audiences and performers will continue to seek out.

Chapter VIII

GOULD AS A YOUNG MAN

FAREWELL TO YOUTH

If you can talk with crowds and keep your virtue,
Or walk with Kings—nor lose the common touch,
If neither foes nor loving friends can hurt you,
If all men count with you, but none too much:
If you can fill the unforgiving minute
With sixty seconds' worth of distance run,
Yours is the Earth and everything that's in it,
And—which is more—you'll be a Man, my son!

Rudyard Kipling
(from the poem "If")[1]

In spite of growing pains, one's adolescence is still a privileged phase of human life. An adolescent can bask in the warmth and safety of the parental home while building the stamina to leap forward to the next, more independent stage of personal development. Having to part with the amenities of this youthful decade and face the next ten most exciting years of young adulthood is both challenging and perplexing. By the age of twenty-one, the normative volatile features of adolescence are supposed to settle and give way to a more stable adjustment.

Developmental psychologist Calvin Colarusso proposed the concept of a "third individuation," which is the ability of humans to continue growing and emotionally differentiating in the later stages of life between ages twenty to forty and even into middle adulthood.[2] It is encouraging to know that human growth is a dynamic and ongoing process and that it is never too late to work at one's emotional independence. It is said that in the transition from the teens to adulthood, young individuals suffer from normative loneliness[3] until they are able to form intimate ties and establish a family of their own.

For Glenn, adolescence was most gratifying from the perspective of his musical conquest, as he received much praise from others for his extraordinary artistic advancement. It was on the personal level and within the context of his family of origin that Glenn could not keep pace with his peers. Inevitably, he entered young adulthood with unfinished business from his teens. Ironically, when Glenn was supposed to celebrate his important twenty-first birthday with his friends and have a sense that "the Earth" belongs to him "and everything that's in it," he was more personally insecure than ever before. Parallel to the symbolic loss of his teenage status and emotional distancing from his parents and his music mentor, Glenn had to endure the real loss of another dear person from his past—his paternal grandfather. Tom Gould died shortly before Glenn's uncelebrated twenty-first birthday. This is what was reported in the obituary Glenn saved in his valued "Keepers file:"

> The death occurred on Wednesday, September 9, 1953 of Thomas George Gould, Toronto businessman, and resident of Uxbridge for the past 70 years ...
>
> Mr. Gould was engaged in business in Uxbridge and was an active worker in the early days of the Methodist church of this town where he was Sunday School Teacher and Local Preacher.
>
> In 1908 sensing a need for Christian work among the men of the town, he organized the Business Men's Bible Class, a group of business and professional men which became known all across Canada as the largest and most successful class of the kind. This class with its well remembered teachers, officers and orchestra, continued to give leadership to the town for some 35 years.[4]

Glenn missed his "Papa Gold," as he affectionately called him. The passing of his grandfather stirred up long-repressed emotions of love and loss. Papa Gold was a history buff and an avid reader of war stories and biographies of generals and state leaders. Yet he left Glenn uninformed and puzzled over his own ancestral history. Whether Tom Gold was of Jewish descent remained a vague family secret.

"Do you think that Glenn's grandfather, Tom Gold, was of Jewish descent?" I asked Vera Dobson Gould.

"Well, whenever I went to his fur salon back in the 1930s, he used to wear a black suit and a black hat all day long. I thought to myself he must have had some Jewish blood in him," Vera chuckled.

"This is an interesting story but it still does not prove that he was Jewish. Did you ever talk about that with Glenn's father?" I probed.

"No, not really. I don't think that Bert would have liked to discuss that aspect of his life. I wasn't privy to this information, which I sensed was kept under wraps. I respected his need for privacy. He was fond of his father but as far as Bert was concerned, he himself was a Gentile and that was all that mattered,"[5] Vera opined.

There was another controversy in the relationship between Glenn and his grandfather. Tom was a staunch churchgoer and a steadfast Christian activist. He read the Bible daily and disseminated its teaching through the Bible class he founded in Uxbridge. Meanwhile, his firstborn grandson, Glenn, stopped going to church by the end of his teens and replaced Bible studies by voracious reading of secular writers—Nietzsche, Thomas Mann and Kafka, to name but a few. By departing from his grandfather's strong moral values and practices, Glenn, deep within himself, had to "answer" for his deeds. He lived under the pretence of being emancipated from the overpowering ties with religion and being independent in his thought and social behavior, when in reality he was neither. Through his frequent emphasis on being morally "pure," or being a "puritan," Glenn kept in close touch with the moral values of his staunch Methodist grandfather. This is how he alternated between attempts to be his own person, self-confident and individualized from his elders, and feeling badly for letting them down. The following anecdote illustrates how profound and meaningful their relationship must have been to have affected Glenn six years after his grandfather's death.

Glenn Gould gave his last European concert on August 31, 1959, in Lucerne, Switzerland. He played the Bach D Minor Concerto with Herbert von Karajan conducting the Philharmonic Orchestra. While in Lucerne, Gould paid a special visit to the local museum:

"Mr. Gould, don't you think that it was rather unusual for Glenn to visit museums before his concerts?" I asked Glenn's father.

"Well, on the whole it was. But on that occasion, Glenn heard that there was a painting of Charles I, King of England and Scotland, in their museum and he wanted to see it," Bert answered decisively.

"Why, what was so special about the painting of Charles I?"

"Well, I told you before that my father was an amateur historian, and apparently a replica of this painting hung in our living room in Uxbridge. So I grew up watching King Charles in his glamorous cape, and also Glenn couldn't help seeing the king whenever he visited his grandparents, which was pretty much once weekly,"[6] Bert Gould explained.

One wonders what kind of effect the painting of Charles I had on Glenn? He probably looked at it with curiosity and with some special meaning related to his grandfather. What was this rare painting doing in his grandpa's living room? Glenn probably wondered. It stood there almost out of context, as if the king were the patron-saint of his grandfather. Over the years, Glenn listened to his Papa Gold telling him stories about King Charles I, how he was in conflict with the puritans, and how during his time many of them immigrated to North America. The most tragic part was how the king's life ended. History confirms that Charles I opposed Puritanism, that he also opposed the Parliamentary forces, that he was defeated by Oliver Cromwell and, eventually, was tried for treason and executed. This was the most moving story for Glenn. He was deeply shaken, even appalled, by the fact that a human being, in this case the king, was treated so savagely.[7] Still, why did it matter to Glenn that his grandfather was a fan of royalty, and why did he care about it at this particular time of his life? From the fact that Gould was not a keen tourist nor a historian yet he visited the museum in Lucerne, it can be deduced that he was on some personal mission. Not only did Gould ponder the portrait of Charles I, but he hired a professional photographer[8] to take a picture of him in front of it. Obviously, he wanted to show it to somebody, most likely to his grandmother, another beloved and aging relative. It appears that Glenn's visit to the painting was an act of mourning for his grandfather. Being reluctantly away from home, he was homesick and more reflective. When he found the painting in the museum catalogue, this kindled the memories of home and of his benevolent "Papa." Playing the music of his favorite composer, the grandfatherly Bach, with the fatherly-looking Karajan, Glenn was able to delve into his masculine identity as it related to himself and his male models.

"What happened with the painting of Charles I? Where is it now?" I asked Glenn's father, Bert Gould.

"Funny you should ask, because this is quite a story. After our family home in Uxbridge was sold in the 1970s, nobody wanted it, so I took it to my home and put it in the basement." Bert paused.

"You put it in the basement? What then?"

"Well, it stood there for years and I've forgotten all about it. Then, one day while I was working in the basement, I spotted it. There it was, King Charles looking at me from the canvas," Bert said bemusedly, as if the memory of it was still unsettling to him.

"What did you do with it? Did you tell Glenn? Did he want it for his apartment?" I was impatient to hear the end.

"Well, it was in a pitiful condition, all dusty and the frame was falling apart. So I took it to a store on Yonge Street to restore the painting and change the frame." Bert was looking at me as though he did not want to disappoint me.

"And then?"

There was a long pause as Bert was rubbing his eyebrows. "You wouldn't believe this. I never went back to pick it up. Never. And I don't have any excuse for that. I just let it go."[9] Bert sounded distraught.

This fascinating story reveals the power of a never-ending unconscious intergenerational conflict between Glenn and his father, Bert, and between Bert and his father, Tom, all symbolized in their attitude toward this family painting. Each of the three men had mixed feelings for each other. Bert loved his father, Tom, but not enough to cherish and save his favorite painting. Bert loved his son, Glenn, but not enough to pass onto him the family heirloom. Glenn, on his part, was always ambivalent about both his father and grandfather, about their occupation as furriers and their secrecy and concealment of their heritage.[10]

Gould in his early twenties was at the crossroads. He found himself in the borderland where major decisions had to be made and colossal responsibilities had to be undertaken. A turning point of any kind has the built-in risk of loss and benefit of acquisition. Which way to turn now? Should he stay within the shelter of his family or take off into the untested world of bachelorhood? At home, his parents were early risers and always pragmatic and orderly. Meanwhile, Glenn had a penchant for a diametrically different lifestyle. Once Glenn stopped taking music lessons and consulting with Guerrero, he spent more time indoors, sleeping-in, playing his music, and staying up at night reading the world's literary classics. While Bert complained that Glenn was frittering his life away, Florrie continually worried about her son's health and his public image. Such an atmosphere at home became tedious and countercreative for Glenn. He needed to get away from the intense vigilance of his parents. With this realization in mind, Glenn made conscious efforts to break away from his original family nest. He came up with an intermediate solution to take off to the cottage and spend weeks on end there by himself. This way he did not exactly move out, nor did he stay at home. Glenn took with him to the cottage his old Chickering piano and the collapsible piano chair with a back support. This core equipment was accompanied by other music and mind related paraphernalia, notably stacks of scores and classical music records, his tape recorder, books and knickknacks.

All of a sudden, Glenn found himself in a new scenario that seemingly had no limits and no obstacles. This was his season of content, when nobody told him what to do. More intuitively than deliberately, he restructured his life at the cottage to accommodate his own preferred lifestyle. Having decided on a concert pianist career a decade earlier, here was the prime moment for Glenn to sculpt his music future on his own terms. He filled his days with practicing, listening to music, experimenting and creating different renditions of music works. There were other activities to entertain. His radio was turned on nonstop, day and night, even when he was playing the piano, one of the luxuries that was not permissible at home. When having a break from the piano, Glenn pursued two pastimes tirelessly; he walked through the woods with his new and loyal dog, Banquo, bustling around, while music sounds percolated in his mind; or, when more emotionally charged, the concert pianist indulged in the fairly boisterous activity of crisscrossing Lake Simcoe and Lake Coochiching in his high-powered motor boat, given to him by his father. Just like his boat at his private quay, Gould was securely moored at the cottage like nowhere else.

Glenn loved his newly emerging purpose at the cottage. Nevertheless, he also was going through the phase of "normative loneliness."[11] His contemporaries proclaimed that Glenn withdrew into creative solitude. Indeed, from an artistic vantage point, the pianist needed a measure of quiet in order to actualize his music talent. Emotively, he needed to heal from real and abstract separation and loss. The spacious living-room studio was perfect for incubation of his musicality and became a platform from which Gould propelled himself as an international piano virtuoso.

The love affair with the cottage was a two-edged sword. In an attempt to reorganize his life to his own tune, Gould swayed into the opposite extreme of practicing a rather chaotic life. Having been brought up with a strong emphasis on order and discipline, the quick transition into a free and unrestrained world was for him too much to handle. All of a sudden, there were no "have to's" or "should's;" no prescribed showertime, suppertime, or bedtime. Gradually, the rebel son rephrased his parents' motto of work ethics, "Do it now," into a new one: "I'll do it when I want, or I may not do it at all."

Thus, the quest for dismantling many personal restrictions began. On the surface, Gould came across as a quiet, solitary artist, while underneath he was bursting with dramatic changes. He drove his Chevrolet Impala on dusty back roads at highway speed, acting as though the only purpose of traffic signs was to defy them. Who needs to go to bed before midnight, when the best music on the radio and the wonderful silence of the pitch-dark night were in the wee hours? Gould loved anything to do with sound, from the harmony of silence to the fortissimo of music. Another routine was challenged. Why do we need regular meals when we are not babies anymore? Why can't we just eat here and there when our stomachs are growling? To him, spending time on food preparation was unthinkable. Glenn's eating practices at the cottage became irregular and monotonous. At home, his mother prepared sumptuous hot meals—roast beef garnished with carrots and peas, soaked in gravy, mashed potatoes and Yorkshire pudding followed by mincemeat pie. Glenn's gastronomical skills consisted of opening cans of spaghetti in tomato sauce and preparing scrambled eggs, the only food that he was willing to make for himself from scratch. His favorite snacks invariably consisted of sipping English tea and nibbling on arrowroot cookies. When hungrier, he occasionally ate out at a local Orillia restaurant. He was a finicky eater and an absolute minimalist when it came to his choice of food and his selection of clothes.

His mother equipped him with a stack of V-neck pullover sweaters that were supposed to be worn on chilly days. Glenn wore them in the summertime over a shirt. Then, whenever he was at home, he would put a robe over the sweater just in case the air was to become more crisp. He got for himself a variety of headgear, including a beret and porkpie hats, to protect his health from the winds on the lake. He wore woollen gloves with cutoff fingers, which turned out to be a very practical device. It left his fingers free to play the piano while the rest of his hand was covered. Gradually, Glenn developed his own fashion style, which did not seem to resemble the dress of his father, uncle, cousins or friends. It was remarkably unique. It had a normal function—to protect him from unfriendly Canadian weather conditions. Unlike the majority of other people, it also had a defensive role—to defend him from his ever-anticipated danger of catching a cold and as a partition from the world. Layers of clothes—undershirt, shirt, sweater, undercoat, overcoat, beret, woolen scarf, heavy-knitted gloves—were worn all year round, even in the summer time. Nobody would or could imitate Gould in his fashion. Glenn's evolving half-starvation and peculiar dress were both signs of his individuality, and pointed to his attraction to being unusual.

When many years later Glenn's first cousin John Greig [Jr.] was interviewed in Uxbridge, Ontario, we specifically talked about details of Glenn's wardrobe:

"Mr. Greig, do you remember what kind of hat Glenn was wearing? His father used to wear a three-piece suit and a formal hat with a round brim; I think it is called a fedora. Meanwhile, Glenn wore such an unusual and casual hat," I stated.

"Unusual! I don't think it was unusual at all. Debbie, can you please bring me my hat?" John addressed his request to his daughter, Debbie Greig Dee.

"There you are." To my surprise, John Greig showed me his hat, which was almost identical to the one Glenn used to wear.

"Oh, dear, it's unbelievable." I was shocked. It was as if Glenn was resurrected and was himself present in the room. "How do you call this kind of hat? I mean, is there a name for it?" I asked slightly embarrassed.

"This is a common Scottish hat or a cap with visor. I think Sherlock Holmes used to wear one like that,"[12] John simply explained.

Typically, those who were close to Glenn viewed him sympathetically and embraced him the way he was. To John Greig, his wife Audrey, and their daughter Debbie, Glenn was not seen as unusual compared to how he was seen by other, more distant observers.

While the man was starving and perspiring in layers of warm clothes, the musician in Gould was thriving. He rehearsed, polished and perfected many music pieces in preparation for concerts. On November 19, 1953, two months after the loss of his grandfather, Gould gave a recital at Eaton Auditorium in Toronto, playing like no one before him in that hall. He performed one of his beloved music pieces, *The Lord of Salisbury his Pavan,* and *The Lord of Salisbury his Galliard*, by the English baroque master, Orlando Gibbons. As if in the recesses of his unconscious mind, Gould played the somber Pavan and the cheerful Galliard for *his* Earl of Salisbury, Papa Gold, whose ancestors came from the vicinity of the ancient town of Salisbury in England. He inspired confidence in his music maturity and manifested his genius at the piano. Other music works by Bach and Schoenberg performed by Gould were learned from Guerrero. It appears that Gould was paying silent respect to those whom he loved but to whom he could not express his feelings. Renowned author of works on grief, George Pollock, wrote in his paper, "Mourning and Memorialization Through Music:"

> My thesis is not that musical creativity depends upon object loss, but that given such losses, the direction of musical creativity in general will be influenced by intrapsychic processes of mourning and memorialization.[13]

Pollock studied the life of the famous Austrian composer, Gustav Mahler, and noticed that Mahler's multiple losses through death, particularly the loss of his several siblings, had influenced his music compositions. Mahler suffered greatly upon the loss of his brother, Ernst, who died at the age of thirteen. Four years later, Mahler composed an opera titled *Herzog Ernst von Schwaben*, which was inspired by his deceased brother. Pollock, in his psychological studies of mourning, raised important questions with respect to Mahler's motive for composing this opera:

> What does this mean? Does it serve the purpose of remembering the dead brother? Does it represent an attempt at immortalizing the dead brother? Or, does it represent a continuation of the mourning process for the dead brother?"[14]

In comparison to Mahler, Gould was not a composer, nor was he a typical concert pianist. Most of Gould's music interpretations had a deep personal meaning. In this case, when Gould played Gibbons's *Pavan* and *Galliard* for the Earl of Salisbury, he likely experienced deep feelings of loss and mourning, as well as the pleasant remembrances of his beloved grandfather. This is only one explanation of Gould's greatness as a re-creative music artist—his ability to touch, impress and pass on his own pathos and yearnings, or his own heartfelt love and a sense of tribute to his appreciative audiences. The seriousness and depth of Gould's music, in particular, and the personalized character of his interpretations seem to have an "in memoriam" quality. *Pavan* and *Galliard* by Gibbons remained among Gould's best performing and recording pieces. To observers, the choice of his music for the Eaton recital may have seemed strange, even puzzling. For us, the readers and Gould scholars, it is clear that his music is a personal working-through of his inner dynamics. So, when Gould's numerous personal quirks and his day-to-day disarray are considered along with his choice of music at this time, one can recognize his efforts to grow and individuate; to love and grieve his elders; to produce healing and generative music; and, despite all solitary pretenses, to carry on as a social being.

STRING QUARTET OPUS 1

> It's Op. 2 that counts!
>
> Glenn Gould[15]

Life went on. In the next three years after his grandfather's passing, Gould scored three major musical achievements: he composed String Quartet op. 1; he reached the first peak of his performing music career through his successful international debut in New York in January 1955, and he recorded his bestseller, Bach's *Goldberg Variations.*

Ever since a child, Gould was not gratified enough by being just a pianist. Though his pianistic interpretations were more re-creative than literal, he was always longing for more independent and more complete ways of self-expression—the music composition. His inclination to make new music was noticeable as early as at the age of five; became more prominent in his teens; and culminated in his twenties with the emergence of his String Quartet, op. 1.

The impulse to create comes from within. The wish to compose music comes from awareness of its beauty. The incentive for creation is derived from both an inner aptitude and outer motive or stimulation. In the language of the psyche, the ability to compose music is a form of ego mastery. To organize raw creative impulses from within into a coherent music piece requires many ego strengths, including spontaneity, superb concentration, and an ample sense of self-discipline. Furthermore, the act of composing music requires four sensory perceptions: auditory, visual, tactile and kinesthetic (sense of motion). Gifted individuals are known to have advanced sensory ability, which, combined with their motivation and task mastery, accounts for a distinct end result—a music composition. Gould was a genius who possessed excellent innate ego strengths: music intelligence, supreme memory capacity and extraordinary ability at all four sensory modalities. These cognitive functions were at the base of his natural music endowment. He also had a strong drive to express music and the volition to compose.

Alberto Guerrero composed too. From time to time his compositions were played by the music students at the Royal Conservatory as a matter of choice for their final exams. It is very likely that Glenn was familiar with Guerrero's music pieces and perhaps played them himself, though there is no evidence of it. By embodying the abilities to compose and to perform music, Guerrero always was the most suitable music model for Glenn to emulate. It was the breakup with Guerrero that propelled Gould to get on with his own composing. In the post-Guerrero phase, Gould was free from didactic music classes and could easily take off to the cottage, which became a perfect medium for the incubation and realization of his String Quartet. Solitary activities like walking in the company of his dog in the woods and looking through the picture window at the lake from his piano chair jogged Gould's imaginative impulses. Solitude facilitated the creation of music for him.

The String Quartet was composed between 1953 and 1955, before Gould was internationally acclaimed. This was the time when he was greatly interested in the music of Arnold Schoenberg and Richard Strauss, to which he was introduced by Guerrero. *The String Quartet* reflects the influence of both Strauss and, to a greater extent, the influence of Schoenberg, on whose twelve-tone technique it is based. It is known that creativity is often prompted by loss and that the creation of an art piece, be it music, poetry, sculpture, often serves as a form of psychic repair. Gould's composition followed his separation from home, from Guerrero, the loss of his grandfather and the recent deaths of both Strauss and Schoenberg in 1949 and 1951, respectively. *The String Quartet* became a multi-symbolic vehicle for the expression of love and dedication, as well as for grieving and healing.

Gould had good insight into the emotional meaning of his music composition. When the scores of his String Quartet were published in 1956 by Barger and Barclay of New York, Gould wrote autobiographical liner notes in which he acknowledged his affection for his past influences:

> The Quartet represents a part of my musical development which I cannot but regard with some sentiment. It is certainly not unusual to find an op. 1 in which a young composer inadvertently presents a subjective synthesis of all that most deeply affected his adolescence ... Sometimes these prodigal summations are the harbingers of the true creative life. Sometimes the brilliance with which they reflect the past manages to excel all that their composer will do thereafter. In any event, though the system must be cleansed of Opus Ones, the therapy of this spiritual catharsis will not remedy a native lack of invention. It's Op. 2 that counts![16]

Of course, the presence of Guerrero as the most significant music figure in Gould's life (other than his mother) deeply affected his adolescence. There is no doubt that Gould's quartet was emotionally linked to his teacher. After expressing tribute to positive influences of his past, in his liner notes

Gould also expressed harsh self-scrutiny and concern about the future of his composing. He wondered whether he would have enough natural invention in him to continue composing and concluded: "It's Op. 2 that counts!" It was as if what he had done so far was not good enough, and he would have to keep producing more to prove himself.

The String Quartet is a chamber music piece written in sonata form and modeled after Schoenberg's early-twentieth-century style of composition. The music is marked by tonality and, as Gould put it, is "scandalously melodious." It is a long piece, lasting up to forty minutes. Gould stated that after playing it on the piano he was exhausted and required several days of rest afterwards.

Why would Gould, a piano master, take over the role of a string master? It was Glenn's father who played the violin in his youth and continued to favor strings over the piano. It is evident that Gould's String Quartet is emotionally related to his father, with whom he had something in common at last. Further, Gould's composition is a subconscious attempt to rebel against primary identification with his mother, who was symbolically represented in the piano as a music instrument. Gould's personal, as well as his occupational identity, was heavily dominated by the influence of his mother. The choice of his music instrument, the piano, the concert pianist career, and the way he dressed, spoke and behaved in his childhood and teens were all influenced by his mother. Meanwhile, the composing, conducting, "misbehaving," unkempt demeanor and unorganized life all represented his attempts at assertion as an individual in his struggle against feminine identification. In this sense, Gould's String Quartet is a departure from his dependent emotional ties with his mother, which opened him to the unknown world of self-discovery. The creation of *The String Quartet* served multiple purposes. It was an attempt at separation and at masculine identification. It was also a symbolic marker of Gould's rite of passage, a coming of age. Being able to break away from Guerrero; to spend time at the cottage by himself; to compose his music as opposed to always having to interpret the music of others and to pay respect to his father were all ways for a sheltered boy to make the transition into manhood.

There are other traceable dynamics related to Gould's composing activity and his composition. Gould loved the sound of the cello. His teacher of counterpoint, Leo Smith, with whom he studied for seven years, was a child prodigy on the cello and a renowned cellist in his adulthood. Smith was also a member of the Toronto String Quartet. As a person, he was warm and sensitive. Glenn was fond of him and missed him when he died in 1952. In Leo Smith, Glenn found an erudite man with multiple music interests with whom he had much in common. Hence, Gould's String Quartet is an ode to several important male figures who touched and influenced him in his developing years, like his father and his teachers. Gratitude that could not be spoken in words was expressed in this beautiful music.

Yet another significant dynamic was at play. Gould believed that he was related to Edvard Grieg. Ever since his mother told him that they were relatives through her ancestors, Glenn inadvertently became involved in an emotional web with his "cousin Grieg." Not that Gould championed or adored Grieg's music, but he was certainly in awe of his achievement as a composer. Gould's fascination with the Nordic spirit, which he later portrayed in his radio documentary, "The Idea of North," appears to be subconsciously related to Grieg and Grieg's portrayal of the Nordic spirit in his own music. Both Canada and Norway share the climate of the North. Grieg was the greatest Norwegian musician-composer. In Gould's subconscious mind, he harbored the fantasy of being the Canadian counterpart of his "cousin" Grieg, which was a strong impetus for his composing. Despite his fantasy, Glenn Gould was unable to become the equivalent counterpart of Edvard Grieg, nor was he able to capture the Nordic spirit in his String Quartet. Without conscious imitation, Gould branched out into his individual and original conquest of music.

Once Gould finished his composition, he was anxious to see it recorded. He sent the scores to Otto Joachim, the founder of the Montreal String Quartet and a member who played viola. Earlier on, Joachim had expressed interest in premiering Gould's music, but there was no formal contract signed. Irritated by the delay of recording, Gould wrote this half-humorous, half-angry letter to Joachim:

> Dear Otto, [c. 1955]
>
> Reach for your most reliable sedative. You are about to receive a blast! As you will no doubt recollect—the Quartet has been in your possession for nigh on 2 months. As yet I have no word that work has begun.
>
> ... I have waited with exemplary patience, not usually identified with my temperament. And, in the past couple of months, I have given you guys a helluva lot of free publicity. Your performance of it has been mentioned in numerous interviews on my trips. Naturally, all this stems from motives of the greatest altruism. But even the benign charitability of my nature has plumed its abysmal recess. And now the Gould ire so long sublimated with friendly forbearance gives sign, and symptoms of severe inflammation. (A condition against which terramycin is woefully ineffectual.)[17]

Gould's complaint was effective, and his music was premiered in Montreal on May 26, 1956, by the Montreal String Quartet with Otto and Walter Joachim, Hymann Bress and Mildred Goodman. The piece was also recorded in the same year and released by the CBC International Service Program. It was premiered but not met with enthusiasm. There were some positive individual responses. Marcel Valois, the critic of *La Presse* praised the quartet: "Serious, of high inspiration, pensive rather than lively, bathed in a discreet and slightly saddened coloring, the work ... is of extraordinary interest."[18] The critic picked up on the main features of Gould's work—"pensive" and marked by "saddened coloring"—not even knowing their connection with his grief around the losses. The next and only time *The String Quartet* was publicly performed during Gould's lifetime was on July 9, 1956, at the Stratford Festival. Walter Kaufman, the conductor of the Winnipeg Symphony Orchestra, was in the audience. He wrote to Gould:

> Three days ago I heard your String Quartet ... a most remarkable work. ... You have much to say, and although you may say it differently in the years to come, whatever you say in your Quartet is good, solid, and honest music.[19]

The Stratford performance of Gould's String Quartet was favorably received by *The New York Times* as expressed in these words:

> In his own quartet one found comparable intellectual grasp of the material used, and even though the work had a frankly acknowledged indebtedness to

> Bruckner and Richard Strauss, it was a moving and impressive work. It was in conventional tonality, for the young pianist explained he himself has passed through his twelve-tone phase.[20]

Other than those isolated supportive comments, there was general apathy for Gould's composition. In the period from 1955 to 1956, Gould was thought of as a performing artist whose fame was on the rise. The chief interest of his audiences was really in his pianistic debut in New York and in his release of Bach's *Goldberg Variations*, which by far overshadowed his composing activity. Gould himself was insecure and apologetic about his music composition. He expressed mixed feelings about composing in his letter to David Diamond, the American composer who was at the time staying in Florence, Italy:

> Dear David, February 23, 1959
>
> What are you working on at present? I am struggling with a sonata for clarinet and piano, which I am desperately trying to prevent becoming a quintet. My piano writing always has a habit of getting over-rich and assuming a sort of organ pedal for the left hand which always ends up being unplayable except for the cello. At any rate, it is going along reasonably well. I would like to play it for you some day.[21]

Gould was in dire need of hearing Diamond's scholarly opinion, yet dreading the possible dislike even rejection of his music. He tried to endear himself to Diamond. Though at the pinnacle of his performing success, he did not speak from the point of the piano virtuoso but more as a freshman-composer. Gould never finished the "sonata for clarinet and piano," which became his typical and menacing problem, to start various pieces and never finish them.

Gould was aware that several fine American composers, such as Aaron Copland, Virgil Thompson, Roy Harris, Marc Blitzstein, Walter Piston and even his friend, David Diamond, all studied composition with Nadia Boulanger in Paris, yet he showed no interest to study composition himself. Endowed by the natural talent for creative artistic expression, Gould probably felt that he was entitled to compose fresh and original music without having specific theoretical background for composing. Just as he was able to write a variety of stimulating essays and other literary pieces with serious or humoristic content, he thought that he could replicate the same in music. The thesis here is that Gould was not short of innate talent for both music and literary expression. He had plenty of it. Unfortunately, the ingredients needed for facilitation of such a vast talent were lacking. Simply, the talent for creative expression cannot come to full bloom if things are in its way. Gould's ambivalence and his emotional obstacles were indeed in the way of his artistic expression required for composing. This is well illustrated in the next significant letter to another American composer, Lucas Foss. In this letter, Gould expressed self-criticism and even a degree of shame with respect to his composition:

> Dear Lucas, June 30, 1959
>
> I hope you like the Quartet. It is a work that I am proud of but not altogether happy with. It was my first attempt at writing for strings and my old organist's

> habit of seeing the cello line as a pedal-board induced me to keep it for long stretches on the C string, among many other faults.[22]

Both his tendency for excessive self-criticism and his shame are seen as inhibiting his drive to compose music. In his unsureness, Gould did not give a special name to his String Quartet but left it with its generic name. By relying on simplicity and leaving his work nameless, he humbled himself more than necessary. He thought of his music as not good enough and was absolutely terrified that it might end up being an imitation of someone else's music.

After the initiation in Montreal and Stratford, Gould's String Quartet was recorded in March 1960 in Severance Hall in Cleveland by Symphonia Quartet, with Kurt Loebel and Elmer Setzer, violinists, Tom Brennand, violist, and Thomas Liberty, cellist. Soon after, the same group of musicians recorded Gould's String Quartet for Columbia Records. This recording (ML 5578) was released in the latter part of 1960. Irvin Colodin of *The Saturday Review* wrote:

> Gould's materials have a shape and character of their own (beautifully suited, incidentally, to the medium in which he is working) which stand out clearly no matter how complex his contrapuntal elaborations become. The impulse to 'sing' is strong in him, and it comes as a sample of refreshing esthetic candor to find a composer who dares to write what he feels. As Gould says in concluding the self-exposition of his work, 'It's Opus 2 that counts!' But let it be said that this Opus 1 leaves us impatient rather than apathetic about hearing what follows.[23]

Gould had the unique distinction of being the first Canadian composer to have a major work recorded within the same year by two American companies.

Eric McLean of *The Montreal Star*, who closely followed Gould's pianistic career from its inception, was not ready to accept him as a composer and wished him to stick with his piano playing. This is what McLean reported after *The String Quartet* was released:

> It is touched with genius like everything Mr. Gould sets out to do ... But its faults are great ones too. The string writing is almost completely out of character, with the instruments crowded into a narrow tessitura. Whenever he ventures into such things as double-slopping, tremolos at the bridge, or even pizzicato, the effect is rather self-conscious ... I still believe that the best way to hear this work is to have the composer play it on the piano, singing whatever his fingers cannot encompass, and cursing the page-turner.[24]

What was Gould's take on his major music composition? In the radio interview with a renowned CBC television producer, Vincent Tovell, in 1960, this is how Gould characterized his music piece:

Tovell: What about your String Quartet? Where has it been played?

Gould: It's been played here at Stratford. In fact, its premiere was there. It's been played in Montreal. And it's been recorded by the CBC for their overseas library. [In spite] of its

> many sections, it's really one sonata allegro movement with three very clear sections—the exposition, the development and recapitulation and a coda which alone is three hundred bars long—and as you can imagine, all this takes about thirty-five minutes. It didn't completely come off. Three years of my life went into this thing and I am extremely proud of it. But it didn't completely come off.[25]

What a powerful confession! Though Gould declared the pride he had taken in his String Quartet, he could not hide his self-disappointment. It was as if his entire talent and motivation to compose music were in question. This was his real identity crisis as a composer.

Gould's music friend and conductor, Victor DiBello, enjoyed Gould's composition. This is what he said in an interview at his home in Toronto:

"Have you had a chance to hear Gould's quartet live?" I asked DiBello.

"Of course, at the Stratford Festival many years ago. I told you before that I had conducted the orchestra there and Glenn and I spent much time together."

"How did you like it?" I asked.

"I thought it was a very attractive piece. You can tell Gould was a composer at heart. I congratulated him and we discussed it in detail. He liked my opinion," DiBello recalled.

"Why do you think Gould's quartet was never performed in Toronto?" I asked.

"It wasn't? How could it be?" DiBello was stunned and in doubt.

"I am afraid not. At least not while Gould was alive," I said with regrets.

"Well, I am speechless. Come to think of it, the piece should have been premiered in Toronto soon after the Stratford performance. There must be a mistake here ..." DiBello almost was in agony.

"I wish there was one." I probably sounded helpless myself.

"But, I don't know what to say, it's the mentality, a small-town mentality, I guess. Not to perform his music in his native city, not to honor him, it's pathetic,"[26] blustered DiBello as he stood up for his friend.

Indeed, the Toronto music community was suspicious and obviously not ready to embrace Gould as a composer, which was summed up in the fact that his String Quartet op. 1 was not publicly performed in Toronto during Gould's lifetime. The recording produced at Severance Hall in Cleveland was first presented on the CBC radio in 1961. The CBC *Times* of June 1961 reported:

> Gould's first opus, a romantic String Quartet (completed in 1955 and published the next year) took him 2½ years to write. It is a mahogany-coloured work, with an intensely beautiful grain and richly-coloured shadings, written in one movement that takes little over half-an-hour to perform. Following its premiere at the Stratford Festival in 1956 the New York *Times* described it as "moving and impressive." The Symphonia Quartet of Cleveland gave it its first American performance late in 1959, and the Cleveland *News* reported next day that the work was "lyrical, romantic, suffused with a delicate glow."[27]

If Gould's String Quartet was published in 1956, why did it take another five years to hear it on the radio? What made Torontonians so reluctant to broadcast it immediately after the Stratford premiere in 1956, or why was it not performed live in Toronto? There are no reasonable answers but only clamoring questions. It appears that the music community in Toronto was parochial and not open for something untested and new. Gould's compelling need to champion the Viennese school composers did not help the matter and was met with skepticism, even dismissed as an act of his eccentricity. Unlike Edvard Grieg, who put a signature on his compositions that became typical Norwegian music, and unlike Aaron Copland, who put an American signature on his music, Gould's String Quartet could not be qualified as typically Canadian. On the whole, it was not seen as patriotic and worthwhile to perform in public and celebrate. Had Gould received more praise and encouragement by the press and audiences, this may have been reassuring enough to help him continue his career as a composer.

COMMUNICATION AT A DISTANCE

> All in all, he [Gould] proved exasperatingly normal, and I found it impossible to believe that I was sitting opposite to the world's greatest pianist ...
>
> Jim Curtis[28]

If Glenn lost the potential chance to be admired as a composer, he gained a sizable population of supporters and fans for his performing and recording successes. Among family members, his cousin, Jessie Greig, maintained positive regard for him throughout the years of his growth and took lively interest in his progress. Jessie worked as an elementary school teacher in Oshawa, a small town in the vicinity of both Toronto and her native Uxbridge. Soon after the release of Gould's first record with Columbia, Bach's *Goldberg Variations*, Jessie wrote him this letter that captures her affection that Glenn could always count upon:

> Dear Glenn,
>
> Just a wee note to say how proud I am of you—as are all the Greigs. Glenn I've told you many times that I know nothing of music (as you well know). However, I understand plain English, so when the critics say ("one of the greatest etc.") I want you to know I heartily agree with them—but you were always the greatest, so far as mother, dad and I were concerned. Perhaps we were a bit reticent about telling you, but if we were, just put it down to our stolid, silent Scottish background.[29]

When Jessie said "you were *always* the greatest," she referred to the special status Glenn had enjoyed from the people around him from the time he was a child. By that time, both the Goulds and the Greigs delighted in Glenn's expanding popularity. His presence was constantly felt either through his radio broadcasts, live appearances, or in print. Naturally, it was gratifying and flattering to have him as a relative. Jessie concluded her letter:

> We so enjoyed the spread you received from *Life* magazine. Really, we never expect another member of the family to make its pages—once in a lifetime for that sort of thing. Frankly speaking, I think *Life* should pay me a small fee

for sales promotion (that's my Scottish background too). I have "buttonholed" everyone within speaking distance to show them my famous cousin.

Well, I won't take up any more of your time. Congratulations again and once more.

Sincerely
Jessie Greig[30]

If Glenn received his first letters of admiration at the age of six upon his radio debut, then in the mid-1950s, after his New York debut, the letters of his fans showered him like a true world-famous celebrity. His former school teachers wrote him words of remembrance and praise. Likewise, his former classmates, current friends and acquaintances sent him their good wishes. When the celebrities in the world of entertainment receive letters from their fans, their press secretaries review them and respond. When Glenn Gould received letters from his fans, he felt obliged to answer them personally, never just in a two-line thank you note but always elaborating. Though he did not share much about his private life, he readily spoke about the music. Composing letters took a big chunk from his creative time. He often wrote them in several drafts, sent them by taxi to his secretary who would type them and send them back for him to edit the text until it was ready for a final copy. For some of his business-oriented letters, he had to research the topic, which was a time-consuming process. Often, it took several hours to complete such letters, but Gould still pursued them with fervor.

In the pre-technology era, correspondence was the only way of communicating with others at a distance. Great individuals like Goethe, Beethoven, Freud and many others were known to write hundreds of letters during their lives, which in the course of time became historical and literary treasures for mankind. Gould, who had been in the habit of writing letters since he was a schoolboy, left behind a wealth of copies of letters sent and received.[31] He enjoyed hearing from his fans, particularly when they were sympathetic and supportive of him. Their praise and admiration made him feel safe and reassured that he was okay. His admirers wrote generously to Glenn expressing their love of his music and care for him as a person. Compliments were coming from everywhere and Glenn thrived on them. His childhood friend, Norman Brenan, wrote:

Dear artist Gould, April 15, 1956

You are now an artist, and I am now a dud; but in childhood it seems we had two feelings in common at least.

One, the urge to express ourselves and find our philosophy through the piano.

Two, the urge to consider physical combat is for the birds (nut house type of birds).

You've done something marvelous with your feeling; but I double-crossed mine and concentrated on engineering—hence I am a dud today.

May your wonderful plans succeed all the way. Keep giving the people joys they haven't experienced before; and keep manifesting yourself through music. All the best,

Sincerely
Norman Brenan[32]

In the same year, 1956, after a string of favorable music events, his manager, Walter Homburger, encouraged Glenn to take a break and have a holiday in the Bahamas. Homburger, a shrewd businessman, thought that Gould's sojourn in such an exquisite place as Nassau might be good for publicity. He also wanted to help his client, who never went on a "real" holiday, to be a little more experienced and worldly. To maximize the project, Homburger invited Jock Carroll, photographer and writer for *Weekend Magazine*, to join Gould, not as a chaperon but more as a journalist. *Weekend Magazine*, having a vested interest in this mission, sponsored Carroll in order to report on Gouldian eccentricities and popularize his music wizardry.

Accompanied by Carroll, Gould flew to Nassau for a two-week vacation at the Fort Montagu Beach Hotel. During this short-lived friendship, Carroll, a nonmusical person but a keen observer of human behavior, got to know some deeply personal and never-published details about his star companion. From Carroll's avid pen and photographs, one finds that Gould did not spend time sailing or snorkeling and exploring the incomparable riches of the ocean but spent most of his time barricaded in his modest hotel room with a "Do Not Disturb" sign hung on his door. Carroll wrote in his notes:

> After several days of waiting around the hotel without any word from my wunderkind, I began to get panicky. I knocked on his door. Somewhat reluctantly, he [Gould] let me in. It was a bright tropical day outside but his room was almost dark, the curtains drawn tightly, the two twin beds pushed together in the middle of the room.

"I was afraid you'd died," I said.

> "No," said Gould. "I've been working. I've gotten three bars of my opera written since we got here. I have to be alone a lot. It's going to take me about three years for the opera. I did a radio interview a few weeks ago in which I developed a theme I stole from Thomas Mann—how a creative artist has to be a bit of an antisocial human being in order to get his work done."[33]

From Carroll we learn that Gould practiced piano in solitude at the local nightclub "between the hours of two and four in the morning," showing all his typical mannerisms, sitting low at the piano, being shoeless, sitting with his legs crossed, conducting with the free hand, and humming, though there was nobody there to watch him play. Carroll, who was eavesdropping, concluded that Gould's manners were natural and simply an aspect of his creative mind, not an attention-seeking device. More intimate stories related to his health issues; his nightmares and fears were all candidly shared with Carroll with a strict plea for confidentiality. Gould shared with Carroll a recurrent nightmare about being swept over Niagara Falls. He struggled in the dream "to catch hold of a protruding rock and hang on." Said Gould:

> At this point in the dream, some strangers appear and they begin banging away at my hands, trying to make me loosen my grip. This is where I wake up. My mother says as long as I can keep waking up at this point I'll be all right.[34]

This nightmare bespeaks Gould's insecurity that accompanied him wherever he went. He was not able to totally relax in this Caribbean paradise because he was not able to forget how dangerously distant he was from home. Carroll was the only person he knew. To relieve his unbearable anxiety, Gould let down his guard and told his temporary confidant about his nightmare. Then Gould proceeded to share with Carroll his terrible fear of eating in public and about going out of his way to avoid gatherings, parties and restaurants, which could be potentially embarrassing to him.

Unfortunately, the relationship with Carroll was temporary and lasted only one month after their Bahamas interlude. Apparently, during their last telephone conversation, Gould realized that Carroll was foremost a photo-reporter who wrote down everything he observed and heard, and that he, Gould, had shared too much of himself with a stranger. After Carroll's reports about Gould were published in the *Weekend Magazine*, Gould felt extremely exposed and vulnerable. He realized that public knowledge of the details of his personal life could be damaging to his career. With this in mind, Gould recoiled from Carroll and, from then on, avoided any professional or lay person who was felt to be prying into his private affairs. For the rest of his life, Gould maintained a consistent attitude in relationship to other individuals and to his audiences. He would share and exhibit his creative genius in front of the world but definitely and emphatically insisted on staying distant and anonymous as a person.

It was at the cottage during his self-imposed seclusion that Glenn rediscovered his two faithful inanimate companions, the radio and the telephone. The radio was on at all hours, even during his sleep. Glenn slept upstairs in his attic bedroom, which he had favored since he had been a young boy. The lights were also on at night because he had a fear of the dark. It follows that the radio and lights meant a lot to him. They served to protect him and keep him company, soothe and appease his restlessness and act as vehicles of communication with the world. Though Glenn played his piano while the radio was on, he was not distracted by its "noise." This was possible thanks to his contrapuntal mind, which was capable of concentrating in several directions at the same time. Glenn had an excellent figure-ground ability, to focus intensely on one primary thing that stands out, while focusing less but still being aware of the background qualities. In this sense, he could pay attention to several things at the same time.

When Glenn needed to have contact with others, he called long distance. At first he called his mother, who always had words of advice for him. She wondered if he ate on time and whether his clothes were freshly pressed. She arranged for her neighbor at the cottage, Mrs. Doolittle, to watch over Glenn by tidying up the house and preparing occasional hot meals for him. Glenn was not the type of person who would tolerate any hired help, but he was familiar with Mrs. Doolittle and did not mind her sporadic "supervision." His anxious mother was always worried about him: "How's your health, Glenn? " "Make sure to bundle up, the winds are too strong this season," she would ask and comment, which only raised his own concerns over his health and reinforced the idea of "bundling up." Glenn's curious mind wanted to communicate with a wider choice of people. He called Walter Homburger, with whom he discussed his business goals. Then he called his friends, Oskar Morawetz, Nicholas Killburn, Nicholas Goldsmith and many others, to discuss music. Gradually, the temporary practice of making telephone contacts grew into a habitual need to speak, express feelings and opinions, joke around, negotiate business or to play guessing games—all over the telephone. These telephone calls were quite long, usually about an hour, but not infrequently Glenn stayed on the phone two or three hours or longer. He relished them. Whenever talking over the phone, Glenn came across as being eager, animated and very lucid. Glenn called usually late at night, which was convenient for him since he stayed up late but was inconvenient for his partners in conversation who were getting ready to settle and go to sleep. It seems that Glenn's impulse to socialize over the telephone was so strong that he became a little insensitive to those he had called. Once he was in his element, anxiety-free and safe from being seen and criticized, Glenn felt like staying on the phone forever. Obviously, he had difficulty parting and saying "goodnight." Glenn's evolving insomnia made him delay going to bed rather than making him look forward to it.

Reactions of his friends and associates to Glenn's telephone calls were twofold. Most of them felt good about hearing from him. After all, Glenn was such a versatile personality and a very easy one to engage in conversation. Glenn would usually put forward his guessing games: "Guess what I am preparing for the next recital?" which was supposed to break the ice. Once the quiz was complete, Glenn would initiate another topic. Those who enjoyed Glenn's youthful spirit went along with his ways on the phone and turned into listeners and sounding boards.

Unluckily for Glenn, among his friends and acquaintances there were always those who could not stand his habit of calling late. They also had little tolerance for his lengthy monologues and for what they perceived as his self-centered attitude on the phone. By avoiding his phone calls, or by cutting him short in conversation, these friends risked possible break-up of relationship with Glenn. This very situation happened between Glenn and his friend from childhood, Robert Fulford. Glenn used to call Bob at all hours, disregarding Bob's needs for privacy and his basic need for sleep. Bob pointed to Glenn's insensitivity and asked him not to call late. Instantly, their entire friendship was in jeopardy. From then on, the two friends gradually grew apart.

Thanks to the electronic transmission through the telephone, Glenn's skills for communication with others became very advanced. He was capable of starting and maintaining friendship over the phone and was equally capable of dissolving it in the same manner. Glenn also conducted a variety of business transactions, which were negotiated and planned over the phone. While music was Gould's best mode of emotional and creative communication, the telephone became his most desired medium of verbal communication with others.

While at the cottage, Glenn acquired two other electronic gadgets that consumed a good deal of his attention. Just like his father, who was one of the first local owners of a radio, Glenn was among the first to own a tape recorder. This was an old-fashioned tape recorder in a huge box with two large reels. It stood directly next to the piano so that Glenn was able to tape his piano rendition of a music piece, then get up and push the button of the tape recorder and play it back. Gould's overall success in his piano career owed much to the use of the tape recorder.

Starting in 1952, Glenn was not only heard in the concert hall and on the radio but was also seen playing the piano on the television screen. The Goulds, who were always big on new technology, were among the first ones to have a TV set. By the mid-1950s, Glenn had the pleasure of watching TV both at home and at the cottage, as the family owned two sets for Glenn's entertainment needs.

By pursuing multiple telephone calls and by writing letters on a daily basis, Glenn was communicating at a distance with a network of friends. His correspondence was enormous. In the late 1950s and in the 1960s, Glenn wrote approximately two letters daily, averaging 700 letters and greeting cards per year. This number dropped in the last ten years of his life. The copies of only a little over 2,000 of his letters are preserved and available for research at the Library and Archives Canada.

Two themes are prevalent in Glenn's letters—his personal health and music. He referred to his ailments in terms such as "lethargic malaise," "stomach flu" or "pain in my hand." He apologized profusely for being late in responding to his fans: "I am ashamed of myself for not writing you sooner ..." and in order to make up for his delay he would write in a long and chatty manner. Gould's letters written in the first fifteen years of his adult life are on the whole more lively, humorous and sparkling, as opposed to those produced in the second part, which are dryer in tone and businesslike.

While Glenn predominantly pursued communication at a distance, he avidly maintained another medium of relating to the world. This was his world of relative emotional closeness. In some instances, not so infrequently, Glenn was able to let his guard down and open himself a little more than usual to his friends and fans. In the 1950s, a young Canadian-born harpsichordist, Jim Curtis, became a fervent fan of Gould. From the first time he heard him play, Curtis made a point of traveling to Gould's concerts and talking to him backstage. Their personality mix worked very well, and they developed a degree of social closeness. Curtis, who was at first a student of Greta Kraus, renowned Toronto harpsichordist, and later on her assistant and friend, summoned enough courage to call Glenn at his home in Toronto in the hope of visiting him. Curtis kept a journal of all his contacts with his famous music counterpart, which serves as an invaluable source of insight into Glenn's private life and his capacity for closeness. The following is an entry from Curtis's diary:

> Saturday, November 24, 1956
> ... Late in the afternoon the idea occurred to me to visit Glenn in Toronto ... I phoned Greta [Kraus] for his address and set out. Sure enough, after supper I found him at home, alone, wrapped in a housecoat and nursing a cold he had just caught on the way back from the concert in Texas (Dallas, Beethoven 5)! The next hour and a half still seem an incredible dream. We sat in the living room, he lounging on the couch, two well-punctured socks in full view, gesticulating wildly at times to demonstrate a musical passage ... His dog Banquo proved overly friendly, and kept interrupting our conversation by nuzzling up to me. At one point we went into an adjoining room and he improvised a bit to demonstrate his practice piano ... We discussed many things—his recordings, the critics, Pleasant's book ("silly"), jazz (he has no use for it), his mannerisms, technique ("I've never had serious difficulties"), Schnabel, Kapell ("too slow") etc. He even asked my advice as to what he should play Monday night, and I suggested the 'Italian' [Concerto]. All in all, he proved exasperatingly normal, and I found it impossible to believe that I was sitting opposite to the world's greatest pianist ...[35]

Curtis, who remained Gould's studious admirer, shed much light on this "other side" of the pianist that is often neglected—being warm, sensible and down-to-earth. As it turned out, on Monday, November 26, 1956, Gould appeared in Niagara Falls and played the Italian Concerto. Curtis, who was at the recital, wrote: "Glenn's playing was more astonishing than ever: his technical wizardry verges on the miraculous. Everyone was enthralled." Not only was Gould not aloof nor did he ask Curtis not to attend his concert, but, on the contrary, he made a point of fulfilling his wish by playing the magnificent "Italian." The emotional transaction between the two soul mates was bursting with mutual empathy.

Over the years, Gould developed into a powerful communicator. By using electronic media like the radio for broadcasting his music and related thoughts, by the massive use of telephone and correspondence, by recording his music and, finally, by telecasting it, Gould communicated the products of his versatile mind at long distances. When the Toronto-based philosopher Marshall McLuhan introduced the concept of the "global village," Gould was already practicing the very concept by communicating his music to the world at large.

THE KING IS TO BLAME

> Look not mournfully into the Past. It comes not back again. Wisely improve the Present. It is thine. Go forth to meet the shadowy Future, without fear, and with a manly heart.
>
> Henry Wadsworth Longfellow[36]

The period from 1959 to 1960 was emotionally painful for Glenn. His first cousin and cohort from childhood, Barry Johnson, tragically died in a boating accident in June 1959. When interviewed, Barry's younger brother, Dr. Tom Johnson, a dentist from Lindsay, Ontario, described:

T.J. Barry was a game warden working for the Department of Lands and Forestry in Northern Ontario. Once during the inspection of Tamagami Lake, he fainted on the boat, fell overboard and drowned.

H.M. He was only twenty-five years old. Why did he faint? Did he have any illness, something like epilepsy, that would account for his fainting?

T.J. No, as far as I know he didn't. I was told it was an accident.

H.M. Do you know whether he was depressed? I understand that your mother, Freda, was quite depressed, wasn't she?

T.J. Yes, but that was only after Barry's death. She took it so hard. She was never the same afterwards.[37]

The tragic event happened upon Gould's return from his triumphant series of concerts in London, England, where he performed Beethoven's concertos with Josef Krips and the London Symphony. Glenn, who by that time rarely attended any family gatherings, appeared at Barry's funeral at Cannington, Ontario. The news about Barry's death came as a great shock, yet, quite predictably, Glenn was unable to express sorrow and engage in the customary shared grieving. Instead, he had an emotional setback that was manifested in further, more severe social withdrawal and an increase in physical ailments. Glenn was petrified by the loss, which made him feel helpless and reminded him of his own mortality. No amount of fame experienced in London could remedy his deep-seated sense of sorrow related to the tragedy of his younger cousin. There was also a great deal of unresolved and unfinished family grief that stretched through three generations of the Gould family, making Glenn more vulnerable to loss. When Barry perished, a long-repressed emotional pain was stirred up and relived, particularly by Barry's mother who was Glenn's favorite aunt, Freda. Decades earlier, Freda's paternal uncle, Freddy Gold, drowned in the local pond. From then on, the family of Tom Gold never fully resolved the grief and guilt over Freddy's death.

Upon Barry's death by drowning, his mother, Freda, entered into inconsolable mourning. "After my brother's tragedy, my mother was never the same. She became depressed and required shock treatment,"[38] recalled Dr. Tom Johnson. Unresolved family grief, just like any other unfinished family business, is liable to surface and to become compounded by the newly arisen grief over recent losses. In this example, the Gold family could never quite work through their grief and successfully master the mourning-liberation process. More than seventy years after Tom's baby brother Alfred "Freddy" Gold drowned, Barry, the grandson of Tom and nephew of Bert, succumbed to an identical destiny.

Barry's mother, Alfreda "Freda" Gold, was named after her uncle Freddy. Such were the deep attachments in the Gold family. Without knowing, Glenn was a subject of cumulative grief, the past grief in the family of his grandfather and the current one experienced upon the loss of his peer-cousin. This event was so distressing that it had a negative subterranean effect on Gould's concert career. Following Barry's death, Gould became more frail and phobic. He made only one mini-tour to Europe by giving concerts in Salzburg and Lucerne. It was in Lucerne that he was compelled to see the painting of Charles I that both he and Barry always viewed in the living room of their grandfather, Tom. This marked the end of Gould's European performing career.

Gould did not even get through this bereavement when another major loss occurred. On November 9, 1959, Alberto Guerrero, Glenn's principal music teacher, died unexpectedly from acute heart failure. Gould, who in 1951 took part in the commemoration of the composer, Arnold Schoenberg, through a personally written speech and interpretation of his music before a school audience at the conservatory, missed taking part in any type of visible memorial service upon Guerrero's passing. It was John Beckwith, another one of Guerrero's students, who paid special honor to Guerrero on behalf of the music community. On the day of Guerrero's death, Gould gave a recital in Rock Hill, South Carolina, as a part of his extensive American tour. The program consisted of music works that Gould years ago perfected in the presence of his teacher, such as Bach's Partita no. 1, in B-flat Major; Berg's Sonata for piano, op. 1; Mozart's Sonata no. 10, C Major, KV 330; Schoenberg's Piano Pieces and Beethoven's Sonata in A-flat major, op. 110. Glenn's concert tour, which started on October 25, 1959, in Berkeley, California, continued through Denver, Colorado to Atlanta, Georgia, and Rock Hill, South Carolina, where he was on November 9. His next concert was in Cincinnati, Ohio, on November 20. Technically, if Glenn really had wanted to attend Guerrero's funeral event, he could have squeezed it in between his Rock Hill and Cincinnati appearances. Though it would have been a tight squeeze, it would have been useful for him to have honored and mourned his teacher's passing more directly.

In the fall of 1959, Glenn was struggling with a bout of depression. Upon Guerrero's death, he was in the grip of an inner conflict of love and hate in relation to his music mentor. None of these powerful feelings of deep love and attachment, as well as anger and hurt, were ever sufficiently expressed outwardly. The grief, on top of Glenn's underlying depression, compounded with Glenn's inertia and reluctance to travel, caused him to make such an unfortunate decision to refrain from paying respect and saying a final goodbye to Guerrero. Instead, Glenn's love of his teacher was reflected through his positive identification with the music and personality aspects of Guerrero. Glenn's father was also unaware of Glenn's innermost feelings about Guerrero, as portrayed in our following dialogue:

"What was Glenn's reaction to Mr. Guerrero's passing?" I asked Bert Gould.

"Honestly, I can't remember," Mr. Gould replied briskly.

"Was Glenn present at Mr. Guerrero's funeral?" I persisted.

"Oh, I am sorry but I wouldn't know." Mr. Gould did not favor the question.

"What about yourself, were you at Mr. Guerrero's funeral?" I asked.

"Well, of course. My wife and I went to the Humphries Funeral Home where Mr. Guerrero's remains were laid out and we paid him respect," Mr.Gould vividly recalled.

"To refresh your memory I can tell you now that Glenn was not present at the funeral, simply because he was out of town making an appearance in the States. I am interested whether you remember his reaction to his teacher's death after he had returned home." I was grappling for an answer.

"Funny thing, I can't remember much more. I suppose Glenn was shaken but I don't remember that he said anything to me,"[39] Mr. Gould was anxious to get on to another topic.

There is no doubt that the Goulds regretted Glenn's emotional distancing from his one-time valued and beloved teacher. When Guerrero died, they would have preferred Glenn to have honored him with more feeling and dedication. Finally, when Mr. Gould was asked to reflect on this sad event, more than thirty years after Guerrero's death and more than ten years after Glenn's passing, his memory of the true feelings was blunted by his need to keep up with good public relations, as well as by his need to defend Glenn's interpersonal emotional flaws.

Studies of the early lives of great performing artists show that a favorable relationship between a principal music teacher and a student is one of the key factors in the future adjustment of the student as a musician. A good example would be that of the great twentieth-century pianist, Joseph Hofmann, who had a gratifying relationship with his music mentor, Anton Rubinstein. Hofmann reminisced on their memorable relationship and the effects of parting in the following heartfelt confession:

> The effect that his death had upon me I shall never forget. The world appeared suddenly entirely empty to me, devoid of any interest. My grief made me realize how my heart had worshipped not only the artist in him but also the man; how I loved him as if he were my father.[40]

Hofmann referred to Rubinstein with affection and honor as "my master," whereas Rubinstein composed a Polonaise in E-flat minor and dedicated it to his exceptional student, his future pianist-successor. The student-teacher transaction, but more importantly the person-to-person relation, was complete and fair, ending in mutual love and respect. Hofmann's identification with his teacher did not preclude his ability to individuate from him into a great world virtuoso.

In the Gould-Guerrero example, the interpersonal emotional transaction between them was incomplete and unsatisfactory. Gould could not weep or tell stories, nor reminisce about his teacher upon his passing. He simply was unable to express any feelings about his Signor Guerrero. Yet the loss of his mentor was a developmental milestone that, in its meaning, was comparable to the losses of other relatives. In the absence of appropriate emotional catharsis, Gould was at heightened risk of being sickly and indisposed.

In the 1960s, people were becoming more aware of the role of stress in their lives. Sociologists Holmes and Rahe[41] found a correlation between recent life events, like death, separation and various life changes and losses and the onset of illness. It was further observed that psychosocial stressors that occur in rapid succession are taxing on our well-being, as they do not allow enough time to adapt and attend to them.[42] A prerequisite for a concert pianist of Gould's calibre is to be able to endure a highly eventful life full of rapid unions and separations, the interpersonal effects of fame, and myriad concerns and apprehensions that all call for good coping mechanisms and social adaptiveness. Even under the best of circumstances, performing artists invariably suffer from anticipation anxiety and are at heightened risk for a personal crisis of some sort. It is said, "the show must go on," and indeed, no matter how the performers feel, they are expected to perform at their maximal capacity and be perfect. This is why job burnout is so common among touring performers. It was not accidental that famous pianists like Vladimir Horowitz and Van Cliburn disappeared from the concert stage for a block of twelve and eight years, respectively, before they were able to make a comeback. In their cases, the emotional "burnout" and breakdown of their ability to cope with the high demands of their careers led to the lengthy withdrawal from the performing scene. In Gould's case, his withdrawal from public concerts was at an early age and was permanent, which was suggestive of the magnitude of his life stress and inability to continue his performing career.

Gould appeared to be predisposed to situational crises and emotional stress in that period of his life. In 1959, on top of fifty-one major concerts given and over and above the traumatic loss of Barry and Guerrero, Gould experienced a major life change—he had to move out of his birth home. This new undertaking was prompted by rising tension in the relationship with his father. While during the 1950s Gould was an eminent music personality in the eyes of the world, at home he was still treated as a delicate and difficult child. His parents spent their entire lives trying to be "normal" and proper citizens but ended up having such an unusual and controversial son. Glenn's finicky eating habits, the way he dressed, his daring driving practices, his singular posture at the piano, many interpersonal misgivings and ailing health were all perpetual sources of concern and bewilderment to his parents. They both often were exasperated by Glenn's oddities and erratic habits, but they each handled them differently. Bert was at the end of his tether with Glenn. He was critical, and he expected Glenn to change. While his mother was subtler and more conciliatory in her expectations, she still wished Glenn to be "normal." On his side, Glenn felt entitled to parental love and approval without having to conform to their desires. He had a healthy need to move out and be his own independent person.

From his mid-adolescence on, Glenn and his father continued to grow further apart. Open clashes, prolonged silences, mutual avoidance, and the lack of good times together typified their relationship. Glenn was in constant opposition with his totalitarian father. He resented his occupation as a furrier, his conventional behavior, strong masculinity and patronizing manner. There was a great deal of competitiveness between the two men, stemming from their personal differences. Gould's lifelong philosophy against competition, including sports, music contests, and even competing at school for the best marks, derived from his unresolved father-son, love-and-hate relationship and inability to come to terms with his father.

It turned out that for Glenn the act of moving out was harder than he ever anticipated, for this meant emotional separation from his home and his mother. Ever since a lad, Glenn always fantasized about owning his own personal country home where he would establish a domestic atmosphere full of pets and other pleasantries. Of course, he wanted to duplicate early experiences at his home and at the cottage. Once the decision to move out was made, Glenn went through a brief episode of elation about making his dream come true. He had a short-lived grand fantasy to move into a large country mansion with the pretty name of "Donchery." In his letter to Edith Boecker, dated January 27, 1960,[43] Gould described his ordeal of moving out in his humorous but extremely honest manner:

> ... Several months ago I began to develop a longing for grandeur which my establishment at Lake Simcoe was not fully able to satisfy. So, more or less on a whim, I became a tenant of an estate some fifteen miles above Toronto, known as "Donchery." It was love at first sight and lasted until the day after the lease was signed! The estate, let me tell you, had 26 rooms, if one counts the seven bathrooms, the breakfast room, the scullery, the dog kennel ...[44]

Gould proceeded to praise other amenities of the estate—"a river running through it, a swimming pool and tennis court, a four car garage,"—adding that "at night with flood lights was like looking at Salzburg castle." Gould continued to tell his intimate story in minute detail:

> Anyway the lease was signed on December 13 and on December 19 I was suddenly struck with the realization of what I had done as well as with the intriguing puzzle of what I would ever do with 26 rooms in the first place.[45]

This is for Gould a most unusual outpouring of feelings about his very private business, all shared with a casual acquaintance, Edith Boecker. Gould met Boecker in Hamburg, Germany, during his European tour two years earlier and carried on with her a sporadic correspondence. This letter is a rare example of an open but rather impulsive confession of a personal and disastrous undertaking. Gould, as the good story teller, offered a lively description of his euphoria around shopping for kitchenware and other necessities for "Donchery:"

> On the second day of the lease, I set out on a gigantic buying spree in a vain attempt to furnish 26 rooms in two days..[46]

Gould then insightfully described how his excitement switched into the state of self-doubt:

> The following day I was back at "Donchery" to welcome the movers as various purchases began to arrive. I was alone at that time in the twenty-six rooms at first, as the larger items such as the refrigerator and the stove arrived, I was grateful for the space which they filled and optimistic about the possibility of polishing off the other 25 rooms. But then suddenly it happened—the brooms and Pyrex dishes arrived and I was filled with all the horror of the domestic idyll I had been courting.[47]

Gould brought his innocent adventure to a dramatic conclusion:

> Only last week, at considerable expense to the management, was I able to purchase my release and so now, when not occupying a newly acquired apartment

in Toronto, I return with my tail between my legs to Lake Simcoe which somehow seems quite grand enough.[48]

This key document reveals how complex Gould's situation was at the time of moving. In a sincere and unguarded manner, he gave the account of the rise and fall of his enthusiasm and self-confidence into the recesses of defeat and shame. By setting his eyes and wishes on the beautiful "Donchery" estate, Gould briefly felt worthy of making it his home. The short-lived feeling of self-confidence was quickly replaced by personal insecurity, which prevented him from completing his goal. In the background of this change was his plaguing separation anxiety and fear of change. Gould was stunned by his own realization that he was just not ready for such a big move and for such a leap to freedom; that he lacked the skills to run any household let alone an elaborate one; that he was neither a handyman like his father nor a gardener like his mother, and even less of an interior decorator. He obviously did not have the approval nor support of his parents for this undertaking. On the contrary, the amount of shame that followed—"I return with my tail between my legs to Lake Simcoe"—is suggestive that his parents may have chastised him for his immodesty and lack of thoughtfulness. Gould's temporary euphoria and aggrandizement seemed like manic behavior, but it was not prolonged as in manic-depressive illness. It was rather short-lived and merely served as a defense mechanism defending against his high separation anxiety.

The empathetic reader is probably right now wishing that Gould had gone ahead, moved to "Donchery" and made it a Salzburg castle à la Gould with his own gazebo overlooking the river; and that he took on the challenge of overcoming his anxieties and guilt feelings over having grand aspirations for the beauty and luxury that life offers. The truth is that Gould, had he been independent enough and sure enough of himself, could have moved wherever he pleased without owing explanations to anybody and with no need to feel guilty. Unfortunately, he was not ready for such a reach. His original dazzling fantasy about moving to "Donchery" was shattered and replaced by his somber inner reality of feeling unworthy. Incidentally, he still moved out into a rental apartment but with a different set of feelings. With a sense of indifference, dreariness and humility, Gould eventually moved into a six-room penthouse at 110 St. Clair Avenue West in Toronto. This was to become his permanent but unloved and never enjoyed dwelling.

In that same critical December of 1959, when Gould was gathering the momentum to build his own nest, another stressful event unfolded that impaired his well-being and had a negative impact on the outcome of moving out. This event was well researched by Gould's earlier biographer, Otto Friedrich,[49] and could be summed up as follows: On December 18, 1959, following the end of his tiring tour in the United States, Gould made a stopover at New York Steinway. During his meeting with the manager, Winston Fitzgerald, the chief piano technician, William Hupfer, entered and greeted Gould by touching his shoulder. When Hupfer left, Gould said to Fitzgerald: "He hurt me." From then on, Gould was convinced that Hupfer had caused him the "shoulder injury." This event at Steinway Hall triggered a six-month-long period of depression and preoccupation with his purported illness. Gould entered extensive treatment, including painful cortisone shots, physiotherapy, and even an upper-body cast for his "shoulder injury." The spurious ailment was responsible for his numerous recital cancellations and litigation against Hupfer. The following is a reconstruction of several episodes of a situational crisis in a certain period of Gould's life, which in the long run contributed to his decline and eventual withdrawal from the concert stage:

PSYCHO—SOCIAL STRESS IN GOULD'S LIFE IN 1959-1960

1959	
June 6	- cousin Barry Johnson drowned
November 7	- music mentor Alberto Guerrero died
November/December	- preparations for moving out of the parental home.
December 13	- lease signed for Donchery Estate
December 14	- buying spree to furnish the mansion
December 17	- concert in Oklahoma City
December 18	- business trip to New York; "incident" at Steinway Hall; purported shoulder injury
December 19	- realization and panic over moving out of parental home and moving into a 26-room mansion
December 25	- Christmas—emotional tension at home over moving; sense of shame and guilt over being grandiose and ungrateful
1960	
January	- canceling the lease on Donchery; hastily moving into an ordinary apartment
January-April	- Gould's last dog, Banquo, who was in the care of his father, was run over by a car and killed instantly
	- being ill and receiving treatment for the shoulder injury; high anxiety and depression
	- all recitals canceled; continued performing at concerts as a soloist with an orchestra, as follows:

March 2	Baltimore, Maryland
March 18	Toledo, Ohio
March 27, 28	Victoria, B.C.
April 5	Washington, D.C.
April 9	Rochester, New York
April 19	Montreal, Quebec
April 24	South Bend, Indiana

May	- Orthopedic treatment in Philadelphia, upper-body cast, rehabilitation
July	- partial relief from the separation crisis and psychosomatic body pain; returned to concerts and recitals;
July 29 and August 2	- triumphant concerts in Vancouver
October	- success in Detroit, etc.
December	- filed a lawsuit in Federal Court, claiming $300,000 in damages against Hupfer and Steinway & Sons
January 1961	- settled out of court; received $9,372.35 for damages.

Here is one possible psychological explanation of Gould's separation crisis and alleged physical pain. Gould was prompted to move out of his parental home because of his strained relationship with his father. It follows that he likely felt pushed out by his powerful father, with whom he had always competed for the love of his mother. Not only did Glenn feel emotionally defeated and injured by his father, he also had to endure the pain from having to separate from his mother, with whom he was emotionally intertwined. Chronologically, Gould was twenty-seven years of age, which means old enough to be moving out, but emotionally he was not ready. In the end, he was not able to successfully handle his separation crisis, which resulted in a breakdown of his existing strengths. Amid the high separation anxiety, there was a short-lived upsurge of overconfidence and grandiosity represented in his attempt to move into a luxurious estate mansion. This grand undertaking was an unconscious compensation for his losses and associated pains. While Gould was victorious on the world stage, he could not win his Oedipal victory over his father. Worse, he was filled with a profound sense of humiliation over losing this battle. Gould used to abhor competition of any kind in the course of his entire life. He said: "Competition is at the root of all evil." He was not conscious of saying that unresolved conflicts in the son-mother-father triangle of his dysfunctional family were at the root of his many "evil" experiences and personal sufferings.

The incident at Steinway Hall involving the piano technician, William Hupfer, stood for Gould's unconscious projection of his inward rage with his father onto an outsider. In Gould's mind, Hupfer was like a bad and critical father, as in the past, on several occasions, he refused to tune and adjust Gould's piano to his liking. Hupfer, the reputable piano tuner who used to tune pianos for the pianistic elite like Paderewski and Rachmaninov, tuned the piano for Gould too but set the limit about altering the properties of Gould's pianos. Gould, the piano master, was hurt and angry by being doubted by Hupfer. According to Gould, Hupfer was supposed to listen to his wishes and fulfill them unconditionally. In reality, Gould was fundamentally injured by his father, and very slightly and inadvertently by Hupfer but reacted as if Hupfer was the main culprit. Gould subconsciously chose Hupfer to bear the brunt of his enormous anger that he could not express toward his father. It appears that Gould's acute left shoulder pain had a strong emotional component and was psychologically determined. There is no doubt that he felt it as real and that he genuinely suffered, but there is a strong case for a psychosomatic origin of his pain. If the pain is psychosomatic or psychogenic, that means there is no hard evidence of physical or organic injury causing the pain, while there is abundant evidence of the corresponding emotional stress that could be easily related to it.

During the six-month-long crisis, Gould was deprived of many joys. His pleasure at moving out was spoiled; he was totally preoccupied with his sickness, with litigation, and he canceled all recitals. More deprivation was to follow when he canceled his entire European tour, which robbed him of deserved applause and fame. In this episode, Gould's self-defeating or masochistic personality traits emerged in their full force.

Shortly after moving out, Gould's last dog, Banquo, who stayed at home in the care of his parents, was killed on the street by a car. A detailed description of this sad event was given by Otto Friedrich. Apparently, Gould's father took Banquo for a walk. Suddenly Banquo "dashed across the street. He ran right in front of a car and was killed on the spot."[50] The death was quite stressful as it compounded the previous losses of his cousin and teacher, and it came at the time of Glenn's recuperation from his separation crisis. Gould held his father wholly responsible for this new loss. With Banquo's death, Gould closed his twenty-seven-year-long chapter on his pets and moved into a petless, more austere phase of life. He continued to harbor deep affection for animals, particularly for members of the canine species. Glenn sublimated his love of dogs by collecting pictures and interesting published stories about dogs and by joining the Humane Society, which in due course he named as his beneficiary.

Gould compensated for the loss of his dog by voracious reading. He developed an insatiable need for the world's cultural knowledge and satisfied it by studying international classical literature. His reading as a hobby started earlier in his boyhood when Glenn read everything from *The Magical Land of Noom* through the more down-to-earth *Book on Dogs*, to the classic *Great Expectations*. In his teens, he became fervently involved in reading poetry, which paralleled his rapidly evolving grasp of music. As a young man, he adored Shakespeare and the poetry of Tennyson and Rilke. He enjoyed reading the novels of Thomas Mann, the plays of Strindberg and the Russian novelists like Tolstoy and Turgeniev. This is when Glenn also experienced thirst for stories and biographies of the world's composers, ranging from Bach and Mozart to Beethoven and everyone else whose music he played. Reading became his second nature, his second-best friend, a runner-up to music and a forerunner to people. As time went on, the stress of life and losses gradually building, his reading practices became more compulsive in nature. The emerging piano virtuoso was not only gobbling up loads of intricate music scores but had swallowed volumes of classical literature and stored them in his memory bank, which like a present-day computer hard disk, held for him a wealth of cumulative information from which to draw. As an adult, Glenn hardly ever read belles lettres. It was always the serious content that interested him; the exploration of philosophy, religion, architecture and fascination with human psychology. He studied the works of Sigmund Freud and owned Freud's *The Origin and Development of Psychoanalysis*. In his future writings, Gould often referred to various Freudian and psychological terms. More poetry, more social sciences and a heavy focus on the deep human drama of lonely individuals were to follow. The austere tragic tales of troubled but noble heroes, avengers, the wounded and disillusioned men always fascinated him. Along with Glenn's growing collection of sheet music and records, he owned over 600 volumes of books that were personally selected and usually purchased at Albert Britnell's, Toronto's oldest book store, located on Yonge Street, just steps north of Bloor Street. While Gould the legendary musician and the brilliant author will be met elsewhere, here the recesses of his unconscious mind will be explored through the choice of his reading repertory.

In his twenties, the young and prosperous Gould developed a friendship with John Lee Roberts, distinguished music radio producer. Roberts immigrated to Canada from Australia in 1955 and moved to Toronto in 1957. He became a music director of the Canadian Broadcasting Corporation (CBC). The two musicians collaborated on several music projects and established a fairly close rapport, as close as Gould was able to tolerate. Inspired by John's enthusiasm for drama, Gould joined a small, informal group, self-titled "The Lower Rosedale Shakespeare Reading Society," which he attended from time to time whenever he was in town. The group consisted of a few friends who congregated in John's apartment for sessions devoted to reading and reciting Shakespeare's plays. Gould, with his photographic memory, was quickly able to reproduce verses and act them as if he were a professional actor. Shakespeare's *Hamlet* became one of the favorite reading and acting pieces for the "society."

Hamlet is a drama that portrays the complex human psychology of the family triangle between the father, mother, and son. It is a derivative of the Greek legend of King Oedipus, told by Sophocles in his famous classic drama *Oedipus Rex*. Hamlet is a drama about a young Danish prince who loves his mother and hates his stepfather, with whom he is a rival for his mother's love. Hamlet also attempts to avenge his natural father. He has asexual feelings toward Ophelia, daughter of Polonius and sister of Laertes. Hamlet kills Polonius, and his son, Laertes, seeks revenge. In the final scene, there is a duel between Laertes and Hamlet, the two avengers of their fathers, in which Laertes mortally wounds Hamlet with a poisoned rapier. Gould loved playing the role of Laertes, which he knew by heart. Here is the final dialogue after Hamlet and Laertes mortally wounded each other:

> Laertes: ... Hamlet, thou art slain;
> No medicine in the world can do thee good,
> In thee there is not half an hour's life;
> The treacherous instrument is in thy hand,
> Unabated and envenom'd: the foul practice
> Hath turn'd itself on me; lo, here I lie,
> Never to rise again: thy mother's poison'd:
> I can no more: the king, the king's to blame

After Hamlet mortally stabbed the king, Laertes begged him for forgiveness:

> Laertes: Exchange forgiveness with me, noble Hamlet:
> Mine and my father's death come not upon thee,
> Nor thine on me![51]

The repeated reading and acting of roles of Hamlet and Laertes was cathartic for Gould. He was intuitively reliving his own unresolved Oedipal drama of loving his mother and wanting her to himself, and at the same time competing with his father for her love. In Gould's subconscious mind, his father was split into a good father, akin to Hamlet's father-ghost, and a bad father, akin to Hamlet's king-stepfather. Gould identified with the positive and good aspects of his father but fought his "bad father" and competed with him for his mother's love. Laertes's exclamation that Gould played so well, "the king, the king's to blame," summed up Gould's feelings about the image of his "bad father." In reality, Gould indeed blamed his own father for a number of personal hardships. The impact of Gould's unresolved Oedipal complex resonated throughout his life to the very end. Freud discovered "that Hamlet was written immediately after the death of Shakespeare's father (in 1601), that is, under the immediate impact of bereavement ..."[52] Just like Shakespeare, who worked through his relationship with his father through the inner dynamics of his personal drama, Gould worked through his relationship with his father in a variety of ways, one of them being to act out his feelings through the roles of imaginary characters.

Gould's choice of literature is strikingly consistent with his own personality features and beliefs. He was generally able to relate well to lonely heroes, portrayed in literature as socially isolated, eccentric, but always exquisitely gifted men. He was absolutely consumed by Santayana's masterpiece, *The Last Puritan*, to the point of identifying with its main characters. He found himself in all three solitary, rich and resourceful men, who were harshly deprived of love and affection. The three relatives, Nathaniel, Peter and Oliver Alden, were raised as puritans, and they each led a schizoid and destitute existence that inevitably ended in premature deterioration of their mental well-being. "Puritanism is a natural reaction against nature," said Santayana.[53] Oliver Alden was "the last puritan," who embodied the internal struggle between a puritan identity passed on to him by his elders and his need to be worldly, free, and loving. Gould referred to Puritanism in several of his writings. At one point he stated: "I, rather than Mr. Santayana's hero, am 'the last puritan.'"[54] The similarities between Gould's life experiences and those portrayed in Santayana's book are uncanny. For example, in the description of Oliver, he was educated at home apart from other children; his father was uninvolved in his upbringing; and his mother was mainly concerned with his physical health. This all applied to Gould. Even Gould's nanny, Elsie, who was affectionate and loving, was comparable to Oliver's nanny, Irma, the only compassionate person in his life. The tragic end of all three unhappy and lonely men was a result of transgenerational and cumulative emotional problems. The poignant emotional triad—abandonment, shame and guilt—was responsible for the gradual but inevitable destruction of the protagonists. Gould, with his profound experience of loneliness, riddled with shame and continuous self-reproach, could relate to Oliver Alden very well.

Gould was interested not only in the lives of the literary characters but in the plights of authors. He was quite impressed by the figures of Feodor Dostoevski and Friedrich Nietzsche and their philosophies. They were geniuses full of personal discontent, hardly understood by their contemporaries. Yet these dark, solitary humans had the power to enlighten the world. While they themselves were not brought up to experience their own feelings and to express them, they inspired others to get in touch with their inner selves. Don't we recognize Gould in this summary? He mirrored himself in those dark, exceptional literary fathers who became his symbolic role models. In some aspects, many musical and nonmusical children and adults of the present day mirror themselves in Glenn Gould.

Chapter IX

THE GOLDBERG VARIATIONS

THE ESSENCE OF CREATION

The music that can deepest reach
And cure all ill, is cordial speech.
Ralph Waldo Emerson[1]

Never before was a music piece so celebrated, promoted and powerfully delivered single-handedly to the wide public masses as Bach's *Goldberg Variations* by Glenn Gould. Through the force of his artistic originality, this charismatic pianist represented one of the three greatest composers of all times in the most original and the most stimulating way, both to audiences and to critical scholars. Gould resurrected and enlivened Bach's Variations played on the piano more than anybody ever managed to do in the past two centuries since this monumental piece was composed and first published. The questions are, why and how was this fruitful liaison made possible between a German composer and a Canadian music performer, whose births were separated by 247 years?

Johann Sebastian Bach was by far Gould's favorite composer. Gould loved Bach deeply and genuinely, as if Bach were his living relative, someone very close and dear to him, such as a benevolent and affectionately loved grandfather. Gould could not be more personal and more explicit in this notice of dedication:

> For Mendelssohn, Bach represented a perfection of musical architecture ... To the Victorians, Bach represented the sonorous glory of the age when faith still held sway over reason. For the post-Wagnerian, Bach represented a prescription for the contrapuntal ideal ... For the neoclassicist, Bach represents the clarity and perfection of the miniaturist ... For the jazzman, he represents the optimism ... For the spiritual man, he represents the embodiment of the providential inspiration; for the agnostic, the realities of earthbound determinacy. All things to all men![2]

Short of saying it directly—"Bach is my ideal and the universal music ideal of mankind"—Gould summed up his feelings and his music perception of Bach in a more elaborate way. Either way, his message is crystal clear, Bach is all things to all men! Glenn Gould not only perfected his piano interpretation of Bach's prolific keyboard compositions, but he also managed to identify both cognitively and artistically with the inner workings of this music, its content and meaning and its universal message. This is an opportunity to examine some of the history and dynamics of Bach becoming such a sustained symbol of love and admiration to young Glenn Gould.

Johann Sebastian Bach was born in the small German town of Eisenach, located north of Frankfurt and west of Bonn, in the year 1685. He became the central and most prominent music figure of the fabulously talented Bach family, in which more than fifty members through several generations achieved a status of distinction in music. During Bach's lifetime, his contemporaries were not aware that he was a genius but thought of him as a reputable church organist, a gifted composer and a crafty player of several other instruments, clavichord, harpsichord and violin. Having been orphaned at the age of ten, Bach studied music under the auspices of his older brother, Johann Christoph, whom he by far surpassed, becoming the greatest master of the Baroque period of music. The Baroque period began in the late sixteenth century and lasted into the middle of the eighteenth century. According to Walter Piston, an expert on counterpoint, "Baroque music, most highly developed in the work of J. S. Bach, introduced a strongly rhythmic and instrumental style and a new harmony based on the principle of tonality."[3]

In the period between 1703 and 1707, Bach worked as an organist in Arnstadt at St. Boniface church. He became a fervent composer of spiritual music, aiming to "... employ music as a vehicle for the exaltation of God's glory ..."[4] Bach composed a wealth of vocal music, including more than 200 cantatas and four passions, which became incorporated into the sacred services of Christian churches all over the world; generations of church goers have been comforted by their solace and beauty. Bach was greatly inspired by his contemporary, Dietrich Buxtehude, the famous organist of Lubeck in Germany, whom Bach visited in 1705 for a period of four months to study his organ technique. This is what evolved from this fruitful liaison:

> [Bach] brought back to Arnstadt from his contact with Buxtehude a newly acquired virtuosity which greatly perturbed his congregation. He accompanied the hymns with unconventional freedom and set his hearers agape at the audacity of his improvisations. The Consistory vainly admonished him, and his relations with that body became increasingly uncordial.[5]

Hence, those scholars who study Gould's approach to Bach's music need to include Buxtehude's direct influence on Bach and, by inference, his indirect impact on Gould. Indeed, Gould's innovative interpretations of Bach's music and his unparalleled virtuosity of the *Goldberg Variations* are, for the most part, his original creation, yet influenced by those two grandfatherly mentors of Baroque music.

Bach is to be credited for composing and disseminating music not only among spiritual audiences but also for the secular world. Over the past century, Bach's music became more popular and more accessible to all interested individuals as well as to wide public masses. At the present time, his music is universally played on the piano, organ and harpsichord; it is admired by students of music regardless of their age, class or religious denomination.

Among the treasures of Bach's work, the *Goldberg Variations* take the place of a special and distinct jewel. This majestic music piece is the fourth and final of Bach's extensive four-part project, which he titled the Clavier-Ubung, meaning "keyboard exercise." It opens with an aria from which springs a chain of thirty variations. It is said that:

> ... they formed the largest-scaled single keyboard work published at any time during the eighteenth century, indeed until the publication of Beethoven's Hammerklavier Sonata and the Diabelli Variations. And, like the B-minor Mass and the Well-Tempered Clavier, the "Goldberg" Variations, too, constitute an encyclopedic compendium, which this time, as Manfred Bukofzer had suggested "sums up the entire history of Baroque music."[6]

According to the original story, first recorded by Bach's biographer, Johann Nicolaus Forkel, in 1802, and later retold by generations of writers, the Variations were commissioned by Graf Hermann Karl von Keyserlingk for his own harpsichordist, a former pupil of Bach's, Johann Gottlieb Goldberg (1727-1756). Here are Forkel's words verbatim:

> The Count once said to Bach that he should like to have clavier pieces for his Goldberg, which should be of such a soft and somewhat lively character that he might be a little cheered up by them in his sleepless nights. Bach thought that he could best fulfill this wish through variations, which, on account of the constant sameness of the fundamental harmony, he had hitherto considered as an ungrateful task.[7]

Apparently, Keyserlingk served as a Russian ambassador to the Saxon court in Dresden where Bach was posted in the function of Court Kapellmeister. The story goes that Keyserlingk commissioned Bach by paying him the most generous honorarium that he ever received, a golden goblet filled with gold coins. Bach responded to Keyserlingk's plea by producing an aria with thirty variations, a potpourri of music that indeed was of lively character yet soft and soothing in its overall effect. It was said that Goldberg, who learned counterpoint from Bach, played the Variations repeatedly for Keyserlingk at his bedtime. Those thirty keyboard music pieces, which were professed to be a lullaby for an adult man who reportedly sponsored them, should have been duly called the Keyserlingk Variations. Instead, in the nineteenth century, long after Bach and Goldberg were deceased, they spread into the world of music history under the new and permanently engraved official title, the *Goldberg Variations*.

Christoph Wolff, through his meticulous research published in his recent biography of Bach, challenges the accuracy of Forkel's story. Wolff contends that if the Variations were commissioned they would have had "an official dedication in its published version."[8] Meanwhile, "the original print contains no trace of a dedicatory inscription."[9] Wolff proposes a new educated version of the Goldberg-Keyserlingk anecdote. He says:

> It can be proven that Bach stayed at Keyserlingk's Dresden house in November 1741, and it seems highly plausible that Bach gave him on that occasion a presentation copy of the last part of the Clavier-Ubung hot from the press.[10]

Once Keyserlingk was presented with the music copy, Goldberg may have frequently played a few variations at a time to help his master relax and fall asleep. Wolff concludes:

> All internal and external clues indicate that the so-called Goldberg Variations did not originate as an independently commissioned work, but were from the outset integrated into the overall concept of the Clavier-Ubung series, to which they constitute a grandiose finale.[11]

Gould only had access to Forkel's story, which means he believed the Variations to be specifically geared to relieve a person with sleepless nights and restless moods. Such a belief contributed to Gould's positive identification with both the music and the story behind it. This is not to say that Gould, had he known Wolff's version, would be less fascinated by the *Goldberg Variations*, which in themselves and regardless of external motives had a profound positive emotional and creative effect on him.

Having gone through the very basics of Bach and his Variations, it is safe to return to Glenn Gould, for whom Bach, as a music figure, pater familia, innovator and educator became a significant object of love and admiration. This enormous inclination and attachment to Bach did not happen by chance but was deeply and meaningfully rooted in the recesses of Gould's psyche. It appears that Gould was attached to Bach and his music through four distinct intra-psychic types of ties: Christian roots, family ties, academic connection and personal ties.

The Christian Connection

Glenn listened to sacred songs being practiced at home by his parents, as well as to those performed during countless church services he attended in his formative years. His musically intelligent mind quickly was able to grasp both the lyrics and the music of many hymns and cantatas. Bach's cantatas are built into the worship of both the Catholic and Anglican churches and his cantatas, motets and other works are often played within the context of prayer. The song "Jesu, Joy of Man's Desiring" from cantata 147 is among the most popular of Bach's sacred songs, with perpetual use in church services. The music of cantatas represents Bach's phenomenally creative mind, his versatility and endless innovativeness in the world of sound. The beauty of his melodies and the hypnotic power of the lyrics that breathe in the peace and harmony of the inner human self are unmatched when it comes to his sacred compositions. Glenn was fully able to relate to this music quality because he himself was in possession of similar auditory tonal acuity and sensitivity to the very style of Bach's music. While Glenn was able to fly on the music wings of cantatas in the world of artistic esthetics and imagination, he often was oppressed by the content, morality and projected message in some of the lyrics and the acting drama of the vocal performers. Here is a typical text of Bach's cantata BWV 131, which is used to demonstrate Glenn's ambivalence about and dichotomy between the music and the morality of the songs. The full analysis of this song and the impact on Glenn is beyond the scope of this biography, but the reader's attention is directed to the guilt-enhancing and self-depreciating content of this song:

... I perish in my sins
And lose hope forever
... I too am a grieving sinner
stricken by my conscience,
and wish to be washed
of my sins in thy blood ...

Glenn's lifelong struggle was centered around being made to feel guilty, to which he responded with defiance. His defiance extended to rejecting the concepts of sin and guilt. He also resented the need to submit and lose the freedom of thought and expression of feelings. Frankly, he did not favor lyrics that in any way encouraged guilt, repentance and suffering. The fact that Glenn stopped playing the organ and stopped going to church at the expense of the bitter disapproval of his parents and grandparents, and the fact that he concentrated on the piano as an instrument, on which he portrayed secular, more worldly music, are very telling of his attempts to distance himself from religious influences. This took place at mid-adolescence when he was about seventeen years of age and began to rebel against the morality and philosophy projected through much of the sacred music. Gould's rebellion could be illustrated by the following example from his correspondence. In his adult life, Gould made acquaintance with Reverend William Glenesk of Spencer Memorial Presbyterian Church in Brooklyn, New York. Apparently, Reverend Glenesk invited Gould to lecture on Bach and Bach's influence on religion in his music. In his letter of May 31, 1960, to Glenesk, Gould at first spoke extensively about his shoulder injury. Then he briefly addressed Glenesk's invitation in this way:

> I was very interested to read about the series of lectures you are arranging and very impressed with the list of lectures. I must say, however, that in order to say something individual on the subject of ecclesiastical influence on Bach, or on the Baroque music generally, I feel that a more specialized study is necessary than that which I have devoted to Bach.[12]

Then he preceded to say that he is more interested in the musico-technical qualities of Bach's music:

> I have been involved the last couple of years in a study of Bach from the particular angle, that of disposition of modulation in Bach's music ... this subject is one which is more readily available to me than the quasiphilosophical one you propose. I really feel that for your purposes you need someone much more experienced and knowledgeable in the command of the 17th century church-state-social concepts.[13]

Clearly, Gould declined in a polite but direct way Glenesk's invitation, saying that his interest and knowledge were in the esthetic qualities of Bach's music rather than in its religious meaning. Had Gould been interested in the subject of religiousness of Bach's music, there is no doubt that he would have approached it as studiously as he approached many other subjects in music and socio-cultural history. Gould refrained from being more expressive and negative toward Glenesk's invitation but, at a certain point, almost could not suppress his anger by saying that his proposed topic was "quasiphilosophical."

A few years later, in 1966, Glenn's friend, the famous German harpsichordist Sylvia Kind, visited Toronto. He arranged a recital for her, which took place in a local church in a small Ontario town. Kind reminisced on Gould's behavior:

> We went directly to the church where all concerts were held. Glenn immediately went up to the pulpit and began to "preach" in a voice of earnest moral exhortation. Of course his words were nonsense, but what he said sounded immensely real ... We laughed so much that we almost fell off our chairs.[14]

Obviously, in this serious church setting prior to a recital Gould felt like joking, even caricaturing the practice of preaching from the pulpit. This behavior is diametrically opposite to the one proposed by Rev. Glenesk to give a serious lecture on the church music of Bach. Glenn, by that time, had developed mixed feelings of respect and resentment for everything that was church-like and moralistic. Hence, his deep concentration on the esthetic, technical and contrapuntal, social and worldly aspects of Bach's music. Gould was at peace when he performed the *Goldberg Variations* because to him it was a beautiful, non-moralistic and sincere music piece without religious strings attached to it. The Goldbergs were produced with purely humanistic intentions to entertain and relax their listener. They project a deeply human message in the form of concern for someone's well-being. Here, there is no manipulation of the audience in any shape or form by exhortation or admonishment, as could be seen in sermons. Gould knew it and concentrated on this piece of music with all his being. This state of mental resoluteness helped him enhance the music of Bach, rather than being rebellious and reckless, as he often was in relationship to music of some other composers, such as Mozart.

Gould's Family Ties to Bach

Gould's ties and closeness to Bach went beyond his mother's influence. One may recall his paternal grandfather, Tom Gold, who was a dedicated lay preacher and Sunday school teacher in his home town of Uxbridge, Ontario. In his early childhood, Glenn felt warm feelings for his Papa Gold. This sense of kinship was unspoiled until Glenn was six years of age, when he became aware that his beloved Grandfather Tom was a furrier, a profession that was in Glenn's mind associated with cruelty to animals. Glenn's feelings toward his grandpa lost their purity and became contaminated by more ambivalent feelings, those of love and those of disapproval. In due course, through his incrementally increasing love of music, particularly the music of Bach, Glenn subconsciously transferred his originally pure feelings for his grandfather onto his new and more ideal object of love—Johann Sebastian Bach, the ideal creator of the ideal music. In other words, since his close family member, Grandfather Tom Gold, failed to be an ideal love object by being a furrier, Glenn discovered and added to his life another more pure object of love, Bach, the man and the musician. Bach, in Glenn's mind, had produced the music of peace, the music completely free of conflict and free of aggressive strivings.

Another dear relative was Tom's wife, Alma Rosena Gold, Glenn's Grandma Ally, who played Bach's organ music in their Methodist Church. She was a true fan of Bach's music and is to be credited for playing the same music on the piano. As an educator and the town socialite, Alma Rosena played

Bach's music on the piano at her home for her many guests and students. This is how the residents of Uxbridge had a chance to hear Bach's music played on the piano earlier than most other Canadians. As to her influence on Glenn, there is no doubt that Glenn was inspired by her love of Bach and her courage to play his music on the piano. Glenn the child and Glenn Gould the virtuoso continued to favor Bach's music and to play it on the grand piano, just as his grandmother did on her piano in his childhood.

On the maternal side, Glenn's grandfather, Charles Holman Greig, was a precentor in church who was well versed in the songs of worship. Though Grandpa Greig had died before Glenn's birth, the stories about his vocal talent and his knowledge of Bach's cantatas survived and became a part of Glenn's heritage. Hence, Glenn was born into a family of cantors and church organists, and through his exposure to their playing and singing of Bach's music, he himself became preconditioned to be involved with it.

Much was said earlier about Florence Greig Gould, whose own musicianship and love of Bach's music was passed on to her son. From his infancy on, Glenn was continually exposed to Bach's music by listening to his mother's piano practices of Bach's compositions and her vocal interpretations of Bach's cantatas. This, at first precocious fascination with Bach's tricky keyboard pieces, gradually matured in Glenn's musically gifted mind into a profound sense of kinship and resulted in recreative mastery of Bach's music. Many of the personal qualities of Florence, such as her deep religiosity, her stern deportment and her role as a church vocalist, were also true of Bach's second wife, Anna Magdalena. Bach dedicated many of his music pieces to Anna Magdalena, who bore him thirteen children and was a loving and loyal companion to him as a wife and musician. She was a well-trained singer who professionally performed in the royal court and often premiered her husband's music in local churches. Moreover, she was Bach's right hand as "a neat and accurate copyist of his music." According to Malcolm Boyd, Bach's monumental piece, the *Goldberg Variations*, "was first published by Balthasar Schmid of Nurenberg in 1741 or 1742, but the theme itself, a thirty-two bar saraband in binary form, is much earlier. It is found in the second Clavierbuchlein for Anna Magdalena (1725) ...[15] It appears that in Gould's subconscious mind, his mother represented the condensed images of both Bach and Anna Magdalena. As a pianist she represented Bach, and as vocalist of sacred music and as a loving maternal figure she was akin to Anna Magdalena.

The Academic Connection to Bach

Glenn's first scholastic exposure to Bach's music was inseparable from the family and church connection to the same, as his mother was his first piano teacher. By the age of ten, Glenn had a full knowledge of Bach's *Well-Tempered Clavier, Book I*, which he interpreted with a personal inclination and fondness for this type of music. When Glenn was in his developing years, the main living authority and interpreter of Bach's music was harpsichordist Wanda Landowska. She "played a Pleyell instrument that was the next thing to a concert-grand piano ... [and] her registrations and musical approach were highly romantic."[16] Glenn studied Bach's music on an upright piano at first and then on his Chickering concert grand piano. By comparative listening to Landowska's harpsichord music broadcasted on the radio and his mother's and grandmother's interpretations on organ and piano, which he heard live, he noticed the differences in their personal approaches to Bach's music and the differences with respect to the choice of keyboard instrument. He developed a clear preference for his mother's playing of Bach on the piano over Landowska's harpsichord production of the same music. Gradually and securely, Glenn was falling in love with Bach's keyboard compositions played on the grand piano. Though the first forte piano was created during Bach's life in 1709 by the Italian harpsichord maker Bartolomeo Christofori, Bach never made a transition from his familiar keyboard instruments—the organ, clavichord and harpsichord—to playing and composing on the forte piano. Wanda Landowska, known as the "revivalist" of Bach's music works, which she played on the harpsichord, also never showed any great interest in playing them on the piano. The appearance on the music scene in the 1930s of American pianist Rosalyn Tureck was of historical importance because she chose to perform Bach's music on the concert grand piano. Tureck, who was born in 1914, was one of the best-known pupils of the famous piano teacher, Olga Samaroff, at the Julliard School in New York. She was also trained in harpsichord and clavichord, which made it possible for her to explore Bach's music comparatively on three keyboard instruments. As a musically gifted student of Bach's music, Glenn was fascinated by Tureck's efforts at playing Bach on the piano.

Glenn's second music teacher, Alberto Guerrero, was himself a fervent admirer of Bach's compositions interpreted on the piano, and often played them publicly in his recitals. Admittedly, Glenn was initiated into Bach's music by his mother; then trained in it by Guerrero and further inspired by the achievement of Rosalyn Tureck. This all contributed to his impressive background as a scholar of Bach. Such cumulative music acquisitions, filtered through his innovative and talented contrapuntal mind, resulted in his own original concept of Bach's music played on the modern piano. The more Glenn grew to like Tureck and the more he developed his pioneering style of interpretation of Bach's music on the piano, the less he was tolerant of Landowska's conservative and romantic style on the harpsichord. Wanda Landowska, by being Glenn's "non-model," inadvertently helped him to develop his own academic approach to Bach, which then became critically acclaimed world-wide. Both Tureck and, to a greater extent, Glenn Gould, through their pioneering work, managed to popularize and elevate Bach's keyboard music to a higher and more appropriate level to his genius.

The Personal Connection to Bach

Gould's personal ties to Bach's music are long-standing and deeply private in nature. They could be traced as far back as his boyhood, when he was already besieged by many anxieties. Glenn simply dreaded the act of going to bed at night and being left in the room alone. Worst of all was the act of parting from his mother at bedtime, which often led to his frequent nightmares. What Glenn liked the most was for his mother to entertain him at bedtime by playing the piano and by singing suitable songs for him. He was practically hypnotized by her gentle soprano voice and the calming lyrics of the poems and songs she chose. Modern child psychology recognizes the value of child-parent attunement. In other words, the parents, through their constant observation and understanding, become aware of the child's emotional vulnerabilities and do their best to alleviate them. Reassuring dialogues, little stories and songs told by loving caretakers are proven to be particularly helpful at bedtime. One of many nursery rhymes told to Glenn by his mother was "Little Piper of the Hill,"[17] which reads as follows:

> Oh, will you play a tune for me,
> Little Piper of the Hill

A tune of elves and fairies small
That dance when all is still.

"O, yes," the little Piper said
"Just close your sleepy eyes
And go with me to Dreamland, child
Beyond the hill it lies.
For there you'll meet a hundred elves
And bright-winged fairies too
And on our way to Dreamland, child
I'll play a tune for you."

Glenn, a child of imagination, through his mother's presence and voice was able to picture himself as a Little Piper in the land of benevolent tunes and creatures. These bedtime rituals between mother and son, woven with melodic sounds, helped him ease his severe separation anxiety. His mother's lullabies became represented in Glenn's mind as a symbol of their mutual love.

The way Glenn's life unfolded from his boyhood onward left him with relentless fears and anxieties that were carried into adulthood. One of these problems was intractable insomnia. The connection to Bach around Glenn's difficulty with sleep is manifold—through direct listening of Bach's tunes that his mother played and Bach's songs that she sang for him, as well as through Bach's humanness of being able to relate to the plight of insomnia sufferers. Bach, who fathered twenty-one babies, was well aware of the power of vocal and instrumental music to soothe them. His music creation did not stop with his children or the children of the world, but he fervently composed and dedicated his music for every stage of life; for individuals and for groups; for every season and occasion; for secular audiences and spiritual believers. Bach's psalms and requiems are for adults what lullabies are for children. By producing thirty nameless variations as a lullaby for a grown man with insomnia, Bach inadvertently became a forerunner of music therapy, for his Variations played by Goldberg were able to turn the ugly anxieties and insomnia of Count Keyserlingk into a more relaxed state of mind. According to the legend, Keyserlingk depended on Bach's music for his sleep, and this need was akin to children's needs for a favorite teddy bear or other soothing object. Bach's Variations became an emotionally charged necessity, a specific object of love, known in human psychology as a "transitional object." The music could soothe, reassure, relax and help the count cope with the stress of life. Similarly, the music of Bach that Glenn grew up with filled him with a sense of familiarity and serenity. Bach was, in Gould's mind, the chief Piper of the Hill. In the twentieth century, Glenn Gould evolved into Bach's emissary. While Goldberg played only for the count, Gould played and will continue to play through his recordings for millions of people of all ages and all walks of life. Gould plays for our morning needs; for afternoon relaxation or our bed time; for our insomnia; for our spiritual enrichment and for our worldly entertainment. Bach, as an immortal chief Piper of the Baroque period, was 200 years later succeeded by his brilliant disciple, Glenn Gould.

THE GREATEST LIVE PERFORMANCE

His heart was in the performance as it always is ...
George Kidd[18]

The quadruple ties to Bach got their fullest expression in Gould's masterful interpretation of thirty variations. By comparative listening to Bach's music played on the harpsichord, on the radio, Tureck's recording and Guerrero's live version of the *Goldberg Variations*, Gould could discern their similarities and differences. Hence, he took this music in, note-by-note, bar-by-bar. This process of listening helped him create his own rendition. The first time Gould heard the *Goldberg Variations* played live was at the age of fourteen when his friend, John Beckwith, who was five years his senior and also a student of Guerrero, performed them in the small basement auditorium at the Royal Ontario Museum in Toronto. Don't we all wish that Gould kept a journal or at least wrote belated memoirs to tell us about the process of falling in love with this music masterpiece? What was really going through Glenn's mind when he first studied it, when he gave it a major overhaul or performed it for the world at the pinnacle of his success? Was it a sense of pleasure, kinship, curiosity, or perhaps a twinge of envy and hypnotizing awe? The *Goldberg Variations* are famous for their:

> ... devilish, hand-crossings, passages in thirds, trills in inner parts, rapid arpeggios and runs, etc. There is nothing like these extroverted acrobatics in any of Bach's other keyboard music. In fact, demanding and idiomatic keyboard writing at this level of difficulty can be found in the works of only one other composer of the time: Domenico Scarlatti.[19]

What was the driving force behind this colossal project of learning by heart a sequence of, say, 15,000 music notes, mastering them to absolute technical perfection and then weaving into them his own recreative talent? In the absence of a diary and memoirs, all that is left for us is to imagine and safely assume how Gould must have felt in the company of the Goldbergs. One can conjecture that Gould's enormous drive to promote and perform the *Goldberg Variations* was in that massive, multi-dimensional attachment to Bach. This intra-psychic force became a source of strong and unwavering motivation and inspiration for this daring project of representing the great composer. Bach, the original and great master of music, became Gould's ego-ideal. By re-mastering Bach's greatest work, Gould felt at one with Bach, as if he were his music son and natural heir to his wealth—the *Goldberg Variations*.

In his pre-fame period, Gould was well acquainted with the concept of music variations produced by different composers. At the age of sixteen, he publicly played the Czerny Variations and Mendelssohn's *Variations Serieuses*, and soon after he performed the famous Beethoven's *Eroica Variations*. But it was not until his early twenties that he premiered the *Goldberg Variations* in Toronto at the Royal Conservatory of Music and, soon after that, in Ottawa in a modest recital held on March 14, 1955, at the Technical School Auditorium. Though these two performances received very little publicity, they were important as a dress rehearsal for his pending first recording of the Variations, which was soon to come in June 1955. The first showing of the *Goldberg Variations* as a major concert event was in Montreal on November 7, 1955, at Plateau Hall. Two years later on November 11, 1957, Gould delivered them to the long-awaiting Toronto audience at Massey Hall; whereas the Americans saw him first play this piece in Pittsburgh, Pennsylvania, and Cincinnati, Ohio, on November 16 and 20, and then in New York City on December 7, 1957. From then on, most of the major cities in North America had an opportunity to hear Gould's rendition of the *Goldberg Variations* in live performance. Altogether, the virtuoso played them publicly dozens of times in full and countless times in part for encores.

The publicity that Gould received, related to his interpretation of the *Goldberg Variations* is so extensive that when compiled and edited it would comprise two sizable volumes. The critical reviews on Gould's Goldbergs became a standard of excellence in the art of pianism. Even the sternest and most adversarial critics were disarmed by his mastery of Bach's Variations. Frankly, Gould earned permanent laurels by interpreting them with his special and unparalleled expertise. Here is one of the earlier professional commentaries of Gould's performance in Montreal on March 23, 1958, as expressed in a lengthy report titled "The Gould Conquest" by Thomas Archer of *The Montreal Gazette*:

> The Goldberg Variations rank in height and depth with anything in the repertory. They also require the highest possible capacity of execution and artistic comprehension if they are to come off properly. Mr. Gould did everything the right way.
>
> His conception of the work on the whole is magnificent in its grasp on Bach's unique way of using all the complex resources of the contrapuntal technique available to him and yet stating what is basically a simple case. Mr. Gould stated that case completely in all its aspects. He knit the variations into a gigantic whole complete in all its parts, observing contrast while never once breaking the continuity of the structure. He is a master of the art of contrapuntal playing, so much so that he makes you quite forget that the piano is not naturally adjusted to this kind of musical writing.[20]

It took Gould close to forty minutes of this Montreal recital to play the whole set of Variations, during which time the audience was invariably transfixed by his virtuosity and emotional amalgamation with the music he produced. The end of this performance was greeted by a storm of applause that broke like thunder. He touched his viewers, who then wanted more of him and recalled him over and over again. From the audience's point of view, this entire concert was a unique emotional affair never experienced before nor expected to be ever duplicated by another music artist.

It was the same or an even better reception in Vancouver, where Gould was already known from his previous appearances. George Kidd, the correspondent of *The Toronto Telegram*, captured the emotional and technical quality of Gould's playing there on July 23, 1958:

> Following intermission, Gould turned to the now quite familiar Goldberg Variations. His heart was in the performance as it always is, and the work came vividly alive with the amazing dexterity of the young soloist.
>
> In his complete understanding of each of the 30 variations, there was a mature freshness that never wavered and an overall intelligence that was beautifully controlled.[21]

In the Soviet Union, Gould made the history pages as a Bach scholar, for which he was even more hailed than in North America. The news of his success after the release of his first record of the *Goldberg Variations* in 1956 reached Russian music circles prior to his tour. Though only a handful of music lovers could afford the ownership of Gould's album, many more knew about his music by word of mouth and passionately waited for him to appear in person. When Gould arrived in Moscow, he was already surrounded by an aura of preconceived fame, so that at his concert on May 8, 1957, featuring Beethoven's Fourth Concerto played with the Moscow Philharmonic, the public response was overwhelming. Walter Homburger, who witnessed the occasion, reported for *The Toronto Star* on May 9, 1957:

> I was told that soloists very rarely give encores after playing a concerto. However, after Gould had taken innumerable bows at the end of the concerto, the rhythmic applause began so Gould sat down and played a couple of the Goldberg Variations by Bach.
>
> But if Gould thought this was enough the audience definitely thought otherwise. In the end I lost count as to how many of the Goldberg Variations he played as encores. Each time he left the stage the rhythmic applause started again. After about 15 minutes of encores we were finally able to get a message to the concert master so that the members of the orchestra left the stage.[22]

Three days later, on May 11, Gould rewarded the loyal Moscow public by playing for them a full set of the *Goldberg Variations*. This time he definitely stole the hearts of those lucky spectators who got tickets for this recital. The leading Moscow newspaper, *Pravda*, known in the 1950s for its serious and highly censored content, gave this generous review:

> The rich creative nature of the young pianist—practically a youth—responds with equal penetration to power and tenderness, sorrow and jest, grace and brilliance. Gould dominates the instrument. His rare virtuosity and range of sounds, are completely subjugated to the creative idea. The ovations after the performance of the thirty variations were unbelievable ... Glenn Gould, particularly in his interpretation of Bach, is a bright and shining event in the musical world.[23]

Gould was told that Moscow fell in love with him. When he appeared for his last recital in the famous Bolshoi Hall, the oversized audience first listened to his music breathlessly and then broke into an outpouring of rhythmic clapping and ovations. He played Bach's fugues and partitas, and the director of the Moscow Philharmonic complimented him backstage: "We never heard fugues played like that." But the audience clamored for more. Gould graciously kept returning and playing *Goldberg Variations*, two or three at a time as an encore. The more he played, the more exhilarated and frenetic the audience became. In total, he played eleven variations. The audience would not part from his physical and musical stage presence. Again Homburger reported to *The Toronto Star*:

> Still the audience persisted in their applause, so in the middle of receiving congratulations Gould was rushed out on the stage once more and as a final encore he played another five of the Goldberg Variations. Having thus played over one-third of the variations as encores the concert ended in a veritable triumph.[24]

In all, the *Goldberg Variations* became Gould's trademark of performance and the benchmark of his pianism. It made him world-famous, and it raised the public's awareness of this type of classical music, evocative of warm feelings in the music-minded and even in those who knew little about music. Before Gould, one could hear the *Goldberg Variations* played by Wanda Landowska or Ralph Kirkpatrick on the harpsichord, or by Rosalyn Tureck on the piano. When Glenn Gould came along, "his convulsive rendition swept the attention of the musical world."[25] Gould's music audiences simply became spellbound by this music piece, be it when they heard him perform it live or on his first recording. From the time he first played the *Goldberg Variations* before the public in the early 1950s, for the next half of the twentieth century, Gould is still considered to be the supreme interpreter of this outstanding baroque composition.

GOULD ON THE "GOLDBERGS "

> The music, yearning like a God in pain.
>
> John Keats[26]

The more Gould played Bach's music, and specifically the *Goldberg Variations*, the more audiences wanted to hear him play it. By rule Gould's concerts were sold out, but in the 1960s there were fewer performances to attend. If Gould's fans could no longer hear him live, they purchased his recordings. Indeed, by 1968, about twelve years after the first recording of the *Goldberg Variations* was released, over 100,000 albums had been sold, which was an unprecedented achievement in the annals of the classical recording music industry.

Gould's love of Bach's *Goldberg Variations* provided a strong impetus for him to record them twice: the first time in 1955, which was released in 1956, and the second and final time in 1981, which was released in 1982. According to Gould's own explanation as to why he re-recorded Bach's *Goldberg Variations*, it seems that he had not been fully satisfied with his first rendition which compelled him to perfect it and deliver his new musical and psychological insights one more time. Gould argued that his first recording was done at the height of his performing career when he had to behave like a piano virtuoso and please his spectators, not only with his interpretative skill but also by delivering the music with charismatic showmanship. Gould said, referring to his first recording: "In those days, my tempi were souped up and rather breakneck." This is why he produced the second recording, which would be less dramatic and attention-seeking and more objective and introspective. Gould made it clear that his tactile piano technique was the same in both renditions.

In his liner notes provided for the first recording of the *Goldberg Variations*, Gould summed up not only his view as a budding music critic, but also his deep, subconsciously rooted ties to this very masterpiece and, in a broader sense, to the music of J. S. Bach. After decoding Gould's convoluted but profound writing, one can notice how much he identified with the Goldbergs. The enthusiasm, the choice of words and warm expressions are but a few indicators of this positive identification. Gould started his ode to the Goldbergs by giving an historical account of the Goldberg-Keyserlingk connection; then he referred to the Variations as "the luxuriant vegetation of the aria's family tree" and expressed his curiosity about its "generative root" and "parental responsibility." By comparing the Variations to a family tree, generativity and parenthood, Gould more than hinted that the Goldbergs symbolize family and familiarity to him; that they stand for closeness, procreation, parental love and parental duty to their children. Then Gould seemingly goes into a musico-technical analysis of individual variations, but under those technical terms, one can again discern the personal and emotional meaning and his deep connection to this music piece. In describing the opening of the Variations by the aria, he refers to it as "a docile but richly embellished soprano line." This description may be motivated by his perception of his mother's beloved voice as "a docile but richly embellished soprano" voice. Gould then concludes his fondness for the aria: "In short, it is a singularly self-sufficient little air which seems to shun patriarchal demeanour ..." It was as if Gould summed up his own personal identification with the aria by defining himself as a "singularly self-sufficient" person, who fought anything patriarchal and conventional and admired the aria as a sturdy, independent and defiant little piece of music. Gould proceeded to emote about Variation 1 and 2, again seemingly as a music critic, but he poured his heart into it. Here is the entire paragraph:

> Nothing could better demonstrate the aloof carriage of the aria than the precipitous outburst of Variation 1, which abruptly curtails the presiding tranquillity. Such aggression is scarcely the attitude we associate with prefatory variations, which customarily embark with unfledged dependence upon the theme, simulating the pose of their precursor, and functioning with a modest opinion of their present capacity but with a thorough optimism for future prospects. With Variation 2 we have the first instance of the confluence of these juxtaposed qualities—that curious hybrid of clement composure and cogent command which typifies the virile ego of the "Goldbergs."[27]

Gould, as a gifted individual, had this ability for "antropomorphisation of inanimate objects," which is the concept of the American psychoanalyst, Phyllis Greenacre. This means that he was able to personify and enliven the music as if it were a person. The words like "aggression," "optimism for future prospects" and "the virile ego of the 'Goldbergs'" have a human and personal meaning. Gould was compelled to let us know that the Goldbergs were not just some mushy, romantic music pieces but were exactly to his taste—an interesting "hybrid of clement composure," human strength and uprightness.

In the next sequence of his poetic writing, Gould proceeds to pay tribute to some specific music qualities of the Variations that he particularly admired, such as the canons and the counterpoint. Gould absolutely adored Bach's canons, interpreting them with glee and a feeling of closeness to them, as if this was his kind of music. He stated that Variations 3, 9 and 21 are full of canons of "surpassing beauty."

Gould enjoyed the G-minor mode of Variation 11 and 14, saying that they were done with the irrepressible elasticity of what was termed "the Goldberg ego." In reference to Variation 25, Gould used romantic language, saying that this "wistful, weary cantilena is a masterstroke of psychology," which provided us with the "languorous atmosphere of an almost Chopinesque mood piece." What did Gould mean exactly? Perhaps, by his comment referring to "a masterstroke of human psychology," he wished to say that he could deeply relate to this music segment, which touched his heart in a very unique way. Gould's comment about the "Chopinesque mood piece" may have been slightly derogatory. It referred to his own interpretation of the Variation 25, which he considered romantic and reminded him of Chopin's music, which he did not favor. Overall, it is evident that Gould liked everything about the *Goldberg Variations*: its virile ego, its variability and richness, along with the affection and loving feelings it incites in the listener. In other words, for Gould the Goldbergs have both the masculine strength and feminine subtlety that gave him a sense of parental completeness. The *Goldberg Variations* evoked in Gould both paternal and maternal images. Toward the end of his liner notes, Gould wrote:

> With renewed vigor, Variations 26 and 29 break upon us and are followed by that boisterous exhibition of deutsche Freundlichkeit—the quodlibet.[28]

In Variations 26, 27 and 29, Gould's virtuosity at the keyboard comes to its full expression. Though Gould spent a good portion of his life denying the importance of virtuosity, which he identified with the music performance and the show-off feature of a music performer, undeniably he was in possession of a rare combination of top music skills and a God-given gift to be a piano virtuoso. So, when he played Bach's Variations 26, 27 and 29, be it in his live performances or for the recordings, he sailed through them in a triumph over oneself and over the intricacies of these music pieces. Nothing stood in his way—the technical difficulties, the hazard of the breakneck speed, the interpretative demands, crossing of the hands, nothing could discourage Gould from its mastery.

The last or the thirtieth Variation is in the form of a melodic burlesque—the famous "Quodlibet." Based on a popular folk song with cheerful and humorous lyrics, it has the following theme:

> I've not been with you for so long
> Come closer, closer, closer,
> Cabbage and beets drove me far away.
> Had my mother cooked some meat
> Then I'd have stayed much longer.[29]

Who would have ever imagined that Bach's sophisticated "Quodlibet" was inspired by the love of a peasant for his chosen sweetheart!

At last, Gould pays the poetic tribute to the final and conclusive part of the *Goldberg Variations*, known as aria *da capo*:

> Then, as though it could no longer suppress a smug smile at the progress of its progeny, the original saraband, anything but a dutiful parent, returns to us to bask in the reflected glory of an aria da capo.[30]

Again, here Gould refers to the aria as a parent who smiles benevolently at his or her children, the Variations being seen as progeny. Then, he explains that the aria is not "a gesture of benediction" but is a suggestion of perpetuity. The very last summary of the deep meaning of the *Goldberg Variations* to Gould is stunning:

> It is, in short, music which observes neither end nor beginning, music with neither real climax nor real resolution, music which, like Baudlaire's lovers, "rests on the wings of the unchecked wind." It has, then, unity through intuitive perception, unity born of craft and scrutiny, mellowed by mastery achieved and revealed to us here, as so rarely in art, in the vision of subconscious design exulting upon a pinnacle of potency.[31]

Keep in mind that these liner notes were written in 1955 when Gould was only twenty-two years old. His writing is exceptionally mature for the young man he was. It reveals his hard and studious work as a keyboard performer, and as a music psychologist, historian, philosopher, music critic and admirer. By reading between Gould's lines, one can see the depth of his personal feelings for the Variations. The images of his parents or parenthood, the relationship of parents to their children, the procession of metaphors and the treatment of that particular music piece as if it were a person is part and parcel of Gould's artistic genius. Great artists differ from the rest of mankind by being able to enliven or anthropomorphize physical objects and make them become alive. Gould animated the *Goldberg Variations* to their possible maximum, building them not only into our record library but into our permanent memory bank and our storage of soothing feelings of affection. Gould's rendition of the *Goldberg Variations* is both thought and reflection provoking. When listening to it, we tend to introspect, feel peaceful, strong and warmhearted, and all that in the span of forty minutes of its flow. Undoubtedly, the *Goldberg Variations* played by Gould transcend the twentieth century and entered the twenty-first century in their full strength and beauty. From this point on, they will march to perpetuity. Bach, immortalized by his music, has an heir in Gould, a loyal adopted great-great-grandson, who assured the revival and adaptation of his music to the needs of modern culture.

The three Gould brothers—Bert, Grant and Bruce. *Personal Gouldiana Collection. With permission of the Glenn Gould Estate and Glenn Gould Limited.*

Glenn, at the age of two, held by his paternal grandfather, Tom, whom Glenn affectionately called "Papa Gold." *Personal Gouldiana Collection. With permission of the Glenn Gould Estate and Glenn Gould Limited.*

Glenn as a baby enjoying happy family moments with his paternal grandmother, Alma, his fifteen-year-old uncle, Grant, and their dog in Uxbridge, Ontario, c. 1933. *Personal Gouldiana Collection. With permission of the Glenn Gould Estate and Glenn Gould Limited.*

Glenn at the age of three with his maternal grandmother, Mary. At this age, Glenn had already started piano lessons given by his mother. *Personal Gouldiana Collection. With permission of the Glenn Gould Estate and Glenn Gould Limited.*

Glenn Gould at the age of five holding a medium-sized pike on a hook. *Personal Gouldiana Collection. With permission of the Glenn Gould Estate and Glenn Gould Limited.*

Glenn Gould at age ten with a neighbor and his fishing trophy, at the cottage in Uptergrove, near Orillia, Ontario, c. 1943. By that time, Glenn had finished grade nine and was introduced to Alberto Guerrero to start the challenge of the senior music program at the Toronto Conservatory of Music. *Personal Gouldiana Collection. With permission of the Glenn Gould Estate and Glenn Gould Limited.*

Tom and Barry Johnson posing with their cousin, Glenn Gould (far right) after swimming, c. 1945. Barry (middle) drowned in 1959. *Personal Gouldiana Collection. With permission of the Glenn Gould Estate and Glenn Gould Limited*

Alberto Guerrero, Glenn's principal piano teacher, socializing with his thirteen-year-old student, Glenn Gould, boating on Lake Simco, c. 1946. Photograph by Bert Gould. *Personal Gouldiana Collection. With permission of the Glenn Gould Estate and Glenn Gould Limited.*

Glenn at age eleven as organist (center) surrounded by members of the junior church choir, c. 1944. Glenn won three medals for the highest standing in the Province of Ontario, in grade ten piano and grades eight and six organ. *Personal Gouldiana Collection. With permission of the Glenn Gould Estate and Glenn Gould Limited.*

Elsie Lally Feeney, Glenn's principal nanny and a friend of Gould's family during Glenn's entire life. On the cabinet there is an enlarged picture of Glenn as a baby. *Photograph by Helen Mesaros (1991). Personal Gouldiana Collection.*

Glenn's wicker rocking-chair kept in the house of Elsie Lally Feeney. *Photograph by Helen Mesaros (1991). Personal Gouldiana Collection.*

Glenn at age sixteen as a fully certified concert pianist, playing the piano in his living room in Toronto, Ontario, in the company of his dog, Nicky. *Photograph by* The Evening Telegram, *Toronto, 1949. Personal Gouldiana Collection. With permission of the Glenn Gould Estate and Glenn Gould Limited.*

Glenn Gould, already a professional performing concert pianist, playing the piano at his home in Toronto, Ontario, c. 1952. *Personal Gouldiana Collection. With permission of the Glenn Gould Estate and Glenn Gould Limited.*

The Town Hall in New York is located on West 43rd Street. This is where Glenn Gould made his New York debut in January 1955. *Photograph by Helen Mesaros (1994). Personal Gouldiana Collection.*

Glenn Gould at age twenty-one during the recording session of Bach's *Goldberg Variations* in New York, on June 10, 1955. *Photograph by Don Weiner. Courtesy Sandra Weiner.*

Glenn Gould and Leonard Bernstein in preparation for a concert in New York in 1957. *Photograph by Don Hunstein. Sony Classical.*

Glenn Gould in a pensive pose at the piano during the rehearsal of Beethoven's 2nd Piano Concerto in New York in January 1957. *Photograph by Dan Weiner. Courtesy Sandra Weiner.*

Glenn Gould in Lucerne, Switzerland, in front of the painting of King Charles I of England, August 1959. *Photograph by Paul Weber. Personal Gouldiana Collection. With permission of the Glenn Gould Estate and Glenn Gould Limited.*

Glenn Gould on Bach.
CBS Still Photo Collection/Roy Martin (1962).

Festival: Glenn Gould on Strauss.
CBS Still Photo Collection/Roy Martin (1962).

Glenn's mother, Florrie Gould, with her niece, Jessie Greig, enjoying a cup of tea, c. 1962. *Personal Gouldiana Collection.*

Glenn Gould in the CBS Radio Station. *CBS Still Photo Collection (1969).*

Glenn's parents, Florence and Bert Gould, in front of their home in Toronto, Ontario, with Bert's brother Dr. Grant Gould in the early 1970s. *Personal Gouldiana Collection. With permission of the Glenn Gould Estate and Glenn Gould Limited.*

Glenn Gould in his typical contemplative pose. *Photograph by Don Hunstein. Sony Classical.*

Glenn Gould in his late forties, playing the piano in his typical low-sitting position. *Photograph by Don Hunstein. Sony Classical.*

The "Hall of Fame" at Steinway in New York, where the portraits of famous concert pianists are displayed. At the time, Gould's portrait was noticeably missing. *Photograph by Helen Mesaros (1994). Personal Gouldiana Collection.*

The four famous concert grand pianos in the basement of Steinway Hall in New York. Concert pianists usually select one of them for their public performances. *Photograph by Helen Mesaros (1994). Personal Gouldiana Collection.*

Russian pianist, Andrei Gavrilov, taking a bow in front of the gigantic poster of Glenn Gould at the Glenn Gould Festival in Groningen, Holland, in 1992. *Photograph by Helen Mesaros. Personal Gouldiana Collection.*

Gould's unique piano chair as it was displayed at the Glenn Gould Conference in Toronto, 1992.
Photograph by Helen Mesaros. Personal Gouldiana Collection.

Gould's Chickering grand piano displayed at the Glenn Gould Festival in September 1992 in Toronto.
Photograph by Helen Mesaros. Personal Gouldiana Collection.

Helen Mesaros in conversation with Glenn's father, Bert Gould, in January 1994. *Photograph by Vera Gould. Personal Gouldiana Collection.*

Helen Mesaros and Gould's first cousin, John Greig, in an interview, in Uxbridge, Ontario, December 2000. *Photograph by Debbie Greig Dee. Personal Gouldiana Collection.*

The Post-Gouldians: (from left to right) Helen Mesaros, Angela Hewitt, Robert J. Silverman, David Young and Ghuslaine Guertin at the Glenn Gould festival in Groningen, Holland in 1992. *Personal Gouldiana Collection.*

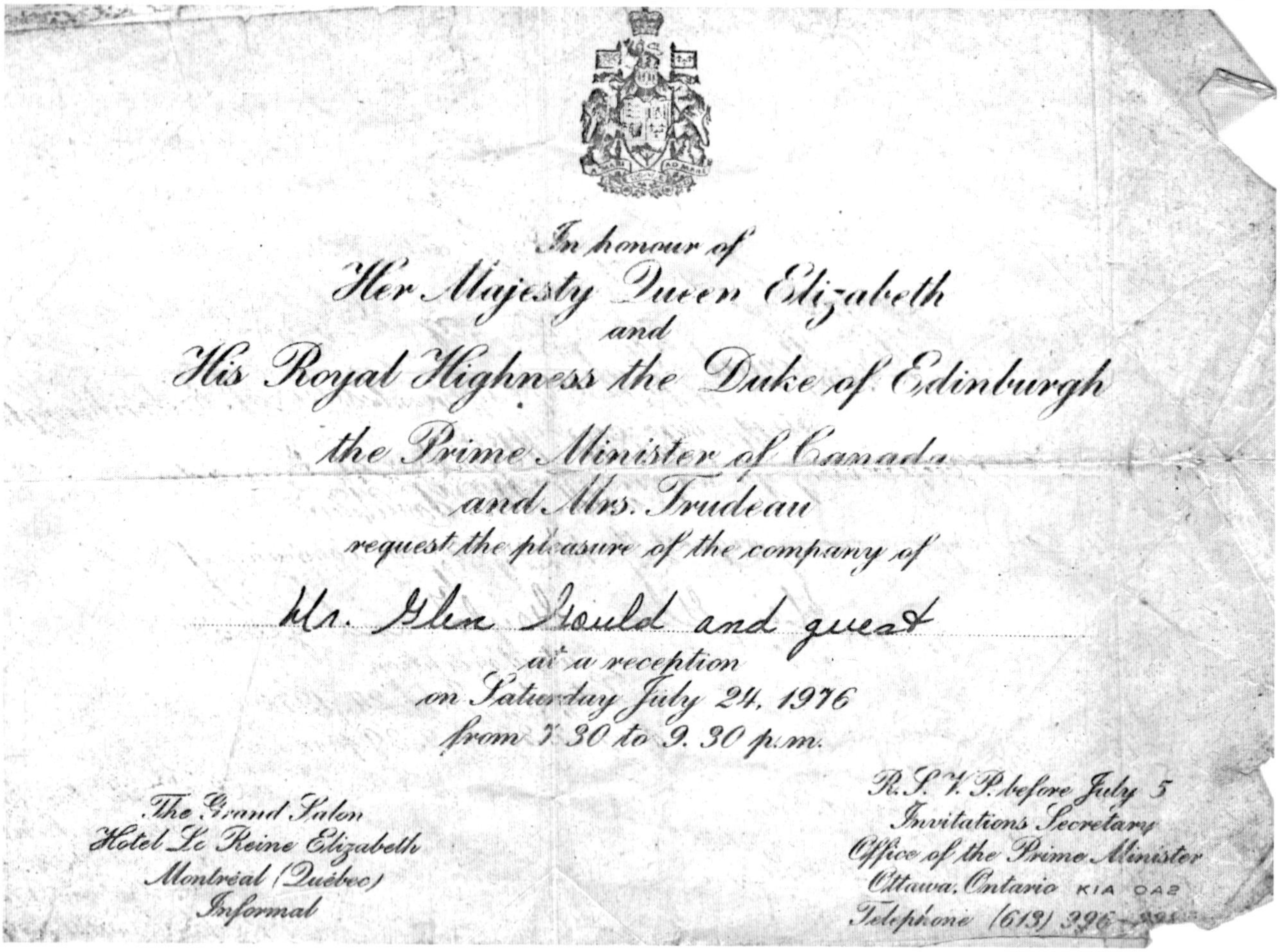

In honour of
Her Majesty Queen Elizabeth
and
His Royal Highness the Duke of Edinburgh
the Prime Minister of Canada
and Mrs. Trudeau
request the pleasure of the company of
Mr. Glen Gould and guest
at a reception
on Saturday July 24, 1976
from 7.30 to 9.30 p.m.

The Grand Salon
Hotel Le Reine Elizabeth
Montréal (Québec)
Informal

R.S.V.P. before July 5
Invitations Secretary
Office of the Prime Minister
Ottawa, Ontario K1A 0A2
Telephone (613) 996-

Invitation from the Prime Minister of Canada, Pierre Trudeau, for Glenn Gould to attend a reception in Montreal, Quebec, in honor of Her Majesty Queen Elizabeth II, in July 1976. *Personal Gouldiana Collection.*

Chapter X

THE CEREMONY OF PERFORMANCE

THAT SPECIAL PIANO CHAIR

> The mannerisms, if they are that, are external and irrelevant.
>
> Louis Biancolli[1]

In February 1961, connoisseurs of music in St. Louis, Missouri, had the rare treat of seeing Glenn Gould as a piano soloist in an array of concerts, performing all five Beethoven concerti. Gould felt relaxed in that old "Gateway to the West," where he was warmly received by his fellow-musicians; Edouard Van Remoortel, the conductor, and the members of the St. Louis Symphony Orchestra. A rather fancy concert program booklet, specially prepared for this historical occasion, presented the pianist in the following way:

> Enough has been written elsewhere about Gould's stage mannerisms and personal idiosyncrasies. Enough attention has been called to his specially built, low piano bench; his habit of soaking his hands and wrists in warm water; his occasional refusal to wear conventional formal dress at concerts, etc. Suffice is to say that these do not detract from his intensely serious approach and scholarly outlook. They are merely Glenn Gould's way of making music—and critics everywhere have agreed that few pianists in the world are Gould's equal in that.[2]

What precisely did the writer mean by Gould's "stage mannerisms"? The answer to this delicate and elusive question lies far below the surface and can be tracked down by way of a meticulous analysis. In the course of his entire music career, Gould displayed remarkable dependence on specific inanimate objects and on repetitive behavior that he was truly unable to change or give up on his own. There was an assortment of predictable habits and manners that he religiously pursued. Worst of all, Gould used to sit unusually low at the piano in a slouch; he was unable to sit up straight or hold still during his piano playing but curved his body and leaned his head over the keyboard. His face was expressive and looked as if he were dialoguing with the keyboard. Almost by rule, Gould's playing was accompanied by audible humming and chanting that could be heard in the back rows of concert halls. Frankly, his whole posture at the instrument was different and diametrically opposite to what it should be according to the tenets of piano pedagogy. Gould's mannerisms started subtly and insidiously as far back as in his grade school years, and they continued to spread throughout his teens. Finally, this extra-musical behavior completely took over and became fixed and permanent in his adult life. At the very beginning, Glenn's mother thought that he was going through a passing stage of naughtiness so typical for young boys. Her dogged efforts to make Glenn sit up straight and hold still were to no avail. Then came Alberto Guerrero, who shook his head at the sight of Glenn's piano manners, giving them the operative nickname—"platform antics." Guerrero, dazzled by Glenn's artistic potential, focused on his music progress, while feeling fairly confident that his student's foreign piano manners were transient and correctable. He could not have been more wrong.

There was more to be concerned about. Glenn was not only fixated on his platform behavior but also on certain physical objects, namely his chosen grand piano and, more importantly, his piano chair. He cogently believed that the two were necessary for the excellence of his music performance. Gould ceremoniously pursued both those objects and his habitual manners with the vehemence of a compulsion, over and over again. A lot has been written so far about human obsessions, which often go hand in hand with compulsive behavior and rituals. Sigmund Freud gave us an early insight into this by asserting that "neurotic symptoms have a sense ... [and] a connection with the life of those who produce them."[3] In elaborating on symptoms of obsessive neurosis, Freud stated:

> A pathological ceremonial ... is unyielding and insists on being carried through even at the cost of great sacrifices; is too screened by having a rational basis and at a superficial glance seems to diverge from the normal only by a certain exaggerated meticulousness.[4]

Freud offered this conclusion:

> On closer examination ... we can see that screen is insufficient, that the ceremonial comprises some stipulations that go far beyond its rational basis and others which positively run counter to it.[5]

In other words, obsessive behavior may at first glance appear to be rational, but upon further observation it can be seen that it differs from what is considered as normative. Gould, as a pianist star, was driven to sit low and slouch at the piano, to sing and ceremoniously conduct with his free hand while performing on stage. The most striking of all his neurotic behavior was his obsessive need for a special piano chair, which played a central role in his elaborate ceremony of performance. It was Glenn's handy-man father, Bert, who provided a temporary, physical remedy for his son's compelling need to slouch and sit lower at the keyboard. Mr. Gould actually went through years of experimentation in designing a suitable low chair for Glenn, and several dining room chairs were subjected to modification in his woodworking shop. The legs of the chairs were sawed off, little by little, in order to adapt the height to Glenn's emerging needs. At the end, the physical manifestation of the effort came to fruition, and the peculiar sitting object acquired its final shape. The Chair was born. By this time, Glenn was in his late teens. From then on, for better or worse, Glenn and this particular Chair were inseparable in his pianistic pursuits.

Joseph Roddy summed up the cumbersome process of creating Glenn's meaningful possession, the Chair, in the following way:

> To accommodate the slouch, his father, a Toronto furrier, sawed down the legs of a high-backed wooden folding chair and tipped the feet with screws three inches long, enabling his son to adjust it exquisitely to the height and angle that suited him best, the height usually being fourteen inches off the floor, a working level from four to seven inches lower than that of most professional pianists.[6] The finished product, looking like a footstool with a back rest, was not a sightly object, but Gould soon found himself unable to do without it, and takes it with him to every concert hall he performs in.[7]

The Chair was viewed by worldwide audiences in Gould's concerts; it was used at almost all recording sessions, radio and TV appearances, as an exalted item that "went on to become his trademark."[8]

It appears that the roots of Gould's attachment to his chair go far back to his early parent-child relationship. Remember the story from Glenn's infancy when he was placed on his mother's lap and encouraged to charge at the keys, as if the piano were one of his phase-appropriate rattles or toys? Glenn got an inordinate satisfaction from this large, noisy box and even more adoration from the cheering, day-to-day audience of his mother, grandmother, Mary, and Elsie, the nanny. Bert, as a part-time spectator, was also bemused by his son's fascination with the piano sounds. This zealous family quartet was the first mirroring audience for Glenn. He thrived in this role of having a "true love affair with the world."[9] Things gradually became more serious when Mrs. Gould assumed the role of a formal piano teacher to her three-year-old son. At the age of six, Glenn had to face the loss of his maternal grandmother, Mary, and to separate from his own mother by having to start grade school. From then on, Glenn's parentless and insecure mother took her own parenting duty even more seriously and to the extreme. The carefree times of having fun before an appreciative audience at home were replaced unfairly by the solemn atmosphere of decorum. Under the circumstances, Glenn became emotionally vulnerable, which led to his behavioral changes.

One of the first signs of his own childhood difficulties was a slouching posture that was noticeable while he sat at the piano and elsewhere. This new "misbehavior" was met with disapproval and annoyance from his mother who, as a piano teacher of Victorian upbringing, put much emphasis on outward appearance and posture. She responded with frequent corrections: "Sit up, Glenn. Sit up straight, please"[10] Several years ago on the *Tonight Show*, the famed Johnny Carson, who had an impeccably vertical posture, stated with his dry humor that his mother was to be credited for the shape of his back. Carson elicited a thunder of laughter from the audience by saying that his mother reminded him so often to keep his back straight that he not only did not slouch forward but went the other direction of slouching backward. The comment was by all means funny, but it inadvertently revealed a deeper meaning. Obviously, Carson complied too much with his persistent and dutiful mother, ending up with a permanently concave back that then became a trademark of his physical demeanor. Metaphorically speaking, his mother was (reflected) on his back.

In Gould's case, his mother's ongoing efforts to have her son stand up and sit up straight were completely ineffective. The more she worked at correcting Glenn's posture, the more he felt unduly bossed around and rebelled by ignoring her. Hence, Glenn's curved posture and convex back gradually evolved through the lengthy battle of wills with his mother. Having lost the round, both as a mother and as a piano teacher, Florence was confronted with two choices. She could either fight the drooping posture of this strong-willed boy, or she could give in to Glenn's idea to sit at the piano in a chair with back support, which would supposedly help correct the slouch. Glenn rationalized that in his childhood, Mozart, as a picture of him portrayed, sat at the piano in a chair with a back support with his legs crossed. So he felt justified to do exactly the same. Mrs. Gould was too impatient to let Glenn work through his own quirks on his terms. Instead, she never quit meddling in her son's life. Glenn's father conformed to his son's needs by building an adequate piano stool for him. Prim and proper Florence was frustrated by this compromise and by being forced to give in to Glenn's capricious need to sit at the classical instrument in such a non-classical and unsightly way. One can sense the power struggle in the mother-son relationship, which Glenn handled by way of defiance of one of his mother's endless rules. Florence was not able to understand the meaning of Glenn's peculiar posture at the piano, nor was she able to leave him alone.

Glenn's father, who "accommodated the slouch," unconsciously endorsed his son's maladaptive behavior. Seemingly, by designing the Chair, Bert showed his acceptance of Glenn's individual differences, when in reality this was a sign of his denial that there was anything wrong. When interviewed, Mr. Gould denied that Glenn in his childhood could have had scoliosis or kyphosis that would have accounted for his hunching posture.[11] It follows that, from the purely physical and body-mechanics point of view, Glenn was likely fully capable of sitting up straight. The slouching and sitting low at the piano are seen as a functional and physiological disorder. In the dynamic framework, this behavior is regarded as the habitual and symptomatic expression of Glenn's inner problems in relationship to his family. His inability to show protest and assert himself more directly with his high-strung mother resulted in his indirect coping style of antagonizing her and other authority figures. Both parties, Glenn on one side and authoritarian adults who tried to change him on the other side, were seized in a psychological deadlock. Was Glenn supposed to please his mother by straining himself, sitting up properly on the standard piano bench; or was he going to stick to his own style and do what was comfortable for him? By developing his unique posture at the piano, Glenn achieved a degree of autonomy from a formidable, interdependent bond with his mother. His dependency needs were transferred onto the Chair, which was an aborted attempt at coping and emancipating himself from inordinate family ties. In the end, all these laborious subconscious maneuvers resulted in a no-win situation. Glenn was unable to resolve his conflicts, and his parents were unable to help him more efficiently. So far, it can be seen that Glenn's posture, as a symptomatic behavior, makes "sense," as Freud suggested, in the light of the subject's life, and, in this case, in the light of Glenn's life vis-a-vis his significant caregivers.

There is another approach to understanding Gould's "stage mannerisms." Bernard Asbell described his initial encounter during the interview with Gould in this way:

> I asked if he objected to the use of a tape-recorder. He didn't at all. He only wanted the microphone placed at the level of his face, explaining that for reasons he could not understand he is uncomfortable addressing anything low. (At the piano, he sits in an uncommonly low chair, the keyboard almost at his chin which has caused him to suffer a certain amount of ridicule).[12]

This paragraph is loaded with meaning, particularly the part referring to Gould's discomfort in "addressing anything low" and his preference for sitting low himself. One of Gould's favorite books, *The Last Puritan* by George Santayana, will be used as a guide to the riddle of his low seating position. In this book the tragic hero, Oliver Alden, was portrayed as emotionally deprived by his remote and unfeeling mother but was still fortunate enough to have affection from his warmhearted German governess, Irma. Once, during a spontaneous loving outburst toward Irma, the four-year-old Oliver surprised her by putting his arms around her neck and holding her tightly. Irma cautioned him gently but dutifully:

> "But do you ever hug your mother like that? And, of course, it would be wrong not to love her ever so much more than you love me, because she is your mother." Somewhat slowly and absent-mindedly, Oliver let go. He certainly never hugged his mother like that. It was all rather discouraging. Irma felt this too, and never stroked his legs again, and gradually ceased to take him on her lap. "You are such a big boy now," she would say. "You must sit up in your high chair," and she would lock him into it with the oval shelf attached on hinges to the back, which could be swung over his head to form a table in front of him. On this she would lay his brightly illustrated Animal Alphabet from Aunt to Zebra, like an open Bible. "There you are, a little angel in a pulpit: If ever you become a pastor—you know my dear father was a pastor—that's what you will look like preaching in a church." A vague apprehension remained in Oliver's mind that he was destined to be a pastor and to be locked into a pulpit with a big book opened in front of him. A pastor would always look like that and always feel like that: because the persons he ought to love best, like his mother and God, would always be impossible to hug and it would always be wrong to hug the others.[13]

Like Oliver, Glenn too was afraid of being "locked into a pulpit." The highchair and the pulpit are high places that prevent the users from being close and intimate with others. Glenn identified with Oliver's deep emotional pain. Both Oliver and Glenn would far more prefer tender and personalized loving care from their mothers. How could they possibly cuddle with them if they were cold, formal and often angry or disapproving? Both boys were in the state of emotional privation for which they blamed authority represented in the codes of religion. Glenn's parents and both sets of grandparents were staunch, churchgoing Presbyterians. The issues of religious orientation and moral commitment were much too confusing to Glenn. There were those religious aspects that he deeply identified with—the inner peace, the "pure' values, the sacred and solemn music played in church. On the other hand, the church was in Glenn's mind symbolically identical to the "high-chair," which he deeply feared and avoided. One goes to church in one's best clothes, punctually and dutifully. One is also supposed to feel a sense of humility and be constantly responsible for one's own sins. Glenn was extremely sensitive to all these moral codes of obedience. He resented the conventional traits of his rule-obeying parents, relatives and neighbors, which made them, in his mind, more emotionally unreachable and estranged. He unconsciously projected his unfavorable feelings toward his moralistic, churchgoing mother and the rest of the throng onto pulpit-like places and preacher-like figures. That, in part, explains why Gould stopped going to church in his late teens and why he avoided all "high-chair" situations by using antithetical "low chair" strategies. Several other illustrations related to Gould and church morality follow.

In 1972 Robert Walker, in one of his promotional letters, noticed quite perceptively:

> ... Gould's idiosyncrasies obscured his musical genius and those people who record [music] as though it were a church service were put off by his manner-isms ...[14]

This means that Gould's unconventional and undisciplined manners as a musician directly clashed with a style of a church service, or in a broader sense, with any orthodox and rigid practice in music and in his private life. Over the years, Gould departed from church-like standards by developing defensive strategies against mother-like and church-like authority. Richard Kostelanetz quoted Gould saying:

> ... Within the last few decades ... music has ceased to be an occasion, requir-ing an excuse and tuxedo and accorded when encountered an almost religious devotion ...[15]

This is again an example of what Gould resented, a "tuxedo" and "religious devotion" as symbols of formality, metaphorically representing the significant human figures in his life.

There is yet another aspect of Gould's habitual low-sitting pose. His piano teacher, Alberto Guerrero, used to sit lower himself at the keyboard than the majority of other concert pianists. But he sat up straight and was quite determined to teach Glenn to do the same. Joseph Roddy beautifully captured the push-pull contest between the two stubborn musicians at the piano:

> While the boy played ... Guerrero would stand behind him and press down heavily on his shoulders. Gould would push up in self-defense, but the teacher would ordinarily win the match by driving the pupil into a slump. One result is that Gould now has a sturdier set of back and shoulder muscles than a good many practicing weight lifters. Another is his singular posture at the piano. After several years of vain effort to sit up straight under the pressure from Guerrero, Gould came to the conclusion that he could play properly only in a slouch with his elbows either pushed out from his sides, practically parallel to the keyboard or dangling six or eight inches below the arch of his wrists.[16]

Guerrero's nagging efforts to have his student sit up straight were so reminiscent of Mrs. Gould's teaching style that they were quickly rejected and defied. Gould could never understand why he, an acknowledged prodigy, had to abide by the rules and orders of his non-prodigy mother, and later on, his teacher. He resented Guerrero's interference with his piano style and constantly rebelled in one way or another. Roddy's concise psychological evaluation, summed up in the sentence "Gould would push up in self-defense, but the teacher would ordinarily win the match," refers to the seriousness of competition between the two. Guerrero, who may have won an odd match, in the end lost the war. Sadly enough, Gould thought he won the war over his teacher, while accomplishing only a Pyrrhic victory[17] by being doomed to assume, for the rest of his life, his singular posture at the piano as a defense and protection from a would-be intruder. Gould clearly had mixed feelings toward Guerrero, whom he emulated and defied at the same time.

While most performing pianists are comfortable sitting appropriately on standard adjustable piano benches, infrequently there would be subtle deviations from the orthodox practices. The late Artur Schnabel, Gould's pianist-model, also showed a preference for sitting lower at the keyboard in a chair with a back support. More recently, the renowned American pianist, Peter Serkin, sits at the piano in an unusually high wooden chair with a back rest. He is practically towering over the keys, with his elbows above the keyboard. Another distinguished pianist, Radu Lupu, is in the habit of sitting at the piano in an ordinary hard chair with a back support. In these cases, though there is a deviation from conventional practices, it is done discretely, and the audience is reassured that there must be some kind of valid reason for the departure from the standard.

Outwardly, Gould's Chair stuck out like a sore thumb, while inwardly, the creation of the Chair was a remedial compromise for him. In his inner world, the Chair was supposed to bridge the emotional gap felt by Glenn in relation to his mother, father and others. The Chair was taken from Glenn's original home. Its presence awakened pleasant images of his parents, their friends and relatives sitting around the bridge table playing cards and chatting. Notice the metaphor—the bridge chair serves to bridge the interpersonal gap. This idyllic image could be retrieved any time and give that homey, soothing feeling of familiarity and security. The emotionally insufficient family triad was unconsciously compensated for and expanded into a tetrad; my father, my mother, me, and the Chair. Gould's underfunctional self-image was enriched when he allied himself with his personified Chair—"me and my Chair are traveling to New York." He was simply addicted to his Chair and could not conceive of performing on stage without it. George Pollock, in his elaborate work on human symbiosis, stated:

> ... the symbiotic person cannot be left alone, but seeks objects to complete the particular dyad resulting from an earlier impasse. We might call these ... patients object addicts, who search constantly for figures with whom they can establish ties.[18]

Pollock specifically referred to dependency and addiction of one person to another human love object, but the same principle applies to reliance and addiction to physical, chemical and other objects. Addiction of any kind, though it may appear to a user as a temporary solution, does not work in the long run. Accordingly, Gould's dependency on his chair only gave an illusion of strength. It was carried too far, masquerading his underlying insecurity and jeopardizing his music career.

Gould's Chair was not only perceived by the world as bizarre, it also produced those absurd, annoying squeaking sounds, heard both at the recitals and on his albums. His recording producer Andrew Kazdin said that "cracking sounds being emitted by Glenn's favorite piano chair had reached an objectionable high level."[19] Both Tom Frost and Andrew Kazdin, who were the recording producers of the set of Beethoven's work, decided to eliminate "as many of these noises as possible, leaving only those that resisted the operation." Kazdin, who was Gould's producer for a period of fifteen years, described that he worked on editing so meticulously that it deserved to be called a "brain surgery." Despite such precise work on editing, the squeak still could be heard on several of Gould's records; the *Goldberg Variations* included. The noises from the piano that Gould called a "hiccup," the Chair and his own guttural throat noises became an integral part of his music recording, as if a new tune (or out of tune) was added to the original piece. In that sense, Gould put his stamp on each of his interpretations. He felt entitled to it. The vehemence of this self-centered pursuit forced others to accept him as he was. Obviously, both recording producers and the consumer audience consented to having final products—the records—contaminated by these alien noises.

Contaminated or not, Gould's playing, in itself, is a commodity, and his records are sought after, not just for the pleasure of everyday use, but also as a collector's item of increasing and lasting value. In the world of philately, the rare stamps with errors end up reaching the highest catalogue price. Likewise, in the world of the recording industry, Gould's records are a bestseller despite many oddities and glitches. It matters only that Gould is playing in person; the method and the process being immaterial to the public. In the course of time, the audience learned to distinguish the bright, fabulously talented figure from the dusky ground of his chaotic personality. The audience delights in his musical qualities. A Columbia Records salesman summed it all up by saying to the recording crew annoyed with Gould's mannerisms, "don't rattle him, he sells like crazy and Columbia has got him."

There is also another dimension in the analysis of the intriguing Chair. This originally odd but tidy looking chair with a seat was transformed into a shabby and fallen apart chair. Over the years the seat turned to shreds, leaving the bare wooden frame to sit on. This very feature, and the height of the chair of twelve and a half inches, makes it strikingly resemble a toilet seat. Richard Kostelanetz wrote:

> ... he made the chair such an integral part of his essential equipment that he had spurned the offers to build him a substitute. Some years ago the hazards of airplane travel smashed its seat and he expended considerable effort finding pieces of green cloth and mattress rag that, he judges "end precisely the same tension and support as the chair originally had."[20]

In truth, Gould tried many times to replace his Chair. Evidently, in August 1956, amid Gould's skyrocketing fame after the release of the *Goldberg Variations*, his manager wrote to an aluminum company in Montreal, Quebec. He wondered about a possibility of designing a light, aluminum chair because the wooden chair posed an "excess baggage bill on airplane." When a potential firm was finally found in New Market, Homburger backed off on a deal:

> Mr. Gould's greatest fear is that a chair made out of aluminum might be so light that when he would play and possibly sit at the edge it might slide away from under him.[21]

These efforts were only halfhearted and the end result was that the Chair was never repaired nor was the missing panel on the top of the seat ever replaced. Kazdin, who depicted the gradual regression of Gould's chair in a lively fashion in seven paragraphs, concluded: "... in the final analysis, his [Gould's] gluteus maximus was positioned directly over an open rectangle ..."[22] Gould and his Chair regressed simultaneously. His subconscious need to reenact the act of sitting on a toilet-like chair is seen as a regression to early childhood, to the so-called anal stage of human psychosexual development. Sitting on the potty at age two may be a pleasurable experience when accompanied by the warm, empathic attitude of the caregiver. The entire process may be internalized and remembered as safe and comforting. By sitting low at the piano where his performance anxiety was the highest, Gould was able to retrieve a tranquil image from his childhood, as an antidote to his menacing stage fright.

Mastering one's own bowel function in the course of toilet training is not only a personal triumph of a child but is also a reward for responsible parental effort. The trap here is that toilet training pursued by a rigid and disciplinarian mother is liable to upset and frustrate the child. The issue of cleanliness was of the foremost importance to Florence Gould. Her fastidious personality traits were manifested in her pedantic style in housekeeping, in the manicuring of the flower garden, and certainly in the unmistakable grooming of her little boy. Glenn experienced these values of his mother as meaningless chores that he rebelled against continuously. He became compulsive and ritualistic, not in pursuance of cleanliness, but in adherence to his many unbending principles and his tenacious need for his Chair. Wearing the traditional performance attire of pianists and the use of a conventional piano chair were experienced as nonsense by Glenn. This is why he changed them both—the formal, lordly tuxedo was replaced with a plain dark business suit, whereas the official black, upholstered and adjustable piano chair was demoted to a wooden, stripped away, toilet-seat like chair. In Gould's mind, the image of the chair as a toilet seat was being used ambivalently. On one hand it symbolized pleasure and peace derived from retentive relief. On another, it stood for his aggressive power against those experienced as oppressive. In common street parlance, the toilet image and associated activities symbolized the notion of "giving them shit" or "dumping on" oppressors of any sort.

This dwarf-like chair may have been unhealthy and unattractive looking, but it survived through hundreds of Gould's concerts. The Chair served multiple purposes. In the first place, it was provocative and defiant. For a beholder, the Chair was a deceptive cover-up of Gould's many anxieties, a decoy to vex and fool his observers. The critics were hooked on it, baffled, often enraged by it. Unknowingly, both the critics and audiences who were exposed to Gould and his platform behavior subconsciously became participants of a dynamic interaction with him. The audience was split into those who admired him unconditionally and those who condemned him. The critics were hopelessly divided, too, according to their subconscious reaction to Gould as a person. Some of them were overprotective of Gould, often idealizing him, while others displayed various degrees of unbridled hostility and bafflement. A small number of critics and music scholars were able to maintain healthy boundaries and an objective stance while filled with empathy and the ability to set apart Gould's neurotic behavior from his music achievements.

Published reports of Gould's Chair and his assorted platform antics invariably exposed subconscious reactions of the writers, more in response to Gould as a person than to him as a creative musician. Joseph Roddy wrote:

> ... mostly, though he plays in a deep slouch, the base of his spine on the forward edge of his low chair, his legs crossed and stretched out around the pedals,

> which he rarely uses, his shoulders hardly higher than the keyboard, his whole posture a scandal to the piano teachers in the audience, who, whatever their differences, agree that a pianist should sit up straight and sit still.[23]

Roddy starts off the paragraph objectively, describing Gould in situ at the piano, only to end it more subjectively, by implications disapproving of Gould's scandalous piano posture. Similarly, Gould's teacher, Guerrero, and many other scholastic musicians and critics suffered empathic failure in relationship to Gould. The transaction between Gould and those music scholars was patterned by the early mother-child transaction, marked by the maternal empathy failure and the use of an approval-disapproval formula. Gould unconsciously invited the disapproving and scandalizing responses of scholars who, in turn, played into his neurotic needs. Unhealthy interaction was self-perpetuating between Gould and the beholder.

The prestigious critic, Donal Henahan, succumbed to his own personalized hostile feelings toward Gould. Following Gould's recital in Chicago on April 22, 1962, Henahan of *The News* wrote:

> ... Music's most successful hipster, Glenn Gould, finally slouched onto the Orchestra Hall stage after three cancellations ... Seating himself at the Ouija board on a sawed-off rickety relic of a chair that was held together with wires, the disheveled recitalist sang and stomped and conducted.[24]

The commentary seems to contain emotions of predominantly ferocious anger and ridicule. Henahan reduced Gould's grand instrument, the piano, into an obscure object of mockery such as a Ouija board. Meanwhile, Gould was so selective of his pianos. Henahan demoted the entire process of selection and mastery of the grand classical instrument to a caricatured status of a non-instrument, the Ouija board. The critic proceeded to be in a sarcastic and unpardoning mood. His rage culminated around the subject of Gould's chair. Henahan was at a loss to understand the onslaught of his impulses to be so insulting toward Gould. His music expertise as a critic was paralyzed as he was consumed by Gould's extra-musical behavior while having a blind spot for him as a whole person and an extraordinary musician. Henahan offered neither insight nor did he leave room for any understanding of Gould's unique approach to the piano.

If Henahan was making a critical commentary about a comedian-pianist such as Victor Borge, then a humorous style may have been appropriate. Benign humor is conflict-free and is supposed to elicit a painless and joyous response. On closer examination of the critical paragraph on Gould, the humor was glib, biting and inappropriate for a serious, classical event. This look-alike humor was harmful to Gould. The critics, in general, by the virtue of their professional authority, serve as barometers of both the music performer and the performance. The audience is sensitive and responds to such barometers accordingly. Superficial and unempathic critics may unduly raise anxiety, trigger depression and lower self-esteem of an artist performer and, in the end, may destroy the artist's potential.

There were more subtle and benign descriptions and criticisms of Gould's piano-related behavior. This one is quoted by Gould's first biographer, Geoffrey Peyzant, from the Columbia liner notes:

> ... But the collapsible chair was the Goldberg (Rube) variation of them all. It's a bridge chair, basically with each leg adjusted individually for height so that Glenn can lean forward, backward or to either side. The studio skeptics thought that this was wackiness of the highest order until recording got underway. Then they saw Glenn adjust the slant of his chair before doing his slightly incredible cross-hand passages in the variations, leaning in the direction of the 'cross.' The chair was unanimously accepted as a splendid logical device.[25]

Here, it is interesting to notice the attitude of the recording staff. The "studio skeptics," initially perturbed by the chair, were relieved to find a rationale for its use, accepting it in the end "as a splendid logical device." The anxiety of the recording crew, related to Gouldian eccentricities, was dealt with through the use of inoffensive humor and understanding.

Interestingly, the lay audience was more receptive to Gould's ceremonial behavior than the professionals. Gould's superb artistry, coupled with his extra-musical behavior, was delivered to his audiences as a package. The public felt stimulated by Gould's originality, enjoying him as a figure and his music as the treat of the season. While in performances of non-classical music there is more freedom for showmanship and imagination, the classicists tend to adhere to more rigorous traditional standards of performance. Gould kept trying to loosen the long-prescribed standards, and the audiences did not seem to mind. Some viewers, who prefer to maintain the illusion of a recital as a "show," experienced the Chair and Gould's platform behavior as a gimmick deliberately used to amuse them.

So far, a variety of insights have been offered into the existence and meaning of the Chair. One question still remains unanswered. Why was it never repaired or replaced by a similar, more attractive and more acceptable chair? The invaluable work of D. W. Winnicott will help in solving this riddle. Because of high emotional dependence and separation anxiety, Glenn strongly relied on his pets and music, which filled the psychological space (or the gap) between him and his mother. In child psychology, this gap is called the "intermediate area of experience." In other words, this was an emotional zone where he could have a shelter and his own individual experience, including the piano-related behavior, all apart from the symbiotic ties with his mother. The rising conflict over his dependency needs generated an intolerable level of anxiety, calling for the employment of elaborate defenses against it. The pets and music served as a desirable comforter, and the interaction between the two, combined with a specific set of Glenn's personal habits, played the role of the space filler. The entire behavioral complex, including the slouching posture, sitting low on his personal Chair, audible singing and conducting, had high subjective meaning and the power to repeat itself in its original, unmodified form, over and over again. Any departure from this ritual would result in increased anxiety and associated frustrations, and therefore was avoided. In Winnicott's words, Glenn's complex extra musical rituals would be called "transitional phenomena," whereas the objects central to that subjective experience, such as the pets and the Chair, would represent "transitional objects." Winnicott holds that the:

> fate [of the transitional object] is to be gradually allowed to be decathected, so that in the course of years it becomes not so much forgotten as relegated to limbo ... It is not forgotten and it is not mourned. It loses meaning and this is because the transitional phenomena have become diffused, have become spread

> out over the whole intermediate territory between 'inner psychic reality' and 'the external world ...' that is to say over the whole cultural field.[26]

In Gould's case, where his early childhood development was interfered with, the space between him and his mother (transitional phenomena) was never successfully negotiated and decathected (never lost its meaning) but carried into his adult life. By this token, Glenn's childhood impasse of not being able to let go of things and holding onto them tightly continued to be meaningful in his adult years. The continuous emotional deprivation led to the reinforcement of an addictive position in relationship to transitional phenomena and his transitional object (Chair). Gould's lifelong dependence on medications, his need to be playful, his ritualistic way of approaching music and the relentless need for a specific piano and specific chair are all considered to be related to the unresolved developmental issues of the transitional phenomena and transitional object.

These dynamics explain why the Chair was neither improved nor replaced. The original transitional object of infancy, such as a favorite teddy bear or a soft blanket, must never be changed by others until the child is ready "to relegate it to limbo." Sensitive, non-compelling mothers don't even wash those smelly, raggedy toys and blankets in order not to change their meaning to the child. True, these mothers may not understand the dynamics of this interesting human behavior, but they are able to recognize intuitively the depth of its meaning to the child. In Glenn's life, the frustrations with his caregivers resulted in his inability to resolve his childhood needs and in his lasting attachment to his transitional objects, which then became permanent. In doing so, he created a new soothing experience that was maladaptive in nature but secured for him a degree of separation from an overpowering bond with his mother. Gould was innocent inasmuch as he truly did not know what drove him to his extra-musical behavior. So whenever asked, he desperately tried to rationalize it and make some sense out of it. As a result of the strong inner dynamics, his anachronistic activities persisted and the Chair, as the central transitional object, survived, even outsurvived, its master.

Another reason for Gould's excessive attachment to his dilapidated piano chair had to do with his narcissistic personality traits. Gould harbored a strong sense of entitlement, and he felt justified to impose his mannerisms and the Chair on others. Public acceptance and unconditional acclaim from his critics and audiences were expected in return. From his childhood on, Gould showed an irresistible need toward the omnipotent control of others, demanding from them uncontested devotion. The message that Gould projected was: "I can do anything and still expect your adoration." He made no concerted effort to change his behavior, for example, through psychiatric treatment. On the contrary, he expected his environment to change its response to him. Alas! When the critics and music professionals withheld their absolute veneration, Gould was the one to suffer a great deal through painful injuries to his self-esteem, which in the scientific literature is often referred to as "narcissistic injuries." The repeated emotional injuries had devastating after-effects, resulting at first in Gould's withdrawal from public performance and later on from life, in general.

Gould was quite aware of the negative feedback from the professional music critics in response to his stage behavior. Even though the audiences on the whole were more welcoming and accepted Gould the way he was, a certain number of individual concertgoers were annoyed by his platform mannerisms. Some of those zealots wrote him critical letters offering their disciplinary tips. One of Gould's anti-fans, who introduced himself as a "tenor, soloist performer," wrote to him:

> To you as a young man I would like to tell you that you would be well advised to forget affectation and perform with quiet and dignified style. First of all, have a hair cut. It [long hair] does not increase your presentation and is in fact "Sissie."
>
> ... You do not need any eccentric actions to impress the audience. Just be yourself. When not actually playing, sit still and place your hands on your knees ...[27]

Gould personally read all his letters and most often responded, even if they were offensive. It is not known whether he replied to this letter, which, under the guise of well-meaning advice, had a moralizing tone. It must have been highly reminiscent of the preaching style of his mother and corrective method of his music mentor, Alberto Guerrero. Worst of all, the unfortunate choice of the word "sissie" must have been a painful reminder of his father's frequent put-downs in Glenn's growing up years. Gould must have felt gravely hurt and humiliated by this scornful fan who could not see the forest for the trees.

In another letter of a dissatisfied viewer and personal friend, the writer was somewhat gentler in lecturing the internationally acclaimed virtuoso:

> Dear Glenn, April 19, 1956
>
> ... All the young people who hope for concert careers, receive the same hard-boiled advice: "Talent is not enough. You must have a lot behind you and also a gimmick to make people notice you."
>
> Now you have proved that it is possible to succeed without a fortune in your pocket but at the same time you have added strength to the argument that a gimmick is essential.
>
> There is no doubt in the mind of any musician I have talked to that your success would have come just as certainly, if a little more slowly, on the strength of your performance alone. I myself am convinced that we hear only a part of your interpretative potential, and that much of the emotional fuel is siphoned off in a meaningless gymnastic display.
>
> Even those of us who recognize your talent as superior have some pride in our ability to become "lost" in a performance, and have found that getting rid of mannerisms is a necessary but painful process during which one has to settle for something less than perfection, musically.
>
> Please work at it. Everyone is very proud of you and it hurts to find your name is greeted first with a smirk and then with a grudging admission that you are a fine artist.
>
> Yours very sincerely,
> Harry [Heap][28]

Some of Gould's contemporaries were convinced that his stage behavior was premeditated. They thought of it as a commercial gimmick or theatrical affectation. After Gould's passing, more than two decades of scientific studies were needed to refute these awkward and superficial accusations. Gould did not use his chair, nor his piano, nor did he rehearse his conducting and singing before his performance in order to fascinate or please his public. He was just unable to separate his beloved music from the emotional clutter of the past.

In short, Gould's ceremonial use of the Chair, grand piano and his "platform antics" are regarded as elaborate, subconscious strategies defending against high anxiety. This behavior, though largely maladaptive and uneconomical in nature, made a lot of sense in the light of his personal psychology. Most of all, it helped him to carry on a time-limited but still very rich concert career. If Gould was not allowed to pursue his ceremonial behavior, his inner peace would be so massively challenged and compromised that he would have given up much earlier. This way his life span was extended till long into his adulthood. The Chair has a polysymptomatic meaning, and it serves as a symbol of distinction among pianists. In a more fundamental way, it represents an unconscious attempt to deal with excessive attachment to his mother. To others, the Chair may have been obsolete and meaningless, but to Gould, it was a pet chair, a dear and inseparable "transitional object," a Linus blanket that bridged the emotional gap between his childhood and adulthood, between him and his family, between him and others. The Chair was Gould's companion that helped him perform brilliantly in Leningrad, New York, Berlin and wherever else he went, and it made it possible for him to actualize close to a hundred recordings of classical music that have sold over seven million copies.

In retrospect, though some of Gould's contemporaries thought his mannerisms were a conscious, attention-seeking device, from the above in-depth analysis it is clear that he could not help it, nor could he have stopped it without professional help. Gould did not consciously plan to "misbehave" and irk anybody, but his behavior was an inevitable end result of the variety of inner psychic forces that were overpowering. In the final analysis, we, the survivors, may have to ask ourselves, why did it matter so much how this great artist behaved beyond making music? If Gould sat at the piano in crimson red attire or in a tank top and a pair of shorts, the audience would be flabbergasted; the keepers of moral standards would be disgusted, but the same quality music would come out of his music genius. The music is not contained in the conventional attire or short pants but stands on its own. The question arising from this essay is: Does one really have to behave to produce good quality music?

The critic of the *New York World-Telegram and Sun*, Louis Biancolli, after a triad of Gould's concerts in March 1960 with Leonard Bernstein and the New York Philharmonic, had put this question in the optimal prospective:

> For all the novelty of Pierre Boulez and the barbaric power of Bela Bartok, the news at yesterday's Philharmonic concert was Beethoven and the reason was Glenn Gould. In the slow movement of the Master's Piano Concerto no. 4 the young Canadian artist outdid himself in beauty and spirituality of playing. For the few minutes it took to perform the Andante, Carnegie Hall was transformed into a place of worship ... Mr. Gould seemed all inner fire and radiance. *The depth and nobility of the playing were extraordinary in one so young. The mannerisms, if they are that, are external and irrelevant. It was the message that came from within and within Beethoven that counted.*[29]

GOULD AT THE GRAND PIANO

> I hope people won't be blinded to my playing by what have been called my personal eccentricities.
>
> Glenn Gould[30]

Having pondered the symbolic meaning of Gould's legendary Chair, equal attention is paid to his special grand piano as the chief instrument of his emotive and musical expression. In the first fifteen years of Glenn's life, several ordinary pianos were used in order to satisfy his rapidly evolving musical skills. The common upright piano, which served for the pleasure and modest practicing needs of his mother, was also at Glenn's disposal for his first piano lessons. In his teens, when Glenn officially became a concert pianist, his parents rewarded him by purchasing an expensive Chickering grand piano, a vintage model of 1895.

Jonas Chickering, the founder of the Boston-based piano manufacturing firm, is considered to be "the father of the American piano and 'the father of the piano as we know it.'"[31] Many great pianists played Chickerings. Franz Liszt owned one in Weimar, and Ferruccio Busoni, Ernst von Dohnanyi and Louis Moreau Gottschalk were all Chickering artists. Music historians recorded this pertinent anecdote:

> Louis Moreau Gottschalk played exclusively on Chickerings. A description of a concert in San Francisco in 1865 gives us a glimpse into this colorful period in American history. Gottschalk and nine other pianists, each one playing a separate Chikering, performed the Soldiers' Chorus from *Faust* and the Pilgrims' March from *Tannhauser*. The enormous hall was soon reverberating with the clang of silver dollars which the audience threw at the strings of ten Chikering grands.[32]

For Glenn, it was love at first sight, and he quickly embraced his new concert grand. He practiced and played it tirelessly with renewed inspiration and a deep belief that the structure of the keys and the sonorous quality of the Chickering were better and more suitable for him than those of any other piano he had played before. For example, Gould was convinced that the space between the Chickering keys was wider than in average pianos, which allowed enough room for the wiggling of his fingers.

Not only was Glenn in his youth closely intertwined with music, but the Gould family dynamics and their whole lifestyle revolved around music and its instrument—the piano. Mr. and Mrs. Gould preferred the leisurely atmosphere of cottage country life to their demanding city home pace. Every opportunity, such as weekends and holidays, was used for a temporary relocation of the family to their cottage in Uptergrove, on Lake Simcoe. Mr. Gould reminisced on these early days:

"Whenever we fled to the cottage, Glenn's piano was shipped along," Mr. Gould stated with an air of pride.

"You mean you had to hire professional piano movers to move the piano to the cottage?" I was stunned.

"Yes, exactly, it was always a nuisance, and it was an added expense, but Glenn's mother thought of it as very important, and I did not question it," Mr. Gould said with a firm conviction.

"What about Canadian weather circumstances? How did you manage them?" I was thinking of winter blizzards and slippery roads.

"That didn't matter. We moved the piano regardless of the weather. In the winter, candles were burned at the cottage to keep the piano warm."[33] Mr. Gould sounded very inventive.

In further conversation, Mr. Gould told me that moving the piano up and down the Toronto-Simcoe trail was very common in their life because "Glenn simply needed his piano." There were monetary expenses and unavoidable frustrations around arranging for the piano movers and tuners. Damage of the precious instrument was habitually incorporated into everyday life. The patterns of "move-and-tune" combined with the "damage-and-repair" were carried into Glenn's adult life, setting the stage for his future piano-related manners. As an established concert pianist, he preferred to take his piano with him on tour whenever possible, enduring all related hazards and expenses. Once in the cottage, the piano was installed in the spacious music room that was custom-made for Glenn by his father. Bert, who was Glenn's stagehand, personally took care of such fine details as acoustics, heating, soundproofing and lighting to secure Glenn's maximal comfort.

While Glenn's piano was being moved from one residence to another, the car trip to or from the cottage was highlighted by classical music on the radio. One may conjure up the typical car scene: the father, by rule, in the driver's seat; the mother peremptorily sitting next to him and the youngster, Glenn, reclining by himself in the roomy back seat of the car. The radio was purposely turned on to enhance Glenn's music education. Selected was the CBC channel with classical music, and often it was the New York Philharmonic performing under the direction of the aging maestro Arturo Toscanini. Glenn's ambitious mother, afraid of "wasting" her son's valuable time on spontaneous chatter, introduced a more didactic tone to their conversation about music matters. Meanwhile, down-to-earth Bert Gould could think of many interesting stories to run by his wife and child, but he chose to refrain in the service of Glenn's education. The mother constantly felt impelled to feed Glenn novel tidbits from the world of music and, for the most part, he absorbed those learned delicacies by internalizing fused images of his mother and music. The repeated trek to and from the cottage became the stage for Gould's emotionally charged psychodrama. For Glenn, the car scene was pleasurable and soothing at times, giving him the sense of specialness and safety. At other times, he felt thwarted and controlled by the formal roles of his parents. Despite the mixed feelings Glenn had about his parents' rigid attitude, the sojourn to the cottage was deeply meaningful to him. It carved into his memory in a somewhat idealized way as a childhood idyll.

Carting the piano up and down the Ontario highways was a complicated task that necessitated diverse mechanical routines. First, the piano was secured, then this essential and highly valued object was carried down the stairs and out of the city dwelling. It was then guided and protected apprehensively during the truck loading. In the next phase upon arrival at the lake home, the whole tedious procedure had to be repeated in reverse, this time the piano being maneuvered into the small cottage. One can sense a ritualistic and compulsive flavor in those activities, which gradually became an integral and ceremonious feature of Gould's personal life.

The piano turned into an object of preoccupation for the Gould trio. The elegant and sizable Chickering was not spared from the rough and frequent move-and-tune rituals. Even when Glenn acquired his second grand piano, which was permanently installed at the cottage, he still insisted on shipping the Chickering, thereby having two pianos lined up side by side in the music room. The Chickering acquired personified meaning and became a highly emotionally charged object. At the time of emotional discord with Glenn's piano teacher, Alberto Guerrero, when Glenn was about eighteen years old, the music played on the Chickering was more than ever needed to appease his inner worries. Gould clung to his piano, which stood for his mother, who obtained it for him, and his teacher, Guerrero, who taught him the secrets of piano mastery. In Gould's subconscious mind, the grand instrument posed for the grand people in his life.

Out of the numerous pianos Gould played during his music career, four of them stood out in their meaning. After his first love with the Chickering, the next two favorites were both Steinway pianos. The first of them was model One-Seventy-Four and the second was model CD 318. Both grand pianos, particularly the latter one, were an integral part of Gould's music fame as a concert pianist. In his youth, Glenn played a Heinzman piano at public performances, only to become an exclusive Steinway artist in his adult years.

Following the deaths of Jonas Chickering and his sons, their piano manufacturing firm was absorbed by the Aeolian American Corporation, which in 1982 permanently closed its doors. The Chickering piano became an antiquity and a collectors' item. During the second part of the nineteenth century, the popularity of the Steinway piano rose dramatically. Steinway & Sons of New York produced a definitive form of the modern grand piano in 1855. From then on, the Steinway piano became one of the finest and most sought-after keyboard instruments in the world.

While on a music tour in New York, Gould was quickly attracted to the Steinway and Sons piano firm conveniently located just across from Carnegie Hall on 57th Street near 6th Avenue. Gould was generally well-received at Steinway's, where he was treated as an exceptional customer. This is where his fascination with the Steinway piano started, which continued to exist for the next quarter of a century. Glenn's fastidious taste and compulsive search for a particular grand piano were well known to the Steinway staff members, who made concentrated efforts to satisfy him. William Hupfer, the chief piano technician, who worked for Steinway for fifty years, was personally involved in discussing with Gould the merits of each piano of his interest. Hupfer was at Gould's disposal for tuning and altering the pianos whenever needed. Gould's persistent piano hunting was rewarded by discovering model One Seventy-Four, which supposedly possessed the desired sonic qualities. He instantly secured the exclusive loan privileges to this special instrument, which then became his principal partner at work in a variety of North American concert halls. Gould, the Chair and his grand piano as a tripartite team toured together. This was a true recreation of the original childhood idyll involving the music-related family trips to the cottage.

Joseph Roddy portrayed the meaning of this particular piano model in Gould's life in the following manner:

> ... in January of 1955 Gould found the closest thing yet to the ideal piano he had been looking for ... The instrument lived up to his expectations; it was tight and puritan and the spaces between keys were generous enough to allow all the wiggling he wanted.
>
> Over the next eight months he carted it up and down the eastern seaboard,

> and the freight bills which, of course, he had to pay personally, came to just under four thousand dollars, not a cent of which Gould considered misspent. ... in March 1957, One Seventy-four simply came apart [after a concert in Cleveland]. ... Gould was in despair ... At first he felt completely off his form with music and out of sorts with himself—a depressive state for which the only therapy he knew was a fast flight home to the Chickering.[34]

Gould seemed to be overwhelmed with sorrow around the loss of his beloved music object. "The Chickering is sick and One-Seventy-four is gone. I guess in a few years I'll retire too," Gould pined. This somber statement, like a bad omen, revealed the depth of Gould's despair in the face of loss. The forceful separation from his beloved piano was yet another stressor aggravating his high anxiety and stage fright, which led to even more obsessive preoccupations and odd behavior. Fortunately, after concerts in Cleveland on March 28 and 30, 1957, Gould embarked on a European tour, where he was unable to transport his favorite piano because of the distance. He was forced to make do with any concert piano made available to him. It appears that Gould made a greater emotional investment in his music objects than in the living people around him. The loss of his enormously cathected or emotionally charged grand piano called for an appropriate mourning reaction.

One of Gould's lasting handicaps was that he could never express his innermost feelings and mourn his losses properly. Gradually, through his incomplete mourning, Gould seemingly managed to overcome the grief; only to transfer his strong needs and feelings onto the next exalted music object, which was the Steinway piano, model CD 318. In the first several years from the early 1960s, this model was loaned and always readily available to Gould for his concert and recording purposes. In 1973, Gould finally purchased this particular grand piano, which thereafter remained in his permanent possession.

In an interview with Johnatan Cott in 1974, Gould described his attachment to the Steinway grand piano model CD 318 in the following way:

> ... I use only one piano and have for the last fifteen years. The piano I do all my recordings on since 1960 is a piano built in '45 but reconditioned by me in '60 and many times subsequently, including last year, when it had to be completely rebuilt—it was dropped by a truck ... this piano has a very light action, as indeed all pianos that I prefer do ... it has the most translucent sound of any piano I've ever played—it's quite extraordinary, it has a clarity of every register that I think is just about unique.[35]

Once again, Gould became emotionally bonded with this Steinway piano. The custom clearance records show that he traveled with this concert grand for nineteen years back and forth to New York for his recording sessions.[36] Gould was even preoccupied with the number 318, which became his lucky number. Whether the traveling virtuoso was plainly attention-seeking or superstitious, the result was still the same. He insisted that his travel agent always book for him hotel room 318. In Toronto, he permanently resided for some time in room 318, at the Hampton Court Hotel across from the CBC building on Jarvis Street. If for any reason his CD 318 was not available for radio and TV appearances,

Gould used to rent a particular Steinway from the CBC, the cost of which in 1975 was $75 per day, whereas the cost of moving the same piano from the Studio to Eaton Auditorium was $95. His quest for a special instrument was monetarily costly and emotionally taxing. In 1973, Gould purchased from Steinway & Sons a Steinway piano model D Grand with Ebonized case, for $6,700. This piano was never able to compete with and replace his beloved CD 318.

Because of frequent relocations and restorations, the Steinway piano CD 318 deteriorated and was no longer in top condition for Gould's refined pianist standards. In his last years of life, Gould opted to purchase a Yamaha piano, Model CF 11. The Steinway CD 318 was only physically replaced by the Yamaha, but emotionally the latter could never compete and earn Gould's deep sense of closeness and compassion as the former did. The loss of the most meaningful object, as well as the broken tradition and emotional ties with Steinway & Sons, once again called for an extensive and thorough grieving process. The loss of such an emotionally over-invested piano was costly. Since Gould was ambivalent in both his love and loss, he was unable to complete his mourning-liberation process. His observers could not understand his chaotic life while he was stumbling through a series of incomplete mournings of frequent losses. For a beholder, Gould was seen to have extravagant and childish stage mannerisms since he had to cling with such tenacity to a particular piano and the Chair.

Other than his compelling need for his special grand piano, Gould also showed a need for special qualities of the piano sound. His piano had to be "tight and puritan," to have a "very light action," "clarity" and "translucent sound." It is worthwhile to analyze this further in order to set apart Gould's real needs as a great pianist from his purely compulsive needs.

Distinguished musicians—composers, conductors and performing artists—differ from the average population by their exaggerated ability for deep sensory perceptiveness and a deep inner experience of music. Advanced musicians know from the very beginning of their creation what the end result of a music piece should be. An orchestra conductor leads a variety of musicians through a maze of cumbersome rehearsals toward a particular end result, in which a perfect match is sought between the mental image of the music and the final performance.

Gould, having had the natural gift of perfect pitch, was able to discern the most subtle gaps between his own mental experience of music and its execution on the keyboard. He resorted to elaborate music theorizing and experimentation, all for the purposes of lessening the discrepancy between the inner and outer experience of music. Often his methods and way of pursuing this goal stood out and seemed odd to other contemporary concert pianists and scholars. Gould, in his quest for maximizing the executive prowess of his grand piano, managed to change the sonic qualities of his instrument to the point of a qualitative distinction from most existing others. Indeed, upon listening to Gould's records even a lay admirer could often notice the uniqueness of the style and sound of his interpreted music. This is largely a function of his distinct music technique; as well as the very modified, distinguishable physical qualities of his grand piano. The "harpsipiano" is what Gould affectionately called his renewed grand instrument. This hybrid-piano satisfied his need for "light action" and the "translucent sound."

He longed for a special music instrument that would optimally represent the beauty and rich nuances of the music experienced in his mind. His prolific correspondence with diverse music personalities shows the extent of thought given to perfecting the piano mechanics and sound. In an interesting letter from a music historian, Avner Carmi,[37] dated February 7, 1960, Gould's search for a special piano was recognized as sensible and justifiable from the musico-technical point of view. From this letter one can find out that Carmi, as a scholar of so-called Siena Piano, authored a book titled *Immortal Piano*. He proposed that Italian masters of music had found that "the jump from harpsichord to piano was harsh," leading to the invention of the Siena as a "missing link between the harpsichord and the emergence of the era of the piano." Carmi, as an expert in the field, was able to relate to Gould's quest for a modified piano. Gould, with his ultra-sensitive auditory ability, perceived the lack of subtlety of the contemporary piano sound, particularly when interpreting baroque music. This may explain why he made concerted, independent efforts to soften the "harsh" piano sound and bring the contemporary interpretations of baroque music closer to the originals.

The following excerpt from Gould's affectionate letter dated August 24, 1961, to a music associate in Leningrad, Madame Kitty Gvozdeva, is a lively portrayal of his original attitude toward the favored "harpsipiano."

> ... I have just concluded a very busy summer with concerts at the Stratford Festival (of which I am a co-director) and the Vancouver Festival and have done a lot of rather interesting programs, most of them for the first time, which included conducting two Bach cantatas from the keyboard (Nos. 51-54) and the Third Brandenburg Concerto in the same manner. For these works where I am continuous player, I have been using a delightful piano which was specially prepared for me. It is a small Steinway with various metallic clips in the end of the hammers which produce a sound very much like a harpsichord but retains the projection of a larger instrument. Many people did not like it and felt that it was neither piano nor harpsichord (although to be honest many more people did like it) but I personally feel that this kind of instrument may provide the proper solution for doing Bach performances in large auditoriums. I may sometime make some recordings on this particular piano.[38]

Having explored the music meaning of Gould's harpsipiano, the next task is to look at the symbolic meaning of his concert grand in the framework of his relations with significant people in his life. Gould became famous on account of his extraordinary pianist ability best embodied in the delivery of Bach's music. His unique interpretation of Bach's *Goldberg Variations* is considered to be his foremost masterpiece. This magnificent, heartwarming music piece was originally championed by the most outstanding harpsichordist of the century, Wanda Landowska. She is credited with the first public performance of the complete *Goldberg Variations* in Paris in 1933, when Gould was one year of age. Furthermore, Landowska pioneered the same piece in New York in 1942 after immigrating to the United States, and her recording of it became one of the bestsellers of that particular music genre. Hence, in Gould's life chronology, the Variations were performed on the harpsichord by Landowska during his infancy and childhood. Gould's music teacher, Guerrero, who was a fervent admirer of Landowska, introduced him to her style of interpreting baroque music. Guerrero, himself, knew the *Goldberg Variations* intimately and taught them to his most gifted student. The pupil, Glenn, took it to perfection and became the world's best pianist master of the piece. Yet Gould publicly denied his admiration for Landowska:

> ... I knew many of the Landowska recordings when I was a kid, but I don't believe I heard any of them since I was about fifteen ... I was much more familiar when I was growing up with the recordings of Rosalyn Tureck ... than I ever was with Landowska. In fact, really I didn't like Landowska very much, and I did like Tureck enormously—Tureck influenced me.[39]

Gould, in the company of Landowska and Tureck, is a part of the most famous North American keyboard trio of interpreters of Bach's work. He eventually surpassed both of them in his repute, technical merit, originality and interpretation. Landowska was one of several musicians who became a source of subconscious conflict for him. Gould harbored polarized feelings for Landowska; those of admiration and those of disdain. He subconsciously identified with the admired aspect of Guerrero, and through him with the famous harpsichordist, thereby subconsciously incorporating many parts of these respectable music elders. Gould, like Landowska, favored pre-nineteenth-century music, especially the music of Bach. His love of the harpsichord-like piano sound is not accidental. Rather, it was directly related to the dynamics of his relationship with his role-models—Guerrero and Landowska. These two significant figures are reminiscent of the subconscious relation with his mother in their musicianship and looming authority. Gould's austere and religious mother favored the solemn aspects of Bach's music. Here, in the subconscious triangle among Gould, his mother and Guerrero, one of the operating defense mechanisms is displacement. Gould's love of his music-minded and solemn mother was displaced onto two more refined and sophisticated music figures, Guerrero and Landowska; and from them onto the harpsichord-like piano that was supposed to actualize such pure and solemn music. This is a moment to recall Gould's compelling need to have his grand piano "tight" and "puritan," which were the original qualities of his primary, love object, his mother, and secondary displaced love objects, Alberto Guerrero and Wanda Landowska.

Contrary to Gould's admiration of Landowska, which, in the final analysis, was reflected in his creation of the "harpsipiano," is his overt denial of her influence on his music identity. This complex intrapsychic transaction had to do with Gould's ambivalence toward accomplished authority figures with whom he was often competitive and who he perceived as a threat. At the point when Gould started being more resentful of Guerrero, he projected some of these negative feelings onto Landowska.

The above illustrated psycho-dynamics indicate the enormous importance of the grand piano and the Chair in the life of Glenn Gould. These objects became literally a part of his day-to-day living, almost as essential to him as the human physiological needs for food and oxygen. Without being conscious of it, Gould elevated the status of his piano-chair tandem into animated love objects. American psychoanalyst, Phylis Greenacre, described a specific ability of great artists for empathic instillation of life into physical objects. In her sensitive paper, "The Childhood of the Artist," she stated:

> ... The increased empathy associated with creative talent would seemingly depend on the sensory responsiveness to the individual's own body state as well as to the external object, and appears as a peculiar degree of empathic animation of inanimate objects as well as heightened responsiveness and anthropomorphisizing of living objects. The difference between empathy and sympathy is here specially conspicuous. Such animation of the inanimate anthropomor-

> phisizing ordinarily is lost after early childhood, but in gifted individuals remains active either in its own right or appears in the form of the ease and wealth of the symbolization.[40]

Gould certainly retained the ability for empathic animation of those needed inanimate love objects, the grand piano and the Chair, as they symbolically represented his most important life figures, his mother and father.

In Gould's case, the amount and perseverance of the emotional involvement with the piano takes on proportions of obsessive preoccupation. We know of another contemporary of Gould who was also preoccupied with the grand instrument. It was the renowned American entertainer-pianist Liberace, whose lifestyle was filled and dominated by piano symbols, piano-like objects and related activities. Liberace owned an extravagant collection of luxurious, dazzling showpiece grand pianos. Furthermore, many parts of his wardrobe, such as ties, shirts, rings and belts, were in a white-and-black keyboard pattern or the piano shape. At his home, certain pieces of furniture, the swimming pool, and even bath tubs were piano-shaped. Undoubtedly, there is plenty of evidence testifying to Liberace's preoccupation with the grand piano and related symbols. Nevertheless, on comparison, there is a clear and dynamic difference between the piano preoccupation of Gould and that of Liberace. The latter was not only enjoying his piano mania but was fostering it deliberately for commercial purposes and showmanship. Regardless of the subconscious motives of Liberace's piano strivings, the outward manifestation of his behavior appears to be consistent with his joy in playing the piano. It is also geared to entertain and is permeated with a good sense of humor.

In contrast to Liberace's exhibitionism, Gould's involvement with a special piano comes across as deeper, more personal and serious in nature. It also appears to be more depressive than enjoyable, and it is not intended to be humorous at all. Gould is more needy and regressive when it comes to his valued object and suffers genuinely when he is deprived of it. The way Gould relates to his piano is more compulsive and ritualistic than deliberate and spontaneous. Carting his piano from city to city was a repetition of the pattern his parents set for him in his childhood. It was done ceremoniously and with a sense of being entitled to behave in such a way. While some of Gould's music associates and the audience accepted his compelling need for the special treatment and particular objects as prerequisites for the music performance, many others were not able to understand and tolerate it. Gould and his chair-piano tandem became a target of local news, music criticism, even lay psychological analysis. He was considered by many to be weird and hopelessly eccentric. Meanwhile, Gould pleaded innocence to those accusations, and kept trying to defend his position by appeal and reasoning:

> I hope people won't be blinded to my playing by what have been called my personal eccentricities. I don't think I'm at all eccentric. It's true I wear one or two pairs of gloves most of the time and take a few sensible precautions about my health. And I sometimes play with my shoes off or get so carried away in a performance my shirttail comes out or, as some friends have complained, I look as though I were playing the piano with my nose. But these aren't personal eccentricities—they are simply the occupational hazard of a highly subjective business.[41]

There is more to say about Gould's attachment and passion lavished upon his grand instrument. Music producer Andrew Kazdin referred to Gould's piano CD 318 as a "mistress."[42] Kazdin likely used the term casually on the basis of observed behavior of his very special client-associate. The word "mistress" has a manifold use. It can designate a female in a position of authority and command; or a woman who had accomplished mastery in her field; or a female lover cohabiting with a man in a forbidden love relationship. This is why the term "mistress," unless qualified, could be quite misleading. Even though Kazdin did not specify his use of the term "mistress," one senses his intention to designate the piano as a love object, a lover, or a substitute for a lover to his master pianist.

In Gould's inner world, the piano represented his mother. Gould loved the good and loving parts of his mother and hated the negative aspects of her authority and commanding power. He was unable to integrate those opposing images internally. Be reminded that Florence was an austere woman lacking sex appeal, for which she compensated with her beautiful singing voice. She subconsciously saw the arrival of her son as an opportunity to express her talent in music through him and to satisfy her need for admiration and glory. Therefore, the piano was highly emotionally charged and became an important nonsexual love object, first for the mother and then for the son. Moreover, the piano as a live-in partner for Gould became a substitute for the important human figures in his life, particularly his grandmother and mother. These significant people were internalized as safe and dependable adult images. In Gould's subconscious mind, the musical images of his mother and grandmother became blended and fused with the piano image. This means that an image of living love-objects was fused with an image of an inanimate but enlivened love object.

What kind of symbolic meaning does the piano have? Elegance and power for sure. Does it have predominantly feminine or masculine symbolic features? Even the term "grand piano" designates its impressive physical size and symbolic domination over other musical instruments. The piano usually takes a central position on the stage. It is a noble, revered and powerful tool of communication. It demands attention via its centrality. The piano is omnipotent; it can survive in solitude or it can be successful in conjunction with one, two or many instruments in the orchestra with or without vocalists. A solo pianist, together with the solo instrument, makes a fully productive and self-sufficient unit. When the piano is combined with other philharmonic instruments, it provides a matrix to weave the music into a majestic symphony of performance. The piano sound is equally psychologically significant. Whether piano-generated music is in the foreground as in a recital or blended with the rest of the orchestral instruments, it influences the audience emotionally. It triggers a wide spectrum of emotions, ranging from pleasant ones to those of sorrow and lamentation to those of triumph and ecstasy. Piano music can elicit emotions of love and rejoicing, which transform into bodily sensations that can be compared in their intensity to the peak of human sexual experience, the climax. This all makes it possible for a pianist, in a partnership with a grand piano, to project an overpowering visual and auditory image in the minds of listeners.

On the basis of this analytical observation, the grand piano could be conceived of as having more masculine or phallic features when considering its potential force and dominance. In Gould's inner experience, his mother was the dominant force in his formative years. The impact of such a force called for subconscious measures and strategies against his mother's supremacy and, subsequently, against power of any kind. The goal of these strategies was to reduce the power of his forceful maternal image by bringing it under control. While it is hard to exercise direct control over one's own real or fantasized mother, it was much easier to master the representative of his mother, the grand piano. Gould was compelled to reduce the masculine meaning of the piano and emasculate its robust sound potency. Indeed, in years of experimentation he managed to decrease the music prowess of his piano to a softer harpsichord-like sound. Gould was the only person alive who needed that kind of altered and controlled instrument. The softer and tamer the piano became, the more Gould's sensitive subconscious mind found it acceptable and easier to love. His entire creative and musico-technical attitude, such as the low sitting position, the "finger technique" and the "soft touch," were all his expressive reactions toward his object of nonsexual love—the piano and the music played on it.

The soft touch is not the only sign of Gould's gentle demeanor. While playing, his face is intimately close to the keyboard, almost touching it. When Gould is in action, or according to his favorite expression, in ecstasy, the piano becomes his irreplaceable object of attachment. There is a part in Gould that truly and genuinely loves his piano. Gould, at his beloved grand piano, is at the height of his demonstrative ability for love and affection. This is not sexual love as Kazdin hinted earlier in his allusions, but nonsexual, creative and platonic love. Together with his instrument and the Chair, they produce an endearing effect where tender touch and translucent sounds weave music to remember. There are those who are amused by Gould's romantic shenanigans, fascinated by his colorful music personality and fully accepting of him on the whole. The famous present-day pianist Emanuel Ax offered us this heartfelt comment:

> I've become not only a fan but a complete apostle, if you will, of [Glenn Gould's] whole philosophy of life—except for the fact that I like to play concerts. Everything about trying to see different points of view, experimenting, splicing, all of that I think is so sane and so wise, that to call him an eccentric? The rest of us are eccentric.[43]

What was perceived by Gould's viewers as eccentric was meaningful to him and made sense in the context of his life, and even more in the context of his inner dynamics. Gould could not do so well with surface "viewers" but needed responses of those who could empathize and understand him from within. This is not to say that Gould was "normal" in his behavior and that viewers were abnormal in their responses, but rather that Gould had emotional problems and emotional assets, all enveloped and intertwined with his fabulous music talent, but all of this was not wholly understood by others who vacillated between idolizing him and rejecting him. The greatness of Gould as a piano virtuoso, and as a music figure in a broader sense, lies in his ability to transform his inner turmoil creatively, to enliven inanimate objects like the Chair and the piano and use them as a powerful medium of mass communication.

Chapter XI

THE MUSIC CIRCLE

GLENN GOULD AND LEONARD BERNSTEIN

Since when was genius found respectable?
Elizabeth Barrett Browning[1]

Creative individuals are, by virtue of their extraordinary ability, usually involved in a broad network of associates, collaborators and admirers. Even when an artist protects his privacy and avoids social contact at any cost, as a proponent of the arts, his solitary creative strivings can be fulfilled only partially. For on the whole, the world of art is a world of inclusion and communication, rather than of exclusion and isolation.

Glenn Gould, for all his professed need for solitude, had a rich interactional life. At his level of music development, networking with contemporary high stature music associates was inevitable and in keeping with his steady artistic growth. Even the soloist, as the loneliest of all musicians, is given to intense association with those figures who serve to promote, manage and buttress his artistic achievement. Interpersonal relations can easily begin and flourish within the realm of such an artistically charged environment. One way to approach this interesting and boundless subject is to analyze the interpersonal dynamics of a few selected dyads between Gould and his corresponding associates/conductors. Out of all distinguished conductors with whom Gould had worked, he had the most dynamic relationship with the celebrated Leonard Bernstein.

Starting from the late 1950s, these two remarkable men conjointly performed six classical piano concertos, which they delivered both before a live audience and recorded for posterity, as shown below:

The Gould and Bernstein Collaboration

Live	Recording		
1957			
Jan. 26, 27	April	Beethoven Piano Concerto no.2 in B-flat Major, op. 19	L. Bernstein Columbia Symphony Orchestra
	April	Bach Piano Concerto no. 1 in D Minor	as above

Live	Recording		
1959			
Apr. 2, 3, 4	May	Mozart Piano Concerto no. 24 in C Minor, KV. 491	L. Bernstein New York Philharmonic (live)
Apr. 5	May	Beethoven Piano Concerto no. 3 in C Minor, op. 37	L. Bernstein Columbia Symh. Orch. (recording)
1961			
Mar. 17, 18, 19	May	Beethoven Piano Concerto no. 4 in G Major, op. 15	L. Bernstein New York Philharmonic
1962			
Apr. 6, 8	Sept.	Brahms Piano Concerto no. 1 in D Minor, op. 15	L. Bernstein N.Y. Phil.

During the time between 1957 and 1962, the two developed a personal relationship through various off-stage modes of communication, mostly private visits and correspondence. At the peak of their productive music liaison, Gould was between twenty-five and thirty years old and Bernstein's age ranged from forty to forty-five. Both of them were quite noticeably handsome men and remarkable as music figures. Gould was allegedly more eccentric but was a music genius; Bernstein was dramatic and controversial but was regarded as the great multitalented music figure of the continent.

The following are Bernstein's reminiscences about his first encounter with Gould's interpretation of Bach's *Goldberg Variations*:

> I remember when during the summer of 1955 ... Felicia was waiting to give birth to our son, Alexander. The doctors had miscalculated, so we had an extra month to wait. It was June; there was a heat wave in New York; she was in her ninth month and very easily tired and disgruntled. One of the great sources of comfort to us during that month was Glenn's first recording of the *Goldberg Variations* which had just come out. It became "our song."[2]

Bernstein's memory was in error, as Gould's recording of the Goldbergs was released in January 1956. Regardless, once he obtained the record, Bernstein delighted in Gould's version of Bach's loveliest collage of music. Filled with the sense of adoration and pressing curiosity, Bernstein could hardly wait to meet this capable, emerging virtuoso. The two musicians made their acquaintance shortly before Gould's orchestral debut with the New York Philharmonic on January 26, 1957, in Carnegie Hall, with Bernstein as conductor. The choice of music for that occasion was made by Gould, who selected his favorite Beethoven Piano Concerto no. 2. Joseph Roddy recorded the following dialogue between Bernstein and Gould on the day of the concert rehearsal on January 26:

> "Glenn, baby!" he called. "In your heart of hearts, do you feel the first movement in a fast four today, or alla breve?"

> "Oh, a fast four by all means," Gould answered. "Like this," he went on, drying [his hands] and heading for the dressing-room piano to illustrate the tempo he liked. "I feel it conducts in a fast four."
>
> "I've never conducted it in four before, because I've never conducted it before," Bernstein said. "This is a Bernstein premiere."
>
> "Good," Gould said "I have an idea—thought of it last night. Let's walk out there together, and you play the piano part and I'll conduct the orchestra. It will be the surprise act of the season."
>
> "Oh no!" Bernstein said, and went on, affecting a pompous manner. "The Beethoven Second is not one of the five glorious concertos in my solo repertoire this season."
>
> "It's been in mine, sir, since I was thirteen," Gould said, bowing low to the conductor.[3]

A playful dialogue, indeed, but ridden with deep meanings. Analysis of this short interplay reveals strong unconscious dynamics operating in both men from the very start of their relationship. Gould challenged Bernstein by suggesting to switch music roles with him. Implicit in this jesting and seemingly benign comment was that, in Gould's mind, he was as good a conductor as he was a pianist. By emphasizing that he was a master of this Beethoven concerto from the age of thirteen, Gould made a point of Bernstein's belatedness in studying the same piece for the first time at the age of forty. Initially, Bernstein was somewhat patronizing toward Gould, while affectionately referring to him as "Glenn, baby." As a contrast to this intimate nickname, Gould responded to Bernstein by calling him "sir," which served a multiple purpose: to express true reverence; to preserve emotional distance and autonomy; and to control Bernstein by way of mockery.

There was also a degree of genuine liking and affection in Gould for Bernstein. A day before the concert, Gould had a pleasant evening in Bernstein's comfortable apartment in Osborne House, across from Carnegie Hall. The two musicians played the piano and engaged in a lively discussion about the concerto. In this spontaneous conversation, Bernstein shared with Gould that he also owned a Chickering piano while he lived in Boston. Gould interpreted this little detail as a good omen of their future relationship and felt a sense of kinship to Bernstein.

Their successful performance of the Beethoven Concerto was followed by a positive review in *The New York Times*:

> Glenn Gould, the spectacular young pianist from Canada, chose an unspectacular work for his debut with the Philharmonic Symphony ... he presented a sharp, clear-cut reading that had decided personality ... his interpretation was musical and logical ... to receive an ovation after a performance of the Beethoven B flat is not something that comes to every pianist.[4]

The critic of *The Saturday Review* was even more generous:

> Glenn Gould's first appearance in New York with orchestra left little doubt

> that in this young Canadian pianist the younger generation of music lovers has found a new idol and prophet.[5]

After the concert, there was a lively discussion among the musicians about the possibility of recording the piece immediately. Abram Chasins, the author of *Speaking of Pianists*, wrote that on this occasion Gould, at some point, made the statement, "Bernstein is not ready," in reference to the recording plan. Both Gould and Bernstein, when afterwards questioned, denied that they respectively had ever heard or uttered such a comment. When the Beethoven Second Concerto was finally recorded in April 1957, with Gould as a soloist and Bernstein as a conductor of the Columbia Symphony Orchestra, the critic B. H. Haggin gave the following review:

> The orchestra's tense, hard-driven harsh-sounding playing makes it evident that Bernstein still wasn't ready, but Gould makes Bernstein's unreadiness glaring with each piano phrase that he articulates and shapes so perfectly and with such repose and executes with such precision and such beauty of sound.[6]

If the strong unconscious forces between Gould and Bernstein began from their first meeting, after the concert they grew even stronger. Apparently, Gould won the laurels and became a new "idol and prophet," as the critic suggested. In the language of competition, Gould won the round. Within the short span, from the rehearsal until after the concert and then after the recording, Bernstein and Gould were torn by strong mixed feelings—those of affection and animosity; kinship and rivalry; and those of respect and envy. As noticed in the earlier dialogue recorded by Roddy, Gould teased Bernstein by offering to replace him as a conductor and by flaunting his own mastery of the concerto. This is why it is quite likely that the comment attributed to Gould, "Bernstein is not ready," was actually uttered and would have been consistent with his sense of supremacy in this concerto and his sense of competitiveness with Bernstein. Regardless of those inner conflicts, their recordings of Beethoven's Second Concerto and Bach's D Minor Concerto got very favorable reviews. Harold Schonberg, the chief critic of *The New York Times* commented:

> The results are beautiful. Both works emerge in clear, unhurried, rhythmically precise manner, overall impression is one of well-balanced plasticity of piano merging with orchestra and veering out again, of fine ensemble and musical finesse.[7]

Only a few weeks later on May 18, Gould triumphantly played the same Beethoven Concerto no. 2 in Leningrad, with Vladimir Slovak and the local philharmonic orchestra. Both the concert and subsequent recording went smoothly, and there was no conflict reported of any kind. Gould was unconditionally accepted as a person both by the conductor and the Russian audiences and was showered with their emphatic greetings. Gould and Slovak did not seem emotionally entangled but held onto their separate roles, maintaining self-respect and mutual respect. Meanwhile, the emotional conflict stirred up between Gould and Bernstein continued to fester over the next few years of their collaboration. It is likely that the fuel for such ongoing mutual psychodynamics was supplied through their transference reactions to each other and their corresponding narcissistic personality traits. Transference is an interesting unconscious phenomenon in which a human subject transfers the original feelings related to significant figures of his/her developmental years onto important people in adulthood. In other words, our feelings and perceptions are often subjectively colored by our original perceptions of our parents, relatives, teachers and other principal people who influenced us in childhood. In Gould's formative years, he often perceived his mother, his father and his teachers in an ambivalent fashion, as all-good and all-bad figures; harboring simultaneous feelings of both love and hate toward them. His adult relationships were patterned on those original feelings and perceptions of his primary elders.

Transference reactions were strong between Bernstein and Gould. Once again we may reflect back to their first encounter when they rehearsed the Beethoven Second Concerto as described by Joseph Roddy. Bernstein asked Gould to make the choice of the tempo: "... do you feel the first movement in a fast four today, or alla breve?" What made a fifteen-year-older, musically more astute conductor allow the supremacy of tempo choice to his keyboard soloist? It appears that some features of Gould's personality triggered in Bernstein a need to please him, even to submit to Gould at times, and to dominate him at other times. Bernstein was caught in a father-son type of transference in which he alternated between being paternally permissive to being paternally dominant toward Gould. In the analysis of Bernstein's life, this writer finds that his key problem was in his relationship with his authoritarian father. In order to understand what happened between Gould and Bernstein, it is necessary to have a few points of comparison of their personal and family histories. Here is a brief summary of Bernstein's personal and family background extrapolated from his three biographies by Joan Peyser, Michael Freedland and Humphrey Burton, as well as from other writings by and about him.

Leonard, affectionately called Lenny, was a first-born son to Samuel and Jenny Bernstein. Both parents were Russian Jews who immigrated to America as children and settled in the vicinity of Boston. Bernstein's early family life was marked by the ongoing marital discord of his parents, by their separations and reconciliations, and frequent moves; which were all associated with changing neighborhoods, schools and friends. This was emotionally too unsettling for Lenny. In order to compensate for emotional pain, he threw himself into a variety of achievements. As a bright child, he grasped with ease the lessons of both the public and Hebrew school that he attended simultaneously. He showed interest in playing the piano, which was well described by Freedland:

> Lenny was not a prodigy but at the age of ten he had discovered a piano and within days was using it to some effect. He taught himself to play by ear 'everything' musical he heard on the radio.[8]

At the age of eleven, after begging his father in vain to get him piano lessons, Lenny went on his own initiative to the New England Conservatory of Music to pursue piano studies. After finishing at the reputable Boston Latin School, Bernstein pursued studies in music; first at Harvard and then at the Curtis Institute in Philadelphia. Throughout Leonard's formative years, his father, Sam, a religious student of the Talmud and a hard-working businessman, wanted his son to join him in business, actively discouraging him from studying music. Both father and son grew widely apart in their respective interests, lifestyles and goals. Having no support from his father, Leonard developed an insatiable need for approval and recognition from him and, in a broader sense, from other important, father-like figures. At the same time, he harbored coexisting hostile feelings toward his father, represented in his constant rebellious and defiant behavior. Hence, Bernstein's subconscious feelings of love and hate were a reflection of his inner split where the good-father and bad-father images were taken in or internalized in a split fashion. Splitting, as a defense mechanism operating in Bernstein's inner dynamics, was largely responsible for his interpersonal failures. He kept going through life by longing and looking for "good fathers" and rejecting the "bad" ones; or by making ongoing efforts to be a good and special "son," or to find "good sons" and reject the "bad" ones. There were deep-seated and unresolvable handicaps in such a relentless quest for an all-good loving figure, which in real life could never be found. Bernstein was compelled to look for an ideal in each man he encountered and reject the non-ideal, without being able to reconcile the two aspects. This is why a good number of Bernstein's relationships with men started with hope and enthusiasm, reached a peak of productivity, and then ended in some form of failure. One can recognize the presence of this very pattern in the relationship between Bernstein and Gould, which will hopefully become clearer in the course of this story.

Initially, Bernstein treated Gould as a "buddy," or he played the role of a "good" father. In the framework of transference, he had a strong need to be a benevolent mentor, permissive and conciliatory, like in an "ideal" father-son relationship. But the role of a father is a peculiar one even under the best and healthiest of circumstances. The unconscious message projected from a father to his son is: "I love you, but you are little and I am big, strong, and experienced, and you must accept my supremacy." In Gould's unconscious memory this message was very familiar, as it was at work in his relationship with his own father, whose supremacy he fought constantly. At the same time, Gould was a child prodigy, a special son and gifted musician, whose status called for a submissive attitude on the part of his ordinary father. So between Gould and his father there was a lifelong issue of competition and a seesaw dynamic of dominance-submission. Gould either felt controlled or in need of controlling his father. Bernstein had a similar problem with his own father. When these two musicians with such conflicted family backgrounds got together, they entered an emotional web of alternating between dominance and submission, as suggested below:

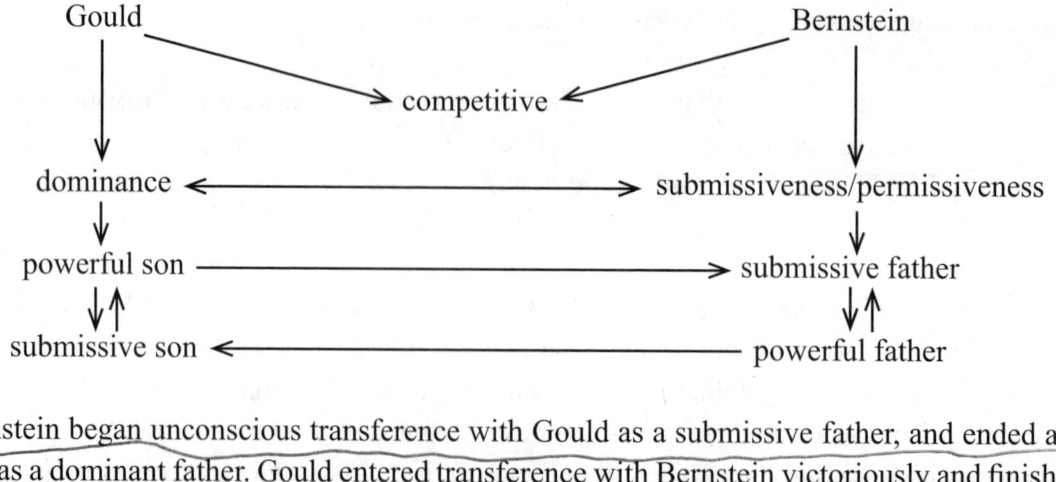

Bernstein began unconscious transference with Gould as a submissive father, and ended after a few years as a dominant father. Gould entered transference with Bernstein victoriously and finished by withdrawing from the working relationship with him. There were no winners in this unfortunate type of interpersonal dyad, and both parties endured emotional injuries.

Other major concurrent psychodynamics in both Bernstein and Gould were their narcissistic personality traits. The chief characteristic of the narcissistic personality is the presence of grandiosity. Bernstein was described in literature as having an insatiable need for attention and centrality; for love and adoration; for conquest and entitlement; for being unique and the best at all times. Peyser wrote:

> The appearance Bernstein gives is one of infinite goodness: Schuller has described him as "a sweetheart." But underneath the apparent sweetness Bernstein's competitive spirit is working around the clock, and while acting like a beneficent god, dispensing blessings to everyone around, he does manage to command center stage to get whatever attention is available.[9]

Bernstein, as an extrovert and a dramatic personality, displayed many behavioral excesses, such as working long hours, smoking heavily, drinking, and socializing intensely. Gould, who also had features of grandiosity, was more inhibited and introverted. He was utterly disgusted by Bernstein's smoking, drinking and party-going, as he was by anybody else with these traits.

When two talented giants of superior intelligence, like Bernstein and Gould, get together they should be able to master any task set for themselves, to their own contentment and to the satisfaction of others. When in the real situation, Bernstein and Gould got together with both of them having a streak of grandiosity and entitlement, coupled with other personal hindrances, they were able to make only partial use of their talents and had to settle for only limited results. In other words, their respective emotional flaws repelled and robbed them of more potential success and pleasure in achievement.

There were other undercurrents in the friendship between Glenn and Lenny. Gould, who was known to be well read and informed, usually was prepared for his future concerts not only musically, but he researched and learned a lot about his future associates. At the point of meeting Bernstein, Gould knew quite a bit from the press and other sources about him. He knew about Bernstein's pianistic ability and music background. Gould looked up to him as a conductor and, particularly, as a composer. He was also aware of Bernstein's adventurousness, flamboyance, and of his promiscuous love life. This pre-knowledge made him somewhat guarded when he met his conductor. Bernstein had a habit of kissing people often on the lips, was physically demonstrative, and socially outgoing. He wore his sexuality on his sleeve, and all of these characteristics were dramatically opposite to the way Gould was. While Gould hid his natural attractiveness and endeavored to stay "pure" and inoffensive, Bernstein was more worldly than spiritual and more sexual than platonic. Did Bernstein ever make a pass at Gould? Did he kiss him or try to, and if so, did he kiss Gould randomly like his other friends, or with a specific idea in mind? By that time, Gould received hundreds of letters from fans making various propositions to him. He was good-looking, extremely interesting, humorous, talkative and, most of all, absolutely astonishing at the piano. What we know is that Gould as a moralist condemned any hedonistic behavior, and according to his standards, Bernstein was a hedonist; that Gould was threatened by Bernstein's emotional and erotic effusiveness; and that he employed his old but effective defense of counter-charm. Gould kept himself unattractive looking, unkempt, sickly, and produced a number of direct and indirect responses ranging from covert defiance to overt rejection. If Bernstein, despite all these protective barriers and warning signals, still made a pass at Gould, then he was rebuked. As the story unfolds, there will be more evidence built up in favor of the last statement.

There was genuine greatness and natural giftedness in these two men, and they each aspired to become the renaissance man of North American music. Both of them in part succeeded. Glenn Gould, master of counterpoint, often referred to as a disciple of Bach, showed supremacy over other fine pianists in his way of interpreting Bach's music. Bernstein was fascinated by Gould's contrapuntal mind and the unparalleled virtuosity of his dominant left hand. Gould brought into the music world new ideas, often original and outlandish but valuable in stimulating novel thinking.

Bernstein too aspired to be a renaissance man, and indeed revolutionized the style of conducting and changed the ways of disseminating music in North America. He introduced the conductor's speech by addressing the public from the podium, thereby diminishing the distance between the audience and the orchestra. In Bernstein, Gould found a multitalented artist, a superman, who was a fine pianist, good conductor, composer, educator, and married father of three children. Inspired by Bernstein, Gould too began addressing audiences from the stage, writing more, and broadcasting his thoughts and music. Gould was dimly aware that he would not be able to keep up with some of Bernstein's qualities—like being a composer and having a family. His major composition, the String Quartet, op. 1, had just been released in the previous year, but nothing had been completed since.

Bernstein, at the age of twenty-five, premiered his own composition—First Symphony—at Carnegie Hall, leading the Philharmonic Symphony Orchestra. "This work, which he calls *Jeremiah*, outranks every other symphonic product by any American composer of what is called the younger generation."[10] *Jeremiah* was dedicated to Bernstein's father, Sam. While Bernstein had vast emotional conflicts in the relationship with his father, he was, to a point, able to work at it by dedicating music to him. Gould was more "paralyzed" by his internal conflicts and was not able to compose a music piece of any size for his father or his music mentor, Alberto Guerrero. He suffered with envy and made attempts to catch up with Bernstein's conducting ability or with his own losses in general. Here is an excerpt from Gould's letter dated August 29, 1958, showing his longing to be a conductor:

> Dear Leonardo,
> ... I see by the *Musical America* that you are conducting in Milan in the middle of November, which is exactly the time that I am playing in Florence, Turin and Rome. If it is at all feasible, I shall descend upon La Scala (or is it Le Scala) and take a few conducting lessons.[11]

As it turned out, Gould felt indisposed and was unable to follow through on his planned recitals in Turin and Rome, which were both cancelled. He also never made it to Milan, and never fulfilled his mother's dream and his own fantasy of visiting La Scala Opera House.

In the 1959-60 season, Bernstein was appointed as music director of the New York Philharmonic, which made him the first American-born conductor to hold such a distinguished position. Before Bernstein, until 1954, maestro Arturo Toscanini dominated the music world as the greatest conductor of his time. In the first half of the twentieth century, Italian-born Toscanini held alternate tenures as the principal conductor of La Scala in Milan and the New York Philharmonic Symphony Orchestra.

The role of any conductor is associated with fame and commanding power; and the role of an outstanding conductor like Toscanini engenders enormous authority and influence in the music world. Since childhood, Gould had misgivings about adults who exercised excessive control over others, and

Gould, as an avid radio listener, was often exposed to Toscanini's orchestral music, which dominated radio programs in the 1940s. While enjoying the music, Gould developed a sense of personal dislike toward Toscanini, thinking of him as too controlling and authoritarian.

As a child, Glenn had ample opportunity to watch his mother in the role of a choir leader in church, where she used to prepare, direct and organize spiritual music programs. For a little boy with a musical ear, his mother's ability to produce beautiful music from scratch made a powerful impression. Incidentally, Toscanini was one of Florrie's early music models as a conductor. She was fascinated by his music that was aired on the radio, and she made a point of educating Glenn about its merits and beauty. Through this type of didactic interaction with his mother, Glenn, who had never met Toscanini, developed mixed feelings of love and hate toward the great conductor. He was fascinated by his symphony music but resented him as a disciplinarian over the orchestra members. Glenn familiarized himself with the stories of Toscanini's temper, his reputation of a tyrannical orchestra leader, and dismissed him in his mind as an oppressor of the powerless. One may sense the transfer of Glenn's feelings for his mother onto the conductor. Just as he resented certain aspects of his mother—her rigid and formal demeanor and a need for order and command—this is how he resented Toscanini.

By the time Gould personally came into situations of being a soloist in the orchestra interacting with a conductor, he was already pre-sensitized to this role of power. If Gould was able to experience a certain conductor as benevolent and supportive, he felt more at ease with him, which helped to turn the orchestral performance into a collaborative success. The converse was also true. This model of relating to others could help us understand why Gould had more interpersonal conflicts with some music associates and fewer with others; and why with some he could create a brilliant orchestral performance, or a substandard one working with others.

Having made this necessary digression, let me return to the Gould-Bernstein relationship. Gould experienced an inner conflict around Toscanini and a real conflict around Sir Ernest MacMillan, Director of the Toronto Symphony Orchestra, described earlier. For the twenty-four-year-old Gould, meeting Leonard Bernstein was quite refreshing. In Gould's initial perception, Bernstein was more liberal and personable than either Toscanini or MacMillan. He took special interest in Gould and gave him generous attention and sympathy. Bernstein, according to his own reminiscences, during their preparation of the Beethoven C Minor Concerto in April 1959 even invited Gould to his home for dinner. Gould reportedly was quite bundled up in excessive clothing and even wore a fur hat. Bernstein's wife, Felicia, persuaded Gould to let her give him a hair cut and a shampoo. Bernstein finished his description of this scene by saying: "He emerged from the bathroom looking like an angel. I have never seen anything so beautiful as Glenn Gould coming out of that bathroom with his wonderful blonde clean hair."[12]

Gould may have come across as pitiable in his layers of clothes, but on stage at the keyboard he was a rivaling partner that threatened to take away the spotlight from his conductor. Bernstein himself had his insecurities and transference reaction vis-à-vis Gould and could never forget how the critics hailed the pianist and dubbed him an "idol and a prophet," the adjectives to which Bernstein aspired. His competitiveness was well known to his associates and was summed up by his biographer, Joan Peyser, in this way:

> Bernstein, while hugely talented, was fiercely competitive; his brother Burton, angered him by beating him in tennis. Through the years he challenged and beat

> practically anyone in musical trivia games identifying musical themes or lyrics. In later years Samuel Barber refused to visit Bernstein in Martha's Vineyard because the playing of such games was too fatiguing for him: Bernstein always had to win.[13]

If Bernstein was competitive with his family members, friends and music associates, he was comparably competitive with Gould, who happened to be dazzling at the piano, which was also Bernstein's solo instrument and Glenn was brilliant in his memory bank of music literature. Competitiveness is closely related to envy. By his insatiable need to win, Bernstein was envious of other high achievers, especially when they were hailed as winners. Feelings of envy have deep roots and can be traced back to one's unfulfilled childhood needs. Bernstein knew that Gould had had piano classes from the age of three and that both his parents had actively supported Glenn's musical development. Meanwhile, Bernstein had the opposite situation to endure—lack of support for his music studies. In his inner perception, Gould was lucky as he had it all made, whereas he, Bernstein, was hard-done-by because of his losses and had to spend his entire lifetime in attempts to recover them. An accomplished pianist himself, Bernstein was well able to estimate Gould's pianistic worth and realize that Gould's type of fame was unreachable to him. This insight may have been a constant cause of injury to his self-esteem and a danger to his precarious ego strengths. Such strong inner dynamics of reverence and envy, of love and hate and irresistible competition with Gould, were invisible to others, yet they existed in the background of their tremendous success and the unfortunate dissolution of their working relationship.

Another major intrapsychic force that influenced the relationship between the two musicians was their respective sexuality. According to Joan Peyser, Bernstein was predominantly homosexual. His life from his teens on was full of intense and voracious sexual explorations. Some of his contemporaries thought of him as bisexual, as he was married and was a father of three children. Bernstein did not hide his prevailing homosexual awareness, which appeared before he was twenty years old. Many of his close friends at that time were also gay. In 1937, the nineteen-year-old Bernstein met the famous conductor, Dimitri Mitropoulos, who had an alleged homosexual orientation. This encounter appeared to have been decisive in Bernstein's coming out of the closet. Bernstein maintained sexual interest in younger males throughout his mature adult years.

The purpose of this study is not to analyze Bernstein's personal history nor his sexuality, but to understand his impact on Gould. By the time the two artists met, Gould was known as sexually inexperienced and unengaged, which placed him on the opposite end of his ebullient and experienced colleague. Attractive, youthful and fabulously gifted, Gould instantly became the subject of Bernstein's artistic, personal and sexual curiosity. Gould had in his personal repertoire a number of defense mechanisms and coping techniques that protected him from falling prey to anyone's sexual advances. Such protective armor diminished his capacity for intimacy and made him impenetrable both emotionally and physically. Therefore, if Bernstein was attracted to Gould, this was a futile and lost cause. Gould was only interested in pursuing music and intellect-based relationships, though playful and creative, but strictly non-erotic, non-threatening and devoid of any hint of sexuality. Gould's total rejection of Bernstein's potential sexual attraction to him, in addition to their other negative transference reactions, contributed to a slow decay of their friendship and partnership in music.

All these complex inner dynamics between the two men culminated around the last project they worked on together—the live performance of the Brahms D Minor Concerto on April 6 and 8, 1962. The following events that took place were motivated by intricate, unconscious underpinnings, which gradually escalated into a full-blown interpersonal drama. Gould, as the chosen piano soloist, proposed to Bernstein some changes in the original tempo, dynamics and concept of interpretation of the Brahms concerto. On the surface, Bernstein agreed to go along with those changes, under the condition that he offer a brief explanation to the audience. Instead of making a concise and professional announcement, Bernstein delivered a long and ambiguous speech, which because of its importance is presented here in full:

> Don't be frightened, Mr. Gould is here, [laughter] will appear in a moment. I am not as you know in the habit of speaking on any concert except the Thursday night previews. But a curious situation has arisen which merits, I think, a word or two. We are about to hear, a rather, shall we say, unorthodox performance of the Brahms D Minor Concerto, a performance distinctly different from any other I ever heard, or even dreamt of for that matter, in its remarkably broad tempi and its frequent departures from Brahms dynamic indications.
>
> I cannot say I am in total agreement with Mr. Gould's conception and this raises the interesting question, what am I doing conducting it [laughter in the audience]. I am conducting it because Mr. Gould is so valid and serious an artist, that I must take seriously anything he conceives in good faith, and his conception is interesting enough so that I feel you should hear it, too.
>
> But the age-old question still remains: in a concerto who is the boss [laughter], the soloist or the conductor? [much laughter]. The answer is of course, sometimes one, sometimes the other, depending on the people involved, but almost always the two manage to get together by persuasion, or charm, or even threats [laughter], to achieve a unified performance.
>
> I have only once before in my life had to submit to a soloist's wholly new and incompatible concept; and that was the last time I accompanied Mr. Gould [much laughter].
>
> But this time, the discrepancies between our views are so great that I feel I must make a small disclaimer. So why, to repeat a question, am I conducting it? Why do I not make a minor scandal to get a substitute soloist or let an assistant conduct it. Because I am fascinated, glad to have a chance for a new look of this much played work; because what's more, there are moments in Mr. Gould's performance that emerge with astonishing freshness and conviction. Thirdly, because we can all learn something from this extraordinary artist who is a thinking performer. Finally, because there is in music what Dimitri Mitropoulos used to call the sportive element, that factor of curiosity, adventure, experiment and I can assure you, that it has been an adventure this week [laughter] collaborating with Mr. Gould on this Brahms Concerto. It is in this spirit of adventure that now we present it to you [much laughter].[14]

This three-minute and twenty-four-second speech is ridden with meaning and is worth analyzing. By the opening sentence; "Don't be frightened, Mr. Gould is here," Bernstein unnecessarily alerted the audience to Gould's tendency to cancel concerts, trivializing it and inviting the laughter of the audience at Gould's expense. By doing so, he drew attention to himself as a central and more competent figure. In the next paragraph, Bernstein admitted to his mixed feelings toward Gould and the issue in question, but the real agenda was to pave a safe way for himself to the hearts of the audience. His ambiguity toward Gould manifested itself in his decision to go along with such a skewed performance and disclaim it at the same time. Once Bernstein made such an unfair opening, he could not stop himself from getting more involved in further controversial themes. He unnecessarily raised another complex issue for the audience: "In a concerto who is the boss, the soloist or the conductor?" This ponderous question would have been more appropriate to raise as a part of one's doctoral dissertation in front of music philosophers; or on the analytic couch as part of free thought association that did not require an answer. Having raised such an emotionally charged question, Bernstein one more time revealed his envy and hostile feelings toward Gould, as well as his own inability to keep them in check. By inviting laughter, Bernstein attempted to endear himself to the audience and guarantee their support and empathy. This was his old psychological ploy that he used to deceive and upstage his opponents. Bernstein then wavered between making a "small disclaimer" and his effusive compliments of being "fascinated by the moments of Mr. Gould's performance that emerged with astonishing freshness and conviction." Tributes followed, again in an ambivalent style, one of them to Mitropoulos, leaving the audience unclear whether he really admired or ridiculed his music friends Gould and Mitropoulos. By the end of Bernstein's speech, the subliminal message was communicated to the audience: "Should you enjoy the concert praise me as an exceptional conductor directing an exceptional soloist; should you be displeased don't hold me responsible, as I warned you in advance."

There were even deeper unconscious dynamics operating in the Gould-Bernstein dyad related to the Brahms D Minor Concerto. In 1962, Bernstein was in his fourth year as a director of one of the most prestigious philharmonic orchestras in the world. His tenure was stable and his fame was increasing steadily. Parallel to his success, he was increasingly exhibiting a number of unfavorable personality traits, both on stage and in his personal life. He was by then seen as a dramatic and histrionic individual with a prominent egocentric style and sense of entitlement played out in his interpersonal relationships. Regardless of his psychological problems, his music talent and abilities prevailed, reaching the hearts and minds of wide audiences. Thanks to his love of music, his excellent public relations, and hard work, Bernstein popularized new American composers and single-handedly expanded the music horizons of the American people. Bernstein was also competitive with long-deceased composers whose music he felt compelled to recompose by adding his own personal touch. Hence, in meeting Gould, Bernstein met an interesting counterpart: a peer, and in many ways an identical thinker, and an identical rebel. Bernstein was quite astonished to find how much he and Gould had in common, an insatiable need to be different and unique, both in music and in personal life, and the need to be the best. Such a strong identification with Gould was particularly noticeable in Bernstein's permissiveness and idealization of Gould at the beginning of their relationship. Idealization, as a primitive defense mechanism, does not really work in the long run and does not make for a quality relationship, as it does not permit true closeness and sincere inter-relatedness. It follows that the mechanism of idealization of Gould by Bernstein was doomed to fail and, finally, it ended in hostility and the destruction of Gould's career.

And where was Gould in 1962? Age-wise he was thirty years old, and a prosperous, internationally acclaimed virtuoso. His music portfolio was rich and impressive, and he worked hand in hand with such illuminating musicians as Herbert von Karajan, George Szell and Dimitri Mitropoulos. At the same time, Gould was increasingly symptomatic and was obviously slowing down in his number of live appearances on stage. He had a reputation of eccentric behavior, which was often commented upon before his music achievement. Bernstein was well aware of all these attributes of his junior colleague. When Gould first announced his experiment with the Brahms D Minor Concerto, Bernstein was amused by his innovativeness and vicariously lived through it himself. Bernstein was not so much interested in distorting this distinguished music piece but rather used this situation to rebel against conventional norms in general. Clearly, in the psychological sense, Bernstein also used this opportunity to defeat Gould, to become an ultimate winner who, once and for all, was able to eliminate Gould from further competition.

In the orchestral, anthropological and dynamic constellation, the conductor is akin to a tribal leader, the pater familias who takes his people through the complex but successful pathways of survival. A pianist-soloist and his conductor could be viewed as a mother and father of the orchestral family. These two parental-like figures predetermine the growth and success of the orchestra for that performance. Therefore, the emotional consensus or, in a psychoanalytic sense, the emotional attunement between a soloist and the conductor is a prerequisite for a successful end result. When the symbolic marriage between the conductor and his solo instrumentalist works, the whole orchestra thrives in its development, reaping the benefits of their mutual music and interpersonal relationships. When the symbolic spouses are in conflict within their own selves and mutually, their discord will inevitably affect the intraorchestral atmosphere. The "interspousal" conflict culminated between Gould and Bernstein in their performance of the Brahms D Minor Concerto.

A virtuoso and maestro are supposed to arrive at a consensus about an interpretation of a music piece; that is, to reach a spoken and unspoken agreement how best to represent the composer's inventions and wishes. Both experts are foremost in the service of art and humanity, and more specifically in the service of their own individual music self-actualization and pleasure. Those artists who unconsciously strive to reverse this order and pursue art more for the sake of art (l'art pour l'art) or mostly to satisfy their personal grandiose needs risk ending up with a variety of complications ranging from projection of an unfavorable, self-centered image onto the audience to causing damage to the music performance. Following this analysis of the Gould-Bernstein tandem around the performance of the Brahms D Minor Concerto, one can safely conclude that both those fine artists became victims of their individual deep-seated, emotional problems which were mutually amplified and resulted in a destroyed music performance.

Bernstein's rivaling behavior toward Gould was predictable on the basis of his previous conflict-ridden interpersonal relations. Through various maneuvers and gestures, Bernstein used to compete and often eliminate his real and imagined rivals-conductors, such as Dimitri Mitropoulos, Fritz Reiner and Bruno Walter, to name but a few. It is recorded that once Bernstein, who despised the long-deceased Richard Wagner as an anti-Semitic proponent, exclaimed: "Richard Wagner, I hate you, but I hate you on my knees,"[15] testifying to mixed love and hate feelings vis-à-vis the great composer. This supports the thesis that Bernstein harbored severe inner conflict in the relationship to significant male figures in his life. Gould happened to have been just a part of his conflicted and split inner world.

As an avant-garde musician, Gould was perceived by Bernstein as a dangerous rival who could potentially jeopardize his specialness and entitlement to fame. When Bernstein and Gould were at work, they each displayed not just excellent musicianship but also extraneous musical behavior as an attention-seeking device. Gould, with his repertoire of oddities, was able to "outmisbehave" Bernstein and become the central figure of their shared music performance. On the other hand, the presence of Gould was a rejuvenating and stimulating experience. Bernstein saw in Gould an opportunity to immortalize some music together, to live through Gould's genius vicariously, and to act out through him his own aggressive impulses toward conventional standards of social behavior. The risk of acting out his own antisocial fantasies through Gould was lower than had he expressed them directly and personally. Bernstein, who was easily attracted to young and handsome males, was equally seductive toward Gould and was angered by Gould's unresponsiveness to his advances. Bernstein, in revenge, permitted Gould to complete his suicidal mission, which was best illustrated by the unfortunate result of the performance of the Brahms D Minor Concerto. Even though Bernstein's assistant-conductor John Canarina was in attendance, Bernstein as the "big boss" kept the privilege of working with Gould to himself. The emotional qualities of this ambivalent liaison with Gould were intense enough to be pursued at all costs. Having already jeopardized Gould's reputation in their previous work together on Beethoven's Fourth Concerto, which received negative reviews as the "wrongest" concerto, Bernstein once again sacrificed Gould in delivering a poor version of the Brahms D Minor Concerto. The critics were perceptively alert to Bernstein's subconscious maneuvering. Eric McLean of *The Montreal Star* wrote: "By going through with the performance he [Bernstein] reduced Gould's chances of ever again playing with [New York] Philharmonic." Akin to that concern, the chief music critic of *The New York Times*, Harold Schonberg wrote on April 7, 1962:

> I think that even though the conductor makes this big disclaimer, he should not be allowed to wiggle off the hook that easy. I mean who engaged the Gould boy in the first place? Who is the musical director? Somebody has to be responsible.[16]

Of course, Bernstein, as the leader of the orchestra, was responsible. He should have responded to Gould's extravagant proposal by accepting or rejecting it firmly and unambivalently. Failing that, the result was predictably catastrophic for Gould and his career, a well as for the music world. The blackest moments were yet to come for Gould. Peyser reported:

> Scheduled to play under Bernstein with the New York Philharmonic the following February in 1963, Gould called in sick. This particular cancellation had felicitous consequences: Bernstein used the opportunity to introduce Andre Watts ...[17]

The consequences were felicitous for the sixteen-year-old Watts but not for the humiliated and despondent Gould.

The "scandal" involving the Brahms D Minor Concerto was unusual and was directly related to the Gould-Bernstein interpersonal problems. This is more obvious by the fact that only six months later, on October 9 and 10, 1962, in Baltimore, Gould delivered an excellent music interpretation of the same piece, together with the Baltimore Symphony and Peter Herman Adler as conductor. Gould had worked with Adler earlier and the two musicians maintained a fair and professional relationship. Clearly, Adler did not stir Gould into "mischief" but was able to bring out the best in him. Fortunately, this Baltimore performance was taped, which permitted us, the fact finders and avid readers, to re-evaluate Gould's pianistic renommé and redeem him from the New York disaster. When the Baltimore concert was released on CD in 1989, the critic, David Breckbrill, in his liner notes for this recording, made a comparative analysis between the reckless Gould-Bernstein rendition and the "normal" and productive Gould-Adler performance. Breckbrill says:

> Listening to that performance [New York rendition] a quarter century after the event, one is struck how dramatically tastes and styles of interpretation have changed in the intervening years, because tempi per se do not seem unreasonably slow—in fact, Bernstein himself turns in a longer performance in his commercial recording with Krystian Zimerman (from the mid-1980's).[18]

Bernstein in a way plagiarized Gould's original idea of playing the Brahms D Minor in a slower tempo, a concept he had ridiculed twenty-five years earlier. Breckbrill concludes:

> Although in many external features the New York performance differs from this Baltimore rendition, the two share an attitude of fundamental disjunction—in New York, the conflict is between breadth and energy. While other imaginative pianists or interpreters might choose more overtly "expressive" and spontaneous means by which to project the ambiguities and uncertainties of the music, it is typical of Gould's potentially perverse iconoclasm that he achieves the same through careful, dispassionate control of tempo, rhythmic profile and textural structure. A gauge of his creativity is the fact that within six months he was able to exploit two completely different parameters of conflict in order to create technical metaphors for basic questions raised by Brahms' first concerto.[19]

Unlike his predecessor-critics who bitterly condemned Gould for his New York performance, Breckbrill in his thoughtful comparative analysis of the two performances recognized Gould's re-creative talent in music. Sadly, Gould did not live long enough to reap the benefit of such recognition.

In 1964, Gould and Bernstein met for the last time in Toronto when the latter came to give a concert. On that occasion Bernstein called Gould and visited him at his St. Clair Avenue apartment. Bernstein described his remembrances of that visit in his posthumous essay on Gould. One of his memories was that Gould's place was cluttered with papers, books and magazines, and that his bathroom was littered with pill boxes. When at one point in the course of surveying Gould's apartment Bernstein exclaimed, "Oh, that must be a bedroom," Gould frantically prevented him from opening the bedroom door. Bernstein assumed that Gould's bedroom was equally messy as the rest of his apartment and that is why he did not want him to see it. There are other possible explanations. One that readily comes to mind is that Gould never recovered from the previous emotional injuries inflicted by Bernstein. He was cautious and he could not fully trust Bernstein, but considered him somewhat of a "traitor." Another one is that being reunited with this successful and flourishing musician may have been threatening for Gould, who had just lost his public career by stopping live performances. Such strong feelings of grief and envy around the loss may have made him even more antagonistic toward Bernstein. The final explanation for Gould's aloofness with Bernstein may have to do with a possibility that the latter made sexual advances toward Gould or, at least, Gould might have imagined so. Whether one condition was true or if all of them were working at once, Gould was more alarmed than relaxed and more sullen than happy about Bernstein's visit. He never played the piano for his distinguished visitor, felt claustrophobic and suggested to take him for a car ride. Bernstein described the car ride with Gould in a humorous way, even while referring to his obnoxious hang-ups associated with his driving practices. The skillful observer can easily discern in his essay that by using exaggerated literary style, Bernstein was out to destroy Gould, who even though deceased, was still experienced as his rival.

Overall, in his relationship with Gould, Bernstein succeeded in a symbolic "castration" of his younger colleague, who, for many real and imagined reasons, posed a serious threat to his self-esteem. Though personally competitive and at times injurious to each other, the liaison between the two musicians was productive for the public who enjoyed their personalities and artistic presence.

OTHER MUSIC ASSOCIATES

> Tomorrow night I appear for the first time before a Boston audience—4,000 critics.
>
> Mark Twain[20]

Notes on Dimitri Mitropoulos

Before Glenn's birth, the Greek-born conductor Dimitri Mitropoulos had already attained an international reputation. In 1930 he was a pianist-conductor of a concert with the Berlin Philharmonic. Mitropoulos immigrated to the United States and became music director of the New York Philharmonic; a position he held from 1950 to 1958. It was in this last year of his tenure that he met and worked with Glenn Gould, the young but established piano virtuoso. Music critic Jonathan Cott reminisced about Gould's rehearsal before a set of concerts with Dimitri Mitropoulos in New York in March 1958:

> I also remember being one of three or four privileged observers at a Carnegie Hall rehearsal session of the Schoenberg Piano Concerto (with Dimitri Mitropoulos leading the New York Philharmonic) at which a shoeless Gould in socks emerged from the wings, almost gliding onto the stage in his stocking feet, wearing a scarf, carrying a bottle of Poland Water, and warming his hands in a basin of hot water in preparation for what turned out to be the most assured and vital performance of this concerto I have ever heard.[21]

The core of Gould's agony prior to the concert with Mitropoulos, to which Cott referred, was his high anticipation anxiety manifested in physical flu-like symptoms. Gould was very anxious and self-conscious in his quest to deliver the perfect performance. His anxiety was augmented by the presence of Mitropoulos, who also strove for music perfection. Gould burdened himself with another responsible task, not only to accomplish an excellent interpretation of Schoenberg's piano concerto but to represent Schoenberg's music as a true and loyal disciple. If Gould was intent on a perfect representation of Schoenberg's music, so was Mitropoulos, who was famous for his interpretations of twentieth-century music. One would think that such mutual dedication to the composer would bring the two music interpreters closer to each other, but not in this case. On the contrary, the younger virtuoso was fiercely competitive with this particular maestro.

Unlike with Bernstein, who was more personable and more approachable on the surface, Gould was in awe of Mitropoulos, who he perceived as distant and shielded with an aura of mystery. It appears that there were two basic sources of conflict in the Gould-Mitropoulos relationship: first, in the area of Gould's competition with Mitropoulos's greatness, and second, in the sphere of sexuality. Gould felt intimidated by the authority of other famous conductors like Herbert von Karajan and George Szell, with whom he had collaborated previously. The same apprehension now reappeared in this relationship with Mitropoulos. The concert pianist perceived those great men with batons as dictators who exercise supreme power and wave their music stick as a symbol of control and punishment. In the unconscious, a baton in the hands of a conductor is not only mesmerizing for the onlookers, but assumes a more ferocious phallic meaning. Gould was always mortified by phallic objects and symbols and spent his lifetime in avoiding and defying them. The conductors inadvertently inspired in Gould mixed feelings of admiration and envy, of cooperation and defiance. According to Cott's description, when Gould entered the stage shoeless, wearing a scarf and holding onto a bottle of water, he was obviously regressed and resembled a three-year-old child that was left all alone to fend for himself. It meant that Gould was unable to relax enough to enter the stage with the mind-set of self-confidence, but was more in the mode of self-pity and suffering.

Another possible reason accounting for Gould's discomfort is that he felt sexually intimidated. Mitropoulos was a homosexual and well-known for his seductive pursuits and multiple love affairs with male partners. If Gould put forward the full force of his natural attractiveness, the experienced Mitropoulos may have made a pass at him. This way, by assuming a panoply of obnoxious habits (shoeless, sickly, holding onto a bottle), Gould subconsciously protected himself from any eventual lustful advances.

There were other interesting dynamics at work during this pre-concert rehearsal between Gould and Mitropoulos. One of them was Gould's long-standing superstitiousness. Gould, very much like his mother, often had premonitions of disaster. Ever since he was a child, Glenn developed certain patterns of behavior in order to prevent bad luck. For instance, he believed that being cocky and self-assured may "jinx" his chances, and vice versa, by downplaying himself by wearing shabby and outmoded clothes and by looking sickly and helpless, he would improve his chances for success. This was a ritual that helped him cope with his stage fright—to suffer first and rejoice later.

In spite of his appearance and behavior at rehearsal, Glenn Gould, the New York Philharmonic and its musical director, Dimitri Mitropoulos, produced a set of three fine music performances on March 13, 14 and 16, 1958. They performed Bach's D Minor Concerto and Schoenberg's Piano Concerto; both of which were Gould's and Mitropoulos' specialties. The audiences, unaware of the turbulent emotional dynamics behind the facade of the two starring musicians, were enchanted. To at least one music critic it appeared that Gould was too boisterous in his interpretation of Bach's D Minor. Hugh Thomson of *The Toronto Star* reported that Gould "cut his thumb on the keys in the excitement of the finale." Thomson described that when in the next sequence Gould played the Schoenberg piece, blood was still "spreading over the keys." "This was probably all to the good, because if there ever was a work that needed some blood, it's Schoenberg's piano concerto,"[22] Thomson concluded.

Only five months later, in August 1958, Gould and Mitropoulos performed Bach's D Minor again, together with the Concertgebouw Orchestra at Salzburg's Mozarteum. Out of two scheduled concert appearances, Gould canceled one of them due to the identical sickness and corresponding underlying dynamics that were operating in New York. The one concert that he was able to perform was quite successful, and the Salzburg audiences enjoyed the grandeur of the occasion of seeing such rare artists—Gould and Mitropoulos. This was their last appearance together prior to the sudden death of Mitropoulos in 1960.

In conclusion, the personality match of Gould and Mitropoulos was somewhat strained and caused Gould bouts of stage fright and associated obsessive rituals and sickness. Yet they managed to produce memorable concerts that were recorded and left us a lasting document of their greatness.

"Tough Love" Between Glenn Gould and George Szell

Gould's relationship with George Szell, the famous Hungarian-born American conductor of the mid-twentieth century, was patterned on how he felt and related to Toscanini-like tyrannical male figures. From a purely musical point of view, Gould regarded George Szell to be "a far better conductor than either" Leonard Bernstein or Eugene Ormandy, and "even more accomplished than [Arturo] Toscanini." Yet on the personal level, the concert pianist antagonized his conductor through defiance and provocation. In his writings, Gould referred to Szell as "martinet," which means someone who is a rigid, military disciplinarian and, as Dr. Cyclops.[23] In Greek mythology, Cyclops were giants who had only one eye in the middle of the forehead. It follows that Gould vented his protest against Szell, whom he perceived as a strict drill sergeant and, even worse, as a gigantic, monstrous and evil authority figure. Not a subtle image at all!

In March 1957, Gould made his debut with the Cleveland Orchestra, of which Szell was the permanent music director since 1946. Originally, the concert program was supposed to include both Beethoven's Second Concerto and Schoenberg's Piano Concerto. In the end, the latter was never played because, according to Gould, Dr. Szell "hadn't learned the piece." (Is this not a tad reminiscent of Gould's later controversial comment, "Bernstein is not ready"?) Szell was known to have had no interest in Schoenberg's music, the very music that Gould adored. This difference in their tastes contributed to their mutual dislike and interpersonal rift. Though the twenty-four-year-old piano soloist had complete mastery of the Beethoven concerto, he did not have full mastery of his resentment and anxiety in the face of the approaching performance. In the course of the rehearsal, Gould was visibly tense, which automatically sparked a number of his extramusical mannerisms. All of a sudden, he panicked that his chair was not low enough for the performance with Szell, so he came up with a strange idea to "raise the piano in lieu of lowering the chair."[24] Gould had the audacity to hire a carpenter in order to build three wooden blocks for him, which were inserted under the piano feet. This event soon was followed by another incident. During the same rehearsal, during the orchestral tutti, while Szell was conducting, Gould unbashfully got down on his knees on stage to adjust the coupling of his adjustable piano chair. By fussing with the chair and fidgeting, Gould was able to work out some of his excessive anxiety, but he also came across as being arrogant and disruptive. Szell was known as an autocratic conductor who fostered rule-abiding behavior in his orchestra members. To his dismay, here was a youth who paid no heed to his traditional authority. Szell was aghast! Yet, aside from raising his eyebrows and asking Gould in his European accent, "vat are you doing?" Szell for some time hid his annoyance and refrained from disciplining Gould.

Szell began his music career as a performing pianist and specialized in the works of Beethoven. He had a personal intimate knowledge of Beethoven's Second Concerto, which they had just rehearsed. At some point during the rehearsal, Szell interjected: "Excuse me, Mr. Gould, I don't understand why you are using the soft pedal. It is not necessary. It makes a very feminine sound. Gould replied:

> Well, Dr. Szell, I am sure I don't need to tell you that Beethoven's piano was certainly not capable of the kind of sound this one is. And I just prefer a very thin sound with reduced climaxes, if I may say so. And if you would like me to come up a little bit, I will, but I still will do so with the soft pedal down.[25]

In reiterating this event many years later to Jonathan Cott, Gould commented:

> So, he [Szell] was a little miffed about that and obviously not at all used to being argued with, especially from a whippersnapper who was on his first American tour.[26]

Though the "whippersnapper" and the patriarch accomplished synergy in their music, they also developed their irreconcilable differences. Szell's choice of the word "feminine" was like a dagger and was intended to punish Gould for his "misbehavior." Daringly, Szell in an indirect way was not only mocking Gould's interpretative style in music but also alluding to his sexuality.

Once the two concerts were executed before the public at Cleveland's Severance Hall, they were an unprecedented success. There were curtain calls and laudatory reviews, as well as the proliferation of fiction stories about the Gould-Szell controversy. After the concert, Szell congratulated his piano soloist but could not refrain from putting in another jabbing comment: "I am sorry to use the word, but it makes a very effeminate sound." Gould retorted: "I am sorry you feel like that, Dr. Szell, but that's the way I play early Beethoven." In retelling the story, Gould, still not fully recovered from being hurt by Szell, said, "What I really wanted to say to him, however, was, 'Why don't you reduce some of your bloody strings! Because you've got too many of them in there.'"[27]

For Gould the word "effeminate" was a sign of personal effrontery. On his side, by frustrating his conductor and resenting his "bloody strings," Gould pursued his ongoing unresolved teenage rebellion against a vicious authority figure. The two men engaged in a real verbal duel, in which their tongues were sharp and hurtful. One more time Gould was unconsciously engaged in a transference reaction with somebody who symbolized power and who he experienced as a tyrant in the same way as he experienced important adults in his childhood. Evidently, Szell also had a strong counter-reaction toward his guest-soloist, which prevented him from maintaining a professional attitude. For example, Szell could have said something more straightforward like this: "Mr. Gould, I would prefer that you did not use the cast under the piano," and then he could have discussed it with him. This was not possible because Szell was in awe of Gould's pianistic brilliance, which prevented him from setting limits. Having lost control and supremacy, Szell resorted to a more devious, passive-aggressive personal criticism of Gould.

This relationship of upmanship between the two musicians, which eventually resulted in their interpersonal debacle, had far-reaching aftereffects and was further exploited by the press, who used it as a gold mine of gossip. Barry Farrell, the music critic of *Time*, gave a biographical profile of Szell upon his death in 1970, in which he exaggerated the incident including Gould. According to Gould's recollection, Farrell wrote something like this:

> During the rehearsal, Mr. Gould, a notorious eccentric who likes to fiddle with a ridiculously low piano chair, began to waste so much of the orchestra's valuable rehearsal time, that the maestro, glowering down from the podium said; 'Unless you stop that nonsense immediately, I will personally remove one-sixteenth of an inch from your derriere, thereby satisfying your need for a lower posture.'[28]

Gould was very upset by Farrell's report and wrote a letter of protestation to *Time*. He adamantly denied that such a sentence as "unless you stop that nonsense ..." was ever said and that if it was said, he, Gould, would have walked out and called off the concert. It appears that Farrell's comment was a product of his imagination and his unsympathetic feelings toward Gould. When personally confronted by Gould, Farrell stated that he only quoted what Szell himself told him. Of course, Szell was no longer alive to corroborate the story. Regardless of who put forward such a rude comment, Szell or Farrell, it appeared to be born out of their negative feelings, disguised in sarcasm and ridicule, all at Gould's expense.

In ensuing years, Gould gave concerts in Cleveland with Szell's assistant conductor, Louis Lane. He loved working with Lane, who was a subtle and pleasant character. Gould said to Cott: "Louis was a very dear guy but he was like a petrified grasshopper."[29] The comment referred to Lane's subordinate role vis-à-vis George Szell. It was recorded that during Gould's next performance in Cleveland, Szell, sitting in the audience as a spectator, exclaimed in reference to the pianist: "That nut's a genius." This phrase summed up Szell's simultaneous mixed feelings about Gould, those of contempt and those of deep respect. As to Gould's feelings, he experienced Szell as an ogre, and their mutual indignance inevitably ruined their potentially much more productive relationship.

Notes on Maestro Herbert von Karajan

Only a couple of days after the two concerts with Szell, Gould embarked on his European tour to Russia, where, relatively speaking, he achieved far more popularity than in North America. On the way back he stopped in Berlin, where he played on May 24, 25 and 26, 1957, the Beethoven Concerto no. 3 with Karajan and the Berlin Philharmonic. Herbert von Karajan was by that time already a superstar among the world's conductors and well on the way to turning into a lasting legend. Born in Salzburg, he was trained and started his career as a distinguished performing pianist and became a conductor of the Berlin Philharmonic in 1955. At the time of their meeting, Gould was twenty-four and

Karajan was forty-nine years old. Harold Schoenberg in his book on famous conductors, *The Glorious Ones*, wrote:

> Karajan presents the Apollonian side in music. Under his baton everything proceeds in a cool, objective, totally organized manner. One of the most polished technicians in history, he strives for a kind of tonal perfection (to which all conductors aspire) and achieves it (which not all conductors do). Clarity and precision are the hallmarks of his work, expressed in a luminous, transparent sound when he is at the helm of the Berlin Philharmonic.[30]

Gould, too, was dubbed Apollonian in his interpretative works. If Karajan strove for tonal perfection, so did Gould, and the two of them found in each other a worthy counterpart. The legendary team—Gould, Karajan, the Berlin Philharmonic—produced the legendary performance of Beethoven's Concerto #3, which was then praised by the critic Stuckensmidt in his fabled comparison of Gould with Ferruccio Busoni. In the following year the same team met again and on September 21 and 22, 1958, they produced a distinguished performance of Bach's D Minor Concerto. This concert was proceeded by a speech from Mayor Willy Brandt, the future Nobel Prize winner for peace, and was attended by many German dignitaries. Uncharacteristically, Gould misread Karajan's cue at the beginning of Bach's D Minor and started a slice of the second earlier, but he quickly adjusted to the orchestra. Gould felt embarrassed afterward and wrote about it in his private diary. Just the same, the response of the audience was characteristically positive in the form of standing ovations. Gould was adored in Germany by the lay listeners as well as by the most erudite music scholars. A year later in Lucerne, in August 1959, Gould and Karajan together with the Philharmonic Orchestra repeated a glorious performance of Bach's D Minor Concerto, which was also Gould's swan song for his overseas concerts. Unfortunately, "the great team" never immortalized their music officially by making recordings.

While Gould was in Berlin, he watched Karajan conducting the Berlin Philharmonic in its premiere of Jan Sibelius's Fifth Symphony. For this occasion Gould did not sit in the audience but in a glassed-in broadcast booth over the stage, which allowed him to see every "ecstatic grimace" on Karajan's face. Gould wrote:

> Karajan tends—in late—Romantic repertoire particularly—to conduct with eyes closed and to endow his stick-wielding with enormously persuasive choreographic contours, and the effect, quite frankly, contributed to one of the truly indelible musical/dramatic experiences in my life.[31]

Karajan was known to have a profound effect on his viewers, who were mesmerized by his stature and by his incomparably beautiful music. Gould, though more competitive and more critical than an average concert viewer, succumbed to Karajan's music charisma. He publicly admitted in his writings that watching Karajan at work was one of the "indelible" musical and dramatic experiences in his life. At the same time, Gould perceived Karajan as a music juggernaut, and he developed toward him a degree of resistance that was later played out when Gould refused to make recordings with him.

If Karajan's personality and music were impressive, so was the Fifth Symphony—the work of the Finnish-born composer Jan Sibelius. What Grieg was for the music life of Norway, Sibelius was for Finland. Sibelius weaved into his music the Nordic spirit of his native Finland. Not surprisingly, his music appealed to Gould. More, Gould was so stimulated and inspired by the Karajan-Sibelius combination that this stimulated a creative chain-reaction in his mind. Ever since childhood, Glenn was fascinated by the Canadian north, its serenity, the solitude and the endless white expanses dotted with evergreens. Watching and listening to Karajan's interpretation of Sibelius's music gave rise to Gould's creation of his radio documentary "The Idea of North." In this work, he incorporated a segment of this very recording, Karajan's Sibelius's Fifth, but "revised the dynamics of the recording to suit the mood of the text it accompanied."[32]

Just as Gould was of two minds with his other great music partners, like Bernstein, Mitropoulos and Szell, here in relationship with Karajan there were also mixed feelings out of which, in the end, negative ones prevailed. There was a strong inner split of love and hate; of positive identification with Karajan's Apollonian style, his tonal perfection and serenity, all coexisting in Gould with his strong disapproval and rejection of Karajan in the end. With the cessation of his European concert tours in 1959 and with the concert in Lucerne, Gould no longer had to worry about public appearances with Karajan. Since his recording career and TV programs continued to flourish, it was quite conceivable that the two musicians could meet in the foreseeable future and tape music for posterity. The opportunity arose in 1976 when Karajan and the Berlin Philharmonic were on tour in New York. The choice of music was Bach's D Minor and Beethoven's Second Concerto. In Gould's private diary he drafted a tentative scenario where the piano part would be recorded separately from the orchestra part, and they would be mixed together in the studio. That way, Gould wrote, "HvK and GG could have a meeting of minds without a meeting."[33] The project fell through because of Gould's health problems at the time. After the loss of his mother in July 1975, Gould's coexisting emotional and physical ailments progressively worsened to the point of more social avoidance and more odd and rigid behavior toward others. In 1978 there was another offer from Karajan's side to record several concertos together. Karajan was going to accommodate Gould and bring the Berlin Philharmonic to Toronto. This was an honor granted rarely, if at all, and if it had materialized, it would have been a great contribution to Canadian music culture, and in a broader sense, to the world's recording history. Gould again obstructed, this time by making an impossible counteroffer that Karajan had no choice but to refuse. In his letter to a potential German producer, Gould wrote:

> As I recall, during our ill-fated attempt to tape with the Berlin Philharmonic in the fall of 1976, two concertos—the Bach D minor and the Beethoven B flat major—were tentatively scheduled and two days set aside. This already seemed a breakneck pace to me but within the realm of the possible, nonetheless. In your recent letter, however, you proposed Beethoven no. 1 and 2 plus Bach's D minor and D major "in a couple of days," and I frankly cannot imagine committing the music to tape at such a pace ... I am not willing to tape an average of more than 10 minutes of music per day.[34]

According to this proposal, recording of the two concertos that would take over an hour would last over six days. This would be far too expensive and impractical to keep the Berlin Philharmonic with its, say, hundred orchestra and staff members in Toronto for that length of time. The question is, why did Gould really turn down such an offer of a lifetime? The most obvious reason is related to his need for perfection. If he was unable to produce perfect live music for live audiences, he could always be an absolute stickler for producing perfect recording music. By that time, Gould was already known to studio producers as a fastidious artist who insisted on making numerous takes and who was in the habit of recording one music piece over a period of several days.

Deeper undercurrents to Gould's decline of Karajan's offer were to do with his personal feelings toward the conductor. Gould was simply unable to overcome his competitiveness with and his surmounting envy of Karajan's music success. Disappointed in himself for not being a composer, Gould was longing to be a conductor, which in his mind would be a wider application of his music gift. Karajan, who was self-assured and stable, was initially his model of emulation but later became an object of envy. Gould could no longer tolerate playing a concerto with an orchestra and his last recording with an orchestra was in 1969 with Vladimir Golchman and the Columbia Orchestra. Indeed, after this failed project with Karajan, in his last year of life Gould recorded Strauss with the Hamilton Symphony as a conductor and not a pianist. This gesture showed that he symbolically abandoned the piano and embraced conducting, which seemed to him to be a higher calling.

Gould ventilated his feelings toward Karajan by inventing a fictional character named Dr. Herbert von Hochmeister. Gould's middle name was Herbert, whereas Hochmeister in the German language would translate as "high master." It followed that Gould created the name of his character by condensing his name with Karajan's name, to whom he referred as "Generalmusikdirektor of Europe." He then used the Hochmeister name as his personal pseudonym for three articles that were published in *Musical America*. Gould's character, Herbert von Hochmeister, was a retired conductor who turned into a stuffy, rigid and blatantly old-fashioned music critic. It seems that Gould included into this character some aspects of Karajan and some of George Szell. This character became his alter ego that allowed him more freedom of expression of anger and criticism than if he had signed his real name.

The Lion from Philadelphia

A number of important individuals Gould encountered in the course of his life left a searing impression on him. Every failed relationship with others led to accentuation of his emotional pain and more social isolation. Repetitive, interpersonal conflicts may cause weakening of the spirit required to carry on. Gould was aware of his over-sensitivity to his colleagues and endeavored to keep away from them. He wrote: "All my life I avoided the company of musicians," and consoled himself that "Artists work best in isolation."

Following the massive social exposure during his first American tour in 1957, highlighted by the clash with Szell and preceded by an even more stressful European tour, Gould was in dire need of peace and equanimity. He practically "overdosed" on people. Music associates, members of the orchestra, fans who wanted to meet him backstage to introduce themselves and shake his hand were all experienced ambivalently. He was flattered by their much-needed recognition but overwhelmed by such social intensity. All he could do was to fantasize about his quiet haven on Lake Simcoe, where he would soon return to hibernate. Gould received enough music recognition from his fans, but he remained unendingly hungry for personal acceptance and unconditional regard of his confreres. His hunger was at least in part met when he found his match in the personality of Leopold Stokowski.

Completely by chance, Gould and Stokowski met in a railway station in Frankfurt in west central Germany while they were independently boarding the Amsterdam-Vienna express. The pianist was still "high" on his conquest in Russia and Berlin and was heading to Austria for his last recital of the tour scheduled for June 7, 1957. Upon spotting Stokowski, who was pacing the platform, Gould as a solitary traveler was suddenly taken by an irresistible urge to join his counterpart. Though Gould never saw Stokowski in person, he was not a stranger to him. Glenn was raised on Stokowski news since his boyhood, and at the age of eight he watched the movie *Fantasia*, for which Stokowski conducted music. Gould summarized his first encounter and the entire artistic and emotional relationship with this great conductor in his sizable article "Stokowski in Six Scenes."[35] This work is his personal literary masterpiece that differs from many of his other writings in its warmth, sincerity and overall positive regard toward the subjects involved. It is as if the whole interaction with Stokowski was smooth and, in the end, coalesced into a total nurturing experience without any interpersonal impasses or hardships.

It is a reader's delight to go over Gould's hilarious and endearing description of his first meeting with Stokowski, of his many funny strategies as to how to introduce himself, and of his childlike fear of making a faux pas before the great man. Finally, just at the time of the boarding call, when the passengers were flocking to the door and Stokowski was quite near him, Gould dropped his ticket, picked it up and, while straightening and apologizing, introduced himself in a stuttering fashion to the maestro. To his surprise, Stokowski recognized him and instantly responded, "I have read that you were recently in Leningrad." Stokowski offered to visit Gould in his train compartment, which he did. They chatted for almost an hour about their mutual reminiscences on Leningrad and their music views. Gould wrote that he was not "star-struck" by this get-together, but certainly his "dream had come true." The two of them developed an amiable and collegial relationship. "This century's most celebrated podium profile," as Gould referred to Stokowski gallantly and affectionately, became one of Gould's rare objects of true admiration, the least ambivalent and unconflicted love figure in the pianist's mind. If one recalls the strong mixed feelings Gould harbored toward other conductors and people at large, this predominantly positive, non-ambivalent relationship with Leopold Stokowski came as a blessing, a bright comfortable reality in his armamentarium of disturbed relations.

Much happened in Gould's life after that historical meeting. In the course of the next few years, Gould gradually withdrew from his performing career and gradually reoriented himself to his recording career and to becoming a famous radio and TV personality. It was in this role that Gould continued his relationship with Stokowski through correspondence, personal meetings and recording collaboration.

Stokowski granted three face-to-face interviews with Gould. For the first interview, according to his personal testimony, Gould visited the maestro in his luxurious Fifth Avenue apartment in New York in November 1965. Gould was a novice as a journalist. He was at that time working on his article "The Prospects of Recording," and by that time Stokowski had spent forty-eight years in the recording studio. Gould's sense of self was fragile and easily imbalanced in the presence of others. Besides, here he also had the role of the interviewer, which was entirely unknown to him. Yet he carried on with the interview, delighted to find in the eighty-three-year-old Stokowski an easy and cooperative partner.

Leopold Stokowski was born in London, England, in 1882. He received the highest education in music at Oxford University and established himself in New York as a chief organist at the church of St. Bartholomew. Stokowski was the music director of the Cincinnati Symphony Orchestra until 1912, when he became the director of the Philadelphia Philharmonic. As an organist, Stokowski was well versed in the works of Bach. He also wrote parts for the various instruments and arranged the music of Bach for the symphony, making it possible to be expressed on a large scale. As a master of one of the best symphony orchestras, he well knew how to propagate and amplify the beauty and greatness of a music piece. In 1936, after twenty-four years of such dedicated work, the major domo of the symphonia went to Hollywood to start a new kind of work—to create and direct classical music for the movie industry. As Gould put it: "He had left Philadelphia, succumbed to the blandishments of Hollywood, and offered what seemed like a lame and fatuous excuse for this heresy." "I go to a higher calling," Stokowski was reported to have said at the press conference that was called to announce his departure.

Roughly, Stokowski is to be credited for two great achievements—first, he raised the Philadelphia Philharmonic to the status of one of the best classical music orchestras in the world; second, he revolutionized the role of music in the film and recording industry by putting art music on soundtrack and popularizing it among the general public. Despite his fame, most of the music scholars and critics frowned upon Stokowski's abandonment of the conventional role of a philharmonic conductor. While his contemporary, Arturo Toscanini, "in academic circles was considered more respectable," Stokowski's move to Hollywood was too innovative to be readily embraced.

Toscanini was known as a "literalist;" "for him, the composer's instructions were gospel." This was precisely one of the reasons why Gould did not favor Toscanini's interpretation, as he thought of him to be inflexible and too formal both as a person and in his music work. Gould listened to Toscanini's radio programs since he was a child, and this is what he as an adult commented on his music: "To my ears, it seemed that the sound was edgy and unbalanced, that Toscanini's interpretations did not carry one forward with the visionary sweep of his fellow literalist Weingartner, and that the playing, by and large, born of terror rather than conviction, was sloppy."[36] If according to this statement, Toscanini did not have such a vision, Stokowski, who left Philadelphia to explore new avenues in music, was a visionary, which was a quality Gould could relate to and support. Gould wrote: "It didn't matter that my colleagues rambled on about Stokowski's eccentricities and deviations from the text and then segued to an account of Toscanini's latest metronome steeplechase; for me, Stokowski had already redefined the role of the interpreter."[37]

So when the thirty-three-year-old Gould, in his role as an interviewer, met the fifty-years-older Maestro, he already looked up to him, not only as a benevolent, grandfatherly figure but considered him perhaps the greatest living musician-conductor. At the end of this meeting, to Gould's greatest astonishment, Stokowski turned to him with this priceless question: "May I ask you why we have never been invited to make records together?" Gould always thought that Stokowski did not like soloists and "that concertos, as a symphonic subspecies, were quite beneath his notice." Obviously, Stokowski desired to make music with Gould, which means that he had positive feelings toward both the concerto as a form of music and this particular pianist whom he well respected. Gould promptly replied to Stokowski's question with an equally worthy proposal to record Beethoven's Emperor Concerto. In March 1966, the two musicians and the American Symphony did record for CBS at the New York Manhattan Center the Beethoven Concerto in E flat major no. 5 "Emperor," which became an historical landmark for their conjoint accomplishment.

Before the recording of the Emperor Concerto, Gould rehearsed at the piano in Stokowski's presence at the Manhattan Center. Gould had two distinctly different renditions prepared. He played them both for Stokowski and asked him which one he preferred. To Gould's delight, Stokowski chose the "slow" rendition. This gesture is so reminiscent of the Gould-Bernstein event of 1962 when they both interpreted Brahms' D Minor, and Gould put forward a slow rendition that Bernstein approved. That project ended in a major drama and press hysteria, which was described earlier. Unlike with Bernstein, Gould did very well with Stokowski, who supported the "slow" rendition and gave his younger soloist full reign and confidence. When Stokowski asked collegially and without any hidden agenda: "What is your tempo?" Gould candidly and gallantly responded: "My tempo is your tempo." Then he added:

> I hope, however, [with] the tempo we can make this piece into a symphony with piano obbligato; I really don't think it ought to be a virtuoso vehicle.[38]

Gould went on to explain in this essay that his intention was "to demythologize the virtuoso tradition." Here Gould was not at war with Stokowski, who was gentle and fair to him, but was at war psychologically with the power of the concerto as a music form and with the greatness of Beethoven as a creator of such a powerful music piece.

In 1969 Gould paid enormous respect to the aged Stokowski by producing a radio documentary about him. Gould interviewed Stokowski in front of the camera and asked him among other things, a long, philosophical "if" question—something about if there were living beings on other distant planets, what would he tell them about the artistic achievements of Earth men? Stokowski answered in an equally tricky and equally philosophical lengthy monologue in which he covered the topic of human destructive tendencies, alluding to the Vietnam War, which was at its peak in 1969. He spoke about touchy subjects with candid honesty and dignity. From this interview it was clear that Stokowski left the great Philadelphia Orchestra for a "higher calling," which was to devote the rest of his productive life—to be exact, another thirty years—to the recording and film industry. This gave him a greater sense of working for humanity at large than for the circumscribed audiences of concert halls.

As the Stokowski legend unfolds, one may notice many points of interest to Gould and his subconscious identification with his older colleague. Stokowski refused "to regard the score, or the material [on which] he had to work, as Holy Writ;" his abandonment of the concert hall for the "higher calling" of technology, his attraction and preference for Bach, but most of all, his innovative spirit all appealed to Gould and served as a model to follow. Gould's psychodynamics ran deeper than observed. His mother, too, admired Stokowski and followed his remarkable music career as she was developing musically. It was she who introduced Glenn to *Fantasia* and taught him about Stokowski's role and his soundtrack music. Glenn incorporated into his mind the image of Stokowski as a benevolent and interesting grandfatherly love object. The maestro was seen by Gould as dear "Stocky" and a familiar man who was strong enough to challenge his elders on many issues in classical music. By doing something new, by putting his most advanced and most refined skills toward the film and recording industry, Stocky managed to reach the hearts not only of the adult public but also wide children's audiences that normally do not attend evening concerts. The part that fascinated Gould was that Stokowski "challenged his elders," which he, Gould, was also continuously doing all his life, except that Stokowski's challenges seemed healthier, as he managed to complete his many projects and live an impressively long life; whereas Gould's challenges backfired at times and were personally unfulfilling. The presence of Stokowski in Gould's life was an excellent model for inspiration and gave him someone with whom he could identify. It gave Gould a reference point, a sense of being justified and the sense of affirmation. Gould finished his tribute essay to Stokowski in this way:

> In his life time he had witnessed the triumph and confirmed the essential humanity of those technological ideas which had inspired his activity as a musician; for him, technology had indeed become a "higher calling." He had understood that through its mediation, one could transcend the frailty of nature and concentrate on a vision of the ideal.[39]

These thoughts are more autobiographical as they apply to Gould's perception of himself. There is a sense of kinship to Stokowski in Gould's statement that "one could transcend the frailty of nature and concentrate on a vision of the ideal," which reflects his need to shrug off his personal frailties and become stronger and happier. In the way of his thinking and in his behavior, Gould really came so close to seeing himself in Stokowski. The difference was that Stokowski may have nearly achieved his life's goals, whereas Gould was constantly hindered from within and from without, which left him only partly fulfilled and able to live up to a fraction of his life's great potential.

Chapter XII

TURNING THIRTY

We thought we were running away from the grownups, and now we are the grownups.

Margaret Atwood[1]

By the time Gould turned thirty years of age, he was a megastar among concert pianists. Yet, for a few years, he considered phasing out his public performances so he could dedicate himself to other creative enterprises. His radio and TV careers were already booming, and he was popular for his unique music commentaries and documentaries. Gould created TV programs in which he explored different themes, with titles such as *Music in the U.S.S.R* or *Glenn Gould on Bach*, or the CBC *Wednesday Night* recitals aired on the radio. These were all well-known programs in Canada.

There were always at least two parallel realities about Gould. The first had to do with what was observed, and the second with what was hidden. On the outside, Gould kept up a rich facade made up of his creative and intellectual talents. He looked busy, keen, even almost happy at times. Simultaneously, on the inside, within the privacy of his inner life, Gould was in a state of languor and enervation. There was nothing he could do to reconcile these two polarities. Most of his contemporaries were not conscious of this split in his psyche, which prevented them from being more sensitive and more understanding of his growing inconsistencies. Though very quiet in his suffering, Gould gave away signs of longing for support and acceptance, which were not granted readily.

For women and men of the late twentieth century in North America, the peak of productivity is in their thirties and forties. This becomes the time to generate, expand, excel and focus on self-development. For Gould, entering his thirties was like retrogressing. His recording and broadcasting career carried on with moderate intensity, whereas his performing career was decelerating. He lost the stamina for the nomadic life of a performing artist and resented having to appear before the eyes of crowds. To make things worse, Gould developed a phobia of flying and stopped traveling by plane. Traveling to foreign places was hard for him even in his earlier years. His mother also had anxieties about going away from home. She had never been on a plane and had a full-fledged phobia of flying. More, she was also anxious about Glenn's prospective long trips, particularly those that may have involved traveling by plane or by a big ship like an oceanliner. It appears that the seeds of Glenn's fear of germs, fear of the dark, fear of the unfamiliar, were all planted in his early childhood and took epidemic proportions in his adulthood. Then, when he was in his thirties, his underlying fear of flying suddenly took over and prevented him from traveling by air. According to Lorne Tulk, Glenn's recording engineer at the CBC, it happened after the concert in Cincinnati, when Gould, upon arrival at the airport, had a panic attack looking at a slew of parked airplanes. He found it unbearable to enter any of them and fly. Gould performed in Cincinnati five times, his last recital being on November 20, 1962. It seems that the event in question happened during this final visit to Cincinnati. Gould's state of panic was so strong that he had to cancel the flight and the rest of his tour to Kansas City, Kansas, and Louisville, Kentucky, as well as his flight back home. In the end, he drove all the way back to Toronto in a rented car. In Gould's life, this form of apprehension and fear of flying meant less mobility for concert tours and more personal isolation through geographical confinement. On a personal level, he was quite insecure, and it was obvious that he was longing for more quiescence and solitude.

Consistent with his inner sufferings, there was a series of mishaps that occurred in 1962. For example, in March Gould had to cancel three appearances in Seattle, Washington, one of which was supposed to be a benefit performance. In a telegram to Milton Katims, the conductor of the Seattle Symphony, the pianist apologized for canceling on account of his ailing health, notably his shoulder pain and stiff neck. The press reported that Gould, in fact, suffered "a kickback from an old injury," alluding to the Steinway incident of December 1959.

Shortly after this failed project, there was yet another incident that grew into a notorious music scandal. This was on April 6, 1962, when Gould appeared at Carnegie Hall as a piano soloist along with the New York Philharmonic and Leonard Bernstein as conductor, where he delivered his unusually slow rendition of the Brahms D Minor Concerto. This catastrophic event was partially described earlier, and the speech Bernstein gave before the concert was brought out in full. Here it is worthwhile to touch upon the negative publicity and its emotional effect on Gould. On that critical Friday afternoon, in front of 2,800 viewers, Bernstein denounced Gould's approach to the Brahms D Minor Concerto but still went ahead with its performance. By following through with his extremely slow interpretation of the piece, Gould provoked disapproving, even hostile responses from the music critics. The American press rose in defense of what was considered a standard of music performance and attacked Gould for his sacrilege of the Brahms piece. A few critics became overly critical in their wrath, and they lost touch with the reality of Gould's worth as a musician. It did not matter to them that on the next day, Saturday, he delivered at the same Carnegie Hall, with the same orchestra and the same conductor, what was expected from him—a "normal" rendition of the Brahms D Minor Concerto. As far as the critics were concerned, Gould "sinned" and had to be severely punished for it. One of those condemning critics was Harold Schonberg of *The New York Times* who, on April 7, 1962, gave a brash evaluation of Gould's first performance without waiting to hear the second interpretation. His critique was in the form of a sarcastic letter to his long-deceased friend, Ossip Gabrilowitsch, a renowned pianist at the turn of the century:

> **Music: Inner Voices of Glenn Gould**
>
> Such goings-on at the New York Philharmonic concert yesterday afternoon! I tell you Ossip, like you never saw ...
>
> First the conductor comes out to read a speech. He says he doesn't like the way the pianist will play the concerto.
>
> I mean this, Ossip, Glenn Gould is waiting in the wings to play Brahms,

> and has to listen to Leonard Bernstein saying that this was a Brahms he never dreamed of ...
>
> So then the Gould boy comes out, and you know what, Ossip? Now I understand. I mean, a conductor has to protect himself. You know what? The Gould boy played the Brahms D Minor Concerto slower than the way we used to practice it. (And between you, me and the corner lamppost, Ossip, maybe the reason he plays it slow is maybe his technique is not so good).[2]

At first, Schonberg was mildly critical of Bernstein, but Gould caught the brunt of his snide criticism. He mocked the virtuoso in a patronizing tone by calling him repeatedly "the Gould boy." In his writing, Schonberg became so emotionally entangled with Gould that he not only lost basic respect for him, but he also lost his critical distance and objectivity. This is why his letter to Ossip looked more like an exercise of gossip than a fair musical critique. The concertgoers, on the other hand, filled Carnegie Hall on both days, vigorously applauded and enjoyed both performances. The audiences, on the whole, never completely lost their enthusiasm for and confidence in Gould as a performer.

Gould himself proved that he did not play "so slow" because "his technique is not so good" but because he was a re-creative artist of infinite curiosity who liked to experiment and try different modes of musical expression. It was already well-known that Gould was capable of producing two or more different renditions of the same music piece, which was one of the features of his music greatness. The problem here is not so much with Gould's musicianship but with his intricate personality. Resourceful as he was, he also had a number of liabilities that happened to be operating in this case. Driven by his need for innovation, Gould acted over-confidently and too daringly. By pursuing his slow and mellow rendition of the Brahms concerto, he did the unexpected and trampled on many a critical ear, which got him into trouble.

The question that arises here is whether Gould's deed was a transgression or the gift of music interpretation. Musicians on the public stage, by delivering a music piece, are primarily the messengers of the composer's wish. Undeniably so, they are also the conveyers of their own music emotion. Together, the composer's wish and the performer's skill-and-emotion are presented to the audience as a gift of music interpretation. It follows that a gift given by musicians, be it small or large, has an implicit positive meaning. It encompasses good wishes and the efforts of interested parties. It is likely that Gould offered a gift of an experimental music interpretation to the audience.

Much like Schonberg, another critic, Harriet Johnson of *The New York Post* did not see Gould's behavior as a trial or gift-giving but expressed in a rather perverse way her personal exasperation with him. She wrote:

> **Gould, Bernstein at Odds in Brahms**
>
> Pianist Glenn Gould's eccentricities in the past have struck way out into left field but now they've gone over the fence ...
>
> Friday his piano was raised on blocks as usual, a rug went under it, his shop-worn chair was properly adjusted and his glass of water within reach. During rest periods he was bent over enough to look like a question mark facing right instead of left, or turned toward the orchestra conducting vigorously with his

> left hand. Underneath his pants on his right hip was a bulge as if a cushion or heating pad had been tucked therein.
>
> The brooding introspection of the Brahms masterpiece was not illuminated by Gould's heavy deliberation in the initial movement. He was Atlas carrying a heavy-laden world. The Adagio was also far too slow and rhythmically unpredictable but there were times when the depth of his musical comprehension brought forth a rare beauty in contemplative passages. His technique is, of course, prodigious, and his inherent musical gifts magnificent.[3]

After a lengthy introduction of over three hundred words, in which Johnson drew attention to the chasm between Gould and Bernstein and quoted some of the highlights from Bernstein's speech, she became fixated on Gould's physical appearance at the concert. This was a perennial trap in which the majority of music critics fell when writing about Gould. Johnson lost her critical objectivity by making an odious description of Gould's demeanor. What does, for example, a supposedly bulging right pocket have to do with Gould's musicianship? Gould never claimed to be a fashion model nor a student of a school of charm. Perhaps he stuffed his pocket with handkerchiefs needed to wipe the sweat off his forehead during the performance. If so, one would expect more empathy for the artist at work. Meanwhile, Johnson showed little empathy and even less professionalism. It was only at the end of her article that she offered a word of praise: "His technique, of course, is prodigious ..." but even this was done half-heartedly. As if the prodigious piano technique is a matter of fact; something that could be anybody's possession.

Both critics missed the mark. Theirs was a myopic view of an illustrious and brilliant character, who being so exceptionally musically gifted could not play by the rules of the average world. Even if he stepped out of line in this concert, as great as he was, could he not be forgiven?

It is noted that the majority of music critics are unfulfilled musicians. They study instrumental music and often their ideal is to become performing artists. When their dreams fail, these scholars often stay in a related field of music such as music journalism and critique.

Having studied the critical responses to Gould's interpretation of the Brahms D Minor Concerto in New York, Eric McLean of *The Montreal Star* produced a lengthy article on April 14, 1962, titled "L'Affaire Gould." He introduced some sobriety among the critical abandon of the press and attempted to heal the rift between Gould and his observers. McLean wrote:

> Apparently the performance was very slow (the first movement is a long one even at normal speed) and the tone produced by Gould was almost inaudible, which caused one of the critics to suggest that perhaps Gould was incapable of playing it any louder or faster. Whatever else he may be accused of, I believe that anyone who has followed Gould's career will know that his technique is up to just about anything written for the keyboard. In this instance the critic was a little wide of the mark ...[4]

Without mentioning the name, McLean referred to Schonberg's accusation of Gould. McLean took Gould under his wing and rose to his defense in a seemingly fair and objective way. He concluded:

> Actually, there are a number of precedents for Gould's behavior. When Liszt or Paganini appeared as soloists with an orchestra, it seems unlikely that either one of them would give a fig for the opinions of the conductor who happened to differ with them on the interpretation. He was there to wave a stick and co-ordinate the musicians with whatever the soloist was doing.[5]

There are other possible explanations for Gould's choice of a slow rendition. These could be found in the realm of interpersonal psychology. Had Bernstein adamantly disagreed with his rendition, Gould may have given up on the idea. Gould was not trying to be blatantly uncooperative with Bernstein. If Bernstein said, "Glenn, your slow rendition of Brahms is interesting but I don't think it is a good idea to put it forward in front of the fastidious New York critics on the first day. Let's save it for later," Gould would have backed off. It was well known about Gould that whenever he collaborated with others, such as playing chamber music with Oskar Shumsky and Leonard Rose in Stratford, he was quite cooperative with respect to the tempo and the style of interpretation. If Bernstein did not have any underlying neurotic agenda vis-à-vis Gould, he should have adamantly disagreed with Gould's choice of tempo and insisted on a performance proper. Or, if he had genuine respect for Gould's rendition, he should have gone along with it without a trace of ambivalence. He could have been quite straightforward in his speech by saying: "Mr. Gould and I are very united in our decision to try this rendition as an experiment even though we are aware that our esteemed critics may not agree with it." Realistically, Gould can not be singled out alone and faulted for his slow performance of the Brahms concerto. It was a mutual effort of Gould, the New York Philharmonic and Leonard Bernstein at its helm. Therefore, it was either their mutual disaster or their mutual victory.

Did Gould have a death wish by throwing himself in front of the highbrowed New York critics? Was he not able to control his protest against authority figures? These and other underlying psychological reasons may have been at work. This is precisely why Gould's behavior cannot be judged or successfully evaluated in a stroke of a pen but has to be pondered sensitively and analytically.

For Gould, turning thirty was an invisible trauma. Among his other fears, Gould had a fear of aging and dying, and each birthday, particularly those anniversarial ones, like turning twenty or thirty, raised these very fears to panic proportions. If Gould in his twenties was already showing a distinction in his dress by lack of color coordination and by wearing winter clothes in the summer time, then in the next decade he was becoming even more strange in his appearance. His clothes were oversized. As time went on, his pants were becoming more loose and baggy. Along with his avoidance of tight clothes, Gould usually did not wear a belt, which added looseness to his pants. His contemporaries frowned at that habit. Today, we understand that those unfortunate individuals who struggle with ever-present anxiety tend to gasp and swallow much air, causing them to feel bloated and distended. This renders it necessary for them to make their clothes looser and more comfortable.

If the anxiety was in the background of Gould's manner of dress, then his rising depression was largely responsible for his poor eating habits. After Gould moved out from his parents' home and began living on his own, he declined in both the upkeep of his living space and of himself. His meals were irregular and scarce. His belated breakfasts, which took place in the mid-afternoon, consisted of a glass of grapefruit juice, a muffin and a pot of weak tea with a spoon of honey. The tea-drinking, coupled with munching on arrowroot cookies, would then continue for the duration of the entire day.

Gould's mother believed them to be the best to prevent constipation. Gould, assuming his mother's preferences, devoured arrowroots with much gusto and to the exclusion of other sweets. At the same time, he began skipping meals, and his lunches gradually disappeared, leaving him only with very late dinners after midnight. He was extremely reluctant to prepare his dinners and, if he happened to be at home, he would invariably open a can of spaghetti with tomato sauce or prepare scrambled eggs for himself. He ate somewhat better when he happened to be at a restaurant at night after a recording session. In his thirties, Gould used to eat an occasional lamb chop with a serving of green salad and potatoes, whereas in the future he avoided eating meat and became a "virtual vegetarian."[6]

Along with irregular eating habits, Glenn was becoming more squeamish at the sight of certain foods, particularly meat. He could not overcome the fact that meat was a derivative of slaughtered animals, and he could certainly not forgive humans for killing them. The old childhood conflict around his father's fishing hobby and his occupation as a furrier was played out in the form of aversion to eating. He refused to eat fish and ate very few meat products, which was all colored by his inordinate sensitivity to animals. Glenn's father confirmed those observations:

"Mr. Gould, when Glenn turned thirty in 1962, were you still in the fur business?" I asked.

"Of course, this was our bread and butter. When Glenn was younger, we bought piano after piano, we had to roll them [the pianos] to the cottage in all kinds of weather. The main expense, as far as I was concerned, was providing pianos. That was costly."

"What happened in terms of your work once Glenn became famous and financially independent?" I pursued the interview with some risk to impinge on Mr. Gould's sense of privacy.

"Well, when Glenn became famous, I still had to work to catch up with things. We repaired the house and the cottage. Also, I liked my job very much, and the business was booming. My wife and I, we were very active at the time and we needed the money," Mr. Gould elaborated.

"Yet, Glenn was never too happy about you working as a furrier?" I asked cautiously, trying not to hurt Mr. Gould's feelings.

"Glenn seemed to have a natural hatred for the fur business. He loved animals so much that he could not love the fur business. When he got older he wouldn't even eat meat for the same reason." Mr. Gould was slightly exasperated.

"What is your philosophy with respect to the animal fur industry?" I asked.

"I differed with Glenn on that. Canada is a frontier country. People depend on animals for their survival. I gave up fishing for Glenn's sake because it would have broken his heart if I hadn't, but I could not give up my job. I had to support my wife and the property, and Glenn knew it,"[7] Mr. Gould conceded.

As always, there was a lack of mutual understanding between the father and his son. Mr. Gould made numerous sacrifices for his son, even giving up one of his oldest hobbies—fishing. He was pragmatic, a matter-of-fact person who often could not relate to the inner world of his only child. Glenn dealt with his father by avoiding face-to-face contact with him. It got to a point that they stopped seeing each other. Glenn kept in touch with his mother by visiting her in secrecy. Both parents had mixed feelings in response to Glenn—those of extraordinary pride and care for him. At the same time, they experienced frustration, anger and a sense of shame. Glenn met his parental expectations only in part, and they, on their side, were not flexible enough to accept him as he was. This type of interaction was as old as Glenn was, and it had never improved but instead led to more tension in the small triangular Gould family. Failing to change their son and make him more "normal," Glenn's parents turned to their own specific interests. Mr. Gould immersed himself in his work and community functions. In 1967, he became the president of the Kiwanis Festival, the same one where Glenn won the first prize years earlier. Mrs. Gould threw herself into her charitable work in church and with unwed teenage mothers. By playing the piano and singing for the young mothers and their newborn babies, Mrs. Gould was reminded of Glenn as a baby, which helped her deal with her sense of sadness about not having a grandchild. Already in his thirties, Glenn showed absolutely no signs of interest in getting married and settling down as a family man.

Gould too was generous and giving in his own way. George Gibson, who worked at Eaton's in the early 1960s in the piano repair department, was "fascinated by the pianist Glenn Gould, who often came to try our concert grands and select them for his performances." Gibson recalled:

> We used to punch a hole in the wall to watch him play. He was so good and we were breathless. He used to borrow a little leveling stool from us to sit on at the piano. He was so generous that he gave the guy a five-dollar tip for lending him the stool.[8]

Gibson also remembered that in 1963 Gould had a piano mechanic by the name of Donald MacDonald.[9] Since the piano keys are set for a certain depth of touch, the conversation between Gould and MacDonald was very specific. Gould would say to him, "the key is too shallow" or "too deep," and MacDonald would adjust the piano keys accordingly. Gibson recalled that MacDonald also went to New York to tune Gould's pianos for recording sessions at the Columbia studios. Gould used to give the following advice to MacDonald: "When you get to New York, make sure to take a taxi there and make sure to give the driver a good tip."

"You seem to have vivid memories about Gould. Do you think that he was strange, or eccentric or even a little weird?" I asked Mr. Gibson.

"Not at all. He was a great artist, and artists live in their own world which we may not be able to relate to. He was such a generous man. I can never forget him. Can you imagine, to give a guy five dollars just for the leveling stool? That was a goodly sum of money in those days. I have nothing but highest regards for him,"[10] Mr. Gibson concluded.

As usual, Gould's music was at the center of all of his strivings. In his thirties, he acquired two major figures that accompanied him in his creative achievements in the next fifteen years—Verne Edquist and Andrew Kazdin. Edquist became Gould's steadiest piano tuner and Kazdin his closest music producer. This famous trio worked together to create successful recordings of classical music.

Born in Saskatchewan to parents who were Swedish immigrants, Edquist lived his early years as a farm boy. With only ten percent of his vision left, he was sent to the Ontario School for the Blind in Brantford, Ontario, where he learned the trade of piano tuning. In Toronto, where Edquist settled and established his family, he initially worked for the Heintzman Piano Factory tuning new pianos and the showroom instruments. After twelve years of such work, in 1961 Edquist became the concert piano tuner at the Timothy Eaton Company, which had the Steinway agency. In this capacity, he tuned the Steinway concert grand pianos being used by the artists performing at the Toronto Massey Hall and Eaton Auditorium. Edquist tuned piano for Mona Bates, a renowned piano teacher of the day, as well as concert pianos for a number of famous visiting pianists such as Artur Rubinstein, Rudolf Serkin, Vladimir Ashkenazy, Liberace, Victor Borge and, of course, Glenn Gould, for whom he faithfully worked for about seventeen years.

It all started when Edquist was asked by a booking agent, Muriel Musson, to tune Gould's Chickering piano. Edquist reminisced:

> When I played it, I found that it was quite out of tune—as it would happen to older pianos that were exposed to cottage environment and then brought to a warm apartment. The wood would shrink and the tuning pins would get loose, thus making it impossible to stay in tune. Others had attempted to solve the problem by muting off the strings that wouldn't stay in tune. But there were so many strings in this condition that I just pulled out the mutes and explained [to Gould] that the piano would have to be taken in to the repair shop and have larger tuning pins installed.[11]

Edquist described that he felt very awkward when Gould insisted on tuning the piano "as it was." The tuner said no, and the following sharp interaction occurred:

Gould impatiently: "You mean you refuse to tune the piano?"
Edquist calmly: "That's correct because new tuning pins are required."
Gould hastily: "Then I'd better order a taxi for you to get you back to Eatons."[12]

Eventually, once Gould's temper cooled down, he agreed to transport his beloved Chickering piano to the repair shop at Eaton's. Edquist dutifully replaced the tuning pins, and they are still in the piano to this day. From then on, Verne Edquist tuned Gould's pianos for his recording sessions, as well for his radio and TV appearances in Toronto.

Andrew Kazdin arrived on the scene in 1964. This is when he joined Columbia Records at the Masterworks Department in New York, where Glenn Gould had already been recording for about eight years. At that time, the staff consisted of the director of Masterworks, John McClure, with three record producers—Tom Frost, Tom Shepard and Paul Myers with Richard Killough as associate producer. Kazdin, the newly hired music editor, gradually worked his way up to become a renowned American music producer.

In the period from 1962 to 1964, Gould was recording for Masterworks with Paul Myers as his music producer. Together they turned out several of Bach's compositions including Bach's *Well-Tempered Clavier, Book I*, with its twenty-four music pieces, and Bach's *Inventions*. Their artist/producer relationship came to a halt for unclear reasons. According to Kazdin, Gould was prone to periodic cancellations of recording sessions, but he liked to use up the time in the booked studio for practicing the piano. He asked Paul Myers to stay with him and watch him practice. Myers politely declined the invitation on account of being busy. Gould appeared hurt but Myers stuck with his decision to leave. On one occasion, Myers "stated that this may have been 'the beginning of the end' for their working relationship."[13] It is noteworthy that Gould and Myers continued to enjoy an amiable relationship. When Myers moved to London, the two friends carried on a viable relationship at a distance through correspondence. Myers contributed to Gould's career by propagating his recordings in England, where Gould was much less popular than in North America.

After the work partnership with Myers had dissolved, Gould switched to working with Tom Frost as his new producer at Masterworks. They began working on a massive project including the works of Schonberg and the simultaneous recording of the set of Beethoven's sonatas, beginning with Sonata no. 10. Kazdin, who was assigned to assist Frost, worked on the editing of the Beethoven set. Kazdin recalled:

> It was during this period of snipping extra notes and creaks out of the opus 10 sonatas that my friendship with Glenn began to develop. We were thrown together for extended periods of time working on Frost's record, and we seemed to get along amicably. Because of this, it was most natural for Frost to think of me when, on short notice before a scheduled session to record some more Schonberg Lieder (specifically the Book of Hanging Gardens, opus 15), Frost could not direct the sessions and had to provide a substitute producer. It was the first time Glenn and I recorded together. With only one exception, this launched an exclusive collaboration that lasted through 1979 and produced over forty records.[14]

Gould in his thirties, was a seasoned, world-class piano virtuoso; he was a number-one broadcaster of classical music and one of the most prolific North American recording artists of classical piano literature. Yet in his personal life he was rather frail and inconsistent. There was another side of Gould, the one that was defiant, incorrigible, even wild in some of his behavior. These characteristics came to their full expression when Gould was at a steering wheel. He would then transform into a daredevil personality who had no tolerance for rules and regulations. In that, he was more like the typical North American rebel, like the character that movie actor James Dean played in *Rebel Without a Cause*. This character was idolized by the teenage population as their young and restless hero. This rather impulsive side of Gould will now be explored.

GOULD IN THE DRIVER'S SEAT

> Man is sometimes extraordinarily, passionately, in love with suffering.
>
> Fedor M. Dostoevski[15]

The image of the concert pianist is usually associated with a variety of subtle and refined qualities and not with high-risk activities. Aside from Gould's overall delicate demeanor, he showed strong masculine tendencies, represented in his need to control his environment and the people around him. Sometimes, this need for control was expressed in aggressive and forceful ways. Remember that Gould drove his motorboat at high speed on Lake Simcoe, scaring the fish away from fishermen on the shore. At the age of twenty-nine, Gould described the scene spontaneously and candidly:

> I have a motorboat now, called the *Arnold's*, after Arnold Schoenberg, the composer. Whether it is true or not, I don't know, but I've heard fish are frightened away by noise. So wherever I see any fishermen when I am out in the *Arnold's*,

> I make it a point to roar around them as close as possible, as part of my anti-fishing campaign. I get some pretty dirty looks. I am probably known as The Scourge of Lake Simcoe.[16]

In his mind, Gould believed himself to be a benefactor of the innocent fish, but in the fishermen's view he was a bully. The term "scourge," used by Gould depicts a severe noxious force. An anti-fishing campaign also means an anti-fishermen campaign. While he purported to be a defender of fish, he was at the same time an aggressor to humans. Interestingly, Glenn thought of himself as a pacifist and was not aware of the aggressive tendency in himself.

It was Glenn's father who introduced and taught Glenn how to navigate motor boats and drive a car. Bert Gould had a passion for technology and technical amenities. He enjoyed driving long distances and made several long trips to the United States and remote places in Canada by car. Mr. Gould reminisced:

"When Glenn was four years old, I sat him on my lap in the car and taught him how to navigate the steering wheel. He loved it more than anything else. Even when he played in the living room, he played with toy-cars or he'd grab a pot lid, pretending it was a steering wheel." Bert smiled benevolently.

"Glenn must have been very imaginative at play," I remarked.

"Are you kidding? He'd produce such funny motor noises to simulate the car engine. At such a young age, Glenn could tell you twenty different types of automobiles, and when he was a little older, he could tell you the history of the Cadillac, Chrysler, Lincoln Continental, you name it." Mr. Gould obviously shared his son's fascination with cars.

"When did Glenn start driving on his own," I asked.

"Well, when Glenn was about fifteen, I let him drive my Buick at the cottage, usually on the back roads. In those days, there weren't that many cars on the roads and I thought he was pretty safe. But we couldn't tell his mother, it was kind of a hush-hush between us," Mr. Gould said somewhat mischievously.

"Oh really, how long did that last?" I was doubtful.

"Well, that didn't last too long, and she eventually found out from our neighbors." Mr. Gould made a somewhat guilty face.

"What was Mrs. Gould's reaction once she had found out?"

"Well, she was not amused to say the least. She thought it was all my fault and that I was pushing Glenn to get out there to drive, but I really wasn't, he had a natural interest in cars. He asked me to help him get his driver's licence and I did. He was just a young lad, but he was ready, I thought,"[17] Glenn's father remembered.

Bert always owned large, powerful vehicles. Naturally, he tried to pass some of his passions and skills on to his only son. He also encouraged Glenn to handle a boat and provided several types of boats for him, ranging from a skiff with oars to a top-of-the-line motorboat. Glenn, who remained a bachelor all his life, continued his father's tradition by owning and driving large cars. Brands like Chevrolet Impala, Cadillac, Buick and Lincoln were among the cars Glenn owned. By enjoying the cottage built by his father and by favoring the driving of motorboats and cars, Glenn identified with these masculine aspects of his father.

Nevertheless, unlike his father, Glenn showed an early tendency to drive erratically and hazardously. From the beginning of having his driver's licence and throughout his entire life, Glenn remained a fast and careless driver. Several witnesses testified to his imprecise and daring driving habits. His oldest friend, Robert Fulford, remembered an event when Glenn gave a ride to him, his mother and sister:

"What was it like to be in the car with Glenn as a driver?" I asked.

"It wasn't fun at all. He was turning corners sharply, squealing his tires, stopping abruptly, and through all this he was speeding and talking non-stop." Bob made no excuses for Glenn.

"What did you do?" I asked.

"I simply asked him to please slow down but he didn't pay attention to that. It got to a point that I gave him an ultimatum. I said, 'Glenn, look, either you slow down or we won't drive with you.'"[18] Bob was obviously annoyed. Glenn reluctantly slowed down.

Elsie Feeney, Glenn's nanny in childhood and his housekeeper in adulthood, was often given a ride home by Glenn after her day's work at the Gould's home. She reminisced how Glenn's father used to caution him beforehand: "Watch your driving; don't you rush up that hill to cause trouble and get Elsie scared."[19]

What were the roots of Glenn's recklessness at driving? While Bert was a good, relaxed and steady driver, his wife Florie did not drive at all. In reality, she was insecure about driving in general. "She was a nervous wreck; she didn't travel very well,"[20] said Glenn's nanny, Elsie, who often accompanied the Gould family in their car trips to the cottage. In his childhood and teens, Glenn was frequently a witness of his mother's apprehension in the car. She used to watch her husband's driving and make critical remarks: "Watch out, Bert, there is an oncoming car," or "C a r e f u l! Slow down, there is a horse-buggy ahead of you," or "Bert, you are racing again."[21] Glenn's mother insisted on slow driving, kept warning her husband about speed limits, and constantly drew his attention to road conditions. Glenn, who was invariably sitting in the back seat, felt irritated by his mother's nagging, wishing for a more agreeable atmosphere in the car. This was a rare situation where he took sides with his father and rose to his defense. After all, Glenn admired his father's debonair role at the steering wheel, while at the same time he resented his mother's controlling force. Ever since a child, Glenn became so sensitized to anything that symbolized control and authority that he rebelled and defied it whenever possible. Even traffic regulations, which are necessary and protective measures for society, were perceived by Glenn as oppressive ways of thwarting him. He resorted to massive counter-defenses against those in power and became a relentless violator of traffic regulations. So, in his adult life, Gould was blessed with the joy of driving and cursed with the misery of risk-taking.

Following Gould's triumphant recital in Vancouver on July 29, 1960, *The Toronto Telegram* correspondent, George Kidd, cabled a long report, which centered not on the virtuoso and his music but on his driving practices in the following fashion:

> July 30, 1960
>
> Vancouver—Yesterday I took my life in my hands. I went riding the rugged rockies, 3,400 feet up, with pianist Glenn Gould, who already has had three Ontario traffic offenses this year.
>
> The provincial police who stopped us were very polite about the whole thing ... but they were also very firm.

> Certainly Mr. Gould, who has stunned an audience of more than 2,000 persons on the previous night, could not know that the speed limit on the main drive was 30 and not 40 miles per hour ... So there was no ticket. The unsmiling policeman just gave a gentle warning, but it was an emphatic warning in clear, unmusical terms.[22]

Kidd went on describing this uncomfortable and anxiety-producing trip in the mountains. Glenn made frequent remarks such as, "There is a terrific draft," calling for hermetically sealing the windows and the air vent. Glenn also pointed to the unsafe road conditions: "Funny thing they don't put guard rails around. People are liable to get killed." Kidd finished his over inclusive report on this note:

> We rode into Horseshoe Bay, where the mountains dipped to the edges of the water, covered with small boats.
>
> "I am as good at boats as I am with cars," said Glenn. "Perhaps tomorrow we could go for a ride in a boat."[23]

Glenn's remark to Kidd that he, Glenn, was as good a navigator of boats as of cars is quite interesting. Glenn derived great satisfaction from his perceived excellent driving ability, while Kidd shivered in fear in the car! Was Glenn making fun of himself and admitting that he had a problem around operating a motor vehicle? It appears that he was not fully conscious of his recklessness, which accounts for the fact that he could never improve his driving. The following document reveals how serious Glenn's inner conflicts over aggression were, which rendered him dangerous to himself and to others:

> November 15, 1961
> Ontario Department of Transport
> Driver Control Branch
>
> Dear Mr. Gould,
>
> The records of this Branch show that you accumulated 8 demerit points as a result of convictions for the driving violations described below:

Speeding	January 21, 1960	3 points
Wrong Way on one way street	July 28, 1960	2 points
Speeding	November 2, 1961	3 points

> This record merits your careful attention. We urge you to examine your driving practices and to give special care to the observance of safe driving standards whenever you are in charge of a motor vehicle in future.
>
> Research has shown that driving violations increase the risk of accidents. A driving offense, even a minor one, may endanger lives. By observing the traffic laws, drivers can check the needless waste of life, health and property on our streets and highways. Your cooperation will help to do this.

The points you have accumulated will remain on your record for two years from the date of each conviction. By good driving, you can restore a clear record. If violations continue you may require at 9 points to attend an interview to discuss your driving record. Suspense of your licence is automatic at 12 points.

Yours truly
W.A Groom
Chief Review Officer[24]

This firm letter did not inspire Gould in the direction of positive change. Consistent with his inner turmoil, he continued to violate traffic regulations and lose more demerit points. At the age of thirty-one Gould had to repeat his driver's exam. The record states:

October 21, 1963 Record of driver reexamination—passed
Remark— "fails to complete turn in proper lane"
"continuously drives in passing lane"[25]

Gould passed this exam, but even here he was unable to curb his own rebellion and still made two errors. A virtuoso who could produce the most precise piano acrobatics at the keyboard was imprecise and heavy-handed behind the steering wheel. While these two activities appear to be contradictory, in the psyche they made sense. Notably, Gould, despite his polite and amiable facade, harbored deep aggressive impulses for which he had few outlets—one of them being his daring driving practices.

Another interesting detail is that Gould never drank alcoholic beverages and he made all his driving errors in the state of total sobriety. As a teetotaler, he completely and consistently refrained from drinking. He never smoked and never used street drugs, which made him an atypical offender. In his mature years, Gould's driving habits never mellowed and he continued to be careless, causing a number of minor accidents. His future friend, Ray Roberts, who appeared on the scene in the last ten years of Gould's life, often helped him out from embarrassing situations after Gould bumped into moving or parked vehicles. Gould was caught in a never-ending, incorrigible rebellion against authority.

THE PLAYFUL PURITAN

He was outcast from life's feast.
James Joyce[26]

If Gould at the piano and in his social behavior revealed a serious and puritanistic demeanor, when at ease he showed a fabulous sense of humor and playfulness. The blend of the serious and comical, the stern and playful, the morose and high-spirited, made him such a distinct and colorful personality. The quality of his humor is like his music—inimitable, unpredictable, often impetuous and quickly recognized as uniquely Gouldian. There is a wide range to his humor, which spreads from the point of being comical and grotesque, to sober and thoughtful, to more sarcastic, provocative and even offensive.

The Range of Gouldian Humor

comical	absurd	witty	cynical
innocent	grotesque	thoughtful	sarcastic
clowning	ludicrous	inventive	boorish
entertaining	parody	imaginative	offensive

This other side of Glenn was not only fun-loving but also fantasy-prone and playful in words and manner. Being witty and playful was an enduring feature of Gould's communicative life skills. From his childhood, he had retained a habit of engaging in guessing games with his partners in conversation. He would start his dialogues over the telephone or in person by using "A Game of Twenty Questions." Gould would say: "In twenty questions or less, can you guess which book I am reading?" or "In twenty questions or less, can you guess which music piece I am playing?" Of course, there are endless possibilities as far as the choice of questions is concerned. Again, Gould would pursue his quiz: "Guess who called me today?" or "Can you guess what's my next TV program?" Whoever was on the other end of the telephone line had to engage in this child-like play. The person would say something like this: "O.K. Let me try. Is your TV program focusing on a composer?" "Is this a nineteenth-century composer?" "Is he a European composer?" "Is he a German-born composer?" "An Austrian-born?" By this time, Gould was cackling and rubbing his hands in glee over the mystery he created. Who would have guessed that the composer in question was Dimitri Shostakovich? How interesting and playful? For Gould, it was like playing with crayons and colorful marbles, except in his case the words were used as imaginatively as crayons and marbles.

Gould's guessing games were often combined with another type of mental exercise. He would ask his favorite "If " questions. For example, "If you were a fish what kind of fish would you be?" or "If you were playing a music instrument what sort of instrument would you play?" Once Gould got a response, such as "If I were a fish I'd be a pickerel," the next question would be, "Why? For what reason would you be a pickerel rather than a catfish?" If Gould's friend had some knowledge about the qualities of the freshwater fish, he may have responded by saying: "Because I'd prefer to have sharp teeth like a pickerel." If he didn't, Gould would then proudly declare a victory as a fish expert. Gould got quite a kick out of this quiz. He played the role of an educator and an entertainer at the same time. Altogether, the entire game was quite amusing for both Gould and his friend, and the two of them would laugh themselves silly.

For Gould, creative joking and witticisms were like using a relaxant for both mind and muscles in order to enhance the mood between two playmates. While others may use a drink or smoke cigarettes as their social booster, Gould pursued guessing games, playful rhymes and a variety of jokes. Once Gould put on an air of bluster and bravado, he would get "high" on it. His humor was unique and entertaining to his listeners, who often chuckled or burst into irrepressible laughter.

Today Gouldian jokes survive in his letters, published works and in the living memory of his friends and associates. To a friend who announced that she was to be married, Gould wrote this humorous letter.

February 18, 1957

Herbert Gould Agency
Escort Services, Marriage Counseling, Divorce Attorney

Our motto: "low fidelity and high frequency"

Dear Miss McLean:

It is with great pleasure that this office received the announcement of your imminent betrothal. We shall do all in our power to render those services—our specialty—which constitute such an invaluable aid to those contemplating the state of matrimony. Further, we shall plunge into any investigation that you might wish us to undertake with the vigor and intensity only possible to those who wish to mask their personal desolation in seeing you withdraw from circulation at so premature a time.[27]

In this letter Gould clowned around to the point of euphoria. He amused himself and probably made his friend laugh to tears. His motto, "low fidelity and high frequency," is hilarious. It means that the comedian in Gould did not mind such grim things in life as marital infidelity and divorce. In reality, he could not fathom such serious subjects and shied away from addressing them. Gould often made fun of his own name, disguising it by using colorful pseudonyms. At times he signed as Herbert von Gould, imitating the name of Herbert von Karajan. In this letter, he only used his middle name, Herbert, as he probably felt it to be Germanic and funny. Offering his "Escort Services and Marriage Counselling" is equally comical. After Gould's return from the U.S.S.R., he added to his Germanic imitations many Russian words and accent, addressing male friends as "gospodin" instead of "sir." He referred to himself as Vladimir Guldovski—Vladimir being a common Russian name but also the name of his contemporary colleague, Horowicz. At one point, he addressed his manager, Walter Homburger, as Gospodin Gomburger.

Gould was a master of quip. In criticizing Mozart, he compared him to the French composer, Camu Saint-Saens, and said: "I like Saint-Saens especially when he does not write for the piano."[28] In saying that, Gould managed to shock his interviewer and at the same time express a sarcastic attitude toward Mozart and Saint-Saens. In a similar playful way, he described one of his favorite composers, Arnold Schoenberg: "Schoenberg does not write against the piano, but neither can he be accused of writing *for* it."[29]

Once when Gould received a very small honorarium for his radio commentary for the broadcast of his String Quartet, he wrote this jocular letter to John Lee Roberts, his friend and a music producer for the CBC:

I cannot tell you, sir, how much this assignment and its colossal attendant fee means to myself, my good wife, my ill-clad children and my dog. This will be our first cheque in five months and will be such a relief to provide for them for the month of June, or possibly July should the cheque be delayed, the bare necessities of life. I am sure you, as a family man yourself, will appreciate the

> emotion now surging in my breast and I beg you to express my humblest thanks and most sincere appreciation to the CBC for their generosity.
>
> Yours sincerely,
> G. Herbert Gould
> Freelance Writer and Composer[30]

This letter is full of exaggeration and unabating humor that carries on and on till the point is clear. Of course, Gould was unmarried and he made up the story of ill-clad children to tease Roberts.

To his friend, Dr. Peter Ostwald of San Francisco, Gould wrote:

> Dear Peter—you dog:
>
> What the h--- do you mean by announcing your marriage two months after the fact. The nerve! ...
>
> Now that I have let off steam, let me say seriously how delighted I am to hear of your marriage and compliment you on having the good taste to marry a Canadian.[31]

In an ongoing correspondence with Roma, the wife of his friend Wilfred Riddell of the CBC in Windsor, Ontario, Gould went from the state of friendliness and humor to the state of annoyance. In September 1957, Gould wrote in response to the arrival of her newborn baby girl, happily discussing a selection of names for the baby. He suggested names like "Glennella," "Glennette" or "Glennovna," which in his opinion "would have begun the child on a life of emulation of a noble spirit ..." He signed: "Affectionately, G Herbert von Gould."

Less than a year later, Gould was quite dismayed by Mrs. Riddell's delay in returning the Schoenberg recording that he had loaned to her earlier. When his intervention failed to bring the record back, Gould resorted to a serious but funny way of handling his friend's procrastination. He wrote her a letter pretending that he hired an agency, "Albert Arnold Ames, Private Eye Inc.," to recover his valuable possession:

> Mrs. Wilfred Riddell June 4, 1958
>
> ... Mr. Gould is of the opinion that since you have retained this recording for fully one month, you should now have been able to saturate yourself with all the niceties of it and, indeed, that you should be able to duplicate your once rather auspicious feat of singing the whole thing through in your sleep every night for the rest of your life. While this may not be the most desirable soporific, it will certainly be one that will keep our thoughts on a relatively high level and it may in the long run be instrumental in avoiding psychological trauma and other marital disturbances.[32]

Gould was in a biting mood. He finished his letter in the form of a humorous diatribe:

> ... Furthermore, we would simply wish to add that if we do not have an immediate reply to this present note, we shall send one of our Detroit representatives to you directly who will create such fracas as to alarm all the neighbors and irritate all the tenants that you will never be welcome in your present place of residence again and Mrs. Riddell, let me remind you that not even Zippy, the Magic Carpet, can save you.[33]

Gould's piano tuner, Verne Edquist recalls that the pianist really enjoyed grass-roots humor. Edquist wrote:

> Knowing that I came from Saskatchewan, Gould asked me whether I knew some western humor. At that time, he was thinking of going west to film the life of Dukhobors. I told him that, where I came from, the farmers often have very heavy accents and speak improper English. This is how one farmer phrased his sentence: "Son, throw the cow over the fence some hay." Glenn laughed a lot. He thought it was very funny and repeated the phrase after me.[34]

Gouldian humor could be very sophisticated and, at times, difficult to follow. In 1974, in an interview with Jonathan Cott, at some point, Cott compared Barbra Streisand, whom Gould adored, to the Beatles, whom he did not like, and the Italian composer, Bellini, to Gould's favorite composer, Arnold Schoenberg. Gould protested. Cott, sensing his irritation made another mischievous comparison in order to tease Gould: "I should have compared the Beatles to Anton Webern?" Gould, who detested the Beatles and favored Webern, replied with an artillery of mixed fury and humor:

> Listen, if you have done that, I would have trotted out all my alter egos and enlisted all my exotic Doppelgangers and barraged *Rolling Stone* with a Letter-to-the-Editor campaign for the next ten years. I think I'd send my letters off to Vienna, perhaps, or to London. Sverdlovsk maybe, or for the benefit of Teddy Slotz, Brooklin Heights. I'd get them postmarked accordingly, and they'd all contain the same message: "This idiot Cott has done it again."[35]

Impersonations were another aspect of Gould's humorous and imaginative disposition. His father recalled: "Ever since he was a child, when alone with his mother, Glenn liked to clown around and imitate the Scottish accent and manners of people. He'd pretend that he was a radio reporter and he'd grab something, a can or a bottle, and he'd speak into it as if it were a microphone.[36] Obviously, the idea was to attract the attention of his mother, but the initiative came from his natural ability to notice every detail in the behavior of others and from his irresistible need to play out whatever he perceived. Like the proverbial Professor Higgins, Glenn was a little linguist capable of spotting the subtlest nuances in speech of those around him. Combined with this auditory gift was his ability to see the funny side of things and people. While imitating the Scottish accent he rolled his R's and teased his mother, who was of Scottish descent. By watching black and white war movies, and more after the arrival of Walter Homburger in his life, Glenn became fascinated with the German accent, and he used it from then on for his funny skits.

Glenn the child and Glenn the adult played with words as if they were toys. He was a jolly and harmless joker, but in more tense social situations Glenn used humor to ridicule and parody his opponents in order to relieve personal hurt and anger. Gould's talent for drama and acting was innate, and together with his gift of speech and intonation, they accounted for his very interesting demeanor.

As an adult, Gould went one step further by not only imitating a variety of accents but by inventing and impersonating fictional characters. This helped him to express his own negative thoughts and feelings, for which he did not have other outlets. Gould called these newly created characters Doppelgangers or his alter egos. He became the creative father of several such imaginary characters, but two of them deserve particular attention: the stuffy and pretentious conductor, Herbert von Hochmeister, and the hippie character, Theodore Slotz. Glenn used to simply lapse into one or the other character, or he would recall them on the radio amid the conversations with his friends and in his writings. Gould eloquently described the birth of Herbert von Hochmeister in this way:

> I, for instance, was incapable of writing in sustained humorous style until I developed an ability to portray myself pseudonymously. I started this in the mid-sixties. I wrote a few articles for *High Fidelity* in which I turned up a critic named Herbert von Hochmeister who lived in the Northwest Territories. The reason for that metaphor was that Herbert could thereby survey the culture of North America from his exalted remove, and pontificate accordingly. The character was also vaguely based on Karajan; von Hochmeister was a retired conductor and was always spouting off about Germanic culture and things of that nature. At least, that's how I got into the character. Once having got into it, I had to make him sufficiently aware of them and more recent innovations so that he could speak of them with some authority. But in any event, once I did that, I found it no problem at all to say what I wanted to say in a humorous style. Until then, there was a degree of inhibition that prevented me from doing so. But then the floodgates were open, and subsequently I developed a character for every season.[37]

In the 1960s, Gould was the witness to the roaring changes in Western society. The postwar, restrained, parochial culture underwent a massive face lift. Under the backdrop of propulsive technology, the new face of society shunned its inhibitions and became more animated. One byproduct of the societal changes was the hippie movement among youth and young adults. Its proponents were out to dismantle societal conformism and particularly to tear down what they perceived as an outmoded social system of moral values. The hippies had no regard for prim and proper demeanor and clean aesthetic looks. They refused to speak properly, infiltrated the language with a wave of new colloquialisms, and had disregard for proper grammar. Men and women grew long hair and refused to work hard, but hung around in groups and played music instead. The quest for pacifism, free love and sex became their new motto. This epidemic rebellion of Western society seemed to border on social anarchy. The young of the previously regimented and subdued world became interested in using mind-altering stimulants to defy personal and societal inhibitions built up over nineteen centuries of Christianity. At the same time, the rock 'n' roll pandemic spread in North America and Europe. Soon, the rock 'n' roll culture became a synonym for the hippie generation. The proponents of rock 'n' roll music—Elvis Presley, Jerry Lee Lewis, Chuck Berry, Little Richard and others—literally shocked and shook the world with their electrifying new music. At the same time when Gould rose to stardom in the mid-fifties, his two-year-younger counterpart Elvis Presley, evolved into a superstar of popular music. As gifted artists, each of them became a music phenomenon of their times. As individuals, they embodied a one-man uprising against oppression and succeeded as rebels in challenging and defying old standards in classical and popular music, respectively.

Though Gould openly denied any interest in rock 'n' roll and never joined the hippies, he invented a fictional hippie character, Theodore Slotz. The man who never wore jeans or fancy leather clothes suddenly wore a black leather jacket when playing Teddy Slotz. When in this role, his pure, slang-free English language would suddenly transform into a street vernacular that lacked proper grammar and was filled with double negatives and colloquial expressions. Gould explained that a New York City taxi driver who once gave him a ride from the Columbia studio to his hotel served as a model for this fictional character. In this imaginary dialogue, Gould reenacted the taxi driver in the character of Teddy Slotz:

> "Sir, who do you think is going to do pretty good in the election, Mac?" And I said, "Well, I don't know, I guess the Governor's got a pretty good chance"—Rockefeller was running for re-election—and he looked at me (he had initiated the subject) and said, "Yah don' expect me to talk politics wit yah, do yah, Mac? I mean, like, there're two things I don't never talk about in this cab, one's politics and other's religion, know what I mean? I never talk about that, man. No offense to you personally, man. I don't know if you're a Democrat or a Republican" Well, I'm Canadian, so I'm not really either of those things."[38]

Teddy Slotz may be an unpolished and flippant character, but he is also witty, endearing and surely capable of making others laugh. By persisting to wear worn-out clothes and shoes, by neglecting personal order and cleanliness and by having a passion for Teddy Slotz, Gould seemed like a hippie. Glenn longed for the uncensored, and the impersonation of Teddy was the epitome of the type of social freedom that he sought. Though the weightiness of his puritanistic upbringing never allowed him to fully bloom into a hippie, his comedy and imagination brought him closer to it. This was his way of testing, amusing and exploring his self and the world. Gould's lifelong question, "Who am I when I am neither my father nor my mother?" came to the fore in this very decade when he relinquished his concert career and made other choices. His answer was: "I am for once my own person."

Puritanism is the exact opposite to the lifestyle of hippies. Puritans start from the premise that everybody is guilty of original sin. It follows that one has to work hard and behave in certain prescribed ways to expiate the ever-present guilt. The Puritans lived under the credo of hard work, moral purity, prohibition of pleasure and emphasis on religious pursuits. Glenn was brought up in the Presbyterian spirit, which was influenced by puritanism. Though in the course of his life Gould repeatedly tried to defy some aspects of his moral legacy, he still predominantly was a puritan. All his playfulness, humor, his Doppelgangers and the love of theater were but a temporary relief from his fundamental austerity.

At the same time, when Gould joked around with his friends and impersonated Herbert von Hochmeister and Teddy Slotz, the rest of his behavior indicated deep seriousness. This was best reflected in his writing. In 1966 he published a tribute essay to the man he vastly admired, Jehudi Menuhin. In this work, Gould used his paternal grandmother as a reference point, alluding to her musicianship and austerity. On the whole, the essay ends up being a tribute to the Alma Gold—Jehudi Menuhin duo of Gould's admired puritan elders. This double tribute is written with brilliant originality of ideas interspersed with sophisticated humor. Gould says about Menuhin: "Puritans approved his endless capacity for work, his clearly focused sense of mission." It is as if this sentence is an autobiographical summary in which he says that his grandmother and his elders, in the broader sense, approve of hard work and that he, Gould, also subscribes to this puritan ethos. The essay is illustrative of both Gould's dour, over-intellectual side and the freshness of his humor:

> His is a household name to Americans ("So help me, Theodore, get back to your practicing or you'll never be a Mischa Menuhin!") In the United Kingdom, he is the protean patron saint of self-effacing soloists and interchangeable chamber players ("I say, Cecilia, my dear, I see by the *Times* that Mr. Menuhin is sitting in with Amadeus this evening. Does seem a bit odd; string quintets at the Royal Albert?"). He has been rescued by wandering tribesman in the Sahara who, having helped to dislodge his auto from drifts which had blown free since last they felt the tread of Romel's Afrika Korps, suddenly exploded with incredulity "C'est Menuhin, c'est lui!" And if, as I hope, and as I have urged him to, he someday visits the outpost communities of Arctic Canada, I have no doubt that he will return with a trunkful of ethnographic tabulations, the sketch for an improved system of Eskimo shorthand, and the manuscript of a lecture detailing the nutritional deficiencies of the barren-ground caribou.[39]

Notice the length of the last sentence, with some fifty-nine words. This was a Gouldian trait to produce lengthy and over involved sentences that simultaneously express mixed feelings of love and hate toward the subject. It developed into a cognitive problem, which because of its importance will be addressed in more detail later.

At the same time when Gould was one of the top-ranking piano virtuosi in the world, Jasha Heifetz and Jehudi Menuhin were the greatest living violinists. Gould regarded Menuhin with idolatry. Earlier during his concert-giving days, he tried to persuade Menuhin, when they met in New York, to record something together. Menuhin on principle agreed but could not make a specific commitment because of his extremely busy schedule. This left Gould to fantasize about their possible future collaboration. Menuhin, born in the United States, but residing in England, was knighted for his music and humanitarian activities in 1966 by Queen Elizabeth II for his fiftieth birthday. This very period from 1966 to 1967 was a pinnacle of personal and creative relationship between Gould and Menuhin. At Gould's persistent instigation, the two great musicians got together in Toronto and produced a TV show in which they played works of Bach, Beethoven and Schoenberg and discussed each of them. The show was aired on May 18, 1966. Though this endeavor stood out in the public eye and in the press, the interpersonal tension between the two artists was less obvious. Under the veneer of politeness and cooperation, there was an air of competitiveness and intellectual coolness. Both individuals were headstrong and not used to being told what to do. Gould insisted on putting a work of Schoenberg on the program, knowing full well that Menuhin had no particular interest in this composer. Challenged by Gould, Menuhin agreed but came to Toronto for taping unprepared. He virtually had no pre-knowledge and never rehearsed the Schoenberg piece, which left him with only one day to learn it from scratch. In the end, in Gould's words, "Jehudi had absorbed that extraordinary piece overnight and played it with absolutely reckless virtuosity." Having held Menuhin in high esteem and considering him a paragon of virtue, this episode finished on a positive interpersonal note.

Gould's initial adulation of Menuhin was augmented by his amiable rapport with Lady Diana Menuhin, whom he met in person and with whom he corresponded. In his tribute essay to Menuhin, in describing Jehudi's life as "incessant travel," Gould added: "Depressingly uniform hotel suites became less austerely antiseptic on those occasions when his wife, the incomparably irrepressible Diana, accompanies him ..." Gould wrote it from his own heart and personal experience of antiseptic loneliness. The feeling was mutual, and Diana Menuhin responded eagerly by writing a twelve-page letter to Gould. In his letter of April 25, 1966, Gould referred to Sir Yehudi's fiftieth birthday celebration and benefit performance in his honor:

> One more thing dear Lady Diane: I have chosen not to comment directly upon Sir Yehudi's elevation to the Knighthood because frankly, my nose is out of joint ...
>
> With much love to you both.
>
> Sincerely,
> G. Herbert Gould
> Treasurer and Principal Beneficiary
> Knightly Musicians' Benevolent Fund[40]

Gould's respect for Menuhin, enveloped in good-spirited humor, was dappled with the sense of personal loss and child-like envy, for he was never equivalently honored in Canada. In the ensuing years, Gould distanced himself from Menuhin, as he did with Leonard Bernstein, Lucas Foss, Peter Ostwald, Eugene Ormandy, Winston Fitzgerald and some other of his former friends.

Chapter XIII

THE TALES OF STRATFORD

The audience listened with their nerve-ends, and what they heard was a performance of which no other living keyboard artist ... is capable.

Eric McLean[1]

From 1953 to 1963, almost each summer, Gould participated in music performances at the Stratford Festival in Stratford, Ontario. During most of this time, he was also engaged as one of the music directors at the Stratford Festival. His work as an administrator and organizer, as well as his prolific performing career at Stratford, have not been much explored in the literature. This is a story of a productive decade in Gould's life on the extraordinary Stratford scene.

The Stratford Festival became a household name in Canada. Its founder, Tom Patterson, a strong-willed visionary, conceived of the idea to establish an annual festival in Stratford, Ontario, akin to the one in Shakespeare's birth town Stratford-on-Avon in England. Supported by Stratfordites, Patterson's seemingly outlandish and far-fetched idea was nursed into reality. Against all imaginable odds, like extravagant costs and bleak predictions, the Stratford Festival successfully opened in July 1953.

In the pre-festival era, Stratford was a small half-farming and half-industrial town with a population of about 18,000. It is situated on the Avon River within a hundred miles west-southwest of Toronto. The story goes that Stratford originated from the Shakespeare Inn built in 1832 and the little community that grew around it. In time, this settlement of pioneers expanded into a town, which from the beginning adopted the practice of giving Shakespearean names to the streets, schools and other structures. In 1864, the town celebrated Shakespeare's 300th birthday with a huge "Commemorative Festival."[2] Soon after, in 1885, on achieving city status, Stratford dubbed itself the "Classic City."[3] Gradually, Stratford evolved into an attractive town featuring elegant parks with majestic swans populating the Avon River. There is some resemblance between Stratford, Ontario, and its predecessor model city, Stratford-on-Avon in Warwickshire, England.

Stratford-on-Avon is famous as the birthplace of William Shakespeare. This is where the poet was baptized, grew up, went to grammar school, which is still preserved, and was buried together with his wife in the old Church of the Holy Trinity. This quaint town is full of historical sites. The half-timbered Tudor-style homes, the parks with their elegant weeping willows, and the Avon River with its busy water traffic full of all kinds of boats are but some of the main features of Stratford-on-Avon. The first Shakespeare Memorial Theatre, which was built in Stratford-on-Avon in the nineteenth century, was destroyed by fire in 1926. It was rebuilt by public subscription and reopened in 1932. Since then, it stands as a permanent memorial and cultural-historical attraction where visitors from all over the world gather to honor the great bard.

Tom Patterson was inspired by the stories about Stratford-on-Avon and by the historical background of his own hometown, Stratford, Ontario. Born and raised in Stratford, Patterson was an independent-minded person. He was a maverick, an indefatigable optimist guided by intuition and fantastic dreams. Fortunately, unlike some other wild dreams that cannot be translated into reality, Patterson's grand dreams had substance. They were contagious enough to have engaged a fair number of great individuals, and even masses of citizens, until it turned into a worthwhile reality. Patterson proposed his festival project to the city leaders, who, after many fierce meetings and deliberations, endorsed it. An executive festival committee was formed with Harry Showalter as president. "For Showalter as for Patterson and many others, a unique world-class Shakespearean festival in Stratford was a once-in-a-lifetime opportunity, worth any amount of fuss and worry and hard work. It was exciting. It was exhilarating. It was, in fact, intoxicating."[4] The people of Stratford embraced Patterson's brain child with cheers and faithfully supported the project through their untiring volunteer work.

Many civic-minded Torontonians also contributed to this worthy cause by offering ideas and monetary support. Vera Dobson Gould recalled that she attended a dinner in the early 1950s at Hart House in Toronto, where Tom Patterson delivered an enthusiastic speech soliciting support for the festival. "Patterson completely sold us on the idea,"[5] said Dobson.

One of many hallmark events was the engagement of Tyrone Guthrie, the renowned British director, as a professional consultant. Guthrie was in Canada in 1931 when he was hired by the Canadian National Railway (CNR) to produce the radio series *The Romance of Canada*. As a reward for this work, Guthrie received a free ride across Canada by train from the CNR. During this project, Guthrie met Edward A. Corbett, an eminent Canadian educator from Edmonton, Alberta, and a member of the Canadian Radio League. More than twenty years later, in 1952, Tyrone Guthrie was back in Canada. Remembering his old friend, Ned Corbett, who by that time had relocated to Toronto and had become director of the Canadian Association for Adult Education, Guthrie telephoned him, and the following historical conversation between the two men took place:

Corbett: "Well, what brings you to Toronto, Tony?"

Guthrie: " I've been asked by some people in Stratford to put on two Shakespeare plays next summer, and we must put up a theatre of some sort, so I'm here, looking about for an architect."

Corbett: "Well, well, now that's a coincidence, because I have a son-in-law who is an architect."

Guthrie: "Jolly good, perhaps I could meet him while I'm here."[6]

This is how the gifted, Toronto-based architect, Robert Fairfield, was discovered and entrusted by Guthrie with this responsible project—to design the future Festival Theatre in Stratford, Ontario. Under Guthrie's guidance, through many hours of intensive creative thinking and innovating, Fairfield concocted an architectural plan of a theatre for which he had no prototype. Considering the shortage of funds, Fairfield and Guthrie came up with a congenial temporary solution to build only an auditorium bowl covered by a canvas tent, which would save money and fit into their modest budget of $150,000. The famous thrust stage was built with tunnels allowing the actors to appear on and disappear from the stage. A rust-colored canvas tent purchased in Chicago from a famous tent-master, Skip Manley, was erected over the amphitheater. Several months before the box office opened, the requests for reservations poured in from all over Canada, the United States and Europe, from as far away as Miami, Florida, Hollywood, California, and the British Isles. The prominent British actor Alec Guinness accepted the leading role in Shakespeare's Richard III.

"It's hard to believe that Guinness even considered coming to Stratford, Ontario," I said, inviting Irene Bird, a native of Stratford and a friend of Gould's, to comment.

"It all had to do with Guthrie. Once he agreed, and he was such a famous director, others just followed him,"[7] Mrs. Bird explained. Hence, the great Alec Guinness, intrigued by the newly opened Stratford Festival in Canada, chose to participate in it over and above his potentially greater engagements in this historical Coronation Year in England. It has been noted that the British press was rather mystified if not miffed by Guinness's decision. In response to their criticism, Guinness commented:

> I do not consider accepting an invitation to go to Canada to play in a theatre in the round, not yet built, in a town with a population of only 18,000, with a program quite impossible to present commercially in the West End, to be entirely unadventurous. The possibilities for disaster are quite formidable.[8]

One can imagine the high anxiety of all those involved, both the anonymous activists and, in particular, the internationally famous artists and Stratford pioneers—Tyrone Guthrie and Alec Guinness. Another famous believer in this exceptional project who contributed to its grandeur and success was British designer Tanya Moiseiwitsch. She developed the festival stage. According to *The New York Times*, her original design, when the theatre was under the tent, was described in this way:

> Miss Moiseiwitsch ... did design a five-sided apron stage that jutted out into the audience, a stage with a few simple columns, a trap and a balcony.[9]

The opening night, July 13, 1953, was a true climax of the collective efforts of energetic fundraisers, as well as the dedication of the art community and wider public. The celebratory mood took over and the entire town was in a state of jubilation. The lavish festivities organized around the opening of the festival had never been seen before in this corner of Ontario. The Shakespearean flag, as a symbol of the good wishes of the Shakespeare Memorial Theatre in Stratford, England, toward the success of the festival in Stratford, Ontario, was presented by Dr. Tyrone Guthrie to the president of the Festival Foundation, Dr. H. Showalter. A fanfare for trumpets, composed by the Canadian composer Louis Applebaum, commemorated the event. The sense of extraordinary pride and dignity ran through those present at the opening. The throbbing sound of cannons followed, a gigantic brass bell rang out and the Stratford Shakespearean Festival was officially proclaimed open.

Glenn Gould played an active part in this festival milieu both as a viewer and participant. Being artistically-minded and an avid admirer of Shakespearian literature, Gould passionately followed through the media the planning and inception of the Stratford Festival. Specifically, the festival offered a wealth of music events, in addition to its theatre activities, which interested him even more. From the very beginning of the Stratford Festival, Glenn was the star in its music section.

Personally, Glenn was absolutely delighted to be in Stratford during the opening season. He hung around for days, watched the plays and developed a real fascination for Shakespearean theatre. The man who ordinarily avoided crowds did not mind them in Stratford. He socialized, made friends and even enjoyed performing on the thrust stage. On July 31, 1953, he made his Stratford debut in a performance of Beethoven's Trio op. 70 and Brahms's op. 101, with Albert Pratz playing violin and Isaac Mamott playing cello. This was his first experience performing under the tent before the audience in the circular play theatre. Glenn very much enjoyed that set up because it was less formal than in the conventional city music halls where he had played thus far. Vera Dobson Gould remembered:

"In the summer of 1953, there were many thunderstorms and rainy days which jeopardized the integrity of the tent and even caused some leakage. During one such day, while I was in the audience with Murray, there was a terrific electrical storm which almost burned down the tent."

"How do you think Glenn experienced this situation himself?" I asked.

"I don't know because I never asked him but I know that he was there. My husband, Murray Dobson, was a distant cousin of Bert [Gould] and we always followed Glenn's career. Now, if you want me to guess how Glenn had felt, I think he was ecstatic about the festival," Vera answered.

"How do you think Glenn felt about the rain?" I asked.

"Oh, about the rain, I think he was amused rather than aggravated by it. He always preferred rainy weather,"[10] said Vera Dobson Gould.

On a rainy August 4, 1953, Glenn Gould drew substantial attention to himself during his first solo Stratford recital. He presented a selection of his best interpretative music pieces: Bach's Sinfonias and Partita no. 5, Beethoven's Sonata in E Major, op. 109 and the Berg Sonata. This young pianist displayed his music maturity along with his very youthful persona, which captivated the audience. The feeling was mutual and Glenn, despite this potentially claustrophobic artist-audience closeness, was able to enjoy these relaxed and appreciative spectators. This initial positive chemistry determined Glenn's future fondness for the festival and his growing role there.

"Were you present at Glenn's recital?" Again I asked Mrs. Vera Dobson Gould to share her valuable memories.

"Oh, yes, of course. We were his fans. Besides, he was Murray's relative. But we were not musicians. I only remember that Glenn was so famous at that age that audiences loved him and we clapped so hard after each piece he had played,"[11] Mrs. Gould answered enthusiastically.

Overall, the first Stratford Festival was a stunning success. Gradually, the festival facilities improved, and in 1957 the tent was replaced with a permanent festival theatre that was also designed by the founding architect, Robert Fairfield. Looking from the outside, the permanent festival building resembles a gigantic carousel. "The Fairfield roof" is of exceptional architectural beauty. This fluted roof with its zigzag edges and sloping panels gathering at the top, rises to an impressive apex that is adorned with a coronet and pennant mast. Together with festival flag, the entire building with its umbrella-like roof looks quite spectacular. It is one of a kind. Surrounded by serene parks with weeping willows, this man-made festival setting in Stratford, Ontario, somewhat resembles Stratford-on-Avon in England.

Something is to be said about Fairfield's dedication to building the Stratford Festival Theatre. His wages were so negligible that he was unable to hire a secretary or a drafting assistant for this job. Instead, Fairfield had to do every detail by himself, from the most menial groundwork to the finest tasks. Tom Patterson, Tyrone Guthrie, Robert Fairfield and Tanya Moiseiwitsch could be rightfully dubbed "the founding quartet" of the Stratford Festival Theatre. Moiseiwitsch designed both the original and the permanent stage. This is what *The New York Times* reported about the new stage of the Stratford Festival Theatre:

> Miss Moiseiwitsch's stage has undergone a few alterations. Because of the building height she has been able to add two windows leading out to two balconies, and the orchestra "pit" has been raised to an upper floor ...
>
> ... But this [stage] isn't the only playing area in the design of the theatre. Seven aisles through the auditorium as well as two tunnels that rise out of the auditorium bowl are used to heighten effects as players can surge to or retreat from the stage as required, thereby again helping to make the audience part of the play's events.
>
> Altogether, it is a masterpiece of design. Shakespeare probably never had it so good.[12]

Eventually, the Stratford Festival innovators and builders were adequately recognized for their lifetime accomplishments. The founding architect, Robert Fairfield was awarded a Massey Gold Medal for his exceptional architectural achievement in designing the Stratford Festival Theatre. In 1961 Tyrone Guthrie was knighted by Queen Elizabeth II for his supreme artistic achievement as an art director, as well as an artistic founder of the Stratford Festival Theatre. Guthrie earned the reputation of the greatest director of his time in English-language theatre. In 1967 Tom Patterson, as a founder of the Stratford Festival, was made an Officer of the Order of Canada.

As for Glenn Gould, he became a central music figure at the festival over the next decade. Gould was thrilled by the wealth of artistic events and the presence of famous individuals at the festival. He also liked the abundance of chamber music and the fact that the musicians were at more liberty to choose what they wanted to play. Gould particularly enjoyed audiences in Stratford, who seemed to him more relaxed and unassuming than their counterparts in major cities. Often, before the matinee performance, the concertgoing public made an excursion to the parks to watch the swans and ducks idling around or to even have a picnic-style lunch on the grass. Because of the pleasant and welcoming atmosphere, Gould kept coming back to Stratford.

In total, Gould participated in seven Stratford Festivals, and scores of North American audiences had the opportunity to see him in a different light than in concert halls. Gould, supported by the management, deliberately created a specific approach to the music part of the festival. Though there was some music by Bach and Brahms played, the focus was on playing the contemporary music of twentieth-century composers.

Following his Stratford debut in its first season, Gould next appeared at the festival in the summer of 1955, after he had been internationally acclaimed in New York. On this occasion, he played what was to become his opus magnum—Bach's *Goldberg Variations*. This was an extraordinary performance, almost too grand for his undemanding audience. It generated enormous positive aftereffects—the spread of his fame and instant loyal fans. From then on, Gould affirmed for himself the special status as one of the festival's most interesting performers.

In 1956, Gould gave a recital at Stratford with this esoteric choice of music:

Sweelinck	Fantasia for Organ
Krenek	Sonata no. 3
Gould	String Quartet
Schoenberg	Ode to Napoleon Bonaparte (Gould conducting)
Berg	Sonata for Piano

Gould's fervent admirer and friend, Jim Curtis, described his authentic experience:

> He [Gould] strolled onto the [Stratford] stage in his usual unconcerned manner, dressed very plainly in a nondescript outfit. This time he wasted no time before beginning and was into the Sweelinck Fantasia as soon as he sat down. It was a marvel of clarity and intensity. He made a few program emendations before continuing with the Krenek sonata (No. 3). He turned this into a deeply moving experience, despite its complexity and unfriendliness of structure ...[13]

At this concert, Gould presented himself as a multi-talented artist. He was a solo concert pianist; his own composition was premiered; and he conducted the work of Schoenberg. This was a triumph of a special kind—to join his favorite, handpicked composers as a composer himself.

Just as Gould was allowed by Columbia Masterworks to write liner notes for his own records, here at the Stratford Festival he was encouraged to prepare the program notes. Among his elaborate notes for this concert, where he introduced his own composition, Gould wrote:

> It may strike one as odd that a work of such *fin de siecle* romantic breadth as Gould's String Quartet should find its way into an evening of such esoteric fare as Schoenberg and Krenek.[14]

As always, Gould's language is a bit haughty. What is fin de siecle? How many average music listeners know this French phrase? Were the average audiences familiar with the names of Schoenberg and Krenek? Perhaps Gould's intention was to educate the audiences and share with them some history of music. After all, music critics always use a lot of technical language. Or maybe Gould was just using his own style regardless of the preferences and music sophistication of his respectful fans. If so, one cannot exactly say that Gould showed enough sensitivity toward them.

In 1956, Gould was given the post of music director of the Stratford Music Festival, which was a position shared with the distinguished American artists Oskar Shumsky, violin, and Leonard Rose, cello. This triumvirate worked marvelously together. Being the creative organizer, Gould exercised great influence on the festival's music program selection. He included the songs of Richard Strauss, the works of Hindemith and other contemporary composers in the program. He introduced a number of Bach's works, featured numerous chamber music pieces and even presented the rarely played Russian music of Michail Glinka and Sergei Prokofiev.

Many years after, Mr. Rose reminisced in the interview with Daniel Kunzi:

Kunzi: Can you describe your collaboration with Glenn Gould?

Rose: Glenn, of course, was a genius. There is no question of that. He was also a little bit "wacky." He was a real character. Although he always played at the [Stratford] Festival during the summertime, one didn't dare to open the window, even in the hottest weather imaginable. Glenn Gould had a dreadful fear of catching colds. Playing music with him, recording music with him was a sheer joy![15]

In this modestly paid administrative position as music director at the festival, Gould played the multiple roles of program maker, writer, performer and stage director. On top of that, he had the benefit of practicing public relations. It was in this capacity that he hired guest musicians, enlarged professional correspondence and acquired many friends and associates. Here is a sample of correspondence with the renowned British composer and pianist Benjamin Britten:

> Dear Mr. Britten, November 30, 1962
>
> I am writing to you on behalf of the Stratford (Ontario) Music Festival, of which I am now co-director. We hope that we can persuade you in the near future to reserve your association with us, since we remember with greatest pleasure your visit of 1956.[16]

Gould's friendships with Victor DiBello, a Toronto-based conductor, Lucas Foss, an American composer and conductor, and many others were enhanced by their collaborative work at Stratford. DiBello remembered: "Leonard Rose was a fine musician but a quiet man, he kept to himself. So it was left up to Glenn and Oscar to manage everything."[17]

The period from 1961 to 1963 was the busiest for Gould as a participant in the Stratford Music Festival. In his fruitful 1961 Stratford season, Gould appeared in three interesting concerts:

July 16	Brahms Cello Sonata no. 1 Violin Sonata no. 1; Trio no. 3 Oscar Shumsky, violin Leonard Rose, cello
July 23	Strauss songs Violin Sonata, op. 18 Capriccio (arr. Gould) Ellen Faull, Victor Braun, Oscar Shumsky
August 13	Bach Concerto in D Minor Sonata no. 3 for gamba and harpsichord Leonard Rose, cello National Festival Orchestra

At Stratford, Gould was given liberty to do some stage directing. As always, his creative mind conceived many novel ideas that at times were quite extravagant and baffling. One could never predict whether the critical audience would embrace or reject them. The event of July 8, 1962, was a case in point. On that day, before his brilliant interpretation of Bach's *Art of the Fugue*, Gould asked the audience to refrain from applauding. Eric McLean of *The Montreal Star* reported avidly:

> Glenn Gould told the audience in the Stratford Festival Theatre that he had a favour to ask of them. He admitted that his request was an unusual one, and that it was the sort of thing associated with memorial services for royalty, not with an ordinary concert. At the end of the seven fugues he would play the chorale which Bach composed on his death bed, after which the audience was asked not to applaud.[18]

To his satisfaction, this unusual and daring request was met with acceptance by most of the viewers. One of Gould's avid fans, Deanne Bogdan, was in the audience:

"Do you remember what happened on that occasion?" I asked her at the Glenn Gould Gathering that took place in September 1999.

"Yes, I do. Glenn was being almost priestly when he asked us to refrain from applauding. He was very serious about it," she recalled.

"What was it like to sit there and not be able to applaud?" I asked.

"The public has great difficulty with silence. They need to express their feelings and they would have liked to honor Bach's music. But not just that. They applaud in order to defend against their own loneliness and isolation. Applause is a form of joining together,"[19] Deanne reflected.

Another loyal and passionate fan was Jim Curtis, a harpsichordist from Fenwick, Ontario, who traveled with his wife, Audrey, to most of Gould's Ontario performances and even to some in the United States. Curtis described the actual concert with enthusiasm:

> ... The concert (Stratford) was a triumph, both in conception and execution, since it scaled the Olympus of the Bach oeuvre: the *Musical Offering*, scored beautifully for English horn, bassoon, viola, cello, violin, flute, and Glenn's "harpsichord-piano;" the "Chaconne" violin partita, which Shumsky performed with consummate mastery despite the handicap of constantly flickering lights due to a flash storm; and the *Art of Fugue*, from which Glenn chose seven fugues, in a performance which confirmed once more his supremacy among Bach players. He requested that we refrain from applause, on the grounds that it is "an easily induced mob reaction, indicating nothing but momentary hysteria." Everyone complied ...[20]

If the banishment of applause was bewildering, Gould's music was not. Eric McLean was astounded by the excellence of Gould's performance. He paid him a tribute in this landmark review:

> The effect was electric ... It was an attention-getting trick, but one which cannot be altogether condemned since it attracted as much attention to Bach as it did to Mr. Gould. The audience listened with their nerve-ends, and what they heard was a performance of which no other living keyboard artist, to my knowledge, is capable.

> The complex tangle of voices unraveled under his fingers, each line of the writing standing out clearly and in proper relation to the rest. It was a masterly demonstration of those things which have managed to sustain the high reputation of Glenn Gould despite his eccentricities and despite such irritating stage habits as stomping his foot for the tempo, or CONDUCTING the music, whether he happens to be playing it or someone else.
>
> Although there were other fine things in this concert, they seem rather pale now in comparison with Mr. Gould's musical wizardry.[21]

Gould's music was flawless, whereas his habit of "stomping his foot for the tempo" was inappropriate and distracting. Jazz pianists and pop musicians tend to stomp their feet during performances, but in classical pianism the same behavior is taboo. American pianist-entertainer Liberace stomped his fancy leather boots to the tempo of classical music. But Liberace was a Las Vegas-type piano performer whose affectation was in the service of showmanship. Meanwhile, it was incongruous for Gould to be stomping his foot while playing Bach's music. One explanation for this behavior would be that Gould was driven by his deep-seated need to show off. Under his puritan exterior, he harbored an entirely different character, one that he tried to conceal—an outgoing, even flamboyant one. Another explanation would be that his foot stomping was a physical extension of the pleasure he took in rhythm. This type of body language helped him compensate for the lack of physical expression through dance and exercises. The stage in Stratford, better than any other, provided an outlet for those repressed qualities of his expansive personality.

The year 1962 represented a zenith in Gould's performing career at the Stratford Festival. He appeared in four concerts: opening with his beloved Bach and then continuing with the performance of another, newer contrapuntal composer, Paul Hindemith. On July 29, Gould appeared at the piano, accompanying Canadian soprano Lois Marshall in an interpretation of *Das Marienleben.* This epic song cycle was composed by Hindemith to poems by Reiner Maria Rilke. The composition is extremely long and requires endurance of both the performing artists and the audience, which is why it is so infrequently performed. *Das Marienleben* is not exactly a cantabile melody listened to with ease or with an urge for foot-tapping. Yet the audience broke like thunder into a prolonged applause at the end of the performance. Marshall and Gould clearly were the dominant stars of the music festival. They accomplished what was virtually unaccomplishable. To attract such overwhelming adulation after performing Schubert's *Ave Maria* is expectable. The majestic but ultra serious *Das Marienleben*, interpreted before the informal and picnic-loving Stratford audience, mostly succeeded because of the incomparable performers. The press also was more than pleased. Jacob Siskind, the Montreal-based critic who on the whole was unsympathetic to Gould's platform behavior, disregarded it completely in this case. Siskind was quite touched by the performing duo and summed it up in this sentence:

> It would be hard to imagine more persuasive interpreters than Glenn Gould and Lois Marshall for whom this was obviously a labour of love.[22]

In the latter part of the concert, Siskind was obviously mesmerized by Gould's solo performance of the Hindemith Sonata. He wrote:

> The afternoon closed with a staggering performance by Gould of the Third Piano Sonata. If I have any quarrel with the interpretation, it is that accelerando in the third movement did not seem to be wholly convincing. But this was in every other respect a remarkable piece of piano playing and music making. Gould's ability to unravel the strands of the most-involved contrapuntal writing was never more taxed, nor more fully exploited, and the limited emotional involvement of the music kept his expressive tendencies under control.
>
> This was a rare piece of music making, one I should be glad to travel another 500 miles to hear again.[23]

For Gould, this was not only a time of harvesting music compliments, it was a summer of his personal content. The man who usually avoided intense social scenes and was mildly depressed at best, seemed to have perked up at Stratford. This environment was somehow different, invigorating and nonthreatening to him. He spent a fair amount of social time with his old music associate from the east side of Toronto, Victor DiBello, who conducted the National Festival Orchestra in Stratford. DiBello was a music coordinator, so he and Gould were doubly connected, as program participants, organizers and as personal friends. DiBello reminisced that in the 1960s "it was in vogue to use the word coordinate." Meanwhile, he loathed the role. Glenn knew it and teased him on purpose: "Vic, why don't you coordinate ... this or that." And I would say: "Glenn, I am sick and tired of coordinating." Subsequently, DiBello's title was changed to his satisfaction into "music administrator."[24] As Gould was ready to step down from his directorial role, he encouraged Victor to be his successor. Indeed, DiBello maintained his role as music administrator at Stratford until 1969.

At the same time, while Gould was Stratford's music star, Christopher Plummer was its super star of the theatre. He appeared in the lead roles in Shakespeare's *Macbeth* and *The Tempest* and in Edmond Rostan's *Cyrano de Bergerac*. Though it was against his principles to sit in the audience, Gould made an exception and watched the famous actor doing Shakespeare's great soliloquies, which he himself often knew by heart. Gould was seemingly happy. Everything went smoothly that summer, his social life, his artistic conquest and even the press reviews; until his last and disastrous concert on August 8, 1962. This is when things started to deteriorate to a point of no return. Having organized and participated in three successful concerts of classical music—presenting Bach's *Art of the Fugue*, then works of Hindemith and Mendelssohn's beautiful chamber music—Gould was impelled to fill his fourth and last concert with something very different. He put on the program works of Igor Stravinsky and combined them with some humorous acting and narrating. Knowing Gould's long-standing dislike of Stravinsky's piano music, one may question his motives for putting it in his repertoire. It appears that Gould's choice was not determined by his admiration of Stravinsky's music. He parodied it out of personal disdain.

The concert was titled "Panorama of Music of the Twenties." In the first part, Canadian pianist Marek Jablonski and violinist Lea Foli, dressed in flannels and straw hats, performed "Pulcinella" by Stravinsky. Gould was on the stage too, acting as a stand-up comedian. His humor appeared for the most part to be innocuous. As soon as Gould entered the stage, he turned to the audience and said wryly: "Who did you expect, Plummer?" The press reporters were infuriated by both his humor and his stage directing, which they thought was in bad taste. Joyce Goodman of *The Montreal Star* gave a particularly grim account of what she observed. Here are the highlights:

> During their [Jablonski and Foli] performance, Mr. Gould sat on the piano, and at one point stretched out on top of it, his knickered legs dangling over the piano lid. He rolled, he writhed and he commented on the works. Sample: "Are you sure you are finished?"
>
> ... The audience began to leave, one by one, then by rows.
>
> [After the first part was complete:]
>
> Mr. Gould brought up the rear. He wore a raccoon coat this time, carried a sign proclaiming "Intermission" and planted it midstage.
>
> ... For the second half of the program, Mr. Gould wore tails, and he played the piano: "Angels" by Carl Ruggles and "Suite for Piano" by Schoenberg. He accompanied Miss Ilona Kombrink in her performance of "Der Wein" by Alan Berg.
>
> People continued to leave the Auditorium.[25]

The Toronto reviewers too were unpardoning. John Kraglund of *The Globe and Mail* denounced Gould's comical strivings:

> Seen through the eyes of Mr. Gould ... it was a time of unmitigated boredom. And thanks to his humor about as light and frothy as a tub of wet cement ...[26]

Again, Gould's friend, Jim Curtis, recorded his perceptive observations about the concert:

> ... what a concert! Glenn's idea was to present the significant musical activity of the 1920's (Schonberg, Berg) against the sterile nonsense that the era inspired. He devoted the first half to the "chaff," the second to the "wheat." He appeared in plus-fours, a tweedy, brown English hunting outfit and beret, pretended to be Christopher Plummer (as Sherlock Holmes?), then sat on top of the piano lid and expounded his theories at length. He couldn't be heard very far back, and this tended to put much of the audience into an impatient frame of mind. He then presented a pianist and violinist [Marek Jablonski and Lea Foli] (in vaudeville get up) and had them perform, "robot-fashion," works by Stravinsky and Hindemith (he said he was "too proud" to play such things) while he lolled on the piano, at one point stretching right out, taking a bottle from his coat and imbibing (saying to the audience "purely medicinal!") Then followed a parody of musical comedy by William Walton called Facade, admirably done by John Horton and a gorgeous blonde named Ilona Kombrink, but there was just too much of it and hordes of people headed for the exits. Glenn appeared from the trapdoor, housed in a huge fur coat, and planted a sign announcing the intermission. Afterwards he appeared in formal dress for the masterworks. But the sympathies of the house were already estranged.[27]

On August 22, 1962, *The Montreal Star* published a letter of protest to the editor written by a pair of teachers in response to Joyce Goodman's critical report. They signed with initials E. B. and E. S.

Their perception of Gould's music and stage behavior was entirely positive. These two fans stood up for Gould and explained not unreasonably what in their opinion he had tried to convey:

> The purpose of the first part of the concert appears to have been to show the sterility of some of the music of the twenties. In order to show attention to this point, and connect it with the life of that time the performers were suitably attired in the blazer, plus fours and raccoon coat of the time.
>
> ... The concert-goer is all too often present at the concert as a spectator without background knowledge of the compositions he is hearing. Mr. Gould not only performs, but educates his public to listen intelligently and critically.
>
> ... As for the repeated statements about people leaving the concert during the performance, it may be that as many as one hundred of the two thousand people in the auditorium walked out. We didn't notice, being too engrossed in the marvelous performance.[28]

Today, almost half a century after the fact, when the memory of the authentic witnesses is faded, it is left up to us, the post-Gouldians, to try to understand what actually happened. As implied earlier, one of the reasons why Gould lasted so long and blossomed at the Stratford Festival was because he felt a sense of freedom. He was free of restraints to create and innovate, to be spontaneous and more sociable. This all served as an incentive for a variety of experiments which were legitimate to some and were condemned by others. As a pianist-expert, he provided versatility in music selection. He spiced it with humor, which he personally enjoyed and believed others would too. Often, he miscalculated because his inner conflicts spoiled his sincere conscious planning. As a child, Glenn was short of ordinary play, refrained from sports, dance, jazz and other popular music. He was often reminded not to "make a spectacle" of himself and to suppress his need for attention. Yet he was also raised to be a performing artist, which implicitly meant to entertain, to attract attention and to be spectacular. These were conflicting messages that accounted for his inner duality. Gould simultaneously harbored two identities—one of a serious classical musician and another of a clowning rascal. This was confusing to some observers who could not reconcile his clashing realities.

Some spectators of the "Panorama" program were so accustomed to Gould as a classical pianist that they could not adapt to his sudden transformation into a comedian. It was hard to conceive of Gould lying on top of the piano or seeing him in a gaudy, full-length raccoon coat! Yet his entire behavior had some hidden meaning. On the Stratford stage, Gould was able to release some of those repressed and hidden aspects of himself, his need to show off, to attract attention, to be mischievous and comical. He also expressed a degree of mockery toward the piano, to which he committed most of his life. Lying on the top of the piano was a form of light acrobatics that he used to express his self-deprecating humor. In this instance, it is clear that under the mantle of the seriousness of a classic pianist, there was a repressed and unfulfilled lighthearted slapstick comedian.

At the present time, audiences are much more receptive and flexible in their relationship to performing artists. For example, British actor Dudley Moore was known as a fine classical pianist but was even more famed as a movie comedian. It follows that in the public's mind these two roles were successfully integrated and accepted. The end result was seamless. When people watched Moore play at the piano George Gershwin's Rhapsody in Blue, they normally did not burst into laughter, nor while watching his movies did they feel he was betraying his gift of music.

In the end, we have to concede that some aspects of Gould's behavior were not appropriate for a virtuoso. At times, Gouldian humor was capable of being banal, annoying, cynical, even rough at the edges. During the "Panorama" show, Gould made tactless and derogatory remarks about Stravinsky's music. He said that playing it was beneath his dignity. It was meant as a joke, but the critics were not amused. Indeed, Gould was not able to hide his unfair, loathsome attitude toward his fellow musician, and the critics must have sensed Gould's real contempt, which dampened the humor.

Ever since he was eight years old, Gould had always had an "attitude" toward Stravinsky and his music. At that time, Glenn watched the movie *Fantasia* where Stravinsky's music "Le Sacre du Printemps" was played. Glenn did not like the music, as he found it too harsh for his sensitive music taste. He got sick to his stomach and developed a severe headache, which he associated with both the violent scenes in the film as well as the music. The effects of the movie were so powerful that Gould not only remembered them but carried his personal dislike of Igor Stravinsky and his music for the rest of his life. Subconsciously, Gould projected his personal frustrations onto Stravinsky in the form of holding a grudge. When Gould's friend, John Lee Roberts, tried to arrange a meeting with Stravinsky for the purpose of Gould recording Stravinsky's piano music, Gould adamantly refused. Saddened, Roberts reminisced on the event in question:

> On one of his visits to Toronto, Stravinsky asked me to invite Glenn to lunch. Columbia was going to make a recording of the Capriccio for Piano and Orchestra by Stravinsky and the old man's dearest wish was that Glenn should be the soloist. The lunch took place in the Park Plaza Hotel where Stravinsky and Craft always stayed. Stravinsky hinted, but Glenn avoided any proposal coming into focus and confessed afterwards that the event had been an ordeal. He had no interest in thc Capriccio. I felt it was a work he simply did not know and begged him to look at a score I had of it, but to no avail. Once Glenn had made up his mind about something there was no changing it.[29]

In his writings, Gould showed mixed feelings toward Stravinsky by calling him "a spiritual emigre" who "has never learned to synthesize his experience." On the positive side, according to Gould, Stravinsky is "full of curiosity" and has "this kind of lovable, childlike wonder."[30]

If Gould's "Panorama" program of the previous year was "offbeat" as the critic put it, so was his next concert in 1963. This was also his final year of performing at Stratford. In the first all-Bach concert, Gould accompanied Oskar Shumsky on harpsichord in a performance of the B Minor Violin Sonata. Eric McLean was much disappointed in Gould's avoidance of playing the piano. He reported with deep concerns:

> Between Glenn Gould and his public, there is a gap that has been widening in recent years. They are still very much his public, as I am, but he persists in doing things to annoy and distract them, and he is neglecting more and more the very thing which won him admiration in the first place.

> They want to hear him play the piano.
>
> In the opening Stratford concert he did everything but. He sang, he conducted, he emoted, and he played the harpsichord.[31]

The question still persists—what really went wrong in the last two Stratford seasons, 1962 and 1963? Gould was a crowd-puller, never short of the public's adoration. Stratford was his preferred environment over other bigger and worldlier cities. Why did such a beautiful experience have to be ruined? Did Gould, as a maker of the "Panorama" show, subconsciously sabotage himself, or was his ingenuity misunderstood and unappreciated at the time? Was this show a product of his destructive mind or creative spirit?

In the rest of his life, Gould was showing signs of social withdrawal. One remembers that the spring of 1962 was emotionally traumatic because of the disaster with the Brahms performance in New York in connection to his slow interpretation of Brahms' Second Concerto. Turning thirty in that year was an undesirable milestone that meant more responsibility and more "behaving" as an adult. Instead of going along with his emotional growth, Gould resisted it with vehemence. In Stratford's 1963 performance, his conflict with the public escalated by depriving them of the pleasure of his piano music. What made him play the harpsichord at the summer festival? Why did Gould put a cantata on the program? Why did he play such deeply serious, esoteric music as opposed to the down-to-earth and more popular music that audiences would cheer?

On the outside, Gould seemed defiant toward the world. On the inside, he was falling apart. This was nothing new. Glenn had had symptoms of an emotional disorder since the age of six, but his enormous resources drove him ahead. The balance of energy was anabolic—more creation than destruction. Here, upon entering his thirties, the balance was tipped in the direction of gradual decline of his mental health—more illness, more social clashes, more seclusion and more self-destructive behavior. Gould was clinically depressed. He entered the grey zone of his life marked by high anxieties and social phobia; by pessimistic views and self-doubts. He resented having to be away from home and having to perform before crowds. The more demands on him, the more he panicked and resisted. This very panic in the face of public performance pushed him away from it. Gould developed a so-called negative transference reaction toward his live audiences. He perceived them as demanding, critical and hard to please in the same way he had perceived his elders earlier on. He compensated for his insecurities and apprehension by being more controlling and defiant. This was reflected in his inner terror at the thought of having relatives and friends in the audience. Gould could not bear their possible disapproval and rejection. His close friend John Lee Roberts remembered:

> ... I often accompanied him on car trips to and from Stratford attending what were for me spellbinding concerts. However, it was in either 1962 or 1963 that he begged me and my wife, Christine (by that time I was engaged), to accompany him but not to attend the performances, a request we respected.[32]

Obviously, Gould's stage fright was so high that he could not bear to be watched by those whom he knew well. Bereft of inner peace and ashamed of himself, particularly in the eyes of his mother, who wished him to continue his concert career, Gould closed his performing career chapter at the

Stratford Festival by passing his role of music director on to his friend, Victor DiBello, in 1963. He appeared in two last concerts. On July 7, he played the beautiful Bach Violin Sonata op. 1 with Oskar Shumsky on violin, and the Bach Concerto no.6 with Mario Bernardi conducting the National Festival Orchestra. On July 28, Gould devoted the concert to the Russian composers Glinka and Prokofiev. He performed Glinka's *Trio Pathetique* with Oskar Shumsky, violin, and Sol Schoenbach, bassoon, and Prokofiev's Violin Sonata op. 94 with Oskar Shumsky playing the violin.

Studying Russian composers for Stratford appearances helped Gould in his literary-scholastic work. He wrote a monumental article titled "Music in the Soviet Union," which he delivered at Convocation Hall of the University of Toronto upon receiving his honorary doctoral degree in 1964. Perhaps, by honoring Russian composers, Gould was saying a belated "thank you" for his memorable experience on his tour in the Soviet Union years before. Canada's number one musician was also saying goodbye to his performing life in Stratford without consciously knowing it.

Stratford was Gould's connection to Shakespeare's literary works and his bridge to his parental ancestors who all resided in the British Isles. Best of all, a decade in the Classic City meant that Gould was pursuing classical music with less formality, relatively free from stage anxiety, which is perhaps the most gratifying state of mind for which any performer can hope. The tireless concertmaster, who was not in the habit of idling and vacationing, was able to relax and even have a holiday in this serene place. Gould's life at Stratford was full of innovation and whimsical spirit. He behaved as if he had permission to deviate from the usual standards of concert performance. His good feelings and creative mind, blended with his impeccable piano virtuosity, came to fuller expression in this pleasing and unpretentious Ontario town in front of keen and appreciative music audiences.

Chapter XIV

BOWING OUT

THE END OF GOULD'S PUBLIC PERFORMANCE CAREER

Mr. Gould shines with incomparable brightness.
Robert Offergeld[1]

In his early twenties, Gould was making off-handed remarks about the strain of his performing career, hinting at his likely retirement at the age of thirty or thirty-five at best. Following the emotional stress that descended upon him in the period of 1959 to 1960, the idea of retirement was more frequently expressed. Gould was uttering numerous complaints to his manager and associates with respect to his public performance career, which he had been experiencing as a burden. He was becoming increasingly more weary of traveling, during which his old and never-healed separation anxiety always reoccurred. As time went on, he was coming across as more sickly and hypochondriacal, which was reflected through more frequent concert cancellations.

If becoming a world-class pianist is a Prometheus-like task, quitting the art of pianism so early in one's life ought to be the emotionally hardest and most trying of all music-related decisions. The stage, unlike any other medium of communication, provides the live and exclusive, one-time experience for both the performer and the audience. It was not as if Gould wished to resign from the stage by choice and out of a clear mind, but he rather *had* to stop pursuing his performing career that was draining him. Should he carry on or should he quit his performing career once and for all? This was the question that was gnawing at him. So, in the period from 1961 to 1964, Gould was gradually consolidating his idea of retirement from performing and changing his focus to a recording and broadcasting career. One of the earlier documents was his letter to a fan, Mrs. H. L. Austin of Quebec, written on February 15, 1961, where he spontaneously formulated the problem:

> Strangely, I have always preferred working in a studio, making records or doing radio or television, and for me, the microphone is a friend, not an enemy and the lack of an audience—the total anonymity of the studio—provides the greatest incentive to satisfy my own demands upon myself ...[2]

"The microphone is a friend" could be interpreted that Glenn's recording activity caused him less anxiety because this way his music was heard while his platform mannerisms remained unseen. It is not so much that Gould avoided the audience but that he needed to avoid the escalation of his inner tension triggered by public performance.

Only a few days after writing this letter, Gould's ailing grandmother, Alma, passed away in Uxbridge, Ontario, on February 24, 1961. She was the elder musician in the family, the pianist and organist, the teacher and propagator of music. Glenn could always rely on her unconditional love and admiration. He counted on her letters of support while he was on his long and tiring concert tours. Grandma "Allie" was Glenn's emotional hub, a strong connection with his past, with the Goulds and with music. At her death, Glenn was bogged down and grief-stricken. On the day of her passing, Gould gave a concert in Tulsa, Oklahoma where he was a piano soloist for the Beethoven Concerto no. 4, with the Tulsa Philharmonic conducted by Franco Autori. He rushed back home to Toronto to join the family for the funeral. His father, Bert Gould, recalled this sad event:

"Mr. Gould, what do you remember about your mother's last days of life and about Glenn's reaction to her passing?" I asked.

"My mother lived a long life, she was almost ninety [years old], and she was quite sickly, so we all knew that the end was nearing. But Glenn used to say: 'Grandma's gonna be all right.' He always counted on her being there for him." Mr. Gould captured his son's denial.

"What was his reaction once she passed away?" I needed to know more.

"I was at peace to know that the good Lord took her with him, but Glenn was not at peace at all. He was so restless and pale, I told my wife to watch him, to give him a proper lunch and talk to him." Mr. Gould showed his own sorrow.

"Do you mean that he was withdrawn? I asked.

"Well, whenever Glenn was deeply distressed he went speechless. This time it was even worse. He was quiet and shaken. He wouldn't talk much with anybody. I kept looking for him. Frankly, we were more worried about him than about the funeral,"[3] Mr. Gould said.

This sad and irreparable loss of a rare soulmate in his family had a negative impact on Gould's performing career. In the spring/summer season, he was at the height of bereavement but was unable to show his grief and distress to others. Instead, he was sickly in an obscure way, which reflected outwardly in more separation anxiety, in more fear of traveling and in an increased number of concert cancellations. Gould's unexpressed and unresolved grief inevitably contributed to the demise of his performing career.

Shortly after the loss of his grandmother, Gould wrote a letter to his friend, Kitty Gvozdeva, on April 27, 1961, in which he spelled out his strong feelings with respect to public performance:

> As I think you know, there are many aspects of the concert world which do not appeal to me very much—traveling, for instance, which I hate—and it is sometimes easy to assume that these disenchantments represent a certain ennui for music itself.[4]

Here Gould disclosed to us the awareness of his hate of traveling, which caused "a certain ennui for music itself." Hence, his inner anxieties caused by the loss and grieving were projected on to his music achievements, threatening to compromise them. To Gould, having to part from his family, having to travel to distant and unhomey places in order to entertain others seemed so alien and meaningless. Such deep feelings of futility caused in him listlessness, loss of interest in practicing the piano and more stage mannerisms. In turn, this all led to frequent concert cancellations, program substitutions, the outrage of critics and, finally, to a sense of giving up.

Nonetheless, it was not time to give up yet, and in the period involving the years 1961 and 1962, Gould demonstrated his enormous efforts to sustain himself at the level of public performance. Consistent with this, he created memorable performances in St. Louis, New York, Stratford, Vancouver and many other places across North America, totaling about sixty appearances in two years. His undertaking in St. Louis was a monumental one and surpassed those in London, England, Russia and Israel, where he offered high output over a short period of time. In St. Louis, where Gould was sincerely welcomed, he graced the audiences by playing for them six Beethoven concerti in a succession of three double-bill concerts with the St. Louis Symphony and Edouard Van Remoortel conducting. On February 5, 1961, the virtuoso played Beethoven's Concerti no. 2 and 4 on February 8, no. 1 and 5, and on February 11 he performed Beethoven's Concerto no. 3 and the Triple Concerto op. 56 for piano, violin and violoncello with Harry Farbman and Leslie Parnas at the last two instruments, respectively. Each time Gould brought down the house. Here Gould was at the pinnacle of his success, a triple hero so to speak. If the concerts in St. Louis were a part of the music Olympic games, the maestro of pianism would have won three gold medals, for virtuosity required, for artistic interpretation and for the colossal capacity to memorize and deliver this music to the audiences.

The next major event was Gould's successful appearance in New York over three consecutive days, when from March 17 to 19, he played Beethoven's Concerto no. 4 with the New York Philharmonic and Leonard Bernstein conducting. On April 25, 1961, Gould appeared in a recital in Los Angeles, where he performed Webern's Variations for Piano, Op. 27 and Bach's *Goldberg Variations*. In August of the same year, Gould performed for the last time for the Vancouver audiences. On August 17, 1961, he played the Brahms Concerto in D Minor with the Vancouver Symphony and Zubin Mehta as conductor. Gould had played this piece once before, in Winnipeg on October 8, 1959, with Victor Feldbrill and the Winnipeg Symphony Orchestra. This beautiful and technically demanding music piece, which Gould played eloquently in Winnipeg and Vancouver, stirred a torrent of negative criticism in the following year, 1962, when Gould played a very slow rendition of the Brahms concerto in New York with Leonard Bernstein conducting the New York Philharmonic. The results were catastrophic as the press descended upon Gould with venomous criticism. This was a cut off point. From then on, there was a steady decline of Gould's health and the number of his performances.

In Canada, Gould's public career was curtailed earlier than in the United States. The last two concerts were in Toronto where on December 6 and 7, 1960, Gould performed the Schoenberg Piano Concerto and Mozart's Piano Concerto in C Minor with the Toronto Symphony Orchestra and Walter Suskind as conductor. Gould's last appearance in Montreal was in a recital on April 9, 1961, when he played Bach's Partita no. 3 in A Minor, Haydn't Sonata no. 59 in E-flat Major, Krenek's Sonata no. 3 and Beethoven's Sonata in A-flat Major, Op. 110. Yet he kept performing in the Stratford Festival beyond this, and appeared there both in 1962 and, for the last time, in 1963 in several concerts. Interestingly, during the same last four years of his performing career, Gould gave a number of concerts from coast to coast for American audiences. Hence, the Canadians, particularly Torontonians, had to travel long distances to see Gould live, though they were able to see him on television. The message that

Gould tried to relate to his countrymen was: "If you are so critical of seeing me and my performance behavior, I may as well disappear from the scene, but you can always turn on the radio to hear my music." Gould was indeed making a transition from being seen to being heard through the electronic media. By switching from a performer to becoming a recording artist, he was able to save some of his scarce energies and was out of sight of those most critical observers. Meanwhile, in Stratford, Ontario, unlike in the major cities, Gould was more at ease giving concerts, as he encountered there more relaxed and informal circumstances conducive to his emotional needs.

Similarly, Gould stopped playing for his previously faithful New York audiences earlier than in the rest of the United States. His last concerts in New York were on April 6 and 8, 1962, when he performed as a piano soloist the Brahms D Minor concerto with Leonard Bernstein conducting the New York Philharmonic. A few days after this event, on April 17, 1962, Gould wrote a letter to Humphrey Burton, a television producer with the BBC describing his state of mind:

> I am not, at the moment, planning any tour in Europe, or indeed at the moment for any season. This is due to the fact that, as of two months ago, I decided that when the next season is over, I shall give no more public concerts. Mind you, this is a plan I have been announcing every year since I was 18, and there is a part of my public here that does not take these pronouncements too seriously, but this time I think I really mean it. One of the things I will not, however, give up is television.[5]

As part of his last efforts to perform for the people one more time, in 1962, Gould appeared in a stream of performances in American cities that he perceived to be more receptive and friendly to him, such as Toledo and Columbus, Ohio, Chicago, Illinois, and Lexington, Kentucky. In Baltimore, on October 9 and 10, Gould gave a successful performance of the same Brahms D Minor Concerto with Peter Adler leading the Baltimore Symphony. In Atlanta, on October 23, he performed the Beethoven Concerto no. 5, and on November 8 the Beethoven Concerto no. 3 in Detroit, Michigan; both being his last performances of these respective music pieces. After this, Gould gave three recitals in rapid succession from November 20 to 27 in Cincinnati, Ohio, and Kansas City, Missouri, concluding the season in Louisville, Kentucky.

In 1963, the stream of Gould's public appearances dried up, leaving the puddles of only eight performances; three of them were in his favorite San Francisco. On February 13 and 14, Gould played at the War Memorial Opera House, and he played at Foothill College in Los Altos Hills on February 15. This is where he gave the final masterful piano demonstration of Bach's D Minor and the Schoenberg Concerto and where he performed with conductor Enrique Jorda and the members of the San Francisco Symphony for the last time. Two weeks later, on March 5 in Denver, Colorado, Gould played for the last time the Brahms D Minor Concerto and completed the last orchestral performance ever to be done publicly by him in a major concert hall. During the rest of the year, there were two last concerts in Stratford and, finally, two recitals; the first one on April 16 at the Eastman Theater in Rochester, New York, and the second on October 16 at the Masonic Temple Auditorium in Detroit, Michigan. In both recitals, Gould presented an almost identical program—Bach's *Art of the Fugue* (four), Beethoven's Sonata in E Major, op. 109 and Hindemith's Sonata no. 3.

It behooves us to try to understand Gould's choice of Bach's *Art of the Fugue* for his last appearances. This music piece is one of Bach's greatest compositions, comparable in its magnitude to his work called *Musical Offering* and to the *Goldberg Variations*. The *Art of the Fugue* was likely composed in 1749, only a year before Bach's death. Because of his eye disease, Bach had to spend his last days in a dark room unable to read and write. Sensing death, he dictated to his son-in-law the finale of the *Art of the Fugue* and told him to entitle it "I Draw Near Onto Thy Throne." The *Art of the Fugue* was Bach's personal statement, a music diary and a confession of profound meaning of the human search for inner peace. It is an artistic form of greeting where the words "hello" and "goodbye" are spoken simultaneously. Bach's son, Carl Philipp Emanuel, referred to the *Art of the Fugue* as "the most perfect practical fugal work." The recent biographer of Bach, Christoph Wolff, concludes that "the Art of the Fugue, in spite of the fact that it is not Bach's very last work, represents the attainment of an ultimate goal, the 'be-all and end-all of an extraordinarily strong-willed artistic personality.'"[6]

For us, the readers and analytic observers of his inner dynamics, Gould's choice of playing the *Art of the Fugue* at his farewell recital was equivalent to producing a requiem or a mass for the repose of the souls of the dead. On the personal level, it was an act of symbolic mourning of the loss of Bach, an act of real and prolonged mourning of his grandmother, Alma, who was dedicated to Bach and, on a more general level, an act of mourning different symbolic losses, including his waning concert career and his ailing mental health.

Gould, in 1964, was in the process of parting from his performing music career. In March, his manager, Walter Homburger, scheduled him to perform in New York but this plan was canceled. The same fate followed two other prearranged appearances, one in San Francisco on April 5, and in Minneapolis, Minnesota, on April 27, both of which were called off because of Gould's poor health. Fortunately, Gould was able to follow through with the remaining two scheduled recitals. On March 29, he played in Chicago at the Orchestra Hall his trademark pieces: Bach's *Art of the Fugue* (four), Bach's Partita no. 4, Beethoven's Sonata in A-flat Major, op. 110 and Krenek's Sonata no. 3. On April 10, he presented the same program before a Los Angeles audience at the Wilshire Ebel Theater with the exception of Krenek's sonata, which he replaced with Hindemith's Sonata no. 3. This piano recital was Gould's swan song of public performance. He was only thirty-one years of age. Like Bach, he too made a personal statement of an unconscious search for inner peace, respite and restitution. Scores of Gould's fans, music lovers, music critics and Gould's opponents turned up for these two concerts completely unaware that they had just attended his last, historical, live performances. At that time, no one realized that Gould the stage persona was fading and being transformed into a living legend. There was no retirement party, no farewell words said and no special honors given. Gould made his exit from the concert platform quietly and inconspicuously. He entered the music annals of permanence. The following words of Robert Offergeld of *High Fidelity* best capture the essence of Gould the musician at the point of this career change:

> One cannot imagine Lipatti,[7] for example, playing anything unbeautifully but neither can one imagine him being particularly interesting in the strangely cryptic fifth Contrapunctus of the Art of the Fugue, or even in the big and somber five-part fugue (number 4) of The Well-Tempered Clavier. But it is just here that Mr. Gould shines with incomparable brightness. Where others find chilly

> enigmas, he produces hushed and mysterious moments of an ineffable poignancy—lonely intellectual abstractions too architectural, too purely musical, for anybody's verbalization.[8]

On this note: "Mr. Gould shines with incomparable brightness," the great artist himself completed this most dynamic and challenging chapter of his life as a concert pianist and more fully embraced a new mode of self-expression through the electronic media.

GOODBYE STAGE FRIGHT

> My voice had a long, non-stop career. It deserves to be put to bed with quiet and dignity, not yanked out once in a while to see if it can still do what it used to do. It can't.
>
> Beverly Sills[9]

Less than a year after the harpsichord concert in Stratford, and two years after the New York debacle, Gould's performing career ended. The fear of his close friends that he indeed might stop playing in public came true in 1964, when on April 10 Gould gave his last public recital ever. This was a watershed event. Just as Gould never received the red carpet treatment during his performing music marathon, he was not honored with the fanfare at closing it. For example, when Gould returned from his triumphant concert tour in Europe, in June 1957, where he was celebrated in Russia and Germany, he received modest publicity in the press but there were no special receptions made to honor him. As opposed to that, when one year later, in 1958, the American pianist Van Cliburn returned from his piano competition in Russia, he was given a ticker-tape parade in Washington, D.C., to celebrate his success. At the closing of his career, Gould simply made a few faint bows in front of the Los Angeles audience and then permanently bowed out.

Nobody believed it; his mother, his relatives, his music friends, nor his fans. Walter Homburger, too, was in the state of disbelief. "Most of us thought maybe he will have a hiatus of several years"[10] Homburger commented. In order to quell his panic, Homburger continued to advertise and search for new engagements for his boss as if nothing had happened. On August 7, 1964, four months after Gould's closing recital in Los Angeles, Homburger wrote this letter to the U.S. Department of Justice, Immigration and National Services in New York: "... the last petition approved by your office for Mr. Gould has expired. I, therefore, enclose herewith a new petition to cover Mr. Gould's concerts and lectures in the United States up to the end of January 1965."[11] Homburger was in the state of denial, not to mention anger, with Gould, who in addition to being stubborn and difficult, was also breaching a contract with him as manager. There also was a financial loss. At that time, the fee for Gould's concerts rose to $3,500 for a single appearance, and the fee paid to his manager was twenty percent. Gould did not mind the monetary losses as long as he was able to relax from the menacing stage fright. While Walter was petitioning, Gould was writing this very clear and definite letter to Lord Harewood:

110 St. Clair Avenue West
August 13, 1964

The Right Honourable The Earl of Harewood
c/o Edinburgh International Festival Office
29 St. James Street, London, S.W.C. England
Dear Lord Harewood,

Thank you very much for your letter of July twentieth, and for the invitation to take part in the Edinburgh Festival.

The programs that you outline are very tempting indeed which are really no great surprise to me since as an occasional festival director myself I have followed with the greatest interest the marvelous things you have been doing at Edinburgh in the last four seasons.

I am afraid, however, that for the moment at least I shall have to take a rain check on your kind invitation. In the past few years I have given very few public concerts in order to conserve as much time for composing and writing as I possibly can, and this has meant that I have not ventured to Europe for the last four seasons.

However, should I become disenchanted with semi-retirement in the near future, I can think of no place that I should rather give concerts than at the Edinburgh Festival.

With best wishes

Yours sincerely,
Glenn Gould[12]

The Edinburgh International Festival is considered the biggest arts festival in the world, where about four hundred thousand people show up for its remarkable performances. Had Gould summoned enough energy to attend, he would have had an opportunity to reconnect with his Scottish heritage, and the audiences would have enjoyed him tremendously knowing that he reversed his retirement for them.

Still hoping that Gould would eventually come back to his senses and get back in the concert-giving business sooner than in "several years," Homburger negotiated two concerts for Gould. The first one was supposed to take place in Cincinnati, Ohio, on January 10, with the Cincinnati Symphony and the second was to be in Baltimore, Maryland, on March 17, 1965, with the Baltimore Symphony. On both occasions, the chosen music piece to be played was Gould's favorite, Bach's Concerto no. 1. Reluctantly, Homburger had to cancel these appearances, as Gould was not nearly ready to return to the performing circuit.

Officially, Gould stopped performing in order to devote himself to composing, writing for music magazines and working in electronic media on recording and broadcasting. In other words, according to him, he only shifted gears and changed direction from public performance to media performance. In reality, Gould's withdrawal from the stage was a result of his ailing mental health. For some years he struggled with depression and pursued odd behavior; his anxiety was high and he required sedatives; he was misunderstood and criticized, which was a source of ongoing injuries to his self-esteem. His health was withering, and he had to stop plundering his precious emotional reserves. At that point, in April 1964, Gould was at the end of his beleaguered road of live performance. He was increasingly weary of piano practicing, yet public concerts are impossible to carry on without constant piano practice. He felt that he shared enough of himself with live audiences. Having given something beautiful to the world, it was now his time for respite and relaxation from the tribulations of a performing career.

While Gould was in the early 1960s heading toward the cessation of his public concert career, it would have been customary to announce his retirement due to health reasons. In that case, the press would have had time to accept it, and the public would have had time to deal with the grief around the loss of the opportunity to see him in person. This practice of planning and announcing one's retirement is common among famous performing artists and sportsmen who after their great performances and Olympic victories at some point have to part from the demanding competitive scene. In the end, after the grief and anger are expressed, the relationship between the performer, the press and the public usually becomes resolved at some point.

In Gould's case, he spoke about the retirement for years, so nobody took him seriously. There was no official date-setting for the last concert; nor was there a manifesto issued explaining his health problems as the main reason for retirement. There was no anniversary celebration where the audience had a chance to honor him and properly part from him, nor a social gathering in the form of a party thrown for him. Gould resorted to a more passive way. Like a locomotive approaching a train station and decelerating its speed to the point of stopping, so was Gould's career slowing down until halted. Simply, after his last concert in Los Angeles, he never went back to the live stage. His was a clandestine and lonely way of bowing out, painful for all those involved.

Instead of relaying a clear message to the world: "I have to take a break from performing because of my health reasons," Gould invented elaborate theories to justify and rationalize his behavior. In his quest for reduced personal stress, he went overboard by not only denying the satisfaction of public appearances to himself, but to the world at large. Guided by his ill-fate, Gould proposed that public concerts would disappear by the year 2000. This anti-concert campaign started much earlier when he was in his twenties. At first, he lobbied in subtle ways. For example, he personally refrained from concertgoing and expected from his friends to refrain from attending his concerts. In 1962, Gould asked audiences to refrain from applause in a performance at the Stratford Festival, which was another subtle subversion against the practice of concerts. In the next sequence, Gould personally stopped performing. He continued his one-man rally until finally, in the year 1966, he published an article, "Prospects of Recording," where he clearly stated his extreme position with respect to public concerts:

> ... I herewith reaffirm my prediction that the habits of concert going and concert giving, both as a social institution and as a chief symbol of musical mercantilism, will be as dormant in the twenty-first century as, with luck, will Tristan de Cunna's Vulcano; and that because of its extinction, music will be able to provide a more cogent experience than is now possible.[13]

In this article, which is regarded to be one of the best he had ever written, Gould elaborates on the advantages of recording, saying that the future of music is closely connected with technology and, frankly, it lies in the recording industry. The listener, according to Gould, will have the benefit of sitting at home and not passively enjoying the music but actively participating by modifying its tempo or mixing the music of two or more performers/conductors. Gould suggests;

> Let us say, for example, that you enjoy Bruno Walter's performance of the exposition and recapitulation from the first movement of Beethoven's Fifth Symphony but incline toward Klemperer's handling of the development section, which employs a notably divergent tempo ... you could snip out these measures from the Klemperer edition and splice them into the Walter performance.[14]

Gould encouraged the connoisseurs of music to be their own tape editors and to graft music of one performer onto another. Then he went on praising background sound in movies and TV shows, which he regarded as a marvelous new way of electronic expression, saying that the identity of a musician creating the music is not important and that "distinctions that separated composer and performer and listener will become outmoded." In the end, Gould not only denounced the importance of live concerts, individual composing and individual music performance but also denounced the role of art and the creative process in general. He took a firm stance that the future of music is in the hands of electronic technology. He concluded his thesis:

> In the best of all possible worlds, art would be unnecessary. Its offer of restorative placative therapy would go begging a patient. The professional specialization involved in its making would be presumption. The generalities of its applicability would be an affront. The audience would be the artist and their life would be art.[15]

At first glance, Gould's article is a well-written piece that consists of a brand new view of the future of music. It is more philosophical than musical; it is more radical than negotiable. Gould, in one stroke of his pen, proclaimed that the future of music is in the recording industry. The crux of Gould's radicalism is that the art created by individuals on the whole will be unnecessary and that the masses would be the artists.

Such a philosophy is reductionist because it diminishes the importance not only of current concert practices but disregards the importance of centuries of music, architecture, visual and performing arts. Earlier, Gould banned the applause; now he banned the people from concertgoing and concert giving. He placed people in their rooms, suggesting them to play with their electronic gadgets, tape recorders, record players and more sophisticated electronic splices that are so far used only in recording studios. It appears as if Gould worked in the best interest of people, trying to make things easier and more accessible to them. In reality, his philosophy was self-serving and helped him work through his own deep-seated emotional issues. Concertgoing is not dead because it is outmoded and not of benefit for audiences, rather this idea was a product of Gould's depressive and negative outlook. Gould's stage fright around concert giving, the sense of humiliation, apprehension, and exposure to what he thought was the shallow interest of the audiences who do not understand music and who are there for sensational and trivial reasons, were all in the background of Gould's philosophy of the future of music. His extremist view was more defensive than constructive. By defending his own beliefs, Gould built the Maginot Line to help him attack the philosophy of performing and, more importantly, to help him protect and defend his severe resentment toward it. This blitzkrieg article looks very interesting and engaging at first sight, but hides the enormous pain of an artist who can no longer perform and a potential composer who cannot compose. Personally, for Gould's mental health it was beneficial to have written such an article, which helped him sublimate his inner aggression into something creative and useful as a new concept. Though Gould's concept was not accepted by the world, certain aspects are worthy of its attention.

A couple of years after this article was published, Gould revealed some of his emotional pain that he had experienced in his performing career, and his relief upon its cessation. In 1968, in an interview with John McClure,[16] which took place in New York, Gould said, "the role of a concert artist in our society is an exalted one;" that "it is a great liability to have an audience," that he had to "take tranquilizers to sedate myself," and that he often played Bach's Fifth Partita at his concerts not only because it was his favorite but because it was comforting and familiar. In other words, Gould opened his heart and told the world that a concert pianist has a highly responsible task; that he was no longer feeling well enough to keep up with the task of such high expectations on him, and that he had to stop performing. He went one step further into mild paranoia by accusing audiences for their "lust for blood," waiting for the conductor to forget his lines, and his horror is reflected in the statement, "I don't have concertgoers as friends." This was not true. Gould's music friends, John Lee Roberts and Victor DiBello, both loved to go to concerts and his future friend, Robert Silverman, was an avid concertgoer. In stating this, Gould was neither manipulative nor was he lying on purpose but was simply unconsciously defending himself and rationalizing his act of quitting. His guilt feelings over letting others down were overpowering. His mother and grandmother took such pride in his public stature. Above all, he betrayed his wide audiences, his cheerleaders and fans who felt so privileged to see him in person. In order to expiate surmounting guilt, Gould withdrew into solitude and lived an ascetic life in the state of self-deprivation.

In the interview, McClure of Columbia Masterworks stated that there was a "great deal of ruefulness" around Gould's refusal to play in public; that "half a dozen of impresarios" were waiting for him to change his mind and engage him for concerts, and that it did not make sense that Gould, as "one of the most talented and most controversial artists and certainly a unique one, suddenly does not want it"[17] [to perform in public]. It was as if McClure was not only lacking compassion for Gould's plight of not performing but was almost irritated by Gould and possibly angry with him. McClure's interview was taped and sold as a disc titled: *Glenn Gould, Concert Drop-Out*. In general, the term "dropout" has a negative connotation. The commonly used phrase "a high school dropout" refers to one's failure to complete the task of going to school. Though Gould was the first one who used the term self-critically in reference to the abrupt end of his concert career, others took over and continued to use this rather punitive choice of word. It appears that those who continue to refer to Gould as a concert dropout subconsciously perceive him as a failure for not performing in public.

When other great pianists, like Vladimir Horowitz and Van Cliburn withdrew from live performance for a period of several years, they were not referred to as concert dropouts. When recently, in the 1990s, one of the most famous American pianists, Murray Perahia, disappeared from the concert stage, nobody in the press referred to him as a dropout, but it was widely understood that he suffered finger injuries. What is different in our perception of Gould's cessation of public concerts? In truth,

Gould achieved enormously and generously shared his music products with the world. According to this, the world was supposed to be grateful for what was received, rather than to grumble for what was not. Just as the American pianist William Kapell cannot be accused for dying in a plane crash that cut his promising piano career short, Glenn Gould cannot be responsible for having an emotional crash that reduced his vitality for public performance. It appears that our different perception of Gould is greatly influenced by his own perception of himself, which was negative and self-punitive. Those who continue to refer to Gould as a concert dropout seem to do it for commercial or sensational purposes, or out of a deeper experience of annoyance followed by their dismissal of him. This view is biased in relationship to our view of similar problems of other great pianists and does not leave room for deeper understanding and compassion.

What did Gould do with his time when he stopped playing concerts? He kept very busy. In 1964, he went to New York every two or three weeks to record the works of Beethoven and Schoenberg. He was extremely immersed in the preparation of four TV shows titled *Concert for Wednesdays*, where he appeared as musicologist and pianist by interpreting music and speaking of its merits.

In May of the same year, Gould published an article in *The Saturday Review* titled "Strauss and the Electronic Future," in which he reinforced the importance of solitude:

> By far the most important contribution to the arts is the creation of a new and paradoxical condition of privacy. The great paradox about the electronic transmission of musical sounds that as it makes available to the most enormous audience, either simultaneously or in a delayed encounter the identical music experience, it encourages that audience to react not as captives and automatons but as individuals capable of an unprecedented spontaneity of judgement. This is because the most public transmission can be encountered in the most private circumstance ...[18]

On June 1st, 1964, Gould was awarded an honorary doctorate at Convocation Hall of the University of Toronto. In the ceremony it was said: "The president will request the chancelor to confer the degree of Doctor of Laws, honoris cause, upon Glenn Herbert Gould." In November, Dr. Glenn Gould delivered a speech at the Royal Conservatory of Music in Toronto with the title "Advice to a Graduation," in which he said, "if I could find one phrase that would sum up my wishes for you on this occasion, I think it would be devoted to convincing you of the futility of living too much by the advice of others."[19] Out of all possible suggestions given to the young graduates, Gould put forward one that was deeply meaningful to himself. It was as if he had been living his own life on advice from others and resented it bitterly.

Though quite satisfied with some aspects of his life, such as writing and broadcasting, Gould personally suffered for not being able to carry on his performing career. After all, he was raised to be the central figure on the world stage, always in the foreground, whereas then, in semi-retirement, it was like stepping down into the underworld. At one level, Gould acted as if he were relieved, yet on another level he grieved his loss and felt badly about letting his family down. In 1974, ten years after his last public appearance, Gould wrote an autobiographical article[20] in which he revealed how torn and restless he was around his performing career. He analyzed the role of an artist vis-à-vis the public and concluded that "the artist should be granted ... anonymity," that "he should be permitted to operate in secret ... unaware of the presumed demands of the marketplace," and "the artist will then abandon his false sense of 'public' responsibility and his 'public' will relinquish its role of servile dependency." In the same article, Gould revealed that he was haunted by "a traumatic experience in the Salzburg Festspielhaus," where he was supposed to perform in 1958 but could not because of his chest congestion. He confessed: "... my tracheitis was of such severity that I was able to cancel a month of concerts, withdraw into the Alps, and lead the most idyllic and isolated existence."[21] In both vignettes, Gould referred to his quest for anonymity versus exposure, which represented his old childhood conflict between his inner inhibitions and need to show and share his gift with others.

By stepping down, Gould was relegated into the realm of a living legend. Though as an artist he continued to exert powerful presence, as a person Gould was literally invisible. The term "living legend" is flattering and reverential and has to do with idealization of greatness. At a second glance, being a living legend during one's lifetime also has to do with the denial of the strength and potential of the real person.

By and large, for Gould giving up his performing career was necessary and adaptive. It lessened the tension between inner conflicts, notably his many inhibitions clashing with his personal need to display his musical greatness. He felt it was time to withdraw. Old, unresolved childhood issues, such as separation anxiety, a variety of fears and phobias, distrust of the world and the feelings of personal shame and doubt were all reenacted in his early thirties. At that point, Gould felt sick before, during and after each performance. Much has been said so far about Gould's stage fright and very little has been said about his profound sense of shame.

Gould was filled with shame. In correspondence with his friends, he often expressed apologies, a sense of embarrassment and humiliation. "I am terribly ashamed of myself that I did not reply sooner to your greetings," he wrote in February 1965 to his Russian friend, Kitty Gvozdeva. To his German friend Silvia Kind, he lamented, "I feel very ashamed of myself that I have not written long ago to thank you for your marvelous Bach autograph, which I am very proud to have ..."[22]

According to the findings of Erik Erikson, shame originates in early childhood. Erikson divided human psychosexual development into eight stages and referred to the second stage, which takes place in infancy, as the stage of "Autonomy vs. Shame and Doubt." He proposed that in this stage children gain the sense of self-control, the ability to hold on and to let go. If the child in this developmental phase is not well-guided, he may develop a deep sense of shame and self-doubt, as well as a tendency to doubt others. Erikson says: "He who is ashamed would like to force the world not to look at him, not to notice his exposure. He would like to destroy the eyes of the world. Instead, he must wish for his own invisibility."[23] This is all so true of Gould. He realized that he was not able to change and that the only solution for him was to withdraw. This helped him to decrease the overwhelming shame over not turning out to be the man he was expected to be. Erikson summed it up:

> This stage, therefore, becomes decisive for the ratio of love and hate, cooperation and willfulness, freedom of self-expression and its suppression. From a sense of self-control without loss of self-esteem comes a lasting sense of good will and pride; from a sense of loss of self-control and of foreign over control comes a lasting propensity for doubt and shame.[24]

The wide sense of shame and doubt that Gould experienced made him very insecure and hypervigilant. He doubted the importance of public concerts; he was suspicious and avoidant of his friends, even of his family members. In other words, nothing and nobody was totally trustworthy. "From a sense of self-control ... comes a lasting sense of pride," said Erikson. The loss of self-control by being unable to handle one's concert career cannot be associated with the sense of pride. Gould absolutely had to set himself apart from the squalling critics and the masses. This evolving paranoid-like attitude toward others was both uncomfortable and unproductive. Gould had to keep his guard up most of the time, and the moments of unguardedness and spontaneity were progressively diminishing. His distrust referred not only to the distrust of others, but also to his fear and avoidance of the untrustworthy world he thought was against him and/or after him.

There are other, more positive ways of explaining Gould's untimely separation from the concert stage. As a child, Glenn witnessed the evolution of electronic technology represented in the phonograph, radio, tape recorder and television. He was fascinated and consumed by it and, in that sense, he resembled his father. It would not be stretching it to say that had Glenn been left alone to emerge into the occupation of his choice, perhaps he would have become an electronic engineer, a capable CBC music director, or maybe a famous disc jockey. Instead, he was launched on the very narrow but steep pathway of a concert pianist. Now that he was in his thirties, he felt it was time to change his orientation and vocational identity. He was tired of the unpredictable stage escapades. The radio seemed to him a more enticing and far(ther)-reaching medium. Gould confessed: "Radio ... is a medium I've been very close to ever since I was a child, that I listen to virtually non-stop; I mean it's wallpaper for me—I sleep with the radio on ...[25]

It all came together at this point of his life—his background as a radio buff, his knack for electronics, the long-felt concert fatigue and the need for solitude. When the momentum was gained, Gould made a transition from public performance to an electronic media career. On this pathway, he was inspired and encouraged by the thought of his contemporary, Marshall McLuhan. The Toronto-based philosopher, McLuhan, put forward innovative ideas that had both stimulating and shocking effect. His famous dictum, "The medium is the message,"[26] opened up doors of endless debates. Gould subscribed to the age of technology and in this vein his first love, the piano, became overtaken by his second love, the radio. Though he had mixed feelings about McLuhan and often disagreed with his concepts, he was stimulated by his challenging ideas. McLuhan says, "the medium is the message" because "it is the medium that shapes and controls the scale and form of human association and action." He also divided media into hot and cold, radio being a hot medium with a "high definition," whereas the telephone and the television are cool media. Here are some typical excerpts from McLuhan's writings:

> And as for the cool war and the hot bomb, the cultural strategy that is desperately needed is humor and play. It is play that cools off the situations of actual life by miming them. Competitive sports between Russia and the West will hardly serve that purpose of relaxation, such sports are inflammatory, it is plain.[27]
>
> ... One way to spot the basic difference between hot and cold media uses is to compare and contrast a broadcast of a symphony performance with a broadcast of a symphony rehearsal. Two of the finest shows ever released by the

> CBC were of Glenn Gould's procedure in recording piano recitals, and Igor Stravinsky's rehearsing the Toronto Symphony in some of his new work.[28]

McLuhan's ideas emerged in the 1960s and applied to his experience of the world of media. Gould found it encouraging to put emphasis on media communication as opposed to close interpersonal relationships. McLuhan's favoring of Gould's recording sessions, rather than watching his public recital in a concert hall, was a justification for Gould that he was on the right track making a transition to the media—radio and recording.

Gould's industrious needs found their full appeal in technology and telecommunication. On the radio, he could broadcast both his music and his views without taking an interpersonal risk. Radio provided this peculiar atmosphere for him to be heard and not seen, which was a reversal of the Victorian attitude toward children in whose spirit he himself was raised. Good riddance! No more formal, stuffy attire with a starched white shirt and deplorable black tails. Enough of the abrasive comments on his piano chair and his piano posture. Gould's unspoken message was: "Goodbye stage fright, I never have to sweat again around each performance." The radio was perceived as a safe haven that allowed him to be creative while healing from many injuries to his self esteem, from his phobias and from endless contacts with people. At last, Gould was able to relax from public demands and practice introversion when necessary or be outgoing and expressive when he felt like it.

Chapter XV

LOVE AND SEXUALITY

TOUCH ME, TOUCH ME NOT

Abstinence is as easy to me as temperance would be difficult.

Samuel Jonson[1]

By a gift of nature, as a young man Gould was quite handsome and in possession of many attractive physical traits typical of the males on his father's side. Those who were touched by the looks of his face spoke in romantic terms about his "blueberry eyes," and about lockets of misbehaving dark blond hair falling over his forehead during his dynamic piano performances. Gould was sexy-looking and photogenic, and whenever posing for promotional pictures, he had a pensive and captivating aura about him. Press-released photographs, be it on his records, concert programs or in magazines, summoned attention and even infatuation in female audiences. Women fans showered him with letters full of appreciative comments about his looks and music. What Gregory Peck was for women as a motion picture artist, Glenn Gould was as a classical music star.

On closer examination, it can be seen that Gould was going through a rapid transition with respect to his self-image during his early twenties. While in his childhood and teens he wore elegant, custom-made clothing, as a young man he was less stylish. Gould started wearing an obsolete wardrobe without any flare or design. By the time he became fully responsible for his self-care, he not only was not interested in adorning his body but actively neglected it. Everything from self-grooming to nutrition and recreational practices gradually declined. The turning point appeared to be the time when he stopped going to school and stopped contacts with Guerrero, but more conspicuously when he went away from home and began isolating himself at the cottage. With the loss of the structure of school and home, Gould's style seemed to change from being formal and au courant to casual, even shabby. He no longer cared for color coordination, and his new preferred colors, charcoal and dark blue, were symbolic of his inner somberness. Another distinct feature of Gould was that he wore his clothing loose, oversized and tent-like, which disguised his natural beauty. Not only were his clothes subdued and unattractive but he developed a habit of wearing excessive layers of clothing. Items like sweaters, long overcoats, knitted scarves and gloves, and a choice of hats like porkpie hats and berets, which are normally used only in winter weather, became constant in his wardrobe year round, even on the hottest summer days. This is how a paradox gradually was formed about Gould. As a virtuoso, he had that universal appeal and attractive image projected through the media, but as a person he projected this vulnerable and non-attractive side of himself. His family defended him outwardly when it came to his external looks. His first cousin, Jessie Greig, did not think he had a major self-image problem:

"Do you think that Glenn was attractive in the eyes of the opposite sex?" I asked her while we were sitting side-by-side on her sofa.

"Very much so. I thought he was very attractive as a man, and women were crazy about him. A friend of mine asked me to introduce her to him, but I told her Glenn was too busy to go out on dates." Jessie protected her famous cousin.

"Of course, there was more to Glenn than just good looks?" I asked.

"That's given. Glenn gave away a sense of importance, regardless whether he was joking or being serious. But above all, there was this aura of intelligence around him. He was very special to me. I felt so blessed to have had him in my life."

"Yet, Glenn used to wear layers of clothes and was often described as old-fashioned, even bizarre in his appearance. Don't you think his clothes made him look less attractive?" I asked.

"Well, the whole idea about his outside looks seems overblown to me. Sure he dressed differently and his clothes were somewhat austere. Sometimes I asked him, 'Aren't you hot, Glenn, 'and he said very decisively, 'No, Jessie, it's good for my joints. Besides, I have a different metabolism than you people.' And I was very satisfied to know that he was O.K. The clothes did not make him less attractive, not to me, anyway,"[2] Jessie said adamantly.

The history of religious and ethnic traditions shows that clergy, monks and nuns throughout the centuries have worn rather plain and monotonous-looking clothing. The major component of this practice is to de-emphasize the importance and looks of the body and stress the importance of one's spiritual being. Often, those who serve God are expected to curb their desire and pleasure-seeking activities and do away with their libidinal temptations. The clothes worn by the clergy serve as a partition from the physically invested sensual world. Once libidinal desires are under control, one could dedicate oneself to God and to spiritual life. By wearing dark and austere garments, Gould created a sort of imaginary divider between himself and all others. His entire life took on a character of solitude and avoidance of face-to-face interactions and physical touch.

On the pathway of introversion, Gould found comfort in fictional characters who also were lonely and repressed men. He was fascinated by Santayana's portrayal of solitary men in his novel *The Last Puritan*. In a similar way, he identified with another even more stern and dramatic character named Adrian Leverkuhn in Thomas Mann's novel *Doctor Faustus*. Adrian, a musically gifted man of brilliant intelligence, lived a life of a theologian, morally "pure," socially reclusive and emotionally self-depriving. Here is a portrayal of Adrian by Thomas Mann, which, to a great extent, can apply to Gould:

> There has always been in his nature something of NOLI ME TANGERE. I know that his distaste for too great physical nearness of people, his dislike of "getting in each other's steam," his avoidance of physical contact, were familiar to me. He was in the real sense of the word a man of disinclination, avoidance, reserve, aloofness. Physical cordialities seemed quite impossible to associate with his nature, even his handshake was infrequent and hastily performed. More plainly than ever this characteristic came out during my visit and to me I cannot

> say why, it was as though "Touch me not! Three paces off" had to some extent altered its meaning, as though it were not so much that an advance was discouraged as that an advance from the other side was shrunk from and avoided—and this undoubtedly was connected with his abstention from women.[3]

The fictional Adrian and the real Gould were both "touch me not" people who shrank from human touch through their counter-social behavior. "Even his handshake was infrequently and hastily performed," Mann said of Adrian. Gould shunned shaking hands whenever possible by keeping his hands in his pockets, by wearing gloves or simply by avoiding receptions and other forms of social situations. While a number of pianists do not hesitate to shake hands with the public and give autographs after concert receptions, it may be reasonable for a virtuoso to exercise caution and escape en masse handshakes in order to protect his hands from possible micro-injuries. Gould, in his manner of evasion, went beyond the reasonable. His avoidance of shaking hands was not just an occupational safety measure but was a sign of inhibition that served to protect him from the potential "hazard" of social closeness.

Gould was in possession of two major faculties that made it possible for him to become a supreme virtuoso at the keyboard: first, he had a natural excellent sense of touch, and second, his sense of touch was systematically trained into a perfect piano touch, or more specifically into his piano technique. The critics often referred poetically to Gould's amazing sense of touch, without quite being aware of the complexity of its background. Here is one early reference to Gould's capable sense of touch, reported in the *Uxbridge Times Journal* on February 1, 1951, following Gould's performance of the Beethoven First Concerto at Massey Hall:

> **Gould At TSO Shows Genius In Piano Touch**
>
> Piano entry after orchestra prelude was touchingly beautiful—such gentle singing tone rare as genius itself.
>
> His piano touch is creative as well as interpretative. He is one of Canada's greatest pianists—young as he is.[4]

The piano touch, not the human touch, became emotionally invested, or in more psychodynamic terms, cathected with libidinal energy. When the music critic said that Gould's "piano entry" was "gentle" and "touchingly beautiful," it sounds as if he were describing a romantic relationship between two mates involved in an intimate love scene. Music and human love are two separate and distinct activities that often become intertwined. The content of one may blend with the content of the other. Melody and lyrics are frequently related to human love in that music may portray, facilitate and help perpetuate loving emotions.

If music and love go hand-in-hand, then music, love and human touch are even a more complete and compatible trio. If Gould wore heavy knitted gloves and long tent-like topcoats, it was not because he was literally cold but because he was afraid of warming himself up toward another human being. The same principal was at work in his avoidance of shaking hands. Just as a kiss on the lips can stimulate densely spread nerve endings and produce an emotional response, a handshake has to do with tactile stimulation ending in a similar way. The handshake is a significant symbol of social contact, friendship and mutual respect between individuals. It could mark a beginning, continuation, or the end of relationship, and it may open a freeway of uncharted interpersonal opportunities.

The above trio becomes a quartet by adding to this synchrony of music, love and human touch another parameter, human sexuality. A sexual relationship in a concrete sense of sexual intercourse, or in a broader sense as a synonym with love and intimacy, is the most emotionally charged tactile stimulation. The handshake, the kiss and lovemaking are three tactile experiences that are emotionally charged (cathected), and together they account for the vitality and perpetuity of human life.

Gould was lucky in being able to apply his exquisite tactile abilities to music, which for him on the conscious level was the center of his emotional gravity. At the same time, the importance of human closeness and touch was denied. He was terrified of having bodily pleasures. If he allowed himself to feel one moment of body lust, it may have opened him to another, and he feared that before he knew it, he would not be able to control his pleasure needs. This was the crux of Gould's inner plight, where the presence of rigid moral values forbade him to engage in love and intimate relations. By the time Gould was in his twenties, his whole inner psyche was geared to repudiate any sexual desire for fear that he may easily end up as a moral reprobate.

Gould's distancing from others was deeply subconsciously programed and inescapable. Coming from an emotionally reserved family, Glenn himself became nondemonstrative of his feelings very early in his life, to the point of emotional guardedness. This feature of his character became more exaggerated as he grew older. In his upbringing, there was a real paucity of closeness expressed through overt gestures of endearment. Glenn was simply not used to receiving hugs and kisses. On the contrary, he was trained to refrain from yearning for physical intimacy. That is why his pets, notably the series of dogs he had, meant so much to him. Unlike people, they could always be affectionately cuddled as a substitute for human touch. Once deprived of engaging in human intimacy with its corresponding physical touch, the young man was left with limited tactile choices. He still had the option of the tactile pleasure of playing the piano as an imaginary love object; of touching his own body or permitting health professionals—doctors, chiropractors, masseurs—to touch and handle him in a socially accepted and justified way for the purpose of looking after his well-being.

From what is known about Gould, it is unlikely that he could afford to touch himself freely and pleasurably, sexually or nonsexually. When having to bathe and groom himself, he pursued it quickly and negligently. In his private diary, Gould referred occasionally to taking extended hot baths in his bath tub for medicinal purposes. He did not so much look for erotic pleasure but rather struggled with the consequences of not having it, which was then reflected in his overall restlessness and tension.

Prohibition from erotic and autoerotic sexual and emotional discharge was identical with practicing asceticism. Indeed, Glenn's ascetic phase was very noticeable in his adolescence, when he did not show the usual pubertal interests. He never dated like other boys and never had a sweetheart. Once this phase of development was not appropriately mastered, its consequences were carried into adulthood in their unresolved form. As a man, Gould went so far in his self-denial of libidinal needs and love responses that he developed a conceited rationale of dividing people into two groups: those who are secular and hedonistic and those who are spiritual. Even his intense dislike of Mozart as a person was related to his profound conviction that Mozart was hedonistic and overindulgent. This attitude robbed him of the ability to fully enjoy Mozart's music, which according to Gould was not "pure" enough, since it was composed by a hedonist. Gould modeled himself after those dramatic characters who are gifted yet are in denial of their love needs. For example, the character of *Hamlet*, who Gould studied and to which he aspired, had asexual feelings toward Ophelia, whom he urged to go to a nunnery.

A part of Gould's mystery has to do with his fastidious selectiveness of music, marked by strong preferences and even stronger repulsions. The entire Gould phenomenon is related to his repressed sexuality. The music that he could experience cerebrally and spiritually, like baroque music, appealed to him. He was able to embrace, master and recreate it, and the fame he earned by interpreting it immortalized him in return. The payback for playing the music that did not give rise to his unconscious conflicts was maximal and unequivocal. This is not true of the romantic music for which Gould showed distaste and removed from his interpretative repertoire. As a master of piano music, he was supposed to be less biased and more receptive to music works by such great composers as Chopin, Shumann, Schubert and Liszt. This attitude created confusion and hostility around him. Gould was not aware that his music bias was not his asset or a product of his healthy and creative self but was rather an unconsciously determined hindrance, a product of his deep insecurities about love and pleasure. He dealt with this impediment by justifying and defending his position and making it look like a conscious choice. In the interview with Tim Page, Gould provided the following rational for his feelings about romantic music:

> The music of that era is full of empty, theatrical gestures, full of exhibitionism and it has a worldly, hedonistic quality that simply turns me off.[5]

A little further in the same conversation, Gould was full of praise of the music of Richard Strauss:

> *Metamorphosen* is my favorite Strauss piece because in it he has finally come to terms with the abstract nature of his own gift. In a way, it's Strauss's *Art of the Fugue*. It's an asexual work if you like, a work that has no gender.[6]

Short of explicitly saying that he perceived romantic music as sexual and immoral, during his entire life Gould hedged around this topic that gave him tremendous anxiety and discomfort. As far as his awareness went, romantic music was a synonym for love and sexuality, whereas spiritual and, particularly, cerebral music were devoid of it; which in his mind proved them safe from worldly temptations. Though this defensive attitude was, for the most part, operating during his manhood, there were a few challenging exceptions. In the next story, there can be found a spark in Gould for the popular music of his time and for a singer, Petula Clark, who awakened his love interests.

IN SEARCH OF LOVE

> Face, figure, discreet gyrations, but, above all that voice ...
>
> Glenn Gould[7]

Gould maintained a surprisingly large correspondence with his female friends. In some way, in his letters to women he was able to be more chatty, more expressive and even personal at times. One of the first examples of an expressive letter was the one written to Edith Boecker in January 1960.

Gould wrote this particular letter shortly after his attempt to move out of his parents' home and move to a twenty-six-room country mansion, Donchery. The concert pianist genuinely confided to Boecker as if she were his close friend or a therapist, when in reality he only met her casually during his German tour in 1958. While the story about Gould's moving out was already told earlier, here the focus is on how he perceived the reaction of others to the Donchery episode. In one humorous sentence he alluded to the people around him as being doting and possessive:

> Homburger, I think, was terrified that I was giving up the piano to devote myself to the role of country squire and his secretary was convinced that I was having an affair with the upstairs maid (who hadn't yet been engaged—to do housework, that is) and my mother, I'm sure, was convinced I was secretly married."[8]

Gould obviously felt that his mother was uneasy about his moving out. She was afraid of letting him go. Florrie Gould often voiced her fears of Glenn abandoning his piano career, of being involved with the wrong crowd and developing other interests. With respect to this, falling in love and getting married could be a distraction that may have taken Glenn away from the mission she had wished for him. Contrary to this, Glenn's father appeared concerned and often irritated by his son's "abnormal" lifestyle, so poignantly empty of love relations. Even so, when long after the fact Mr. Gould was asked how he felt about his son's love life, he defended him in this way:

"Mr. Gould, Glenn was a permanent bachelor. How do you explain the fact that he never got married?" I asked.

"Oh, that's very simple. Glenn was a very busy man. He was an artist and artists don't have regular lives. He worked at night and slept during the day. The last thing he needed was to go out on a date. He hadn't got time for that." Mr. Gould was quite frank about this.

"How did Mrs. Gould feel about Glenn not having a girlfriend?" I was looking for a less-defensive answer.

"If you mean whether she urged him to get married, she didn't. She would never interfere with Glenn's life. She wanted what's best for him," said Mr. Gould.

"Yet, Glenn was attractive and one of the most eligible bachelors in town. He must've had a lot of fans?" I expected a more elaborate answer.

"Oh, yes, his women fans bothered him all the time. They asked him out, wrote him long letters and even harassed him. And, you know something, he answered all these letters in person. That distracted him from his creative work. It led nowhere. So I can see why he kept away from getting involved."[9] Mr. Gould dismissed the importance of love and intimacy in his son's life.

By saying that women were merely a distraction from Glenn's creative achievement, Mr. Gould perhaps tried to put a stop to further questions about Glenn's love life. He gave an example of an older woman who used to drive several summers in a row from Boston to the Goulds' cottage in Uptergrove on Lake Simcoe, hoping to see Glenn in person:

> I remember, she parked her station wagon right across from our gates. She had a photo camera, and she was watching our door like a hawk, looking for Glenn to show up. She even went to the shore, to see whether Glenn was coming by boat.

> She was so obsessed by him. Once, I remember, she began walking toward our door. I was watering the front lawn with a hose and I kept making bigger circles, not paying much attention to her. I guess, she noticed she was not welcome and she went back to her car. The whole thing was so disgusting.[10]

By only referring to those casual contacts, Mr. Gould evaded the issue of love in Glenn's life. Several questions come to mind. Why was Mr. Gould so defensive about Glenn with regards to women? Perhaps this woman-visitor was only a curious fan who was justly fascinated by Glenn Gould as a great musician. Why didn't Mr. Gould let Glenn deal with his fan instead of taking the matter into his own hands and making her unwelcome? Why didn't Mr. Gould, who was a very articulate person, talk to this woman and find out what she was after? Instead, he reacted as if he were threatened by her. It seems that Mr. Gould was unable to cope properly with his son's manhood or with his fame. He had mixed feelings about Glenn's love life and inadvertently contributed to Glenn's insecurity about love and intimacy. The father remained "loyal" to his son by maintaining an aura of secrecy. This was detrimental to Glenn as it discouraged him from getting in touch with his love feelings.

On the whole, Glenn's ability to fall in love was inwardly thwarted and outwardly restrained, until he encountered the songs of the British pop singer Petula Clark. Though Glenn had been familiar with the singer ever since her first hit, "Downtown," was released in 1964, he really discovered Petula and his own feelings about her two years later, when he accidentally heard her fourth hit, "Who Am I ?" This took place during one of his random car rides when his radio was turned on as usual. When Glenn was bored by the seclusion at home or in a hotel room, wherever he resided at the time, he entertained himself by driving along Ontario highways. Ironically, for him this appeared to be a less solitary activity and a way of reaching out. One of his favorite destinations was Marathon, a small town on the northern shore of Lake Superior. His itinerary consisted of heading north from Toronto to rural Ontario; then following the east side of Georgian Bay until he reached the mining country around Sudbury. At that junction, Glenn would take Highway 17 west to the northern shore of Lake Superior. Glenn absolutely delighted in driving overnight from Toronto to Marathon, or other nearby towns like Wawa and Terrace Bay. Though it took well over a thousand kilometers (or 655 miles) to get there, he drove with demonic energy and speed, with very few stops on the way. The usual scenario was that having reached one of these places, he would check into the local motel to find his peace and the hope that he would be able to fall asleep. After a day or two, the ritual of driving back home would repeat in reverse. This route was not accidental but was rather emotionally significant as a heritage trail for him. Passing by Lake Simcoe, where Glenn spent the best years of his young life, then edging on Port Severn, where his mother was born, and driving through Sault Ste. Marie, where she took piano classes in her youth, was familiar and soothing. Radio music was always turned on to entertain him. Glenn's many excursions to small Ontario towns were a reenactment of the original comfort felt in his boyhood when he was with his parents.

On one such occasion when Glenn took this same route to Lake Superior, he heard Petula Clark singing one of her greatest hits, "Who Am I?" Glenn was instantly jolted and awakened by this song. Everything about it appealed to him, the lyrics, the music, the content to which he was so able to relate, and most particularly the voice of the songstress. The young man driving alone in the dark and exposed to a lovely female voice was a perfect candidate for a love fantasy. Though Glenn was not consciously looking for it, he certainly set himself up for that kind of a response. All of a sudden, his long repressed romantic strivings came to the surface. Petula's song became a catalyst for the emergence of strong amorous feelings. In common parlance, Glenn was "turned on."

This raises a number of questions. Why Petula Clark? Why not Edit Piaf or Mireille Mathieu, the leading French proponents of love chansons? Why not one of the teen idols like Connie Francis or the very popular movie star and singer Doris Day, who were so much more known in North America? Doris Day was dedicated to animals, particularly dogs, which would be one more reason for Glenn to have liked her. Why did it happen on this particular trip and not ever before? The answers vary from a simple possibility that these songs were not on the CBC program as "the pop picks from *Billboard* magazine"[11] at the time when Glenn was in such a receptive mood, to more intricate and deeper emotional reasons. The latter appears to be more true. This working hypothesis suggests that Gould was not so much captivated by Petula's song in a narrow sense but that he was rather charmed by her voice, which to him had a personal meaning.

Having stopped his public performance career in 1964, Gould felt as if a big weight was lifted off his shoulders. The doors to the next, more exciting chapter of his life seemed to be wide open. He was then free to rearrange his busy schedule and have more spare time. The pressure in his inner world and the need for constant guardedness and control were all temporarily decreased. Gould was more than ever at liberty to make long and adventurous trips. Being less defensive and less inhibited also meant that he was more open for change. So, at the point of Glenn taking that particular ride on that long Ontario highway, when Petula's song happened to be aired, he was predisposed not only to enjoy the song and the voice of the singer but to be lovestruck. Empowered by the command of his eight-cylinder Lincoln Continental, appeased by the endless space around him and deeply touched by Petula's seductive voice, Glenn was in the state of ecstasy. In scientific language, he was able to "genitalize" his romantic state of mind without having to put it to the test. His genital excitement was probably associated with some erotic masturbatory fantasies. Glenn allowed himself to experience those gratifying feelings of power, pleasure and even sexual arousal without feeling too guilty. He was in the car by himself and no one was there to censor him. Even if he felt embarrassed by his own erotic response, he could always rationalize that it was only the voice that aroused him and not the presence of a real woman.

Petula Clark, the honey-blonde singer with the pop-and-jazz voice, reached fame in the 1960s with the release of "Downtown." Other hits followed—"My Love," "Don't Sleep on the Subway," and in 1966 it was "Who Am I?" Glenn's excitement upon hearing Petula's songs was not momentary but sustained him through the stretch of several years. During that time, he learned about her biography, took pleasure in her voice and studied the music she sang, composed for her by Tony Hatch. Gould confessed: "I never bought a pop record in my life. But after that [hearing Petula on the radio] I picked up every record she'd ever made."[12]

What was so special about Petula's songs? Here is the first stanza of the song "Downtown:"

> When you're alone and life is making you lonely,
> You can always go, Downtown,
> When you've got worries, all the noise and the hurry,
> Seems to help, I know, Downtown,

Just listen to the music of the traffic in the city,
Linger on the sidewalk where the neon signs are pretty,
How can you lose? The lights are so much brighter there,
You can forget all your troubles, forget all your care,
So go, Downtown, things will be great when you're, Downtown,
No finer place for sure, Downtown,
Everything is waiting for you.[13]

The song is a social invitation for lonely men and women, encouraging them to come from their dull suburbia to the lively downtown. In most urban communities, downtown is seen as a circle of potential excitement, a magnetic powerhouse that seduces all kinds of people to gather there for fun, for business or simply to be where the action is. But the song ignores the dark side of a downtown. Indeed, it can be a black pit for many, a place of temptations and a trap for lost souls. Its mystery makes it an undying object of curiosity and a source of potential danger. The acts of violence and crime, the sleazy bars that foster human indulgence and vice of every kind, the vendors and buyers of sex are to be found here. Frankly, in a downtown there is potential for both pleasure and pain. It is a place where inhibitions and sorrows are magically unfastened; for some, it is a symbol of blackness and despair, and a place of bright lights and excitement for others.

Petula's voice and her optimistic song became a secret aphrodisiac to Glenn. After listening to "Downtown," he could no longer maintain his lily pure demeanour to himself but, reluctantly, had to give up his mental virginity. This partial sexual awakening became a modest addition to his inner fantasy of love and, in a broader sense, to his overall inner sexual experience. In spite of that, Glenn never mustered enough energy to let himself go "downtown" to enjoy its offerings. Instead, he practiced the opposite, getting away from social stimulation and pleasure. He thought of downtown as a metaphor for evil, a moral purgatory rather than a social paradise.

This entire experience of falling in love with the voice and the pop-songs served as an incentive for Gould to write and publish an article, "The Search for Petula Clark," which may as well have been titled "The Search for Love." Gould subconsciously channeled his sexual energy into intellectual achievement and into the creation of this literary piece. He was embarrassed about delving into a topic of love and made sure to disguise his personal feelings through his highly intellectual and convoluted style of writing. Even so, he was not quite able to hide his outpouring emotions that escaped him here and there in little bursts of adoration. Gould says: "Pet Clark ... is pop music's most persuasive embodiment of the Gidget syndrome," and "Her audience is large, constant and possessed of enthusiasm which transcends the generations." Gould not only loved Petula's songs but studied their lyrics and music and even made a lay analysis of their deeper dynamics. He says:

> ... Each of the songs contrived for her by Tony Hatch emphasizes some aspect of that discrepancy between an adolescent's short-term need to rebel and long-range readiness to conform. In each the score pointedly contradicts that broad streak of self-indulgence which permeates the lyrics. The harmonic attitude is, at all times, hymnal, upright and relentlessly diatonic.[14]

By characterizing the song as "hymnal, upright and relentlessly diatonic," Gould braced himself with his preferred moral values in which he happened to identify with his mother. By suggesting that the lyrics are self-indulgent, he shows his disapproval of anything frivolous and pleasure-seeking, which are symbols associated with downtown. Gould was of two minds. He liked the music and voice of the singer but rejected her symbolic invitation to social pleasure. By saying that Petula is "pop music's most persuasive embodiment of the Gidget syndrome," he was referring to the series of light movie-musicals that portrayed teenagers having fun on the beach. Gould used to watch these movies in his late twenties when he had a chance. For onlookers of any age, it is uplifting to see youth dancing, singing, suntanning and falling in love while spending happy days on the beach. The message of the Gidget movies refers to the joys of adolescence and to the importance of socializing and pursuing a love life.

Glenn, who literally grew up in the Beaches of Toronto, missed out on the entire age-appropriate fun that he was supposed to experience at such a popular "hangout" place for youth. By hanging around together as a group, by playing beach volleyball, by swimming, splashing, joking around and touching each other, young men and women practice togetherness and social intimacy. Growing up, Glenn was not encouraged by his family to dash away to the beach, which was only a few blocks south from where he lived. The whole experience passed him by. This is why many years later, in his adulthood, he had such a craving for watching the Gidget movies and soon after to listen to Petula's pop music. At least on some personal level, Glenn was aware that he had a lot of catching up to do. Watching the teen-idol movie stars and listening to popular music was for him a new form of personal fulfillment. In his article on Petula Clark, Gould referred to "Downtown" as "that intoxicated adolescent daydream," giving us a hint of his own pleasure at fantasizing about his teens many years later. In reality, the beach and downtown are the special fun-loving places for people of all ages but are particularly attractive to the young and affluent. By encountering Petula's voice and songs, Gould was able to recapture some of his missed adolescent emotional needs. For Gould, partial sexual awareness was helpful in his overall psychosexual adjustment.

Petula's fourth released hit, "Who Am I?" triggered in Gould a bout of creative spirit and cemented his love of her voice. He studied her entire music achievement to date and produced an article about it. Gould particularly loved the lyrics that in his words deal with "identity crisis." He says that "Who Am I?" is "but a modest acceleration of the American teen-ager's precipitous scramble from the parental nest," which was exactly the trauma he had personally experienced at moving out from his family home. Here are the poignant verses Gould identified with:

> The buildings reach up to the sky,
> The traffic thunders on the busy street,
> Pavement slips beneath my feet,
> I walk alone and wonder, Who Am I?[15]

And after much wondering in an attempt to discover oneself among the skyscrapers, the song offers a semi-solution of being loved by somebody, which makes one's identity problems easier to bear:

> Maybe I am reaching far too high,
> For I have something else entirely free,
> The love of someone close to me,
> Unfettered by the world that hurries by,
> To question such good fortune, Who Am I?[16]

Gould's positive identification with the theme of this song is extended to the music composition by Tony Hatch. In a comparison of "Downtown" and "Who Am I?" Gould said that the two songs play the "similar game of reverse" in which "Downtown" is associated with "infectious enthusiasm," whereas "Who Am I?" is "somnambulistic."[17] When Gould commented on Tony Hatch and his work, he made a pun by saying that he "hatched" these songs specially for Petula. This is a typical Gouldian joke.

In analyzing Petula's songs, while being fascinated by her voice, Gould compared her favorably to the Beatles. The more he idealized Petula, the more he rejected the art of the Beatles, to the point of brutal dismissal. He accused them of having "little regard for the niceties of voice leading," and for "the indulgent amateurishness of the musical material."[18] Gould was simply livid about the fact that the Beatles were "in" while Petula was relatively "out." He was completely unaware that his evaluation of their vocal artistry was heavily colored by his private feelings of hate and love respectively. When at the peak of his bias and castigation of the Beatles, Gould became vile, he said: "Theirs is a happy, cocky, belligerently resourceless brand of harmonic primitivism."[19] Gould did not like the Beatles because he harboured deep personal intolerance toward their exhibitionism. While he thought of Petula Clark as a decent, family-oriented, down-to-earth performer, he regarded the Beatles as more flamboyant, more sexually suggestive and more hedonistic; behavior that he had always condemned. Gould was a black-and-white person who either glorified others or showed intense dislike for them. Often, it could have been the same person observed at different points of time, idealized at first and demoted from the pedestal status and rejected later. Petula Clark was an exception to the rule and remained in Gould's good graces permanently as an object of veneration. He liked her modesty and covert sexuality, "but, above all, that voice." Gould looked at Petula through the shiny glasses of reverie that he had for a certain type of idealized women. He mused:

> To her more mature public, she's comfort of another kind. Everything about her onstage, on-mike manner belies the aggressive proclamations of the lyrics. Face, figure, discreet gyrations, but, above all, that voice, fiercely loyal to its one great octave, indulging none but the most circumspect slides and filigree, vibrato so tight and fast as to be nonexistent ...[20]

It was as if Gould came out of his longtime sexual repression and suddenly declared his love of Petula's voice and her other qualities. Gould was taken by the voice, and he fell in love with it. But the voice is only an extension of a person and not the person itself. Falling in love with the voice is equal to falling in love with a person's eyes, foot or even the shoes or the clothes worn. Petula's voice, and to a lesser degree her songs, became a cherished fetish to Gould. The voice touched a sensitive spot in him in the same way as his mother's voice touched him in his boyhood. Not to say that his mother's and Petula's voices were identical in color or texture, but Glenn's experience of Petula's voice was reminiscent of the original pleasure felt at hearing his mother's "angelic" voice.

Apart from the infatuation with Petula Clark's voice, which went on for a few years, Gould's sexuality in his thirties continued to be under siege. By that time, he had never seen a live striptease nor had he ever gone to a stag party, though he watched many of his male friends get married. Fearing retribution from within, he obeyed the demands of his puritan moral values. The motto of puritans with respect to love and sex is chastity and fidelity, to which Gould not only faithfully subscribed but took it to the extreme and added another stringent value—virginity. In his eyes, sex was a liability that was unaffordable even for the purpose of procreation. Along those lines of inner prohibitions, Gould could not allow himself to use any devices, such as reading pornographic literature, that would even remotely stimulate sexual excitement. This he would instantly consider sinful. The lifestyle of the hippies who put emphasis on pleasure and sexual freedom, the lyrics and rhythm of rock 'n' roll and the inception of Playboy magazine, which were all the unstoppable social phenomena of the 1960s, were in Glenn's mind met with severe disapproval. For many, rock 'n' roll was considered as the "devil's music." Glenn thought of it as a form of exhibitionism that had always put him off.

Andrew Kazdin recalled an episode that is a clear example of Gould's austere sexual morality. According to Kazdin, his wife Genevieve once casually picked up a copy of *Cosmopolitan* magazine. Much to her surprise, she found there a music review of Gould's recently released recordings in 1969 of Scriabin and Prokofiev. Kazdin, himself excited about her discovery, broke the news to his music friend and asked him to guess the name of the publication. Gould habitually lapsed into the game of Twenty Questions, ferociously going through his mental list of possible American magazines. When finally with some difficulty Gould found out that it was *Cosmopolitan*, he was not pleased at all, but instead he became alarmed by Genevieve's choice of literature. He responded with panic and admonishment:

> What's Gen doing reading *Cosmopolitan*? ... Well you may tell her for me that I disapprove, I strongly disapprove ... I think that Gen should end her subscription immediately ...[21]

When Kazdin tried to defend his wife by saying that she was really not a subscriber but more of an occasional reader, Gould was still unforgiving: "I am very disturbed with Gen. I really think that's got to stop."

Kazdin's story, though colored by his personal feelings of love and hate toward his famous client, is consistent with Gould's long-standing tendency to idealize others at first and then to reject them at some point after, because sooner or later they could no longer meet his impossibly high expectations. Glenn disapproved of *Cosmopolitan* because he thought of it as pornography. His prudishness was transferred onto Genevieve Kazdin, who as a woman engaged in reading of "obscene" literature became instantly de-idealized in his mind.

This brings us to the prototype of an idealized woman created by the Christian religion, the Virgin Mary, mother of Jesus. She is often referred to as the Madonna, which in Italian means "My Lady." Mary became a female ego ideal to many generations of Christianity. She is a consecrated figure who stands opposite to anything that is profane and secular. It is said that the Madonna conceived through the act of immaculate conception rather than in the way of ordinary lovemaking, which accounted for her lasting virginity.

Gould unconsciously perceived women in an idealized fashion as sacred and untouchable. This view was influenced by the role of religion in his life and could be traced back to his relationship with his staunchly religious mother. Be reminded that Florrie gave birth to Glenn when she was forty-two years old and that she regarded this event as a miracle. Glenn was treated by his mother with solemn devotion, as if he was a God-given gift and her holy child. Reciprocally, in his mind, she too became idealized and akin to the religious symbol of the Madonna.

In visual arts, the myth of the Madonna has been particularly explored through the Renaissance period. Painters perpetuated this serene, human ego ideal embodied in the visual image of the Madonna. The famous Italian painter, Raphael Santi, painted several portraits of the Madonna. Other great art masters like Leonardo da Vinci, El Greco and post-Renaissance Dutch master Rembrandt all immortalized the Madonna on canvas.

Gould may be regarded as the music painter of the Madonna. By championing Renaissance composers Orlando Gibbons and William Byrd, by idealizing women and rejecting anything romantic, sexual and boisterous in music, Gould symbolically represented the spirit of the Madonna, or in an extended sense, the spirit of anything that is pure and virginal. Indeed, the purity of Gould's music and his special touch make him both revered and untouchable. It is as if Gould, through his music, personally identified with the ego ideal of the Madonna.

Having followed this line of analytic thinking, it is easier to understand why Gould was not free to engage in common, worldly and fully represented love; for in his unconscious mind he was not a commoner but rather he was special. Perhaps he was meant to be a monk or a priest and be wholly dedicated to a deity. But in real life, Gould fell in love with music, which stole him away from practicing religion. This is how he stopped halfway between the extreme of religion and the extreme of worldly living and was not quite able to enjoy either. Gould was not a monk but neither was he a playboy. In many ways, he was more worldly than his parents, but in some other ways he was far less experienced than they. In love and sexual matters he was virtually a virgin. While his parents and grandparents were dutiful churchgoers, they also enjoyed the state of matrimony. Gould lived most of his life in privation and celibacy.

The "Madonna complex" robbed him of engaging freely in mature love relations. He was able to love certain parts of the world like music, poetry and other 'higher callings," but was really unable to fall in love with a whole person and follow through. In Gould's mind, genital and platonic love were set apart. He thought of lust and lovers as immoral and separated love from desire. Gould went so far in this philosophy that he condemned all those who came across to him as indulgent and hedonistic. He hated those men who flaunted their masculinity and more specifically those he perceived as lewd, obscene and "dirty old man" types.

One wonders when and how Glenn got the idea that sex is immoral and that men are "dirty?" Was it at home watching the relationship of his parents? This question leads us to the psychodynamics of the primal scene. The act of seeing one's parents for the first time in lovemaking is psychologically significant and is referred to as the primal scene. It is known that young children may become quite upset by seeing their parents in the sexual act. To them, the lovemaking may look like an act of force and aggression in which the mother is being attacked or hurt by the father. A child exposed to the sight of the sexual act is frightened and feels personally threatened. Those parents who have enough sensitivity to the child usually find sensible ways of preventing and handling the child's distress. In the opposite situation, when the parent does not pay attention to their child's reaction, this may be a source of permanent psychological trauma to the child.

Glenn's father was an epitome of masculinity, he was the hunter, the fisherman, even the lady's man, whereas Glenn not only did not identify with such a strong macho model but actively rebelled against it. Gould lived his adult life as if he had been subjected to psychological injuries at the level of the primal scene. His perception of sex as brutal and his avoidance of physical intimacy stood as unbridgeable barriers to falling in love with a person. All that he could afford was partial love of a person's voice. This was his secret fetish.

THE MYSTERY OF FETISHISM

> The fetish, an inanimate object, is immutable and permanent ...
>
> Janine Chasseguet-Smirgel[22]

A fetish, by definition, is any object regarded as having mysterious powers. It usually refers to any inanimate object or part of the human body, not including the reproductive system, which arouses sexual interest. Fetishism is a form of sexual preference where sexual excitement is achieved not necessarily in the presence of another person but rather in the presence of inanimate objects to which one assigns the mysterious power of love. For men, a common fetish is female lingerie such as underwear and brassieres, or other feminine apparel that acquire a deep psychological meaning and are capable of stimulating and eliciting sexual pleasure. The fetish becomes a pleasant addition to ones incomplete life, a mode of self-satisfaction and a protective device against one's own inadequacy in pursuing a more wholesome and complete relationship. What a fetishist fears the most are the genitals, both the real ones and their symbolic meaning. The original fear is of the masculine power of one's father experienced in childhood. A child that cannot overcome such fear will have to learn ways of coping with it. Any little boy that has been exposed to a trauma of the primal scene and has been unable to come to terms with it may find it difficult to manage the reality of genital sex. Such a person is forced to create "a new reality in which the father and his attributes are disqualified and in which the genital level of sexuality is disavowed."[23] The fetish represents a magic solution and a substitute for genital sex. The fetishist is stuck at the level of being too emotionally enmeshed with his mother but prohibited from pursuing a love relationship with her. At the same time, he rejects the masculinity and genitality of his father. In this conflict, the only way to turn is to inanimate objects or to parts of the human body rather than to the total person.

Gould's adoration of his mother's voice outweighed any feelings that he might have had in relationship to his father. In the language of inner dynamics, his mother's voice became a symbol of power to the point of exceeding the masculine power of his father. A need for a fetish is not necessarily connected with a quest for sexual satisfaction but could simply reflect a longing for general pleasure and wellbeing. According to this,

> ... fetishism aims at overcoming separation anxiety through a feeling of complete union with the mother obtained by means of the introjection of the good object. The ultimate aim of the fetishist is not to get genital satisfaction, but to feel a state of elation linked to that union with the good object."[24]

Gould, who had a high degree of separation anxiety all his life, developed a number of coping mechanisms to help preserve his sense of well-being. By this token his fetishism, which included the female voice regardless of whether it happened with or without sexual arousal, served the purpose of alleviating his high personal anxiety and producing temporary pleasure and comfort. In the absence of a full-scale, mature love relationship, this was the best that he could hope for, a partial experience of love from a distance.

One can look at fetishism as non-mainstream sex or as sexual perversion. Sigmund Freud, who extensively studied human sexuality, concluded:

> Perversions are neither bestial nor degenerate in the emotional sense of the word. They are the development of germs, all of which are contained in the undifferentiated sexual dispositions of the child, and which, by being suppressed or by being diverted to higher, asexual aims—by being sublimated—are destined to provide the energy for a great number of our cultural achievements.[25]

This was so true in Gould's case. Most of his libido as a drive was "diverted to higher asexual aims," notably his music and literary achievements. Only a small part of such energy was available for romantic pursuits, including his favorite fetish—the female voice.

Despite the universality of human love expressed in ordinary life, glorified in poetry, mystified in love stories and thoroughly studied and published in scientific literature, the phenomenon of love is still not sufficiently understood. The current consensus is that the capacity for mature love is a complex human asset that is determined by multiple inner dynamics. These dynamics start operating in the early years of human development and accrue in the course of emotional growth. Emotionally balanced individuals have the benefit of mature love, which encompasses the ability for genital satisfaction coupled with the capacity for tenderness. Here, the tenderness is not just a momentary show of affection but a more substantial and sustained capacity to be loving and caring. The ability to be tender is deeply rooted in early childhood and derives from oral and body surface eroticism and its integration together with libido as a drive and ability to relate to others.[26] Once the first stage of psychosexual development is achieved in the first two years of life, it is followed by the next period, known as the Oedipal or phallic stage. This is a time when male children accomplish sexual identification with their fathers and female children identify with their mothers. If all goes well, in the next sequence of emotional growth, there is a "full integration of genitality into love relationships—achieved by resolving oedipal conflicts."[27] Stable sexual identity, which in healthy individuals occurs toward the end of adolescence or in young adulthood, includes the ability for genital pleasure and tenderness and the capacity for mature idealization of the love partner. Mature idealization is based on one's ability to mourn personal losses, on empathy for others and on the realistic awareness of the love partner. It is said that "parents who deprive the child of opportunities to mourn over the loss of loved objects contribute to atrophy of the capacity to love."[28] The achievement of long-term intimacy between two adults is possible only if they have accomplished a stable identity in the previous stages. Normal sexual identity is a consequence of normal identity formation. It cements ego identity and gives it depth and maturity.[29]

Those individuals who do not have satisfactory psychosocial and psychosexual development may end up with a variety of conflicts from early childhood, which will then interfere with their capacity for mature love relationships. Gould was certainly one of them. He was enormously emotionally attached to his mother and unable to complete the task of individuation. At the same time, there was a relative emotional distance and ambivalence toward his father, which interfered with healthy identification. Out of those unsettled and unresolved relations with the most significant love objects in his life, separation anxiety remained a constant and plagued him for the rest of his life. Glenn was unable to mourn real and abstract losses and to celebrate his achievements and anniversaries. During his formative years, when the capacity for love was being shaped, Glenn was overinvolved with inanimate and abstract objects, the piano and music. He avoided discussing love matters with his peers but held onto artistic and intellectual themes. As a grown up, when he had a choice of changing and catching up with emotional and sexual growth, Glenn practiced social isolation. All these developmental impasses were damaging to his social and sexual adjustment. This is how Glenn was cheated out of the capacity for mature love.

Gould had an extraordinary capacity, not common in the general population, to enliven inanimate objects, and he indeed treated his concert piano, his piano chair and music in general as if they were alive. Otto Kernberg draws attention to "the 'coming alive' of inanimate objects:"

> This reaction to inanimate objects, as well as to nature and art, is intimately connected with the transcending aspect of a full relation in which the capacity for a total object relation and capacity for genital enjoyment are integrated.[30]

This is another feature of Gould's love life to transcend "ordinary" interpersonal love and devote himself to the love of music as a higher calling. Kernberg wrote:

> ... the capacity to experience in depth the nonhuman environment and to appreciate nature and art, and to experience one's self within a historical and cultural continuum, are intimately linked with the capacity for being in love ...[31]

In this case, Gould's extraordinary love of music is regarded as his personal strength and is equivalent to the quality of interpersonal love.

Gould's fetishism was not recognized during his lifetime, and most of his observers interested in his love life focused on his heterosexual dynamics. Some of Gould's contemporaries wondered if he were a homosexual. In San Francisco, at the Mozart Symposium in 1991 after a "Kaffeeklatsch" discussion about Glenn Gould,[32] several participants asserted their belief that he was gay. The "believers" mainly relied on their "hunch" and the obvious evidence that Gould was unmarried and spent most of his social time in the company of men, but they were still not able to offer any specific proof. In New York and Toronto, many close and peripheral observers also pondered the same question. This attitude was fueled by the reality that many contemporary music artists, both composers and instrumentalists, were practising homosexuals.

Jock Carroll[33] penned down a story Gould told him in 1956 that shows how Gould's physical appearance had a baffling impact on his contemporaries. Apparently, in one of his visits to Stratford, Ontario, for the summer festival, Gould appeared at a private house party. For this occasion, the twenty-three-year-old concert pianist wore a long black raincoat, a standard black cap that was pulled down to his eyebrows, a woollen scarf wrapped around his neck, and black gloves. A woman at the party, astounded by his exotic garb, charged at him: "Are you a fairy? Or aren't you a fairy? Are you a man or a mouse?" Perhaps her motive was more humorous than malicious but Gould was not amused. Though he did not say anything at the time, he was bothered by her abrasive questions. Later on, while he was relating the story to Carroll, he said that only after the party an idea came to his mind that he should have retorted to this woman: "Are you a harlot? Or aren't you a harlot? Or do you come with a house?" This was one of Gould's uncommon confessions of anger. It follows that Gould felt very offended by the woman's question, "Are you a fairy?" and wished to have fought back. The choice of his word "harlot" reveals that he interpreted her word "fairy" not as an imaginary supernatural being commonly portrayed in fairy tales but more as an offensive sexual slur that refers to a male homosexual. Ever since a pre-pubescent boy, Gould had always been oversensitive to any allusion to sexual issues, obscenities and smutty remarks. To him, the word fairy was not facetious but was rather obscene and abhorrent. It was reminiscent of the word "sissy" commonly used by his father. This was more a matter of self-esteem than a matter of sexuality. Gould's self-esteem was injured in his boyhood to the point of having widespread effects on his sexual identity.

Gould's closer friends did not see him as gay. Ray Roberts adamantly negated the possibility but admitted that sexual themes were a taboo, and he never dared to ask Gould about his love life. Andrew Kazdin referred briefly to the topic of Gould's sexuality, concluding that Gould was asexual, a kind of a sexual neuter:

> Was Gould a homosexual?...Gould was such a master at keeping control over exactly what he would allow one to know about his private life that I cannot make a definitive statement. I can only reply that in the fifteen years I knew him, never did I see any evidence to that effect. Of course, never did I see or hear evidence to the contrary. My own conjecture was that he was a kind of neuter. His own emotional involvement with his music ... was so intense that one might conclude that the piano was his mistress ...[34]

The assertion that "the piano was his mistress" adds to the theory of Gould's fetishism. The piano and the music sound elicited from this instrument are akin to the female voice in a sense that they are all inanimate. Only a sexually neutral person, a neuter, as Kazdin put it, would be able to prefer the love of physical and inanimate objects to falling in love with a whole human being.

In reality, sex according to Gould was a taboo. Sex in the form of sexual intercourse was not seen as love making but as fornication or something indecent and forbidden. While Gould's mother was alive until he was forty-three years of age, he only allowed himself to practice love fantasies and avoided real involvement in any type of love relationships. After Florence Gould died in 1975, her son was much too grief-stricken and despondent to afford falling in love. Gould was too socially removed, too puritanistic, too inept and too defensive in the sphere of interpersonal intimacy to be able to indulge in full, mature love relations. He experienced a degree of sexual excitement and possibly orgasm in the presence of the fetish—the female voice—but not within an interpersonal relationship, rather apart from it. For Gould, celibacy was a higher calling and his libido as a drive was sublimated or channeled in the direction of higher callings, intellectual achievements and artistic pursuits. Gould pursued celibacy relentlessly. He allowed himself genital arousal and infatuation with adult females in the form of platonic love or a romance free of sexual intercourse. Gould remained a genital virgin throughout his life inasmuch that he never experienced interpersonal sex. Having stopped short of genital sex, Gould stayed in the realm of idealized, platonic love with women, and in the domain of love of inanimate objects, the piano, the music, and the female voice. Gould was neither asexual, a neuter as Kazdin had suggested nor homosexual as some had wondered. His strong emotional reaction to Petula Clark is proof that he had a capacity to experience both romantic and erotic feelings toward women.

REAL LOVE STORIES

> Mature sexual love implies a commitment in the realms of sex, emotions, and values.
>
> Otto Kernberg[35]

Glenn frantically wrote in his journal:

> How good is our friendship? In my opinion it is so good that it has created an almost tensionless atmosphere. Because; we met and den.[ied] it when we were seemingly of one mind—one purpose; we both fell in love (63) talking about tranquility of spirit and we reinforced each other's determination to find that quality and bring it into our lives. ... I talked about hierarchy of friendship but I hadn't believed in them. I said that there are moments of intensity which have nothing to do with longe.[vity], intimacy, proximity etc. We, in my opinion reached that plateau very quickly and till now have maintained ourselves there in a marvelous fashion. We've also reached that plateau because, like all good Navajo cafe customers, it hasn't made any sense to play games, to employ strategies of any kind; we've behaved, I think, as though we really might never see each other again ...[36]

This emotionally powerful diary, which mentions no names, refers to Gould's romantic involvement with a married woman who was fascinated by him both as an artist and as a person. Led by strong passion, she temporarily moved to Toronto with her two children and settled in Gould's neighborhood. Their special blend of friendship and a platonic romance lasted about four years, until her reconciliation with her husband. Just like Ludwig van Beethoven, who wrote about his "Immortal Beloved" without mentioning her name, which posed a task to the generations of historians, Gould poured his heart out in this diary without once mentioning the name of his object of love. "Let the biographers chafe," said Sigmund Freud referring to the massive body of personal archives that he had destroyed in order to protect his privacy. Many great men like Freud, even without having lurid lives, still dread the exposure of their most intimate details of life. Guarding one's own privacy is a preventive measure against potential misuse of information and sensationalism. Likewise, both Beethoven and, then much later, Gould wrote in riddles about their love life in order to achieve a degree of privacy. In doing so, they did not so much intend to be difficult to future researchers but to protect themselves and their reputations from the nosy tabloids, which may, by way of being indiscreet and insensitive, hurt or ridicule them.

The moral dilemma for this biographer is whether to reveal or not the identity of Gould's partner in their mutual love story. If either of the two participants ever wished the world to know about their love affair, they would have spread the news themselves. Instead, both of them were surrounded with a wall of silence and discretion. What right do the writers, journalists and researchers have to pry into their intimate lives? The opposite argument would be that Gould, as a public figure, is a subject of curiosity and veneration, as well as the subject of analysis and inquiry into his life. By the same token, his partners in love also become a subject of public interest. This is how, for right or wrong, Gould's life and his life's achievement become a public domain to study and ponder; to admire and provide constructive critique; to enjoy and develop in-depth understanding and empathy for him. In that spirit, here are some bare details of Gould's love story.

Gould's friend and collaborator for the period of fifteen years, Andrew Kazdin, was the first one to reveal the name of Cornelia Foss as the person with whom Gould was intensely infatuated in the mid-1960s.[37] Cornelia was the wife of Gould's music friend and renowned American composer, Lucas Foss. Apparently, Gould invited Lucas to premiere his composition at the Stratford Festival in 1962. On July 13, Foss played the piano in the Schoenberg Heritage program organized by Gould, and two days later the members of the National Festival Orchestra featured the Canadian premiere of Lucas Foss's *Time Cycle*. There were also letters exchanged between the two music artists, and Gould entrusted to his friend his own newly composed music of his String Quartet no.1. Gould enjoyed Lucas Foss as a composer and a former student of Arnold Schoenberg. In turn, Foss admired Gould as a musician. Gould's first biographer, Otto Friedrich, described the beginning of their relationship:

> Gould did, in fact, have a long romance with a wife of a rather prominent musician, but she is reluctant to talk about any of the details. It began, in a way, when she and her husband were driving to dinner in Los Angeles, and the car radio suddenly began playing a new recording by an obscure young pianist performing the *Golberg Variations*. The husband pulled up at the side of the road and sat listening, spellbound. The wife recalls that they were very late in arriving at the dinner party. She met Gould at a concert not long afterward, and an elaborate courtship began.[38]

After more than four decades since they met, Cornelia Foss decided to step out of anonymity and speak up about her relationship with Glenn Gould. Quite recently, on August 25, 2007, *The Toronto Star* published a sizable article by Michael Clarkson about the Gould affair as it was seen by Cornelia

Foss. Still withholding the details, Foss made the following general statements: "I think there were a lot of misconceptions about Glenn and it was partly because he was so very private ... But I assure you, he was an extremely heterosexual man. Our relationship was, among other things, quite sexual." The fact that Cornelia's photograph from 1963 was published on the front page of *The Toronto Star*, which is usually reserved for the most important news, speaks for itself. The press could hardly wait for an opportunity to rehabilitate this Canadian idol into the state of normalcy. Or perhaps, the press is looking for fresh, sensational news in this special, anniversarial Glenn Gould Year. The rest of the story shows that Gould and the Fosses, who resided in Buffalo at the time, developed a friendly relationship and exchanged frequent telephone calls. In 1967, Cornelia Foss, driven in part by her marital difficulties but also by her growing tender feelings toward Glenn Gould, made a radical decision to leave her husband, Lukas. She took her two children, Christopher, age nine, and Eliza, age five, and moved to Toronto, where she purchased a house near Gould's residence. This is how the relationship between Glenn and Cornelia was made possible, by him visiting her and her children at their home. One wonders about a number of complications encountered and how Gould, who had no family skills, dealt with them. How did Gould cope with Cornelia's children, who were longing for their father? Was he feeling responsible for the breakup of his friend's marriage? Was he filled with shame vis à vis his parents?

Looking at Gould's private diary, which appears to be unfamiliar to Cornelia or to the press, Gould showed that he was in a quandary with respect to his loving feelings but clearly denied having any sexual relationship:

> I took a little too much for granted, I just assumed that my prevailing interest in a relationship life style was understood and I didn't realize how hurt I am and [whether] to interpret it as rejection. But I think now we reach a larger problem and a more urgent need for clarif.[ication]. Because our rel.[ationship] has, no doubt about it, escalated. There's a psychic intensity which is really quite extraordinary—it's also prod.[uctive] and comforting and reassuring. But it can resemble—if one wants to let it,—a physical intensity,—or, if not that one can easily convince oneself that its rational course is in the direction of physical intensity. And that isn't necc.[essarily] so, in my opinion and if there is a confusion of purpose between us and a corres.[ponding] need for clarif.[ication] that's where it's going to arise. Because nothing that's happened, or is going to happen in our relationship is going to change this way of life that I've decided many years ago, to lead.[39]

This last sentence is very telling about Gould's commitment to celibacy, to the life of moral purity and sexual chastity. Instead of being able to open up to his lover and say in so many words, "I am madly in love with you," Gould was worried about how to handle and disguise his emerging sexual feelings. Here is Gould's greatest dilemma:

> Theories of physical relations = psychical deterioration
> Years of prep.[aration] for this way of life-change would be destructive

> and produce the kind of resentment that would rather awefully cause our relationship to plunder. Therefore = no change is contemplated, can you live with that?—is psychic energy per se hard for you to deal with?
>
> I tell you this now only to avoid the kind of confusion that could add even a moment's uneasiness to what is really a remarkable relationship. I intend that, if you are willing to continue, we will bring each other such a peace as "passeth understanding."[40]

This paragraph is striking! Gould actually spelled out his greatest misconception—that physical relations inevitably lead to psychical deterioration. Further, he mentioned the "years of preparation for this way of life," which confirms that he had always lived in celibacy like a monk. Gould concludes very emphatically: "Therefore no change is contemplated. Can you live with that?—is psychic energy per se hard for you to deal with?" In one sweeping sentence, Gould excluded any possibility of a sexual relationship with the woman he loved. All he could offer was his fidelity and incomplete, platonic love. Cornelia Foss was worldly enough not to be able to "live with that." According to her, Gould was too sick with "paranoia" and "phobia" for her and her children to be exposed to him. After more than four years of waiting for Gould to relax in love matters, she returned to her husband and family life.

Glenn Gould was initially inspired by Petula Clark. She was his muse, a source of his positive energy, an object of love, devotion and creative spirit. By comparison, Cornelia Foss may have served as another muse to Gould. Their relationship may have been poetic, romantic, platonic, based on seduction, artistically inspirational or all of the above with or without a sexual relationship proper.

We, the post-Gouldians, cannot assess with certainty the quality of the love relationship between Glenn Gould and Cornelia Foss on the merit of her testimony alone. Future reaserchers may need another few years of reviewing Gould's papers and other sources that may have been privy to his secrets and then match the findings with reminiscences of Cornelia Foss. There are many remaining questions to be answered in order to determine the truth. What happened with Gould's admiration of Lukas Foss once he became involved in the triangle with his wife? What about Gould's parents? Were they aware of their son's involvement with a married woman, and if they were, how did they manage to deal with this reality? The new discoveries will guide us into more objectivity and fewer suppositions.

As a strong contrast to these brooding personal notes, Gould also wrote a very humorous and sexually suggestive piece in the form of a newspaper advertisement, which was never published. This note is undated, but may have been written during his romance with Cornelia Foss. This is how much Gould was in need for female companionship:

> WANTED: By [this word was crossed off by Gould] Friendly, companionably reclusive, alcoholically abstinent, tirelessly talkative, zealously unjealous, spiritually intense, minimally turquoise, maximally ecstatic, loon seeks moth or moths with similar qualities for purposes of telephonic seduction, Tristanesque trip-taking and permanent flame-fluttering. No photos required, financial status immaterial, all-ages and non-competitive vocations considered. Applicants

> should furnish cassette of sample conversation, notarized certification of marital disinclination, references re. low-decibel vocal consistency, itineraries and sample receipts from previous, successfully completed out-of-town (moth) flights. All submissions treated confidentially. No paws need apply. Auditions for all promising candidates will be conducted with and on.[41]
>
> Anaton Penisslow
> Nfld

The Gouldian sense of humor is original, fresh and unabating as always. It is also metaphoric and creative. Gould refers to himself as a "loon" looking for "moths" for the purposes of telephonic seduction. The loon is a bird and a symbol of northern loneliness. Gould was simply unable to write directly, "An attractive male-musician in his thirties is looking for a woman for dating purposes," but hedged around the topic of dating while trying very hard to disguise his longings for a female partner. The more Gould was writing the more his anxiety was on the rise, as is reflected in his handwriting, which was becoming more unclear. At the very end of his would-be-ad, Gould panicked at the thought that some male applicants may respond. He wrote an obscure sentence: "No paws need apply," which is quite hard to decode. Is it an abbreviation or his personal neologism? If Gould used the word "paws" the sentence would read, "No dogs need apply." Did Gould mean "No men need apply"? If so, this may be suggestive of his possible homophobic feelings. Gould's father often alluded to and used ridicule terms like sissy-boy and Peter Pan, meaning boyish, immature, possibly gay men. Gould's pseudonym signature is even more convoluted and secretive. He signed his ad as "Anaton Penisslow" Nfld, which speaks for his highly sexualized state of the mind. Words "penis" and "slow" are easy to recognize. The last item, "Nfld," stands for Newfoundland. It may be that Gould wrote this note while he was in Newfoundland in 1968 during his research for his radio program called *The Latecomers*. This was the second part of his *Solitude Trilogy*. By using the term "latecomers," Gould referred to the Province of Newfoundland, which was the last to join the Canadian federation in 1949. He may have subconsciously referred to himself as a "latecomer" meaning a late or "slow" bloomer in a sexual sense.

This ad was just a momentary eruption of Gould's fantasy and enigmatic humor used to cover up his shyness, but most of all the real agenda—how to find a partner in love. The need to fall in love, the wish for courtship and romantic dating was on Gould's mind all along, only to be overcome by his ever-present moral inhibitions.

In the 1970s, Gould met two very attractive women, Margaret Pacsu and Roxolana Roslak. Pacsu has been long associated with broadcasting and had her own radio music program called *Easy Street*. She was assigned to work with Gould on his Silver Jubilee Album. She came from an intellectual and artistic family. Her father was a professor at the prestigious Princeton University in New Jersey and her mother and aunt were pianists. Pacsu was an excellent partner in conversation with Gould. Of Hungarian descent, Margaret was very good at using the accent of her mother tongue, whereas Gould was forever fascinated by the intricacies of the German language, which he relentlessly imitated. During their breaks from very serious and focused music recording, they behaved like two teenagers, sharing laughter, funny anecdotes and imitating different language accents.

"How did you feel about Gould at that time when you were working with him," I asked Margaret during her visit to my home.

"I liked him instantly. We had so much in common. I was very comfortable with him as a person," she replied.

"How did you like him as a man?" I sensed that she might have been attracted to him.

"Well, he was very good looking." Margaret smiled.

"Do you think women loved him to the point of going all the way with him?" I pursued the topic of Gould's love life.

"I am sure of that. Women would definitely go to bed with him if he only gave them a hint." Margaret was quite decisive.

"What happened between the two of you once your working contract was finished?" I questioned her.

"Nothing. Absolutely nothing. Sorry to say that, because I admire him so much, but he never wrote me a note and never asked me for a dinner to celebrate our successful business partnership. Come to think about that, he may have called once to thank me but this was very formal,"[42] Pacsu concluded.

In 1976, Gould embarked on a recording of Paul Hindemith's vocal music *Das Marienleben*. A soprano diva was to be selected. Gould heard a young opera singer, Roxolana Roslak, singing on the radio. The next morning he called Mario Prizek, the producer of his *Musicamera* series *Music in our Time* on CBC television, and said to him, "Get me that girl!" This is how Miss Roslak was promptly hired to sing the *Ophelia Lieder*. Gould was at the height of his bereavement after the loss of his mother, and the arrival of the attractive opera singer with a glorious soprano voice was like a soothing remedy for his grieving soul. The instant the two artists saw each other they developed mutual feelings of admiration. Gould, master at interpreting Hindemith's music, and Miss Roslak, so skillful at interpreting the somber lyrics in a very fine German, quickly became compatible teammates at work. Roslak reflected with devotion: "Gould was my wonderful and great colleague. He would create a very special world, deep within the music and then he would invite you to join him there."[43] She was obviously taken by Gould, like many of his friends and followers. Roslak reminisced more spontaneously: "Over the years we became close friends. I remember once, Ray [Roberts], his young son, Wayne and I decided to help Glenn resurrect his garden. Glenn had such a beautiful terrace off his penthouse where the garden became quite neglected. Glenn just sat there, watching, while the three of us worked up the sweat,"[44] Roslak laughed. Of course, Gould was not used to any manual labor and never had dirt under his fingernails since his early boyhood.

The cover photograph for the Hindemith recording made by CBS photographer, Don Hunstein, is striking. It shows Gould and Roslak together. She is in a romantic dress with ruffles and he is in a dark business suit in a pensive pose, both elusive but unable to hide their mutual attachment. It also shows Gould sharing his fame with a lovely woman who had such a pleasing voice. This was suggestive of substantial progress in Gould's capacity to love, from only adoring Miss Roslak's voice as his fetish to having a wider interest in this attractive-looking, unmarried lady-friend. As far as we know, this favorable liaison was the last one of the kind in Gould's life.

Chapter XVI

REAL AND IMAGINED ILLNESS

TO BE ILL OR TO BE HEALTHY?

> To be or not to be; that is the question;
> Whether 'tis nobler in the mind to suffer
> The slings and arrows of outrageous fortune,
> Or to take arms against a sea of troubles,
> and by opposing end them.
>
> W. Shakespeare
> (Soliloquy from *Hamlet*)[1]

Dr. John Percieval was Glenn's steadiest home base physician from 1971 onward. He practiced general medicine on St. Clair Avenue West, within a five-minute walking distance from Glenn's residence. Dr. Percieval reminisced on his famous patient amiably: "Gould came frequently to see me; he was delightful to talk to because he had such a good command of English. His general health was excellent and I never found him seriously ill."[2] Gould usually asked for the doctor's last appointment at 6:00 p.m., and he invariably got it. From the beginning of their professional relationship, Dr. Percieval was supportive of Gould. His approach was to downplay the illness and to bolster his client's existing health and positive attitude. When Gould complained of his many symptoms, the doctor consoled him and reminded him of his normal findings. Dr. Percieval was aware that Gould suffered with hypochondria, which involves a persistent conviction of being seriously ill. He stated that as the primary caregiver, he often physically examined Gould but never had a reason to diagnose him with arthritis or fibrositis, which Gould was convinced he had. Furthermore, Dr. Percieval insisted that Gould's blood pressure was within normal range and that he found evidence of hypertension and treated him for it only at the end of Gould's life. Dr. Percieval stated that he did not know at the time that his famous patient had also been seeing several other health professionals on his own initiative. Gould also took a great variety of medications without letting Dr. Percieval know about it, which was quite unwise and risky because of possible undesirable drug interactions. Here is a pertinent excerpt from the interview with Gould's physician:

Q. Dr. Percieval, do you remember whether Gould told you anything about seeing Dr. Logan at the same time when he was seeing you?

A. No. He never told me about Dr. Logan, and I never received any medical report from him.
Q. Gould used to go to him. Dr. Logan prescribed antihypertensive medications for Gould in 1976. What about Dr. Philip Klotz? Do you know that Gould periodically had consulted with him?
A. I had no idea.
Q. Are you aware that Gould went to see Dr. Dale McCarthy, who prescribed for him medications for arthritis?
A. No, I had no idea he went to him. I never found signs of arthritis in Gould.
Q. Gould also went to Philadelphia to see Dr. Irvin Stein, orthopedic surgeon. Did you have anything to do with this referral?
A. No, I didn't. I knew that he saw a neurologist from time to time after this guy at Steinway slapped him on his back. Smart ass with no proper manners.[3]

The degree of miscommunication between Gould and Dr. Percieval was striking. The patient withheld vital information from his primary physician, whereas the latter was not able to fully engage and reach his patient. This is because Dr. Percieval looked after Gould's physical health, which was for the most part adequate but disregarded his emotional problems. Though he noticed Gould's hypochondria, he took it lightly and tried to talk him out of it. Several years after the fact, Dr. Percieval admitted that he never referred Gould to psychiatric treatment and thought at the time that Gould's problems were not necessarily related to his mental health but were more circumstantial in nature.

Hypochondria is a serious psychiatric disorder that may start as early as in childhood; it usually takes a chronic course and reaches its peak in middle-age. The most common feature of patients who have hypochondriasis is a marked preoccupation with their body symptoms. Those who suffer from hypochondria usually are obsessive and have narcissistic personality traits. They show narcissistic behavior by craving attention and sympathy from others, and then get what they need through their professed illness. It is said that hypochondriasis is a paradigm of narcissism. The patients, who tend to be controlling of their treatment, are likely to be dishonest, self-righteous, nonconformist and have an inordinate need to defy others. Sufferers with hypochondria are often hard to get along with because they are blatantly self-centered, attention-seeking and totally preoccupied with the tedious topic of their illness. Their complaints are referred to in pejorative terms and are frequently ignored as they are emotionally overtaxing to listeners. Ironically, men and women with hypochondria tend to search for wellness through their heavy indulgence in illness. They are known to shop around for perfect remedies that, in the end, can never be found. Their attachments to health professionals are as fickle and tenuous as they are with their friends and associates. Prognosis or outcome of illness in terms of cure is not promising.

Gould, being a hypochondriac, used to shop around for medical findings and medications without informing all those involved in his care about his other concurrent therapies. A major component of this behavior is a lack of cooperation. Gould was simply compelled to control both his treatment and all his caregivers. Deliberately withholding crucial health information is manipulative and potentially self-harming. It prevents involved health team members from working together toward a common and optimal treatment goal.

Physicians who treat patients that shop around, if they spot their behavior, are often in a dilemma as how to handle them. Should they confront them, which may lead to an abrupt cessation of treatment by the patient, or should they concentrate on building a therapeutic relationship and set the limits later? Some patients are more subtle in their quests for simultaneous therapies because they are impelled by their deep-seated insecurity and childlike need for frequent reassurance, whereas others that are self-righteous could be quite aggressive and bold in their demands. In both cases, such patients impose extra pressure on the caregivers and are considered to be difficult to work with, which interferes with the best therapeutic efforts. There are other complicating factors. For example, if the patient happens to be a famous personality, this may have a "blinding" effect on the caregivers who, out of fascination, may try too hard to please them. This situation works at the expense of objectivity and the neutrality of the caregivers, which are two basic principles of effective treatment.

Using the above scenarios as guidelines, one may be better able to understand the nature of the Gould—Dr. Percieval relationship. Gould went to Dr. Percieval more often than to any other physician, yet he was not sincere and open with him. It follows that Gould was satisfied with some aspects of what his doctor had to offer but also had a whole hidden life that he kept from him. Notably, Dr. Percieval provided reassurance and a clean bill of health, but Gould fancied ill health and needed confirmation of the same. Gould required much attention for his psychosomatic symptoms, particularly his body pains, headaches and stomach discomfort. Dr. Percieval did not yield to these complaints but pursued his agenda, to rule out major medical illness. There were also deeper undercurrents to their relationship that remained unrecognized. Gould, upon moving to his St. Clair Avenue residence, had to endure the emotional pain of estrangement from his father, which he compensated for by having various levels of friendship with other males. Dr. Percieval, more than two decades Gould's senior, was seen by Gould as a benevolent father-like figure. He was readily available, easy to talk to, and he provided parental succor. Gould harbored deep ambivalent feelings of love and hate toward his father, which he subconsciously projected onto Dr. Percieval; whom he in part liked and relied upon but in part also ignored and defied.

To be ill or to be healthy, this was a perpetual question in Gould's inner mind. Glenn's preoccupation with his physical problems was long-rooted in his childhood. Some of his symptoms were incubated when he was a toddler, then hatched and clearly recognizable by the age of six (phobias, posture problems), and some others by the age of eight (headaches, being sick to his stomach and swallowing soda mints as antidotes to nausea). By the time of young adulthood, Gould already felt subjectively sick and obsessively began looking for answers and solutions to his malaise. Soon his virtuoso career became heavily intertwined with his obstinate habit of frequenting physicians and chiropractors in those cities where he performed when he needed therapeutic contacts and potions to fortify himself for each combat with his colossal enemy—public performance. In some paradoxical way, Gould's sick role helped him to stay afloat and carry on with his stressful and demanding occupation as a pianist. Retrospectively, one can easily guess that his menacing stage fright was at the core of Gould's subjective suffering, but in those days neither he nor most of his contemporaries had any concept of how advanced his anxiety was. The following is an illustration of Gould's typical sickness and his way of coping: On November 7, 1955, Gould gave his historical recital in Montreal's Plateau Hall, where he played his best music piece ever, Bach's *Goldberg Variations*. But it did not really matter how well he was prepared. He was still anxious and jittery to the point of feeling sick and needed medical help at once. A few hours before this recital, Gould rushed to the office of the Montreal-based psychiatrist Dr. A. E. Moll, who was not blinded by his fame nor sidetracked by his "physical" illness, but accurately noticed and addressed the scope of Gould's emotional distress. As a result of this empathic encounter,

Gould was able to deliver a world-class performance. Dr. Moll, a psychoanalytically trained psychiatrist, strongly encouraged Gould to seek psychiatric help in Toronto. On his prescription pad, Dr. Moll wrote the names of four prominent Toronto psychiatrists: Dr. Alan Parkin, Dr. Arthur M. Doyle, Dr. B. M. Allan and Dr. Aldwyn Stokes.[4] This referral was supposed to be a clear and nonambiguous indication to Gould that his vulnerability was in the area of mental health.

Nevertheless, Gould relentlessly steered himself in the direction of looking for concrete physical illness and for hands-on treatment. On the day of October 30, 1956, before his successful performance of Bach's D Minor Concerto with the Montreal Symphony and Milton Catims as conductor, Gould checked into the Montreal General Hospital and received physiotherapy for his tense and achy muscles. Just two weeks after, on November 16, 1956, he sought help from Dr. Bierman in New York City, hours before his outstanding recital at the Metropolitan Museum. Gould was on a circuitous path of treatment, visiting different medical practitioners but not mental health professionals. This pattern of pursuing the sick role and shopping around for physical treatment became recurrent and deeply entrenched through Gould's entire music career, both public and recording.

Gould's hypochondria was also reflected in his habit of hoarding every bit of medical information—physicians' reports, pharmacy labels, doctors' bills and his elaborate personal health journals. Gould even purchased the *Merck Manual*, which is a professional medical textbook, in order to study his own symptoms and anticipate physicians' findings. This was all superfluous and energy-consuming. Gould was locked into a self-perpetuating circuit of obsessions and compulsions. The obsessive, self-focused worries and compelling repetitive rituals and mannerisms, like those earlier described around the use of his piano chair and the piano, were becoming more troubling as he grew older. Some of Gould's behavior, such as his eating and grooming practices, were not only obsessive but were also unnatural, even bizarre, which had a baffling effect on those around him.

This preoccupation with the intricacies of real and imagined illness permeated Gould's lengthy telephone calls and his voluminous correspondence. Often, good portions of his letters were devoted to various health issues. Sometimes, he was so taken by medical problems that he pretended to be a doctor to his friends. By role-playing and jesting around the serious subject of illness, Gould managed to assuage his inner terror and his sense of helplessness. Here is Gould in the role of doctoring his music friend, Leonard Bernstein:

> Dear Leonardo December 13, 1961
>
> I am so terribly sorry to hear that you are suffering at the moment, though I have no doubt that you are suffering with elan. Moreover, it is, my spies tell me, an exotic ailment and that is worthy of you—but do you have a title for it? If you are stuck in that department, I have several titles for diseases which I am expecting to have in later life, but have not yet had occasion to make use of. I always find that a good disease title will impress your average concert manager to no end, and this I have long felt has been largely responsible for my modest success.[5]

This good-spirited letter was written before the rift with Bernstein in 1962. In this letter, Gould candidly revealed that he consciously considered an "exotic ailment" as a useful tool for coping with the stress of a performing career. He also put himself down by saying that a "good disease title" "had been largely responsible" for his "modest success," which was suggestive of his lack of awareness of his self-worth. Behind the jovial wittiness, there was the poignant reality of a twenty-nine-year-old, world-famous virtuoso dwelling on illness, as if he were an octogenarian.

Another, less benign example of doctoring was Gould's behavior with his fellow pianist, Tom McIntosh. The story goes that McIntosh shared with Gould that he had suffered insomnia and stage fright in the face of each concert. Gould, who carried a supply of his own medications with him, opened his briefcase and gave McIntosh a handful of tablets, not naming them, but only indicating their purpose and the manner of use. McIntosh wrote in response to this gesture:

> Dear Mr. Gould, January 14, 1957
>
> I wish to thank you for the pills out of your supply. The sleeping pill helped, and the others which I took just before the recital, worked wonders. I have never felt as relaxed as I did for this recital. Therefore, could you possibly give me the name, contents or directions as to what kind of pill I should ask my doctor for in order to get some of the same kind of pills?[6]

Six weeks later in his next letter, McIntosh actually referred to his famous colleague as "Dr. Gould:"

> Dear "Dr. Gould," February 27, 1957
>
> This is a letter of belatedness. First of all my belated thanks for your "prescriptions." I am sure they will help greatly in the future. I do, however, resent being called a "neurotic artist." After all, my psychoanalyst says it won't be too long before I am almost normal.
>
> Tom McIntosh[7]

The pills Gould gave to McIntosh were from the barbiturates family used for sleep and sedation. By doctoring his friends, Gould showed a degree of moral irresponsibility. Dispensing his medications to another person was entirely unwise and potentially harmful. Gould knew nothing about his friend's health status and possible allergies to barbiturates, not to mention the long-term risk of negative effects. Had Gould wanted to be helpful, he could have encouraged his friend to discuss his anxiety and need for medication with his physician.

As noticed in the above letter, McIntosh resented Gould for calling him "neurotic." Gould not only scoffed at his friend but often referred to himself as "neurotic" as part of his humorous, self-depreciative behavior. Gould was fascinated by human psychology and was well read on the subject, which afforded him a degree of intellectual insight into his psychological problems. Still, on a deeper emotional level, he was more invested in denial of mental illness and believed that he was physically ill. When Gould used the term "neurotic artist," he used it as a synonym for outlandish and as a trademark of his own personal fame. It follows that he mistook the state of being "neurotic" for being flamboyant and artistic, rather than thinking of it as being sick. This type of thinking was partly shaped by his time. From the 1950s to the 1970s, mental disorders were looked upon as a stigma and were often hidden and denied.

Gould also experienced numerous psychosomatic symptoms. He was known to complain and seek treatment for various body pains such as throbbing headaches, wandering pains in his joints and extremities, steady ongoing pain in his upper back, and severe muscle tension. Yet his X-rays and other laboratory tests and physical findings were often normal and not consistent with his complaints. He also reported to have stomach-related symptoms like nausea, vomiting and bloating, without having any major illness diagnosed. This would be suggestive of the presence of psychosomatic disorder, in which emotional problems are expressed functionally through various organs in the form of somatic or physical sensations like pains and discomfort. This condition is not deliberate and the symptoms in those who suffer from it are felt as real and are not feigned. The psychosomatic overtone has to do with an inability to express feelings directly by crying or being angry. Instead, these individuals become physically ill when in mental or emotional anguish. A contrast to psychosomatic disorder is malingering, which is a conscious and willful behavior of avoiding responsibility by staging and simulating illness.

Gould did not plan or act his illness but felt genuinely ill. He believed that he had rheumatoid arthritis in several joints that caused him pain. As seen earlier, Dr. Percieval adamantly denied that Gould had arthritis or any kind of muscular or skeletal condition. If so, then why did the other physicians prescribe for Gould anti-inflammatory medications like Naprosyn and Indocid? It appears that these drugs were prescribed for him because of his complaints rather than based on objective findings. By being given medications, Gould felt appeased and reassured.

Gould also believed that he suffered with the condition called "fibrositis," which he felt was responsible for pain and stiffness of his hands. The following is a description of a medical disease referred to as "fibrositis:"

> Although no definite organic pathology has been associated with this musculoskeletal disorder, fibrositis patients frequently complain of stiffness and localized areas of nonarticular pain which is worse in the morning. The patients are chronically fatigued, emotionally distressed and their sleep is usually disturbed.[8]

Toronto psychiatrist Dr. Harvey Moldofsky discovered in his sleep research studies that there are specific sleep abnormalities in patients with "fibrositis syndrome." Following his discovery, it was proposed that the fibrositis syndrome be considered a "non restorative sleep syndrome" that may be triggered by several factors including psychologically stressful situations. At present, the medical term "fibromyalgia" is in widespread use to designate the diffuse body pains that go with fatigue, depressed mood and poor sleep. All information considered, it is most likely that Gould suffered from chronic mood swings with bouts of depression and insomnia, which made him sensitive and prone to subjective feelings of pain.

The pains in his joints and muscles, to which he referred as "fibrositis," started as early as in Gould's teens, when an idea was born in his mind that there was something wrong with his hands. His music teacher, Alberto Guerrero, played into it by suggesting that this may have been a rheumatic condition and encouraged him to soak his hands in warm water. Hence, Guerrero helped set the stage for Gould's very characteristic habit of soaking his hands in hot water before each public performance. While Guerrero harbored a layman's idea of his pupil having rheumatism, Gould himself believed that he had a circulatory problem. He used to say convincingly: "If I don't take pills, I don't circulate." Nothing was further from the truth for young Gould, who neither had rheumatoid arthritis nor a circulatory condition of his hands. He had a pair of healthy and agile hands, but he was panic-stricken before each performance, and his rituals of soaking and draping his hands in woollen gloves served to ward off his pre-concert terror.

Gould had frequent flare-ups of his "fibrositis syndrome," which usually occurred prior to major concerts. At times, he was able to overcome his emotional and physical terror and go on with a concert. At other times, when many of his strategies and rituals did not work, he was forced to cancel and postpone his music engagements. This invariably got him into feuds with often-annoyed concert negotiators and the press. Meanwhile, Gould's muscle pains and aches were like a vicious circle. The more he was preoccupied with his pains, the more negative impact it had on his music career. The more concerts he had to cancel, the more losses and humiliation were self-inflected upon him. This all led to a new set of physical symptoms, and the vicious circle became self-perpetuating.

Gould's preference for heat application, in the form of wearing excessive clothes, the frequent use of hot baths and soaking his hands in hot water, as well as the use of physiotherapy, massage and ultrasound, were all derivatives of his obsessive conviction that he was ill. He often went out of his way to prevent the onset of would-be illness and took even greater and more elaborate measures once he felt ill. For example, in 1960 following the "Steinway incident" and subsequent shoulder malady, Gould had no fewer than 117 physiotherapy sessions from January to October in Toronto; not counting those he received in Philadelphia in the month of May. On some days there were even two physiotherapy sessions. Given the fact that Gould slept through the morning, it must have been quite difficult for him to fit so much treatment into one day. This pretty well took up his entire day and put a strain on the rest of his productive schedule. In September 1960, Gould was alarmed by an episode of pain in his right shoulder. In his letter to a fan, he wrote:

> I am happy to say that the right shoulder was nothing serious, merely the result of thoughtlessly carrying a suitcase. I guess I am just too delicate for this world.[9]

In less than four months from this confession, Gould wrote to another friend, Sylvia Kind, more about the same theme:

> Dear Silvia, January 25, 1961
>
> I travel now mostly with my own physiotherapist in attendance—and I have once again been able to resume all my activities although occasionally I still have to cancel a concert when there is some difficulty with my shoulder.[10]

From 1961 onward, Gould substituted physiotherapy with his newly purchased portable Ultrasound Therapy Unit, which he kept at home for self-application.

In the 1960s, a Dutch-born massage therapist, Cornelius Dees, came to Toronto and opened his practice. Gould became his steady client. It happened that Dr. Percieval knew Dees well and spoke to him from time to time. When Gould performed his last concert in Los Angeles in 1964, he felt tense and achy and urged his massage therapist over the telephone to come and treat him. Dees flew instantly from Toronto to Los Angeles and gave Gould a massage treatment before the recital. Later on, Dees commented to Dr. Percieval that there was nothing much physically wrong with Gould and his request was unwarranted.[11] Looking at the same case from the psychological point of view, Gould was in a pre-recital panic, and he needed human support and reassurance from Dees, which in turn helped him follow through with his stage performance. At present, a wide variety of touring entertainers and stage performers have at their disposal health clubs on the hotel premises where they could pursue exercises or relax through massage and hydrotherapy. Hence, what Gould had practiced and was ridiculed for decades ago has become a fully recognized method against stage fright and fatigue, particularly for this sensitive group of touring artists.

Gould's obsession with his musculo-skeletal condition went beyond his subjective experience of the "fibrositis syndrome." At several stressful junctions of his life, he complained of traumatic injuries. One such purported injury was described earlier and was attributed to the so-called "Steinway incident," when Gould in December 1959 claimed that one of the Steinway employees, William Hupfer, slapped him on the left shoulder. Following this incident, Gould sought consultations with several specialists, one of them being Dr. Irvin Stein, an orthopedic surgeon in Philadelphia. This is how a lengthy doctor-patient interaction began between Stein and Gould. Here is a list of their most important contacts:

Treatment With Dr. Irvin Stein

Date	Treatment Prescribed
1960 April/May—6 weeks of therapy	- Cortisone tablets - body cast, left arm cast x 4 weeks - physiotherapy x 2 weeks - metal cervical collar
1966 October 4	- Stelazine 1mg three times daily x 100 tablets
1968 ?	- Vitamine B, 100mg - Vitamine B12 1000 micro x 3wks
1971 August 17	unknown
1974 October 2	unknown
1981 December 8	- X-ray of the hands, lumbar spine, cervical spine[12]

With respect to the "Steinway incident," it appears that Dr. Stein did not find x-ray evidence of a fracture or shoulder dislocation, but based his treatment plan on Gould's convincing description of pains and discomfort. Dr. Stein likely assumed that Gould suffered a soft tissue injury, such as tendinitis or synovitis, which is not detectable on an x-ray. He resorted to a now rarely used body cast; by which Gould's left arm was raised above his head and immobilized. The end result was that Gould's trunk above the waist, his left shoulder and arm were all plastered in a cast. Cortisone tablets were prescribed by Dr. Stein and were supposed to reduce possible inflammation of the soft tissue. Dr. Stein endeavored to cure troubling symptoms of his client at any cost. Retrospective evaluation of the Gould-Stein involvement cannot precisely answer the question of whether the treatment Gould received had a placebo effect or whether it was the treatment of choice that led to the actual cure. Dr. Stein certainly "looked after" his vulnerable patient for six weeks through frequent physical check-ups. He gave him considerable attention and respect, took him seriously, helped him allay his anxiety and met his emotional needs. In some way, their doctor-patient relationship was psychologically reassuring; but in another way, Dr. Stein's approach contained an engendered iatrogenic risk that proved to be real when Gould developed severe panic disorder because of the confinement in the cast. Being in Philadelphia for six weeks of treatment also meant being far away from home in an alien room in an alien city. His arm being in a cast was alarming to Gould as for the first time in his life he could not use his dominant, precious left arm and hand. He could not play his piano to which he was attached. His father was disapproving of his obscure illness and his eccentric treatment in Philadelphia; his mother was overly worried, which made him feel badly. He was a world-famous pianist who was supposed to shine on the stage. Instead, he was confined in a dismal prison-cast. Gould, in fact, was quite lucky that after such a protracted immobilization of his left arm he was able to return to his virtuoso career and still perform bravura and other intricate piano techniques. The treatment with Dr. Stein was costly in comparison to the insured treatment he received at home. The Philadelphia experience triggered attacks of panic and left him with a permanent phobic avoidance of public appearance in that city. Indeed, Gould canceled his potentially great concert in Philadelphia in December 1961 and never played there again.

In his letter to Leon Fleisher, who had his right hand injured and was in treatment earlier with Dr. Stein, Gould wrote on November 14, 1966:

> I was down visiting our friend Dr. Stein, in Philadelphia, about a month ago because I threw my left leg out of whack.[13]

Gould empathized with Fleisher regarding his hand injury and with respect to his making an "orthopedic trail" by visiting the specialist. This time, however, it was not Gould's shoulder or hand hurting but his leg. The result of this visit to Dr. Stein was that he prescribed for Gould on October 4, 1966, Stelazine 1 mg. tablets three times daily. Stelazine is a major tranquilizer, which when prescribed in higher dose of 10 to 20 mg. daily is used to treat major mental illness like schizophrenia. In lower dose, it is infrequently given to nonpsychotic individuals who are highly nervous and agitated. It follows by inference that Dr. Stein, by giving Stelazine to Gould while he complained of his "left leg out of whack," saw him as being agitated and somewhat out of touch with reality. By this time, Dr. Stein noticed Gould's hypochondria and the tendency to obsess about his physical pain.

A good deal of Gould's diffuse body pains and aches, which he attributed to fibrositis or circulatory problems, had to do with his muscular tension. Gould's muscles were quite tense and rigid, particularly in his back, neck and shoulders. One of Gould's Toronto-based chiropractors, Dr. Glen Engel, described his findings in minute detail:

> Gould appeared to be of ectomorphic type with thin limbs not well muscled, chest somewhat depressed and pendulous abdomen. The most conspicuous problem was Gould's "kyphotic back," a hunch-back with cervicogenic dorsalgia and severe tightness in his mid-back. The tightness of muscles made his back feel like a piece of cement. His back muscles were hyper tonic, ropy and he complained of a great deal of periscapular pain. His suspensory musculature of the upper back and shoulders was strained with a considerable muscle reduction and "frozen shoulder syndrome." There was a severe postural deficit with no large excursion motion allowed and fixation in his mid-back. There was a devitalization of the chest capacity. The skin appeared fragile, baby-like, pale and tender. He could be helped a little with his neck, but his back was untreatable. I felt I could not break down this wall of cement other than palliative. He was "welded" into "kyphotic posture." His midback was one of the tightest I ever treated.[14]

This straight and poignant expert statement of Dr. Engel demonstrated vividly how sadly derelict Gould's body was. Could it be that when Gould claimed his shoulder was injured by Hupfer it was nothing but a flare-up of his already preexisting "frozen shoulder syndrome?" The references Dr. Engel made to Gould's "kyphotic posture," fragile, pale skin and muscle reduction are shocking. After many years of hunching over the piano and an unhealthy lifestyle, Gould in his thirties was "welded" and beyond repair. When the era of jogging and working out began in the early 1970s, Gould was only forty years of age; young enough to be able to take up selected physical exercises. Yet he did not even do light calisthenics or stretching of any kind, which would have been helpful for his taut nerves and muscles. His long professed walks through the woods were rare and in the form of leisurely ambling rather than being vigorous aerobic exercise.

Remember that the year 1961 was not only the year of his cast and confinement but also the year of the death of his paternal grandmother, Alma. This benevolent woman was his music elder, a model of a dedicated pianist-organist and a pen pal with whom he exchanged letters while traveling on tours. Frayed by the loss of his grandmother, unexpressed grief and by his shoulder malady, Gould was more self-preoccupied and subjectively ill. In that year he started a very long course of treating himself with his portable ultrasound machine, which opened the chapter of self-administration of physiotherapy and other modes of self-help.

At the same time of the shoulder misery, another condition was brewing. Gould's rising separation anxiety, which plagued him through his entire life, gained another bizarre form of expression, a phobia of flying. The year 1962 was stressful. This was the year of the scandal in New York around the performance of the Brahms concerto with Leonard Bernstein as conductor, which left Gould with a profound sense of humiliation. This was yet another scar among many scars to his psyche. After 1962, the terror of flying prevented him from using the airplane for traveling and reduced his options to the use of car and train. Gould's mother, Florence, had a phobia of flying and exclusively traveled by car or train. Evidently, the son identified with his mother's illness and developed similar symptoms.

Related to Gould's nonspecific body pains and aches was his chronic unabating insomnia. From the time of Gould's retreat to the cottage, after he quit high school, and from the time of his broken liaison with Guerrero, he began a habit of staying up late reading and listening to the radio. It was as if Glenn had to engineer a new coping mechanism to help him overcome his pre-formed fear of darkness (nyctophobia) and his rampant anxiety disorder. It is known that people with anxiety suffer with initial insomnia. They tend to worry at bedtime and to toss and turn for some time before they are able to settle. Gould invented a remedy for his initial insomnia by staying up late and keeping himself busy until he would tire himself out. By being a night owl, Gould inadvertently caused to himself a disturbance of his natural, circadian sleep-wake rhythm. Noise and light also contributed to sleeplessness as he played the piano or listened to the radio. By keeping the lights on, he alleviated his childhood fears of the dark and his sense of loneliness. Gradually, Gould's bed time was postponed from 1:00 a.m. to 3:00 a.m. He stayed up longer and longer until by his late twenties, he finally went to bed at the crack of the dawn.

Sleep happens to be disturbed in depressive disorder. This is why, through the use of antidepressants, sleep becomes improved both in its quality and quantity. Unfortunately, Gould's anxieties, depression and insomnia started before the advent of antidepressants, the first of which, Imipramine (Tofranil), became available in North America in 1963. Hence, in the 1950s Gould had to rely on a choice of sedatives from the chemical group called barbiturates; which in those days were in broad use as anti-anxiety drugs and as hypnotics to facilitate good sleep. A very popular medication for insomnia was a short-acting Nembutal Sodium, which came in 100-mg. capsules. Barbiturates are known to be habit-forming when taken over a prolonged period. They are addictive, and users find that they need to increase the dosage over time. When discontinued, the user is left with symptoms of withdrawal, which could be life-threatening in extreme cases. Because of their addictive nature, today barbiturates are rarely used to combat insomnia and are replaced by safer hypnotics.

Gould was taking Nembutal as a prescription drug. He was not judicious in his use of prescribed sedatives but was in the habit of self-medicating, which means he took slightly higher doses than prescribed in order to cope with his emotional distress. To date, there is no evidence whatsoever that Gould took large doses of barbiturates nor that he was physically dependent on or addicted to them. He genuinely required these medications to help him retire to bed, rather than to get high on them or to be "stoned." By the same token, there is no evidence that Gould ever overdosed on barbiturates or on any other medication for the purposes of harming himself or destroying his life. This means that even in the face of his prolonged depression, Gould held onto substantial personal and creative strengths, which protected him from suicidal ideation and from taking his own life.

On top of using barbiturates, Gould also took various other sedatives from the chemical group called benzodiazepines. Two of them most consistently taken were Librax and Diazepam. Librax is particularly useful in those individuals with stomach symptoms such as irritable stomach, nausea, feelings of "butterflies," all secondary to emotional stress. Diazepam (Valium) is a well-known anti-anxiety medication and an excellent muscle relaxant, which is very effective when used appropriately as prescribed. Unfortunately, it is often abused, which is a reason why doctors tend to prescribe it sparingly. Though Gould was not addicted in the medical sense of the word, he latched on to the barbiturates and diazepam with the vehemence of daily necessity.

If the antidepressant Imipramine was not available earlier, the sensible question is, why was it not recommended to Gould in the late 1960s and 1970s, when it became readily available? Imipramine would have helped him battle his depressive moods, would correct his sleep and improve his obsessive worries about his illness. Dr. Percieval already confessed that he had not considered Gould as being depressed. Other consulting physicians missed it too. Granted that Gould did everything possible to control his own treatment, that he projected an image of being very lucid and always in charge of his faculties, it may have been hard to confront him. There is no evidence that any of his physicians, other than Dr. Moll of Montreal, discussed with Gould his psychiatric condition. Dr. Peter Ostwald, admitted that he never referred Gould to see a psychiatrist.

"Why not?" I asked Dr. Ostwald during my second visit to San Francisco.

"We mostly played and discussed music when we met. I saw him as being "great" rather than being "sick," Dr. Ostwald explained.

"Was there anything about Gould that you were genuinely concerned about?" I inquired.

"In hindsight, there were all sorts of unusual things about him. It bothered me when he called me after midnight in the privacy of my home. I thought to myself: 'Doesn't he care about my sleep and that I have to get up early in the morning?'" Dr. Ostwald shared his deeper annoyance.

"Could it be that your fascination with Gould's greatness prevented you from noticing his clinical depression and that's why you have not discussed it?" I was looking for subconscious meanings.

"Well, that's a good point. Perhaps, by focusing on his music, I did not want to see him as a patient, neither did he volunteer to talk with me about his mental state," Dr. Ostwald noted.

"What happened in due course?" I asked.

"I helped Gould to connect with my good friend, Joe [Dr. Joseph Stephens], psychiatrist from Baltimore, but not for a psychiatric consultation but more for music dialogues. I guess, what it boils down to is that I did not want to pathologize Gould, period,"[15] Dr. Ostwald summed it up.

Gould, who corresponded with Ostwald from time to time, also never asked Dr. Ostwald for his opinion as a psychiatrist with respect to his depression, stage fright or hypochondria. Typically, Gould "blinded" his friends with his stature, massive denial and need to be in control rather than allowing others to see him clearly and help him accordingly.

When Dr. Ostwald published Gould's biography in 1997, he expressed his belief that Gould sought some type of psychiatric treatment. Though he did not have any hard evidence for it, he made the conclusion on the basis of reports from Jock Carroll, with whom Gould went to the Bahamas for two weeks in 1956. According to Carroll's recollection, Gould told him that he had seen one of the four psychiatrists recommended to him by Dr. Moll from Montreal. Gould revealed that his psychiatrist, whose name he did not mention, had tried him on two tranquilizers thus far, such as sodium amytal and belladanill. Gould opened up to Carroll about his numerous fears—fear of eating in public, fear of vomiting during a public performance and his fear of crowds, which he referred to as "agoraphobia."[16] In the absence of any other evidence, this hearsay story is still very valuable in finding out about Gould's obscure ailments.

The psychiatrist Gould saw was most likely Dr. Arthur Doyle, who was very popular in the 1960s as a psychiatrist skillful at combining medications with supportive counseling. He worked out of St. Michael's Hospital in the downtown of Toronto. Gould was very familiar with that hospital from his visits to other medical specialists. If Gould saw Dr. Doyle in consultation and for brief follow up, then Dr. Doyle only had a chance to try different sedatives rather than to pursue a long-term psychotherapy, which would challenge Gould's obsessive personality traits and his high anxiety. Dr. Doyle has been long dead, and there is no way to confirm this supposition.

Several of Gould's relatives, including his father, cousin Jessie and cousin Betty, denied that Gould was ever involved in psychiatric treatment. Among Gould's elaborate medical documentation, there are no references or even hints with respect to any possible psychiatric treatment. His friends and associates from the 1960s, Andrew Kazdin and John Lee Roberts were not aware of Gould being involved in any such treatment, whereas they knew about his physical problems, chiropractic treatment, and also were aware of his emotional problems. The more important conclusion on the basis of this in-depth research is that Gould never had a sustained and systematic psychiatric treatment over a period of time, like a year or longer of psychotherapy or psychoanalysis combined with the use of antidepressants. There is absolutely no evidence for that. The type of complex and profound psychiatric disorder that Gould developed over the years required a prolonged and intensive treatment, such as intensive psychotherapy, which had he had it would have been readily noticed by his friends. Gould's premature death also speaks in favor of his inadequate psychiatric and medical care.

DETRIMENTS OF NARCISSISM

> ... grandiosity is the defense against depression and the depression is the defense against the real pain over the loss of the self.
>
> Allice Miller[17]

Having described some of Gould's obvious psychological problems—anxiety, hypochondria and depressive mood swings—the focus now will turn toward studying the many shades and vicissitudes of his personality. The strengths of Gould's personality, his artistic and intellectual genius, his rapid progress in music and charismatic impact on the general public has permeated this book. Gould's personality weaknesses and anomalies will now be addressed. This large topic in psychiatry falls under the general heading of personality disorders. While some psychiatric ailments are more obvious and easily recognized by the lay public, such as depression, mania, panic attacks and phobias, abnormalities of one's personality structure are mostly diagnosed by the experts in the field and not readily understood and recognized by non-professionals. Personality disorders are obscure deviations and hindrances of personality that evolve in the early formative years. They are shaped by the psychological, socio-cultural environment, as well as by genetic influences, and leave a permanent, unfavorable stamp of maladaptation on individuals. Several types of personality disorders are described in the literature and seen in clinical practice, such as passive-aggressive, schizoid, borderline and antisocial types. Here the focus will be on narcissistic personality traits, which are relevant in this study of Gould's personality.

Pathological narcissism is a psychiatric condition seen in adult men and women, showing typical behavior such as great need for attention and admiration by others; an unusual degree of grandiosity; constant quest for control, power and brilliance; the quest for a variety of ideal values, such as perfect love, perfect success or achievement and perfect morality. Individuals with narcissistic traits tend to be very self-centered, self-righteous and feel entitled to everything they want. Yet, underneath their self-inflated facade, they are quite fragile and insecure. Their self-esteem is tenuous and contingent on how they are regarded by others. Their emotional life lacks depth and there is a marked inability to feel empathy for others. These people are often emotionally exploitative in relationship to others and expect special favors and privileges. Commonly, narcissistic persons are depressed, sickly and preoccupied with body pains and aches. In their relations, these people show a pattern of alternating between idealizing and devaluing others; sometimes experiencing those opposite feelings at the same time toward the same person. One of the wicked features of narcissistic persons is their tendency to be dishonest, to distort truth and even lie outright, which they justify by feeling that they have every right to do so. Alice Miller, in her recognized work on depression and grandiosity, offered this concise summary:

> Whereas "healthy narcissism" can be characterized as the full access to the true self, the narcissistic disturbance can be understood as a fixation on a "false" or incomplete self. This fixation can be seen as the intra psychic heir to the narcissistic cathexis of the child by his parents. In order to maintain the object's love, these children developed only those capacities which they felt their parents needed and admired. The unacceptable feelings had to be hidden from the environment and from themselves in order to avoid rejection or shame.[18]

Narcissistic individuals are doomed with a "false" sense of self. They may be successful and may project themselves as strong, haughty and influential, when, in fact, they are deeply insecure and unhappy at their core. As children, such individuals were narcissistically invested by their parent(s), who valued and reinforced some qualities of the child but openly rejected or downplayed other qualities, which created an internal split in the psyche. In Glenn's childhood, his music talent, intelligence and physical health were valued at the expense of his other abilities, other needs and potentials. He was never accepted and loved as a whole person but rather certain parts and aspects of him were loved and admired. Subsequently, he walked through his entire life as an incomplete individual, emotionally stunted, far too often anguished and unfulfilled. Retrospectively, after studying Gould through observation and analysis of his behavior, it is easier to understand and solve the riddle of his personality, because we, the post-Gouldian observers, have achieved a degree of emotional distance from him, which helps our objectivity. Another positive factor that evolved in the past twenty years is that psychiatry as a science became more sophisticated and effective, and psychological education of the public has resulted in increased tolerance and acceptance of mental health problems. The stigma of having those problems, though not disappeared, is gradually lessening. Several celebrities publicly speak about their depression, about their need for medications, and about their experience of counseling, taking stress management courses, and being involved in psychotherapy or psychoanalysis. So living in North America with mental health problems in the first decade of the third millennium is different from what it was in the 1950s and 1960s, when mental health services and education were scarce. Still, it cannot be denied that Gould had at least some access to professional help by living in a city where there were a number of experts in the field of mental health and human psychology, but he did not use these resources adequately.

There is a tendency of famous individuals with narcissistic personality traits to feel that they know more about their disorder than their prospective professional therapists. There is a defensive attitude, distrust, skepticism and fear to enter treatment and admit to their "failure" of not being able to overcome their disorder on their own. They feel that having diagnosed themselves and having read everything there is to know about their condition, they no longer need professional help. In current psychotherapeutic practice, a number of ordinary individuals with narcissistic personality traits receive appropriate treatment. It is always a challenge to treat such people because they resist changes and often show their obnoxious side, which is taxing on the therapist's empathy. The outcome of treatment is good for those who last long enough to change their extreme behavior into a more flexible and moderate behavior. The outcome is worse in famous individuals because their busy and unpredictable lives make them unavailable for steady and intense treatment. These individuals, by being haughty and self-righteous, are hard to reach and are often deemed untreatable.

Narcissistic individuals have a self-centered perception of reality, and when they speak or write they seem self-involved rather than concerned about the listener or the reader. This problem was characteristic of Gould and was responsible for his bad reputation as a critic of music. Gould, in his frantic need to become a music philosopher, writer and critic, took upon himself the unthankful task of evaluating great composers and their compositions. In this, he went so far as to challenge the standard views and glorify or devalue major music works in his self-centered manner, which caused a conflict between him and music scholars. The most deviant examples of this perception are those of how he perceived composers like Mozart, Beethoven and nineteenth-century composers of romantic music. Unlike other mainstream critics, Gould perceived them with strong love and hate feelings, going from extremes of idealizing them to devaluing them. Though this aspect of Gould is so intriguing and calls for a separate study, here only some provocative details of his unusual views and distortions of reality are described.

Gould's perception of Beethoven was ambivalent, with a range of feelings from love, admiration and affection of his music to indifference, dislike, animosity and open rejection. In order to deal with those opposing, inner conflicts of love and hate, Gould wrote a number of articles where he attempted to "work through" those tormenting, mixed feelings toward Beethoven. These articles became a sort of substitute for therapy, a form of self-analysis in order to come to terms with his own polarizing emotions. In his liner notes for his 1970 recording of Beethoven's popular sonatas *Pathetique*, *Moonlight* and *Appassionatta*, Gould launched a narcissistic, no-win war with the world and with himself by trying to prove that the *Appassionatta* is not a great music work after all. At first, he glorified the *Moonlight* Sonata as a "masterpiece of intuitive organization." He concluded his praise by saying, "because of its cumulative zeal, the 'Moonlight' Sonata is deservedly high on the all-time eighteenth-century hit parade." The next part of Gould's psychological agenda was to express mixed, uncomplimentary feelings about the *Pathetique*, by stating that the opening allegro is marked by emotional "belligerence" and that the concluding Rondo "scarcely pulls its own weight."[19] The worst accusation fell on the Sonata, op. 57, known as *Appassionatta*, in which Gould loathes the finale as a virtuoso piece:

> ... prior to whipping up a frenzied stretto for the coda, Beethoven interpolates a curious eighteen-bar gallop that, with its souped-up tempo and simplistic rhythmic format, provides the compositional equivalent of those heroic gestures by which the experienced virtuoso gathers—even for the most illconceived interpretation—frenzied approval from the balcony.[20]

Gould resents the idea of virtuoso exhibitionism in piano performance, equating it with something immoral and indecent. Behind this open attack, there is a covert envy of Beethoven's geniality expressed in this sonata. This is the concluding paragraph of Gould's liner notes:

> For at this period of his life Beethoven was not only preoccupied with motivic frugality; he was also preoccupied with being Beethoven. And there is about the "Appassionata" an egoistic pomposity, a defiant "let's just see if I can't get away with using that once more" attitude, that on my own private Beethoven poll places this sonata somewhere between the *King Stephen* Overture and the *Wellington's Victory Symphony*.[21]

In 1972, in his article "Glenn Gould Interviews Himself About Beethoven," he enlisted his favorite Beethoven compositions: the String Quartet op. 95, the Piano Sonata op. 81, the Piano Sonata op. 31, the "Moonlight" Sonata and the Eight Symphony. In a juxtaposed position, which was consistent with Gould's negative feelings toward Beethoven's music, he listed his unfavorite pieces, saying, "I'm less fond of the Fifth Symphony, the "Appassionata" Sonata, or the Violin Concerto."[22] Gould proceeds to discuss with himself the pros and cons of Beethoven's music, only to reveal more confusion. He says to himself:

g.g.: When you reject Beethoven ... you're rejecting the logical conclusion of the Western musical tradition.

G.G.: But he isn't the conclusion of it.[23]

And further in the article, Gould agonizes over whether to reject or embrace Beethoven's works such as his "Emperor" Concerto. He says that Beethoven himself "vacillated." Meanwhile, it is patently obvious that it was Gould who vacillated between his love-and-hate feelings. He recognized it himself:

G.G.: Hmm. Well, do you mean, then, that if I do reject Beethoven, I'm on my way to being an environmentalist or something like that? I mean, I think John Cage has said that if he's right, Beethoven must be wrong, or something of the sort. Do you think I'm harboring a sort of suicide wish on behalf of the profession of music?[24]

Yes, of course. Gould was harboring a death wish by uttering such discrediting and disparaging comments in order to challenge and defy others. His Don Quixote act of tilting at windmills alone against the world was self-destructive. In the end, his comments backfired, and he suffered from the injuries to his self-esteem whenever he was repeatedly attacked by those who he first challenged and provoked. Gould lost many battles and certainly lost the war when it came to his ambivalent attitude about Mozart, Beethoven, and his blanket condemnation of the romantic composers of the nineteenth century, Shubert, Chopin, Liszt, Shuman and Tchaikovsky. His public image was tainted by such an attitude, not enhanced. Gould suffered whenever he was confronted with losses. He was literally sick whenever rebuked by the critics for his outlandish opinions. Every fall from grace was followed by more throbbing headaches and more social isolation. Gould was on a merry-go-round of being compelled to devalue standard views in music.

Another feature of narcissistic individuals is their tendency toward the self-centered use of language. Gould, who was lucid and had a superior verbal intelligence, was often criticized for being evasive, for the "unintelligible" use of language, for being a devil's advocate, for talking about subjects beyond his expertise and for an unfriendly use of language. For example, liner notes attached to recordings are meant to be read by a wide variety of record listeners and are supposed to appeal to them. Liner notes written by Gould for his recordings looked more like excerpts from a doctoral dissertation, inasmuch as they were highly philosophical, overly researched, at times hostile and always controversial. The same occurred in his published works. Gould's application of language was not user friendly. His words were often oblique and his sentences long and cryptic. Almost by rule, his writings stir up controversies, the content is fatiguing and makes readers feel inferior, baffled, and finally causes them to give up reading them. This, too, is a mode of Gould's self-destructive bent.

It is time to return to the topic of Gould's mixed feelings toward Beethoven and to demonstrate his unfriendly use of language. Angry as he was with Beethoven and his Fifth Symphony and depreciating romantic composers, including Franz Liszt, Gould still recorded Liszt's piano transcription of Beethoven's Fifth. Not only did Gould need to make a point of how bad the piece was musically, he also wrote four imaginary reviews under different pseudonyms in order to underline all the perceived flaws of this music work. Losing himself in wrath toward Beethoven and Liszt, courteous as he was, Gould wrote this very long and sarcastic sentence:

> What would you think, beloved Franz [Liszt], were you to know that your most noble and most charitable enterprise, the product of your love and faith in man, that zealous undertaking through which you sought to bring acquaintance of the master's work to those poor blighted souls, depressed, restricted by the ducal overlords for whom they labored and whom you, too, so heartily despised, who had no private orchestra to play for them, who had no means by which they might encounter princely pastimes, who had no way of knowing that from Bonn had come a prophet of rebellion—a man of music born to bear the burdens of the masses, to issue proclamations with his harmonies and labor on at themes which served as harbinger of that relentless day of wrath to come—what would you say, if you could know that this, your work, your enterprise, distorted, serves only to enrich the few, impoverish the many.[25]

This may very well be one of the longest sentences ever written, with 157 words. It could be that Gould was euphoric and flighty in his thoughts and that his grandiosity expressed in this sentence was a symptom of his affective instability. His long, complicated, difficult-to-follow sentences were not aimed toward helping his readers to understand them but were in the service of the writer's need to express and unburden himself from those overwhelming affects. Gould went on:

> You played for them, good Franz. You did it all yourself because you had to. No glory did you seek, nor profit either. But eighty men denied the right to work, dear Franz. Eighty men whose cold and sickly children will be colder still tonight. And all because one timid, spineless pianist sold his soul to the enslaving dollar, and his lustful quest exploited yours.[26]

This leaves the reader confused between how much humor, anger or truth there is in this writing. Should the readers be upset about eighty members of a symphony orchestra losing their jobs because of the piano transcription? Are they supposed to be angry at Liszt and agree with Gould or are they just supposed to smile benevolently at Gould's wittiness? Nothing is clear. On the contrary, Gould is evasive while trying to pace his anger and express it in small and tolerant doses. The wicked trappings of narcissism, the lack of empathy for the reader, pernicious comments, grandstanding, are both repelling to others and destructive to the self. Gould was daunted by his inner emotional dynamics, which made him bushwhack projects and attack conventional opinions often in a malicious way. Narcissism is deadwood that needs to be pruned, relinquished or at least brought under some control, which could be accomplished in psychotherapy or psychoanalysis. Gould did not have the benefit of being engaged in an intensive, in-depth psychotherapy over an extended period of time, which could have challenged and eased his narcissistic behavior.

IN SEARCH OF TRUTH

Let us accept truth, even when it surprises us and alters our views.

George Sand[27]

Going back to Gould's predecessors, it is obvious that there is a strong family history of mood disorder on the side of both his parents, in the Greig and in the Gould family. Though Glenn's father had been spared from the gene of depression, all of his three siblings, Freda, Bruce and Grant, as well as his son, Glenn, had bouts of despondent mood at various stages in their lives. Glenn's paternal aunt, Freda, never recovered from the grief and deep mourning following the premature death of her beloved son, Barry, in 1959. At the age of 56, she became severely depressed and required electric shock treatment.

According to witnesses, Glenn's uncle, Bruce, used to drink too much and suffered from a mood disorder. He had medical consequences to his circulatory system from alcohol abuse to the point of his arm having to be surgically amputated. Bruce Gould was naturally gifted for music and played several brass instruments. Music was a palliative remedy for his depression, and after the loss of his arm, Bruce Gould continued to play saxophone with only one arm. His dejected mood and need for alcohol led to the break-up of his family life. Toward the end of his life, he lived by himself at his deceased parents' home in Uxbridge.

Glenn's youngest uncle, Grant, though intellectually brilliant and successful, had a number of downfalls, including his marital break up and prolonged and painful divorce process. This personal tragedy became compounded with his depression, alcohol abuse and a degree of social withdrawal. He became isolated from friends and severed ties with his ex-wife and their three children. When we met at his home in New Port, California, in 1992 for an interview about his nephew Glenn, the seventy-four-year-old surgeon was still working part-time in an outpatient clinic. He loved his job and took pride in being a surgeon even though he had stopped doing hospital-type surgeries. Dr. Gould lived by himself, as a recluse in a large house in which the basement had a walkout patio overlooking a wide hilly area. He spent most of his time in that basement, surrounded by his piano and electrical keyboard standing side by side and a state-of-the-art stereo system with an impressive collection of records and CDs. Just like his mother, Alma and his older brother, Bert, Grant Gould enjoyed flowers and dedicated his time to looking after numerous potted flowers on his patio. He asked my daughter, Dr. Marianne McKinley, who accompanied me on that trip to California, to water the flowers for him and to help make a salad for our buffet-style dinner. Starved for human contact, Dr. Gould explained that he was "sick-and-tired of having to prepare meals" by himself and that he would rather leave some time to talk to us, particularly to Marianne, to whom he felt some kinship, as she had studied medicine at the University of Toronto as he had done in the early 1940s. Dr. Grant appeared to be a very unhappy and lonely man. He looked strained and inebriated and proceeded to sip on his cocktails throughout the afternoon. He very much needed alcohol to carry on and confront the stress of his lonely existence. His mood was markedly depressed, pessimistic and irritable. He was reluctant to talk about his family of origin, saying that the past is of no relevance to him and should be forgotten. On the subject of his famous nephew, Glenn Gould, he felt that he did not know him well enough to answer my detailed questions. He felt quite disconnected from Glenn, which he attributed to geographical distance.

The medical history in the Gould family, as in most other families, showed a tendency to repeat itself. Like his beloved Aunt Freda and two estranged uncles, Bruce and Grant, Glenn too was depressed. The patterns of loneliness, leaning on music as a personal asset and remedy, and dependency on alcohol are patterns that Glenn's uncles had in common. Though Glenn condemned alcohol abuse and became a teetotaler, he could not escape the need for medication, which he overused to the point of being dependent on prescribed medication, paralleling the alcohol dependency of both his uncles. Glenn, like his aunt and uncles, was an unwilling recipient of a genetic overload for mood disorder.

Did Glenn Gould suffer a unipolar depression, meaning recurrent bouts of depression, or a bipolar mood disorder, also known as manic-depressive disorder, which is marked by mood swings and where the episodes of depression alternate with manic or hypomanic states? Glenn's father, Bert, described his own mother, Alma, as a "bundle of energy." "My mother did not just simply walk, she ran wherever she went, and when she was going upstairs in the house, she skipped the steps, running up like a young boy. It seemed to me that she was never tired. And she was chirpy and ready for a joke at any time."[28] Bert was amused by his own mother. Was Alma Gold just a fortunate person with a healthy dose of elation, or was she slightly overactive in the sense of being "hyper"? These are speculative questions that remain without definitive answers.

Bert, like his mother, was blessed with robust energy and zest for life. There is no firm evidence that he had periods of either depression or being "high," as in a hypomanic state. When it came to his work, Glenn had prolonged periods of high productivity, creating music recordings, producing written text for publishing and spending hours of his days on correspondence and telephone calls. He was an insomniac and, on the whole, slept less than an average person, about six to seven hours per day, always with the help of medication. Yet in other aspects of his life, Glenn was mostly in a slump, dragging his feet with respect to social events and being rather slovenly in his housekeeping. It follows that Glenn went from feeling "low" to feeling "high," often within the same day. He used his energy mostly for his creative achievements, whereas he fell short of it for other activities such as sports, socializing or entertaining. Worst of all, Glenn was burned-out sooner than his relatives. Both his father, Bert, and his grandmother, Alma, lived well into their mid-nineties, whereas his aunt and uncles also reached an elderly age. By dying at the age of fifty, Glenn had the shortest natural life span of all of the relatives on his father's side.

Glenn's relatives on his maternal side are more unclear when it comes to their mental health. Glenn's mother was a sickly individual who kept her problems to herself. Florence Greig believed in self-healing and God's will rather than in medical help. She had numerous prejudices and was inflexible in changing her attitudes and beliefs. There were evident fears and phobias in her ways of coping. Some of these fears were excessive to the point of reaching clinical proportions. These were: fear and avoidance of seeing doctors, fear of germs, fear of unknown places, fear of traveling far away from home, which is a form of agoraphobia, and fear and avoidance of flying. It appears that she may have been depressed several times in her life—once before Glenn's birth when she had to quit the choir leadership in 1923, then during her mid-pregnancy with Glenn around the loss of her younger brother, Ruel, and again when Glenn was five years old. Also, there are some indications that she may have been depressed in the last two years of her life. There is no evidence that Florence Greig was ever overactive or hypomanic. Both of her parents, John and Mary Greig, appeared to have suffered with mood disorders. John used to drink to excess, was irritable and often in a "foul mood." Mary was reserved, stern and an obsessive worrier. She likely struggled with a lifelong, low-grade depression. Their oldest son, Glenn's Uncle Willard, suffered with depression in his older age following the loss of his wife, Blanche. Glenn's first cousin, Jessie, reported about her father, Willard Greig: "When my mother died from cancer, my father took it really hard. He retreated into the house and let himself go. Though he later remarried, he was never the same. He was not as approachable as he was before."[29]

With such a visible genetic overload of bipolar mood disorder in both paternal and maternal relatives, Glenn was predisposed to it himself. Glenn had the worst case scenario. He did not have just bouts of depression once or twice in his lifetime but was progressively depressed from his late teens on. It did not help that Glenn also had a long-standing anxiety disorder marked by multiple phobias, including his debilitative social phobia, which was deeply rooted in his early childhood. Glenn's obsessive rituals came to full bloom during his performing career when his stage fright, as a form of anxiety disorder, was most severe. These piano-related mannerisms and rituals developed as a defense mechanism against his strong stage anxiety. Glenn's obsessive-compulsive disorder, commonly abbreviated as OCD, was marked by his compulsive hoarding of things, particularly papers, books, documents, notes, drafts of his writing materials, pill bottles and magazines. In Gould's apartment on St. Clair Avenue West, one of his bedrooms was turned into an archive where the window was barricaded and multiple shelves were built on all three walls of the room. Gradually, all available space, including the shelves and the floor, was filled with stacks of papers and books, left there casually in an unorganized fashion. Compulsive hoarders are known to collect things for the sake of fulfilling their emotional needs to be attached to objects rather than to other human beings.

In his teens and young adulthood, Glenn was relatively physically healthy. He did experience early body pains, which he referred to as fibrositis. These signs and symptoms were manifested in the form of muscle aches, mild stiffness of his limbs and hands, and disturbance of his sleep rhythm. This condition developed along with his performing career, and it was strongly connected to the rising level of stress in Gould's life. It appears that during Gould's performing career he was able to cope with the pain in his hands, which did not seem to interfere with his piano technique. The pain, therefore, at that time may have been purely functional, meaning that his stage fright and muscle tension were largely responsible for it. In his later life, notably in 1977, Gould referred in his note pads to experiencing some numbness in his arms and fingers. This caused him growing concerns. American neurologist Dr. Frank Wilson wrote that a "musical career is hazardous" and that musicians often suffer "symptoms and injuries associated with playing." He specifically pointed to the hand injuries in professional pianists in this way:

> The more carefully we study the history of early giants, the more we can see how commonly such problems have occurred from the very beginning: this could have been the case with Liszt himself, who stopped giving solo piano performances in his thirties; Chopin rarely played the piano in public; Robert Schumann's hand, Glenn Gould's hand, Gary Graffman's hand, Leon Fleisher's hand, possibly even Horowitz's, all failed when these phenomenally gifted and successful pianists were at the height of their careers.[30]

Whether Gould had an occupational condition such as damage to the motor or sensory nerves enervating his fingers is inconclusive for the time being and requires a more focused set of studies. What is readily observable on the video from the second recording of the *Goldberg Variations* in 1981 is his brilliant and fluent virtuoso technique, which would not have been possible had he suffered substantial soft tissue damage to his hands. True, Gould was jesting and cursing about certain passages of music for their treacherousness, but he showed no signs of cramps or fatigue whatsoever and was still able to execute them perfectly.

The next physical illness plaguing Gould in his adult life was essential hypertension, which means high blood pressure. This condition was diagnosed in 1976, shortly after the loss of his mother. Gould was fully aware that both his parents were diagnosed and treated for high blood pressure. Moreover, his father survived two attacks of stroke. At first, Gould's hypertension was mild averaging 130/90. The first figure stands for systolic blood pressure (BP), and the second for diastolic. Obviously, it was the diastolic blood pressure which was elevated. Any figure over eighty stands for blood pressure over and above what is considered normal. As time went on, as early as in 1977 or 1978, Gould's diastolic blood pressure was on the rise despite treatment with medications, such as Aldomet. Gould was so scared that he kept a log of his blood pressure readings. In 1979, he became quite obsessed by taking his own blood pressure almost hourly, ten to thirty times daily:

> Friday, September 10, 17 takings, BP = 146/108 to 160/116 (prior to Valium).
> Saturday, September 11, 30 takings:

A.M.	12:00	12:15	12:30	12:45	1:00	1:30	2:00	2:45	3:30	4:15
BP	144/104	136/100	138/100	136/100	132/98	etc.				

As if he were a dutiful nurse, Gould kept a record of his intake of medications as seen in the following sample of his diary:

Sunday, September 26, 1979,

Aldomet I	1:15 A.M.	BP=120/90
Hydro D I	8:30 A.M.	126/88
Aldomet II		
Hydro D II	2:30 P.M.	122/84
Allopurinol		
Aldomet III	7:30 P.M.	120/88
Aldomet IV	10:00 P.M.	126/90

This kind of obsessive self-monitoring and self-doctoring must have been so time-consuming! Gould was unable to relax and go to sleep, to enjoy music or daydreaming, but was compelled to watch over his illness. Abnormal readings invariably threw Gould into a state of panic and social withdrawal but did not change his lifestyle into a healthier one.

While Gould recognized, even indulged in his physical illness, he had only limited insight into his mental state. He thought of himself as "mildly neurotic," when in reality, he had obstinate and multiple mental health problems. It was these problems that were responsible for his piano-related mannerisms and destroyed his promising concert career. While in hindsight we have little problem diagnosing Gould's mental illness and decoding his strange behavior, his contemporaries had great difficulties making sense of them and coined them as eccentricities. Being called "weird," "eccentric," "idiosyncratic" by the press and associates was deceiving and disparaging. At times, it may have been flattering and contributed to the saga of Gouldian kinks. At other times, when Gould was attacked for his piano-related mannerisms, it was hurtful and humiliating. Sharp criticism of his behavior, mistaken as eccentricities, caused him new emotional problems, more withdrawal from the world and more damage to his self-esteem.

Like other mortals, Gould suffered a very common combination of mood disorder and high blood pressure, and it is no longer adequate to call his behavior "weird" or "mysterious." It is more that his overwhelming intelligence and artistic talent made him so unusual among his contemporaries that they were unprepared to accept him as he was. Instead, they were compelled to analyze him, dissect him and misinterpret their findings about him. Somewhere in that process, Gould's observers lost their goal to assess and enjoy the strength of his offerings rather than to be bamboozled by his tricky personal foibles. Most adults do not have perfect adjustment and are expected to have some emotional frailties. But it is not these personal quirks that make the richness of our world but the strength and uniqueness of its individuals. Despite his thick medical records, Gould had a healthy and positive influence in the world. His audiences and fans can still sit back and enjoy his music in the privacy of their homes, which Gould always hoped for, and accept him with awe and appreciation.

Chapter XVII

THE VOLLEY OF CREATIVITY

GOULD AS A DISTINGUISHED CANADIAN BROADCASTER

> I am a Canadian writer, composer and broadcaster who happens to play the piano in his spare time.
>
> Glenn Gould[1]

In his productive broadcasting career, Gould created or participated in up to 200 broadcasts, out of which forty-two shows were for television; whereas the rough estimate of his radio shows, which are hard to track down, is over 150. Radio is a medium that could accommodate entertainers of every ilk. By being a creator and a script writer, a pianist, broadcaster, researcher, educator, narrator, composer, often interviewer, actor, comedian and impersonator, Gould played the role of a universal entertainer. Some of his shows were quite involved, in terms of preparation and research time. According to this, a body of 200 shows for radio and television is equivalent to the time and work of writing several books.

Glenn had been a radio star since he was six years of age, a track record that very few of his fellow contemporaries could have claimed. The CBC archives, established in the 1950s, do not have any record of Gould's childhood radio career. It is not known whether any audio tapes survived in private collections. One can learn about his early radio activity only from the living memory of those who heard him play and from the letters of his fans. Gould himself reminisced:

> In January 1950 I took part for the first time in the CBC broadcast and made a discovery that influenced in a rather profound way my development as a musician. I discovered that in the privacy, the solitude and where the Freudians would stand clear, the womb-like security of the studio, it was possible to make music in a more direct, more personal way than any concert hall ever would permit. I fell in love with broadcasting that day and I have not since been able to think of the potential of music or for that matter of my own potential without some reference to the limitless possibilities of the broadcasting and recording media.[2]

Fascinated by the "womb-like security of the studio," Gould remained dedicated to broadcasting for the rest of his life.

The Canadian Broadcasting Corporation (CBC) had been housed since its inception in a massive, red-brick building at 354 Jarvis Street in Toronto. This gradually became Gould's second home where he spent long hours working on radio programs. Lorne Tulk, Gould's future recording engineer, recalled how he first met Glenn. Tulk's father, who retired from the CBC in 1950, opened his private radio station in Midland, Ontario, working out of his living room. Lorne, who was fascinated by radio technology, became his father's assistant and, eventually, his disciple. When Lorne was twelve years old, his father allowed him to make a copy of Glenn's CBC broadcast recital debut. In this connection, Glenn, at age eighteen, met his six-year-younger coworker at his home-studio in Midland on Christmas Eve 1950. Bonded through the radio, Glenn and Lorne went on being kindred spirits and associates within the realm of electronic transmission.[3]

In September and October 1952, Gould's radio career was heralded for his twentieth birthday, and he performed for listening audiences in five subsequent recitals. In the "Distinguished Artists" series, he played works of Beethoven, and in the CBC Concert Hall series, he championed the little-known piano music of the recently deceased Arnold Schoenberg and his student, Alban Berg. His taste for the unusual and search for something new and different was already obvious. From the beginning Glenn was a restless music star. More Beethoven, Bach and Hindemith was to follow on the radio in the next two years, all of which was a warm-up period before Gould's internationally acclaimed piano debut in New York in January 1955. Radio stardom was a forecaster of his performing fame that was to come. In 1952, Canadian television made its debut, and Gould was present at the opening night playing Mendelssohn's Rondo Capricioso. Despite this solo appearance, his official television debut is considered to be two years later, in December 1954, when at the age of twenty-two Gould performed as a soloist the opening movement of Beethoven's Concerto no.1 in C Minor with an unidentified orchestra conducted by Paul Sherman. Gould played his own cadenza. The footage of this performance is the only video of Gould before a live audience. In April 1956, Gould was interviewed for the first time on the radio by Eric McLean of Montreal, who was to become one of his most important scholarly critics.

In February 1961, Gould's show, "The Subject is Beethoven," was aired on television as a part of the *Festival Series*. The response from the audience was extraordinary. Letters of praise and telephone calls to the CBC-TV station represented the positive feedback of the viewers to a point that the program had to be repeated shortly afterward. Gould performed Beethoven's *Eroica Variations* and Mandelsohn's Variations serieuses, as well as Beethoven's Sonata for Cello and Piano, no. 3 in A Major, op. 69, with Leonard Rose, cello. John Lee Roberts described the enthusiasm of the audience in response to the show:

> Many people wrote to say that they had never encountered so-called concert music, classical music or whatever you want to call it, before. They hadn't encountered it at school; they hadn't encountered music at home, and by chance they found it on television. Those people went on to say that ... they were beginning a whole new exploration of a new world they didn't realize existed.[4]

In March of the same year, Gould signed a contract with the CBC to star in four one-hour television spectaculars. The first telecast was in January 1962 as a part of a Sunday concert series; the program was titled "Music in the USSR." Gould wrote the program, narrated it and played Prokofiev's Sonata no.7 in B-flat Major, op. 83, and Shostakovich Piano Quintet, op. 57, with the Symphonia Quartet.

In October 1962, Gould's show, "Richard Strauss: A Personal View," was aired on television as part of the CBC-TV *Festival Series*. In this program, he spoke about his love of Strauss's music, and accompanied on the piano Lois Marshall, soprano. Strauss's works, like Four Last Songs: no.3 and Three Ophelia Songs, op. 67, were interpreted with Miss Marshall, and the Violin Sonata in E flat, Major op.18 with Oskar Shumsky, violinist. The show provoked the outrage of Roy Shields, a critic of *The Toronto Star*, who castigated Gould. He raised the question as to why Gould was allowed to "exercise his ego for an hour on prime time." In criticizing Gould, Shields contended: "It is difficult to understand why Mr. Gould was allowed to write his own script," and concluded: "His use of language ... is quite unintelligible."[5] It is true that there was a stuffy side to Gould's esoteric speech, but this was a minor and innocent flaw in comparison with what he had to offer in return, a thoughtful and edifying show on Strauss.

In the following two arid years, Gould was in a creative slump and made only one show per year. On October 15, 1963, his monumental show for the *Festival* titled "The Anatomy of Fugue" was aired. He presented as a scholar of Bach by first discussing the history of the fugue and counterpoint as forms in baroque music and then illustrating it by two fugues from *The Well-Tempered Clavier* by Bach. Gould then introduced his own composition, *So You Want To Write A Fugue*, and conducted the four vocalists of the quartet "Concert Singers."

Why was the year 1963 a nadir of Gould's broadcasting career? His live recitals were slowing down following the Brahms-Bernstein fiasco in New York in October 1962. Brutal criticism by the New York press and the pejorative critique by Roy Shields compounded with his own inner dilemma, whether to continue his concert career or not, resulted in a crisis of self-confidence and depression, which affected his interest in broadcasting adversely.

On November 27, 1964, seven months after his last public recital in Los Angeles, Gould was interviewed on the radio by an unidentified woman. He glorified the electronic media, which, according to him, changed the course of music by making ideas available to a wider audience and said that "recordings have this marvelous ability of saying 'no, let's hold in abeyance our judgements, let's decide twenty years from now ...'" Short of pleading directly with the critics, "Please bear with me and don't judge me harshly but rather try to really understand me and my art," Gould made every effort to relate his message. He also put forward a novel idea that it would be useful for composers and engineers to get together so that the former could write more effectively for the microphone and stated unequivocally that he preferred the recording studio to the concert hall.

Once he was sure that his concert career was over and that he was over his temporary setback, Gould threw himself into broadcasting and recording. In January 1965, eight months after his last live recital, one of Gould's major programs, "Dialogues on the Prospects of Recording," was aired on the *CBC Sunday Night* radio. By then, the pianist was lobbying his self-serving idea that public concerts would disappear by the year 2000. In this inventive radio show, there was a lively discussion between Gould and eight distinguished personalities: Schuyler Chapin, the assistant director of the Lincoln

Centre for the Performing Arts; John Hammond and Paul Myers, producers at Columbia Records; Marshall McLuhan, a professor at the University of Toronto; Diana Menuhin, the wife of violinist Jehudi Menuhin; Robert Offergeld, a music editor of Hi-Fi Stereo Review; Leon Fleisher, an American concert pianist; and Ludwig Diehn, a businessman of Norfolk, Virginia, whose hobby was to write symphonies. Their discussion centered on the future roles of artists, tape editors, critics and engineers, and the degree of satisfaction the artist is likely to derive from performing for an invisible audience. This show was Gould's personal "working through" of his inner conflicts between performing and recording, and like many other shows was autobiographical and self-therapeutic.

The zenith of Gould's broadcasting career was 1969 when he created twenty-five shows—one for TV and the rest for the radio. Gould had a gale-force mind whirring with new ideas, and his only difficulty was finding time to materialize them. He took his broadcasting work seriously and could not do anything in a cursory way. His work schedule was very demanding, winning him a reputation of a workaholic artist.

His tireless mind was responsible for the creation of such a timeless, monumental radio series, "The Art of Glenn Gould," featuring classical music, commentaries and interviews. This series was sold in the United States to one hundred stations of the National Educational Radio network. The first show of the series of four was aired on November 11, 1966, and was titled "On Records and Recording." In this broadcast Gould presented excerpts from his several recordings of the works of Bach, Beethoven, Schoenberg and Strauss, offering a commentary on the question of honesty in recording as opposed to live performance. In the second and third show aired in March 1967, Gould combined the works of Bach with his own compositions. He discussed the structure of his String Quartet no. 1 and *So You Want To Write A Fugue*. In the fourth show aired on April 2, 1967, titled "Conference at Port Chillkoot," he presented a satirical documentary about a music critics' conference and illustrated it with the music works of Bach and Schoenberg. "The Art of Glenn Gould" was so successful and popular that it needed to be expanded. In the span of two years, in 1969, it reappeared in a twenty-one-part weekly series. The music critics responded with an outpouring of admiration and praise, and the fans reacted with enthusiastic letters and telephone calls to the radio station. One of Gould's most inspired and dedicated fans, Elizabeth de Roode, penned out these eloquent and sympathetic words to the editor of the *CBC Times*:

> Good Grief! It takes gumption to gush like Glenn Gould. He can be galling and garrulous, but always great, glorious, and generous. From gossoon to gentleman he is a genius. He is gargantuan, gesticulative, genuine, a grandee, a gem, a giant, gracious, glowing and obviously golden. Glory to Gould! In gratitude to the weekly series "The Art of Glenn Gould" and the tv concerts.[6]

The Art of Glenn Gould reappeared for the second time as a weekly series from May 20 to October 7, 1969, and encompassed a vast array of music-related topics ranging from Gould playing the works of great composers to discussing music with his co-host, Ken Haslam. For example, *The Art of Glenn Gould* "Take Four" was dedicated to Arnold Schoenberg, "Take Five" to Mozart and "Take Six" to Bach. "Take Eight" was in honor of the pianist Artur Schnabel and Beethoven's Fourth Concerto. For this program, Gould interviewed Claude Franck, a former pupil of Artur Schnabel, and inserted on the master tape a portion of Schnabel's rendition of the same work. This all was combined with Gould's 1961 complete performance of the Fourth Concerto taped with the New York Philharmonic with Leonard Bernstein conducting. The program was fabulous! Preparation for this show was, like all others, very demanding. A press reporter who sat in on the taping stated: "The atmosphere is tense as the end of the long process comes into view. The technician [Lorne Tulk] and producer [Richard Coulter] show signs of weariness. But Gould, who appears indefatigable, watches the final processing with keen and continuing interest ..."[7]

Gould and his announcer, Bill Hawes, spent time in the control room listening to what was recorded and laughed over Gould's witty writing. The atmosphere in the studio was hot and humid with the air-conditioning being switched off at Gould's request. He wore a black jacket, blue Oxford shirt and a woolen vest. He also played with his sunglasses, which he either pushed up on the top of his head or held and waved in the air while talking. Throughout the work session, there was humor and a pleasant amiable interchange.

In "Take Nine" Gould interviewed over the telephone his friend, Dr. Joseph Stephens, a psychiatrist and harpsichordist from Baltimore, on the subject of the psychology of a virtuoso on stage. The two of them discussed the question of whether it is "morally right" for a soloist to upstage the orchestra. Gould asserted that Romantic music is "sinful" because it celebrates the performer's virtuosity rather than inspire "inward lookingness" in the listener. Dr. Stephens maintained that individual virtuosity can be uplifting to the listener. In "Take Nineteen" Gould presented his interpretation of Bach's *Art of the Fugue* followed by Gould's composition *So You Want To Write A Fugue* and discussed with Haslam the fugues composed by Bach, Mozart, Bartok, Buxtehude, Verdi and Beethoven. In "Take Twenty" Gould and Haslam conducted a lively conversation on music critics and their criticism, and in the final "Take Twenty-one" Gould discussed the Moog synthesizer and Walter Carlos's electronic recording of selected Bach works. The recording was released under the name "Switched-on Bach," in which Carlos performed on the electronic instrument, a synthesizer, designed by Robert Moog. In describing the historical importance of Carlos's professional performance of classical music, Moog said:

> [Carlos] has shown that the medium of electronic music is eminently suited to the realization of much traditional music, and in doing so has firmly brought the electronic medium into the historical mainstream of music.[8]

Glenn Gould, who "modernized" interpretations of Bach's music by playing it on the contemporary concert piano, made a historical contribution to the professional performance of classical music. Gould made a quantum leap from performing Bach's music on the organ or harpsichord to performing it on the grand piano. Walter Carlos made the next chronological leap by performing it on an electronic synthesizer. In his radio program, Gould was extremely complimentary toward Carlos's daring undertaking, as he himself was delving into electronic media of radio and TV transmission of music as well as recording music.

The Art of Glenn Gould is a unique radio biography. It portrays Gould as the piano virtuoso, musicologist, conversationalist, comic, but, most of all, a creator and an explorer of new pathways of communicating classical music to the general public. It is his personal salute to those who directly or indirectly shaped his music development and his life. He paid tributes to great composers, to contemporary composers, to baroque music, to Schnabel, Strauss, to the recording industry, and to his country of birth. Gould loved working on that show. For each hour of the show, he put in two to six hours of writing it longhand and up to twenty hours of recording in three studios with his team—producer Richard Coulter and three technicians.

On November 15, 1967, Gould starred in *Centennial Performance* in the last of three special TV concerts for Canada's 100th birthday. He was a piano soloist with the Toronto Symphony Orchestra conducted by the guest conductor, Vladimir Golschmann. They played Bach's Concerto no. 7 in G Minor and Strauss's Burleske for Piano and Orchestra in D Minor. The choice of music was typically Gouldian, and Golschman, a friend and admirer of the virtuoso from his performing days, deferred to his music repertory. Gould hailed Strauss and made such public statements as follows:

> "[Strauss is] the greatest man of music of the twentieth century. I've always been addicted to his music the way some are addicted to chocolate sundaes. I find it absolutely irresistible. And I find that my perspective on music of the twentieth century seems infinitely clearer for having known rather than ignored Strauss."[9]

Gould's *Solitude Trilogy* consisted of three radio documentaries: "The Idea of North," "The Latecomers" and "The Quiet in the Land." Janet Somerville, a founding producer of a popular night show, *Ideas*, provided for him a compatible medium for his radio creations. This is where Gould developed his famous and original concept of "contrapuntal radio" or "aleatoric radio." This is a radio program where people's voices are overlapping. Somerville, who was Gould's associate but also a loyal admirer, was the one who recognized that "he had more than 88 keys in him."[10] In order to accommodate Gould in his creation of the show "The Idea of North," Somerville wrote numerous memos to her superiors pleading for more finances. On June 24, 1969, she wrote to N. Gardiner, radio technical director, asking for extra equipment—six pan pots (phantomers) to make it possible for Glenn Gould to do the mix he wanted.[11] Her persistence paid off and funds were obtained for Gould to embark on his trips to Ottawa and Winnipeg to interview several individuals about the north. He spoke with Marianne Schroeder, a nurse, who spent several years in a mission in the North; Frank Vallee, a retired sociologist and author of a book on the Eskimo; Robert Phillips, the author of a book, *Canada's North*; James Lotz, an anthropologist; and Wally Maclean, who served as the narrator of the documentary. These five characters never met, but their monologues were taped and their voices were combined in contrapuntal fashion, two or three voices talking simultaneously. In the space of one hour of the show, Gould "layered" their voices so that they were overlapping each other. This is Gould's contrapuntal radio.[12] The setting was on an imagined train where the five individuals met and talked about their journey north. The background sound is that of the train as basso continuo. The five individuals familiar with the northland engaged in lively descriptions of the north. In his letter to John Culshaw of the British Broadcasting Corporation, Gould explained that his show about the North "was really an exercise in the techniques of radio."[13] The following is an excerpt from Gould's radio show, which is representative of Gould's innovative radio technique as well as of his philosophy on the Canadian North:

M.S.: And as we flew along the east coast of Hudson's Bay, this flat, flat country
F.V.: *I don't go—let me say*

M.S.: frightened me a little, because it just seemed endless.
F.V.: *this again—I don't go for this northmanship bit at all.*

M.S.: We seemed to be going nowhere, and the further north we went
F.V.: *I don't knock those people who do claim that they want to go*

M.S.: the more monotonous it became. There was nothing but snow
F.V.: *farther north, but I see it as a game, this northmanship bit. People say, "Well,*

M.S.: and to our right, the waters of Hudson's Bay.
F.V.: *were you ever up at the North Pole?"*

M.S.: Now, this was my impression
F.V.: *and "Hell, I did a dogsled trip of twenty-two days,"*

M.S.: during the winter, but I also flew over the country
F.V.: *and the other fellow says, "Well, I did one of thirty days"* -

M.S.: during the spring and the summer, and this I found intriguing,
F.V.: *you know, it's pretty childish. Perhaps they would see themselves*
Robert Phillips [third voice]: And then, for another eleven years, I served the North in various capacities.

M.S.: because then I could see the outlines
F.V.: *as more sceptical*............[fade]
R.P.: Sure, the North has changed my life; I can't conceive

M.S.: of the lakes and the rivers, and on the tundra,
R.P.: of anyone in close touch with the North, whether they lived there all the time

M.S.: huge spots of moss or rock -
R.P.: or simply traveled it month after month and year after year -

M.S.: there is hardly any vegetation that one can spot from the air....[fade]
F.V.: ..... *more sceptical about the offerings of the mass media* ..... [fade]
R.P.: I can't conceive of such a person as really being untouched by the North.[14]

Gould described this *Centennial* project as "a vocal symphony ... a sort of psychedelic jigsaw of sound, voice and thought, an emotional impression that isn't so much listened to as absorbed."[15] He referred to the voices in "specifically 'baroque' musical terms" "as a trio-sonata." On another occasion, he said: "There is something Delphian about the North West Territories—the idea of its symbolic stance in relation to the rest of North America, the idea of being able to brew positive thoughts in negative nature."[16] Pride and patriotism instilled by his mother are also elements reflected in Gould's fascination with the North, which, with the exception of Alaska and Greenland, belongs to Canada. William Littler wrote in *The Toronto Star*: "The Pianist has turned radio producer and is fashioning his own far-out documentary on—who would have guessed it?—the Canadian North."[17] Littler visited Gould at the CBC studio where he had worked tirelessly on the project. On that occasion he worked till 5 a.m. Gould told Littler: "It's beginning to catch up with me. I usually get by on seven or eight hours [of sleep] and can make it on four or five for a stretch. But I've stretched the stretch to the limit. Shall we call it a night?"[18]

By writing about the Canadian North, Gould contemplated a life in solitude. The northern climate is a metaphor of serene, quiet, unurbanized, solitary living. Yet Gould shows an obvious ambivalence about the topic of solitude vs. people. By favoring telecommunication, by reaching people in the intimacy of their homes, entertaining them and enriching their lives, Gould showed his devotion to them. Radio was a halfway house between solitude and the people. It made it possible for him to be heard but not seen. Half-anonymity and half-public exposure appealed to this conflicted artist. "The Idea of North" does not have anything to do with his love of the climate—on the contrary, Gould hated frigid weather, dreaded the winter even in Toronto and never enjoyed winter sports. Hence, this is a purely social concept, defensive in nature and idealizing the nonsocial, crowd-free environment.

In his biographical book about Gould, Geoffrey Peyzant quoted a passage from the book *Dynamics of Creation* by Anthony Storr, pointing to the "relation between creative genius and the need for solitude [such as] in the case of the schizoid creative personality."[19] By implication, Peyzant and many others may have thought of Gould as a schizoid artist. Meanwhile, Gould was a vigorous communicator with the ability to feel strong affects of love and hate; of pleasure and displeasure; of sadness and envy. His quest for creative solitude was largely conscious and was determined by his preference. Avoidance of others in the form of social withdrawal was due to his depressive disorder. Gould was capable of experiencing a range of angry feelings but for the most part he showed a tendency to hide his anger. Hence, he defended against any demonstrative expression of feelings but he had the ability to feel them. Schizoid individuals by definition have flat affect and are unable to experience deep feelings.

Back to Gould's *Solitude Trilogy*. In the same enthusiastic way in which Janet Somerville assisted Gould in realizing his first radio show, she supported him generously in his second radio show, "The Latecomers." For this show, Gould had to spend one month of his life in Newfoundland and then had to spend 336 man hours putting it together. Somerville wrote in her notes: "Glenn Gould is going to Newfoundland on an imagination-jelling trip," and in her memo to one of her superiors, she wrote: "... for a genius he's very cooperative."[20] "The Latecomers" was aired on November 12, 1969, in Ottawa, Winnipeg and Vancouver only. This too is a contrapuntal documentary in which there is a euphony of voices of fourteen people which are "layered" and become the characters of this drama. The background sound is that of surf. It was done in a more advanced stereo technique as opposed to monaural. Gould commented: "... each character and situation has its own sound, so its rather Wagnerian in that respect. The surf, a hypnotic continuo, is so much a part of Newfoundland. It isolates the characters and draws them together in their isolation."[21] Janet Somerville summed up his motive: "Gould decided upon Newfoundland because of its special relationship to the twentieth century, it's not quite in it, not quite out of it. It is universal—a picture of the human condition."[22]

The choice of the title "The Latecomers" had a deep historical and personal meaning. It referred to Newfoundland as the last province to join Canada in 1949. In the same year Canada gained independence and stopped being a dominion. For Glenn personally, this was an event that his grandfather, Tom Gold, greatly enjoyed. Tom was born in 1867, the year of Canada's birth, when the four provinces, Ontario, Quebec, New Brunswick and Nova Scotia, joined in confederation and became the Dominion of Canada. Tom, who happened to be an amateur historian was extremely proud of this event and particularly about being a first generation Canadian. The story was often retold at Glenn's home while he was growing up. In 1949, Tom rejoiced and celebrated Canada's independence from the crown. Glenn was at that time a restless seventeen year old. By paying tribute to "The Latecomers," which directly meant to Newfoundland and its people, he indirectly expressed the love of his country and, on a more intimate level, the tender feelings for his grandfather.

Gould's *Solitude Trilogy* was a grand project that required a tremendous amount of personal research. Since Gould proclaimed it at the beginning to be a trilogy, he was expected to create a third part. This commitment was hard to follow. As time went on, he developed new interests whereas some of the old ones dwindled. Also, it is safe to conjecture that at some point Gould realized he did not quite believe in his solitude concept. He enjoyed communicating with people, and he spent an inordinate amount of time on the telephone talking with others or in the CBC studios working with his colleagues. Clearly, solitary living was either a sign of social withdrawal whenever he was depressed or Gould pursued it by choice for the purpose of creation and hard work. Because of his change of heart, there was a considerable gap between the time when Gould finished "The Latecomers" and the time when he finished the third and final part of the trilogy, "The Quiet in the Land." This program was aired on April 25, 1977. It portrayed the lives of Mennonites at Red River, Manitoba. In his letter to Elvin Shantz, Gould described what he wanted to accomplish in this Mennonite project, saying: "... what I hope to achieve, primarily, is a 'mood-piece' – a radio-essay dealing with the degree in which, as one of my interviewees put it, the Mennonites are able to remain 'in the world but not of the world.'"[23]

Thus, in the span of ten years of work on the *Solitude Trilogy*, Gould was working through his personal conflict—people vs. solitude. The trilogy served as a framework for his self-analysis. Should he isolate himself and disappear from the scene and the sight of others, or should he maintain a degree of communication with people and continue to create within the human medium? This was Gould's persistent dilemma in which the second part of the question prevailed. He indeed turned more to people, even though in his characteristic, distant way.

Gould was fascinated by the seclusive life of Mennonites. There are only about 60,000 Mennonites in Canada, concentrated mostly in Ontario and British Columbia. They are the members of a Protestant Christian group and are also known as Amish or Anabaptists. The Mennonites lead a simple lifestyle, wearing traditional plain clothes, farming and living off the land, rejecting luxuries and modern inventions like electronic appliances. They practice adult baptism and obey the strict teachings of the Bible. By studying and producing a show on the Mennonites, Gould attempted to understand their social isolation from the world and through them to understand his own differences.

Fascination with the northland, with Newfoundland and with the community of Mennonites, all portrayed in his *Solitude Trilogy*, served as a powerful creative impetus. Gould liked the symbolism of the North and isolation but not sufficiently to want to practice it himself by living in the North or in Newfoundland.

In the 1970s, there were two great series created by Gould among many other shows. One was the *Schoenberg Series* of ten shows aired on radio in 1974, and another was an unfinished TV series about twentieth-century music, decade by decade, and given in the program *Musicamera* as "Music in Our Time." The *Schoenberg Series* is probably the most extensive and best radio account ever produced about Schoenberg's life and music. In the first show, Gould commemorated the 100th anniversary of the composer's birth. Gould wrote the script and narrated the program. In the next sequence, he covered all major works, such as Schoenberg's songs, sung by Helen Vanni, soprano, Ellen Faull, soprano, and Donald Gramm, bass-baritone. He included excerpts from his valuable interview in 1962 with Gertrude Schoenberg, the composer's wife, and lead a lively discussion with Eric Leinsdorf about the composer's American period. More interviews with John Cage, a former student of Schoenberg and Ernet Krenek followed; all of this material was presented in Gould's contrapuntal technique.

Gould was not only an interpreter, admirer and scholar of Schoenberg's music, but in a way, he was his biographer. He single-handedly propagated Schoenberg's music more than any other musician in North America by performing and recording it and by his analytic writing about it. Gould created a little literary collection of writings on Schoenberg. In his monograph, "Arnold Schoenberg – A Perspective," published by the University of Cincinnati in limited edition in 1964, he put forward an incredibly insightful evaluation of the half-century of a rich music career. Gould was very touched by the fact that Schoenberg, shortly before his death, in a lecture given in Los Angeles, opened by saying: "I wonder sometimes who I am." He compared Schoenberg to other great men: "... the name of Arnold Schoenberg is known very widely indeed—is in fact almost as frequent a drawing-room reference as Freud or as Kafka ... yet many people remark that apart from a few of his docile and romantic early works, his compositions have so far failed to attract any large share of public response."[24]

Schoenberg was an innovator and inventor of the twelve-tone technique and atonality in music, and he spent "fifteen years awash in a sea of dissonance" but returned to tonal composing, or as Gould calls it, "quasi-tonal work." Schoenberg's Violin and Piano Concertos were written in that "more conventional twelve-tone discipline." Gould concludes his study of Schoenberg by raising a question—"What sort of influence has he wielded upon our world?" Gould answered: "... if you want my guess ... I would guess that we will someday know indeed "who he was;" we will someday know that he was one of the greatest composers who ever lived."[25]

The real question is, why was Gould so fanatically devoted to Schoenberg and his music? As the idealist, he once again over-idealized somebody with whom he identified. Gould, who was not quite sure of his own identity, deeply empathized with the displaced composer. Schoenberg was hated, ridiculed, dismissed, but also revered as a knowledgeable and talented composer. Just like Schoenberg, Gould, too, was a subject of controversial views. Gould's identification with Schoenberg is twofold—with the man who felt persecuted by others, and with his music, which was mutinous and contrapuntal, defiant, modern, and unlike any other music. Gould wrote other articles about Schoenberg. In his liner notes prepared for his piano recording with Columbia, he stated:

> Experiment was the essence of Schoenberg's musical experience, and we can be grateful that in carrying out his experiments he turned on five occasions to the solo piano. ... But during crucial moments of the most significant experiments in his career, during the years when Schoenberg was reworking the contemporary musical language, the piano—inexpensive to write for, instantly able to demonstrate the dangers and the possibilities of a new vocabulary—was the servant. Schoenberg repaid it with some of the great moments in its contemporary literature.[26]

Again, Gould like Schoenberg was given to experimentation of trying to improve and communicate through contemporary music language. Gould used Schoenberg to an extent as one of his models, but he was not his copycat.

Back to Gould's grand TV series *Music in Our Time*. The first telecast, titled "The Age of Ecstasy," encompassed the period of music between 1900 to 1910 and was illustrated by the music of Berg, Debussy, Schoenberg and Scriabin. In the next show, titled "The Flight from Order" and aired on May 2, 1965, he presented the music between 1920 and 1930 of Prokofiev, *Visions Fugitives*, no.2, op.22, his transcription of Ravel's *La Valse* and Strauss's Three Ophelia's Songs, op. 67, with Roxolana Roslak, soprano. The third show of the *Music in Our Time* with a name "New Faces, Old Forms, 1920-30," dealt with the music of Hindemith, Poulenc, Schoenberg and Walton. In show no. 4, "The Artist as Artisan, 1930-40," Gould presented the music of Hindemith, Casella and Krenek. The show was aired on December 14, 1977. After this, Gould's interest and energy were wearing down, and he could not finish the series and face the music of the 1940s and 1950s.

One may wonder how much Gould was paid for his enormous effort at broadcasting? For his series of four radio programs, *Glenn Gould in Recital*, which ran in 1968 and 1969, Glenn Gould Ltd. received $2,500 each, or $10,000 in total. For the telecast *Music in Our Time*, part three, which aired in 1975, Glenn Gould Ltd. negotiated the price of $8,000 and $3,500 upon re-telecasting. Gould was best paid for the films he worked on. His company received $20,000 for *Glenn Gould's Toronto*. His average annual income in the 1950s was $50,000, which doubled in the 1960s. The film-making and his work for television were more lucrative than his former performing career and his work for radio.

For the "negative" critics, Gould was a sitting duck; for his fans, he was an endless subject of astonishment and adoration. For curious and empathic music appreciators, he was a gold-mine of interesting ideas and invaluable talent, always keen to give something to his listeners and observers. Gould's popularity was on the rise. Offers and requests for interviews were common, several of them granted, most of them declined. The first aired interviews in Canada were by Eric McLean in 1956 and Hugh Thompson two years later. In 1959, two biographical films were made by the National Film Board, titled *Glenn Gould On the Record* and *Glenn Gould Off the Record*. In April 1969, a TV show called "Variations on Glenn Gould" was aired within the program *Telescope*. Director Perry Rosemond endeavored to present Gould's portrait during his recording session at Massey Hall, at the radio studio while working on a documentary, and in the Ontario north where the artist went to reflect and create.

RECORDING PHILOSOPHY AND FAME

Music is a malleable art, acquiescent and philosophically flexible ...
Glenn Gould[27]

After nine years on the international circuit of public performing, Gould realized that his search for immaculate performance was in vein. He decided that he had enough of public appearances and that time had come for him to withdraw and streamline his energies toward recording music and propagating it for larger audiences. He threw himself into more broadcasting, more writing and more recording than ever before. Gould confessed that he was uncomfortable with having only one chance to perform at the concert and prove his goodness at the piano. He often had an urge to stop in the middle of performing a music piece and say "take two," meaning having another chance at playing it perfectly. To him, the music performance was a case of "non-take-twoness," or a regrettably ephemeral event, and he was longing for more lasting forms of self-expression. Radio tapes may or may not survive for posterity but music records are real survivors and the most precious documents of one's own musicianship. The scores of, say, Bach's music are mute while lying on the shelf; they get a beautiful voice while they are performed in front of the audience, but this one-time experience of music may be quickly forgotten afterward. It's only when the music is recorded that it can be played over and over again, enjoyed and remembered to a point of ringing in the listener's ear.

The interpreter is the voice of a composer. According to Gould, an interpreter does not need to be seen but his music needs to be heard. Music is the message to be delivered to wide masses and not only in front of the limited number of audiences of the concert hall. Music is also a personal experience unique to an individual and should be played in the privacy of one's home. The recording studio is a much more personable enclave than the concert hall, which is a place of potential fame but also of a potential disaster. Gould compared the recording studio to a maternal womb, dark and safe. This womb-like security, which he obtained during the recording sessions, was diametrically opposite to being in the limelight on the concert stage. In Gould's own words on the advantages of recording:

> To harbor nostalgia for a medium is one thing but to carry its limitations into a new medium is quite another. I firmly believe that recording is an autonomous medium and could profit one only if it's treated as such.
>
> The microphone does encourage to develop attitude to performance which is entirely out of place in the difficult acoustics of the concert hall. It permits you to cultivate a degree of textural clarity which simply does not pay dividends in the concert hall.[28]

If radio represented his father, the old phonograph and its derivatives, like the modern record player and recording equipment, represented Gould's mother. Hence Glenn's love for these electronic wonders comes from the symbolic marriage of the radio and tape-recorder as represented in the real marriage of his parents. Gould, as the product of that union, became an heir to those technological devices with endless passion and devotion toward them.

Columbia Masterworks treated Gould as if he were their only child. The management of CBS Masterworks gave Gould a limitless mandate by letting him do what he wanted, to record music of his choice whenever it was convenient for him. He was a privileged asset and certainly a very lucrative artist. Having so much freedom at his hand was a two-edged sword. It helped Gould create a unique array of records. Because of this very freedom, he gave to the world Bach's *Goldberg Variations*, which his producers were reluctant to record but he persuaded them. On the other hand, freedom in Gould's hands also meant that he could easily misuse it. In altering tempi and concept of music he recorded, and in writing at times disdainful liner notes for his own records, Gould went too far and created controversies. A good example of that controversy would be Gould's recording of the last three Beethoven sonatas early in his career, in 1956. Gould summed up the problem in his letter to John Roberts, who was at the time music producer for CBC Radio and assistant music director for CBC Television in Winnipeg:

> Dear John:
>
> ... I am delighted to hear that you are doing the two programs of my recordings. In regard to the Beethoven Sonatas, they have, as you know received both extravagant praise and devastating condemnation. I can only say that those alterations of dynamic or tempo indication with which I took license were the result, not of whims, but of rather careful scrutiny of the scores and bear, up to the moment at any rate, an optimistic conviction. Since so many listeners and critics (trustworthy ones too) have taken exception to my conception of late Beethoven I cannot claim that it is the most convincing recording that I have made. However, I do feel that, if only as a personal manifesto, it is the most convinced.[29]

Both the music scholars and audiences were confident that Gould knew how to interpret Beethoven's sonatas in an orthodox way but could not overlook the fact that he delivered them to the public in a form of a permanent document, a recording, in an unorthodox way. Gould claimed that he did not do it out "of whims" but upon a "rather careful scrutiny." He labored on the sonatas, studied them in depth, made conceptual changes, and then recorded them for permanence. Not only that, but he wrote extremely unusual liner notes that accompanied his records in which he glorified Beethoven's Sonata op. 27, no.2—Moonlight Sonata, whereas he was disenchanted, even contemptuous of Beethoven's Pathetique and Appasionata sonatas. Gould's conclusion in his liner notes was quite challenging to the reader:

> These sonatas are a brief but an idyllic stopover in the itinerary of an intrepid *voyageur*. Perhaps they do not yield the apocalyptic disclosures that have been so graphically ascribed to them. Music is a malleable art, acquiescent and philosophically flexible, and it is no great task to mold it to one's want—but when, as in the works before us now, it transports us to a realm of such beatific felicity, it is a happier diversion not to try.[30]

Readers may wonder who the voyageur was. Was it Beethoven or Gould or both of them together? Gould recorded twenty-three of Beethoven's thirty-two sonatas. Out of those recorded only nineteen were released during his lifetime. He vacillated between a benevolent, "good" inner representation of Beethoven and his music, and a malevolent, "bad" representation without being able to integrate them. This is why he was compelled to distort Beethoven's text or stopped short from recording the entire body of Beethoven's sonata.

After the smash hit recording of the *Goldberg Variations* followed by the controversial recording of the last three Beethoven Sonatas, Gould scored another top success by recording Bach's Partitas no. 5 and 6. Joseph Roddy, who was present in Gould's recording session of Partita no. 5, described it in detail in his biographical essay "Apollonian." Recording took place in 1957 at the CBS studio on East Thirtieth Street in New York. Gould had available to him three pianos for practicing and recording. Roddy vividly described him as "shoeless and wearing a heavy muffler around his neck." There were other typical aspects of Gould's preferred recording environment. A portable heater was turned on and there was a little rug under Glenn's feet to keep him warm. On the piano there were pills that he took from time to time. The recording star sat on his low piano chair and hummed while playing the parts. Recording director Howard Scott called him from the studio control room:

> "Glenn, we can hardly hear the piano because you are singing so loud."
>
> "Look, Howard, it's the piano, not me," Gould replied and for a minute he looked hurt. Then he lighted up with a solution. "Suppose I wear a gas mask while I play?" he said. "Then you won't hear me sing."
>
> "Glenn," Scott answered wearily, "suppose we take a break for lunch now, and you start all over again on another piano this afternoon."[31]

Scott's professional intervention, which was aimed toward extinction of Gould's noisy behavior, did not come to fruition. In the end, Gould's voice is heard on the record accompanying his playing. He did not really like to be told what to do. His comment about the gas mask is in part funny, as if he made a joke to lighten up his anger, but it was also a sarcastic warning to Scott that nobody sets limits with Gould. His personal intolerance of anything that even remotely looked like faultfinding and chastising, reminded Gould of his original censors, his mother and his music teacher, Guerrero. Of course, the people like Scott and other producers did not know about Gould's deep-seated dynamics with those he perceived as oppressive. The end result of such high interpersonal sensitivity was that he had to keep himself apart from those who caused him emotional hurt. This in part explains many falling-out episodes and rifts between Gould and those with whom he was at one time close. The alienation from friends and music associates had a deep emotional precursor dating back in his earlier formative years.

When Gould's recording of Bach's partitas was released in January 1958, it won him a distinction as one of the best of Bach's interpreters. The *Houston Post* reported:

> Glenn Gould is not only one of the nation's brilliant young pianists, he is one of the most studious and an artist to be commended for undertaking a good many projects in recordings which are far from the easiest roads to the popular fancy.

> ... These partitas are the work of a greatly devoted and prodigiously equipped pianist."[32]

In the next decade, Gould was increasingly focusing on recording though he was still performing in public until 1964. His output was broad and impressive. Practically all his live performances were recorded and became lasting documents of his music greatness. In the recording studio, Gould recorded music works of Bach, Beethoven, Mozart, Schoenberg, Strauss, Hindemith, Prokofiev and Scriabin. More productivity and more fame was yet to come. In 1968, four years after abdication from his concert career, Gould's masterpiece, the first recording of Bach's *Goldberg Variations* was re-released. The press raved:

> The other release is historic. It is Bach's appallingly difficult "Goldberg Variations," the first recording Gould ever made, twelve years ago, now rechanelled for stereo. It made him famous, sold more than 100,000 copies and intimidated a generation of young pianists. Hearing it again, the annunciation of greatness is loud and clear, the baroque tension between mind and heart memorably taut.[33]

In the same year, Gould graced his music public with several records. First was a recording of Bach's Well Tempered Clavier, Book 2, with a dazzling performance in Gould's détaché style. The next was a recording of the first five piano sonatas by Mozart, also done in a marvelous, decisive classical style. Beethoven's Fifth Symphony, transcribed for the piano by Franz Liszt, was recorded with Gould's brilliant interpretation. Though Gould ridiculed Liszt as a bombastic piano virtuoso, he also referred to him with respect as "the man who never pulled a false note." The set of recordings was concluded by the piano works of Schoenberg, which Gould delivered with intimate knowledge and affection.

Gould was not a stickler for traditional performance. He said: "If there is any reason to play the same piece twice, this is to do it differently." He was a stickler for technical perfection while recording. He was precise and punctilious both in playing the piano for taping and in editing the tapes with a fine-tooth comb. Yes, he often ignored composer's wishes by changing tempi and the concept of interpretation. This is to be seen more as a matter of his curiosity and re-creative talent rather than as sloppy music interpretation. Another element in his unorthodoxy is the fact that Gould was a polyphonist. He hated anything "linear," be it in music, radio programs or in literature. He had a contrapuntal mind that had a capacity to combine things and to do different things simultaneously. Contrapuntal music keeps the left hand very involved or equally busy as the right hand, which was another reason it appealed to left-handed Gould. In the TV interview with Humphrey Burton of the BBC in 1966, Gould in discussing Mozart's music said:

> I have inordinate fondness for all music that is in the least contrapuntal, and if it isn't contrapuntal I try to make it contrapuntal. I try to invent happenings for inner voices even when they don't really exist ... I think it somehow adds vitamins to the music. ... What I am really trying to do is to make Mozart into a baroque composer."[34]

Gould also explained that he played organ in his earlier days, which made him very conscious of the baseline, and he developed a "pedal thinking." His fascination and cognitive predilection for contrapuntal music determined his love of Bach and modern composers Strauss and Schoenberg, who applied counterpoint in their music compositions.

Gould's contrapuntal mind was responsible for a secondary phenomenon called "diagonal" listening. This is how Claus Steffen Mahnkopf in his studious essay, "Glenn Gould's Pianistic Aesthetics," explained the concept of "diagonal" listening:

> Gould's instrumentalistic achievement is that he has raised to a principle the punctualistic non-legato-playing, which is essential for the piano. His radical polymorphous approach which, as it were, never tires of the multiplicity of voices, his endeavours to intensify the expression by enlarging the structural and the achieved measure of complexity changes the ear, which cannot become comfortable neither in the vertical aspect, nor in the horizontal one as the lines are too much individualized, because too much is presented at the same time. The result is a "diagonal" listening, which permanently mediates between both dimensions, in which occur new unexpected sensory perceptions. "Diagonal" listening is Gould's musical achievement.[35]

In conclusion, Gould made strong claims to the synchrony between the composer, the performer and listener. He wanted to see them at one with each other and at one with music. Gould resented the concept of a virtuoso. He was ambivalent about live audiences who, he thought, were often phony and go to concerts for wrong reasons. Gould's recording philosophy was very clear and consistent over the years. In the recording medium, there is no audience and there is no particular need for virtuosity and ambition for standing ovations and encores. This is why he proposed for the applause to be banned. Gould went so far that he even predicted that public concerts would gradually phase out by the year 2000, only to be replaced by the private experience of music at one's own home by listening to records or to the radio and television. This kind of bitterness toward concert-going was colored by Gould's depressive outlook and his distancing from any social stress that might aggravate his mental pain.

Chapter XVIII

THE LAST TEN YEARS

ANDANTE SOSTENUTO

Life is like a piano concerto. It contains many beautiful variations on the theme; with strong solo parts and even stronger group responses and their interactions. The Concerto of Life is full of tutti, with occasional marvelous cadenzas and energetic scherzos or it could be more relaxed and lapse into an adagio with the inevitable finale. No matter what themes or tempos are included, the concerto of one's life is always grande and majestic.

In the 1970s, Gould continued his creative work at a moderate pace. He had to contend with his many illnesses, which he fought vigorously with the help of various medications. Gould was on the circuitous path of treatment. He was visiting different health practitioners, but he still was reluctant to see a psychiatrist. This meant that he just could not see his countless physical symptoms as possibly linked to his underlying emotional problems. In order to conserve his waning energy, which was constantly drained through depression and somatic ailments, Gould had to make some amendments in the way he worked. He made a proactive decision to stop traveling to New York for his fatiguing recording sessions. Instead, he decided to record in Toronto. This is how, for a period of almost ten years from 1970 onward, the artist stayed in his native city, where he produced several records for the CBS Masterworks and a number of shows for the CBC, Canada's National Radio and Television Broadcasting Company. The shift in schedule also meant that his recording producer, Andrew Kazdin, had to keep coming to Toronto for recording sessions. Kazdin was dissatisfied, to say the least, about having to go out of his way to accommodate Gould, who he thought acted like a prima donna. Besides, he too did not like flying, yet he had little choice in the matter. The famous recording trio, Gould, Kazdin and Edquist, had unlimited potential and could produce anything together. Personally, there was a rising, silent tension among them. Gould never praised his coworkers and behaved as if he had the exclusive right to fame. This is where the chasm between Gould and Kazdin first appeared, the former was increasingly controlling and the latter was more resentful of his subordinate position.

Being in competition with Kazdin, Gould, as a multimedia star, decided to try himself in the field of record producing. This is how he emerged as a record producer for the Toronto pianist Antonin Kubalek, who had recently immigrated from Czeckoslovakia. Gould produced Kubalek's first commercial

North American recording, Erich Korngold's First Piano Sonata. When Kubalek was asked what it was like to work with Gould, he answered:

> Fine. Excellent. He [Gould] was always complimentary, and he did not really insist on too many takes. The only problem was the time of the recording sessions. He was a night person, and the recording sessions were always in the afternoon, from two o'clock on.[1]

On this occasion, as usual, Verne Edquist was on the set tuning the piano, except this time for Kubalek. Edquist recalled with his wry sense of humor:

"Once we had a recording session with Kubalek doing [Erich] Korngold. Everything was all right except Glenn showed up wearing a kimono and trying to play the part of the composer," Edquist chuckled.

"Why would he wear a kimono? Just for fun?" I asked.

"Maybe he wanted to look like Korngold," Edquist answered, shrugging his husky shoulders.

"Did Korngold wear a kimono?" I pursued this comical conversation.

"I have no idea. But Glenn was very serious about it. I didn't laugh; if I laughed I'd be gone ... Glenn was totally focused once he got going on something,"[2] Edquist finished his humorous reflections.

Edquist's words, "if I laughed I'd be gone," show that he lived in fear of making a mistake in Gould's eyes and being fired. Though he was Gould's steadiest and most loyal piano tuner, he was not appropriately acknowledged by his boss. Gould never mentioned Edquist in his literary work nor did he give him any credit on jackets of his numerous recordings. Under the guise of humor, Edquist hides his resentment for not being valued as Gould's best piano tuner.

Despite the interpersonal tension with his associates, Gould completed several other major projects at that time. In 1973, Gould's portrait of Maestro Pablo Casals was aired on the radio. This ninety-minute show was a product of his dedication to the ninety-seven-year-old music veteran. Gould loved him as the cellist who "discovered" Bach and practiced his *Six suites for solo cello* for twelve years, until he perfected them and performed them publicly. Casals and Gould had much in common. They were musicians first and instrumentalists second; they resurrected, modernized and popularized Bach's music. Catalan-born Casals was a man of principles and patriotism who once denounced public performance in protest against fascism. Gould had a deep respect for many of the characteristics of the great man. He specifically went to Marlboro, Vermont, to see him in rehearsal sessions as a conductor. By now, Gould paid generous tributes to his great contemporaries, performing legends Stokowski, Menuhin, Casals and a number of famous composers. Interestingly, the fee Gould received from the CBC for his passionate tribute to Casals was $1,500 for the research, preparation and written script. This is an example of the ultimate bargain (or thriftiness) of a major broadcasting company but speaks of Gould's generosity and earnest devotion to a fellow artist. It took him a great deal of time to work on such monumental projects that would be saved for posterity. By propagating these immortal music masters, Gould reaffirmed his own greatness. The idea of immortality by virtue of artistic achievements was more appealing to Gould now that he was in his forties.

In the 1970s, Gould acquired two new friends, Robert Silverman and Ray Roberts. Silverman, the publisher of the *Piano Quarterly* for twenty-two years, was stunned when he was first introduced to Gould's recording of Bach's *Goldberg Variations* by his friend, Gloria Ackerman. He was at the time just entering the publishing business, and Ackerman suggested to him that he get in touch with Gould and ask him to write something for his publication. Silverman wrote to Gould saying that he was starting a small magazine with a circulation of 1,600 copies, and would he, Gould, be interested in contributing articles. Much to Bob's delight, the musician said "yes." Over the next decade, Gould submitted fourteen articles to Silverman, and they were all published. Gould's satirical essay "Conference at Port Chillkoot," his controversial interview with Bruno Monsaingeon published under the title "Mozart and Related Matters," and one of his best works, "Stokowski in Six Scenes," were all published in the *Piano Quarterly*.

Born in New Jersey, Silverman spent part of his childhood in Toronto, only to return with his family to Long Island, New York. Bob showed an early interest in piano music. At the age of eight, he begged his father to buy him a piano. Money was scarce and his father consoled him by getting for his two sons, Bob and Saul, a set of five scotch terrier puppies instead of the piano. At the age of nineteen, Silverman enlisted and, as an American soldier, was sent to Germany during the Second World War. Upon returning home, Silverman pursued his childhood dream of studying piano and composition at the Julliard School in New York. Inspired by his older cousin, the famous ballet choreographer Jerome Robins, Silverman wrote music for several ballets. As a young man, he temporarily dated the famous Hollywood actress Ava Gardner and hung around with Jerome and his friend, Leonard Bernstein. "We used to sit in Jerome's living room and play music games of recognition"[3] Bob reflected with nostalgia. After getting married, Silverman built for himself and his wife, Ingrid, a mountain chalet-like residence in Wilmington, Vermont, which became his permanent home. It was in this hillside residence where Bob Silverman began his publishing work for the *Piano Quarterly* and from which he conducted countless telephone conversations with Glenn Gould.

"How would you describe your relationship with Glenn," I asked Silverman while hiking through the thick woods surrounding his house in Vermont.

"We had many touching points in our lives. We both came from a middle-class family; we both loved to play the game Monopoly. One day Glenn asked me whether I could name all the figures in the Monopoly. He was quite competitive. But we always got along very well," Silverman replied.

"What was it like for you to be his publisher?" I asked.

"I published his works with minimal editing. He liked the fact that I was not critical. He too never made any unfavorable criticism of me in ten years of our friendship,"[4] Silverman answered with a sense of pride.

Bob, who devoted his adult life to writing and publishing about the greatest world pianists, went on to tell a sad story about his best childhood friend, a gifted pianist, Lawrence Chaikin:

"When his mother, who was not musical, was pregnant with Larry, she said that she wanted her child to be a concert pianist. When Larry was sixteen, he was supposed to make his piano debut. He woke up in the morning and his hands were paralyzed from anxiety before the concert." Bob was reliving a deeply repressed grief.

"It seems your friend was stricken with a very bad panic attack," I noticed.

"Yes, he certainly was. His family rushed him to the hospital. Larry was devastated. He never made his debut and his pianistic career was over. He became a philatelist and died a disillusioned man at the age of fifty. What a waste. I still miss him," Silverman concluded his painful story.

"Would you say that Chaikin's tragedy had anything to do with your empathy toward Gould?" I persisted in trying to find the key to the successful relationship between Silverman and Gould.

"I wondered about it myself. I love art music and I appreciate the effort the performing musicians make to make good music. I understand the sacrifices and pain they go through," Bob spoke with compassion in his voice.

"Do you recall the trials and tribulations of some other concert pianists you came across in your musical and publishing career?" I asked.

"Oh, these problems are fairly common. For example, Rudy [Rudolf] Serkin used to be very nervous to the point of throwing up before the performance. Giving concerts is a nerve-wracking feat," Silverman said seriously.

"Do you know how was Mr. Serkin able to control his nervous tension before the performance?" I was curious about techniques of coping with stage fright.

"Well, I interviewed him for the *Piano Quarterly*, which was the first interview he granted in fifteen years. When I approached him at the end of the summer for the second part of the same interview, Rudy could not do it because of his very intensive piano practice." Bob was reliving the drama of the piano related hardship.

"Perhaps he was getting ready for a special piano concert," I said.

"Yes, that's precisely what I am trying to say, except that Rudy was very busy practicing in the summertime for the upcoming concert with [Herbert] von Karajan, which was in December of the same year. Do you realize, it took six months of his life to prepare for that performance?" Bob was visibly distressed by recounting Mr. Serkin's story.

"You mean it took six months of rehearsing to achieve flawless music?" I echoed Bob's distress.

"You bet. As I said, being a concert pianist is the most stressful occupation ever. So I always understood Glenn from this point of view."[5]

Gould had an intricate personality. Often, his friends could not put up with his views and demands. Most of his friendly liaisons waxed and waned, and only a few survived. The relationship with Silverman not only survived but remained untainted for the rest of Gould's life. These two men were soulmates who shared several aspects of their lives. For Gould, Silverman was a positive personality who was able to offer fraternal and unconditional regard. As a businessman, Silverman was informal and gave Gould carte blanche with respect to the choice of writing. Notably, whatever article Gould submitted, Silverman accepted for publishing. In at least one case, Gould betrayed Silverman's benevolent attitude toward him. It had to do with Gould's monumental paper "Stokowski in Six Scenes," which was published in the *Piano Quarterly*. At the same time, Gould sold the same article to *The New York Times* for ten thousand dollars, where it was published in the magazine section in a slightly shortened version. Eventually, Glenn called Bob to confess his wrongdoing, saying, "We're in trouble." Bob "played it cool" and the crisis over double-publishing was averted. By not chastising Glenn, Bob protected him from self-harm and helped him save face.

At the same time when this long-distance relationship with Silverman was in progress, there was another relationship incubating in Gould's life on the Toronto scene. Lorne Tulk was a recording engineer at the CBC with whom Gould closely worked for a number of years. Lorne had a childhood friend, Ray Roberts, who periodically visited him in the studio. This is where Glenn and Ray met in the early 1970s. From this time on, they gradually developed a fairly close friendship. Ray, by nature a friendly man, at first helped Gould in small, menial chores such as carrying and moving music equipment and giving him tips in car management. Ray was a native of the area known as Cabbage Town in Toronto, not too far from the beaches where Glenn was born and raised. He was the son of divorced parents. His mother left him when he was nine years of age to live in the United States. Ray remained in the care of his auto-mechanic father. The caring son maintained a loyal relationship with his temperamental father and looked after him in his old age. Growing up without his mother, Ray learned from his early life how to fend for himself. He was pragmatic and street-wise. After dropping out of grade eleven, Ray worked diligently at various jobs, mostly in sales. At the point of meeting Gould, Roberts worked for Coca Cola, and he finished his career as an insurance salesman. He married early and became a father of three sons.

Glenn and Ray felt a sense of kinship, and over time they developed a degree of closeness. Ray gradually became an irreplaceable figure in the life of his new friend. There were days when Glenn and Ray spoke over the telephone three times daily; first thing in the morning before Glenn went to sleep, then around four in the afternoon when Glenn woke up, and late at night starting around eleven till one or two o'clock in the morning.[6] In his teens, Glenn was too busy to spend time on idle telephone calls, a behavior that is so typical in adolescence. Talking with Ray several times daily was like catching up with what was missed earlier. Like teenagers, they never ran out of things to say. They delighted in telling jokes and in Glenn's favorite game of Twenty Questions. They also pursued more sophisticated themes of the stock market, investments, the merits and shortcomings of certain cars, politics and the daily news. Ray was Glenn's rare nonmusical friend. Ray Roberts shared the following in one of several conversations with this author:

R. R. A couple of times it was apparent that I couldn't always be there for him [Glenn]. So, we tried to replace me but it was not possible. He was to a point dependent on me to get things done. I knew so much about his finances and other things that nobody could replace me. A degree of trust developed.

H. M. You seem to have been quite protective of Glenn, almost like his bodyguard?

R. R. Well, yes. Glenn was furious at people at times, but he preferred me to take care of things on his behalf. Once he bumped the bumper of somebody's truck. I had to play a secret agent for him. I spoke with the owner, told him that somebody accidentally damaged his car but this person doesn't really want to be known. I asked him to please estimate the damage and he'll be paid cash. He agreed and it worked out real well. But please don't misunderstand me. When push came to shove, Glenn was able to do anything. It was always clear to me that he was the one in control.

H. M. Despite his trust in you, were there things that he would not discuss with you?

R. R. Well, he didn't want me to ask him about his private life. When he lived on St. Clair Avenue, my son used to go there to help him with his garden. At that time he had a relationship with a lady. My son knew it and I knew it. But I never asked a word about it even when it ended. He never said thank you, but I had a distinct feeling that he was very grateful that I never asked him anything on that subject.

H. M. Glenn was protective of his music and always very sensitive to criticism. Have you ever discussed his music?

R. R. I am not a musician but I enjoyed his records. He talked and I listened. But if I ever criticized his music it would be gonzo. That was an absolute no-no.[7]

Glenn and Ray developed a multifaceted relationship. Ray felt privileged to be sought after by this famous man, and the lonely musician felt comforted by his new friend. Glenn interacted with Ray on a daily basis, something that he did not feel comfortable doing with his own father, cousins or other friends.

"What kind of attitude did Glenn have toward money?" I asked.

"Oh, he was a first-class capitalist," Ray answered laughing. "He made a lot of money and the money was coming to him from everywhere, but mostly from the [Columbia Records] royalties and from the stock market." Ray knew so much about Gould's financial affairs.

"Do you remember what kind of stocks he owned?" I asked.

"Well, he had some standard stocks with Bell Canada, Massey-Ferguson, Petro Canada, you name it. He played the stock market very well, and he liked to do it," Ray observed.

"What was he like in paying those who worked for him?"

"He was always on time. Usually, when the taping session or recording session was over, he'd write a check to each person working for him," Ray stated.

"What was Gould like at paying his staff?" I asked.

"He was quite fair. In my case, he paid me very well for the work I've done for him. At one point when I was buying a house, he even loaned me a substantial sum of money, and this really helped us a lot. I will never forget that, as long as I live,"[8] volunteered Ray.

Ray became a replacement in Glenn's subconscious mind for his insufficient father and for the brother he never had. He was also a jack-of-all-trades, Glenn's private secretary and his friend. In Ray, he had found precisely what he wanted, a discrete, "good enough," non-critical person who was there for him when needed but without meddling in his private affairs.

The need for privacy, to the point of secrecy, dominated Gould's life. His telephone number was only given to a few trusted friends and his whereabouts were known to even fewer. Victor DiBello took pride in saying: "I was one of the four people who had Gould's phone number.. We always spoke at night, time didn't matter, when and how long. It could be three or four hours or more in one sitting. I had a great respect for him and he knew it."[9]

Though it appears that more than four people earned the privilege of having Gould's unlisted telephone number, there was an aura of secrecy Gould had deliberately created around himself. He was preoccupied with themes of rejection by or withdrawal from society. Working for the underdog, cast-aways and outcasts gave him a distinct pleasure. He referred to himself as a "hermit" and, of course, hermits are those loners who are either actively rejected by society or those who find it painful and intolerable to be sociable. Having been in conflict with the world, Gould wrote an unusual essay, titled "Glenn Gould Interviews Glenn Gould About Glenn Gould," which was published in February 1974 in *High Fidelity*. This was a display of Gould's untiring and lucid mind, which never fell short of authentic wit. Who would ever think of interviewing himself and publishing it in a serious form? Gould did, mainly driven by his genuine and creative need for self-expression blended with his phobic distrust of others, who, he thought, might misinterpret or ridicule his ideas. The essay is also autobiographical in nature and reveals Gould's pessimistic views about the artist-society relationship. Here is a sample of the two sides of Gould having a dialogue with each other:

G.G. I simply feel that the artist should be granted ... anonymity. He should be permitted to operate in secret ... unaware of the presumed demands of the marketplace which demands ... will simply disappear. And given their disappearance, the artist will then abandon his false sense of "public" responsibility, and his "public" will relinquish its role of servile dependency.

g.g. And never the twain shall meet, I daresay!

G.G. No, they'll make contact, but on an altogether more meaningful level than that which relates any stage to its apron.[10]

In this essay, Gould is skillfully discussing the pitfalls of a performing career, pointing to his concept of the "creative audience" and expressing a need for creative isolation. Also in this article, Gould raises his lifelong issue of hating competition of any kind, concluding that "physical and verbal aggression are ... simply a flip of the competitive coin." He identifies the public performance with "martyrdom" and that going back to his performing career would mean to "achieve the martyr's end."

Showing the tendency toward social isolation in the service of creativity is not only necessary but is also a healthy striving. Occasionally, those artists who avoid social contacts are mistakenly thought of as being "schizoid," meaning very poorly adapted to their social environment. Being "schizoid," i.e., sick, or being artistically accomplished, i.e. productive, communicative and drawing the attention of the world, are almost mutually exclusive. Gould was capable of having deep feelings for others, for his mother and grandmother, for his music, for animals and the underprivileged; for his cousin, Jessie, and even for a number of his friends, which, despite all of his social avoidance, still does not put him in the category of "schizoid" personality. Being socially isolated is seen here more as a function of his ongoing social anxiety and depression, which still allowed him to communicate, to create and to have a variety of friends.

While Robert Silverman was Glenn's musical friend, Ray Roberts was his friend for all seasons. Gould's life was further enriched by the arrival of two television associates, Bruno Monsaingeon and John McGreevy. Monsaingeon started his artistic career as a performing violinist and expanded into TV directing and film-making. In the mid-sixties, when Monsaingeon spent some time in Russia, he came across Gould's records, which were extremely popular there ever since his concert tour in 1957. Monsaingeon was mesmerized by Gould's music. He had a sort of spiritual experience of deep kinship with Gould and became his instant devotee. Inspired by Gould's records, Monsaingeon wrote him a letter in which he invited Gould to make a series of biographical TV shows for the French national television. Gould, who thought of himself as "francophobic" and often declined proposals, or sometimes did not even respond to some of them, accepted Monsaingeon's offer at once. In July 1972, Monsaingeon arrived in Toronto for preliminary meetings with Gould. On the first day, the two men spent eighteen hours talking. Gould "clicked" with this Frenchman, and the two of them became quickly emotionally attached to each other, which made their professional relationship very successful. After three days of talking and planning, Gould gave Monsaingeon a ride to the airport.[11] In 1974, the two artists met in Toronto to materialize their mutual project. Monsaingeon, who at that time represented the German firm Classart, came to Toronto with a filming crew of ten members. Gould made himself available for hard work on a daily basis starting at 2 p.m. until well after midnight and into the morning hours. His old friend and recording engineer, Lorne Tulk, and his piano tuner, Verne Edquist, were both engaged to work on the project. The industrious team produced a series of four TV shows, which Monsaingeon titled *Les Chemins de la Musique*. Gould generously played a wide range of music from his repertoire. In the first show, called "La Retraite," he interpreted the works of Bach, Byrd, Gibbons and Schoenberg and excerpts from the Wagner/Gould transcription of *Meistersinger*. This was followed by "L'Alchimiste," where Gould played more Bach and Scriabin and was portrayed as a person with a multitude of skills and interests in recording technology, splicing and directing. The third show introduced Gould as a composer, centering on the discussion about his composition *So You Want To Write a Fugue*. In the last and conclusive show, Gould played Bach's Partita no. 6 in E minor, BWV 830, with its beautiful and introspective opening "Toccata" and somewhat tragic "Sarabande" and "Gigue" in the end. This last of the partitas and the last show with Monsaingeon produced in Glenn an uneasy feeling of pending separation.

For Glenn, working with a compatible team and producing wonderful music gave him an emotional "high," and having to part from Bruno, who was his loyal sympathizer, was a great let down. At the end of the project, when the filming crew arranged a small party, Gould simply could not bear to stay but left in a hurry and without a proper parting ritual.

"Why do you think Gould did not stay for the party?" I asked Verne Edquist.

"He did not like to hang around. He simply disappeared. A few times, Glenn gave me a lift home after the recording, but he would never come to the house. He kept a certain professional distance"[12] Edquist said.

Be it a professional or an emotional distance, Glenn avoided social closeness and particularly avoided saying "good-bye." He was not trying to be a fair-weather friend but was genuinely unable to tolerate separation from those to whom he was emotionally attached. Glenn's instant emotional attachment to Bruno probably had a deep, subconscious meaning. Bruno, as a violinist may have aroused in Glenn some personal feelings that had been originally experienced in relationship with his father. Bert Gould, who played violin in his youth only to stop playing it soon after, never discussed or played violin for Glenn, who enjoyed the instrument very much. It appears that Gould transferred some of these rare positive feelings for his father and for violin music onto his new music associate, Bruno Monsaingeon, which then served as a source of their productive and friendly relationship.

LENTO: LAMENT FOR THE LOST MOTHER

> That's my last Duchess painted on the wall,
> Looking as if she were alive.
>
> Robert Browning[13]

Unlike her son, Florence Gould was reluctant to see doctors. She believed in the power of natural healing and God's will. By the time she was in her eighties, she was visibly becoming feeble from the aging process. The Greigs traditionally died from strokes and heart attacks. Having long survived by far both her brothers, Florrie was at peace with the idea that her time was coming. Even as her health failed, she was always happy to hear from Glenn over the telephone and discuss his reviews and future music plans. Still, the two of them avoided sharing anything personal. In 1974, Glenn moved to Hampton Court on Jarvis Street, a hotel across from the CBC. Florrie disapproved. She could never come to terms with her son's lifestyle. Why was he so eccentric? Must he live in hotels? Couldn't he just have his own home and be normal like Artur Rubinstein, whom she admired, or like Glenn's music peers, whom she knew. On top of this, she had to endure that vile criticism of him, which she had to see in print. Florrie had a very different idea of an ideal son. Her son had pleasantly surprised her in the magnitude of his music talent and his artistic achievements but fell far short in fulfilling many of her ordinary expectations.

Her youthful-looking husband, Bert, was away all day for business, and she withdrew into the house to ponder and pray. She could no longer maintain her exemplary lawn with the small rose garden at the entrance of their Simcoe cottage, and it was increasingly difficult for her to look after two households. Bert was in favor of selling the cottage in Uptergrove. According to Mr. Gould, he offered the cottage to Glenn to purchase but Glenn declined. Since the 1950s, Glenn had been in a silent war with his father, which stopped him from negotiating any business with him. Glenn's cousin, Jessie, asked Glenn whether he was interested in buying the cottage. "At first Glenn said that he wanted the cottage, but later on he said he was not sure he'd be able to look after it. But he never said he didn't want it," Jessie remembered.[14]

The reality is that Glenn was unable to approach his father and say: "Dad, please don't sell the cottage, I want it for myself. I'll hire someone to look after it." His troubled relationship with his father kept Glenn from taking any action. It is curious that Mr.Gould, who made good money from his fur business, would even consider selling this family property that was paid for and was not expensive to maintain. The house on the waterfront that was their haven for over forty years was sold in haste early in 1975. Both parents seemed to overlook the fact that they had an heir to their estate. They had been disappointed in Glenn and did not trust his ability to take care of the property. Perhaps the cottage, which had such emotional significance for Florrie and even more for Glenn, could have been rented out or simply locked until a more satisfactory decision could be reached. Incidentally, Mr. Gould went to another cottage for his own vacations after his wife's death.

Florrie was always known as a stoic woman who did not complain even when she was most distressed. When she was younger, she was the strong one, but now, in her old age, her husband took over and she obeyed. Selling the property to which she was so attached and disposing of the contents, which were supposed to be enjoyed by her son, were harder on her than Mr. Gould had ever expected.

Four years earlier, Bert's younger brother, Bruce, died in Uxbridge in the family home of their parents. Again, Mr. Gould, as the head of the family, was in a rush to dispose of the family home. It appears that Mr. Gould did not have a problem severing emotional ties with his own birth home or the cottage he built with his own hands. In 1980, he even sold the house where Glenn was born. He was a strong-willed man who liked changes, who mourned his losses quickly and went on looking forward to the future. As the perceptive man that he was, and very financially astute and well-off, surely he could have thought of some ways to save the cottage for Glenn's future comfort. After all, Glenn was only forty-three years of age and, being a late bloomer, could still have had a family. Glenn felt displaced. To appease his sense of disinheritance and nostalgia for the cottage, he frequented alien motels in remote cities like Wawa and Terrace Bay, located on the shores of distant lakes, when he simply could have gone to his family cottage, which was so conveniently close to Toronto.

What indeed made Mr. Gould sell the cottage? Being the oldest son, Bert took a great deal of responsibility for his family of origin. The same was replicated in his nuclear family, where he often had to defer to the needs and demands of his overbearing wife and the strange son to whom he was unable to relate. It follows that Mr. Gould could hardly wait to be free from the hampering ties with the past. He was longing for more latitude from such long-standing demands on him. Though this is quite understandable, in the eyes of the beholder, Mr. Gould may still be held responsible for not being farsighted or sensitive enough to Glenn's emotional needs. In search of his own personal freedom, Mr. Gould sold the cottage, inadvertently causing Glenn unnecessary heartache and separation anxiety.

Not surprisingly, Florrie was excessively worried about family affairs, particularly those involving Glenn. She had a history of hypertension that was getting worse. On the critical day of July 21, 1975, Mrs. Gould did not feel well but did not call for an ambulance. Instead, she called her husband at work. When he arrived home, she opened the door for him but lost her balance and fell down as a result of having a massive stroke from which she never regained consciousness. Mr. Gould rushed her to the nearest medical facility, Toronto East General Hospital, where she was in a coma for the next few days.

Glenn was in a state of panic when he heard about his mother's condition. He kept calling his father, who was at the hospital sitting with his moribund wife. According to Jessie Greig, Glenn drove to the hospital, parked his car, sat in it in desperation and had an anxiety attack. Perhaps he wailed and prayed for forgiveness, but he could not bring himself to go into the hospital to see his mother. He had long suffered a phobia of germs and had an inordinate fear of hospitals. Ashamed of himself and distraught, he drove away. He called Jessie and, for the first time in his life, he was short of words. Jessie tried to console Glenn, but he was more bewildered than grief-stricken. She offered to go with him to the hospital on the next day; Glenn tentatively agreed but was still very distraught.[15] Glenn kept swallowing pills to numb his terror. Bert, who preserved a sense of calm, was much more needed by his son to reassure him than by his comatose wife. He was just not capable of reaching out to Glenn and giving him some comfort and absolution from guilt.

After four futile days at the hospital, Florence Greig Gould passed away on July 26, 1975. Thus, the life of Florence Greig Gould ended quietly. The medical diagnosis was: Left CVA (cerebro-vascular accident), Cerebral hemorrhage, hypertension.[16]

Glenn was shocked and emotionally paralyzed. He never managed to visit his mother at the hospital. He was pale, sick-looking and disheveled. The guilt of not seeing his mother on her deathbed hounded him. Never before could he sufficiently mourn his losses, and there were so many deaths of close relatives in the course of his life. Glenn dealt with death and other losses by avoidance of grieving and by refraining from customary rituals for the dead. When he absolutely had to be at a funeral, he was their in body but was emotionally removed. And when his mother died, he was equally remote, stunned and dissociated from the pain of it. He summoned energy to write a five-page eulogy in praise of his deceased mother, in which he gave a biographical account of her best qualities:

> Florence Gould was a woman of tremendous faith and, wherever she went, she strove to instill that faith in others.
>
> For the last few years, she devoted her talents to a group of unprivileged mothers in a large downtown church where weekly, she tried, through music

> and inspiration, to make their lives a little more meaningful. She kept up this weekly contact as long as her strength permitted and was hoping to be able to continue the contact with the mother's group during the coming season.[17]

Even while eulogizing his mother, Glenn was unable to express his tender feelings for her. He could not simply say how much she meant to him in his personal life and how much he missed her. Above all, he could not express his gratitude for the gift of music she had given to him, for being his first teacher and a passionate admirer of his music. It is not that Glenn wanted to hide his affection for his mother but he was mortified at the prospect of blurting out his less favorable feelings of anger and frustrations toward her. On her side, she had mixed feelings toward Glenn. She loved his music but disapproved of him as a person; she indulged his musical brilliance but resented his strange lifestyle and his unholy attitude toward his performing career. In some ways, Glenn's mother was not only his fervent admirer but also his most severe critic. Her charitable work, which she pursued for the sake of undoing the sins of her family, had an implicit message for Glenn. By working for the young unwed mothers and their babies, Florence tried to cope with her own grief about her son's childlessness. Glenn, on his side, by not having offspring, did not secure descendants for the Greig family, which his mother would have wished the most. All these ambivalent feelings between mother and son remained unresolved and continued to burden Glenn for the rest of his life.

The viewing of Florence Gould was held at Humphrey's Funeral Home on Bayview Avenue. She was buried at Mt. Pleasant Cemetery in section thirty-eight. Glenn's nanny from infancy, Elsie Feeney, was at the burial:

H.M. "How did Glenn handle his mother's death?"

E.F. "He took it very hard. I stood right behind him at the grave. He just went silent. His face was still and pale and he never shed tears. But deep down he suffered so much. I knew that for sure. She was all he'd got."[18]

This false sense of calm, accomplished through emotional numbness and the use of sedatives also was reinforced by Glenn's belief in an afterlife. Ever since childhood, Glenn had always subscribed to the supernatural. He believed in the power of premonition, clairvoyance and telepathy. His staunchly religious mother believed in the survival of the soul in heaven or hell. Though Glenn spent his adult life in active denial of religion, his religious indoctrination in his childhood and early teens never faltered, and deep down he too, like his mother, was religious. This may explain why Glenn, when he stood at his mother's casket, was seemingly calm and tearless. Perhaps he was consoled by the theological belief of immortality of the human soul and his mother, by being a good Christian, certainly was worthy of eternal life. In Glenn's mind, she died and went to heaven.

Glenn was sheltered and overprotected by his mother and other adults in his early years and was consumed by music and intellectual achievements. He never learned to express feelings of sorrow. This made him feel helpless in the face of each loss and highly vulnerable to new losses. Not only did Glenn not mourn his losses, but he was equally handicapped by not celebrating happy events like birthdays, holidays, weddings and anniversaries. He was shrouded in his duties, defensive lifestyle and many abnormal habits, which he was incapable of changing. Glenn was not able to adapt well to major changes. Had he more actively challenged those problems in himself by facing his emotional pain, he would have been more relieved. Glenn handled the loss of his mother by withholding feelings about her. He did not open up even with his friends and associates. Verne Edquist recalls that he did not know anything about Gould's mother's illness and death.

H. M. "Did Glenn ever tell you about his mother's illness?"

V. E. "Never. Even when she died, he never told me. He never said a word. I heard it from Andy [Kazdin]. That was O.K. by me."[19]

Glenn's best friend, Ray Roberts, was not invited to the funeral. Andrew Kazdin, who at that time was regularly coming to Toronto for the production of Gould's records, found out much later when Gould mentioned it in passing.

"How much did you know about Glenn's relationship with his mother?" I asked Andrew Kazdin when we met in New York.

"I never met his mother nor did I know anything about her illness. Glenn never spoke about his family life. He never invited me to his home or his parents' home. He kept me away from his private life. In the same way, he kept me from others." Kazdin seemed disappointed.

"Can you think of an example?" I asked.

"Certainly. When [Geoffrey] Peyzant wrote a biography of Gould, he mentioned me only in a footnote and he never interviewed me." Kazdin got this pain off his chest.

"What were his [Peyzant's] sources, then?" I understood Kazdin's sense of unfairness.

"I suspect that he wrote the book on the basis of Glenn's outpourings, his writings and what was written about him. Glenn controlled everything and kept everybody from knowing what was going on in his life." Kazdin was clearly hurt.[20]

The same is true for Gould's correspondence. In his voluminous letters, he rarely wrote about his private life, and the loss of his mother was certainly a personal affair. In 1975, he worked on the project of celebrating the seventy-fifth birthday of Ernst Krenek. He wrote to him in Palm Springs, California, just weeks after the funeral:

> Dear Mr. Krenek,
>
> ... I had particularly looked forward to a casual intermission-style "interview" with you, but, as Larry Lake perhaps told you, the sudden death of my mother necessitated a change of schedule during the last half of July.[21]

This was as far as Gould could go in sharing his personal loss with a music colleague. He did it dryly and swiftly. The rest of the letter is business-like. Another interesting thing to observe here is that Gould was eager to celebrate Krenek's birthday, while he never paid attention to his own and avoided celebrating others' birthdays.

Not nearly recovered from the loss of his mother, Gould had to contend with yet another stress. In the 1970s, he had to face the task of making a will. By that time, he had accumulated substantial assets in the form of liquid funds, stocks and holdings, material possessions such as concert pianos, and the steady cash flow from his recording contracts and broadcasting. Being a single person in his forties, and a daring car driver, Gould's new attorney, Stephen Posen, legally advised him to make a will. Victor DiBello testified:

"Gould was quite reluctant to make a will. He thought that there was plenty of time for it in the future. Once he offhandedly said: 'O.K., if I have to make a will, I'll leave everything to the Humane

Society,'" DiBello recalled.

"What made him so averse to making a will? After all, making a will is a form of good planning of one's own finances," I commented.

"Well, yes, when you look at it this way. But it wasn't so easy for him. The truth is that Gould was very superstitious, and he saw the will-making as a bad omen. After the loss of his mother, he couldn't care less about what might have happened to his assets. He had too much on his mind," DiBello explained.

"Would you go so far as to say that he was depressed?" I asked.

"I didn't know that at the time, but now that I have some problems of my own, I'd say that he must have been very down. He looked jaded. Yes, he was in a sort of a deep, blue funk,"[22] Victor DiBello concluded this poignant dialogue.

If making of the will was such a stressful task, Gould could always have it postponed. Instead, he felt obliged to do it without delay. Like his mother, Gould was generous, and he made monetary contributions to many good causes. For instance, when his colleague-pianist, Antonin Kubalek, immigrated to Toronto in 1968, Gould met him at the CBC studios and quickly recognized the stress of his immigration. Gould simply sent him a check of $1,000 as a contribution to a fellow musician who was just starting life in a new country. Gould was good-hearted with all those with whom he was not in conflict. With his pets and animals in general he was never in conflict. So, when his lawyer brought up the will, Gould hastily decided to name the Toronto Humane Society and the Salvation Army as his major beneficiaries. He left to his father a token income of $50,000 payable on a monthly basis. His last will and testament was made on October 24, 1979. Though Gould had plenty of time to change it in the next three years of his life, he never seemed to get around to it. This rather impersonal will left out Gould's first cousin, Jessie, and several other cousins. In designing the will, Gould was obviously motivated by his disappointments in humans and his love of animals, which do not hurt and are capable of unconditional love and loyalty. His choice of the Salvation Army as a beneficiary was rooted in his deep-seated guilt feelings over many personal "sins" and a need for salvation and redemption. He left nothing for the advancement of music or the arts in general and no scholarships for gifted students. Had Gould lived longer, he might have changed this will, subject to overcoming his disillusionment with others.

In April 1976, Howard Hughes died after twenty-six years of self-imposed seclusion. Formerly a flashy billionaire, Hughes's life was sadly destroyed by his untreated mental illness. He suffered from an extreme case of obsessive-compulsive disorder, marked by rituals in day-to-day living, by an inordinate phobia of germs and an addiction to non-prescribed painkillers. Gould was always fascinated by "Hughesian secrecy," the term he used to justify his own reclusiveness. The tycoon spent almost the last ten years of his life in the "Desert Inn Hotel" in Las Vegas. Inspired by stories like this and guided by his own need for solitary living, Gould also moved to another hotel, "Inn on the Park" in Toronto, where he spent the last years of his life.

In November of the same year, Gould embarked on a recording of one of his favorite modern composers, Paul Hindemith. He selected Hindemith's vocal piece, *Das Marienleben*, which Gould performed in collaboration with Toronto-based soprano Roxolana Roslak. Back in the early 1960s, Gould presented *Das Marienleben* to a live audience at the Stratford Festival together with soprano Lois Marshall. This time he decided to resurrect the song and immortalize it by recording it. The poem *The Life of the Virgin Mary*, written by the famous German poet Erich Maria Rilke, for which Paul Hindemith composed the music piece Das Marienleben, op. 27, is biographical in nature. Gould owned Rilke's book of poetry and was very aware of this particular poem, which consists of fifteen parts. In the first part, "The Birth of Mary," the poet introduces the ancient biblical theme:

> Oh, what restraint it must have cost the angels
> not to burst suddenly into song, as one bursts into tears,
> because of their knowing: that this very night
> will witness the birth of the Mother, she who is destined
> to bring forth the son, the Saviour, who shall appear.[23]

In "The Birth of Christ," the poet celebrates this most divine and the most glorious of all births:

> Had you a greater vision in your mind of Him before?
> How can one fathom greatness? ...
> ... But look! Behold! For there upon your lap,
> wrapped lovingly in swaddling clothes, lies He ...[24]

It almost seems that this poem encapsulates the specialness Mrs. Gould felt around the time of her pregnancy and delivery. Did Glenn identify with the story of the Virgin Mary and Christ as a mother-son story and, in the final analysis, as his story?

"How can one fathom greatness?" the poem says. Glenn's own mother always felt that her child was a God-given gift and that she had a mission to deliver a son of greatness. These feelings of being special were powerfully re-enacted in Glenn at this point of his life. In the part "Pieta," the poet laments over the mother's loss of her son:

> Now is my suffering complete as pain
> unutterable fills my entire being.
> I stare, am numb and rigid as a rock
> is rigid to its very core.
> Hard as I am, I do remember this:
> You grew to boyhood—
> ... grew in height and strength,
> you stood apart and overshadowed me,
> became too great a sorrow, far beyond
> the limits of my poor heart's understanding.
> Now you lie, stilled in death, across my lap;
> now I no longer can bring back your life
> through birth.[25]

In the final part, "The Death of Mary," the mother and son became reunited in heaven.

> ... Yet the heavens high above are trembling:
> Man, fall on your knees, watch my departure, and sing.[26]

In Glenn's story, his mother died somewhat earlier and "waited" for him to join her in heaven. After her death, Gould artistically may have been active and alive but, as a person, he was progressively more depressed and reclusive. He was in a state of pining and longing for reunion with his mother and seemed to become more numb and deadened by her absence.

As always, music helped to ease his inner pain. In the 1970s, Gould began working on the *Glenn Gould Silver Jubilee Album*. His new associate was Margaret Pacsu. When interviewed, this is what Ms. Pacsu had to say about their working relationship:

H. M. What was it like to work with Gould at that time?

M. P. It was fascinating. After all, he was a Canadian superstar.

H. M. Was there an aura of him being a boss?

M. P. Oh, yes, that too. He was very controlling. He wrote the script, both the questions directed to him and answers. He did many takes, ten, fifteen, twenty-five, sometimes I thought that he did them just to show off, to show his power and simply to live up to his trademark.

H. M. Was there anything that stood out about him?

M. P. It was noticeable that he was eccentric, not just as a famous star but it went beyond that. He soaked his hands in hot water prior to playing the piano for a radio program. I pointed it out to him, this was not a concert, we can always do it again. He said: "Well, you may say that I am mildly neurotic, aren't I."[27]

Being a middle-aged man was frustrating and burdensome. The person in Gould was in a gridlock, while the musician was unfinished and unfulfilled. In the 1970s, he no longer played his piano daily but practiced his music cerebrally and only now and then would he rehearse it at the keyboard, usually in preparation for recording. Once he bragged to Ray Roberts that he had not touched the piano for almost six months. Three years after his mother's death, Gould received an offer from John Fraser, a correspondent of *The Globe and Mail* in Peking, to make a documentary on China. This is how he opened his heart to Fraser:

> ... I think the prospects for a China documentary are fascinating, even though the prospects for a visit by me to the Orient are nil. As you know I don't fly—haven't for sixteen years—and no assignment, no matter how enticing, will get me aloft again. Furthermore, with each passing year, I become more committed to a sedentary existence and unwilling to contemplate any form of travel. An auto trip to N.Y.C. is a major event in my life these days and even if a slow boat to China did exist, I would not be on it.[28]

What happened to this forty-six-year-old man who used to love boats, who was full of energy and untiring curiosity? In this post-mortem period of his mother, Gould was in a state of pathological mourning and melancholy.[29] In unresolved mourning, the energy that is required for living is diminished and cannot be readily invested into new objects of love. The mourner tends to identify strongly with the deceased, to feel guilty for the death of the loved one and to deprive oneself of a good life in order to ease the guilt. Gould's private diary from the 1977-78 season illustrates the agony of his self-deprivation manifested in his day-to-day living. He was alone in his hotel room, feeling wretched and sitting up all night watching TV weather reports. As the epitome of the tedium of his life, he kept a log of temperatures in various Canadian cities. On January 1st, 1978, he recorded:

Sleep 4 + 1 ½ hr.	Nembutal, meal period 4:30—12:30		
Temp. 2pm	-9		
Av.(erage)	-12		
High (Windsor)	-2		
Low (Prince George)	-22	Whitehorse	-28

January 2nd, 1978:

Sleep 5 ¾ hr	meal period 4:30—10:30
Temp. am.	-10 (-6)
Av.	-13
Hi (St. John's)	+6
Lo (Timmins)	-31 Yellowknife

January 3, 78:

Sleep 5 ½ + Nembutal which did not work[30]

His sleep was worse than ever and he required sleeping pills. He was prescribed Nembutal for insomnia, a strong drug from the chemical group of barbiturates. There were other problems noticed. Gould neglected his personal upkeep and was quite slovenly in his dress and at housekeeping. His personal contacts with others were diminishing, and he was spending days on end by himself. Even his interest in writing letters to others was greatly decreased, and the telephone remained one of his rare means of communication. Gould was viewed by his compatriots as the odd man out, the recluse, the eccentric. All this pointed to the fact that he was clinically depressed, but none of his observers truly recognized it. Gould never had the benefit of taking the antidepressants that were available at that time. Ironically, the man who was ready to try any remedy recommended to him by his lay friends was not given an antidepressant by professionals, which was indicated as a drug of choice.

Though Gould did not accept the invitation from Fraser to film life in China, he accepted a closer-to-home undertaking to produce a film about his native city. Five months after his mother's passing, on Christmas Eve 1975, Gould received a telephone call from John McGreevy, a young Englishman and a film director at the CBC. The two men knew about each other, but they had never met. McGreevy introduced himself and asked Gould to help him solve a certain problem in his current filming project. Against all odds, Gould suggested that they meet instantly at the CBC studio. Startled, McGreevy, who never expected to see Gould on Christmas Eve, took up his offer immediately and the two zealous artists met at the studio. This is how Gould acquired a new creative associate. In the course of the next couple of years, McGreevy ambitiously conceived of a plan specifically for his famous friend to make a documentary film titled *Glenn Gould's Toronto*. This was supposed to be a part of a larger project called *Cities*, on which he worked for some time. With all his remaining energy, Gould threw himself into the project. He vigorously researched the topic and made sterling efforts to prepare a good script for the film. In doing this he went overboard, and instead of preparing a manuscript of about 4,500 words, he produced a ten-times-more-sizable document on Toronto with 45,000 words. Of course, the text had to be downsized to its desired minimum, which was very difficult for Glenn, as he did not want to part with any detail of his material. In his published essay on the same theme, Gould showed unwavering fondness for the old Toronto and his disapproval of the modern city. He said:

> When I was a child, and indeed until very recently, this city was referred to as "Toronto the Good." The reference was to the city's puritan traditions: one could not, for example, attend concerts on Sunday until the 1960's; it was not permissible to serve alcohol in any public place on the Sabbath until very recently; and now a furor has developed at City Hall over the issue of whether Torontonians should be permitted to drink beer at baseball games. But you have to understand that, as an anti-athletic, non-concertgoing teetotaler, I approve all such restrictions. I, perhaps, rather than the hero of George Santayana's famous novel, am 'the last puritan.' So I always felt that "Toronto the Good" was a very nice nickname.[31]

Florence not only loved the old Toronto, she had embodied it. The above paragraph written by Glenn is his oath to his mother. Glenn followed in the footsteps of her moral values, particularly her humbleness, piety and purity. In his subconscious mind, Glenn was at one with his mother. Here is his next monumental attestation about his birthplace, which is inevitably related to his mother:

> In my youth, Toronto was also called "the City of Churches," and, indeed, the most vivid of my childhood memories in connection with Toronto have to do with churches. They have to do with Sunday-evening services, with evening light filtered through stained-glass windows, and with ministers who concluded their benediction with the phrase "Lord, give us the peace that the earth cannot give." Monday mornings, you see, meant that one had to go back to school and encounter all sorts of terrifying situations out there in the city. So those moments of Sunday-evening sanctuary became very special to me; they meant that one could find a certain tranquillity even in the city, but only if one opted not to be part of it.[32]

Glenn and his mother were connected through their love of music, dedication to religion and their high, even rigid moral standards. In his teens, Glenn emancipated himself from the religious ties to his mother. He concluded this memoir:

> Well, I don't go to church these days, I must confess, but I do repeat that phrase to myself very often—the one about the peace that the earth cannot give—and find it a great comfort. What I've done, I think, while living here, is to concoct some sort of metaphoric stained-glass window, which allows me to survive

> what appear to me to be the perils of the city—much as I survived Monday mornings in the schoolroom. And the best thing I can say about Toronto is that it doesn't seem to intrude upon this hermit like process.[33]

In McGreevy's film called *Glenn Gould's Toronto*, Gould acts like a tour guide and takes his audience to various places in Toronto. He visits the Toronto Zoo, and he sings to the giraffes and a herd of elephants the tune from the music of Gustav Mahler. It is quite humorous and charming to see Glenn imitating an operatic voice in German. He looks as if he had fun doing it. The purpose was to reiterate his love of animals and to show off as a comedian and parodist of operatic singing. Then Gould takes his viewers to the Toronto Eaton's Centre, located in downtown Toronto on Yonge Street. There, in front of the camera, he acts out his dislike for this ultra-modern shopping mall by uttering: "This is absurd, I can't believe it." What he could not believe was that people actually enjoyed being there. More, they did not mind the noise, nor were they bothered by the hustle and bustle of the city. For Gould, who had agoraphobia, the space and the high ceilings of the Eaton Centre seemed nonsensical and totally opposite to his need for a more modest space and for tranquillity. He simply could not relate to other parts of Toronto, such as the contemporary architecture of metallic skyscrapers and the modern business district with the fifty story bank buildings. He considered them a menace and an absurdity.

When the film was completed in 1979, the preview was organized at the new City Hall, two concave, tall buildings in Nathan Phillips Square in the heart of Toronto. Gould had never been to either the Eaton Centre or the City Hall before. He asked McGreevy to usher him in and show him the film in the empty hall. "I'd just love to see myself thirty feet high," Gould exclaimed. He was elated to see himself on the big screen as long as there were no people around. When the film was finally previewed in front of hundreds of special guests, Gould did not show up. He was a producer, actor, writer and a distinguished citizen of Toronto, yet he found it impossible to be a celebrity at that gala party. Representatives of the press were outraged in response to Gould's absence, which was misinterpreted as his arrogance. Bob Pennington of *The Toronto Sun* accused Gould of being a "pretentious recluse" who was "cursed with intellectual snobbery." He continued: "Failing to show at last week's party in his honor at City Hall seemed just another example of the [Greta] Garbo syndrome being used as an excuse for poor manners."[34] Don Downey of *The Globe and Mail* thought that Gould "sneers at the city's foundations" concluding: "There is little, in fact, that escaped Gould's acid tongue."[35] The peak of offensiveness was achieved in *The Toronto Star*, where the TV columnist Ron Base, under the headline "Dracula Lives As Tour Guide To Toronto," made a travesty of Gould:

> Gould announces that he does not arise until after dark. Nosferatu indeed lives! He skulks around Toronto and its shady suburban environs, his hatchet-sharp face shadowed by a floppy cap, his gaunt form swathed in formless overcoat and dark scarf, his wispy hands covered by gloves. Dracula is alive and well and showing us the view from the CN Tower.[36]

This sounds more like an angry diatribe than constructive feedback. Again, Gould was misjudged for his external behavior. Once more, he was subjected to loathsome criticism and even personal attack. His native critics attempted to defame him rather than to show some levity or deeper understanding of Gould's inner mind and his motives behind the project. The famous line that is attributed to Jesus after he was rejected in Nazareth, "A prophet is respected everywhere except in his home town and by his own family,"[37] can be well applied here in the case of Glenn Gould, who was rejected in Toronto. Those who paid heed to Gould's life had realized by then that he was a man of solitude and that his account of Toronto was painted from that very angle. Gould suffered what is called today social anxiety disorder, also known as social phobia, which forced him into social exile many years earlier. His absence was not out of arrogance and snobbery but because he had an involuntary health problem. He was in the state of disease, for which he needed more compassion and objectivity.

In fairness to the press, perhaps Gould should not have taken the *Toronto* project upon himself. Perhaps he could have said to McGreevy: "Your offer is enticing, but I don't think that the audiences are interested in my conservative version of Toronto." By this token, Gould was not infallible. By accepting the work, he inadvertently got himself into "hot water." In more academic language, "hot water" stands for his sadomasochistic relationship with his critics. Driven by the dark forces of his subconscious mind, Gould set himself up for abuse in the form of moral flagellation.

The making of the will, its deep emotional meaning and his ominous premonition that went along with it, added to Gould's consternation. At the end of 1979, he was in the midst of contention with his father, who decided to get married for the second time, which aggravated Glenn's old separation fears. Unexpectedly, another stressful separation was to happen before the year was over. Gould's music collaboration with his producer, Andrew Kazdin, which had been steady and fruitful in the previous fifteen years, was to come to an end. Apparently, at the beginning of December 1979, Kazdin was terminated by Columbia Records Ltd. because of insubordination. According to his story,[38] Kazdin made a certain recording in a conventional manner as opposed to applying the digital method recommended by his superiors. Paul Mayers, the head of the music division, disapproved of his noncompliance, which led to his employment termination. Kazdin was still allowed to keep producing records with Glenn Gould on a freelance basis because of their lengthy partnership. The two of them had a tentative recording session scheduled on the day after Christmas in 1979. When Kazdin called Gould a couple of days before, this ill-fated conversation between them followed:

Gould: "Well, as you know, I've been in discussion with Paul about this whole matter. He tells me that Simon Schmidt absolutely refuses to have you continue producing my records. So, Paul tells me that I have only two options: Either I accept another CBS producer, or I produce the records myself. Naturally, I chose the latter."

Kazdin: I was a bit stunned and asked, "Does this mean that our association is over?" He answered in a very hurried fashion:

Gould: "Yes. Now, don't be a stranger. Let's talk from time to time. Maybe I'll see you if I ever get down to New York. Look, I've really got to go. Goodbye."

Kazdin: All I could utter were the two syllables, "Goodbye ..."[39]

Kazdin was at first gravely hurt about suddenly being "dumped" and emotionally cut off by his famous client. In due course, he became very angry, which gave him an incentive to write a book about Gould in which he dealt with his personal mixed feelings toward him. The executives of the CBS Masterworks traditionally deferred to Gould's needs and wishes rather than challenge them. This is why Myers and Schmidt would never give that kind of ultimatum to Gould, as he was one of their best recording artists. It is more likely that Gould, in his distress and outrage related to his father, took out his anger on his producer. Gould unconsciously acted in a grandiose manner to defend against personal wretchedness. The more he was unhappy, the more grandiose and controlling he acted. As a long-standing habit, he prepared scripts for his prospective interviewers, both the questions and answers. This way, he played a "be-it-all" role in which he tried to be his own judge and jury at the same time. Here, in the case with Kazdin, Gould aspired to be his own producer and recording artist. He deprived himself of an easier option of relying on Kazdin as one of the best and most experienced producers of his time. In an attack of personal fury, Gould sacrificed a long-term productive relationship by severing ties abruptly. From the emotional point of view, this newly arisen situation was not helpful to either of the twosome. The pianist burdened himself with more responsibility and created one more reason to feel guilty over hurting a friend's feelings. Gould also added a clumsy separation to his long list of unfinished emotional business. Once again, there was no appropriate expression of feelings, no proper mourning, and no proper goodbye was expressed. Kazdin was too injured, and he retaliated by writing a book in an angry tone about Gould, which robbed Kazdin of credibility. Verne Edquist and his wife, Lillian, observed:

> We never presumed a friendship [with Gould] and Andy [Kazdin] did, and that's why he was so hurt when Glenn let him go ... Glenn was focused so much that he neglected personal relationships.[40]

There were other psychological dynamics operating in the Gould-Kazdin parting finale. Kazdin followed up with Paul Myers on the truthfulness of Gould's story and Myers "made it clear that Glenn himself opted to work without"[41] Kazdin. It follows that Gould distorted the story, which was less traumatic for him than to pursue termination of the business partnership in a more direct and fair way. As described earlier, Gould's episodic dishonesty and truth evasion was a part of his defensive personality makeup. It was a self-destructive way of coping. One can imagine how poorly Gould felt on that Christmas 1979 upon wrecking the relationship with Kazdin and upon declining the invitation to his father's upcoming wedding.

Avoiding relationships by running away from one's own friends and relatives is a common sign of depression. By the late 1970s, Gould could no longer maintain his amiable ties to Kazdin. He also shed himself of his relationship with Peter Ostwald, who was in the process of writing a biography of Robert Shumann. Gould, who did not admire Shumann's music, saw Ostwald as being disloyal and stopped communicating with him.

Gould allegedly moved out of his parental home in his late twenties because of his antagonistic relationship with his father. The only son did not see eye to eye with his elder. His bittersweet feelings became worse after his mother passed away. Following her death, Bert Gould unleashed his outgoing nature and became socially involved with different women. Bert resented being at home alone and went out on dates. Though in his late seventies, he was still at the helm of his successful fur business located on the premises of the prestigious King Edward Hotel. Women always adored him for his taste in fashion, his personal elegance and style, but most of all for his manliness. He was sort of a suppressed bon vivant whose moment had finally come.

In his search for a prospective partner, Bert Gould called Vera Dobson and asked her to dinner. Vera was the wife of his distant cousin, Murray Dobson, who passed away in 1977. The acquaintance between the two families dated back to the 1930s, when Murray took Vera to Gould Standard Fur and bought for her a Hudson seal coat. The Dobsons followed Glenn's developing music fame with much interest through the media. So, when Bert gave this critical telephone call to Vera in the late 1970s, she was not a stranger to him nor to Glenn. Vera and Bert renewed their long-neglected social ties. One day when she invited him for dinner at her house, Bert offered her a diamond engagement ring and Vera said "yes." According to Vera's recollection, Bert asked Glenn for his opinion, and it looked to him that Glenn had approved.[42]

Meanwhile, Glenn not only did not approve of his father's future plans but felt devastated. He was unable to see anybody as an adequate substitute for his mother. In the absence of a workable relationship with his father, Glenn was not able to share his concerns with him but committed his innermost feelings and thoughts to his journal. He wrote in his journal: "Relationships are addictive just as much as alcohol or tobacco," alluding to his father's intention to marry again. Glenn did not want his father to get married at all.

Had Bert stayed by himself in the house where Glenn was born, perhaps there would have been a better chance for their reconciliation. The two of them would have had a chance to get closer, and maybe Glenn would have paid visits to his father and not felt so estranged. Instead, in Glenn's eyes the worst had happened. The headstrong father, despite his son's emotional torment, chose to get married.

Once Bert decided to enter this nuptial relationship, he sold the family home at Southwood Drive, one of the few places where Glenn ever felt comfortable and moved into his new wife's home. Glenn felt displaced and gravely hurt. He could not imagine his father in a conjugal union with someone other than his mother and saw his father as lecherous and disloyal. Again, he spewed wrath into his diary: "You are of grandmother's age at the time of grandpa's death." This clearly meant that Glenn wanted his father to settle down rather than to begin a new life. Most of all, he could not imagine himself as anybody's stepson. Lacking awareness of Glenn's emotional pain, Bert unbashfully invited him to be his best man at the wedding. For Glenn, to accept this invitation would mean betrayal of his mother; not to accept it inevitably would be followed by feelings of guilt over hurting his only surviving parent. Glenn simply could not win in this grievous emotional dilemma. He kept writing numerous drafts of a would-be letter to his father turning down the invitation. Other more fortunate fathers and sons would personally discuss such a delicate matter and come to some workable solution. In Glenn's case this was not possible, as his relationship with his father was always cold and distant. Glenn wrote in his diary:

> And that's why late marriages such as Uncle Willard's for ex.[ample] seldom work, when you've been married to somebody for a long time the communic[ation] changes and the more normal pattern emerges but when a relationship is new there's much often intensity and the emot.[ional] engines are overtaxed. Now I hope you know what you are doing.[43]

Glenn behaved as if he were an expert in love. Current geriatric sociology encourages intimate relationships in old age as an antidote to loneliness and sickness. Glenn did not speak from the point of logic but from his inner turmoil that he disguised in a rational manner. Glenn ended up rejecting his father's wedding invitation. Bert asked his nephew, Dr. Tom Johnson, a dentist from Lindsay, Ontario, to be his best man and he agreed. Mr. Russell Herbert Gould and Mrs. Vera Dobson married on January 19, 1980. The happy couple departed to St. Lucia for their honeymoon. They were happily married for the next sixteen years. Ironically, Bert celebrated his second wedding at the age of seventy-eight, while his son, aged forty-seven, had never been married.

Had Glenn stood at his father's side as his best man, it may have been a step closer toward a more amiable relationship. Between the father and son there existed mutual emotional tension and animosity. Theirs was a fierce competition. In the animal world, the battle between two contenders like caribou over a female may cost them their antlers, meaning their life. In the civilized world, the strife between two rivals is more symbolic but equally serious. Originally, Glenn's battle was also over a female (his mother) and over his father's masculine supremacy. The son clearly lost all rounds in his childhood, teens and young adulthood in competition with his father. Again, in his middle age, Glenn lost the final round by having to see his father married to another woman.

Indeed, from his mother's death, and more from his father's wedding on, Gould's health was failing. Glenn found his St. Clair apartment too depressing, so he moved to the Inn on the Park located at Leslie and Eglinton, which happened to be within a stone's throw from his father's new residence at Lawrence Avenue and Leslie Street. The difference was that Bert moved into the beautiful and spacious home of his new wife, whereas Glenn moved alone into an ordinary hotel room. At the Inn on the Park, Glenn also had extra space for his studio, which was furnished with electronic equipment but without a concert piano. Glenn, the poor rich man, was now truly homeless. He never considered his St. Clair residence a real home, and hotels are not to be confused with home. Having lost his mother, the family home, the family cottage, his concert career and the hope of reconcilliation with his father, Glenn was despondent on the inside. Though he no longer lived in his penthouse, he still rented and maintained it as a sort of a mental anchor and as a shelter for his two concert pianos. All his scores, books, trinkets and other memorabilia necessary for his soul were left behind. Once in a while, Glenn went to this music shrine to rehearse or to simply play the piano for his emotional sustenance. As a hotel dweller, he was more in a state of limbo than in a state of stability, which a home could offer. Gould literally withdrew into a darkened hotel room where the window was almost hermetically sealed and covered with heavy drapes. This was the self-made, psychological grave of a deeply disillusioned and abandoned man, whose spirits were predictably dying a little each day. His body and mind were breaking down. It was only a matter of time before a total and irreversible giving up.

Breaking up with Kazdin not only had a negative emotional impact on Gould but had consequences with respect to his music career. The famous troika team of Gould, Kazdin and Edquist, which turned out a decade's worth of recordings, was then broken. Gould, who did not like change nor did he like traveling, found himself again in the situation of having to go back and forth to New York for recordings. He also had to get used to a new producer and to a different piano tuner, as Verne Edquist did not have a work permit for the United States. Gould was miserable! Fortunately, Ray Roberts was willing to travel with him. They would drive Gould's Lincoln filled with his equipment, the piano chair, a basin for hand-soaking and a stack of towels and shirts. Once in the New York studio, Ray helped in setting up the microphones for his boss, and he also took care of his food and clothes. Ray was a loyal companion who also fulfilled the role of a business assistant and valet.

The popular superstition that losses and mishaps come in threes became a reality in Gould's life. After that most awkward breakup with Kazdin and soon after his father's wedding, Gould's most important inanimate love object, his Steinway CD 318 concert grand piano, was no longer able to meet his pianistic needs. Having traveled back and forth to New York for nineteen years and having survived many concerts, recordings, hundreds of tuning sessions and reparations, the 318 was irreversibly worn out. It was time to give it up. Gould was very attached to this piano, which he played, caressed, restored and exalted to the point of treating it as if it were his intimate companion. Glenn's grief over the "death" of his beloved piano was proportional to his great emotional investment in his "she-piano" while she was still "alive." Remember that the Piano in Glenn's mind represented his mother, while the Chair represented his father. Although Glenn over the years went through many pianos, only the Chickering in his childhood and the Steinway 318 in his adulthood reached the emotional distinction of the Piano. So then, in the year 1980, five years after the death of his mother and shortly after the wedding of his father, Gould had to face another grave loss. His grief over the loss of the Piano was augmented by the unmourned loss of his mother.

Loss or not, the show must go on. In the mid-1970s, Gould renewed his contract with CBS. There were many recordings yet to be done. Still mourning the loss of his beloved piano, he reluctantly embarked on a search for another one. He reached out to Robert Silverman, who became instrumental in this search:

"Gould called me in Vermont and told me that his [piano] 318 was 'dead' and could not be fixed anymore. So, he needed a new piano. He asked me whether I could help him," Silverman recalled.

"What was your response?" I asked.

"I simply said, 'Sure. I'll call Peter Perez [president of Steinway & Sons] and ask him for assistance,'" Silverman recounted his dialogue with Gould.

"What happened afterwards?" I was anxious to know every detail.

"Well, I called Perez and explained Glenn's situation. He told me that they had some fine pianos for Glenn, but there was one in particular for him in the lobby of the Steinway Long Island Factory," Silverman took a deep breath while we were walking through the woods near his house in Vermont.

"Please go on." I was waiting to hear more.

"Well, I called Glenn and told him the story. Glenn agreed and soon after he came to New York. He visited the familiar basement at Steinway Hall where there is one of the best assortments of concert grands in the world. He tried a few pianos and eliminated one by one saying, 'It's not for me.'" Bob looked moved, as if he was reliving this crucial event.

"It appears that Glenn's piano search was not an easy task for either of you. Please tell me what happened then." I empathized with Bob.

"Right on," Bob exclaimed. "Well, Glenn went to Long Island City searching some more. He called me from there saying that one grand was very nice and he liked it, but then he tried it again and didn't like it. He decided that it was not for him." Silverman spoke with great compassion toward Gould.

"It sounds to me this was an emotional affair rather than an ordinary purchase of a concert grand. Was it not?" I asked.

"Of course it was an emotional affair for all of us. Peter [Perez] called me and told me: 'I don't know what else to do, Bob.' And, I myself was at my wit's end as to what to do." Bob sounded a bit helpless.

"How did you bring yourself to solve this ordeal?" I asked.

"I pulled myself together and called Glenn to tell him that there were other great pianos in New York and in the world and that he should just keep looking."

"Who was the first one to think about the Yamaha piano?"

"Well, it was me. I remembered that in the early 1960s I played a Yamaha piano. So I recommended to Glenn to try a Yamaha and he agreed. At that time, the Ostrowsky Yamaha piano firm in New York was located opposite the back end of Carnegie Hall. Borys Ostrowsky died and his wife Debbie took over," Bob recalled in detail.

"What were your ties to her?" I asked.

"I knew of Debbie because her brother worked as one of my editors. I called her saying that Glenn Gould was interested in trying the Yamaha pianos but would like to do it as anonymously as possible. She said she'd do her best," Bob said.

"Please carry on." I showed Bob my undivided attention.

"When Glenn got to Ostrowsky's, Debbie hung sheets in the window to ensure his privacy. He tried several pianos and was not satisfied, although he found one that he somewhat liked." Bob stopped walking to show me a couple of beavers building a dam in the local pond.

"Normally, Bob, I'd like to watch these busy beavers in action, but right now I'd prefer to hear the end of your story." I was gently persuasive.

"Yes, I understand. To get back to Glenn, as he was getting ready to leave, he suddenly spotted a piano that was not tuned. Debbie did not even want him to see it. Glenn rushed to it, played it briefly, saying he wanted this particular one and also was interested in buying the one from the window that he somewhat liked."[44]

From then on, things developed very fast. Gould wrote a check for the two pianos on the spot. Subsequently, the Yamaha CF SE Grand Piano, Serial 3020900, which cost $21,000, was shipped to the Columbia studios on Thirtieth Street. Thus, the twenty-five-year-long love affair with the Steinways, marked by many victories but spotted with occasional frustrations, abruptly ended. In the world of the piano business, this was an historical event. The great pianist made a drastic decision bordering on a scandal. In the world of human psychology, Gould's impulsive decision to switch from the Steinway to the Yamaha piano was not motivated so much by the "real" technical limitations of the Steinway piano but by his anger at the Steinway management. Years before, in 1958, when Gould was on a concert tour in Sweden, he played a Bechstein piano out of spite, causing an uproar in immediate music circles. Not since that time had he departed from his deep commitment to the Steinway piano. Until that summer of 1980, Gould had always been known as a Steinway artist. It is not likely that Gould absolutely could not find a suitable concert piano for himself at Steinway Hall, but it is more likely that he was unable to overcome his old emotional injuries related to the Steinways. Obviously, the emotional chasm with the Steinways, dating back to 1959 was never healed, and Gould simply could not bring himself to do another major business transaction with that particular firm. First, he was literally sick about having to separate from his model no. 318, and second, from the Steinway piano in a broad sense. On August 12, 1981, one day before the Yamaha piano was purchased, Gould went to Philadelphia to see Dr. Irvin Stein, which turned out to be his last visit. Gould complained of pains in his hands and diffuse body pains, and Dr. Stein ordered an extensive laboratory investigation. Don't forget that Gould most successfully had completed his second recording of the *Goldberg Variations* just three months earlier in May of the same year and had shown no indication of any pain or abnormality of his hands. It was his depression and separation anxiety over the loss of his beloved piano and the scandal of changing piano firms that manifested in physical symptoms.

For Gould, music was always a valuable antidote to depressive feelings. In the period 1979 to 1980, Gould undertook a major project of recording all of Bach's preludes, fugues and fuguettas. When the record was released, Jacob Siskind wrote a critical review titled "Gould excites and infuriates," which typified the old, worn-out, ambivalent attitude toward the artist. Siskind argued:

> [Gould's] playing is unquestionably unique. There's that incredible clarity of texture and concept, that single-mindedness that makes all of his performances fascinating from first to last.
>
> But, as always with Gould, there are those "personal" touches that seem to be tacked on gratuitously, almost like a small child deliberately smudging the edge of the family's favorite coffee table.
>
> He picks a dozen of those Preludes from the 18 that Bach composed at various times, and the performances are brilliant—except when he decides, at some of the most unexpected moments, to inject a bit of emotion into his performances, exaggerated retards, distended phrase lines, adding individualism where it is often least needed ... There are performances that will delight amateurs and other professionals but must be hidden from young students.[45]

One wonders about Gould's reaction to this critique. How did it make him feel? He must have felt that no matter what he did he could not win with some critics. Until that time, Gould had hidden himself from the public, and then he learned that his music should also be hidden from some sensitive segments of the population. Why hidden? Siskind made it seem that Gould's music was wicked and a bad influence on children. Let the students develop their own taste and judgment about music. This is highly reminiscent of the infamous reaction to Elvis Presley, whose dance and stage behavior were deemed indecent to the point that he was forbidden to be filmed from his waist down. Decades after the fact, Elvis is an American idol. This says that the views of the critics are relative reflections of their time and their momentary dispositions. Gould could not rationalize that way or share this perspective. He was exasperated. He always had the same, painful visceral reaction to ambivalent criticism—he became physically and emotionally sick whenever he felt rejected and humiliated.

BRAVO FORTISSIMO

I have immortal longings in me.
William Shakespeare [46]

When depressed or hurt by others, Glenn turned to music as an inanimate love object for solace. Music, not people, was like an oxygen supply that kept him alive. After his father's wedding, Gould's broadcasting career slowed down. His last TV show during his lifetime was in December 1979, and his last radio appearance was in December 1981 in the program *Booktime*. In it, he presented the book *The Three-Cornered World* by Natsume Soseki, the Japanese novelist and philosopher who fascinated him. Gould absorbed Soseki's philosophy of life in which he resents the secular world and embraces the world of art as the only one that counts. Soseki writes:

> Strip off from the world all those cares and worries which make it an unpleasant place in which to live, and picture before you a world of graciousness. You now have music, a painting, or poetry, or sculpture.[47]

This truly appealed to Gould, denial of the necessity of love toward another person in exchange for a perennial appreciation of the arts. Gould practically learned Soseki's book by heart. At the same time, his own writing career came to a halt. This shutdown of Gould's other-than-music artistry was in the service of his primary love, piano music. The piano artist in him was fervently working on the preparation and recording of six Haydn sonatas, in which he reinstated his love of solo classical music, particularly of the sonata form. Gould became consumed by the notion of recording his most beloved music piece, Bach's *Goldberg Variations*, for the second time. By that time, he had the music maturity of more than thirty years, from the time when his mentor Guerrero taught him the piece, and he had refined and saved his instrumental brilliance for something truly exceptional and monumental. The choice in his mind fell on the Variations. The creator in him was compelled to develop a different concept of the Goldbergs by adding to them more of his reflective and interpretative power.

In April and May 1981, Gould once again recorded Bach's Thirty Variations with his co-producer, Samuel Carter. The recording took place in New York City, in the Columbia Masterworks studios on Thirtieth Street. It was filmed by Bruno Monsaingeon for the firm Classart. Monsaingeon was engaged for this special occasion because Gould trusted him. Ray Roberts accompanied Gould to New York and stayed on the premises during the entire session. This was an optimally supportive environment of friends with whom Gould was a good personality match.

Watching the eight-hour video of this recording[48] is probably as exciting as sitting in the orchestra of the Roy Thompson Hall and seeing Gould live in performance. His appearance is astonishing; his playing is breathtaking. Gould is full of energy and good humor. His piano technique is brilliant. Everything "typical" of him is there. His dark blue shirt, his crouching posture and, of course, his piano Chair. The proverbial Chair does not have a seat, and Gould is sitting on its frame. His right leg is crossed deliberately. An attending make up artist approaches the pianist periodically to powder his sweaty face and balding forehead. Gould plays one variation at a time, each of them in several takes. He is alert, excited and highly motivated to make it work. His hands are healthy looking and beautiful; the skin is smooth with no aging marks. He conducts with his free hand. His conducting, which during his pianistic career was branded as redundant and distracting, appears to be quite purposeful, a sort of a substitute for a metronome. When playing, he is sitting so low that the keyboard is at the level of the upper third of his chest. The virtuoso is quite bent over and his chin and nose are three to six inches from the keyboard. He is gazing at his own fingers with the wonder of a child, as if he is talking to them. His lips are rhythmically moving as if they are singing in tune with music—ta-ta-ra, ta-ta-ta-ta. Then, there are times when Glenn is audibly singing or calling on others. "Ray, Ray," he cried twice. There is an ongoing commentary between the takes on the pieces he just played. "I don't like it. I'll try one more in the faster persuasion," Glenn contended. Then there are brief conversations between Glenn and Sam [Samuel Carter], his co-producer. When Glenn masterfully finished Variation 3, take 4, he yelled: "How about that?" The voice from the control room responded: "F a n t a s t i c, f a n t a s t i c." After the seventh take of Variation 2, Glenn became a little exasperated. "Damn it," he swore under his breath. For Glenn to use swear words was unthinkable in the past. And then he did it, perhaps on purpose, in front of the camera. It looked completely spontaneous though and appropriate to his frustrations around playing this technically difficult part. After this cursing interlude, Gould's mood picked up again. When he went back to work on Variation 4, take 1, there was some skin redness noticeable over his knuckles. He likely just soaked his hands in hot water. "I heard a note that is not quite bang on," he uttered. It was worth getting angry because the Variation 4, take 6 came out beautifully. This piece was played with rare vigor and in those crystalline, Gouldian tones. "Sam, if you would like to have the heat put on just for a second?" Glenn pleaded. "Right, Glenn, will do." Sam was supportive as always. Sam announced: "Variation 9." "Do you realize this is the only chance in this piece I get to conduct?" Gould was astonished. During all this time, the piano master was in his socks, and there was a square rug under his feet. The voice announced: "Variation 10, take 10." "A sloppy trill in the end," Gould says, then he played some more. "Oh, shit ," he yelled at the point of tonal imperfection. This was progress for Gould, being able to use street slang to express his frustration or his excitement. "Very weird rash."[49] Gould spotted redness on his second left finger.

It occurred to me while watching the tape that this century should have exercised more flexibility in accepting Glenn Gould the way he was for his own good and for the benefit of his audiences. Gould was unable to clearly relate his message and his wishes to his contemporaries. He did it in a convoluted, disguised and often spiteful way. He wanted to be unconditionally loved and approved of as he was. He was hungry for attention and love and could not handle anything less. Had he been understood, perhaps he would have been around longer and been more productive. This is not to say that the ultimate acceptance of Gould and his behavior by his critics and the public would have cured his underlying misery, but it certainly would have made his life and music production much more comfortable. Here in the studio, it is so obvious that he responds well to gentle and positive feedback from Sam and Bruno. He practically is bursting with contentment.

"Variation 13, take 1," the voice said, and Gould performed the segment. "Oh, shit, that was so good." Glenn was rejoicing in his newly discovered word; he decided he may as well use it while he was in such a good mood and in the presence of his worthy friends. He raised his arms and stretched them out in the air. "All right, stand by, please," the calm and soothing voice of Sam Carter says for the umpteenth time. "Variation 13, take 3." This is a very soft and gentle variation with frequent pianissimo. Gould played it flawlessly. "Let me do one more," Glenn proposed tirelessly. "One more, you really want one more?" Bruno repeated the question in disbelief as to him it felt perfect. "Yeah," Gould said decisively. "Variation 13, take 4," and then "Variation 14, take 2," the voice kept announcing. Glenn played them with incredible speed and clarity. His cross-passages are a thrill to watch and probably a torture to execute. My eyes are glued to the TV screen, and this part leaves me totally stunned. No one else noticed a flaw, but Glenn said that three notes were a little shaky, so he wanted another take. "Variation 15, take 3," the voice went on. My mind wanders deep. An idea occurred to me: *There is so much to say about Gould, this truly amazing and unique individual, that he deserves his psychobiography to be written in three volumes.*

"Glenn, stand by please, whenever you are ready. Variation 16, take 1," the voice was relentless. Good grief, I thought to myself. This variation appears to be very hard. How could Glenn possibly memorize all this? Perhaps his singing helps him to remember the music and makes it easier to go through with it. "The first half is terrific, the second is not. Just for my own amusement, I'll do it once more." Glenn was determined to make it perfect. "Variation 16, take 2," the voice of the producer announced. The make-up artist approached Gould, touching his moist forehead and scalp. Glenn kept going with a demonic force. "Oh, shit, not very well," said Glenn, throwing his hands up and then clapping them on his thighs. "Sam," he asked for help. "Yes," Sam responded calmly. "All right, Glenn, please stand by, sir" Sam seemed to know how to quell the fire in the piano master. "Variation 16, part 2, insert into take 2," Sam's voice declared. "I keep doing that, damn it." Glenn let off steam one more time. Surely, it is not easy to make one of the best recording music pieces ever, the thought went through my head. "Variation 17, take 1." Cross passages flow. "Oh, shit, let me do it once more." "Variation 17, take 2 and then 3," the voice said and Glenn played gloriously. "How about that, isn't it nice?" Glenn was in the state of ecstasy. "W o n d e r f u l," responded equally ecstatic Bruno. "Stand by please. This is Variation 18, take 1," then 2 through 9 followed. What a painstaking business. Who wants to be a concert pianist anyway? "Variation 18, take 10," the voice again. "How about that?" Glenn was amused by his own mastery. "Perfect," the voice was cheerful. "Let's come and listen." Everyone was invited to a listening feast. The entire crew meticulously listened to the whole thing from the beginning to the present. Glenn was back at the piano. "Variation 19, take 1," then 2 through 6 followed. "Bruno, is that all right for you?" Glenn asked in a voice of a school boy. "Absolutely, it's beautiful!" Bruno was totally satisfied. "Let me do it one more time." Glenn yearned for perfection. "This is Variation 21, take 1," the voice carried on. "This is a helluva good take but there was a wrong note in the end," Gould said insightfully. "Variation 22, take 1," the voice uttered, then 2, 3. Gould protested that the recording machine was not running in the first half of this variation. "Sorry, we had a bit of confusion over here," the voice from the control room was apologetic. "Next time if it happens try to stop me," Gould was direct. "We tried to but at least the video was running," the voice persisted.

It is getting tiring for me to follow this superhuman effort. How could Glenn keep up with it? He must have enormous love of the Goldbergs to want to do them over and over again. "Variation 24, take 1," the voice stated. This is a soft piece in a slow tempo. It is a sad melody, and Gould sang it audibly. When Gould sings, he subconsciously gets reconnected with his mother and her best asset, her voice. At that point of Gould's performance, it became noticeable that his right thumb had a brown mark as if the skin over its base was cut. Also, the tip of his third left finger appeared injured. This proves that playing the piano could be hazardous to one's health. "Variation 26, take 1," and then 2 through 12. This one was done at a horrendous speed. Glenn stopped several times, laughing. He was not satisfied at all. "Okay, we will leave this to later. There is no point doing it 'cause I will just keep making a mistake," he said conclusively, and the recording session was over for the day.

By allowing himself to be filmed during the recording session of Bach's *Goldberg Variations*, Gould opened the door to the wide audiences of the world. Through this precious video, his interpretative music gift is seen and heard one more time, as if this time, Gould had no fear of judgement by the critics. He openly shared with the world his special piano technique, rejuvenated and exalted in this interpretation. Even though Gould was not seen in public performance since 1964, seeing him on that recording video is very close to seeing him perform live. Samuel Carter reminisced on this filming and recording session:

> I often felt that he was being excessively nit-picking, only to discover in the intensive listening and editing sessions that followed that he had known precisely the difference he wanted in every case. He is a man who is very reluctant to accept anything short of the absolute attainment of his artistic goal.[50]

It is true that Gould strove for music perfection but, more important, is the profound emotional meaning of the recording. It was his swan song into which he poured all shades of his emotive expression—his love of music, his courage and jolliness, his vibrancy and vitality, his loss and sorrow and the inevitability of parting. Listen to Variation 25. In his first recording of the *Goldberg Variations*, Gould felt that he interpreted it in a romantic style and made it into a "Chopinesque mood piece." He felt somewhat ashamed as it stood against all his principals. This time, he delivered Variation 25 with a renewed vision, ridding it of romantic features. Variation 25 is still very emotional and touches the deepest recesses of the soul. While his opening aria is felicitous, Gould's closing aria da capo is wistful and equally hypnotic. It is the epitome of Gould's emotional and reflective power at the keyboard. His rendition of Variation 30, *Quadlibet*, represents Gould's capacity for buoyance and playfulness. For Gould, the *Goldberg Variations* are his joie de vivre. As a music piece, this is the holder of all his dreams—a dream of being a music prophet, a renaissance man; a dream of ennobling the music and freeing it of all that is trivial and romantic. If Bach surpassed himself at composing such a rich music piece, Gould surpassed himself in playing it for the widest audiences in the world. Gould did not play for a church congregation or for the local aristocracy and their subjects, but for the audiences of the globe. Gould is heard in countries like Japan and Saudi Arabia, and much more often in North America and European countries, where generations of music students were raised on Bach's music but never in the resplendent manner and style delivered by Glenn Gould.

Chapter XIX

FINALE

REQUIEM FOR A CANADIAN

> I had managed by degrees to reach an enchanted land from which I could look down on the world with complete detachment, but I felt now as though someone was demanding that I return the clock of immortality.
>
> Natsume Soseki[1]

The last two years of Gould's life brought to the fore his lifelong struggle between personal problems and creative achievements. Gould was practically invisible to the public and, except for a few friends with whom he remained in contact, his life was devoid of closer relations with people. He kept in touch with Jessie, his cousin, whom he called almost daily. There were even more frequent contacts with Ray Roberts. He called his father periodically, usually late at night but never visited him and his wife at their home on Norden Crescent, less than a mile from his hotel. There were professional calls to a few of his remaining business associates. The long telephone calls with Bob Silverman survived Glenn's depressive mood. Bob recalled:

> We talked about many things over the years: mysticism (he was a strong believer in telepathy and "coincidence"), hunting (he abhorred the concept), music, Shakespeare, the game called Monopoly, technology, Jack Benny, growing up, getting old, pianos, recording techniques, books, his new film, politics, an article or interview ... always with humor, sans malice or cynicism and rarely with negative comments about other musicians. Horowitz was the exception.[2]

Even though they spoke over the telephone for more than eight years before they met, Glenn and Bob saw each other in person only twice. The first time was in mid-July 1981, when Bob visited with Glenn at the Inn on the Park, where Bob rented a room. For the next three days, the two friends engaged in marathon conversations in Gould's studio in the basement of the hotel, listening to music and viewing video tapes. Bob Silverman recalled:

> It was both stimulating and exhausting because we went at it for stretches of upward of sixteen hours. When I finally had to call it quits he asked if I was sure I had to leave. Now, given a little stimulation I love to talk and share ideas, but I realized I'd more than met my match. What unrelenting energy!"[3]

Typically, Gould had difficulties engaging in social relations, but once he was connected, he had a hard time separating and going back to his lonely existence. In Bob, he had an avid listener, a valued music personality and a supportive friend. At one point, the two men encountered a crisis in their relationship. This was when Gould played a record of his String Quartet no. 1 for his friend, and after half an hour of attentive listening, he asked Silverman what he thought of the piece. Silverman said that he was not amused by it and proceeded to comment on the weaknesses of the piece. At the end he asked Gould: "Oh, by the way, who composed it?" "I did," Gould answered briskly but seriously. "After this there was a deadly silence. I was speechless. This was the longest and the loudest silence in my whole life,"[4] said Silverman. In some other situation, Gould would have likely clammed up and the relationship with his critical partner would be over. In this case, the momentary tension with Silverman was overcome, and Gould recovered from the injury to his self-esteem. The two men continued in their music discussions and friendship. Eventually, in the summer of 1982, Silverman paid his second visit to Gould. This time he arrived to Toronto with his wife, Ingrid. They met with Gould at the Inn on the Park, spending one and a half days together. On this occasion, the conversation started at 4 p.m. and ended at 5 a.m.

"How did he come across to you?" I asked Silverman.

"I am embarrassed to say, but he was rather dishevelled. His hair was ruffled and his pants were wrinkled, with a gaping hole in the back showing his white underpants. Somehow, he looked drawn and I wondered what was wrong."

"Did you ask him if something was wrong or whether he was ill?" I was looking for clues of Gould's illness.

"Funny you should ask me this. No, I didn't ask him anything on this occasion, but my wife [Ingrid] said to me afterwards that Glenn looked as if he were not well," Silverman said candidly.[5]

Clues of Gould's ill health, emotional and physical, were everywhere but were not recognized by others. Gould himself carried on his business as if nothing was wrong. In the early spring of 1981, he recorded six Haydn sonatas, which earned him the highest mark from critics for his performance and artistic merits, comparable to the highest quality of his Bach's *Goldberg Variations*. Gould co-produced these works with Samuel H. Carter. He was compared to Horowitz and Weissenberg in his technical and music control over his articulation and the rhythmic intensity. Here is a scholarly evaluation of Gould's brilliant piano technique at this stage of his life:

> A key focal point of Gould's playing is his individualized use of articulation in its broadest, deepest sense. It is an approach that goes much deeper than an occasional reordering of a few slur or staccato signs. With Gould's incredible control of touch, articulation is elevated to an expressive device of the highest order. Though split-second precision of key attacks and releases are present, his control of articulation is further used to project rhythmic pulse and tension

> virtually from note to note and even within rests. This, coupled with a rhythmic and technical control which allows him to maintain the most precise degrees of evenness, infuses his playing with a rhythmic tension and vitality that gives it a unique sinewy, taut quality even in passages taken at the most deliberately slow tempi.[6]

In 1981, Gould was interviewed by Tim Page, the music writer and critic, who wanted to find out whether Gould changed some of his radical views:

T.P. Glenn, it's now about seventeen years since you left the concert stage. I am not going to ask you why you left or whether you will return, both questions that you have answered eloquently on a number of occasions. But when you quit the stage, you stated rather unequivocally that the live concert was dead, period, and that recordings were the future of music. Since 1964, however, we have seen a tremendous resurgence of interest in the concert hall ... while the recording industry is in serious trouble. Any second thoughts on this subject?

G.G. Well, I did give myself the hedge of saying that concerts would die out by the year 2000, didn't I? We still have nineteen years to go, and by that time I will be too old to be bothered giving interviews (laughs), and I won't have to be responsible for my bad prognosis ...[7]

By admitting that he made a bad prognosis, Gould showed some flexibility on the subject. He rationalized that electronic technology would eventually prevail over the interest in live concertgoing. Page persisted in drawing from Gould his most interesting thoughts:

T.P. I know you have a dim view of concerts in general. You once told *The New York Times* that you found all the live arts "immoral" because "one should not voyeuristically watch one's fellow human beings in testing situations that do not pragmatically need to be tested."

G.G. Yes, I confess that I always had great misgivings about the motives of people who go to concerts, live theatre, whatever. I didn't want to be unfair about this, in the past, I have sometimes made rather sweeping generalizations to the effect that anybody who attends the concert is a voyeur at the very best, and maybe a sadist to boot! I'm sure that this is not altogether true; there may even be people who prefer the acoustics in Avery Fisher Hall to those in their living room. So, I don't want to be uncharitable. But I don't think that the whole business of asking people to test themselves in situations which have no need of their particular exertions is wrong, as well as pointless and cruel.[8]

There is no doubt that Gould had improved his public relation skills by the time of this interview. In a way, he apologized for accusing all concertgoers for being voyeuristic. His unwavering identification of performing in public with competition and testing of the performer's skills is striking. How horrible Glenn must have felt in his boyhood when he was urged to go from one music exam to another in rapid succession, to be left with such a strong and lasting repulsion toward any exam-like or testing situation? Glenn's skewed views that human aggression is equal to competition, that concertgoers are voyeuristic and sadistic and that the live arts are immoral, have all been motivated by his repeated childhood trauma.

In February 1982, Gould recorded in New York the Brahms's op. 10 – the Four Ballads. Three weeks later, he was interviewed by David Dubal, who asked Gould to discuss the subject of how he practiced the piano. Gould used the ballads as an example, saying that he "never played them before—not even sight-read them," and that it took him six weeks to study the score and to develop a clear conception of how to approach them. In illustrating the process of studying the ballads, Gould said that he found the last of the ballads to be difficult and that he found it hard to get a handle on them. He further commented on the last ballad:

> It's very beautiful in its way—hymnal almost, and what endears me to it is that it is one of those relatively few works where Brahms lets his imagination—a sort of stream of consciousness process really—prevail over his sense of design, of architecture. But for that very reason it's difficult to bring off and I found myself inferring constantly, instrumental groupings of notes of many episodes, until I felt I had found an acceptable tempo.[9]

After the six weeks of searching for an acceptable concept and tempo, it took Gould another two weeks, prior to the recording, to practice the ballads at the keyboard. On an average, he practiced one to two hours daily during these two weeks, but at the same time he ran them in his head "many dozens of times when driving along in the car or conducting them in my studio."[10] Though Dubal found it unbelievable that Gould practiced as little as an hour a day, Gould insisted that the mental image of music and the purity of conception were more important to him in relationship to the keyboard than the actual manual practicing on the piano. Gould summed it up:

> What it all comes down to is that one does not play the piano with one's fingers, one plays the piano with one's mind. That sounds like an easy, even trite cliché, but it's true.[11]

Following the completion of recording the monumental Bach's *Goldberg Variations*, Gould threw himself into another demanding and challenging task. While his father was in a state of matrimonial bliss, traveling, vacationing and having a love affair with life, Gould pursued his austere, monk-like existence. The two men remained guarded in their businesslike relationship. Gould's new project was bringing to the audiences of piano music the works of Richard Wagner. Not everybody could go to Bayruth in Germany or other European cities to listen to Wagner's magnificent operas. Gould was at heart an educator of the people. He made piano transcriptions of Wagner's *Die Meistersinger* and *Gottedamerung* and prepared them for recording. Another idea born in his mind was to record the original chamber version of Wagner's Siegfried Idyll in his arrangement and conduct it himself. Gould sensed that the moment to try himself as a conductor had finally come. His lifelong desire to become a conductor came to realization in July 1982, in Toronto, when Gould conducted a music orchestra of fourteen instrumentalists in their performance of Wagner's Siegfried Idyll. This was his conducting debut in recording. He also recorded his two piano transcriptions of Wagner's *Die Meistersinger* and *Gottedamerung*. Music transcription is not an equivalent to composing but requires composing ability. By making those piano transcriptions, Gould recreated Wagner's music, which was as close as he could come to innovation at that very unhappy period of his life. Gould asked his old friend from the 1960s, Victor DiBello, conductor, to help him:

"When Gould approached you for this recording, what did he expect from you?" I asked DiBello in one of our several conversations.

"He wanted me to be his music manager, a sort of music contractor to him. I've been around myself as a conductor from the time I was eighteen years old, and I knew the musicians in town," DiBello said.

"What was your job?" I asked.

"My job was to select a few distinguished musicians from the Toronto Symphony, which was very easy for me to do because I knew most of them. I contracted them and booked the refurbished studio on the second floor of the St. Lawrence Hall for the recording,"[12] DiBello remembered with pleasure in his voice.

Dr. Timothy Maloney played clarinet in the orchestra. When interviewed in 1991, he provided this valuable account of the event:

H. M. "What was it like to be with Gould in his new role as a conductor?"

T. M. "It was a special experience. I knew I was in the presence of greatness ... Gould did not play a prima donna. He was very relaxed, as relaxed as one can be. Each section was done several times changing expression and articulation ... There was no doubt whose project it was. He [Gould] changed position of the microphone, he listened and discussed the music with the engineer."

H. M. "How did he look physically?"

T. M. "He looked sick, paunchy, and a lot older than forty-nine. His skin was pasty, and he looked like he hadn't taken care of himself ... He was dragging a green plastic bag with him. But he was quite warm and collegial and in the end he shook everyone's hand."[13]

Apparently, the recording was done from 8 p.m. to 11 p.m. over two evenings. As the evening went on, Gould grew more animated, and he started to tell jokes to make it as light as it could be. The musicians were discussing the possibility of starting their own music orchestra in the future since they were so good together. Maloney recalled:

> We joked about a name for the ensemble and Gould came up with two of the best. He suggested "The Academy of St. Lawrence in the Market," which we all thought was tremendous, and, based on Maxwell Davies group "The Fires of London," Gould also suggested "The Ashes of Toronto." There were others floating around like "The Siegfried Idlers," so there were moments of levity and good fun, and he was certainly available to all of us to discuss details on interpretation.[14]

On September 3, 1982, just a month before his death, the pianist completed his final recording at RCA Studio "A" in New York. It was the piano music of Richard Strauss—Five Piano Pieces op. 3 and Sonata in B minor op. 5. Samuel Carter, who was a co-producer along with Andrew Kazdin and Glenn Gould, recalled:

> The [recording] sessions were particularly enjoyable, as Glenn had great enthusiasm for Strauss's youthful Sonata, as well as for Five Pieces, op. 3. He was both delighted with and challenged by the sonata's technical exuberance and its beautiful, unbashedly romantic themes.
>
> I remember his commenting that he often wondered why more concert pianists didn't play the sonata, since it is such a fine showpiece and ends in a great octave-chasing finale that is a guaranteed crowd-pleaser.[15]

At least, Gould's fans can take comfort in knowing that despite his many problems, he was still able to enjoy music. Though the piano master was in good spirits around recording Strauss's music, he was not feeling well overall. Gould was gradually heading toward his fiftieth birthday, yet he felt as if he were an incomplete musician and an unfinished person. He maintained himself on the level of subsistence. The parsimony of his daily diet was at its worst. In response to the letter from Virginia Katims, who had asked him to contribute some recipes to her cookbook, Gould summarized his plight with food:

> ... I'm almost totally indifferent to the process of eating and, quite frankly, can just barely manage to open cans. Furthermore, my basic attitude toward food is that it's a time-consuming nuisance—I have, by the way become virtually a vegetarian in the past decade—and I would be only too delighted if one could effectively sustain oneself with all necessary nutritional elements by the simple intake of X number of capsules per day. I realize that this sounds forbiddingly ascetic, but it's a fair reflection of my attitude toward the subject, and I beg to request exclusion from your [cookbook] volume accordingly.[16]

His friends sensed that he was not doing well, yet there were no major interventions on their part to help him. "He looked haggard," said John Roberts. "He called me every day over the telephone, two and three times, he needed me, " recalled Ray Roberts. Glenn's cousin, Jessie, was in the transition of moving from one place in Oshawa to another. She recalled: "I was busy moving and I haven't heard from him for a few days but before that he called me every day, sometimes even twice a day. I had no idea that he was so seriously ill." His voice over the phone appeared normal, and Glenn knew how to cover up his depression by putting forward an air of bravado and his eloquent speech. Glenn avoided emotional upheavals by living as a recluse. He spent nights reading anything that came his way—reviews, Soseki's book, even passages from the Bible—when he was most restless. His thoughts were only interrupted by monitoring of his blood pressure. Nobody was quite aware of the depth of his mental anguish, and he himself was in a state of denial of it. Physicians, whom he saw regularly, missed it. Friends and relatives missed it. His father, living in close physical proximity but worlds apart from his only son, missed it totally. Gould was terrified of his upcoming birthday. He was never keen on celebrating anything, let alone this fiftieth birthday. To him, it sounded so ominous and so final. At such an advanced age, he felt so late at everything and so unfulfilled. He was superstitious. Praise and celebration felt like a curse or a jinx. Yet, these very rituals are healthy, as they help to express one's own happiness or worries, fears of aging and despair. Birthday parties are cathartic, as they help social closeness and cohesion; they honor our past, acknowledge the present and prepare the platform for the future. Gould deprived himself of all the possible benefits of celebrating this major event in his life. By detaching himself from his feelings, he triggered inner tension and felt like he was sick. He told his father over the telephone that he was "coming down with a cold." As usual, this "cold" was a somatic expression of his inner tension and deep-seated feelings. He felt them in his body.

Gould's fiftieth birthday was on Saturday, September 25, 1982. He spent it by himself in the confines of his hotel room and partly in his studio. There were telephone calls from well-wishers who had his "hot-line" or private number. His first biographer, Geoffrey Payzant, called to wish him happy birthday. Edward Rothstein, whose profile of Gould was published the next day, called; as did John McGreevy, his CBC producer-buddy, and Schuyler Chapin, his friend from Columbia Records. On the day of his birthday, Glenn called Robert Silverman, in Vermont, to alert him to Rothstein's upcoming article. On Sunday, Bob called back to discuss with Glenn the details of Rothstein's article:

"We discussed it sentence by sentence. Glenn seemed to be in a good mood, cheerful and very involved," Bob recalled.

"How did you like the article itself?" I asked.

"I was displeased with the first part. It had to do with Gould's idiosyncrasies, which were written about so much that I found them boring. But the second part was quite laudatory. Rothstein was always very sympathetic to Gould," Bob responded.[17]

Gould's father, Bert, along with his wife, Vera, drove to Glenn's hotel, and while she stayed in the car, Mr. Gould went in and spoke briefly and formally with his son. Glenn did not receive his father inside his hotel room but downstairs, which bespeaks the level of their emotional guardedness. Such a cold and distant emotional encounter between the father and his only son was not new at all. In Glenn's youth and adult years, it was neutralized by the presence of his mother. Then, when she was gone, the two men set themselves apart from each other.

On Monday, September 27, Gould woke up at two o'clock in the afternoon and felt numb on the left side. Having known the details of the fatal stroke of his mother and lesser stroke of his father, Gould made his own diagnosis of stroke. Yet he was in denial of the seriousness of his condition. Like his mother seven years earlier, he too did not call an ambulance. Instead, he called his friend, Ray Roberts, at work. When Roberts arrived, Glenn got up from his bed to unlock the door for him. Roberts called Dr. Percieval's secretary and asked for Dr. Percieval to pay an urgent home visit to Glenn. Dr. Percieval could not be instantly located, so there was more delay. Finally, Dr. Percieval responded by phone and urged Roberts to rush Gould to the hospital without further delay.[18] Apparently, Dr. Percieval could have called an ambulance himself had he sensed the urgency of Gould's condition. Just as Dr. Percieval was in denial of Gould's lifelong psychiatric condition, he was also in the state of disbelief about the seriousness of this critical moment. Roberts, still not calling an ambulance, arranged with the hotel manager to bring a wheel chair. With great difficulty, Gould was placed in the chair and wheeled to his Lincoln, where Roberts managed to place him in and drive him to the Toronto General Hospital in downtown Toronto.

At least six hours elapsed from the time when Gould awoke and noticed his one-sided numbness until he was first seen by the casualty officer in the emergency room. In the past several years of their friendship, Roberts made great efforts to go along with Gould's wishes without challenging him. He showed the same approach in Gould's illness, except, this time Gould was in a life-threatening situation that warranted quick action. Glenn's father, who was his next-of-kin and who lived within one kilometer distance, was not notified. Having survived a stroke himself, Bert Gould would have handled this decisively and more appropriately by calling for emergency help. If Ray Roberts or Mr. Gould took charge and hired an ambulance, Glenn could have been hospitalized ten minutes after his first phone call at the nearby Sunnybrook Hospital, which was about two kilometers away. The choice of the Toronto General Hospital, which is located in downtown, was obviously determined by Gould. His need for being in control and his fears and prejudices proved to be lethal in this case. Whatever the reasons were, Gould arrived to the hospital too late to be rescued.

The current state of the art is that a stroke should be treated as a medical emergency. Acute stroke care is to be administered immediately, starting from the time of arrival of an ambulance. Paramedics begin treatment by performing ABC (airway, breathing, resuscitation) measures and by support and monitoring of blood pressure and temperature. There are available medications called thrombolytics (TPA) used against blood clotting. In some cases, brain surgery may be needed to relieve the brain from the inner pressure. The goal of acute stroke therapy is to reduce brain tissue necrosis (death of cellular tissue) and ischemia (localized anemia of tissue). Intravenous thrombolytic therapy improves the outcome of many patients, but it can be applied only within the first three hours from the onset of the stroke. Mortality from stroke and complications are significantly reduced by prompt hospitalization and treatment.

Gould was out of luck. The combination of his high blood pressure, poor eating habits, chronic depressive disorder, need for control, lack of exercise and high stress were all poor prognostic factors. Moreover, the combination of his denial and delay of hospitalization proved to be fatal in the end. He suffered a carotid artery blockage that caused damage to his brain. While at the hospital, he had throbbing headaches and periods of lucidity alternating with confusion. Ray was at his bedside. His father visited every day and held his hand. Mr. Gould maintained composure and never shed tears.[19] Jessie visited on Wednesday, while Glenn was still conscious. She gave him support and told him her old line: "We, the Greigs, we are the fighters. You must try, Glenn, try harder and do not give up." Glenn responded: "I know, Jessie, but now it's too late for me."[20] Bob Silverman called from Vermont wanting to visit his ailing friend. Ray Roberts discouraged him by saying that Glenn was too sick to handle visitors. Ray obtained a color tv for Glenn and tried to provide a comfortable environment for him. Glenn, in turn, wanted to give Ray his power of attorney. This did not happen because Glenn's condition was unstable with long episodes of somnolence and confusion. Glenn did not want to die. He was scared to be left alone. The presence of Ray felt very safe and comforting, as well were his thoughts about his mother. She was so good with prayers and would certainly have prayed for him, perhaps one of the psalms from her Psalter, which Gould inherited from her:

> 23 The Lord made me weak while I was still young;
> he has shortened my life.
> 24 My God, do not take me away now,
> before I grow old.[21]

Unfortunately, there came another stroke, after which Glenn fell into a coma. Mr. Gould agreed earlier with the hospital staff not to do "heroic measures" on Glenn should he be in grave crisis. In consultation with Jessie Greig, Mr. Gould authorized Glenn's attending physician to "pull the plug," if indicated. After a futile week of progressive decay, on Monday, October 4, 1982, Glenn's life supports were discontinued at 11:30 hours, and he was pronounced dead. May peace be with you, Glenn Gould.

In death, Glenn followed the same pathway as his mother. He died of a stroke like she did, and he was layed out at Humphry's Funeral Home. Mr. Gould decided on a private, family funeral. Ray Roberts, who was instrumental during Glenn's hospital stay, had a proxy to take care of his apartment and his car. Having been so busy with errands, Ray was somewhat emotionally removed around the funeral until a few days after, when he drove Glenn's car out of town for storage. While in the car, he suddenly burst into uncontrollable tears. He had to pull over and park on the side of the road. He wept over the loss of his friend. "I couldn't bear to think that I will never see him again and that we will never drive together to New York."[22] This is when he became profoundly aware that Glenn's life had ended.

The funeral service was held on October 15 at the magnificent St. Paul's Anglican Church on Bloor Street East. St. Paul's is known as the largest church in Toronto according to the number of seats—over 2,000. This is why the important services and celebrations for various religious denominations are held there, and dignitaries arriving to Toronto, such as the Pope John Paul II, are received there. Gould, a native of Toronto and a music citizen of the world, was also appropriately given the honor of St. Paul's.

Nothing could be more sad than Gould's funeral service. His contemporaries were unprepared for his death. In all his seclusion and eccentricity, they had lost sight of Gould in the past decade of his life. Though the publicity about him was intense all along, Gould, the person, was not adequately celebrated during his lifetime. Here, at St. Paul's, he was remembered and honored like royalty would be. Perhaps for the first time, everybody around him was uncritically and totally dedicated to Gould. Collective sorrow, collective empathy and collective guilt prevailed among the mourners. The organizing committee exercised enormous sensitivity to Gould and took into consideration his preferences. The choice of music was determined by what he liked. Bach's music was played and sung as a matrix of the program. Bach's Prelude and Fugue in B Minor BW544 were played on organ by John Tutle. The famous Elmer Isler Singers were conducted by their founder, Elmer Isler, who personally had collaborated with Gould. They performed Brahms's Motet for Double Chorus op. 110 and Bach's Jesu Meine Freude from The Motet no. 3, BWV 227, which was done in German. Reading was done by Rabbi James Prosnit and by a captain of the Salvation Army, Robert Redhood. People wept, even those who never met the deceased. Jessie Greig was grief-stricken: "I had the images of Glenn when he was a child. I kept thinking of our many times together, his jokes, his many fears that he had shared with me. And everything was over. I will never hear Glenn's voice again. When they played his aria I could not bear it. I thought I'd die of sorrow and despair."[23] She was involved in his life from his infancy to his last moments. Gould's old music friend, contralto Maureen Forrester, sang "Have Mercy Lord" from Bach's St. Matthew Passion and the Orford String Quartet played "Cavetina" from Beethoven's String Quartet in B Flat Major, op.130, which Gould admired. Glenn's personal friend, John Lee Roberts, paid him a tribute. In a memorable biographical speech he highlighted the best of Glenn:

> Glenn Gould has passed across the horizon of the twentieth century like a dazzling meteor ... thanks to Glenn's farseeing use of mass media, his musical

> performances touched the hearts and minds of millions of people. ... Glenn carried the burden of genius all his life. ... it is most fitting that in his professional career he went full circle by beginning it with a recording of the Goldberg Variations by Bach and ending it with a second recording of the same work even more astounding than the first. Glenn felt that many people did not leave enough space in their lives for things of the spirit. ... Through his legacy he will continue to invite us to look into ourselves and to pace ourselves with him, to extend ourselves beyond the opening gray clouds of our own consciousness, to journey North.[24]

At the end, Bach's aria da capo from the *Goldberg Variations* was played from Gould's record. This was the emotional pinnacle in this ceremonial mourning; the most moving two minutes were dedicated to Gould, but also were touching for any human soul.

Ironically, it is the memorial service that makes us introspective and profoundly aware of the importance of life. A memorial service can evoke emotions of compassion and sorrow, a sense of humility and mortality; inner peace and hope of forgiveness. Gould, who had a deceased mother and no wife or children of his own, was mourned by the rest of his family and by friends, associates and countless listeners of his music. During his performing career, Gould was known for delicacy of his health and his poetic qualities compared to the English poets, John Keats and Thomas Chatterton. In his death, Gould's many mourners may borrow some beautiful verses from John Keats to express their pain and sorrow:

> Shed no tear! O shed no tear!
> The flower will bloom another year
> Weep no more! O weep no more!
> Young buds sleep in the root's white core.[25]

For his admirers, Gould was like a ghost even during his lifetime. But his music presence on the Canadian scene and on the world stage was very real during his life and continues to fascinate and delight us after his death. Gould will be remembered as a brilliant, recreative music artist who created music that touched the world and became immortal. Ours is a sophisticated generation living in a high-tech society. We prefer to enter the twenty-first century with a more relaxed attitude toward life and toward ourselves in the service of living longer and enjoying life to the fullest. Wouldn't we all like to have Gould alive and let him play for us, even in his socks if he so desired?

Chapter XX

PHOENIX RISING

GOULD AS THE MOST FAMOUS CANADIAN ARTIST

> I can no longer listen to Gould's playing as a detached critic. I have become, I confess, a fan.
>
> Edward Rothstein[1]

The death of a loved one may serve as a powerful impetus for further achievements in survivors. Humans honor the dead through traditional rituals and ceremonies, but individual gifted mourners have their unique ways of paying homage. They may compose music dedicated to deceased relatives and friends. Essays, books and creative epitaphs abound. Survivors mourn to liberate themselves from the most doleful feelings and save the best memories of the one who perished. Memorials and other rituals that follow the death of a loved one are irreplaceable tools in acute grief, but art pieces like requiems and laments, odes and elegies, and other artistic creations are timeless testimonies of love and loss.

A flurry of commemorative articles appeared in virtually all Toronto papers in response to the death of Glenn Gould. For the writers, this was not just a matter of a professional assignment, but they personally mourned the loss through their sensitive writing. On October 5, *The Globe and Mail* reported:

> In the 50 years of his life, Glenn Gould did little that was bland, much that was brilliant and provocative. His death yesterday—from a severe stroke suffered a week earlier—robs the world of more than a superbly gifted pianist, more than a great interpreter of the music of Bach, more than a perceptive writer and caustic commentator. As both critic and artist, he provided a vital cultural stimulant to the arts simply by being a creatively disturbing influence.[2]

John Fraser, the man who a few years earlier offered Gould the possibility of making a documentary about China, wrote with pathos:

> Death can be proud today. It has claimed a titan in his prime ... How many people, for example, did he personally introduce to the wonder of Johann Se-

> bastian Bach? Who else could ever humanize Hindemith? Why did it seem to a new generation that Haydn's piano works never before existed until Glenn Gould brought his enthusiasm and impeccable sense of musical drama to bear on them?[3]

Some writers remembered the deceased for his sense of humor. Composer and music teacher Oskar Morawetz shared some pleasant anecdotes about Glenn, whom he knew from the time Glenn was thirteen years of age. Morawetz was amused by Glenn's sense of humor and ability for acting and imitating others, including him. He recalled a fabled event that so typically portrays Glenn's precociousness:

> During the rehearsals for a television broadcast of some Beethoven trios, Mr. Gould, then nineteen, told the violinist he was misinterpreting the music. The violinist, who was known around the world, said to Glenn, "Look here, young man, don't tell me how to interpret this. I've played it 500 times before."
>
> The trio proceeded to go on camera with Mr. Gould playing the piece from memory and the two other musicians closely following scores.[4]

Another more recent friend, John McGreevy, stated for *The Toronto Sun*:

> Gould was the wittiest and most inventive mind I've had the good fortune to be involved with ... To no longer have access to his wit and his spirit is a tremendous loss.
>
> But people were always harping on his eccentricities when the actuality was much more than those clichés. Glenn had a quality of human warmth that one doesn't normally ascribe to genius. He cared terribly about the struggles of his friends and was fascinated to hear about one's latest endeavors.[5]

John Kraglund of *The Globe and Mail*, who followed Gould's performing and recording career for many years, wrote a well-researched, critical article titled "Glenn Gould: Eccentric Genius of the Keyboard Courted Controversy." He said:

> It was not only Gould's superiority as pianist and interpreter that gained him wide recognition at home. His concert mannerisms were so casual and extraordinary that they drove some music lovers to distraction, also driving them away from his concerts because they found it impossible to focus on the sound, while others, less musically inclined, flocked to see him in performance.[6]

The Toronto Star grieved his death through several lengthy and in-depth reports encompassing the musician's life and achievement. *The Star* also conducted telephone interviews with distinguished individuals all over the world who knew Gould personally and had collaborated with him. Harold C. Schonberg, music critic of *The New York Times*, commented with respect to Gould's death:

> What can one say? Brilliant but eccentric. He had a phenomenal linear ability at the keyboard and his hands were born to play Bach, but sometimes his ideas were, to put it mildly, arbitrary. Anyway, he was a personality, a powerful individualist, and we are going to miss him. I mean that sincerely.[7]

"Brilliant but eccentric." Schonberg was among the first critics to set a precedent for "Yes-But" ambivalent criticism about Gould. Perhaps Schonberg became repentant and realized that he was much too harsh on Gould during his concert career, which contributed to its dissolution. As his contemporary, Schonberg treated Gould as if he were a l'enfant terrible, but in the long run, observing his career from a more objective distance, it appears he grew to slightly change his mind in Gould's favor.

Lord Yehudi Menuhin, who was tracked down in Tel Aviv, was shocked by the news of Gould's death and told *The Toronto Star*:

> Oh no, I can't believe it. This is awful. He was one of my most beloved colleagues. He was admired, respected and loved. It's remarkable that so many people will miss someone who appeared so little in public.[8]

Conductor Leonard Bernstein, who was contacted in New York by *The Toronto Star*, offered this rather diplomatic and sugarcoated reply:

> I am grieving the loss not only of an irreplaceable pianist but of a true intellectual among performers. Glenn had one of the most original minds I have ever known in the world of music, both in his playing and in his writings. We shall all miss him sorely.[9]

Many years before, Bernstein "sacrificed" Gould in the Brahms D Minor Concerto scandal, and soon after he had no problem replacing his music colleague in the next scheduled concert and distancing himself from him.

Soprano Elizabeth Schwarzkopf, who was reached in Zurich, appeared to be genuinely saddened by the news of Glenn's passing. She gave *The Toronto Star* this reply:

> I'm very, very sorry. He was an artist with such a future. At 50, he was still young as an artist. We had several sessions together and he accompanied me in three [Richard] Strauss songs. He wasn't really an accompanist, he was a fellow musician. We didn't see eye-to-eye, he was fantasizing about Strauss, which is not what you should do.
>
> He could just as easily have been a conductor as a pianist. He regarded reading music as only a means of creating what he wanted to produce. It worked with Bach but it didn't work with Strauss. He was a musician of incredible flexibility. He had such a range of sonorities. In Europe, where he didn't perform often, people were in awe of him.[10]

Andrew Davis, conductor of the Toronto Symphony; jazz pianist Oskar Peterson; famous American pianist, Van Cliburn; Walter Homburger, Gould's former manager and several well-known personalities also paid tribute to Gould through their comments in *The Toronto Star*.

William Littler, music critic of *The Toronto Star*, who wrote so extensively about Gould that his articles could fill a book, had a hard time accepting the reality of his passing. If music critics were to be divided into two groups, Littler would belong to the category of constructive and empathic critics as opposed to subjective and destructive ones. His long-lasting admiration of Gould did not seem to impair his critical judgment. On October 5, a day after Gould's death, Littler supplied an article titled: "His Curiosity Made Label Of Pianist So Inadequate," alluding to Gould's versatile creative mind.

> In a country that hasn't always valued the quality, Glenn Gould was an original. He played the piano like no one else, thought like no one else, and probably lived like no one else ... What did matter was the quality of his mind. He challenged us in a way few performing musicians either would or could. To him, nothing was worth doing the same way twice ... But if we didn't fully understand him, we learned from him. I remember a couple of years ago in Moscow meeting a Soviet musician who said, and meant it, that before Glenn Gould came to Russia there was one way of playing Bach. After he left, there was another.[11]

The CBC radio and television mourned too. One of Gould's favorite TV broadcasters, Barbara Frum, acknowledged him on screen on the day of his death. Frum, who never met Gould in person, interviewed Canadian contralto Maureen Forrester, who worked with Gould on several occasions starting from his pre-fame period when he was only twenty-two years old. "He was an odd young man and I was in awe of him." "He had a warm and friendly side as well." Forrester recalled that once when she had a tea with Vincent Massey, who was the governor general at the time, he suggested that somebody should "stop this young man singing and making gestures in front of the audiences." Having personally known Gould, Forrester defended his mannerisms at the piano, saying that they were genuine expressions of his inner world of music.

Accolades have no purpose whatsoever for the deceased but are exclusively geared to the needs of survivors. They are a source of comfort, facilitators of grief and accomplices in denial. Upon Gould's death, the press became more generous, more remorseful and apologetic. It was a sort of plea for forgiveness and absolution. While Gould was alive, he was referred to in ambivalent terms ("yes, his playing is great but he is a bad boy"), whereas upon his death he was mourned less ambiguously, more objectively and more empathically. Coupled with that was an air of acceptance. Gould, a legend, became much easier to accept than Gould, the real individual. Legends are godly, celestial, untouchable and beyond our real grasp. One cannot embrace a legend and kiss its cheek. Do we really prefer Gould only as a legend or as a real human being with all of his natural talents and neurotic foibles?

Overnight, Mr. Bert Gould became the center of public attention. He received hundreds of condolences from all over the world, from his friends and business associates, but much more from his son's admirers. Among them was this distinguished telegram:

It was with deep sorrow that I learned of the sudden death of your son. His unique and inspirational interpretations combined with his awesome technical proficiency thrilled audiences around the world. Even though he was one of the world's foremost pianists, he never ceased his search for newer and better ways to give expression to the music he loved. Canadians have lost one of their most famous sons. The world has lost a great artist. I sincerely hope that you will take solace in knowing that the memory of Glenn Gould's musical genius will live on. I extend my heartfelt sympathy to you and your family in this time of sorrow.

Pierre Elliott Trudeau, Prime Minister of Canada[12]

Another dignitary telegram came from the leader of the opposition and was signed, Right Honorable Joe Clark. Music schools, symphony orchestras, music students and nonmusical fans offered their deepest condolences. Personal notes from the pianist, Rosalyn Tureck, and the conductor of Boston Symphony Orchestra, Seiji Ozawa, were among the many precious letters from fellow musicians. Mrs. Wanda Horowitz wrote from her personal experience of loss:

Dear Mr. Gould, New York, October 14, 1982

Both Mr. Horowitz and I wish to express our deepest sympathy to you at your very sad and sudden loss.

Words never adequately can express what one really feels at such a time, nor can they give the comfort so badly needed by a bereaved parent.

We can understand what you are experiencing at this time, since it is only a few years since the sad and untimely loss of our only daughter.

Please be assured, Mr. Gould, that all the world grieves with you at the untimely death of Glenn.

With our warmest thoughts to you,
Wanda Toscanini Horowitz[13]

Stunned by Glenn's untimely death, Herbert von Karajan furnished this telegram:

Dear Mr. Gould,

The terrible news came to me as an immense shock. Just now we were discussing the possibility to do some recordings in Canada with Glenn at the end of our forthcoming tour to America. My deep sorrow is now that we will never again be able to make music together and Glenn certainly was the artist I admired most because our understanding was like a common thought. His work will live on in his records.

To you and his friends, please accept my heartiest and deepest thoughts of condolence.

Sincerely yours,
Herbert von Karajan[14]

Before Glenn's death, Mr. Gould watched his son's fame from a respectable distance, whereas now he participated in it. By being showered with letters and invited with his wife, Vera, to commemorative meetings, celebrations and awards as an honorable guest, Mr. Gould had an opportunity to catch up with getting to know his son through the experiences and feelings of others. The press and prospective biographers descended upon Bert with insatiable questions: "What else can you remember? Can you tell some stories from his childhood? What was his mother like as a music teacher?" Mr. Gould, who was Glenn's spokesman only in his teens, once more played the same role. It worked out to a point. He was able to provide some valuable reminiscences and global answers to many questions asked, and some interviewers were satisfied. Often, though, he offered platitudes. Mr. Gould did not have enough insight and empathy for his son. He lacked an in-depth understanding of Glenn and could not relate to either his tragedy or his genius. Mr. Gould always insisted that Glenn had a normal childhood. He was unable to connect Glenn's many troubling habits, such as slouching in the chair, intolerance of fishing, temper tantrums or his use of a very low piano chair with any family dynamics.

Just as Mr. Gould's denial affected Glenn negatively during his developing years, this is how misleading it became after Glenn's death. Denial of reality is obstructive and defensive. By unconsciously denying rather than admitting to certain problems in Glenn's childhood, and by fostering secrets and silence, Mr. Gould left the world at a loss to understand and appreciate his son properly. Gould's other relatives, like his cousins Jessie Greig and her older sister, Betty Greig Madill, though quite protective of Glenn, were still able to be more forthcoming about various traumatic influences in their cousin's life. They both agreed that Glenn had an unusually difficult work schedule in his childhood, that he did not play enough with other children, and that he could not be a "kid like others," which then affected him adversely in the long run.

Gould's sudden and untimely death was followed by a small, private funeral, by a magnificent memorial service, and from then on by the perennial mourning-celebration process of those left behind. Mourning has to do with our lasting sadness about his tragedy in life and death, while celebration is related to his unforgettable victory in his creative life. His passing unleashed a torrent of creative activities and creative products that continued into the next century. No other concert pianist of the twentieth century was graced in the first ten years after passing away by a dozen books written and published about him, and no other master-pianist was honored by several thousand essays which, if compiled, would account for another ten books. The greatness of Gould as a music figure is not only determined by music scholars but also by the general public. People from all over the world, those who liked Gould and his music, purchased two million of his albums by the time of his death. This is a lot considering his Calvinistic music repertoire, full of serious, cerebral music and devoid of romantic, people-pleasing music. Shortly after his passing, Gould was awarded a Juno Award. The certificate reads: "Be it known that 'Bach: The Goldberg Variations,' Glenn Gould, Columbia, 1956, has been elected to the National Academy of Recording Arts and Sciences Hall of Fame, Honoring Recordings of Lasting Qualitative or Historical Significance in the year 1983."

During his lifetime, Gould was nominated a few times but was never awarded the Grammy for the best solo performance, until 1983, when his new recording of the *Goldberg Variations* won Grammy awards in both "Performance" and "Record of the Year" categories. Why wait to award an exceptional artist until after he died? Posthumous awards are a sign of a tardy response to a gifted artist who had been outstanding for more than thirty years. Had Gould won any of these awards during his lifetime, he probably would have not shown up for the ceremonial evening, but deep down he would have been gratified and certainly capable of enjoying the entire experience.

Institutions were formed after his death. The Glenn Gould Estate became an official body governing the Gould affairs. The same lawyer, Stephen Posen, who represented his famous client during his life, continued to represent him in death by presiding over the board of the estate. In 1983, the estate supported the establishment of The Glenn Gould Foundation. Gould's friend, John Lee Roberts, became the founding president. Another close friend and supporter, Ray Roberts, became a member of the board and continued to work for Gould with untiring dedication for the next twenty-five years after Gould's death. An expert archivist, Ruth Pincoe, was hired to examine the contents of Gould's penthouse at 110 St. Clair West. All his papers, books, periodicals, tapes, records, concert programs, music scores, correspondence, trophies, medals, photographs and personal possessions, like felt-tip black pens, scarves, gloves and alarm clocks, were sold to the National Library of Canada in Ottawa and delivered in 226 boxes to its music division, where this treasure was classified and organized into the unique Glenn Gould Archives. According to the agreement between the estate and the library, the famous piano, Steinway CD 318, and the piano chair became possessions of the music division. The piano could be seen displayed in the niche of the central foyer of the library, but from time to time it is used for recitals. The Yamaha piano ended up on permanent display in the lobby of Roy Thompson Hall in Toronto, where concert audiences can view it and ponder its history.

Under the leadership of Helmut Kallmann, the chief of the music division, and his assistant researcher, Ruth Pincoe, and other fine staff members, selected objects and materials were used for the first Glenn Gould Exhibition in 1988 at the library. This exhibition became the first hypermedia information tool for popularizing and spreading knowledge about Glenn Gould. The blown-up photographs from various developmental stages of his life, manuscripts, personal memorabilia like his work desk, brown leather briefcase, passport, keys from hotels and his medals were all on display. Gould's music, ranging from his interpretations of Bach to Siegfried Idylls, was played in the background of the exhibition. It was like a sacred shrine where thousands of visitors in a slow procession over several months had a chance to deepen their awareness and sensitivity to Gould.

Still not recovered from the shock of Gould's death, John McGreevy organized activities to help him and the wide public to mourn. At the St. Lawrence Center in Toronto, where Gould made his conducting debut and his last recording of Siegfried Idyll, McGreevy paid cinematic tribute by showing three movies—*Glenn Gould's Toronto* and two films made much earlier by the National Film Board titled *Glenn Gould on the Record* and *Glenn Gould Off the Record.*

Education about and popularization of the Gould phenomena was on the rise. McGreevy engaged Gould scholars, partners at work and enthusiasts to write their reminiscences of him, which he then edited and published as a first post-mortem book about him in 1983—*The Glenn Gould Variations: By Himself and His Friends*. Leonard Bernstein; Joseph Roddy of *The New York Times*; John Beckwith, composer, educator and Gould's friend; Robert Silverman and Richard Kostelanetz all contributed their compassionate tributes. Mourning indeed gives impetus to creation and opportunity for personal expression of tender feelings. Disturbed by Gould's tragedy but inspired by his spirit, the young Canadian composer, Alexina Louie, composed a music piece in the weeks immediately after his death—*O Magnum Mysterium: In Memoriam Glenn Gould*, for string orchestra. Louie confessed: "It was written very quickly which is extraordinary because I don't write orchestral music quickly as a rule. It was wrenched from me and almost wrote itself."[15]

Not only was Gould immortalized in poems, essays and music compositions, but his name and work were sent to another solar system 30,000 years away. The *Pioneer 10* space probe loaded with pictures of men and women, several mathematical formulas and Gould's recording of Bach's prelude were sent into the solar system. In this sense, Gould became an ambassador of the planet Earth in the galaxy. British critic Paul Richardson of the *Observer* wrote:

> Among the objects chosen to represent our species on the *Voyager's* 1977 space mission was a recording of the Canadian pianist Glenn Gould playing the Prelude in C Major from Bach's *Well-tempered Klavier*. Whichever NASA executive decided to include the recording in the space probes ought to be praised for his or her good taste—Gould's playing of the tiny prelude is a model of poise and fastidious phrasing. I suspect NASA should also be commended for its musical wit, for Gould was just the sort of musical alien who might be expected to appeal to little green men.[16]

McGreevy's *Variations*, as the first major printed document, was followed by a major visual biography—*Glenn Gould: A Portrait*—a two-hour documentary produced by Vincent Tovell and Eric Till, which was premiered and telecasted in 1985. This film captured the essence of Gould—the person and creator in a proactive manner. In the same year, a few other major events took place. Columbia Masterworks commemorated 300 years of Bach's birth by launching a fifteen-volume *Gould/Bach Series* and the five-volume *The Glenn Gould Legacy* series. Canadian pianist Angela Hewitt won the International Bach Piano Competition held at Toronto's Roy Thompson Hall. Television producer John Coulson, proud of his work for the competition, realized that Gould hated the concept but hoped that "if he could have witnessed this he would not have been disdainful."[17] Ironically, the proceeds from the competition were allocated to the Glenn Gould Memorial Foundation.

The interest in and curiosity about Gould was not showing signs of diminution, or even signs of leveling off. On the contrary, it showed a linear growth. Several more books were published, which were accompanied by a slew of reviews, analytic articles and additional biographical information appearing in major newspapers and magazines all over the world. Otto Friedrich published the first full-scale biography in 1988, while Tim Page compiled Gould's best writings into a sizable book, *The Glenn Gould Reader*. Gould was a virtuoso, music philosopher, broadcaster, even a zany comedian. From the book published by Tim Page, one can easily discern that Gould was also an accomplished writer. His sentences were crammed and often too long, but he was a master of words and a super inventor of fresh ideas.

In 1987, upon the initiative of the Glenn Gould Memorial Foundation, the international triennial Glenn Gould Prize was awarded for the first time. Established in perpetuity, the prize represents a tribute to Glenn Gould's life and work from the people of Canada and is intended to recognize an exceptional contribution to music and its communication. This award, in the amount of $50,000, was first given to the accomplished Canadian composer, R. Murray Schafer, who was Glenn's music peer and who also studied piano with Alberto Guerrero. In 1990, Sir Jehudi Menuhin, a former associate of

Gould, received the honorable prize. In 1993, the famous Toronto-based jazz pianist, Oskar Peterson, was the lucky winner. In 1996, Japanese composer Toru Takemitsu received the Gould prize when he was on his death bed, and in 1999, Yo-Yo Ma, the celebrated cellist, was honored as a winner. In the year 2002, Pierre Boulez won the Glenn Gould Prize, and in 2005, famed pianist and conductor Andre Previn was the winner. Gould would have had many reservations about the choice of laureates. In his lifetime, he distanced himself from both Lord Menuhin and R. Murray Schafer. Another reality is that Gould never championed jazz music. It could be said with more certainty that, as a japanophile and an admirer of new music, Gould would have likely approved of Takemitsu, as well as of the choice of Yo-Yo Ma, because he loved cello music, but he would most likely disapprove of the prize itself. Though the Glenn Gould Prize is a demonstration of the good will of several major contributors, it is not in accord with Gould's doctrine. He was reluctant to attend ceremonial awards given to his friends and received only a few in his adult years. Most certainly, Gould never received a prize in an amount as high as $50,000. One can argue that the founders of the Glenn Gould Prize were not sensitive to what he stood for or that they took liberty in creating an image by modifying his attitude of challenging social standards into an attitude of social niceties and compliance. By this token, the founders reacted like Gould's mother, who always tried to make him look better in public relations.

Bert Gould enjoyed a very happy decade after his son's death. Having survived two strokes without major consequences, he was remarkably healthy afterward. He was a man of physical prowess and vitality. At the age of eighty-two, Mr. Gould removed a 900-pound fountain from his property all by himself. He and his second wife extensively traveled abroad. They went to England, toured Alaska, took a cruise to the Panama Canal and went to Florida on a yearly basis. At the age of eighty-six, Mr. Gould was photographed in Florida holding two young women up in the air, sitting on his outstretched arms, which was consistent with his robust physique and his enthusiasm for life. In November 1991, Mr. Gould celebrated his ninetieth birthday at the Toronto Hunt Club, surrounded by his friends and family members. In contrast, Glenn would have hated the idea of the Hunt Club and a birthday party. This ceremony was videotaped to serve as a lasting souvenir. Bert's childhood friend, Harry Middleton of Uxbridge, Ontario, reminisced on their school years saying that "nobody would ever mess around with Bert." Of course, Glenn tried to challenge, provoke and "mess around" with his father, which worked in many instances but not in the end. The father won the battle by surviving his son. By the law of nature, the young and strong son is supposed to survive his weakened and aged father. There are aberrations from that law and, in a lesser number of cases, there is a reversal when the strong, masculine father outlives his enfeebled, unhealthy son. In human psychology, sensitive-enough parenting is geared toward the quality survival of the offspring. By being sheltered, lonely, defiant and unable to come to terms with his father, Gould remained vulnerable to the inimical conditions of life. In the end, the oversensitive son succumbed prematurely to his inner frailties and physical illness.

In 1992, a double anniversary took place—the sixtieth anniversary of Gould's birth and tenth anniversary of his death. This event was celebrated in Toronto by an international Glenn Gould Conference, which was titled Music and Communication in the 21st Century: Variations on Themes of Glenn Gould. It drew visitors from all over Canada, the United States, Great Britain and from as far as Japan. The Glenn Gould Studio was officially opened at the new CBC building on Front Street in Toronto. This studio, with its 341 seats, has become one of the most important cultural centers in Gould's native city. He dedicated his life to piano music and CBC broadcasting, and now his ideals live on through the music activities in the studio named after him. Many of Gould's friends were there as visitors or participants. Some of those attending were John Lee Roberts, former music director at the CBC; Robert Silverman, still at the helm of the *Piano Quarterly*, which published many of Gould's articles and those about him written upon his death; Victor DiBello and R. Murray Schafer, who both took an active part at the conference; Ray Roberts and Stephen Posen, who represented the Gould Estate. The Canadian astronaut, Roberta Bondar, spoke about the interface between arts and interplanetary science. A number of piano recitals and chamber music performances took place at the Glenn Gould Studio, entertaining guests but also propagating Gould's heritage in the world of music. At last, the Toronto audiences got to hear Gould's String Quartet live, played by the Glenn Gould String Quartet and performed in the studio that also bears his name. On the same occasion, his other less-known compositions also were presented before the public. Gould's composition for vocal quartet, *So You Want To Write A Fugue*, was performed. *O Magnum Mysterium: In Memoriam Glenn Gould* by Alexina Louie was successfully premiered at Roy Thompson Hall with Samuel Wong conducting the Toronto Symphony. Patrons of the conference wondered what Gould would have said to all this. One can be sure that he would not have attended the festivities, even if they were chiefly prepared in his honor, unless he could hide somewhere in the wings. There is no doubt that he would have disagreed with many aspects and ideas put forward and, more importantly, he would have had great ideas himself to contribute. On the whole, the conference was a way to honor Gould but also was representative of a growing curiosity and understanding of Gould and of his tremendous ability to inspire and to enlighten audiences.

A few days after this successful conference in Toronto, there was another anniversarial celebration of Gould held in an unlikely location—a small town in Holland by the name of Groningen. Though Gould never performed in Holland, he had many fans there. In fact, the first *Bulletin of the International Glenn Gould Society*, published biannually, was not formed in Toronto but in the Netherlands town of Groningen. The publisher, Cornelius Hoffman, was a fervent admirer of Gould. Hoffman wrote to Gould, who approved of the idea of the International Society. Ironically, the society officially began its international activity on October 1, 1982, when Gould was on his death bed. Eventually, Groningen became the epicenter of all Gould-related activities in the Netherlands.

Groningen is a city of some 60,000 inhabitants, out of which about half are university students. This charming historical town opened its gates to over 300 festival participants from European countries, North America and Japan. The festivities took place in the large Cultuur Centrum de Oosterpoort overlooking the Verbindingskanal, which is crowded with picturesque houseboats. The delightful central town square, Grote Markt, dominated by Martinitoren (tower) and Martinkerk (church), gives a specific quaint tone to the city. The church bells rang every hour on the hour as a pleasant reminder of the reality of time. Song and music traditions are interwoven into the cultural fabric of the community.

Sponsored by the International Society, a three-day Glenn Gould Festival was held in Groningen's music hall De Oosterpoort from October 2 to 4, 1992, celebrating Gould's double anniversary. The festival was attended by dignitaries from Canada and Holland. The festival stage of the amphitheater was dominated by a gigantic poster of a silhouette of Glenn Gould, surrounded by majestic flower arrangements. The opening ceremony was followed by the piano recital of the Australian concert pianist, Geoffrey Douglas Madge, who performed Bach's *Goldberg Variations*. Listening to this music piece was like a recapitulation of Gould's entire life—the Aria, which opened his marvelous music career and marked the closure of it, with several lively and several subduing variations in between. During the festival a procession of international pianists followed, among them were several Russian pianists. The internationally acclaimed Andrei Gavrilov graced the festival by performing the works of Schubert, Ravel and Prokofiev's Sonata no.8. Pianist Angela Hewitt gave a remarkably beautiful demonstration of Bach's music works. Her poise, clean technique and meticulous approach to music marked Angela's performance of the same pieces that were earlier perfected and favored by Gould. The festival was punctuated by memories of Gould throughout.

There was more excitement to follow in the appearance of the multi-talented Bruno Monsaingeon. He presented his film *Art of the Fugue*, in which he masterfully portrayed Gould at the piano, playing and commenting on Bach's music. Glenn at the piano and Bruno the filmmaker and interviewer came across as a congruent duo capable of creating timeless artistry. Monsaingeon pleased the audience one more time by presenting Gould's String Quartet, op.1. He played the violin along with three colleagues: Jean-Marc Apap, Gilles Apap and Marc Coppey. It felt as if Gould were there behind the curtain, waiting to come out and take a bow. In the course of the next few years, Monsaingeon honored his famous friend by publishing three books with Gould-related material.

Lectures were held in the auditorium by John Lee Roberts, Kevin Bazzana and Peter Ostwald. Roberts, who knew Gould for twenty-seven years, felt that Gould was the first major musician to develop a total relationship with the electronic media. Ostwald referred to Gould as a genius, stating that it is important "for all of us to keep our geniuses alive and healthy." Bazzana observed that Gould put himself in the position of a composer, a role of which the pianists and musicologists are critical but composers are not. Bob Silverman honored Gould in his dinner speech, saying: "Glenn was a complicated human being, and maybe in the next century there will be another form of understanding him."

Poet James Strecker of Hamilton, Ontario, presented one of his poems dedicated to his great compatriot, titled "At the Grave of Glenn Gould." He pined:

> ... The trees, too far apart,
> cast no shadow on your name;
> nearby, a squirrel, a robin,
> and, at another grave, mourners
> who mourn a death the first
> time. Overhead, some Canada
> Geese make petulant sounds.
> ... You wouldn't be part
> of the world unless you
> had your way;
>   ... You
> seem too cautious to weep
> and defied emotion the best
> you could, as if the heart
> intended some clarity of brain.[18]

Silvia Kind, the famous harpsichordist and Glenn's loyal admirer and friend, who appeared at the festival despite her failing health, commented:

> The Glenn Gould Estate is controlling and stifling the image of the great artist. Canada must open the door to the world and allow a more cosmopolitan approach to Glenn Gould. His fame is not private property to which every interested individual would be a trespasser. The estate cannot be a private business of a group of people but an open and objective forum. We owe that to Glenn Gould, who struggled all his life to shrug off a number of insensitive rules and practices.[19]

The festival was successfully concluded with a recital of the Russian pianist, Grigory Sokolov, who not too long before the festival made his spectacular debut in the Amsterdam Cocertgebouw as the replacement for the indisposed Alfred Brendel. Sokolov played works of Brahms but finished with Chopin's Sonata no. 2 in B-flat Minor, better known as the *Funeral March*. Chopin wrote it shortly before his own death and never saw it published.

With the advent of computer cybernetics, Gould's achievement became vastly accessible to the world. In 1990, a Montreal computer firm, YYIATS, designed an interactive system, The Glenn Gould Profile, which explores his ideas and music. The president of YYIATS, Louise Guay, explained:

> The system we have developed is very much like Gould himself, who loved to mix media, and made collages of sound and text. What we are doing here is allowing the viewer to edit with video, sound and words ... Technology becomes an instrument for creating your own image of the man. Rather than being just a passive consumer, you become an explorer.[20]

Apparently, by pressing keys the consumer can get into the system of Gould's photographs, videos, music and writings and mix and match them freely. It is an "archeological dig" and the users can dig as deep as they wish. The Glenn Gould Profile opened a new door to Gould's multi-artistic gift. Gould would have liked it not only as an adult toy but as an embodiment of his artist-consumer philosophy. With popularization of the Internet in the mid-1990s, consumers have access to thousands of sites on the topics of Gould and related subjects.

The love affair of Columbia Masterworks and Gould during his lifetime continued with Sony Classical in his death. After the takeover of CBS Masterworks in January 1989, Sony Classical inherited not only the entire stock of recorded music by Glenn Gould but also the highest appreciation for one of its most astonishing stars. Old unpublished recordings were dusted off from the vaults of CBS Masterworks, then remastered, repackaged and released on records, audio tapes and discs to appease "hungry" collectors and grieving fans. The advent of the VCR in the early 1980s and the use of the compact disk shortly after Gould's death and the laser disk a little later made it possible for his survivors to see him on video and listen to his music on CDs through stereo sound systems that sound so much better than LP records. In the 1990s, Sony used state-of-the-art technology, High Definition 20-bit Sound, which transfers sound sources from the twenty-bit digital recorder onto CD by using the latest signal processing technique called Super-Bit Mapping (SBM). This technique makes it possible to reproduce original recordings into lasting recordings with excellent quality that captures far more color and hidden details than the previous sixteen-bit CD.

The artist is gone, but his music has become more alive in his death. This phenomenon is unique to great men and women, who being ahead of their peers are not well understood during their lives but their achievements earn increasing value and fame after they die. Among those many records released posthumously are two gems. Beethoven's piano sonatas—no. 24 in F-sharp Major, op. 78, "A Therese," and no. 29 in B-flat Major, op. 106, "Hammerklavier." German musicologist, Michael Stagemann, assisted Sony Classical in rescuing Gould's recordings from storage and releasing them for market use. He also supplied well-researched liner notes. The critics are no longer interested in condemning Gould's renditions but are simply content to have them.

Along with the quantum upgrade of its recording technology, Sony Classical modernized its vision of Glenn Gould that was to carry into the twenty-first century. In 1992, upon Gould's double anniversary, Sony Classical launched its mammoth collection of practically all of his recordings with Columbia Masterworks, both previously released and unreleased ones, under the name of the *Glenn Gould Edition*. This special edition was planned to be released in forty-nine disks. The first round of the *Glenn Gould Edition* was issued in 1992 for commemoration and consisted of seventeen CDs and ten videotapes. The rest of Gould's works were released over the next two years. In 1997, there were only three recordings yet to be released.

Jacob Siskind of the *Ottawa Citizen*, wrote in reference to Sony's Edition: "To some, this all seems to be fitting; to others it smacks of hucksterism." Sony Classical and hucksterism? Not likely. Sony and the Glenn Gould industry—more likely. Sony treats Gould with due respect and credibility. Sony Classical, which was situated next door to the Inn on the Park, where Gould resided, held a discrete but steadfast admiration for its respected star-client. Gould's large posters, CDs, vignettes, cassettes, pictures of all sizes and clippings spread out on the working desks of the staff spoke of an honest commitment to the artist. Sony's Gould-related industry is a fair instrument of his music. Gould, who was originally championed by CBS Masterworks, has another loyal propagator and benefactor in Sony.

In 1993, Francois Girard's acclaimed biographic film *Thirty-Two Short Films About Glenn Gould* was released with an overwhelming response from the public. The role of Glenn was played by Canadian actor Colm Feore, who is known for his Shakespearean interpretations at the Stratford Festival in Ontario. Gould, who adored Shakespeare's plays and identified with some of his heroes, would have found an acceptable representation in Feore, a master of dramatic roles. The script for the *Thirty Two Short Films* was written by the Quebecois-born and Montreal-based Francois Girard and co-authored by Don McKellar. The film won four Genie Awards (the Canadian Oscar) including Best Picture and Best Director.

Robert Fulford provided a critical overview for the film:

> ... Gould liked to challenge, fracture, and reshape the forms of communication he worked with. He would have been fascinated by the way Girard, McKellar and their producers have stretched the limits of biographical film. They could have made a drama, they could have made a documentary based on interviews, or they could have made an art film interpreting Gould. Instead, they have done

> all three, mixing these elements unpredictably, keeping the audience off balance and always curious about what's coming next.[21]

Sony Classical released the soundtrack for the film consisting of excerpts from Gould's best recordings. Anthony Lane of *The New Yorker* wrote:

> Gould's capacity to inspire and to estrange, to aggravate and to soothe, has yet to die down, and is unlikely to do so as long as people keep listening to Bach. His peculiar genius has now been accorded a suitable memorial—a movie that lies somewhere between an act of homage and a public inquiry.
>
> "Thirty Two Short Films About Glenn Gould" is exactly what it sounds like.[22]

Richard Natale of *The Chicago Tribune* quoted Girard's summary of the biopic:

> ... The interspersion of documentary footage and fictional elements creates a unique animal and opens up the possibilities of our notions of biography. But the way Girard views it, "there aren't that many differences between biography and fiction. Look at 'Hamlet.' He has become a character in our collective memory. Glenn Gould has too. There could be 40 films on Gould and there'd still be new things to say."[23]

The British press was also more than satisfied with the film and reminisced most fondly about Gould. *The Guardian* deemed Girard's film as "one of a half dozen best ever made about a musician" and the *Daily Telegraph* succinctly evaluated both the film and its hero:

> By far, the most original film of the week, and the most entertaining, is Francois Girard's Thirty Two Short Films About Glenn Gould. Don't be put off by the austere title, nor by what might seem a specialized subject, the life of the brilliant, eccentric and reclusive Canadian pianist, who retired from live performance at 32 and died at 50 in 1982. This is an exemplary study of a complex, essentially solitary man, with much to say about the cult of genius.[24]

In 1995, two important events took place, the establishment of The Friends of Glenn Gould, which is a society that promotes awareness and communication with respect to the great artist, and the inception of the *GlennGould* magazine as a visual forum for expression vis-à-vis the achievement of Glenn Gould. Canadian musicologist and a Gould scholar Kevin Bazzana became the first editor of the *GlennGould* magazine. Admirers from the international community became the members of the society, expressing their insatiable curiosity about the life and work of their idol. Subscribers from all over Canada and the United States, and those from France, Italy, Germany, Austria, Belgium, Australia and Japan, hastened to join The Friends of Glenn Gould. People are interested in both honoring their music hero and expressing what was inspired by his presence.

Glenn's father's health weakened suddenly. Though he still drove his eight-cylinder Buick at Christmas 1995, his health was rapidly failing to a point of no return. Mr. Gould died in January 1996 at the age of ninety-four. He is remembered as a builder, a hard-working, fun-loving and church-going man. His remains were viewed in the chapel of the Bayview Funeral Home, which earlier had housed the remains of his late wife and son. Bert was laid to rest next to Florrie and Glenn at Mount Pleasant cemetery in Toronto. The small Gould family was together again at last.

Jessie Greig, deeply shaken by Glenn's death, took ill and bravely battled her breast cancer until she succumbed to it in the summer of 1996. She believed that stress from the loss of her favorite cousin was responsible for her illness. For the rest of her life, she played a very active role in propagating the memory of Glenn. Two of Gould's biographers, Otto Friedrich and Peter Ostwald, died within fourteen years of his death. Victor DiBello, an eccentric bachelor and Glenn's friend, died in May 1997 from the consequences of depression and loneliness.

The passing of Glenn Gould left an unbridgeable gap in the music community of North America. He is sorely missed in Toronto, at the CBC, in the recording industry, and by his surviving friends and associates. His personal friends, Robert Fulford, from childhood and John Lee Roberts, Robert Silverman and Ray Roberts from his adult life, lived to tell their stories about Glenn.

Gould was a multitalented, pluralistic and multifaceted music artist whose mind traveled in many directions. He was a man of artistic foresight. His concept of music interpretation differed from that of his peers in its enormous range. It varies from orthodox to experimental, from pleasing to provocative, from playful to cynical. While most great concert pianists satisfy themselves to be what they are, Gould strove to transcend his own boundaries. His chief goal was to transmit the music far beyond the concert hall through electronic media. By broadcasting classical music through his famous radio shows, Gould reached millions of listeners in most unlikely places, like small towns, farms and mountain villages across Canada and the United States. Equally powerful were his numerous taped TV shows that were forerunners of the video industry.

Gould is to be credited for spreading the knowledge of music through recording media. He left to the world a treasure trove of over eighty recordings as a lasting legacy. Single-handedly, this piano virtuoso increased the interest of musical and nonmusical audiences in the music of Johann Sebastian Bach. His interpretations of Bach's music are a precious keepsake. Gould's two renditions of Bach's *Goldberg Variations* are his crowning achievements. They became timeless and legendary landmarks in the history of classical piano music. In 1992, Gould's second recording of the *Goldberg Variations* was acknowledged as a megahit and awarded a platinum certificate by Sony Classical, celebrating the sale of 100,000 copies of the 1981 recording in Canada alone. Sales of Gould's records continue to be high in Canada, Italy, Germany and Japan, less so in the United States.[25] Why are the sales low in the States? Is it because of the systematic debasing of Gould's demeanor and his music during his lifetime? Or could it be that the Americans are valuing their own artists more? There are no definitive answers to those questions, only suppositions.

The world cannot afford to be blinded by Gould's neurotic illness but needs to develop a clearer and impartial vision of his music genius. Some of the defining features of geniuses are that they are ahead of their time; that they are born and not made; that they are original and unimitable and that their works are eternal. It appears that there are only three geniuses among performing pianists: Artur Schnabel, Sergei Rachmaninov and Glenn Gould.[26] That itself puts Gould in a class of his own of "chosen" piano artists. Having enriched generations of music connoisseurs with novel ideas and music interpretations, Gould deserves to be viewed with more empathy and to be more appropriately appraised despite his personal flaws. Indeed, the posthumous critical evaluation of Gould's place in music is much more realistic than during his lifetime. *Music Magazine*'s evaluation of Gould's place in the history of music reads:

> Glenn Gould, Vladimir Horowitz and Rudolf Serkin, musicians as dissimilar in personal style and artistic sympathy as can be imagined, form the unlikely triumvirate that has come to represent the "golden era of the piano" at CBS (then Columbia) from the 1950's through the mid-1970's.[27]

Gould was a writer, educator, broadcaster, music philosopher, a visionary and a composer at heart. He was an intriguing and charismatic artist who managed to capture the attention of the music and nonmusic world in the second half of the twentieth century. His popularity is ascending. His musicianship, his music recordings and his overall influence in piano music gracefully carries on in the new millennium. Now, in the twenty-first century, when the world is oversupplied with information, experience and celebrities, it is neither easy nor simple to draw such focused attention as Gould was and still is able to do. Gould's personality demanded to be noticed. He was an original without a blueprint; he was inventive without forcing it, and he was able to both amuse and satiate his audiences. His talent saddled him with the heavy burden of fame. His heritage burdened him with a moral armor too tight to bear, which made him rebel much too often, sometimes at his own expense. He was called names—a "concert dropout," an "anti-hero" and an "iconoclast." He was capable of shocking others, of challenging his peers, provoking his elders and fascinating the masses. Gould's personality had a salutary effect on people of all ages across North America, Europe and Asia who heard his music. Glenn Gould is Canada's genius. Geniuses do not belong to a family, to their hometown, not even to their native land. They are cosmopolitan treasures. During his lifetime, this luminous personality demanded to be heard but not seen. Today, we find he convincingly deserves both. He is really finally heard and really seen.

***

Recently, my colleague introduced me to his wife.

"Hi, I understand that you like Glenn Gould?" said I while shaking her hand.

"Who doesn't?" answered she with a broad smile on her face.

ENDNOTES

Chapter 1, Glenn's Radio Debut

1. Letter to Glenn, December 5, 1938, Glenn Gould Archives, Library and Archives Canada.
2. *The Uxbridge Times Journal,* June 9, 1938, Uxbridge Scott Museum.
3. Winifred Johnson, letter to Glenn, December 4, 1938, Glenn Gould Archives, Library and Archives Canada.
4. Barry Johnson, letter to Glenn, December 4, 1938, Glenn Gould Archives, Library and Archives Canada.
5. At Glenn's birth his family still held the name Gold. The change to Gould took place in 1938. This writer will use the name Gold sparingly and only when historically necessary.
6. Bert Gould, "My Son Remembered" 1986, Glenn Gould Archives, Library and Archives Canada.
7. Bettsy Greig, letter to Florence Greig Gould, December 5, 1938, Glenn Gould Archives, Library and Archives Canada.
8. Jean Flett was a maternal aunt of Florence Greig Gould.
9. Margaret Flett, the daughter-in-law of Donald Flett who was a favorite uncle of Glenn's mother, Florence Greig Gould.

Chapter 2, The Forerunners of Fame

1. Havelock Ellis, *Little Essays of Love and Virtue,* [1922], in *Bartlett's Familiar Quotations,* Little, Brown & Co., Boston 1980, p. 689.
2. According to Bert Gould, his wife, Florrie, was born in Port Severn, Ontario. Her Greig relatives are of the opinion that she was born in Mount Forest, Ont.
3. Jessie Greig, conversations with the author, August 8, 1991.
4. Ibid.
5. Pollock, George H., *The Mourning-Liberation Process*, International Universities Press, Madison, 1989, p. 146.
6. Jessie Greig, conversations with the author, August 8, 1991.
7. Ibid.
8. Uxbridge Scott Museum, Willard Greig Papers.
9. Jessie Greig, conversations with the author, August 8, 1991.
10. Betty Greig Madill, interview with the author, August 12, 1993.
11. Benjamin Disraeli, "Reply to a taunt by Daniel O'Connell," in *Bartlett's Familiar Quotations,* Little, Brown and Co., Boston, 1980, p. 501.
12. Russell Herbert Gould, known as Bert Gould, conversations with the author, December 4, 1989.
13. Alfred "Freddy" Gold, obituary, 1887. Uxbridge Scott Museum.
14. Bert Gould, conversations with the author, December 4, 1989.

15. Bert Gould was of the opinion that the fur business, as well as hunting and trapping in Canada, were an integral part of life and making a living. He thought that Glenn had an idealistic view of nature and animals rather than a realistic one. Bert's younger brother, Dr. Grant Gould, thought that Glenn may have been put off by the stories he had heard, though he himself never saw the raw animal fur at his grandfather's house. Apparently, by the 1930's, the shipment of finished fur bypassed Tom's house and was sent directly to his Toronto workshop.
16. John Greig, [Jr.], conversations with the author, December 19, 2000.
17. Obituary of Thomas G. Gould, *Uxbridge Times-Journal*, September 17, 1953. In "Keepers" file, Glenn Gould Archives, Library and Archives Canada.
18. Bert Gould, conversations with the author, November 10, 1990.
19. Ibid.
20. Ibid.
21. Ibid.
22. John Greig [Jr.], conversations with the author, December 19, 2000.
23. Bert Gould, conversations with the author, November 10, 1990.
24. Ibid.
25. Ibid.
26. W.H. Higgins, *The Life and Times of Joseph Gould,* Fitzhenry & Whiteside, Toronto, 1983.
27. Ibid.
28. Uxbridge Scott Museum, documents on the history of Uxbridge.
29. Letter of resignation written by Florence Greig, April 30, 1923, Uxbridge Scott Museum.
30. Anniversary of Uxbridge Bible Class (25), the *Lindsay Daily Post,* June 5, 1932.

Chapter 3, Childhood of a Concert Pianist

1. William Wordsworth, from the poem *My Heart Leaps Up,* cited in John Bartlett, *Familiar Quotations,* Little, Brown and Company, Boston, 1980, p. 425:7. It reads:

    My heart leaps up when I behold A rainbow in the sky:
    So was it when my life began;
    So is it now I am a man;
    So be it when I shall grow old,
    Or let me die!
    The child is father of the man;
    And I could wish my days to be
    Bound each to each by natural piety.

2. Bert Gould, conversation with the author, August 6, 1991.
3. Betty Greig Madill, interview with the author, August 12, 1993.
4. This is an unedited excerpt from Pearl's original letter. Glenn Gould Archives, Library and Archives Canada.
5. "In a recent Canadian study of 6o fetuses it was found in more detail that maturation of human fetal response to vibroacustic stimulation begins at about 26 weeks gestation, increases steadily over a 6-week period, and reaches maturity at about 32 weeks." Kisilevsky, B.S; Muir, D.W.; and Low, J.A., *Maturation of Human Fetal Responses to Vibroacustic Stimulation.* Child Development, 1992, 63, 1497-1508.
6. Satt, B.J., 1984, Ph.D. Dissertation; Hepper, P.G. 1988 quoted in M. C. Busnel at al: "Fetal

Audition," *Annals New York Academy of Science,* 1992; 662: 118-34, p. 126.
7. Elsie Lally Feeney received Glenn's white wicket chair as memorabilia after Glenn's passing.
8. Elsie Lally Feeney, interview with the author, January 22, 1991.
9. Bert Gould, "My Son Remembered" 1986, Glenn Gould Archives, Library and Archives Canada.
10. Betty Greig-Madill, interview with the author, August 12, 1993.
11. Ralph Waldo Emerson, cited in John Bartlett, *Familiar Quotations,* Little, Brown and Company, Boston, 1980, p. 498:25.
12. Donald W.Winnicott: *Playing and Reality,* Routledge, New York, 1989.
13. Erik H. Erikson: *Childhood and Society,* W. W. Norton, New York, 1985.
14. Ibid
15. Margaret Mahler: (1972) "On the first three subphases of the separation individuation process." *International Journal of Psycho-Analysis* 53: 333-338.
16. Ibid.
17. Leon Fleisher, in Elyse Mach's *Great Contemporary Pianists Speak for Themselves,* Dover Publications, New York, 1980, p. 101.
18. Edna Meyers, interview with the author, August 1997.
19. Ibid.
20. Glenn Gould Archives, Library and Archives Canada.
21. Bert Gould, conversations with the author, August 6, 1991.
22. Joseph Roddy, "Apollonian," *The New Yorker* 36, no. 13, May 14, 1960.
23. Bert Gould, "My Son Remembered."
24. Betty Greig Madill, interview with the author, August 12, 1993.
25. Elsie Lally Feeney, interview with the author, January 22, 1991.
26. Bert Gould, conversations with the author, August 6, 1991.
27. After Mr. Gould's passing in January, 1996, this document was in private possession of his wife, Mrs. Vera Dobson Gould. I first saw the document during my four-hour long visit to Mrs. Gould at her home at 61 Norden Crescent, North York, on June 8, 1996.
28. The term stimmung is borrowed from the German language for the lack of an appropriate word in English. It designates the particular optimal mood or atmosphere within and/or around the person.
29. D. W. Winnicott: *Playing and Reality.*
30. Robert Fulford, interview with the author, August 10, 1989.
31. Robert Fulford: *Best Seat in the House*, Collins Toronto, 1988.
32. Robert Fulford, interview with the author, August 10, 1989.
33. James Friskin and Irwin Freundlich: *Music for the Piano,* Dover Publications, New York, 1973, p. 146.
34. Ibid. p. 84.
35. Glenn Gould Archives, Library and Archives Canada.
36. Vincent Tovell, *At Home with Glenn Gould,* (disc), CBC, 1959.
37. Jock Carroll, *Weekend Magazine* 6, No. 27, July 7, 1956.
38. *Piano Quarterly*, Winter 1977-78.
39. Glenn Gould Archives, Library and Archives Canada.
40. Ralph Waldo Emerson, cited in John Bartlett, *Familiar Quotations,* Little, Brown and Company, Boston, 1980, p. 498:15.
41. Glenn Gould Archives, Library and Archives Canada.

42. Elsie Lally Feeney, interview with the author, January 1991.
43. Ibid.
44. Edna Meyers, interview with the author, August 8, 1997.
45. Dennis Braithwaite, "Glenn Gould," *Toronto Daily Star,* March 28, 1959.
46. John Greig, interview with the author, December 19, 2000.
47. Bert Gould, conversations with the author, February 22, 1992.
48. Betty Greig Madill, interview with the author, August 12, 1993.
49. Ibid.
50. R. Murray Schafer, interview with the author, July 18, 1991.
51. Ezra Shabas: *Sir Ernest MacMillan: The Importance of being Canadian.* University of Toronto Press, 1994. In addition to being knighted, Sir Ernest was awarded by Queen Elizabeth II a companionship in the Order of Canada in 1959. Gould, as the most accomplished and the most famous Canadian musician was never awarded such an honor.
52. Exclamation of the Roman Emperor Julius Caesar, when he made the decision to cross the river Rubicon. It means literally, "The die is cast," i. e., to make a bold and irreversible decision.
53. John Beckwith, "Alberto Guerrero, 1886-1959," *Canadian Music Journal* 4, No. 2, Winter 1960.
54. Bert Gould, conversations with the author, February 22, 1992.
55. Glenn Gould Archives, Library and Archives Canada.
56. Ibid.

Chapter 4, The Growing Pains of Adolescence

1. George Eliot, *The Mill on the Floss,* (1860), cited in *The Beacon Book of Famous Quotations by Women,* compiled by Rosalie Maggio, Beacon Press, Boston, 1992, p. 221.
2. Glenn Gould Archives, Library and Archives Canada.
3. Doris Fisher, nee Townsend, letter to Mr. Bert Gould, October 28, 1992, personal Gouldiana Collection.
4. Bernard Asbell, "Glenn Gould," *Horizon*, No. 3, January 1962.
5. Ibid.
6. *The Globe and Mail,* September 13, 1944, Glenn Gould Archives, Keepers' File, Library and Archives Canada.
7. Dr. Grant Gould, interview with the author, New Port, California, August 2, 1992.
8. Betty Greig Madill, interview with the author, August 12, 1993.
9. Jessie Greig, conversations with the author, August 8, 1991.
10. Erik H. Erikson, *Childhood and Society,* 35th Anniversary Edition, W. W. Norton, New York, 1985. p. 262.
11. Glenn Gould Archives, Library and Archives Canada.
12. Joseph Mazurkiewicz, interview with the author, September 26, 1989. Mazurkiewicz, a contemporary of Gould, ex-student of Malvern and a long-time neighbour and observer of that school, provided a useful description of the school dynamics in the late 1940's.
13. Ibid.
14. Glenn Gould Archives, Library and Archives Canada.
15. Bert Gould, reminiscing on Alberto Guerrero, interview with the author, June 11, 1994.
16. Lilly Mech, "Glenn Gould: memories linger like music," *The Medical Post,* April 13, 1993.
17. R. Murray Schafer, interview with the author, July 18, 1991, Stouffer Plaza Hotel, Rochester, New York.

18. William Aide, interview in *"A Scattering of the Seeds: The Music Teacher."* Canadian Television Documentary about Glenn Gould's piano teacher, Alberto Guerrero. Produced by Patricia Fogliato. White Pine Pictures, episode 46.
19. Gould finished the piano requirements at the age of 12, but completed music theory a little later which then qualified him for the ATCM.
20. Harold C. Schonberg, *The Great Pianists,* Simon & Schuster, New York, 1987.
21. Glenn Gould, "His Country's 'Most Experienced Hermit' Chooses a Desert-Island Discography" *High Fidelity Magazine,* June 1970.
22. Ibid.
23. Ibid.
24. Edward W. Wodson, *Daily Telegram,* May 9, 1946.
25. Augustus Bridle, *The Toronto Daily Star,* May 9, 1946.
26. Allen Sangster, *Globe & Mail,* May 10, 1946.
27. Glenn Gould, "His Country's 'Most Experienced Hermit.'"
28. Ettore Mazzoleni, letter to Glenn Gould, July 27, 1946. Glenn Gould Archives, Library and Archives Canada.
29. Alberto Guerrero, letter to Glenn Gould, August 26, 1946. Glenn Gould Archives, Library and Archives Canada.
30. Mrs. Samuel Jeffrey, fascinated by the news of Gould's success, wrote on her own initiative about him to the Queen Elizabeth, wife of King George VI.
31. Walter Homburger, Glenn Gould Archives, Library and Archives Canada.
32. Glenn Gould stated that Walter Homburger first heard him at the Kiwanis Festival in 1947.
33. Jock Carroll, *Weekend Magazine*, No. 27, July 7, 1956.
34. Peter Blos, The Second Individuation Process of Adolescence, *Psychoanalytic Study of the Child,* 22:162, 1967. Ed. Ruth S. Eissler.
35. Ibid.
36. Ibid.
37. Anna Freud, Adolescence, *Psychoanalytic Study of the Child,* 13: 255, 1958. Ed. Ruth S. Eissler.
38. Bernard Asbell, "Glenn Gould" *Horizon,* No. 3, January 1962.
39. Pearl McCarthy, *Globe and Mail,* January 16, 1947.
40. Ibid.
41. Glenn Gould, Memoirs for CBC Tuesday Night, (Notes by G. Gould regarding his association with the Toronto Symphony Orchestra), aired in 1968, Glenn Gould Archives, Library and Archives Canada.
42. The Latin expression, literally meaning: "not a day without a line."
43. Anna Freud, Adolescence.
44. Ibid.
45. Robert Fulford, 9 Bugle, Glenn Gould Archives, Library and Archives Canada.
46. Ibid.
47. Jessie Greig, interview with the author, August 8, 1991.
48. Dr. Grant Gould, interview with the author, New Port, California, August 2, 1992.
49. Glenn's essay, Glenn Gould Archives, Library and Archives Canada.
50. Harriet Ingham, letter to Glenn Gould, March 12, 1956, Glenn Gould Archives, Library and Archives Canada.

Chapter 5, Inroads to Fame

1. Henry Wadsworth Longfellow, cited in John Bartlett's *Familiar Quotations*, Little, Brown and Company, Boston, 1980, p. 511 #23.
2. E. W. Wodson, *The Toronto Telegram,* January 15, 1947.
3. Robert Fulford, interview with the author, August 10, 1989.
4. Robert Silverman, interview with Claudio Arrau, *The Piano Quarterly,* 31st year, winter 1982-83, No. 120, p. 30.
5. Aaron Copland/Vivian Perlis, *Copland: 1900 Through 1942,* St. Martin's/ Marek, New York 1984, p. 68.
6. Mitsuko Uchida, quoted in "Mozart Pianist Extraordinaire" by Maureen Lennon, *Music Magazine,* June 1989, p. 18.
7. Bert Gould, interview with the author, June 11, 1994.
8. William S. Newman, *The Pianist's Problems,* Da Capo Press, 1984, p. 94.
9. Glenn Gould Archives, Library and Archives Canada.
10. William Newman, *The Pianist's Problems,* p. 43.
11. Ibid. p. 41.
12. Charles Rosen, "On Playing the Piano," *The New York Review of Books,* October 1999, p. 49.
13. Ibid.
14. John Beckwith, "Shattering a Few Myths" in *Glenn Gould: Variations By Himself and His Friends,* Edited by John McGreevy, Toronto, Doubleday 1983, p. 69.
15. Glenn Gould in conversation with Jim Aikin, *The Art of Glenn Gould*, edited by John P. L. Roberts, Malcolm Lester Books, 1999, p. 262.
16. William Aide, "Fact and Freudian Fable," *The Idler* (Summer 1993), p. 59.
17. Tim Page, ed. *The Glenn Gould Reader,* Lester & Orpen Dennys, 1984, in "Of Mozart and Related Matters: Glenn Gould in Conversation with Bruno Monsaingeon," p. 32.
18. Anton Kuerti, interview with the author, May 20, 1991.
19. Glenn Gould, interview with John McClure, "Glenn Gould: Concert Drop-Out" *The Glenn Gould Legacy,* Vol. I, Disc 3, M3K 79358, CBS Records Inc. 1988.
20. Mitsuko Uchida, quoted in "Mozart Pianist Extraordinaire" by Maureen Lennon, *Music Magazine,* June 1989, p.18.
21. Bert Gould, telegram to Glenn Gould, October 29, 1951, Glenn Gould Archives, Library and Archives Canada.
22. Jessie Greig, telegram to Glenn Gould, October 29, 1951,Glenn Gould Archives, Library and Archives Canada.
23. Bert Gould, conversations with the author, January 26, 1994.
24. Glenn Gould, "Schnabelian authenticity" in "His Country 'Most Experienced Hermit.' "
25. Agreement between G. Gould and W. Homburger, April 1st, 1951, Glenn Gould Archives, National Library of Canada.
26. Bert Gould, conversations with the author, January 26, 1994.
27. Anton Kuerti, interview with the author, May 20, 1991.
28. Eric McLean, *The Montreal Star,* undated clipping, Glenn Gould Archives, National Library of Canada.
29. Glenn Gould's poem about Ernst Krenek, quoted by John Beckwith in *Glenn Gould: Variations by Himself and His Friends,* Edited by John McGreevy. Toronto: Doubleday, 1983.

Chapter 6, Glenn Gould Makes Music

1. Paul Hume, *The Washington Post,* January 3, 1955, Glenn Gould Archives, Library and Archives Canada.
2. *Musical Courier,* undated clipping, Glenn Gould Archives, Library and Archives Canada.
3. Paul Hume, *The Washington Post,* January 3, 1955, Glenn Gould Archives, Library and Archives Canada.
4. Telegram to Glenn Gould from his friends, Irene and Baily Bird, January 11, 1955, Glenn Gould Archives, Library and Archives Canada.
5. Telegram to Glenn Gould from his friends, Bernice and Val Hoffinger, Glenn Gould Archives, Library and Archives Canada.
6. Telegram to Glenn Gould, from Lois Marshall and Weldon Kilburn. Marshall was a distinguished Canadian soprano who collaborated with Gould. Kilburn was her voice teacher and accompanist-pianist.
7. Martin Canin, "Looking Back," *The Piano Quarterly,* 31st Year, Winter 1982-83/No. 120. p. 8.
8. John Briggs, *The New York Times,* January 12, 1955.
9. Glenn Gould, Liner Notes to his first recording of the *Goldberg Variations* Columbia, MS 7096.
10. Robert Fulford, letter to Gould and clipping from *The Atlantic,* March 1956, Glenn Gould Archives, Library and Archives Canada.
11. Harold Schonberg, *The New York Times,* undated clipping, Glenn Gould Archives, Library and Archives Canada.
12. The term "counterpoint" is derived from the Latin *punctus contra punctum,* which means "note against note."
13. Jim Curtis, excerpts from his private journal, courtesy J. Curtis.
14. Ibid.
15. Ibid.
16. Philip Spitta, *Johann Sebastian Bach.* New York: Dover Publications, 1951. p. 55-58.
17. Ibid.
18. Ibid
19. *The Herald Tribune,* undated clipping. Glenn Gould Archives, Library and Archives Canada.
20. *The Musical Courier,* undated clipping, Glenn Gould Archives, Library and Archives of Canada.
21. *The Detroit News,* undated clipping. Glenn Gould Archives, Library and Archives Canada.
22. Isai Braudo, report from Leningrad, *The Toronto Telegram,* May 25, 1957, Glenn Gould Archives, Library and Archives Canada.
23. Glenn Gould gave over 300 public concerts and recitals. The three most productive years were: 1957 with 37 performances, 1958 with 37 and 1959 with 52 public performances.
24. Dr. Peter Ostwald, interview with the author in San Francisco, June 8, 1991.
25. Elena Grosheva, report from Moscow, *The Toronto Telegram,* May 25, 1957.
26. Yuri Bryushkov, report from Leningrad, *The Toronto Telegram*, May 25, 1957.
27. Russian words: harasho = good; eshcho = more.
28. Pavel Serebryakov, report from Leningrad, *The Toronto Telegram,* May 25, 1957.
29. Walter Homburger, report from Moscow, *The Toronto Daily Star,* May 9, 1957.
30. Glenn Gould, letter to Yousuf Karsh, July 8, 1958, in *Glenn Gould: Selected Letters,* edited by John P.L.Roberts and Ghyslaine Guertin. Toronto: Oxford University Press, 1992, p. 13. Karsh, the

famous international photographer residing in Ottawa, sent to Gould a list of questions pertaining to his tour in the Soviet Union which Gould duly answered.

31. Glenn Gould, broadcast commentary on Sviatoslav Richter, *Glenn Gould,* Vol. 1, Fall 1995, p. 12.
32. Russian words: spasibo = thank you; Gospodin = Mister; ne zabudte nas = don't forget us; dosvidanya = good bye.
33. Isai Braudo, report from Leningrad, *The Toronto Telegram,* May 25, 1957.
34. Walter Homburger, Newsletter 1958, press releases, Glenn Gould Archives, Library and Archives Canada.
35. H. H. Stuckenschmidt, cited in W. Homburger's Newsletter 1958. Glenn Gould Archives, Library and Archives Canada.
36. Harold C. Schonberg, *The Great Pianists.* New York: Simon & Schuster, 1987. p. 367.
37. Glenn Gould, letter to his parents from Wien, June 3, 1957, *Glenn Gould: Selected Letters,* p. 6.
38. Ibid.
39. Bert Gould, conversations with the author, January 26, 1994.
40. Glenn Gould, letter to his parents from Vienna.
41. Walter Homburger, Newsletter 1958, press releases, Glenn Gould Archives, Library and Archives Canada.
42. Glenn Gould, report from the press conference, *The Toronto Daily Star,* 1958.
43. *The Pittsburgh Post-Gazette,* cited in W. Homburger's Newsletter 1958, press releases, Glenn Gould Archives, Library and Archives Canada.
44. Raymond Kendall, *The Los Angeles Mirror,*cited in W. Homburger's Newsletter 1958, press releases, Glenn Gould Archives, Library and Archives Canada.
45. My friend, Amy Sum, nee Wong, pianist and piano teacher, helped in applying the concept of "demonic" force from within, which refers to an extraordinary or supernatural talent, seen only in very gifted musicians.
46. New York *Herald-Tribune,* cited in W. Homburger's Newsletter 1958, press releases, Glenn Gould Archives, Library and Archives Canada.
47. Harold Schonberg, *The New York Times,* cited in W. Homburger's Newsletter 1958, press releases, Glenn Gould Archives, Library and Archives Canada.
48. Harold Schonberg, cited in W. Homburger's Newsletter 1958, press releases, Glenn Gould Archives, Library and Archives Canada.
49. Irving Lowens, *The Evening Star,* cited in W. Homburger's Newsletter 1958, press releases, Glenn Gould Archives, Library and Archives Canada.
50. Jim Curtis, excerpts from his private journal, courtesy J. Curtis.
51. George Kidd, *The Toronto Telegram,* July 24, 1958.
52. Glenn Gould, letter to Richard O'Hagan, August 29, 1958, Glenn Gould Archives, Library and Archives Canada.
53. *The Toronto Daily Star,* report from Belgium, undated clipping, personal Gouldiana Collection.
54. Dennis Braitwaithe, *The Toronto Daily Star,* interview with Gould, March 28, 1959.
55. *Maclean's Magazine*, Montreal, November 8, 1958.
56. Glenn Gould, letter to C.W. Fitzgerald, September 20, 1957, *Glenn Gould: Selected Letters,* p. 11.
57. Silvia Kind, in Liner Notes for *Glenn Gould: Broadcast Recital, December 1968.* Gibbons, Haydn, Hindemith. CD 652; Music & Arts. Berkeley, Cal.
58. Silvia Kind, interview with the author in Groningen, Holland, October 6,1992.

59. Glenn Gould, letter from Berlin to Walter Homburger, October [?] 1958, Glenn Gould Archives, Library and Archives Canada. Wolfgang Kollitsch, a renowned impresario who had arranged Gould's concerts in Germany.
60. Ibid.
61. Glenn Gould, postcard from Berlin to his grandmother, Alma Gould, September 25, 1958. Glenn Gould Archives, Library and Archives Canada.
62. Walter Homburger, Newsletter 1960, press releases, Glenn Gould Archives, Library and Archives Canada.
63. Glenn Gould, letter to his grandmother from Hamburg, October 27, 1958, Glenn Gould Archives, Library and Archives Canada.
64. Glenn Gould, letter to Winston Fitzgerald, December 27, 1956, Glenn Gould Archives, Library and Archives Canada.
65. Glenn Gould, letter to Winston Fitzgerald, September 20, 1957, Glenn Gould Archives, Library and Archives Canada.
66. Glenn Gould, letter to Graham, July 8, 1958, Glenn Gould Archives, Library and Archives Canada.
67. Ibid.
68. Glenn Gould, letter from Stockholm to Walter Homburger, October 2, 1958. Glenn Gould Archives, Library and Archives Canada.
69. Glenn Gould, letter from Cologne to Walter Homburger, October 24, 1958. Glenn Gould Archives, Library and Archives Canada.
70. Glenn Gould, letter to Walter Homburger from Berlin, October 27, 1958, Glenn Gould Archives, Library and Archives Canada.
71. Ibid.
72. Glenn Gould, letter from Berlin to his grandmother, October 27, 1958. Glenn Gould Archives, Library and Archives Canada.
73. Peter Goodrich, Steinway & Sons, Vice President, worldwide concert and artist activities.
74. Peter Goodrich, interview with the author, in New York, November 1995.
75. Glenn Gould, letter to Walter Homburger from Hamburg, October 18, 1958, *Glenn Gould: Selected Letters,* p. 18.
76. "This decrease of concerts... caused by depressive disorder." Keep in mind that in 1958, biochemical depression was an untreatable condition, with the exception of electroconvulsive therapy (ECT), which was quite unrefined at that time as a procedure. Antidepressant medications were just discovered. Hence, Gould had no true recourse for his mood disorder. Psychotherapy was available to him but he never engaged in it. A steady and prolonged trial of psychotherapy would have helped him for his underlying personality problems and in coping better with his depression.
77. Glenn Gould, letter to Edward Viets, September 9, 1958, Glenn Gould Archives, Library and Archives Canada.
78. Glenn Gould, letter to Benjamin Sonnenberg, January 30, 1959, Glenn Gould Collection, Library and Archives Canada.
79. Walter Homburger, Newsletter 1958, press release from *Haaretz,* Israel, Glenn Gould Archives, Library and Archives Canada.
80. Jonathan Cott, *Conversations with Glenn Gould*, Little, Brown and Company, 1984.
81. Imagery became popular as a psychological treatment technique in the 1980's. One purpose is to, by evoking strong images, bring out repressed emotions and memories in the client.

82. Walter Homburger, Newsletter 1958, press release from *Haaretz*, Glenn Gould Archives, Library and Archives Canada.
83. Artur Minden, report from Tel Aviv, December 2, 1958, clipping, personal Gouldiana Collection.
84. Walter Homburger, report from Jerusalem, *The Toronto Daily Star,* December 6, 1958.
85. Walter Homburger, Newsletter 1958, press release from *Haaretz,* Glenn Gould Archives, Library and Archives Canada.
86. Glenn Gould, letter to Richard O'Hagan, January 30, 1959, Glenn Gould Archives, Library and Archives Canada.
87. Alfred Frankenstein, *The San Francisco Chronicle,* cited in W. Homburger's Newsletter 1959, Glenn Gould Archives, Library and Archives Canada.
88. Silvia Kind, in Liner Notes, for *Glenn Gould: Broadcast Recital, December 1968.* Gibbons, Haydn, Hindemith, CD 652: Music & Arts. Berkeley,Ca.
89. Walter Homburger, Newsletter 1956, press release from *The London Telegraph,* Glenn Gould Archives, Library and Archives Canada.
90. Walter Homburger, Newsletter, 1959, press release from *London Times*. Glenn Gould Archives, Library and Archives Canada.
91. Glenn Gould, letter to Gladys Riskind, June 30, 1959. *Glenn Gould: Selected Letters,* p. 20.
92. Silvia Kind, in Liner notes, for *Glenn Gould: Broadcast Recital, December 1968.* Gibbons, Haydn, Hindemith, CD 652: Music & Arts. Berkeley, Ca.
93. Walter Homburger, Newsletter 1959, Glenn Gould Archives, Library and Archives Canada.
94. Ibid.
95. Kent Bellows, *The Baltimore Evening Star,* cited in W. Homburger's Newsletter 1959, press release, Glenn Gould Archives, Library and Archives Canada.
96. Harold C. Schonberg: *The Great Pianists.* New York: Simon & Schuster, 1987. p. 420.
97. Josef Mossman, *The Detroit News,* cited in W. Homburger's, Newsletter 1960, Glenn Gould Archives, Library and Archives Canada.
98. Glenn Gould, Artist Series, concert program notes, November 15, 1960, Glenn Gould Archives, Library and Archives Canada.
99. Ibid.
100. John Beckwith, *The Toronto Daily Star,* December 7, 1960.

Chapter 7, The Inner World

1. Bette Davis, *The Lonely Life* (1962), cited in *The Beacon Book of Quotations by Women,* compiled by Rosalie Maggio, Beacon Press, Boston, 1992, p. 238.
2. Glenn Gould, poem, cited in *Glenn Gould: Selected Letters,* Edited by J.P.L. Roberts and Ghyslaine Guertin, Oxford University Press, Toronto, 1992, p. 1.
3. Grandiose self is a technical term first used by Heinz Kohut in *The Analysis of the Self,* International Universities Press, New York, 1971. Otto Kernberg used the same term differently. He referred to it as a self-representation that is associated with excessive self-absorption, intense ambition, the wish to be unsurpassed in power, beauty and brilliance.
4. Otto Kernberg, cited in "Overview: Narcissistic Personality Disorder" by Salman Akhtar, M.D. and Anderson Thomson, Jr., M.D. *American J. Psychiatry,* 139:1, January 1982, p. 14.
5. Otto Kernberg, *Internal World and External Reality,* Jason Aronson, London, p. 136. The full sentence is: "The patlological grandiose self does not charge the battery, so to speak, of internal

object representations and internalized value systems."
6. Sigmund Freud, *The Interpretations of Dreams,* 1900, Penguin Books, London, 1988, p. 362-66.
7. Sigmund Freud, *Introductory Lectures on Psychoanalysis,* [1916-17], Penguin Books, 1986, p. 375.
8. Arnold Rothstein, "Oedipal Conflicts in Narcissistic Personality Disorders, *Int. J. Psycho-Anal.* 1979, 60, p. 189.
9. Robert Fulford, interview with the author, August 10, 1989.
10. Arnold Rothstein, *The Narcissistic Pursuit of Perfection,* International Universities Press, New York, 1984, p. 45.
11. Ibid.
12. Edmund Bergler, *Principles of Self-Damage,* International Universities Press, Madison, Connecticut, 1992, p. 247.
13. Hans Selye, cited in *Anxiety and Musical Performance: On Playing the Piano From Memory,* by Dale Reubart, De Capo Press, New York, 1984, p. 141.
14. Jessie Greig, conversations with the author, August 8, 1991.
15. Elsie Feeney Lally, interview with the author, January, 22, 1991.
16. Andrew Kazdin, *Glenn Gould at Work: Creative Lying,* E.P.Dutton, New York, 1989, p. 84-5.
17. Ibid.
18. Glenn Gould, "Stokovski in Six Scenes," reprinted in *The Glenn Gould Reader,* Edited by Tim Page, Lester & Orpen Dennys, 1984, p. 261-2.
19. Ibid.
20. Pierre Burton, interview with Glenn Gould, winter, 1961.
21. Joyce McDougall, *Theaters of the Body: A Psychoanalytic Approach to Psychosomatic Illness,* W. W. Norton & Company, New York, 1989, p. 15.
22. Abraham Lincoln, cited in *The Living Webster:Encyclopedic Dictionary of the English Language,* The English Language Institute of America, Chicago, 1973, Popular Quotations, p. BT 65.
23. Glenn Gould, Liner Notes for Edvard Grieg's *Sonata in E Minor, Op. 7,* The Glenn Gould Legacy, Vol. 3, Disc 2, M3K 42107, produced by Andrew Kazdin, recorded Eaton Auditorium, Toronto, 1971, manufactured CBS/ Sony Inc. in Japan, 1986.
24. Glenn Gould, letter to Carl Little, June 5, 1971, in *Glenn Gould: Selected Letters,* p. 147.
25. Bernard Asbell, "Glenn Gould: An interview," *Horizon* 4, January 1962, p. 91.
26. Glenn Gould, letter to Carl Little, June 5, 1971, in *Glenn Gould: Selected Letters,* p. 147.
27. Andrew Kazdin, *Glenn Gould at Work,* p. 128.
28. Glenn Gould, Edvard Grieg, *Sonata in E Minor, Op. 7.*
29. Maria Callas (1981), cited in *The Beacon Book of Quotations by Women,* compiled by Rosalie Maggio, Beacon Press, Boston, 1992, p. 223.
30. Glenn Gould, Letter to Marjorie Agnew, November 6, 1956, Glenn Gould Archives, Library and Archives Canada.
31. Glenn Gould, letter to his uncle, Dr. Grant Gould, November 22, 1956, Glenn Gould Archives, Library and Archives Canada.
32. Joseph Roddy, "Apollonian" in *Glenn Gould: Variations By Himself and His Friends,* J. McGreevy, ed. 1983, p. 117.
33. Ibid.
34. Robert Silverman, conversations with the author, November 6, 1995.
35. Glen Gabbard, "Stage Fright,"*International Journal of Psycho-Analysis,* (1979) 60, p. 385.

36. Ibid.
37. Glenn Gould, "Let's Ban Applause," reprinted in *The Glenn Gould Reader,* Edited by Tim Page, Lester & Orpen Dennys, 1984, p. 246.
38. Ibid. GRAADAK, p. 248.
39. Ibid.
40. Ibid.
41. Eric McLean, *The Montreal Star,* July 1962.
42. Ibid.

Chapter 8, Gould as a Young Man

1. Rudyard Kipling, from the poem "If" in "One Hundred and One Famous Poems," compiled by Roy J. Cook, Contemporary Books, Chicago, 1958, p. 108.
2. Calvin A. Colarusso, "The Third Individuation: The Effect of Biological Parenthood on Separation-Individuation Processes in Adulthood" *Psychoanalytic Study of the Child*; 1990, Vol. 45, 179-194.
3. Ibid.
4. "Keepers file" - The Uxbridge Times - Journal, September 17, 1953, Glenn Gould Archives, Library and Archives Canada.
5. Vera Dobson Gould, interview with the author, March 8, 1997, at Central Park Lodge, Toronto.
6. Bert Gould, conversations with the author, August 6, 1991.
7. New Standard Encyclopaedia, Standard Educational Corporation, Chicago, Illinois, 1974, Vol. 3, p. C-224.
8. My friend and Gould's fan, Ada Hefter, personally interviewed on my behalf the Swiss photographer, Mr. Hofman, who had taken a picture of Gould in front of the painting of Charles I. The interview took place in Lucerne in 1997/98. Though Mr. Hofman was aware of Gould as a famous Canadian musician, he did not know it at the time of taking a photo of him. It follows that Gould presented himself anonymously.
9. Bert Gould, conversations with the author, August 6, 1991.
10. Subsequent investigation pursued in Lucerne in 1997/98 by Ada Hefter, was not able to prove the existence of the painting of Charles I in the local museum. It is possible that at the time of Gould's visit to Lucerne, the painting of Charles I was temporarily on special loan from another museum.
11. Calvin A. Colarusso, "The Third Individuation."
12. John Greig [Jr], interview with author, December 18, 2000, in Uxbridge, Ont.
13. George H. Pollock: "Mourning and Memorialization Through Music," *The Annual of Psychoanalysis,* 3:423-436 (1975) reprinted in *The Mourning - Liberation Process,* 1989, International Universities Press, Madison. Volume II, p. 482.
14. George H. Pollock: "Mourning Through Music: Gustav Mahler" in *The Mourning - Liberation Process,* Volume II, p. 662.
15. Glenn Gould, "It's Op. 2 that counts!" cited in "Gould's String Quartet, Op. 1." Liner Notes from Columbia MS 6178, 1960, reprinted in *The Glenn Gould Reader,* ed. Tim Page, Lester & Orpen Dennys, 1984, p. 234.
16. Ibid.
17. Glenn Gould, letter to Otto Joachim, [c. 1955], reprinted in *Glenn Gould: Selected Letters,* p. 2.
18. Otto Friedrich, cited in *Glenn Gould: A Life and Variations,* p. 164.

19. Walter Kaufman, letter to Gould, July 10, 1956, Glenn Gould Archives, Library and Archives Canada.
20. Otto Friedrich, cited in *Glenn Gould: A Life And Variations,* p. 164.
21. Glenn Gould, letter to David Diamond, February 23, 1959, Glenn Gould Archives, Library and Archives Canada.
22. Glenn Gould, letter to Lucas Foss, June 30, 1959, Glenn Gould Archives, Library and Archives Canada.
23. Irvin Colodin, *The Saturday Review,* cited in Otto Friedrich, *Glenn Gould: A Life and Variations,* p. 165.
24. Eric McLean, *The Montreal Star,* cited in Otto Friedrich, *Glenn Gould: A Life and Variations,* p. 166.
25. "At Home with Glenn Gould," Gould in Conversation with Vincent Tovell, in *The Art of Glenn Gould: Reflections of a Musical Genius,* ed. by John P. L. Roberts, Malcolm Lester Books, 1999, p. 83.
26. Victor DiBello, conversations with the author, May 30, 1996.
27. CBC *Times,* June 1961, personal Gouldiana Collection.
28. Jim Curtis, excerpts from his personal journal, courtesy J. Curtis.
29. Jessie Greig, letter to Glenn Gould, Glenn Gould Archives, Library and Archives Canada.
30. Ibid.
31. In the Library and Archives Canada there are 2,030 letters written by Gould and 2,798 letters written to him.
32. Norman Brenan, letter to Glenn Gould, April 15, 1956, Glenn Gould Archives, Library and Archives Canada.
33. Jock Carroll, *Glenn Gould: Some Portraits of the Artist as a Young Man,* Stoddart, 1995, p. 10.
34. Ibid. p. 16.
35. Jim Curtis, excerpts from his personal journal, courtesy J. Curtis.
36. Henry Wadsworth Longfellow, *Hyperion [1839],* in *Bartlett's Familiar Quotations* by John Bartlett, Little Brown & Company, Boston/Toronto, 1980, p. 510.
37. Dr. Tom Johnson, Barry's younger brother, interview with the author, May 29, 1994.
38. Ibid.
39. Bert Gould, conversations with the author, January 26, 1994.
40. Joseph Hofmann, 1976, p. 66
41. Holmes, T.H. and Rahe, R.H., "The Social Readjustment Scale" *J. Psychosomatic Res.* 11:213-218, 1967.
42. Ibid.
43. *Glenn Gould: Selected Letters,* John P.L Roberts and Ghyslaine Guertin, Eds. 1992, Oxford University Press, Toronto, p. 27.
44. Ibid.
45. Ibid.
46. Ibid.
47. Ibid.
48. Ibid.
49. Otto Friedrich, *Glenn Gould: A Life and Variations,* Lester & Orpen Dennys Ltd. Toronto, 1989, p. 87.
50. Ibid.

51. William Shakespeare: *Hamlet,* 1963, Academic Press Canada, p. 241-243.
52. Sigmund Freud: *The Interpretation of Dreams*, 1900, Penguin Books, London 1988, p. 368.
53. George Santayana: *The Last Puritan,* 1936, Charles Scribner's Sons, New York.
54. Ibid.

Chapter 9, The Goldberg Variations

1. Ralph Waldo Emerson, cited in John Bartlett, *Familiar Quotations,* Little, Brown and Company, Boston, 1982, p. 495:17.
2. Glenn Gould, "The Universality of Bach" in *The Art of Glenn Gould,* edited by John P. L. Roberts, Malcolm Lester Books, 1999, p. 91.
3. Walter Piston, author of "Counterpoint," *The Encyclopedia Americana,* Grolier Inc. Danbury, Connecticut, Vol. 8, 1999.
4. Charles Sanford Terry, *The Music of Bach: An Introduction,* Dover Publication Inc. New York, 1963, p. 6.
5. Ibid. p. 5.
6. R. L. Marshall, *The Music of Johann Sebastian Bach:The Sources, The Style, The Significance,* Schrimer Books, New York, 1989, p. 46.
7. Nicolas Forkel, quoted in Christoph Wolff's, *Bach:Essays on His Life and Music,* Harvard University Press, Cambridge, Massachusetts, 1991, p. 212.
8. Christoph Wolff, *Bach:Essays on His Life and Music,* Harvard University Press, Cambridge, Massachusetts, 1991, p. 212.
9. Ibid. p. 212.
10. Ibid. p. 213.
11. Ibid. p. 213.
12. Glenn Gould, letter to William Glenesk, in *Glenn Gould: Selected Letters,* Oxford University Press, 1992, p. 34.
13. Ibid.
14. Silvia Kind, 1990 Liner Notes for Glenn Gould Broadcast Recital in December 1968,(Gibbons, Haydn, Hindemith Program), Music & Arts Programs of America, Inc. CD 659.
15. Malcolm Boyd, *The Master Musicians:Bach,* J. M. Dent & Sons Ltd, London.
16. Harold C. Schonberg, *The Great Pianists,* Simon & Schuster Inc. New York, 1987, p. 475.
17. This poem is from the book titled *Happy Hour.* The author and publisher are unknown. Glenn Gould Archives, Library and Archives Canada.
18. George Kidd, *The Toronto Telegram,* July 23, 1958.
19. Robert L. Marshall, *The Music of Johann Sebastian Bach:The Sources, The Style, The Significance,* Schrimer Books, New York, 1989, p. 46.
20. Thomas Archer, "The Gould Conquest" *The Montreal Gazette*, March 23, 1958.
21. George Kidd, *The Toronto Telegram,* July 23, 1958.
22. Walter Homburger, *The Toronto Star,* May 9, 1957.
23. Walter Homburger, "Press Book for Glenn Gould," August, 1961, quotation from *Pravda,* Russia.
24. Walter Homburger, *The Toronto Star,* May 9, 1957.
25. William F. Buckley Jr., "Goldberg Divined," *Esquire,* March 1986.
26. John Keats, cited in John Bartlett, *Familiar Quotations,* Little, Brown and Company, Boston, 1982, p. 476:10.

27. Glenn Gould, Liner Notes for Gould's first recording of the *Goldberg Variations,* Columbia ML 5060, 1956, reprinted in *The Glenn Gould Reader,* edited by Tim Page, Lester & Opren Dennys, 1984, pp. 22 - 28.
28. Ibid.
29. Anthony Newman, *Bach and the Baroque,* Pendragon Press, New York, 1985, p. 171.
30. Glenn Gould, Liner Notes for Gould's first recording of the *Goldberg Variations.*
31. Ibid.

Chapter 10, The Ceremony of Performance

1. Louis Biancolli, *New York World Telegram and Sun,* March, 1960.
2. Concert Program, Glenn Gould Archives, Library and Archives Canada.
3. Sigmund Freud (1916-17 [1915-1917]) *Introductory Lectures on Psychoanalysis.* Pelican Books, 1976. p. 304.
4. Ibid.
5. Ibid.
6. Robert Moore, a Toronto piano tuner who had worked for Gould, informed me that Gould sat only twelve and a half inches off the floor. Moore stated that a person standing behind the narrow end of the piano would not be able to see Gould's head, as he was crouched down behind the keyboard.
7. Joseph Roddy, in *Glenn Gould: Variations. By Himself and His Friends,* J. McGreevy, ed. 1983, p. 104.
8. John Lee Roberts, cited in McGreevy, p. 233.
9. Phylis Greenacre, "The Childhood of the Artist: Libidinal Phase of Development and Giftedness. *The Psychoanalytic Study of the Child,* 12: 47-72. New York, International Universities Press, 1957.
10. Robert Fulford, cited in McGreevy, p. 57.
11. Bert Gould, conversations with the author, August 6, 1991.
12. Bernard Asbel, "Glenn Gould," Horizon 4, mo. 3. 1962.
13. George Santayana, *The Last Puritan,* New York, Charles Scribner's Sons, 1963.
14. Robert Walker, Glenn Gould Archives, Library and Archives Canada.
15. Richard Kostelanetz, cited in McGreevy, p. 134.
16. Joseph Roddy, cited in McGreevy, p. 104.
17. Pyrrhic Victory - a victory gained at too great a cost, like that of Pyrrhus, king of Epirus over the Romans in 279 BC.
18. George H. Pollock, "On symbiosis and symbiotic neurosis" Int. J. Psycho-Anal., 1964, p. 45.
19. Andrew Kazdin, *Glenn Gould at Work: Creative Lying,* New York: E. P. Dutton, 1989, p. 107.
20. Richard Kostelanetz, cited in McGreevy, p. 130.
21. Walter Homburger, letter to New Market, Glenn Gould Archives, Library and Archives Canada.
22. Andrew Kazdin, *Glenn Gould at Work,* p. 107.
23. Joseph Roddy, cited in McGreevy, p. 96.
24. Donal Henahan, *The News,* April 22, 1962.
25. Geoffrey Peyzant, *Glenn Gould: Music and Mind,* Halifax, Formac Publishing, 1978, p. 15. (from Columbia liner notes).
26. Donald W. Winicott, "Transitional Objects and Transitional Phenomena: A Study of the First Not-me Possession," *The International Journal of Psycho-Analysis,* p. 89-97.

27. Glenn Gould, letter from W. G. Symons, April 20, 1955, Glenn Gould Archives, Library and Archives Canada.
28. Glenn Gould, letter from Harry Heap, April 19, 1956, Glenn Gould Archives, Library and Archives Canada.
29. Louis Biancolli, *New York World Telegram and Sun,* March, 1960.
30. Jock Carroll, *Weekend Magazine,* 1956.
31. Harry James Wignall, Chickering's "Old Ironsides," *The Piano Quarterly,* 36th Year/Summer 1989, No. 142, p. 60.
32. Ibid. p. 63.
33. Bert Gould, conversations with the author, August 6, 1991.
34. Joseph Roddy, cited in McGreevy, p. 110.
35. Jonathan Cott, *Conversations with Glenn Gould,* Little, Brown & Company, 1984, p. 47.
36. Custom clearence, Glenn Gould Archives, Library and Archives Canada.
37. Avner Carmi, letter to Gould, February 7, 1960, Glenn Gould Archives, Library and Archives Canada.
38. Glenn Gould, letter to Kitty Gvozdeva, August 29, 1961, Glenn Gould Archives, Library and Archives Canada.
39. Jonathan Cott, *Conversations with Glenn Gould,* p. 63.
40. Phylis Greenacre, "The Childhood of the Artist: Libidinal Phase of Development and Giftedness."
41. Jock Carroll, *Weekend Magazine,* 1956.
42. Andrew Kazdin, *Glenn Gould at Work,* p. 61.
43. Emanuel Ax, Glenn Gould Archives, Library and Archives Canada.

Chapter 11, The Music Circle

1. Elizabeth Barret Browning, cited in John Bartlett, *Familiar Quotations,* Little, Brown and Company, Boston, 1980, p. 507:21.
2. Leonard Bernstein, in *Glenn Gould By Himself and His Friends,* J. McGreevy, ed. 1983, p. 21.
3. Joseph Roddy, in *Glenn Gould By Himself and His Friends,* p. 116.
4. *The New York Times,* January 27, 1957.
5. *The Saturday Review,* January 1957.
6. B. H. Haggin, undated clipping, Glenn Gould Archives, Library and Archives Canada.
7. Harold Schonberg, *The New York Times,* cited in Walter Homburger's "Press Book," August 1961, Glenn Gould Archives, Library and Archives Canada.
8. Michael Freedland, *Leonard Bernstein,* Harrap, London, 1987, p. 15.
9. Joan Peyser, *Bernstein: A Biography,* Billboard Books, New York, 1998, p. 285.
10. Paul Bowles, *The New York Herald Tribune,* cited in *Leonard Bernstein* by Michael Freedland, p. 64.
11. Glenn Gould, letter to Leonard Bernstein, August 29, 1958, Glenn Gould Archives, Library and Archives Canada.
12. Leonard Bernstein, in *Glenn Gould By Himself and His Friends,* p. 20.
13. Joan Peyser, p. 167.
14. Leonard Bernstein, speech given before the audience on April 6, 1962, CD 682, Historic Mono, Music & Arts, 1985, Educational Media Association of America, Inc.

15. Joan Peyser, p. 14.
16. Harold Schonberg, *The New York Times,* April 7, 1962, Glenn Gould Archives, Library and Archives Canada.
17. Joan Peyser, p. 353.
18. David Breckbrill, liner notes, Glenn Gould Archives, Library and Archives Canada.
19. Ibid.
20. Mark Twain, cited in John Bartlett, *Familiar Quotations,* Little Brown and Company, Boston, 1982, p. 622:3.
21. Jonathan Cott, undated document, personal Gouldiana Collection.
22. Hugh Thomson, cited in *Glenn Gould: A Life and Variations,* by Otto Friedrich, Lester & Orpen Dennys, Toronto, Canada, 1989, p. 75-76.
23. Jonathan Cott, cited in *Conversations With Glenn Gould,* Little, Brown & Company, 1984, p. 125.
24. Ibid. p. 127.
25. Ibid. p. 128.
26. Ibid. p. 128.
27. Ibid. p. 129-30.
28. Ibid. p. 131.
29. Ibid. p. 129.
30. Harold C. Schonberg, *The Glorious Ones,* Times Books, 1985, p. 455.
31. Glenn Gould, undated notes, personal Gouldiana Collection.
32. Glenn Gould, ibid.
33. Glenn Gould, ibid.
34. Glenn Gould, ibid.
35. Glenn Gould, "Stokowski in Six Scenes," *Piano Quarterly,* Winter 1977-78, reprinted in *The Glenn Gould Reader,* edited by Tim Page, Lester & Orpen Dennys, 1984, p. 269.
36. Ibid. p. 263.
37. Ibid. p. 264.
38. Ibid. p. 269.
39. Ibid. p. 282.

Chapter 12, Turning Thirty

1. Margaret Atwood, *Cat's Eye* (1988), from *The Beacon Book of Quotations By Women,* compiled by Rosalie Maggio, Beacon Press, Boston, 1992, p. 4.
2. Harold Schonberg, *The New York Times,* April 7, 1962.
3. Harriet Johnson, *The New York Post,* April 10, 1962.
4. Eric McLean, *The Montreal Star*, April 14, 1962.
5. Ibid.
6. Glenn Gould, letter to Virginia Katims, January 20, 1973, in *Glenn Gould: Selected Letters,* p. 193.
7. Bert Gould, conversations with the author, June 8, 1993.
8. George Gibson, intreview with the author, October, 1999.
9. Verne Edquist clarified in conversation with the author, November 24, 2002, that Donald MacDonald was not a piano tuner but rather a sort of a mechanic who worked in the piano repair section.

10. George Gibson. Ibid.
11. Verne Edquist, manuscript, personal Gouldiana Collection.
12. Ibid.
13. Andrew Kazdin, *Glenn Gould at Work: Creative Lying,* E. P. Dutton, New York, 1989, p. 4.
14. Ibid.
15. Feodor M. Dostoevski, cited in John Bartlett, *Familiar Quotations,* Little, Brown and Company, Boston, 1980, p. 581: 17.
16. Jock Carroll, *Weekend Magazine,* 6, No. 27, July 7, 1956, p. 11.
17. Bert Gould, conversations with the author, August 6, 1991.
18. Robert Fulford, interview with the author, August 10, 1989.
19. Elsie Feeney, interview with the author, January 22, 1991.
20. Ibid.
21. Ibid.
22. George Kidd, *The Toronto Telegram,* July 29, 1960.
23. Ibid.
24. Ontario Department of Transport, November 15, 1961, Glenn Gould Archives, Library and Archives Canada.
25. Ontario Department of Transport, October 21, 1963, Glenn Gould Archives, Library and Archives Canada.
26. James Joyce, cited in John Bartlett, *Familiar Quotations,* Little, Brown and Company, Boston, 1980, p. 777:15.
27. Glenn Gould, letter to Miss McLean, February 18, 1957. Glenn Gould Archives, Library and Archives Canada.
28. Glenn Gould, "Of Mozart and Related Matters: Glenn Gould in Conversation with Bruno Monsaingeon," *Piano Quarterly,* Fall 1976, reprinted in *The Glenn Gould Reader,* p. 33.
29. Glenn Gould, "The Piano Music of Arnold Schoenberg," Liner Notes from Columbia M2S 736, 1966, reprinted in *The Glenn Gould Reader,* p. 123.
30. Glenn Gould, letter to John Lee Roberts, April 6, 1961, in *Glenn Gould: Selected Letters,* p. 44.
31. Glenn Gould, letter to Dr. Peter Ostwald, February 17, 1961. Glenn Gould Archives, Library and Archives Canada.
32. Glenn Gould, letter to Mrs. Wilfred Riddell, June 4, 1958. Glenn Gould Archives, Library and Archives Canada.
33. Ibid.
34. Verne Edquist, manuscript, personal Gouldiana Collection.
35. Johnatan Cott, *Conversations with Glenn Gould*, Little, Brown & Company Canada Limited, 1984, p. 119.
36. Russell Herbert Gould, interview with the author, August 6, 1991.
37. Jonathan Cott, *Conversations with Glenn Gould,* Little, Brown & Company, 1984, p. 86.
38. Ibid. p. 83.
39. Glenn Gould, "Jehudi Menuhin" from *Musical America,* December 1966, reprinted in *The Glenn Gould Reader,* p. 299-300.
40. Glenn Gould, letter to Lady Diane Menuhin, April 25, 1966, in *Glenn Gould: Selected Letters,* p. 88.

Chapter 13, The Tales of Stratford

1. Eric McLean, *The Montreal Star,* July 9, 1962.
2. Barbara Reid & Thelma Morrison: *A Star Danced*, 1994, The Beacon Herald, Canada. p. 26.
3. Ibid. p. 26.
4. Ibid. p. 46.
5. Vera Dobson Gould, conversations with the author, June 8, 1996.
6. Robert Calvin Fairfield, "An Address Given at the 1984 Annual Dinner of the Board of Governors and Senate of the Stratford Festival at Stratford." Courtesy Robert Fairfield's daughter, Ms. Leslie Fairfield.
7. Irene Bird, interview with the author, September 24, 1999 at the "Glenn Gould Gathering." Irene's husband, Baily Bird, was a music publisher and Gould's loyal supporter.
8. Alec Guinness, cited in Barbara Reid/Thelma Morrison: *A Star Danced,* p. 66.
9. Ibid. p. 68.
10. Vera Dobson Gould, conversations with the author, June 8, 1996.
11. Ibid.
12. *The New York Times*, undated clipping, Glenn Gould Archives, Library and Archives Canada.
13. Jim Curtis, notes from his personal journal. Courtesy J. Curtis.
14. Glenn Gould, program notes, Glenn Gould Archives, Library and Archives Canada.
15. Leonard Rose, interview with Daniel Kunzi, 1984, *The Glenn Gould Society,* October 1990, No. 14, p. 31.
16. Glenn Gould, letter to Benjamin Britten, November 30, 1961, in *Glenn Gould: Selected Letters,* p. 68.
17. Victor DiBello, interview with the author, May 30, 1996.
18. Eric McLean, *The Montreal Star,* July 9, 1962.
19. Deanne Bogdan, interview with the author, September 24, 1999, at the "Glenn Gould Gathering." Bogdan was a Professor of Philosophy of Education at the University of Toronto.
20. Jim Curtis, notes from his personal journal, July 8, 1962. Courtesy J. Curtis.
21. Eric McLean, *The Montreal Star,* July 9, 1962.
22. Jacob Siskind, *The Montreal Gazette,* July 29, 1962.
23. Ibid.
24. Victor DiBello, interview with the author, May 30, 1996.
25. Joyce Goodman, *The Montreal Star,* August 11, 1962.
26. John Kraglund, *The Globe & Mail,* August 11, 1962.
27. Jim Curtis, notes from his personal journal, August 10, 1962. Courtesy J. Curtis.
28. Letters to the Editor, *The Montreal Star,* August 22, 1962.
29. John Lee Roberts, "Reminiscences" in *Glenn Gould by Himself and His Friends,* edited by John McGrievy, 1982, p. 243.
30. Glenn Gould, "Music in the Soviet Union" from a lecture delivered at the University of Toronto, 1964, in *The Glenn Gould Reader* edited by Tim Page, Lester & Orpen Dennys, 1984, p. 180-2.
31. Eric McLean, *The Montreal Star,* July 8, 1963.
32. John Lee Roberts, "Reminiscences" 1982, p. 235.

Chapter 14, Bowing Out

1. Robert Offergeld, *High Fidelity,* June, 1963.
2. Glenn Gould, letter to Mrs. H.L. Austin, February 15, 1961, in *Glenn Gould: Selected Letters,* p. 43.
3. Bert Gould, conversations with the author, June 11, 1994.
4. Glenn Gould, letter to Kitty Gvozdeva, April 17, 1961, in *Glenn Gould: Selected Letters,* p. 45.
5. Glenn Gould, letter to Humphrey Burton, April 17, 1961, in *Glenn Gould: Selected Letters,* p. 55.
6. Christoph Wolff, *Bach,* 1993, Harvard University Press, Cambridge, Massachusetts, p. 280-281.
7. Dinu Lipatti, the famous Romanian pianist, who died prematurely in 1950, at the age of 33.
8. Robert Offergeld, *High Fidelity,* June, 1963.
9. Beverly Sills, *Time* (1983) in *The Beacon Book Of Quotations By Women,* compiled by Rosalie Maggio, Beacon Press, Boston, 1992, p. 273-4.
10. Walter Homburger, undated clipping, Glenn Gould Archives, Library and Archives Canada.
11. Walter Homburger, ibid.
12. Glenn Gould, letter to Lord Harewood, August 13, 1964. Glenn Gould Archives, Library and Archives Canada.
13. Glenn Gould, *The Prospects of Recording,* from *High Fidelity,* April, 1966, reprinted in *The Glenn Gould Reader* by Tim Page, ed. 1984, Lester & Orpen Dennys, Toronto, p. 353.
14. Ibid.
15. Ibid.
16. Glenn Gould, interview with John McClure, disc *Glenn Gould: Concert Drop-Out.*
17. Ibid.
18. Glenn Gould, "Strauss and the Electronic Future" from *The Saturday Review,* May 30, 1964, reprinted in *The Glenn Gould Reader,* p. 98-9.
19. Glenn Gould, "Advice to a Graduation" Delivered at the Royal Conservatory of Music, University of Toronto, November, 1964, reprinted in *The Glenn Gould Reader,* p. 3.
20. Glenn Gould, *Glenn Gould Interviews Glenn Gould About Glenn Gould,* from *High Fidelity,* February, 1974, reprinted in *The Glenn Gould Reader,* p. 318.
21. Ibid. p. 316.
22. Glenn Gould, letter to Silvia Kind, January 10, 1965, in *Glenn Gould: Selected Letters,* p. 75.
23. Erik H. Erikson, *Childhood and Society,* 1985, W.W. Norton & Company, p. 252-53.
24. Ibid.
25. Jonathan Cott, *Conversations With Glenn Gould,* Little, Brown & Company, Boston - Toronto, 1984, p. 103.
26. Marshall McLuhan, *Understanding Media,* New American Library, New York, 1964, p. 43.
27. Marshall McLuhan, *Understanding Media.*
28. Ibid.

Chapter 15, Love and Sexuality

1. Samuel Johnson, cited in John Bartlett's *Familiar Quotations,* Little, Brown and Company, Boston, 1980, p. 353:19.
2. Jessie Greig, interview with the author, August 8, 1991.
3. Thomas Mann, *Doctor Faustus.* published by Alfred A. Knopf, New York, 1948.

4. *The Uxbridge Times-Journal,* February 1, 1951.
5. Tim Page, "Glenn Gould in Conversation with Tim Page," *Piano Quarterly,* Fall 1981, reprinted in *The Glenn Gould Reader,* edited by Tim Page, Lester & Orpen Dennys, 1984, p. 453.
6. Ibid. p. 455.
7. Glenn Gould, "The Search for Petula Clark," *High Fidelity,* November 1967 reprinted in *The Glenn Gould Reader,* ed. by Tim Page, Lester & Orpen Dennys, Toronto, 1984, p. 303.
8. Glenn Gould, letter to Edith Boecker, *Glenn Gould: Selected Letters*, John P. L. Roberts and Ghyslaine Guertin, Eds., 1992, Oxford University Press, Toronto, p. 27.
9. Bert Gould, conversations with the author, January 1995.
10. Ibid.
11. Glenn Gould, "The Search for Petula Clark" p. 302.
12. Jonathan Cott, *Conversations With Glenn Gould,* p. 108.
13. Petula Clark, "Downtown," 1964, Warner Bros.
14. Glenn Gould, "The Search for Petula Clark" p. 304.
15. Petula Clark, "Who Am I?" 1966, Warner Bros.
16. Ibid.
17. Glenn Gould, "The Search for Petula Clark," p. 307.
18. Ibid.
19. Ibid.
20. Ibid.
21. Andrew Kazdin, *Glenn Gould At Work,* E. P. Dutton, New York, p. 74.
22. Janine Chasseguet - Smirgel, *Creativity And Perversion,* W. W. Norton & Company, New York, 1985, p. 83.
23. Ibid. p. 80.
24. Ibid. p. 83.
25. Ibid. p. 89.
26. Otto F. Kernberg, "Mature Love: Prerequisites and Characteristics," *This Journal,* 1974, vol. 22, p. 748. The paragraph reads: "The first prerequisite for being in love is the full development of oral and body-surface erotism, in the broadest sense, and its integration, together with libidinally and aggressively determined pregenital "part" object relationships, into "total" object relations."
27. Ibid. p. 749.
28. I. M. Josselyn, "The capacity to love: a possible reformulation" *J. Amer. Acad. Child. Psychiat.,* 1971, vol 10, cited in Otto Kernberg, *Love Relations,* Yale University Press, 1995, p. 35.
29. Otto F. Kernberg, "Mature Love: Prerequisites and Characteristics," p. 749.
30. Ibid. p. 756.
31. Ibid. p. 757.
32. Helen Mesaros, Discussion about Glenn Gould at the Symposium "The Pleasures and Perils of Genius, Mostly Mozart," San Francisco, June 7 - 9, 1991.
33. Jock Carroll, *Glenn Gould: Some Potraits Of The Artist As A Young Man,* Stoddart, 1995, p. 11.
34. Andrew Kazdin, *Glenn Gould At Work,* E. P. Dutton, New York, 1989, p. 61.
35. Otto F. Kernberg, *Love Relations,* Yale University Press, 1995, p. 16.
36. Glenn Gould, excerpt from his undated journal, Glenn Gould Archives, Library and Archives Canada.
37. Andrew Kazdin, *Glenn Gould at Work,* E. P. Dutton, New York, 1989, p. 59-60.
38. Otto Friedrich, *Glenn Gould: A Life and Variations,* Lester & Orpen Dennys, 1989, p. 288.

39. Glenn Gould, excerpts from his undated journal, Glenn Gould Archives, Library and Archives Canada.
40. Ibid.
41. Ibid.
42. Margaret Pacsu, interview with the author, August 15, 1995.
43. Roxolana Roslak, speech at the Grave-Site Ceremony, "Glenn Gould Gathering," September 22-25, 2000, published in *GlennGould: A Publication of the Glenn Gould Foundation,* Volume 6, No. 2. p. 76. (This anecdote was first related to the author in 1992, in a personal encounter with Miss Roslak).
44. Ibid.

Chapter 16, Real and Imagined Illness

1. William Shakespeare, *Hamlet,* Act III, Scene I, Academic Press Canada, 1963, p. 107.
2. Dr. John Percieval, interview with the author, August 9, 1995.
3. Ibid.
4. Undated document, Glenn Gould Archives, Library and Archives Canada.
5. Glenn Gould, letter to Leonard Bernstein, December 13, 1961, Glenn Gould Archives, Library and Archives Canada.
6. Tom McIntosh, letter to Glenn Gould, January 14, 1957, Glenn Gould Archives, Library and Archives Canada.
7. Tom McIntosh, letter to Glenn Gould, February 27, 1957, Glenn Gould Archives, Library and Archives Canada.
8. Harvey Moldofsky, at al. "Musculo-skeletal symptoms and non-REM sleep disturbance in patients with 'fibrositis syndrome' and healthy subjects," *Psychosom. Med.,* 37:341-351.
9. Glenn Gould, undated letter to a fan, Glenn Gould Archives, Library and Archives Canada.
10. Glenn Gould, letter to Sylvia Kind, January 25, 1961, Glenn Gould Archives, Library and Archives Canada.
11. Dr. John Percieval, interview with the author, August 9, 1995.
12. Dr. Irvin Stein, notes on treatment rendered to Glenn Gould, Glenn Gould Archives, Library and Archives Canada.
13. Glenn Gould, letter to Leon Fleisher, November 14, 1966, Glenn Gould Archives, Library and Archives Canada.
14. Dr. Glen Engel, chiropractor, interview with the author, 1991.
15. Dr. Peter Ostwald, interview with the author, in Amsterdam, October 5, 1992.
16. Jock Carroll, *Glenn Gould: Some Portraits of the Artist as a Young Man,* Stoddart, 1995, p. 25.
17. Alice Miller, 'Depression and Grandiosity as Related Forms of Narcissistic Disturbance," *International Journal od Psychoanalysis,* Vol. 6: pp. 61-76, 1979.
18. Ibid.
19. Glenn Gould, Liner Notes from Columbia MS 7413, 1970, reprinted in *The Glenn Gould Reader,* ed. Tim Page, Lester & Orpen Dennys, 1984, p. 52.
20. Ibid. p. 53.
21. Ibid. p. 50.
22. Glenn Gould, "Glenn Gould Interviews Himself About Beethoven," in *The Glenn Gould Reader,* ed. Tim Page, Lester & Orpen Dennys, 1984, p. 44. reprinted from *Piano Quarterly,* Spring 1972.

23. Ibid. p. 49.
24. Ibid. p. 50.
25. Glenn Gould, "Beethoven's Fifth Symphony on the Piano; Four Imainary Reviews," Liner notes from Columbia MS 7095, 1968, originally printed in *Rhapsodia, Journal of All-Union Workers of Budapest,* under the pseudonym of Zoltan Mostanyi, reprinted in *The Glenn Gould Reader,* p. 61.
26. Ibid. 61.
27. George Sand, *The Beacon Book of Quotations by Women,* by Rosalie Maggio, Beacon Press, Boston, 1992, p. 328.
28. Bert Gould, conversations with the author, November 10, 1990.
29. Jessie Greig, conversations with the author in Oshawa, Ontario, August 8, 1991.
30. Frank R. Wilson, *The Hand,* Pantheon Books, New York, 1998, p. 218.
31. Glenn Gould, excerpts from his diary, Glenn Gould Archives, Library of Canada.

Chapter 17, The Volley of Creativity

1. Glenn Gould, Glenn Gould Archives, Library and Archives Canada.
2. Ibid.
3. Lorne Tulk, "A Total Mastery of the Studio" by Christopher Harris, *The Globe and Mail,* July 27, 1996.
4. John Lee Roberts,Glenn Gould Archives, Library and Archives Canada.
5. Roy Shields, *The Toronto Star*, quoted in O. Friedrich's *Glenn Gould: A Life and Variations,* Lester & Orpen Dennys Limited, Toronto, 1989, p. 208.
6. Elizabeth deRoode, letter to *The Montreal Star,* October 17, 1962, (letter signed "Mrs. deR Singer.)
7. CBC Archives, Toronto, Canada.
8. Robert Moog, undated clipping, Glenn Gould Archives, Library and Archives Canada.
9. Glenn Gould, "An Argument for Richard Strauss," *High Fidelity,* March 1962, reprinted in *The Glenn Gould Reader,* Lester & Orpen Dennys, Canada, 1984, p. 85.
10. Janet Somerville, June 24, 1969, CBC Archives.
11. Janet Somerville, memo to N. Gardiner, June 24, 1969, CBC Archives.
12. Glenn Gould, contrapuntal radio, from the original transcript from Gould's radio play "The Idea of North," 1967, reprinted in *The Glenn Gould Reader,* p. 389-390.
13. Glenn Gould, letter to John Culshaw, June 22nd, 1968, reprinted in *Glenn Gould:Selected Letters,* 1992, p. 106-7.
14. Glenn Gould, contrapuntal radio, from the original transcript from Gould's radio play "The Idea of North," 1967, reprinted in *The Glenn Gould Reader,* p. 389-390.
15. Glenn Gould, quoted in CBC Times, September 13-19, 1969.
16. Ibid.
17. William Littler, *The Toronto Star,* December 23, 1967.
18. Ibid.
19. Geoffrey Payzant, *Glenn Gould: Music & Mind,* Goodread Biographies, 1986, p. 52.
20. Janet Somerville, June 24, 1969, CBC Archives.
21. Glenn Gould, notes, Glenn Gould Archives, Library and Archives Canada.
22. Janet Somerville, June 24, 1969, CBC Archives.
23. Glenn Gould, letter to Elvin Shantz, January 20, 1973, in *Selected Letters,* p. 193-4.

24. Glenn Gould, *Arnold Schoenberg - A Perspective,*Monograph published by the University of Cincinnati, 1964, reprinted in *The Glenn Gould Reader,* Lester & Orpen Dennys, Canada, 1984, p. 117.
25. Ibid.
26. Glenn Gould, Liner Notes from Columbia M2S 736, 1966, reprinted in *The Glenn Gould Reader,* p. 128.
27. Glenn Gould, Liner Notes from Columbia, "Beethoven's Last Three Piano Sonatas," ML 5130, 1956, reprinted in *The Glenn Gould Reader,* p. 57.
28. Glenn Gould, notes, Glenn Gould Archives, Library and Archives Canada.
29. Glenn Gould, letter to John Lee Roberts, February 15, 1957, *Selected Letters* p. 6.
30. Glenn Gould, Liner Notes from Columbia ML5130, 1956, reprinted in *The Glenn Gould Reader,* 1984, p. 57.
31. Howard Scott quoted by Joseph Roddy in "Apollonian,"in *Glenn Gould: Variations by Himself and His Friends,* Edited by John McGreevy, Toronto, Doubleday, 1983.
32. *Huston Post,* clipping, Glenn Gould Archives, Library and Archives Canada.
33. Hubert Saal, "The Goldberg Variations" *Newsweek,* April 22, 1968.
34. Glenn Gould, interview with Humphrie Burton, 1966, Glenn Gould Archives, Library and Archives Canada.
35. Claus Steffen Mahnkopf, "Glenn Gould's Pianistic Aesthetics" *The International Glenn Gould Society,* March/October, 1991.

Chapter 18, The Last Ten Years

1. Antonin Kubalek, *Music Magazine*, February/March 1990.
2. Verne Edquist, conversations with the author, March 7, 1998.
3. Robert Silverman, conversations with the author, July 19, 1991, Rochester, New York, Stouffer Plaza Hotel.
4. Robert Silverman, conversations with the author, August 5, 1994, Wilmington, Vermont.
5. Ibid.
6. Ray Roberts, conversations with the author, May 30, 1989.
7. Ibid.
8. Ibid.
9. Victor DiBello, conversations with the author, May 1996.
10. "Glenn Gould Interviews Glenn Gould About Glenn Gould" *High Fidelity,* 1974.
11. Bruno Monsaingeon, reflections on Glenn Gould, *Glenn Gould Gathering,* Toronto, September 22-26, 1999.
12. Verne Edquist, conversations with the author, March 7, 1998.
13. Robert Browning, cited in Bartlett's *Familiar Quotations,* Little, Brown and Company, Boston, 1980, p. 540:22.
14. Jessie Greig, conversations with the author, August 8, 1991.
15. Ibid.
16. Toronto East General Hospital, Medical Records.
17. Glenn Gould, eulogy for Florence Greig Gould, Glenn Gould Archives, Library and Archives Canada.
18. Elsie Lally Feeney, interview with the author, January 1991.

19. Verne Edquist, conversations with the author, March 7, 1998.
20. Andrew Kazdin, interview with the author, November 16, 1990.
21. Glenn Gould, letter to Ernest Krenek, [c. 1975] in *Glenn Gould: Selected Letters,* p. 218.
22. Victor DiBello, conversations with the author, May 1996.
23. Hindemith: *Das Marienleben,* lyrics by E.M.Rilke, in Liner notes, The Glenn Gould Edition, Sony Classical, 01-052674-10.
24. Ibid.
25. Ibid.
26. Ibid.
27. Margaret Pacsu, interview with the author, August 15, 1995.
28. Glenn Gould, letter to John Fraser, July 4, 1978, in *Glenn Gould: Selected Letters,* p. 236.
29. S. Freud: *Mourning and Melancholia*, Standard Edition 14: 239-258.
30. Glenn Gould Archives, excerpts from Gould's diary, Library and Archives Canada.
31. *Toronto,* adapted by Gould from his filmscript for a documentary, originally published in *Cities*, edited by John McGreevy (New York: Clarkson N. Potter, 1981) reprinted in *The Glenn Gould Reader,* edited by Tim Page, Lester & Orpen Dennys, Toronto, 1984, p.415-16.
32. Ibid.
33. Ibid.
34. Bob Pennington, *The Toronto Sun,* cited in O. Friedrich' *Glenn Gould: A Life and Variations,* Lester & Orpen Dennys Ltd. Toronto, p. 226.
35. Don Downey, *The Globe and Mail,* cited Ibid. p. 226.
36. Ron Base, *The Toronto Star,* cited Ibid. p. 226.
37. Good News: The New Testament and Psalms, Canadian Bible Society, 1978, The Gospel according to Matthew, Mark 6.1-6; Luke 4.16-30.
38. Andrew Kazdin, interview with the author, November 16, 1990.
39. Ibid.
40. Verne Edquist, interview with the author, March 7, 1998.
41. Andrew Kazdin, *Glenn Gould At Work: Creative Lying,* E.P. Dutton, New York, 1989, p.163.
42. Vera Dobson Gould, conversations with the author, June 8, 1996.
43. Excerpts from Gould's diary, Glenn Gould Archives, Library and and Archives Canada.
44. Robert Silverman, conversations with the author, November 6, 1995, New York City.
45. Jacob Siskind, *The Montreal Gazette,* undated clipping, personal Gouldiana Collection.
46. William Shakespeare, *Antony and Cleopatra,* act V.
47. Natsume Soseki: *The Three-Cornered World,* Henry Regnery Company, Chicago, 1967.
48. Film, Bach's *Goldberg Variations,* 1981, Glenn Gould Archives, Library and Archives Canada.
49. Ibid.
50. Samuel Carter, in Liner Notes for disc Glenn Gould/ J.S.Bach *Goldberg Variations,* BWV 988, CBS Records Canada Ltd.

Chapter 19, Finale

1. Natsume Soseki, *The Three-Cornered World,* Henry Regnery Company, Chicago, 1967.
2. Robert Silverman, "Memories: Glenn Gould 1932 - 1982" in Mc Greevy's *Glenn Gould: Variations By Himself and His Friends,* p. 143.
3. Ibid.

4. Robert Silverman, conversations with the author, August 5 - 7, 1994, Wilmington, Vermont.
5. Ibid.
6. Glenn Gould, interview with David Dubal, "Reflections from the Keyboard" *The Financial Post*, 1984.
7. "Glenn Gould in Conversation with Tim Page" *Piano Quarterly,* Fall 1981.
8. Ibid.
9. Glenn Gould, interview with David Dubal, "Reflections from the Keyboard."
10. Ibid.
11. Ibid.
12. Victor Di Bello, conversations with the author, May 1996.
13. Timothy Maloney, interview with the author, January 1991.
14. Timothy Maloney, *The International Glenn Gould Society*, 15/16, March/ October 1991.
15. Samuel Carter, in Liner Notes for disc MK 38659 Glenn Gould/Richard Strauss, CBS Records/ Masterworks.
16. Glenn Gould, letter to Virginia Katims, January 20, 1973, in *Glenn Gould: Collected Letters,* p. 192.
17. Robert Silverman, conversations with the author, August 5-7, 1994.
18. Dr. John Percieval, interview with the author, August 9, 1995.
19. Ray Roberts, conversations with the author, February 1991.
20. Jessie Greig, conversations with the author, June 1994.
21. New Testament and Psalms, The Prayer of the Troubled Man, Psalm 102.
22. Ray Roberts, conversations with the author, February 1991.
23. Jessie Greig, conversations with the author, June 1994.
24. John Lee Roberts, Glenn Gould Archives, Library and Archives Canada.
25. John Keats, cited in John Bartletts *Familiar Quotations*, Little Brown and Company, Boston, 1980, p. 478:9.

Chapter 20, Phoenix Rising

1. Edward Rothstein, *The New York Times,* October 4, 1992.
2. *The Globe and Mail,* October 5, 1982.
3. John Fraser, *The Globe and Mail,* October 5, 1982.
4. Oskar Morawetz, *The Globe and Mail,* October 5, 1982.
5. John McGreevy, cited in Jonathan Gross': "The Genius was a warm human being," *The Toronto Sun,* October 5, 1982.
6. John Kraglund, *The Globe and Mail,* Tuesday, October 5, 1982.
7. Harold C. Schonberg, cited in *The Toronto Star,* Tuesday, October 5, 1982.
8. Jehudi Menuhin, cited in *The Toronto Star,* Tuesday, October 5, 1982.
9. Leonard Bernstein, cited in *The Toronto Star,* Tuesday, October 5, 1982.
10. Elizabeth Schwarzkopf, cited in *The Toronto Star,* Tuesday, October 5, 1982.
11. William Littler, "His curiosity made label of pianist so inadequate," *The Toronto Star,* Tuesday, October 5, 1982.
12. Pierre Elliott Trudeau, telegram to Russell Herbert Gould, personal Gouldiana Collection.
13. Wanda Horowitz, letter to Russell Herbert Gould, personal Gouldiana Collection.
14. Herbert von Karajan, telegram to Russell Herbert Gould, personal Gouldiana Collection.

15. Alexina Louie, undated clipping, personal Gouldiana Collection.
16. Paul Richardson, *The Observer,* "Preludes to a lonely life," June 5, 1994.
17. John Coulson, TV Guide, June 1st, 1985.
18. James Strecker, *Echosystem,* Mini Mocho Press, Hamilton,Ontario, 1993 p.93.
19. Sylvia Kind, interview with the author, Groningen, Holland, October 5,1992.
20. Louise Guay, undated clipping, Glenn Gould Archives, Library and Archives Canada.
21. Robert Fulford, *The Globe & Mail,* February 16, 1994.
22. Anthony Lane, *The New Yorker,* April 18, 1994.
23. Richard Natale, *Chicago Tribune,* May 1st, 1994.
24. Hugo Davenport, *The Daily Telegraph,* June 17, 1994.
25. Faye Perkins, Sony Classical, interview with the author, August 19, 1997.
26. Hans Keller, cited in "Remembering Glenn Gould" by Donald Dean, *Gramophone*, January 1993.
27. *Music Magazine,* June 1988, p. 35.

INDEX

A

Abbey, Henry 99
Adler, Peter Herman 140, 255, 310
Age of Ecstasy, The 377
Aide, William 54, 65, 92, 93
Alexander, Isabel 23
Allan, Dr. B.M. 348
Ancerl, Karel 96, 161, 162
Applebaum, Louis 293
Archer, Thomas 211
Arrau, Claudio 87, 166
Art of Glenn Gould, The 370, 371
Ax, Emanuel 240

B

Bach, Anna Magdalena 35, 207
Bach, Johann Christoph 202
Bach, Johann Sebastian 26, 65, 107, 110, 112, 201, 202, 206, 208, 213, 424, 437
  Brandenburg Concertos 123, 139, 140, 142, 236
  Concerto in D Minor 108, 124, 297
  Concerto in F Minor 111
  Goldberg Variations 106, 107, 113, 119, 122, 132, 136, 138, 184, 201, 202, 204, 213, 236, 242, 295, 347, 379, 408
  Partita No. 4, 5, 6 101, 108, 112, 139, 294, 311, 380, 390
  The Art of the Fugue 108, 110, 297, 300, 310, 311, 325, 371
Badura-Skoda, Paul 105, 118
Baltimore Evening Sun, The 140
Banquo (dog) 117, 174, 189, 196, 197
Barger & Barclay 178
Bazzana, Kevin 433, 436
Beatles, The 285, 331
Beckwith, John 54, 93, 102, 142, 191, 210, 429
Beethoven, Ludwig van 68, 107, 110, 120, 141, 338, 360
  Apassionata 360
  Eroica Variations 140, 142, 210, 368
Bell, Alexander Graham 9
Bellows, George Kent 140
Berg, Alban 101, 123, 142, 368
Berliner, Emil 9
Bernstein, Leonard 33, 120, 122, 139, 165, 230, 241-247, 249, 250, 252, 253, 255, 258, 270, 271, 273, 289, 309, 310, 354, 371, 385, 425, 429
Beswick, Dr. Christopher 21
Biancolli, Louis 217, 230
Bierman, Dr. 348
Biggs, E. Power 44
Bird, Irene 104, 293
Blitzstein, Marc 181
Bodky, Edvin 92
Boecker, Edith 194, 326
Bogdan, Deanne 298
Boulanger, Nadia 88, 181
Boulez, Pierre 230, 431
Boyd, Malcolm 207
Brahms, Johannes 101, 112, 272
Braithwaite, Dennis 124
Braudo, Isai 111, 115
Brendel, Alfred 100, 118, 434
Britnell, Albert 198
Britten, Benjamin 297
Browning, Robert 390
Burton, Humphrey 245, 310, 381
Busoni, Ferruccio 92, 116, 231, 261
Buxtehude, Dietrich 202

C

Canadian Broadcasting Corporation (CBC) 1, 89, 139, 182, 183, 198, 232, 234, 269, 283, 319, 320, 328, 343, 368, 369, 374, 375, 379, 383, 384, 386, 390, 395, 397, 398, 419, 426, 431, 437
Canin, Martin 105, 111
Carmi, Avner (Siena Piano) 236
Carnegie, Andrew 12
Carnegie Hall 11, 120, 121, 129, 165, 230, 233, 242, 243, 248, 256, 270, 271, 406
Carroll, Jock 186, 187, 337, 356
Carson, Johnny (Tonight Show) 219
Carter, Samuel 408, 409, 411, 414, 417
Caruso, Enrico 12, 151
Casals, Pablo 112, 384
Catims, Milton 348
Chaliapin, Feodor 12
Charles I, King of England and Scotland 173, 191
Chickering, Jonas 231, 233
Christian Science Monitor, The 139
Clark, Petula 81, 151, 325-331, 338
Clementi, Muzio 126
Cliburn, Van 32, 193, 312, 316, 426
Colarusso, Calvin A. 171
Colodin, Irvin 182
Columbia Records 105, 106, 182, 224, 276, 370, 388, 401, 419

Copland, Aaron 88, 181, 184
Corbett, Edward A. 292
Cott, Jonathan 133, 234, 256, 257, 259, 260, 285
Covent Gardens 12
Curtis, James (Jim) 109, 122, 184, 189, 296, 298, 301
Czerny, Carl 12, 44, 67

D

Das Marienleben 299, 343, 395
Debussy, Claude 54, 377
Detroit News, The 111, 142
Diabelli, Antonio 13, 44
Diamond, David 181
DiBello, Victor 183, 297, 300, 305, 316, 388, 394, 417, 432, 437
Disraeli, Benjamin 15, 20, 41
Dobson, Murray 294, 402
Dobson, Vera 172, 292, 294, 402, 404
Donchery Estate 194, 196, 326
Dostoevski, Feodor 200, 277
Doyle, Dr. Arthur M. 348, 356
Dubal, David 105, 416

E

Eaton Auditorium 71, 72, 86, 176, 235, 276
Edison, Thomas 9
Edquist, Vern 275, 285, 384, 389, 394, 402, 404
Eliot, George 57
Ellis, Havelock 8
Emerson, Ralph Waldo 29, 47, 201
Engel, Dr. Glen 354
Erikson, Erik 30, 74, 318

F

Fairfield, Robert 292, 294
Ferrier, Kathleen 101
Fitzgerald, Winston 128, 195, 289
Fleisher, Leon 32, 129, 353, 365, 370
Flett, Boyd 60
Flett, Donald 37, 42
Flett, Flora 13, 37, 59, 60, 148
Flett, Flora Mackenzie 13
Flett, Mary 8-10, 27, 146, 148
Foli, Lea 300, 301
Ford, Henry 11
Forkel, Johann Nicolaus 203
Forrester, Maureen 101, 421, 426
Foss, Lucas 181, 289, 297, 339
Frankenstein, Alfred 136
Fraser, John 397, 423
Freud, Anna 75, 79
Freud, Sigmund 77, 149, 198, 218, 335, 339
Friedrich, Otto 195, 197, 339, 430, 437
Frost, Thomas 224, 276, 277
Fulford, Robert 50, 62, 80, 81, 87, 101, 107, 151, 188, 279, 435, 437

G

Gabrilowitsch, Ossip 270
Gardner, Ava 385
Gershwin, George 303
Gibbons, Orlando 176, 333
Gieseking, Walter 110
Glenesk, Reverend William 205, 206
Glenn Gould's Toronto 377, 398, 400, 429
Glenn Gould Off the Record 140, 377, 429
Glenn Gould On the Record 140, 377, 429
Glenn Gould Reader, The 430
Glinka, Michail 296
Globe and Mail, The 59, 77, 301, 397, 400, 423, 424
Gold, Alma Rosena Horne (Grandma Allie) 3, 15, 16, 18, 19, 22, 27, 36, 38, 44, 66, 126, 206, 288, 308, 311, 354, 363
Gold, Freddy 16, 190
Gold, Maria Proctor 15, 16, 20
Gold, Reverend Isaac 15, 16, 20, 21, 41
Gold, Russell Herbert (Bert Gould) 3, 15, 25, 29, 36, 41, 52, 66, 96, 99, 117, 149, 150, 173, 191, 232, 278, 308, 390, 402, 404, 420, 426, 431
Gold, Thomas G. 2, 15, 23, 104, 172, 174, 191, 206, 375
Goldberg, Johann Gottlieb 203
Goldsmith, Nicholas 187
Gold Standard Fur 47
Goodman, Benny 81
Goodman, Joyce 300, 301
Goodrich, Peter 131
Gould, Dr. Grant 59, 81, 97, 165, 363
Gould, Glenn
  adolescence 57, 65, 71, 74, 76, 82, 87, 89, 148, 171, 178, 193, 205, 324
  childhood 9, 11, 28, 39, 46, 57, 65, 77, 80, 151, 153-155, 158, 160, 163, 167, 179, 185, 206, 207, 219, 220, 225, 228, 238, 245, 259, 269, 274, 279, 318, 347, 355, 358, 364, 404, 428
  depression 77, 82, 127, 140, 157, 191, 195, 273, 313, 350, 355, 356, 362-364, 369, 383, 389, 407, 418
  eccentricities 76, 77, 119, 231, 238, 271, 299, 366, 424
  genius 2, 11, 58, 64, 69, 73, 76, 78, 88, 93, 94, 119, 124, 126, 133, 135, 176, 178, 182, 216, 222, 230, 242, 254, 297, 357, 370, 374, 422, 424, 427, 428, 433, 436, 437
  Glenn Gould at Work (Kazdin) 224
  Glenn Gould Variations: By Himself and His Friends, The (McGreevy) 429
  humor 28, 128, 281-285, 288, 300-302, 342, 362, 384, 408, 424

hypertension (high blood pressure) 345, 365, 366, 420
hypochondria 48, 307, 345-348, 353, 356
individuation 47, 71, 74, 89, 336
phobia 38, 47, 48, 136, 138, 269, 304, 318, 320, 347, 357, 364, 392, 395, 400, 401
press reviews (accolades) 69, 110, 211, 424, 426, 438
press reviews (critical) 138, 226, 270-272, 301, 407, 435
radio and television broadcasts 57, 184, 424
recording in New York 106, 139, 234, 265, 275, 276, 317, 380, 383, 404, 408, 416, 417
recording in Toronto 383, 417
separation anxiety 38, 42, 47, 117, 118, 127, 138, 146, 151, 167, 195, 209, 227, 307, 308, 318, 335, 336, 354, 392, 407
stage fright (performance anxiety) 77, 79, 92, 94, 115-118, 123, 130, 164-167, 170, 225, 257, 258, 304, 312, 315, 318, 320, 347, 349, 352, 364
The String Quartet 102, 160, 178, 179, 182
Gould, Joseph (founder of Uxbridge) 16, 21, 41
Graffman, Gary 105, 116, 365
Greenacre, Phylis 214, 237
Greig, Edvard 13
Greig, Florence E. (Florrie) 4, 8-13, 17, 19, 23-27, 29, 34, 37, 38, 40, 41, 48, 49, 53, 54, 59, 60, 70, 71, 96, 146, 151, 159, 162, 163, 207, 220, 239, 326, 333, 364, 390-393, 399
Greig, Jessie 8, 11, 14, 60, 80, 81, 97, 154, 184, 185, 322, 392, 421, 428, 437
Greig, John 17, 20, 51, 176
Greig, John C. H. 8, 11, 14, 23, 162
Greig, Peter 8, 163
Greig, Ruel Peter 14
Greig, Willard 11, 14, 15, 17, 23, 32, 41, 51, 364
Greig Madill, Betty 14, 26, 52, 162, 428
Grit and Tory (dogs) 17
Grosheva, Elena 112
Guerrero, Alberto 53-56, 61, 64-69, 71-73, 85-87, 89-93, 97, 100, 102, 139, 176, 178, 191, 193, 196, 210, 218, 222, 229, 233, 236, 237, 248, 350, 408, 430
Guinness, Alec 293
Guthrie, Tyrone 292, 293, 294
Gvozdeva, Kitty 114, 236, 308, 318

H

Haaretz (Israel) 133-135
Hamlet 149, 198, 199, 325, 345, 436
Haydn, Joseph 55, 424
Henahan, Donal 226
Herald Tribune, The 110, 120
Hess, Myra 33
Hewitt, Angela 430, 433
Hindemith, Paul 87, 108, 112, 125, 299, 343, 395
Hofmann, Joseph 29, 32, 34, 45, 76, 93, 94, 99, 110, 151, 192
Holmes and Rahe (sociologists) 192
Homburger, Walter 72, 73, 86-88, 98-100, 103, 106, 112, 113, 115, 119, 131, 134, 186, 187, 212, 224, 283, 286, 311-313, 326, 426
Horne, Andrew 18
Horowitz, Vladimir 128, 166, 193, 316, 413, 438
Horszowski, Mieczyslaw 92
Horton, John 301
Hughes, Howard 395
Hume, Paul 103
Hupfer, William 127, 195, 197, 233, 352

I

Ingham, Harriet 83

J

Jablonski, Marek 300, 301
Jochum, George Ludwig 126
Johnson, Barry 190, 196
Johnson, Dr. Tom 190, 404
Jorda, Enrique 111, 136, 310

K

Kapell, William 317
Karajan, Herbert von 115, 125, 138, 173, 253, 257, 260-263, 283, 386, 427
Karsh, Yousuf 114
Kaufman, Walter 180
Kazdin, Andrew 154, 161, 224, 239, 275, 277, 332, 337-339, 357, 383, 394, 401, 402, 404, 417
Keats, John 213, 422
Kendall, Raymond 120
Kernberg, Otto 147, 336, 338
Keyserlingk, Graf Hermann Karl von 203, 209
Khrushchev, Nikita 112
Kidd, George 122, 210, 211, 279, 280
Killburn, Nicholas 87, 187
Kind, Sylvia 125, 126, 137, 206, 318, 351, 434
King Edward VII 14
King George V 14, 53
Kipling, Rudyard 171
Klotz, Dr. Philip 346
Kollitsch, Wolfgang 125
Kombrink, Ilona 301
Korngold, Erich 384
Kostelanetz, Richard 222, 224, 429
Kraglund, John 301, 424
Kraus, Greta 109, 189
Krenek, Ernst 87, 102, 108, 114, 296, 376, 394
Krips, Joseph 137, 190
Kubalek, Antonin 383, 384, 395
Kuerti, Anton 92, 94, 100
Kunzi, Daniel 296

L

Landowska, Wanda 107, 207, 208, 213, 236, 237
Lane, Louis 139, 140, 260
Last Puritan, The 199, 221, 322
Leschetizky, Theodor 67, 91
Liberace 238, 276, 299
Lipatti, Dinu 311
Liszt, Franz 94, 231, 361, 381
Littler, William 374, 426
Logan, Dr. 345
London Telegraph, The 137
London Times, The 137
Longfellow, Henry Wadsworth 85, 190
Lortie, Louis 100
Los Angeles Mirror, The 120

M

Mackenzie, William Lyon 13
Mackenzie King, William Lyon 13
MacMillan, Sir Ernest 45, 53, 62, 71, 86, 98, 249
MacPhail, Agnes 13
Malvern Collegiate 38, 61, 62, 63
Mamott, Isaac 294
Manley, Skip 292
Mann, Thomas 104, 172, 186, 198, 322
Marshall, Lois 105, 299, 369, 395
Martinon, Jean 133
Massey Hall 13, 45, 54, 63, 68, 70, 77, 85, 86, 109, 142, 211, 276, 323, 377
McCarthy, Dr. Dale 346
McCarthy, Pearl 77, 78
McDougall, Joyce 158
McGreevy, John 389, 398, 400, 419, 424, 429, 430
McIntosh, Tom 349
McLean, Eric 101, 170, 182, 254, 272, 291, 297, 303, 368, 377
McLuhan, Marshall 190, 319, 370
Mech, Lilly 64
Mendelssohn, Felix 41, 44
Menuhin, Diana 289, 370
Menuhin, Jehudi 288, 289, 430
Meyers, Edna 34, 50
Miller, Alice 357, 358
Mitropoulos, Dimitri 123, 129, 250-253, 256-258
Moiseiwitsch, Tanya 293
Moldofsky, Dr. Harvey 350
Moll, Dr. A. E. 347, 356
Monsaingeon, Bruno 385, 389, 408, 433
Montreal Star, The 101, 170, 182, 254, 272, 297, 300, 301
Morawetz, Oskar 54, 86, 187, 424
Mossman, Josef 142
Mozart, Wofgang Amadeus 94, 123, 283, 324, 381
Musical Courier 103, 110

N

Neel, Boyd 124
Newman, William 91-93
New York Times, The 105, 107, 116, 121, 180, 183, 243, 244, 254, 270, 293, 295, 386, 415, 424, 429
Nick, English setter (dog) 42, 78, 146, 148
Niece, Stewart 62
Nietzsche, Friedrich 200
Nobel, Alfred 126

O

O'Hagan, Captain Richard (Dick) 116, 123-126, 135
Oedipus Rex 149, 198
Oppenheim, David 105
Ormandy, Eugene 258, 289
Ostwald, Dr. Peter 111, 140, 284, 289, 356, 402, 433, 437
Ozolins, Arthur 54

P

Pacsu, Margaret 342, 397
Paderewski, Ignacy 33, 91
Page, Tim 325, 415, 430
Paray, Paul 111, 142
Parkin, Dr. Alan 348
Patterson, Tom 291, 292, 294
Peck, Gregory 321
Percieval, Dr. John 345-347, 350, 351, 356, 419
Perez, Peter 405
Peyzant, Geoffrey 226, 374, 394
Phillips, Duncan and Marjorie 103
Phillips Collection, The 103
Phillips Gallery 103
Piano Quarterly 384-386, 432
Piston, Walter 181, 202
Plummer, Christopher 300, 301
Pogorelich, Ivo 33
Pollock, George H. 10, 176, 223
Pratz, Albert 294
Prokofiev, Sergei 296, 305
Pyrrhic victory 223

Q

Queen Victoria 10, 14

R

Rachmaninoff, Sergei 93, 96
Remoortel, Edouard Van 217, 309
Richter, Sviatoslav 114, 116, 135
Rilke, Reiner Maria 299
Roberts, John Lee 198, 283, 303, 304, 316, 357, 368, 379, 418, 421, 429, 432, 433, 437

Roberts, Ray 281, 337, 343, 384, 386-389, 394, 397, 404, 408, 413, 418-421, 429, 432, 437
Robins, Jerome 385
Roddy, Joseph 165, 219, 222, 225, 233, 242, 245, 380, 429
Rose, Leonard 273, 296, 368
Roslak, Roxolana 342, 343, 377, 395
Rostan, Edmond 300
Roy, Klaus George 139
Royal Conservatory of Music 64, 178, 210, 317
Rubens, Bernice (*Madame Sousatzka*) 73
Rubinstein, Anton 192
Rubinstein, Artur 29, 32, 92, 276, 391
Ruggles, Carl 301

S

Samaroff, Olga 208
Sand, George 362
Santayana, George 200, 221, 389, 399
Saturday Review 182, 243, 317
Schafer, R. Murray 53, 54, 65, 66, 430, 432
Schnabel, Artur 67-69, 97, 223, 370, 437
Schoenberg, Arnold 87, 97, 101, 114, 118, 119, 137, 141, 142, 160, 178, 191, 257, 258, 278, 283, 285, 289, 296, 339, 368, 370, 376
Schonberg, Harold 107, 116, 121, 141, 244, 254, 270, 271, 277, 424
Schubert, Franz 114
Schumann, Robert 365
Schwarzkopf, Elizabeth 425
Scriabin, Alexander 114, 332, 377, 390
Serebryakov, Pavel 113
Serkin, Peter 166, 223
Serkin, Rudolf 67, 68, 93, 166, 276, 386, 438
Severance Hall 139, 161, 182, 183, 259
Shakespeare, William 149, 198, 199, 291, 293, 300, 345, 407, 435
Shostakovich, Dimitri 282
Showalter, H. 292, 293
Shumsky, Oskar 140, 273, 296, 303, 305, 369
Sibelius, Jan 262
Silverman, Robert (Bob) 87, 235, 316, 384-386, 389, 405, 413, 414, 419, 420, 429, 432, 433, 437
Silvester, Frederick C. 44, 48, 53, 72
Sisely, Dr. 25
Siskind, Jacob 299, 407, 435
Smith, Leo 35, 45, 53, 72, 179
Somerville, Janet 372, 374
Sophocles 149, 198
Soseki, Natsume 408, 413
Spitta, Philipp 109
Stein, Dr. Irvin 346, 352, 406
Steinway & Sons 116, 127-131, 196, 233, 235, 352, 405, 406
Steinway Hall 195, 197, 405
Steinway pianos 93, 127-130, 233, 234, 405, 406, 429
Stern, Isaac 101
Stevens, Dr. Joseph 140
Stillwell, Mary 18
Stokes, Dr. Aldwyn 348
Stratford Music Festival 170, 296
Strauss, Richard 98, 151, 160, 178, 181, 296, 325, 369, 372, 417, 425
Stravinsky, Igor 33, 157, 300, 303, 320
Streisand, Barbra 81, 151, 285
Stuckenschmidt, H. H. 116
Sum, Amy (nee Wong) 120
Suskind, Walter 109
Sweelinck Fantasia 101, 109, 296
Szell, George 253, 257-260, 263

T

Tchaikovsky, Peter Ilyich 157, 360
Toronto Daily Star, The 69, 124, 142
Toronto Star, The 137, 212, 258, 369, 374, 400, 424, 426
Toronto Telegram, The 85, 111, 122, 211, 279
Toscanini, Arturo 151, 232, 248, 258, 265
Tovell, Vincent 182, 430
Town Hall 104, 105
Trudeau, Pierre 427
Tulk, Lorne 89, 270, 368, 371, 386, 389
Tureck, Rosalyn 33, 71, 208, 213, 237, 427

V

Vengerova, Isabela 92
Victorian Age 9, 14, 20

W

Wagner, Richard 253, 416
Walton, William 301
Washington Post, The 103
Webern, Anton 118, 285
Weekend Magazine 186, 187
Wilson, Dr. Frank R. 365
Wolff, Christoph 203, 311
World War I 14, 22
World War II 1, 40, 42, 46, 58, 115